'Nathan Hill's alarmingly good de̶̶̶̶̶̶̶̶̶̶̶̶̶̶̶̶̶̶̶̶̶̶̶ ̶ ̶ ̶ ̶ ̶ ̶ ̶ ̶ ̶ ̶ is both a Great American Novel as well as a great American novel: his 600-page burglar-thumper deftly teams the life of a bored college teacher and his relationship with his mother with a panoramic, astute commentary on America's media and the failures of capitalism. Hill is already being compared to Thomas Pynchon, David Foster Wallace and John Irving; Irving himself compares Hill to Dickens . . . Reading it when Trump is at the helm will undoubtedly make the novel ache with all-new relevance.'

Guardian '20 talents set to take 2017 by storm'

'A stunning debut that resurrects the violence and anger of the 1968 Chicago riots, carrying it forward into the present day through the story of two Midwesterners addicted to virtual-reality games . . . The first book I've read in two decades that earns the title Great American Novel.'

Liesl Schillinger, *New York Times*
'What's the Best Book, New or Old, You Read This Year?'

'There is an accidental topicality in Hill's debut, about an estranged mother and son whose fates hinge on two mirror-image political events – the Democratic Convention of 1968 and the Republican Convention of 2004. But beyond that hook lies a high-risk, high-reward playfulness with structure and tone: comic set pieces, digressions into myth, and formal larks that call to mind Jennifer Egan's *A Visit From the Goon Squad*.'

New York Magazine

'Impressive that a debutant, Nathan Hill, with his scintillating *The Nix* has given us a character who comes close to out-Trumping Trump . . . Just one of the many pleasures of this engaging story of a mother and son whose private travails become front-page news.'

Observer 'New Year Highlights'

'[A] superb debut novel . . . [*The Nix*] touches on the 2008 financial crash, the Occupy protests, the 1968 Chicago riots, academic life, small-town life, fad diets, pointless apps – and much else . . . an original, funny and affecting story . . . The prose is lithe and energetic . . . It seems like Hill is a writer who can do pretty much what he wants.'

Daily Telegraph 'New Year, New Voices'

'This guy has chops.'   Jay McInerney

'I got a big kick out of Nathan Hill's *The Nix* . . . The book feels powered by a palpable intelligence. The droll sections set broadly in the present day (2011; another strand takes place in 1968) are especially sharp, despite the fact that it is increasingly difficult to send up reality during a time when reality seems to be sending up itself.'

Lionel Shriver, *Financial Times* 'Books of the Year'

'Nathan Hill's digressive, scattershot exploration of the boy, the man, his mother and the times that shaped them is a brilliant, heartbreaking glimpse into just one of the casualties that time and memory make of us all.'   US National Public Radio, 'Books of the Year'

'Dazzling . . . rich and multilayered . . . the debut of an important new writer, able to variously make readers laugh out loud while providing a melancholy, resonant tale that argues "there is no greater ache than this: guilt and regret in equal measure."'   *USA Today*

'*The Nix* is a timely mass-media and political satire, a family saga and two bildungsromans rolled into one – and, in each facet, Nathan Hill crafts a hilarious, observant, unputdownable tale.'   *Huffington Post*

'A fantastic novel about love, betrayal, politics and pop culture – as good as the best Michael Chabon or Jonathan Franzen.'   *People*

'Not only dramatising America's great tussle between minority interests and Midwestern grievances, [*The Nix*] even features a rogue presidential candidate who talks about immigrants as though they are coyotes damaging crops . . . But it's the human drama of a relationship between a son and his mother (too busy protesting in the Sixties to bring him up) that will keep you hooked while you think.'   *GQ*

'Book That May Restore Your Faith in Humanity: . . . Flawed characters, as we all are, but well-meaning in their fumbling toward understanding. May engender a good, cathartic cry.'

Chicago Tribune 'Books from 2016 you
should read if you know what's good for you'

THE NIX

A gloriously ambitious, witty, and deeply touching debut novel of fifty years of America and of American radical protest, the story of a son, the mother who left him as a child, and how his search to uncover the secrets of her life leads him to reclaim his own.

Meet Samuel Andresen-Anderson: stalled writer, bored teacher at a local college, obsessive player of online video games. He hasn't seen his mother, Faye, in decades, not since she abandoned her family when he was a boy. Now she has suddenly reappeared, having committed an absurd politically motivated crime that electrifies the nightly news, beguiles the Internet, and inflames a divided country. The media paints Faye as a radical hippy with a sordid past, but as far as Samuel knows, his mother was an ordinary girl who married her high-school sweetheart. Which version is true? Two things are certain: she's facing some serious charges, and she needs Samuel's help.

As Samuel begins to excavate his mother's – and his country's – history, the story moves from the rural Midwest of the 1960s to New York City during the Great Recession and the Occupy Wall Street movement, and back to the infamous riots at the 1968 Chicago Democratic National Convention. Finally, the trail leads him to wartime Norway, home of the mysterious Nix that his mother told him about as a child, a spirit that can take the shape of a white horse, luring children to their deaths. And in these places, Samuel will unexpectedly find that he has to rethink everything he ever knew about his mother – a woman with an epic story of her own, a story she has kept hidden from the world.

NATHAN HILL was born in Iowa in 1975 and lives with his wife in Naples, Florida. *The Nix* is his first novel.

NATHAN HILL

THE NIX

PICADOR

First published 2016 by as a Borzoi Book by Alfred A. Knopf,
a division of Penguin Random House LLC, New York

First published in the UK in paperback 2016 by Picador

This edition first published 2017 by Picador
an imprint of Pan Macmillan
20 New Wharf Road, London N1 9RR
Associated companies throughout the world
www.panmacmillan.com

ISBN 978-1-5098-0785-7

Grateful acknowledgment is made to Wisdom Publications for permission to reprint an excerpt
from *In Buddha's Words* by Bhikkhu Bodhi, copyright © 2005, 2015 by Bhikkhu Bodhi.
Reprinted with permission of Wisdom Publications (www.wisdompubs.org).

For Jenni

There was a king in Sāvatthi who addressed a man and asked him to round up all the persons in the city who were blind from birth. When the man had done so, the king asked the man to show the blind men an elephant. To some of the blind men he presented the head of the elephant, to some the ear, to others a tusk, the trunk, the body, a foot, the hindquarters, the tail, or the tuft at the end of the tail. And to each one, he said, "This is an elephant."

When he reported to the king what he had done, the king went to the blind men and asked them, "Tell me, blind men, what is an elephant like?"

Those who had been shown the head of the elephant replied, "An elephant, your majesty, is just like a water jar." Those who had been shown the ear replied, "An elephant is just like a winnowing basket." Those who had been shown the tusk replied, "An elephant is just like a plowshare." Those who had been shown the trunk replied, "An elephant is just like a plow pole." Those who had been shown the body replied, "An elephant is just like a storeroom." And each of the others likewise described the elephant in terms of the part they had been shown.

Then, saying, "An elephant is like this, an elephant is not like that! An elephant is not like this, an elephant is like that!" they fought each other with their fists.

And the king was delighted.

—*Inspired Utterances of the Buddha*

CONTENTS

THE NIX

PROLOGUE

Late Summer 1988

IF SAMUEL HAD KNOWN his mother was leaving, he might have paid more attention. He might have listened more carefully to her, observed her more closely, written certain crucial things down. Maybe he could have acted differently, spoken differently, been a different person.

Maybe he could have been a child worth sticking around for.

But Samuel did not know his mother was leaving. He did not know she had been leaving for many months now—in secret, and in pieces. She had been removing items from the house one by one. A single dress from her closet. Then a lone photo from the album. A fork from the silverware drawer. A quilt from under the bed. Every week, she took something new. A sweater. A pair of shoes. A Christmas ornament. A book. Slowly, her presence in the house grew thinner.

She'd been at it almost a year when Samuel and his father began to sense something, a sort of instability, a puzzling and disturbing and sometimes even sinister feeling of depletion. It struck them at odd moments. They looked at the bookshelf and thought: *Don't we own more books than that?* They walked by the china cabinet and felt sure something was missing. But what? They could not give it a name—this impression that life's details were being reorganized. They didn't understand that the reason they were no longer eating Crock-Pot meals was that the Crock-Pot was no longer in the house. If the bookshelf seemed bare, it was because she had pruned it of its poetry. If the china cabinet seemed a little vacant, it was because two plates, two bowls, and a teapot had been lifted from the collection.

They were being burglarized at a very slow pace.

"Didn't there used to be more photos on that wall?" Samuel's father said, standing at the foot of the stairs, squinting. "Didn't we have that picture from the Grand Canyon up there?"

"No," Samuel's mother said. "We put that picture away."

"We did? I don't remember that."

"It was *your* decision."

"It was?" he said, befuddled. He thought he was losing his mind.

Years later, in a high-school biology class, Samuel heard a story about a certain kind of African turtle that swam across the ocean to lay its eggs in South America. Scientists could find no reason for the enormous trip. Why did the turtles do it? The leading theory was that they began doing it eons ago, when South America and Africa were still locked together. Back then, only a river might have separated the continents, and the turtles laid their eggs on the river's far bank. But then the continents began drifting apart, and the river widened by about an inch per year, which would have been invisible to the turtles. So they kept going to the same spot, the far bank of the river, each generation swimming a tiny bit farther than the last one, and after a hundred million years of this, the river had become an ocean, and yet the turtles never noticed.

This, Samuel decided, was the manner of his mother's departure. This was how she moved away—imperceptibly, slowly, bit by bit. She whittled down her life until the only thing left to remove was herself.

On the day she disappeared, she left the house with a single suitcase.

PART ONE

THE PACKER ATTACKER

Late Summer 2011

1

THE HEADLINE APPEARS one afternoon on several news websites almost simultaneously: GOVERNOR PACKER ATTACKED!

Television picks it up moments later, bumping into programming for a Breaking News Alert as the anchor looks gravely into the camera and says, "We're hearing from our correspondents in Chicago that Governor Sheldon Packer has been attacked." And that's all anyone knows for a while, that he was attacked. And for a few dizzying minutes everyone has the same two questions: Is he dead? And: Is there video?

The first word comes from reporters on the scene, who call in with cell phones and are put on the air live. They say Packer was at the Chicago Hilton hosting a dinner and speech. Afterward, he was making his way with his entourage through Grant Park, glad-handing, baby-kissing, doing all your typical populist campaign maneuvers, when suddenly from out of the crowd a person or a group of people began to attack.

"What do you mean *attack*?" the anchor asks. He sits in a studio with shiny black floors and a lighting scheme of red, white, and blue. His face is smooth as cake fondant. Behind him, people at desks seem to be working. He says: "Could you describe the attack?"

"All I actually know right now," the reporter says, "is that things were thrown."

"What things?"

"That is unclear at this time."

"Was the governor struck by any of the things? Is he injured?"

"I believe he was struck, yes."

"Did you see the attackers? Were there many of them? Throwing the things?"

"There was a lot of confusion. And some yelling."

"The things that were thrown, were they big things or small things?"

"I guess I would say small enough to be thrown."

"Were they larger than baseballs, the thrown things?"

"No, smaller."

"So golf-ball-size things?"

"Maybe that's accurate."

"Were they sharp? Were they heavy?"

"It all happened very fast."

"Was it premeditated? Or a conspiracy?"

"There are many questions of that sort being asked."

A logo is made: *Terror in Chicago*. It whooshes to a spot next to the anchor's ear and flaps like a flag in the wind. The news displays a map of Grant Park on a massive touch-screen television in what has become a commonplace of modern newscasting: someone on television communicating via another television, standing in front of the television and controlling the screen by pinching it with his hands and zooming in and out in super-high definition. It all looks really cool.

While they wait for new information to surface, they debate whether this incident will help or hurt the governor's presidential chances. Help, they decide, as his name recognition is pretty low outside of a rabid conservative evangelical following who just loves what he did during his tenure as governor of Wyoming, where he banned abortion outright and required the Ten Commandments to be publicly spoken by children *and teachers* every morning before the Pledge of Allegiance and made English the official and only legal language of Wyoming and banned anyone not fluent in English from owning property. Also he permitted firearms in every state wildlife refuge. And he issued an executive order requiring state law to supersede federal law in all matters, a move that amounted to, according to constitutional scholars, a fiat secession of Wyoming from the United States. He wore cowboy boots. He held press conferences at his cattle ranch. He carried an actual live real gun, a revolver that dangled in a leather holster at his hip.

At the end of his one term as governor, he declared he was not running for reelection in order to focus on national priorities, and the media naturally took this to mean he was running for president. He perfected a sort of preacher-slash-cowboy pathos and an antielitist populism and found a receptive audience especially among blue-collar white conservatives put out by the current recession. He compared immigrants taking American jobs to coyotes killing livestock, and when he did this he pronounced *coyotes* pointedly with two syllables: *ky-oats*. He put an *r* sound in Washington so it became *Warshington*. He said *bushed* instead of *tired*. He said *yallow* for *yellow* and *crick* for *creek*.

Supporters said that's just how normal, nonelite people from Wyoming talked.

His detractors loved pointing out that since the courts had struck down almost all of his Wyoming initiatives, his legislative record was effectively nil. None of that seemed to matter to the people who continued to pay for his $500-a-plate fund-raisers (which, by the way, he called "grub-downs") and his $10,000 lecture fees and his $30 hardcover book, *The Heart of a True American,* loading up his "war chest," as the reporters liked to call it, for a "future presidential run, maybe."

And now the governor has been attacked, though nobody seems to know how he's been attacked, what he's been attacked with, who he's been attacked by, or if the attack has injured him. News anchors speculate at the potential damage of taking a ball bearing or marble at high velocity right in the eye. They talk about this for a good ten minutes, with charts showing how a small mass traveling at close to sixty miles per hour could penetrate the eye's liquid membrane. When this topic wears itself out, they break for commercials. They promote their upcoming documentary on the ten-year anniversary of 9/11: *Day of Terror, Decade of War.* They wait.

Then something happens to save the news from the state of idleness into which it has drifted: The anchor reappears and announces that a bystander caught the whole spectacular thing on video and has now posted it online.

And so here is the video that's going to be shown several thousand times on television over the next week, that will collect millions of hits and become the third-most-watched internet clip this month behind the new music video from teen pop singing sensation Molly Miller for her single "You Have Got to Represent," and a family video of a toddler laughing until he falls over. Here is what happens:

The video begins in whiteness and wind, the sound of wind blowing over an exposed microphone, then fingers fumbling over and pressing into the mic to create seashell-like swooshing sounds as the camera adjusts its aperture to the bright day and the whiteness resolves to a blue sky, indistinct unfocused greenishness that is presumably grass, and then a voice, a man's voice loud and too close to the mic: "Is it on? I don't know if it's on."

The picture comes into focus just as the man points the camera at his own feet. He says in an annoyed and exasperated way, "Is this even on? How can you tell?" And then a woman's voice, calmer, melodious, peaceful, says, "You look at the back. What does it say on the back?" And her husband or boyfriend or whoever he is, who cannot manage to keep the picture steady, says "Would you just help me?" in this aggressive and accusatory way that's meant to communicate that whatever problem he's having with the camera is her responsibility. The video through all this is a jumpy, dizzying close-up of the man's shoes. Puffy white high-tops. Extraordinarily white and new-looking. He seems to be standing on top of a picnic table. "What does it say on the back?" the woman asks.

"Where? What back?"

"On the screen."

"I know *that*," he says. "Where on the screen?"

"In the bottom right corner," she says with perfect equanimity. "What does it say?"

"It says *R*."

"That means it's recording. It's on."

"That's stupid," he says. "Why doesn't it say *On*?"

The picture bobs between his shoes and what seems to be a crowd of people in the middle distance.

"There he is! Lookit! That's him! There he is!" the man shouts. He points the camera forward and, when he finally manages to keep it from trembling, Sheldon Packer comes into view, about thirty yards away and surrounded by campaign staffers and security. There is a light crowd. People in the foreground becoming suddenly aware that something's happening, that someone famous is nearby. The cameraman is now yelling: "Governor! Governor! Governor! Governor! Governor! Governor! Governor!" The picture begins shaking again, presumably from this guy waving or jumping or both.

"How do you make this thing zoom?" he says.

"You press Zoom," says the woman. Then the picture begins to zoom, which causes even more focus- and exposure-related problems. In fact, the only reason any of this footage is at all usable on television is because the man eventually hands the camera to his partner, saying, "Here, would you just take this?" He rushes over to shake the governor's hand.

Later all of this blather will be edited out, so the clip that will be repeated hundreds of times on television will begin here, paused, as the news puts a small red circle around a woman sitting on a park bench on the right side of the screen. "This appears to be the perpetrator," the anchor says. She's white-haired, probably sixty, sitting there reading a book, in no way unusual, like an extra in a movie, filling out the frame. She's wearing a light blue shirt over a tank top, black leggings that look elastic and yoga-inspired. Her short hair is tousled and falls in little spikes over her forehead. She seems to have an athletic compactness to her—thin but also muscular. She notices what's happening around her. She sees the governor approaching and closes her book and stands and watches. She's on the edge of the frame seemingly trying to decide what to do. Her hands are on her hips. She's biting the inside of her mouth. It looks like she's weighing her options. The question this pose seems to ask is: *Should I?*

Then she starts walking, quickly, toward the governor. She has discarded her book on the bench and she's walking, taking these large strides like suburbanites doing laps around the mall. Except her arms stay steady at her sides, her fists in balls. She gets close enough to the governor that she's within throwing range and, at that moment, fortuitously, the crowd parts, so from the vantage point of our videographer there's a clear line of sight from this woman to the governor. The woman stands on a gravel path and looks down and bends at her knees and scoops up a handful of rocks. Thus armed, she yells—and this is very clear, as the wind dies down exactly at this moment and the crowd seems to hush, almost as if everyone knows this event is going to happen and so they all do what they can to successfully capture it—she yells, "You pig!" And then she throws the rocks.

At first there's just confusion as people turn to see where the yelling is coming from, or they wince and flinch away as they are struck by the stones. And then the woman scoops another handful of rocks and throws, and scoops and throws and scoops and throws, like a child in an all-out snowball war. The small crowd ducks for cover and mothers protect their children's faces and the governor doubles over, his hand covering his right eye. And the woman keeps throwing rocks until the governor's security guards reach her and tackle her. Or not really *tackle* but rather embrace her and slump to the ground, like exhausted wrestlers.

And that's it. The whole video lasts less than a minute. After the broadcast, certain facts become available in short order. The woman's name is released: Faye Andresen-Anderson, which everyone on the news mistakenly pronounces as "Anderson-Anderson," making parallels to other infamous double names, notably Sirhan Sirhan. It is quickly discovered that she is a teaching assistant at a local elementary school, which gives ammunition to certain pundits who say it shows how the radical liberal agenda has taken over public education. The headline is updated to TEACHER ATTACKS GOV. PACKER! for about an hour until someone manages to find an image that allegedly shows the woman attending a protest in 1968. In the photo, she sits in a field with thousands of others, a great indistinct mass of people, many of them holding homemade banners or signs, one of them waving high an American flag. The woman looks at the photographer drowsily from behind her big round eyeglasses. She leans to her right like she might be resting against someone who's barely out of frame—all that's visible is a shoulder. To her left, a woman with long hair and an army jacket stares menacingly at the camera over silver aviator shades.

The headline changes to SIXTIES RADICAL ATTACKS GOV. PACKER!

And as if the story isn't delicious enough already, two things happen near the end of the workday to vault it into the stratosphere, water-cooler-wise. First, it's reported that Governor Packer is having emergency surgery on his eyeball. And second, a mug shot is unearthed that shows the woman was arrested in 1968—though never officially charged or convicted—for *prostitution*.

This is just too much. How can one headline possibly gather all these amazing details? RADICAL HIPPIE PROSTITUTE TEACHER BLINDS GOV. PACKER IN VICIOUS ATTACK!

The news plays over and over the part of the video where the governor is struck. They enlarge it so it's all pixelated and grainy in a valiant effort to show everyone the exact moment that a sharp piece of gravel splashes into his right cornea. Pundits argue about the meaning of the attack and whether it represents a threat to democracy. Some call the woman a terrorist, others say it shows how far our political discourse has fallen, others say the governor pretty much asked for it by being such a reckless crusader for guns. Comparisons are made with the Weather Underground and the Black Panthers. The NRA releases a statement saying the attack never would have happened had Governor Packer been carrying his revolver.

The people working at their desks behind the TV anchor, meanwhile, do not appear at this moment to be working any harder or less hard than they were earlier in the day.

It takes about forty-five minutes for a clever copywriter to come up with the phrase "Packer Attacker," which is promptly adopted by all the networks and incorporated into the special logos they make for the coverage.

The woman herself is being kept in a downtown jail awaiting arraignment and is unavailable for comment. Without her explanation, the narrative of the day forms when opinion and assumption combine with a few facts to create an ur-story that hardens in people's minds: The woman is a former hippie and current liberal radical who hates the governor so much that she waited in a premeditated way to viciously attack him.

Except there's a glaring logical hole in this theory, which is that the governor's jaunt through the park was an impromptu move that not even his security detail knew about. Thus the woman couldn't have known he was coming and so couldn't have been waiting in ambush. However, this inconsistency is lost in the more sensational news items and is never fully investigated.

2

PROFESSOR SAMUEL ANDERSON SITS in the darkness of his small university office, his face lit grayly by the glow of a computer screen. Blinds are drawn over the windows. A towel blocks the crack under the door. He has placed the trash bin out in the hall so the night janitor won't interrupt. He wears headphones so nobody will hear what he's doing.

He logs on. He reaches the game's intro screen with its familiar image of orcs and elves torqued in battle. He hears the brass-heavy music, triumphant and bold and warlike. He types a password even more involved and intricate than the password to his bank account. And as he enters the *World of Elfscape,* he enters not as Samuel Anderson the assistant professor of English but rather as Dodger the Elven Thief, and the feeling he has is very much like the feeling of coming home. Coming home at the end of a long day to someone who's glad you're back, is the feeling that keeps him logging on and playing upward of forty hours a week in preparation for a raid like this, when he gathers with his anonymous online friends and together they go kill something big and deadly.

Tonight it's a dragon.

They log on from basements, offices, dimly lit dens, cubicles and workstations, from public libraries, dorm rooms, spare bedrooms, from laptops on kitchen tables, from computers that whir hotly and click and crackle like somewhere inside their plastic towers a food item is frying. They put on their headsets and log on and materialize in the game world and they are together again, just as they have been every Wednesday and Friday and Saturday night for the past few years. Almost all of them live in Chicago or very close to Chicago. The game server on which they're playing—one of thousands worldwide—is located in a former meatpacking warehouse on Chicago's South Side, and for lag- and latency-related issues, *Elfscape* always places you in the server nearest your location. So they are all practically neighbors, though they have never met in real life.

"Yo, Dodger!" someone says as Samuel logs on.

Yo, he writes back. He never talks here. They think he doesn't talk because he doesn't have a microphone. The truth is he does have a microphone, but he's worried that if he talks during these raids some wandering colleague out in the hall might hear him saying things about dragons. So the guild knows really nothing about him except that he never misses a raid and has the tendency to spell out words rather than use the accepted internet abbreviations. He will actually write "be right back" instead of the more common "brb." He will write "away from keyboard" rather than "afk." People are not sure why he insists on this reverse anachronism. They think the name Dodger has something to do with baseball, but in fact it is a Dickens reference. That nobody gets the reference makes Samuel feel smart and superior, which is something he needs to feel to offset the shame of spending so much time playing a game also played by twelve-year-olds.

Samuel tries to remind himself that millions of other people do this. On every continent. Twenty-four hours a day. At any given moment, the number of people playing *World of Elfscape* is a population about the size of Paris, he thinks, sometimes, when he feels that rip inside him because this is where his life has ended up.

One reason he never tells anybody in the real world that he plays *Elfscape* is that they might ask what the point of the game is. And what could he say? *To slay dragons and kill orcs.*

Or you can play the game as an orc, in which case the point is to slay dragons and kill elves.

But that's it, that's the tableau, the fundamental premise, this basic yin and yang.

He began as a level-one elf and worked his way up to a level-ninety elf and this took roughly ten months. Along the way, he had adventures. He traveled continents. He met people. He found treasure. He completed quests. Then, at level ninety, he found a guild and teamed up with his new guild mates to kill dragons and demons and most especially orcs. He's killed so many orcs. And when he stabs an orc in one of the vital places, in the neck or head or heart, the game flashes *CRITICAL HIT!* and there's a little noise that goes off, a little orcish cry of terror. He's come to love that noise. He drools over that noise. His character class is thief, which means his special abilities include pickpocketing and bomb-making and invisibility, and one of his favorite things is to sneak into orc-heavy territory and plant dynamite on the road for orcs to ride over and get killed by. Then he loots the bodies of his enemies and collects their weapons and money and clothes and leaves them naked and defeated and dead.

Why this has become so compelling he isn't really sure.

Tonight it's twenty elves armed and armored against this one dragon because it is a very large dragon. With razor-sharp teeth. Plus it breathes fire. Plus it's covered in scales the thickness of sheet metal, which is something they can see if their graphics card is good enough. The dragon appears to be asleep. It is curled catlike on the floor of its magma-rich lair, which is set inside a hollowed-out volcano, naturally. The ceiling of the lair is high enough to allow for sustained dragon flight because during the battle's second phase the dragon will launch into the air and circle them from above and shoot fiery bombs onto their heads. This will be the fourth time they've tried to kill this dragon; they have never made it past phase two. They want to kill it because the dragon guards a heap of treasure and weapons and armor at the far end of the lair, the looting of which will be sweet vis-à-vis their war against the orcs. Veins of bright-red magma glow just under the ground's rocky surface. They will break open during the third and final phase of the fight, a phase they have not yet seen because they just cannot get the hang of the fireball-dodging thing.

"Did you all watch the videos I sent?" asks their raid leader, an elf warrior named Pwnage. Several players' avatars nod their heads. He had e-mailed them tutorials showing how to defeat this dragon. What Pwnage wanted them to pay attention to was how to manage phase two, the secret to which seems to be to keep moving and avoid getting bunched up.

LETS GO!!! writes Axman, whose avatar is currently dry-humping a rock wall. Several elves dance in place while Pwnage explains the fight to them, again.

Samuel plays *Elfscape* from his office computer because of the faster internet connection, which can increase his damage output in a raid like this by up to two percent, usually, unless there's some bandwidth-traffic problems, like when students are registering for classes. He teaches literature at a small university northwest of Chicago, in a suburb where all the great freeways split apart and end at giant department stores and corporate office parks and three-lane roads clogged with vehicles driven by the parents who send their children to Samuel's school.

Children like Laura Pottsdam—blond, lightly freckled, dressed sloppily in logoed tank tops and sweatshorts with various words written across the butt, majoring in business marketing and communication, and who, this very day, showed up to Samuel's Introduction to Literature course, handed in a plagiarized paper, and promptly asked if she could leave.

"If we're having a quiz," she said, "I won't leave. But if we're not having a quiz, I really need to leave."

"Is there an emergency?" Samuel said.

"No. It's just that I don't want to miss any points. Are we doing anything today worth points?"

"We're discussing the reading. It's information you'll probably want to know."

"But is it worth *points*?"

"No, I suppose not."

"Then, okay, I really have to leave."

They were reading *Hamlet,* and Samuel knew from experience that today would be a struggle. The students would be spent, worn down by all that language. The paper he had assigned was about identifying logical fallacies in Hamlet's thinking, which even Samuel had to admit was sort of a bullshit exercise. They would ask why they had to do this, read this old play. They would ask, *When are we ever going to need to know about this in real life?*

He was not looking forward to this class.

What Samuel thinks about in these moments is how he used to be a pretty big deal. When he was twenty-four years old a magazine published one of his stories. And not just any magazine, but *the* magazine. They did a special on young writers. "Five Under Twenty-Five," they called it. "The next generation of great American authors." And he was one of them. It was the first thing he ever published. It was the only thing he ever published, as it turned out. There was his picture, and his bio, and his great literature. He had about fifty calls the next day from big-shot book people. They wanted more work. He didn't have more work. They didn't care. He signed a contract and was paid a lot of money for a book he hadn't even written yet. This was ten years ago, back before America's current financial bleakness, before the crises in housing and banking left the world economy pretty much shattered. It sometimes occurs to Samuel that his career has followed roughly the same trajectory as global finance: The good times of summer 2001 seem now, in hindsight, like a pleasant and whimsical daydream.

LETS GOOOOOOOO!!! Axman writes again. He has stopped humping the cave wall and is now leaping in place. Samuel thinks: ninth grade, tragically pimpled, hyperactivity disorder, will probably someday end up in my Intro to Lit class.

"What did you think about *Hamlet*?" Samuel had asked his class today, after Laura's departure.

Groans. Scowls. Guy in the back held his hands aloft to show his two big meat-hook thumbs pointing down. "It was stupid," he said.

"It didn't make any sense," said another.

"It was too long," said another.

"*Way* too long."

Samuel asked his students questions he hoped would spark any kind of conversation: Do you think the ghost is real or do you think Hamlet is hallucinating? Why do you think Gertrude remarried so quickly? Do you think Claudius is a villain or is Hamlet just bitter? And so on. Nothing. No reaction. They stared blankly into their laps, or at their computers. They always stare at their computers. Samuel has no power over the computers, cannot turn them off. Every classroom is equipped with computers at every single seat, something the school brags about in all the marketing materials sent to parents: *Wired campus! Preparing students for the twenty-first century!* But it seems to Samuel that all the school is preparing them for is to sit quietly and fake that they're working. To feign the appearance of concentration when in fact they're checking sports scores or e-mail or watching videos or spacing out. And come to think of it, maybe this is the most important lesson the school could teach them about the American workplace: how to sit calmly at your desk and surf the internet and not go insane.

"How many of you read the whole play?" Samuel said, and of the twenty-five people in the room, only four raised their hands. And they raised their hands slowly, shyly, embarrassed at having completed the assigned task. The rest seemed to reproach him—their looks of contempt, their bodies slumped to announce their huge boredom. It was like they blamed *him* for their apathy. If only he hadn't assigned something so stupid, they wouldn't have had to not do it.

"Pulling," says Pwnage, who now sprints toward the dragon, giant ax in hand. The rest of the raid group follows, crying wildly in a proximate imitation of movies they've seen about medieval wars.

Pwnage, it should be noted, is an *Elfscape* genius. He is a video-game savant. Of the twenty elves here tonight, six are being controlled by him. He has a whole village of characters that he can choose from, mixing and matching them depending on the fight, a whole self-sustaining micro-economy between them, playing many of them simultaneously using an incredibly advanced technique called "multiboxing" that involves several networked computers linked to a central command brain that he controls using programmed maneuvers on his keyboard and fifteen-button gaming mouse. Pwnage knows everything there is to know about the game. He's internalized the secrets of *Elfscape* like a tree that eventually becomes one with the fence it grows next to. He annihilates orcs, often delivering the killing blow to his signature phrase: *I just pwned ur face n00b!!!*

During phase one of the fight they mostly have to watch out for the dragon's tail, which whips around and slams onto the rock floor. So everyone hacks away at the dragon and avoids its tail for the few minutes it takes to get the dragon down to sixty percent health, which is when the dragon takes to the air.

"Phase two," says Pwnage in a calm voice made robot-sounding from being transmitted over the internet. "Fire incoming. Don't stand in the bad."

Fireballs begin pummeling the raid group, and while many players find it a challenge to avoid the fire while continuing their dragon-fighting responsibilities, Pwnage's characters manage this effortlessly, all six of them, moving a couple of taps to their left or right so that the fire misses them by a few pixels.

Samuel is trying to dodge the fire, but mostly what he's thinking about right now is the pop quiz he gave in class today. After Laura left, and after it became clear the class had not done the assigned reading, he got into a punishing mood. He told his students to write a 250-word explication of the first act of *Hamlet*. They groaned. He hadn't planned on giving a pop quiz, but something about Laura's attitude left him feeling passive-aggressive. This was an Introduction to Literature course, but she cared less about literature than she did about *points*. It wasn't the topic of the course that mattered to her; what mattered was the currency. It reminded him of some Wall Street trader who might buy coffee futures one day and mortgage-backed securities the next. The thing that's traded is less important than how it's measured. Laura thought like this, thought only about the bottom line, her grade, the only thing that mattered.

Samuel used to mark up their papers—with a red pen even. He used to teach them the difference between "lay" and "lie," or when to use "that" and when to use "which," or how "affect" is different from "effect," how "then" is different from "than." All that stuff. But then one day he was filling up his car at the gas station just outside campus—it's called the EZ-Kum-In-'n-Go—and he looked at that sign and thought, *What is the point?*

Really, honestly, why would they ever need to know *Hamlet*?

He gave a quiz and ended class thirty minutes early. He was tired. He was standing in front of that disinterested crowd and he began to feel like Hamlet in the first soliloquy: insubstantial. He wanted to disappear. He wanted his flesh to melt into a dew. This was happening a lot lately: He was feeling smaller than his body, as if his spirit had shrunk, always giving up his armrests on airplanes, always the one to move out of the way on sidewalks.

That this feeling coincided with his most recent search for internet photos of Bethany—well, that was too obvious to ignore. His thoughts always turn to her when he's doing something he feels guilty about, which, these days, is just about all the time, his whole life being sort of barnacled by these layers of impenetrable guilt. Bethany—his greatest love, his greatest screwup—who's still living in New York City, as far as he knows. A violinist playing all the great venues, recording solo albums, doing world tours. Googling her is like opening this great spigot inside him. He doesn't know why he punishes himself like that, once every few months, looking at pictures late into the night of Bethany being beautiful in evening gowns holding her violin and big bunches of roses and surrounded by adoring fans in Paris, Melbourne, Moscow, London.

What would she think about this? She would be disappointed, of course. She would think Samuel hasn't grown up at all—still a boy playing video games in the dark. Still the kid he was when they first met. Samuel thinks about Bethany the way other people maybe think about God. As in: *How is God judging me?* Samuel has the same impulse, though he's replaced God with this other great absence: Bethany. And sometimes, if he thinks about this too much, he can fall down a kind of hole and it's like he's experiencing his life at a one-step remove, as if he's not leading his life but rather assessing and appraising a life that weirdly, unfortunately, happens to be his.

The cursing from his guild mates brings him back to the game. Elves are dying rapidly. The dragon roars from above as the raid unloads all its best long-range violence—arrows and musket balls and throwing knives and electrical lightning-looking things that emerge from the bare hands of the wizards.

"Fire coming at you, Dodger," says Pwnage, and Samuel realizes he's about to be crushed. He dives out of the way. The fireball lands near him. His health bar empties almost to zero.

Thanks, Samuel writes.

And cheers now as the dragon lands and phase three begins. There remain only a few attackers of the original twenty: There's Samuel and Axman and the raid's healer and four of Pwnage's six characters. They have never reached phase three before. This is the best they've done against this dragon.

Phase three is pretty much like phase one except now the dragon is moving all around and opening up magma veins under the floor and shaking loose huge deadly stalactites from the cave's ceiling. Most *Elfscape* boss fights end this way. They are not so much tests of skill as of pattern memorization and multitasking: Can you avoid the lava splashing up from the floor and dodge the rocks falling from above and watch the dragon's tail so that you're not in the way of it and follow the dragon around its lair to keep hitting it with your dagger using the very specific and complicated ten-move attack that achieves the maximum damage output per second necessary to bring the dragon's health bar to zero before its internal ten-minute timer goes off and it does something called "enrages" when it goes all crazy and kills everyone in the room?

In the throes of it, Samuel usually finds this exhilarating. But immediately after, even if they win the fight, he always feels this crashing disappointment because all the treasure they've won is fake treasure, just digital data, and all the weapons and armor they've looted will help them only so long, because as soon as people start beating this dragon the developers will introduce some new creature who's even more difficult to kill and who's guarding even better treasure—a cycle that endlessly repeats.

There is no way to ever really win. There is no end in sight. And sometimes the pointlessness of the game seems to reveal itself all at once, such as right now, as he watches the healer try to keep Pwnage alive and the dragon's health bar is slowly creeping toward zero and Pwnage is yelling "Go go go go!" and they are right on the verge of an epic win, even now Samuel thinks the only things really happening here are a few lonely people tapping keyboards in the dark, sending electrical signals to a Chicagoland computer server, which sends them back little puffs of data. Everything else—the dragon and its lair and the coursing magma and the elves and their swords and their magic—is all window dressing, all a façade.

Why am I here? he wonders, even as he is crushed by the dragon's tail and Axman is impaled by a falling stalactite and the healer burns to ash in a lava crevice and so the only elf remaining is Pwnage and the only way they're going to win is if Pwnage can stay alive, and the guild cheers through their headsets and the dragon's health ticks down to four percent, three percent, two percent . . .

Samuel wonders, even now, so close to victory, *What is the point?*

What am I doing?

What would Bethany think?

3

THE DANCE PWNAGE DOES in his living room looks like a conglomeration of things football players do in end zones after touchdowns. He is fond of this one maneuver where he moves his fists in a wheel in front of him—"churning the butter" is what he thinks this is called.

"Pwnage rules!" somebody shouts. The elves would be giving him a standing ovation if they weren't all corpses. Their approval roars out of the speakers of his home-theater array. All six of his computer screens now show different angles of a dead dragon.

He churns the butter.

He does that fist-pump thing that looks like he's starting a lawn mower.

Also, that obscene dance where it's like he's spanking something directly in front of him, presumably ass.

The elves' ghosts make their way back to their bodies and one by one his friends pop up from the cave floor, resurrected in that special video-game way where you die but you never really *Die*. Pwnage collects the loot at the far end of the cave and hands it out to his guildies—swords and axes and plate armor and magic rings. It makes him feel benevolent and bighearted, like a man on Christmas Day dressed as Santa.

Then the others begin logging off, and he says goodbye individually to each of his guildies and congratulates them on their excellent performances and tries to convince them to stay online longer and they complain that it's too late at night and they have to work in the morning and so he agrees, finally, that it's time to go to sleep. And he logs out and shuts down all his computers and slips into bed and closes his eyes, and that's when his mind starts in with the Sparkles, those hallucinatory blips of elves and orcs and dragons that cascade unstoppably through his head as he tries to rest after another of his *Elfscape* benders.

He hadn't intended to play the game today. He certainly hadn't intended to play as long as he did. Today was supposed to be the first day of his new diet. Today was the day he had vowed to start eating better—fruits and vegetables and lean proteins and no trans fats and nothing processed and reasonable portions and carefully balanced meals of huge nutritional abundance, beginning today. And he launched his brand-new eating-better lifestyle that very morning by cracking open a Brazil nut and chewing it and swallowing it because Brazil nuts were one of the "Top Five Foods You're Not Eating Enough Of" according to the diet book he bought in preparation for today, along with the diet book's sequel books and the diet's associated meal plans and mobile-device apps, all of which advocated a cuisine made up largely of animal proteins and nuts—basically hunter-gatherer. And he thought about all the heart-healthy good fats and antioxidants and metanutrients inside the Brazil nut pouring through his own body doing helpful things like zapping free radicals and lowering his cholesterol and hopefully strengthening his energy levels because *there was so much to do.*

The kitchen urgently needed renovation: The countertop laminate was cracking and curling at the edges, and the dishwasher stopped working last spring, and the garbage disposal died maybe a year ago, and three of the four burners on the stove were useless, and the refrigerator had lately gone insane—the fridge side shutting down unpredictably and spoiling hot dogs and lunch meats and souring milk while the freezer side occasionally went hyperactive and locked all his TV dinners in perma-frost. Also the kitchen cabinets needed to be cleared of various plastic collections of Tupperware gone yellow with age, and the forgotten bags of dried fruit or nuts or potato chips, and the many small, cylindrical containers of herbs and spices arranged in geologic layers formed by his previous attempts to start new diets, each attempt requiring the purchase of whole new sets of herbs and spices because in the time elapsed since the last serious attempt the old herbs and spices fused within their jars into single, unusable, dehydrated chunks.

And he knew he should open up all the cabinets and throw everything away and make sure there were no colonies of bacteria or bugs living in the farthest, darkest back corners, but he didn't really want to open the cabinets and check for bugs because he was afraid of what he might find, namely *bugs.* Because then he'd have to put up plastic and fumigate and clear space elsewhere to create a kind of "staging area" in which to pile the necessary parts (the new cabinetry and planks for the hardwood flooring and the new appliances and the various hammers, saws, boxes of nails, screws, PVC pipes, and other shit necessary for drastic kitchen reconstruction), though looking around the house he understood how difficult this was going to be: The living room, for example, had to be a no-construction-debris zone in case some evening in the future he found himself entertaining unexpected guests (meaning: Lisa) who would not find heaps of tools inviting or romantic; same with the bedroom, also a bad staging-area choice for exactly the same reason, though admittedly it had been quite a while since Lisa had come over, mostly because she insisted they maintain their "distance" during this new phase of their relationship, an edict that did not stop her from asking for rides to work and to various mini-malls to complete various errands, and just because Lisa had divorced him didn't mean he would let her hang high and dry without a driver's license and a car, and while he knew most guys would do exactly that, he was just *raised differently*.

So the only viable staging area for kitchen detritus would be the spare bedroom, unfortunately also impossible because the bedroom was already overflowing with things the throwing away of which was unthinkable— the boxes of high-school awards, badges, trophies, medals, achievement certificates, and somewhere in there that black leather journal that contained the first several pages of a novel he promised himself he'd get around to writing very soon—and so he had to go through those boxes and catalog their contents before he could create the proper staging area necessary for the kitchen renovation that was required if he was going to start his brand-new diet.

Plus there was the matter of budget. As in, how to afford a totally new healthy diet plan when already he was falling into profound debt paying for his many accounts to *World of Elfscape* and his new smartphone. And yes from an outside perspective he could see how the purchase of a $400 smartphone and concomitant unlimited text and data plan might have seemed exorbitant for someone whose livelihood did not depend on the accessibility of electronic communication, and in fact the overwhelming majority of text messages sent to his smartphone after its purchase were from the maker of the smartphone itself—asking him whether he was satisfied with his purchase and offering him insurance plans and encouraging him to try the company's other software and hardware products—with the few other text messages coming from Lisa saying that she was unexpectedly needed at the Lancôme counter or was leaving the Lancôme counter early or was staying late at the Lancôme counter or didn't need a ride because she'd been invited "out" by "someone at work," and these were the texts that made him shudder with jealousy at their infuriating ambiguity and he curled up on the couch and chewed his brittle fingernails and wondered at the boundaries of Lisa's fidelity. And while of course he could no longer expect hegemonic marital monogamy, and while he could acknowledge the divorce created a certain *finality* to their relationship, he also knew that she did not leave him *for another man,* and he was still a major fact in her life, and so a part of him thought that if he was useful enough to Lisa and helpful enough and present enough that she would never actually "leave him" leave him, hence the need for the smartphone.

Also the essential diet- and exercise-related apps available on the phone were indispensable in any new eating-right program, apps where he could record each day's food and drink intake and receive an analysis of how he was doing both calorically and nutritionally. For example, he recorded what he ate in a normal day to set a kind of "baseline" by which his future excellent eating-right diet could be accurately compared, and found that his three espressos for breakfast (with sugar) registered at 100 calories, his six-shot latte and brownie for lunch was another 400 calories, leaving him 1,500 calories shy of his 2,000-calorie daily ceiling, meaning that for dinner he likely had room for two and maybe even three frozen packages of Ocean Bonanza Salmon Fajitas, each kit containing precisely cut french-fry-looking fajita vegetables and a packet of salty red stuff called Southwestern Spices to which he usually added another tablespoon or so of salt (the smartphone diet app registering this as *zero calories,* which he considered a huge flavor victory), and he ate these frozen salmon meals rather quickly and intensely while trying to ignore that the microwave cooked things so unevenly the green peppers could literally burn his tongue while the insides of some of the larger salmon lumps were still so cold they crumbled apart with a texture of something like damp tree bark, all of which made for an incredibly unpleasant mouthfeel but did not prevent him from stuffing his freezer full of salmon fajita kits, not only because the boxes said they were *Surprisingly Low-Fat!* but also because the 7-Eleven was having a consistent and amazing ten-for-five-dollars clearance deal on them (limit ten).

Anyway, the smartphone app analyzed the nutrients and metanutrients he consumed and compared them to FDA-recommended dosages of all the important vitamins, acids, fats, etc., and displayed the results in a graph that should have been a soothing green if he were doing it all correctly but was actually a panic-button red due to his alarming lack of really anything necessary for the maintenance of basic organ health. And yes he had to admit that lately his eyeballs and the ends of his hair had acquired a disconcerting yellowish hue, and his fingernails had become thinner and more brittle and had a tendency, when chewed, to suddenly split right down the middle almost all the way to the base, and recently his nails and hair had stopped growing completely and now seemed to recede in places or even curl back on themselves, and also he'd developed a more or less permanent rash on his arm at the place a wristwatch would go. So while he was typically far under his 2,000-calorie daily maximum, he understood that the calories he needed to consume in order to "eat better" were totally different kinds of calories, namely the organic fresh whole-food kind that were prohibitively expensive given the monthly credit card payments he was making on his smartphone and its associated text and data plans. And he grasped the paradox of this, that it was somewhat of an ironic bind that paying for the device that showed him how to eat right prevented him from having the money to actually be able to eat right, and yes he was putting all this on his credit card, the debt on which was painfully growing and his ability to pay it off fading away from him like a sort of continental drift. Ditto his mortgage payments, which also kept going up because a realtor had convinced him, years ago, before the town (and the nation's real estate market in general) went to total shit, to refinance his house using some "negative amortization" instrument. This was a huge financial windfall at the time and allowed the purchase of an HD television and various elaborate video-game consoles and an expensive at-home computer workstation, but now was a huge financial drain as the mortgage payments kept jumping shockingly higher while his home's value had, at last check, crashed and flatlined at such a confoundingly low number it was as if the house had suffered a catastrophic interior meth-lab explosion.

And this made him feel stressed, this coupled with all the other financial and budgetary problems, so stressed out that his heart was doing funny things, a kind of jumpy-twitchy thing that felt like someone mechanically palpating his thoracic cavity from the inside. And like Lisa said, "You don't have anything if you don't have your health," which was how he justified his investment in things that helped reduce the stress, namely high-end electronics and video games.

Which was where he turned today. Before completing the chores required of his new diet, he decided he would finish his *other* chores, the ones waiting for him in *Elfscape:* the twenty tasks he completed every day that earned him seriously cool game rewards (like flying rideable gryphons and axes of an unlikely size and neat-looking formal jackets and trousers that made his avatar look dapper when he walked around in them). These quests—which usually involved slaying some minor enemy or delivering a message across treacherous terrain or locating some lost important doodad—needed to be completed every day without fail for up to forty days in a row to unlock the rewards in the *fastest time mathematically possible,* which itself was a kind of reward because whenever he was successful at it these fireworks went off and there was this blast of trumpets and he got his name on the public chart of *Elfscape*'s Most Epic Players and everyone on his contact list sent him notes of congratulations and praise. It was like the game equivalent of being the groom at a wedding. And since Pwnage played with not just one character but enough characters to field a whole softball team it meant that as soon as he finished the twenty daily quests on his main character he then repeated them for his alternate characters as well, so that the number of daily quest completions required of him jumped to somewhere around two hundred, or more, depending on how many "alts" he was interested in leveling. This meant the whole daily-quest process took about five hours total—and while he knew that playing a video game for five hours straight represented the outside maximum tolerance most people had for playing video games, for him these five hours were simply the prerequisite to *actually playing the game,* a kind of warm-up for the real play session, something he needed to get out of the way before the fun could really begin.

So by the time he finished the daily quest grind today it was dark outside, and his mind felt so fuzzy and remote and sort of constipationally plugged up after five hours of rote tasks that he did not have the focus or drive or energy for difficult higher-order engagements, like shopping or cooking or a complicated kitchen renovation. So he stayed at his computer and recharged with a six-shot latte and a frozen burrito and kept on playing.

He played for so long that now, as he tries to sleep, he finds the Sparkles especially amped up, and there's no way sleep is going to come anytime soon, and so the only thing Pwnage can really do is get out of bed and fire up the computers once more and check the West Coast servers and go on another raid. Then he joins the Australian servers, hours later, and attacks the dragon again. Then by four a.m. the hard-core Japanese players come online, which is always a windfall, and he teams up with these guys and kills the dragon a couple more times, until killing the dragon no longer feels triumphant but rather routine and ordinary and maybe a little tedious. And around the time that India appears, the Sparkles have morphed into more of a fleeting mushy luminescence, and he abandons the game and he feels all hazy, like his forehead is physically three feet away from his face, and he decides he needs some decompression time before going to sleep, so he pops in one of the DVDs he's seen a million times (the thinking here is that he can let it play and zone out a bit, since he knows the film so well, not having to do any hard work brain-wise), one of his collection of apocalyptic disaster movies where the earth is destroyed in any number of ways—meteors, aliens, off-the-charts interior magma activity—and his mind begins to glaze over within the first fifteen minutes, at the point the protagonist figures out the secret the government's been keeping all this time and now knows there's some seriously heavy shit about to go down, Pwnage zones out and reflects on his day, remembers vaguely his eager and intense desire that very afternoon to start eating better, and maybe because he feels guilty that he did not, in fact, find it the right day to start eating better, he cracks open another Brazil nut, figuring maybe it's best to kind of ease into these things, that the Brazil nut is a bridge between his current life and the eating-better life that is ahead of him, and he spaces out and stares at the television with an empty fishlike quality in his eyes and swallows the thick Brazil nut bolus and watches as the earth is destroyed and he sort of happily imagines a rock the size of California falling into the earth and in a skeleton-melting flash wiping out everything, killing everyone, annihilating it all, and he rises from the couch, and it's almost dawn, and he wonders where the night went, and he stumbles into his bedroom and sees himself in the mirror—his white-yellow hair, his eyeballs red with fatigue and dehydration—and he gets into bed and he doesn't so much "fall asleep" as he plummets into a sudden allover concussive darkness. And the thing he tries to hold in his mind in this near-comatose state is the memory of himself dancing.

He wants to remember what that felt like: a moment of transcendent joy. He had defeated the dragon for the first time. His Chicago friends all cheered.

But now it won't come to him, the feeling that made him dance so exuberantly. Pwnage tries to imagine himself doing it, but it feels detached—it has the quality of something he saw on television, long ago. The way he feels now, it couldn't have been him churning the butter, starting the lawn mower, spanking that ass.

Tomorrow, he vows.

Tomorrow will be the first day of the new diet—the real, official first day. And maybe today was actually a warm-up or dry run or head start for the actual first day of the new diet, which would be very soon. One of these days very soon when he would wake up early and eat a healthy breakfast and get working on the kitchen and clean the cabinets and buy some groceries and avoid the computer and finally, for an entire day, do everything exactly, perfectly right.

He swears. He promises. One of these days will be the day that changes everything.

4

"YOU THINK I *cheated*?" says Laura Pottsdam, college sophomore and habitual, perpetual cheater. "You think I plagiarized that paper? Me?"

Samuel nods. He's trying to look sad about this whole situation, like when a parent has to punish a child. *This hurts me more than it hurts you,* is the expression he's trying to produce, even if he does not sincerely feel it. Inside, he secretly *likes* when he gets to fail a student. It's like revenge for having to teach them.

"Can I just say? Once and for all? I. Did. Not. Plagiarize. That. Paper," Laura Pottsdam says of the paper that was almost entirely plagiarized. Samuel knows this because of the software—the truly exceptional software package subscribed to by the university that analyzes every essay completed by his students and compares them to every other essay in its massive archive of every paper ever analyzed anywhere. The software's inner brain is made of literally millions of words written by the nation's high-school and college students, and Samuel sometimes jokes to his colleagues that if the software ever achieved sci-fi artificial intelligence and consciousness, it would immediately go to Cancún for spring break.

The software analyzed Laura's paper and found it to be ninety-nine percent plagiarized—everything had been stolen except for the name "Laura Pottsdam."

PLURIUM INTERROGATIONUM
(OR, "THE LOADED QUESTION")

"I wonder what is wrong with the software?" says Laura, second-year university student out of Schaumburg, Illinois, communications and marketing major, five foot two or three, dirty-blond hair that in the greenish gloom of Samuel's office looks a pale legal-pad yellow, thin white T-shirt featuring what seems to be promotional material for a party that happened almost certainly before she was born. "I wonder why it's malfunctioning. Is it wrong a lot?"

"You're saying it's a mistake?"

"It's like *so weird*. I don't get it. Why would it say that?"

Laura looks like she showered in a wind tunnel, her hair is so frazzled and disorganized. That she is wearing tiny frayed flannel shorts roughly the size of a coffee filter is impossible to ignore. Ditto her deeply bronze leg tan. On her feet, she's wearing slippers, Muppet-fuzzy, that yellow-green color of cabbage, with a gray-brown film of dirt around the footpads from being worn too often outdoors. It strikes Samuel that she might have come to his office today *literally wearing her pajamas*.

"The software isn't wrong," he says.

"You're saying *never*? It's *never* wrong? You're saying it's infallible and perfect?"

The walls of Samuel's office are dutifully decorated with his various diplomas, the shelves filled with books with long titles, the whole dark place affecting a generic professorialness. There's the leather chair in which Laura currently sits lightly kicking her slippered feet. *New Yorker* cartoons taped to the door. Little windowsill plant that he waters with a pint-size mister. Three-hole punch. Tabletop calendar. A coffee mug with Shakespeare on it. A set of nice pens. The whole tableau. A coatrack with emergency tweed jacket. He's sitting in his ergonomic chair. He's briefly happy about the correct usage of the word "infallible." The musty odor in his office might be Laura's sleep smell, or his own smell, still lingering after staying up late playing *Elfscape* last night.

"According to the software," he says, looking at the report on Laura's paper, "this essay came from the website FreeTermPapers.com."

"See? That's the thing! Never heard of it."

He's one of those young professors who still dresses in such a manner that his students might regard as "hip." Untucked shirts, blue jeans, a certain brand of fashionable sneaker. This is read by some people as proof of good taste, by others as a sign of internal weakness and insecurity and desperation. He also sometimes curses in class so he doesn't seem old and square. Laura's shorts are flannel with plaid bars of red, black, and navy blue. Her shirt is extraordinarily thin and faded, though it is difficult to tell whether this fade is from overuse or whether it was made in the factory to appear this way. She says, "Obviously I'm not gonna copy some stupid paper from the internet. It's like, *no way.*"

"So you're saying it's a coincidence."

"I don't know why it said that. It's so, you know, weird?"

Laura occasionally puts that upward phonic at the ends of her sentences so that even her declarations sound like questions. Samuel finds this, like most accents, difficult not to mimic. He also finds her ability to maintain eye contact and keep her body relaxed and unjittery throughout all this lying remarkable. She does not display any of the involuntary physical indications of deception: she breathes in a normal manner; her posture is relaxed and languid; her eyes remain fixed on Samuel's rather than doing that up-and-to-the-right thing that indicates she's accessing her more creative brain parts; and her face does not seem to be working unnaturally hard to show emotion, as emotions seem to flutter across her face in a well-timed and more or less natural and organic way rather than the usual liar's face where it looks like the cheek muscles are attempting to mechanically excrete the proper expression.

"According to the software," Samuel says, "the paper in question was also submitted three years ago to the Schaumburg Township High School." He pauses to allow this fact to land and sink in. "Isn't that your hometown? Isn't that where you're from?"

PETITIO PRINCIPII
(OR, "THE CIRCULAR ARGUMENT")

"You know," says Laura, shifting in her seat, moving one leg under her in what might be the first outward physical sign of distress. Her shorts are so small that when she moves around in the leather chair the skin of her lower buttocks squeaks against it or pulls off with a moist little sucking sound. "I wasn't going to say anything, but I feel really offended. By all this?"

"You do."

"Um, *yeeee-ahh*? You asking me if I cheated? It's really, like, rude?"

Laura's shirt, which Samuel thinks was indeed artificially faded using dyes or chemicals or perhaps UV light or harsh abrasives, says "Laguna Beach Party, Summer 1990" in bubbly vintage-looking letters with a graphic ocean scene in the middle and a rainbow.

"You shouldn't call somebody a cheater," she says. "It stigmatizes them. There's been studies? The more you call someone a cheater, the bigger amount of times they cheat."

The bigger *number* of times they cheat, Samuel wishes she would have said.

"Plus you shouldn't punish someone for cheating," Laura says, "because then they have to cheat more. To pass the class? It's like"—her finger draws a loop into the air—"a vicious circle?"

Laura Pottsdam consistently comes to class between three minutes early and two minutes late. Her seat of choice is in the far back-left corner. Various boys in the class have slowly shifted their own desk preferences to get closer to her orbit, creeping mollusk-like from the right side of the classroom to the left over the course of the semester. Most sit next to her for a span of two or three weeks before they suddenly shoot away to the opposite side of the room. They're like charged particles colliding and bouncing apart in what Samuel assumes is some psychosexual melodrama playing out extracurricularly.

"You never wrote this paper," says Samuel. "You bought it in high school and then used it again in my class. That's the only thing under discussion today."

Laura draws both her feet under her. Her leg releases from the shiny leather with a wet pop.

APPEAL TO PITY

"This is *so unfair*," she says. The way she so effortlessly and fluidly moved her legs is a sign of youthful flexibility or serious yoga training or both. "You asked for an essay on *Hamlet*. That's what I gave you."

"I asked you to *write* an essay on *Hamlet*."

"How was I supposed to know that? It's not my fault you have these weird rules."

"They're not my rules. Every school has these rules."

"They do not. I used this paper in high school and got an A."

"That's too bad."

"So I didn't know it was wrong. How was I supposed to know it was wrong? Nobody ever taught me it was wrong."

"Of course you knew it was wrong. You were lying about it. If you didn't think it was wrong, you wouldn't have lied."

"But I lie about *everything*. It's what I do. I can't help it."

"You should try to stop that."

"But I can't be punished twice for the same paper. If I was punished in high school for plagiarism, I can't be punished again now. Isn't that, like, double jeopardy?"

"I thought you said you got an A in high school."

"No I didn't."

"I'm pretty sure you did. I'm pretty sure you *just* said that."

"That was a hypothetical."

"No, I don't believe it was."

"I think I would know. *Duh.*"

"Are you lying again? Are you lying right now?"

"No."

They stare at each other for a moment like two poker players who are both bluffing. This is the most eye contact they've ever shared. In class, Laura almost always stares into her lap, where she hides her phone. She thinks if the phone is in her lap she has effectively concealed it. She has no idea how obvious and transparent this maneuver is. Samuel has not asked her to stop checking her phone in class, mostly so he can savage her grade at the end of the semester when he doles out "participation points."

"At any rate," he says, "double jeopardy doesn't work that way. The point here is that when you submit work, there's a basic assumption that it's your work. Your own."

"It *is* mine," she says.

"No, you bought it."

"I know," she says. "I own it. It's mine. It's *my work.*"

It strikes him that if he doesn't think of this as "cheating" but rather as "outsourcing" then she might have a valid point.

FALSE ANALOGY

"Plus other people do worse things than this," says Laura. "My best friend? She pays her algebra tutor to do her homework for her. I mean, that's *way* worse, right? And she doesn't even get punished! Why should I get punished and she doesn't?"

"She's not in my class," Samuel says.

"How about Larry then?"

"Who?"

"Larry Broxton? From our class? I know for a fact that everything he gives you was written by his older brother. You don't punish him. That's not fair. That's *way worse*."

Samuel recalls that Larry Broxton—sophomore, major undeclared, buzz-cut hair the color of cornmeal, usually in class wearing shiny silver oversize basketball shorts and a monochromatic T-shirt featuring the gigantic logo of a clothing chain found in roughly all of America's outlet malls—was among the boys who had crept toward and, later, bolted away from Laura Pottsdam. Larry fucking Broxton, skin as pale and sickly green as the inside of an old potato, pathetic attempts at a blond mustache and beard that looked more like his face was lightly crusted with panko bread crumbs, a kind of hunchiness and withdrawn, inward manner that for some reason reminded Samuel of a small fern that could only grow in the shade, Larry Broxton, who had never once spoken in class, whose feet had outpaced the rest of his body, growth-spurt-wise, and had resulted in a kind of floppy walk, as if his feet were two large and flat river fish, feet on which he wore these chunky black sandal things that Samuel was pretty sure were designed for use only in public showers and pools, this same Larry Broxton who during the ten minutes Samuel gave to each class for "freewriting and brainstorming" would idly and subconsciously and casually pick at his genitals, he could, almost every day, invariably, during their two-week sitting-together period, on the way out of class, make Laura Pottsdam laugh.

SLIPPERY SLOPE

"I'm just saying," continues Laura, "that if you fail me you'll have to fail everyone. Because everyone's doing it. And then you won't have no one left to teach."

"Anyone," he says.

"What?"

"You won't have *anyone* left to teach. Not *no one*."

Laura looks at him with an expression she might also give someone who's speaking to her in Latin.

"It's a double negative," he says. "*Won't* and *no one*."

"Whatever."

He knows it is a graceless and condescending thing to do, correcting someone's spoken grammar. Like being at a party and criticizing someone for not being well-read enough, which in fact had happened to Samuel his first week on the job, at a faculty get-to-know-you dinner at the home of his boss, the dean of the college, a woman who had been a member of the English Department before bolting for her current administrative gig. She had built her academic career the typical way: by knowing everything there was to know about an extraordinarily small field (her specific niche was literature written during the plague, about the plague). At dinner, she had asked his opinion on a certain section of *The Canterbury Tales,* and, when he demurred, said, a little too loudly, "You haven't read it? Oh, well, *goodness.*"

NON SEQUITUR

"Also?" Laura says. "I thought it was really unfair that you gave a quiz."

"What quiz?"

"The quiz you gave? Yesterday? On *Hamlet*? I asked you if there was going to be a quiz and you said no. Then you gave a quiz anyway."

"That's my prerogative."

"You *lied* to me," she says, affecting this injured and aggrieved tone that sounds inherited from thousands of television family dramas.

"I didn't lie," he says. "I changed my mind."

"You didn't tell me the truth."

"You shouldn't have skipped class."

What was it exactly about Larry Broxton that enraged him so much? Why the actual physical revulsion when he saw them sitting together and laughing together and walking home together? Part of it was that he found the boy worthless—his manner of dress, his casual ignorance, his prognathic face, his total wall of silence during classroom discussions, sitting there motionless, a lump of organic matter contributing nothing to the class or the world. Yes, these things angered him, and that anger was magnified at the knowledge that Laura would let this boy *do things to her*. Would let him touch her, would actually nuzzle up willingly to his tuberish skin, let his crusty lips press against hers, allow herself to be felt by him, his hands, his raggedly chewed fingernails that held little purplish globs of goo. That she might willingly remove his oversize basketball shorts back at his squalid dorm room that surely smelled of sweat and old pizza and body crust and urine, that she would allow all these things willingly and not suffer for them made Samuel suffer for her.

POST HOC, ERGO PROPTER HOC

"Just because I skipped class," says Laura, "doesn't mean I should fail. That's really unfair."

"That's not why you're failing."

"I mean, it's just one class. You don't have to go so, like, nuclear about it?"

What made Samuel suffer even more was the thought that what brought Laura and Larry together was likely a mutual dislike of him. That Samuel was the glue between them. That they both found him boring and tedious, and this was enough to make small talk on, enough to fill in the gaps between the heavy petting. It was, in a way, his fault. Samuel felt responsible for the sexual catastrophe that was ongoing in his class, back row, left side.

FALSE COMPROMISE

"I'll tell you what," says Laura, sitting up straight now and leaning toward him. "I can admit I was wrong about copying the paper, if you can admit you were wrong about giving the quiz."

"Okay."

"So as a compromise, I'll rewrite the paper, and you'll give me a makeup quiz. Everybody's happy." She lifts her hands, palms up, and smiles. "Voilà," she says.

"How is that a compromise?"

"I think we need to get beyond the conversation of 'did Laura cheat' and toward the conversation of 'how do we move forward.'"

"It's not a compromise if you get everything you want."

"But you get what you want too. I'll take full responsibility for my actions."

"How?"

"By saying it. Saying that"—and here she puts her fingers in the air to indicate quotation marks—*"I take full responsibility for my actions"*—end air quotes.

"You take responsibility for your actions by facing the consequences for them."

"You mean failing."

"I mean, yes, failing."

"That's so not fair! I shouldn't have to fail the class *and* take full responsibility for my actions. It should be one or the other. That's how it works. And you know what else?"

RED HERRING

"I don't even *need* this class. I shouldn't even be in this class. When am I ever going to need this in real life? When is anyone ever going to ask if I know *Hamlet*? When is that going to be essential information? Can you tell me that? Huh? Tell me, when am I ever going to need to know this?"

"That is not relevant."

"No, it's very relevant. It's like the most relevant thing *ever*. Because you can't do it. You can't tell me when I'm going to need this information. Because you want to know why? Because the answer is *I won't*."

Samuel knows this is probably true. Asking students to examine *Hamlet* in terms of logical fallacies seems pretty stupid. But ever since a certain provost came to power who is obsessed with teaching hard sciences and mathematics in *every class* (the reason being that we have to funnel our students into these disciplines to effectively compete with the Chinese, or something), Samuel has had to show on his annual reports how he promotes mathematics in his literature classes. Teaching logic is a gesture in this direction, and one that he now wishes he taught more thoroughly, as Laura has used, by his internal count, maybe ten logical fallacies in their conversation so far.

"Look," he says, "I didn't make you take the class. Nobody's forcing you to be here."

"Yes you are! You're all forcing me to be here reading dumb *Hamlet,* which I'm never going to need for the rest of my life!"

"You can drop the class whenever you like."

"No, I can't!"

"Why not?"

ARGUMENTUM VERBOSIUM

"I cannot fail this class because I need it to satisfy a humanities credit so I have room in my fall schedule to take statistics and micro so I can be ahead for the next summer when I'll need to get internship credit so I can still graduate in three and a half years, which I have to do because my parents' college fund won't cover four full years even though there used to be plenty of money in it but they had to use it for the divorce lawyer and they explained to me that 'everyone in the family has to make sacrifices in this difficult time' and mine would be either taking out a loan for my last semester in college or busting my butt to finish early and so if I have to repeat this class it'll screw up the whole plan. And my mom wasn't doing very good post-divorce anyway but now they've found a tumor? In her uterus? And they're operating next week to take it out? And I have to keep going home once a week to quote-unquote *be there for her* even though all we do is play Bunco with her stupid friends. And my grandmother who's all alone now after Grandpa died gets confused a lot about which medications to take on which days and it's my responsibility to take care of her and fill her weekly pill cases with the right drugs or she could go into a coma or something, and I don't know who's gonna take care of Gramma next week when I have to serve my three days of community service, which is so stupid because everyone else at that party drank just as much as I did and yet I was the one arrested for public intoxication and the next day I asked the cop on what grounds could he possibly arrest me for public intoxication and he said I was standing in the middle of the street yelling 'I am so drunk!' which I totally do not remember doing. And on top of all this my roommate's a total pig and a total slob and she keeps stealing my Diet Pepsi and not even paying me back or saying thank you and I'll look in the fridge and there's one more Diet Pepsi missing and she leaves her stuff everywhere and tries to give me advice about eating healthy even though she's like two hundred and fifty pounds but she thinks she's some diet genius because she used to be three hundred and fifty pounds and she's all like *Have you ever lost a hundred pounds?* and I'm like *I never needed to,* but she goes on and on about her triple-digit weight loss and how she totally changed her life since she began her weight-loss journey and blah blah blah weight-loss journey this and weight-loss journey that and she's so incredibly annoying about it and even has this giant weight-loss calendar on the wall so I can't even put up any of my posters but I can't say anything because I'm supposed to be like part of her support network? And it's like my job to ask her if she's hit her calorie burns for the day and congratulate her when she does and not tempt her by bringing in quote-unquote *self-destructive food* and I'm not sure why I'm the one who gets punished for what is in reality her problem but still I go along with it and I don't buy Doritos or Pop-Tarts or those individually wrapped Zebra Cakes even though I *love* them because I want to be a good supportive roommate and the only thing I allow myself and like my only pleasure *in life* is my Diet Pepsi, which technically she's not even supposed to have anyway because she says carbonated beverages were one of her food crutches before she began her weight-loss journey, but I say Diet Pepsi has like two calories so she can deal with it. And—oh, yeah—my dad was stabbed at a foam party last week. And even though he's doing fine now I'm finding it hard to concentrate on school because he was *stabbed* and also what the fuck was he doing at a foam party anyway, which is a question he completely refuses to answer and when I start asking about it he just tunes me out like I'm Mom. And my boyfriend went to college in Ohio and he constantly wants me to send him dirty pictures of me because he says it takes his mind off all the pretty girls out there so I'm afraid if I don't do it he'll sleep with some Ohio slut and it'll be my fault, so I take the pictures and I know he likes it if girls are shaved and I'm okay with doing that for him but I get all these little red bumps that are really itchy and ugly and one got infected and imagine having to explain to some ninety-year-old nurse at student health that you need an ointment because you cut yourself shaving your pubes. And besides all of this now I have a flat tire on my bike and one sink in our kitchenette is plugged up and my roommate's gross hair is always all over the shower and sticking to my lavender bar soap and my mom had to give away our beagle because she cannot deal with that level of responsibility right now and there's all these low-fat ham cubes in our refrigerator that are like three weeks old and starting to smell and my best friend had an abortion and my internet's broken."

APPEAL TO EMOTION

It goes without saying that Laura Pottsdam is now crying.

FALSE DILEMMA

"I'm gonna have to drop out of school!" Laura howls. Her words are coming out in a weeping monotone all smashed together. "If I get an F I'm going to lose my financial aid and won't be able to afford college and I'll have to drop out!"

The problem here is that whenever Samuel sees someone else crying, he needs to cry too. He's been this way as long as he can remember. He's like a baby in a nursery crying out of sympathy for the other babies. He feels like crying is such an exposed and vulnerable thing to do in front of other people that he's ashamed and embarrassed for the person doing it, and this triggers his own feelings of shame and embarrassment, all the layers of childhood self-loathing that accumulated while growing up as a huge crybaby. All the sessions with counselors, all the childhood mortifications, they come rushing back at Samuel when he sees someone crying. It's like his body becomes a big open wound that even a slight breeze would physically hurt.

Laura's crying is not restrained. She does not fight the crying but instead seems to wrap herself up in it. It is a full-on eye-and-nose-discharge cry accompanied by the typical sniffles and hiccupy breathing and facial contractions that tighten her cheeks and lips into a grotesque frown. Her eyes are red and her cheeks shining and wet and there's one small pellet of snot that has crawled terribly out of her left nostril. Her shoulders are hunched and she's slouching and looking at the floor. Samuel feels like he's about ten seconds away from doing the same thing. He cannot bear to see someone else crying. This is why the weddings of work colleagues or distant relatives are a disaster for him, because he weeps totally out of proportion to his closeness level with the bride and groom. Sad films at movie theaters present a similar problem, where even if he can't see people crying he can hear their little sniffles and blown noses and fitful breathing and can then extrapolate their particular kind of crying from his vast inner archive of crying episodes and sort of "try it on" for himself, a problem magnified if he happens to be on a date and is thus hyperalert and aware of his date's emotional tenor and mortified that she might lean in for some kind of crying comfort only to discover that he is weeping like ten times worse than she is.

"And I'll have to pay back all my scholarships!" Laura half shouts. "If I fail I'll have to pay them all back and my family will be broke and we'll be out in the streets and going hungry!"

Samuel senses this is a lie because scholarships don't really work that way, but he can't open his mouth because he's trying to stuff back his own crying. It's in his throat now and tightening around his Adam's apple and all of those devastating childhood weeping fits start rushing back at him now, the birthday parties he ruined, the family dinners stopped halfway through, the classrooms sitting in stunned silence watching him run out the door, the loud exasperated sighs from teachers and principals and most especially his mother—oh how his mother wanted him to stop crying, standing there trying to soothe him and rubbing his shoulders during one of his fits and saying "It's okay, it's all okay" in her gentlest voice, not understanding that it was exactly her attention to the crying and acknowledgment of the crying that made the crying worse. And he can feel it pushing up on his larynx now and so he's holding his breath and repeating in his head "I am in control, I am in control," and this is for the most part effective until his lungs start burning for oxygen and his eyes feel like pressed olives and so his two choices are either to burst out with a naked weeping sob right here in front of Laura Pottsdam—which is just unthinkably awful and embarrassing and exposed—or perform the laughing trick, which was taught to him by a junior-high counselor who said "The opposite of crying is laughing, so when you feel like crying try to laugh instead and they'll cancel each other out," a technique that sounded really stupid at the time but proved weirdly effective in last-ditch situations. It is, he knows, the only way to avoid a devastating blubber-fest right now. He's not really thinking about what it would mean to laugh at this moment, simply that anything else would be a million percent better than crying, and so when poor Laura—all hunched over and weeping and vulnerable and broken—says through her wet gurgles "I won't be able to come back to school next year and I won't have any money and no place to go and I don't know what I'll do with my life," Samuel's response is "Hah-hah-hah-hah-hah-hah-hah-hah-haaaaah!"

AD HOMINEM

This was, perhaps, a miscalculation.

He can see already the effect of his laugh registering on Laura's face, first as a ripple of amazement and surprise, but then quickly hardening into anger and maybe disgust. The way he laughed—so aggressively and insincerely, like a mad evil genius in an action movie—was, he could see now, cruel. Laura's posture has become rigid and on guard and erect, her face cold, any hint of her crying erased. It cannot be emphasized enough how quickly this happens. Samuel thinks of a phrase he's seen on bags of vegetables in the grocery store: *flash frozen.*

"Why did you do that?" she says, her voice now unnaturally calm and even. It is an eerie, barely contained composure with a dangerous edge, like a mob hit man.

"I'm sorry. I didn't mean to."

She studies his face for a painfully long moment. The snot pellet from her nose has disappeared. It's really a remarkable transformation, all evidence of her actually physically crying has vanished. Even her cheeks are dry.

"You *laughed* at me," she says.

"Yes," he says. "Yes I did."

"Why did you laugh at me?"

"I'm sorry," he says. "That was wrong. I shouldn't have."

"Why do you hate me so much?"

"I don't hate you. Really, Laura, I don't."

"Why does everyone hate me? What did I do?"

"Nothing. It's nothing. It's not your fault. Everyone likes you."

"They do not."

"You're very likable. Everyone likes you. I like you."

"You do? You like me?"

"Yes. Very much. I like you very much."

"You promise?"

"Of course I do. I'm sorry."

The good news is that Samuel no longer feels in danger of crying, and so his body relaxes and he gives Laura this feeble little smile and he feels so good that the whole situation has calmed down and seems to be at an emotionally even and neutral level now, and he has this feeling that the two of them have just navigated some seriously treacherous shit together, like war buddies or the stranger next to you on an airplane after going through really bad turbulence. He feels that camaraderie with Laura now, so he smiles and nods and maybe winks at her. He feels so free at this moment that he actually winks.

"Oh," says Laura. "Oh, I get it." And she crosses her legs and leans back in the leather chair. "You have a crush on me."

"I'm sorry?"

"I should have known. Of course."

"No. I think you've misunderstood—"

"It's okay. It's not like the first time a teacher's fallen in love with me. It's cute."

"No, really, you've got it wrong."

"You like me very much. That's what you just said."

"Yes, but I didn't mean it that way," he says.

"I know what comes next. Either I sleep with you or I fail. Right?"

"That is not *at all* right," he says.

"That was the plan from the beginning. This whole thing is just to get into my pants."

"No!" he says, and he feels the sting of this accusation, how when you're accused of something it makes you feel—even if you're innocent—a little bit guilty. He stands up and walks past Laura and opens his office door and says, "It's time for you to leave. We're done now."

STRAW MAN

"You know you can't fail me," says Laura, who is definitely not getting up to leave. "You can't fail me because it's the law."

"This meeting is over."

"You can't fail me because I have a learning disability."

"You do not have a learning disability."

"I do. I have trouble paying attention and keeping deadlines and reading and also I don't make friends."

"That's not true."

"It is true. You can check. It's documented."

"What is the name of your learning disability?"

"They don't have a name for it yet."

"That's convenient."

"You are required by the Americans with Disabilities Act to provide special accommodations to all students with documented learning disabilities."

"You do not have trouble making friends, Laura."

"I do. I don't make any friends."

"I see you with friends all the time."

"They are not lasting."

Samuel has to acknowledge this is true. He is right now trying to come up with something mean to say to her. Some insult that would equal in rhetorical weight her accusation that he has a crush on her. If he hurts Laura's feelings deep enough, if he insults her hard enough, he would be exonerated. It would prove that he does not have a crush on her if he says something really mean, is his logic.

"What accommodations," he says, "do you feel entitled to?"

"To pass the class."

"You think the Americans with Disabilities Act was written to protect cheaters?"

"To rewrite the paper then."

"What specific learning disability do you have?"

"I told you, they haven't named it yet."

"Who's 'they'?"

"Scientists."

"And they don't know what it is."

"Nope."

"And what are its symptoms?"

"Oh, they're really terrible. Every day is, like, a living hell?"

"Specifically, what are its symptoms?"

"Okay, well, I stop paying attention in most of my classes after like three minutes and I usually don't follow directions *at all* and I never take notes and I can't remember people's names and sometimes I'll read all the way to the end of a page and have no idea what I just read. I lose my place while reading all the time and skip like four lines and don't even know it, and most charts and graphs make absolutely no sense to me, and I'm terrible at puzzles, and sometimes I'll say one thing even though I totally mean something else. Oh, and my handwriting is really sloppy, and I've never been able to spell the word *aluminum,* and sometimes I tell my roommate that I will definitely clean my side of the room even though I have no intention of ever doing this. I have a hard time judging distance when I'm outside. I totally could not tell you where cardinal north is. I hear people say 'A bird in hand is worth two in the bush' and I have no idea what that means. I've lost my phone like eight times in the last year. I've been in ten car accidents. And whenever I play volleyball the ball sometimes hits me in the face even though I totally do not want it to."

"Laura," says Samuel, who senses his moment now, who feels the insult coalescing and bubbling up, "you do not have a learning disability."

"Yes, I do."

"No," he says, and he pauses dramatically, and he's sure to pronounce these next words slowly and carefully so that they're fully heard and comprehended: "You're just not very smart."

ARGUMENTUM AD BACULUM
(OR, "APPEALS TO THREATS")

"I can't believe you said that!" says Laura, who's now standing with her bag in hand ready to indignantly walk out of his office.

"It's true," says Samuel. "You're not very smart, and you're not a very good person either."

"You cannot say that!"

"You don't have a learning disability."

"I could get you fired for that!"

"You need to know this. Somebody needs to tell you."

"You are so rude!"

And now Samuel notices that the other professors have become aware of all the shouting. Down the corridor, doors are opening, heads are popping out. Three students sitting on the floor surrounded by book bags who might have been working on some group project are now staring at him. His shame-aversion instincts kick in and he does not feel at all as brave as he did a moment ago. When he talks now, his voice is about thirty decibels lower and a little mousey.

"I think it's time for you to go," he says.

ARGUMENTUM AD CRUMENAM
(OR, "APPEALS TO WEALTH")

Laura stomps out of his office and into the hallway, then pivots and yells at him: "I pay tuition here! I pay good money! I pay your salary and you can't treat me like this! My father gives lots of money to this school! Like more than you make in a year! He's a lawyer and he's going to sue you! You just took this to a whole nother level! *I am going to own you!*"

And with that she pivots again and stomps away and turns the corner and disappears.

Samuel closes his door. Sits down. Stares at his potted windowsill plant—a pleasant little gardenia that's presently looking droopy. He picks up the mister and squirts the plant a few times, the squirting making this slight honking noise like a small duck.

What is he thinking? He's thinking that he's likely going to cry now. And Laura Pottsdam will probably indeed get him fired. And there's still an odor in his office. And he's wasted his life. And oh how he hates that word *nother*.

5

"HELLO?"

"Hello! May I please speak with Mr. Samuel Andresen-Anderson please?"

"That's me."

"Professor Andresen-Anderson, sir. I'm glad I reached you. This is Simon Rogers—"

"Actually I go by Anderson."

"Sir?"

"Samuel Anderson. That's it. The whole hyphenated thing is kind of a mouthful."

"Of course, sir."

"Who is this?"

"As I was saying, sir, this is Simon Rogers from the law offices of Rogers and Rogers. We're in Washington, D.C. Maybe you've heard of us? We specialize in high-profile politically motivated crime. I'm calling on behalf of your mother."

"Excuse me?"

"High-profile crime usually of a righteous left-leaning nature, you understand. What I mean is, did you hear about those people who chained themselves to trees? They were our clients. Or for example certain actions taken against whaling ships and then broadcast on cable television—that, sir, would be something right in our strike zone. Or a run-in with a Republican officeholder that's seen by millions online, if you catch my drift. We defend political actors, provided the media coverage warrants it, of course."

"Did you say something about my mother?"

"Your mother, sir, yes. I am defending your mother against the state's action against her, having taken over the case, sir, from the Chicago Public Defender's Office, you see."

"The state's action?"

"I'll be representing her interests both in court and in the press at least until the fund runs out, which is something that maybe we should discuss in the future, sir, but not today, uncouth as it is to bring up money so early in our relationship."

"I don't understand. What fund? Why is she in the press? Did she ask you to call me?"

"Which of those questions, sir, would you like me to address first?"

"What is going on?"

"Well, sir, as you're aware, sir, your mother has been charged with assault and battery. And because of the, well, let's be frank, the overwhelming evidence against her, sir, she'll likely be pleading and taking a deal."

"My mother assaulted someone?"

"Oh, well, okay, let's back up. I assumed you'd already heard, sir."

"Heard what?"

"About your mother."

"How would I know anything about my mother?"

"It was on the news."

"I don't watch the news."

"It was on the local news, cable news, the national news, newspapers, wire services, and many of the comedy and talk shows as well."

"Holy shit."

"Plus, sir, the internet. The assault was widely circulated on the internet. You don't check any of these outlets?"

"When was this?"

"Day before yesterday. It's fair to say she's reached viral status, sir. Meme status."

"Who did she assault?"

"Sheldon Packer, sir. Governor Sheldon Packer of Wyoming. She attacked him with rocks. Several rocks, sir. Thrown rocks."

"This is a joke."

"I probably won't be calling them rocks during the proceedings. More likely I'll call them stones, or pebbles, or actually now that I think of it probably *gravel*."

"You're lying. Who is this?"

"As I said, I'm Simon Rogers of Rogers and Rogers, sir, and your mother is awaiting trial."

"For assaulting a presidential candidate."

"Not technically a candidate yet, per se, but you're in the ballpark. It was on every news channel literally all day and all night long. You haven't heard about this?"

"I've been busy."

"You teach a class, Intro to Lit. It meets for an hour twice a week, sir. I hope you don't find it prying or intrusive that I have that information, but it's right there on the school's website."

"I understand."

"Because what I'm wondering, sir, is what have you been doing with the other approximately let's say forty hours since this story broke?"

"I've been at the computer."

"And this computer is connected to the internet, I assume?"

"I've been, you know, I've been writing. I'm a writer."

"Because the national mood right now on this subject is like: Could we talk about something *besides* Faye Andresen-Anderson please? Total saturation, I'm saying, so I find it surprising, sir, that you've heard exactly zero about this, and it involves your own mother."

"We don't really communicate, she and I."

"They've given her a catchy name: the Packer Attacker. She's quite famous."

"Are you sure it's my mother? This really doesn't sound like her."

"You are Samuel Andresen-Anderson? That is your full legal name?"

"Yes."

"And your mother is Faye Andresen-Anderson, yes?"

"Yes."

"Who lives in Chicago, Illinois?"

"My mother doesn't live in Chicago."

"Where does she live?"

"I don't know. I haven't talked to her in twenty years!"

"So you're unaware of her current whereabouts, sir. That's accurate?"

"Yes."

"So she could be living in Chicago, Illinois, and you just wouldn't know."

"I suppose."

"So the woman in jail is probably indeed your mother, is my point. Regardless of her current address."

"And she attacked the governor—"

"We would prefer less loaded terms. Not 'attacked.' Rather, she was exercising her First Amendment rights using symbolically flung gravel. I assume from the keyboard clacking sounds I'm hearing that you are currently verifying this via search engine?"

"Oh my god, it's everywhere!"

"Indeed, sir."

"There's a video?"

"Viewed several million times. It's also been remixed and auto-tuned and made into a rather amusing hip-hop song."

"I can't believe this."

"You should probably bypass the song, however, sir, at least until the wound is not so fresh."

"I'm looking at an editorial comparing my mother to al-Qaeda."

"Yes, sir. Most foul. The things they've been saying, sir. On the news. Most horrible."

"What else have they been saying?"

"Maybe it's best you see for yourself."

"Why don't you give me an example."

"Tensions, sir. Tensions and passions are running high, you see. Because it's being seen as politically motivated, of course."

"And so they're saying, what?"

"She's a terrorist hippie radical prostitute, sir, to cite one very nasty but for the most part emblematic example."

"Prostitute?"

"Terrorist hippie radical and, yes, you heard correctly, sir, prostitute. She's being rankly abused, if I may say so."

"Why are they saying she's a prostitute?"

"She was arrested for prostitution, sir. In Chicago."

"Come again?"

"Arrested, but never officially charged, sir, I think it's important to add."

"In Chicago."

"Yes, sir, in Chicago in 1968. Some years before you were born and long enough for her to amend her ways and find God, is something I'm likely to argue if this goes to court. We're talking about prostituting herself with *sex,* of course."

"Okay, see? That's impossible. She was never in Chicago in 1968. She was home, in Iowa."

"Our records indicate she was in Chicago during a one-month period near the end of 1968, sir, when she was in college."

"My mother never went to college."

"Your mother never *graduated* college. But she was enrolled as a student at the University of Illinois–Chicago for the fall semester, 1968."

"No, my mother grew up in Iowa and when she graduated high school she stayed in Iowa waiting for my dad to return from the army. She never left her hometown."

"Our records indicate otherwise."

"She didn't leave Iowa until, like, the eighties."

"Our records indicate, sir, that she was active in the antiwar campaign of 1968."

"Okay now that's definitely impossible. Protesting might be the *last* thing my mother would do."

"I am telling you, sir, it happened. There's a photograph. There's photographic proof."

"You've got the wrong woman. There's been a mix-up."

"Faye, maiden name Andresen, born 1950, in Iowa. Would you like all nine digits of her Social Security number?"

"No."

"Because I have it, her sosh."

"No."

"So there's a reasonable chance, sir. What I mean is unless evidence proves otherwise or we're all the victims of an outrageous coincidence, this woman in jail is likely your mother."

"Fine."

"It's very probable. Ninety-nine percent sure. Beyond a reasonable doubt. A lock, as much as you might hope not to believe it."

"I understand."

"The woman in jail, hereafter known as 'your mother.' We will not be having this debate again?"

"No."

"As I was saying, it's unlikely your mother will achieve a not guilty verdict here, the evidence against her being what you might call incontrovertible. Best we can do, sir, is hope for a plea and a merciful sentence."

"I don't see how you need my help for that."

"A character witness. You'll write a letter to the judge explaining why your mother does not deserve to go to prison."

"Why would the judge listen to me?"

"He probably won't, sir. Especially *this* judge. Judge Charles Brown. Goes by 'Charlie.' I'm not kidding you, sir, that's really his name. He was supposed to retire next month but delayed retirement to preside over your mother's case. I'm thinking because it's high profile? A national story. Also he has a pretty appalling record vis-à-vis First Amendment stuff. The Honorable Charlie Brown does not have a lot of patience for dissent, let me tell you."

"So if he won't listen to me, why bother with this letter? Why bother calling me?"

"Because you have a somewhat respectable title, sir, and you've achieved a middling level of renown, and I will leave no stone unturned while there is still money in the fund. I have a reputation."

"What is this fund?"

"As you can imagine, sir, Governor Sheldon Packer is pretty unpopular in some quarters. In certain circles, your mother is a kind of subversive hero."

"For throwing rocks."

"'A brave soldier in the fight against Republican fascism' was written on one of the checks I cashed. The money poured in for her defense. Enough to retain my legal counsel for upward of four months."

"And after that?"

"I'm optimistic we can reach a deal, sir, before then. Will you help us?"

"Why should I? Why should I help *her*? This is so typical."

"What's typical, sir?"

"My mother's whole big mystery—going to college, and protesting, and getting arrested—I never knew any of that. It's one more secret she never told me."

"I'm sure she had her reasons, sir."

"I want no part of this."

"I should say your mother really direly needs help right now."

"I'm not going to write a letter, and I don't care if she goes to prison."

"But she's your mother, sir. She birthed you and, not to put too fine a point on it, suckled you."

"She abandoned me and my father. She left without a word. She stopped being my mother then, as far as I'm concerned."

"No lingering hope for a reunion? No deep longing for a maternal figure in a life that feels hollowed out and void without her?"

"I have to go."

"She gave birth to you. She kissed your owies. Cut up your sandwich into little bits. Do you or do you not want someone in your life who remembers your birthday?"

"I'm hanging up now. Goodbye."

SAMUEL IS LISTENING to cappuccino-related whooshing at an airport coffee shop when he receives the first message concerning Laura Pottsdam. It's from his dean, the plague scholar. *I met with a student of yours,* she writes. *She had some strange accusations. Did you really tell her she was stupid?* And Samuel skims the rest of the letter and feels himself physically sinking into his chair. *I'm frankly shocked at your impropriety. Ms. Pottsdam doesn't seem stupid to me. I allowed her to rewrite her paper for full credit. We must discuss this immediately.*

He's at a coffee shop across from a gate where a midday flight to Los Angeles will begin boarding in about fifteen minutes. He's there for a meeting with Guy Periwinkle, his editor and publisher. Above him is a television, currently muted, tuned to a news program showing Samuel's mother throwing rocks at Governor Packer.

He tries to ignore it. He listens to the omnibus sounds around him: coffee orders shouted, intercom announcements about the current threat level and not leaving one's bags unattended, kids crying, froth and steam, bubbling milk. Just next to the coffee shop is a shoeshine stand—two chairs elevated like thrones, beneath which is this guy who will shine your shoes. He's a black man who's currently reading a book, dressed in the uniform required of his job: suspenders, newsboy cap, a vaguely turn-of-the-century ensemble. Samuel is waiting for Periwinkle, who wants a shoeshine but is hesitating.

"I'm an exquisitely dressed white guy," Periwinkle says, staring at the man at the shoeshine stand. "He is a minority in regressive costume."

"And this matters why?" Samuel says.

"I don't like the image. I hate that visual."

Periwinkle is in Chicago this afternoon but on his way to L.A. His assistant had called to say he wanted a meeting, but the only time he had available was at the airport. So the assistant purchased Samuel an airline ticket, a one-way to Milwaukee which, the assistant explained, Samuel could use if he wanted but was really just to get him inside security.

Periwinkle eyes the shoeshine guy. "You know what the real problem is? The real problem is cell-phone cameras."

"I've never had a shoeshine in my life."

"Stop wearing sneakers," Periwinkle says, and he doesn't look at Samuel's feet when he says this. Meaning that in the few minutes they'd spent together at the airport, Periwinkle had gathered and assimilated the fact of Samuel's cheap shoes. And several other facts, probably.

Samuel always feels this way around his publisher: a little unseemly in comparison, a little derelict. Periwinkle looks about forty years old but he's actually the same age as Samuel's father: in his mid-sixties. He seems to be fighting time by being cooler than it. He carries himself in an erect and stiff and regal manner—it's like he thinks of himself as an expensive and tightly wrapped birthday present. His thin shoes are severe and Italian-looking and have little ski jumps at the tips. His waistline seems about eight inches smaller than that of any other adult male in the airport. The knot in his necktie is as tight and hard as an acorn. His lightly graying hair is shaved to what seems to be a perfect and uniform one-centimeter length. Samuel always feels, standing next to him, baggy and big. Clothes bought off the rack and ill-fitting, probably a size too large. Whereas Periwinkle's tight-fitting suit sculpts his body into clean angles and straight lines, Samuel's shape seems blobbier.

Periwinkle is like a flashlight aimed at all your shortcomings. He makes you think consciously of the image you are projecting of yourself. For example, Samuel's typical order at a coffee shop is a cappuccino. With Periwinkle, he ordered a green tea. Because a cappuccino seemed like a cliché, and he thought a green tea would have a higher Periwinkle approval rating.

Periwinkle, meanwhile, ordered a cappuccino.

"I'm headed to L.A.," he says. "Gonna be on the set for the new Molly video."

"Molly Miller?" Samuel says. "The singer?"

"Yeah. She's a client. Whatever. She has a new video. A new album. Guest appearance on a sitcom. Reality show in the pipeline. And a celebrity memoir, which is the reason I'm going out there. The working title is *Mistakes I've Made So Far.*"

"Isn't she like sixteen years old?"

"Officially seventeen. But really she's twenty-five."

"No kidding?"

"In real life. Keep that to yourself."

"What's the book about?"

"It's tricky. You want it blasé enough that it won't hurt her image, but it can't be boring because she has to come off as glamorous. You want it smart enough that people won't say it's bubblegum pop sold to twelve-year-olds, but not too smart because twelve-year-olds are of course the principal audience. And obviously all celebrity memoirs need one big confession."

"They do?"

"Definitely, yes. Something we can give the newspapers and magazines ahead of the pub date to generate buzz. Something juicy to get people talking. That's why I'm going to L.A. We're brainstorming. She's doing pickups on her music video. Comes out in a few days. Some fucking stupid shitty song. Here's the chorus: 'You have got to represent!'"

"Catchy. Have you decided on a confession?"

"I am strongly in favor of an innocently small episode of lesbianism. An experimental time in junior high. A special friend, a few kisses. You know. Not enough to turn off the parents but hopefully enough to get us some rainbow-flag awards. She's already got the tween market, but if she could get the gays too?" And here Periwinkle pantomimes with his hands something small exploding into something large. *"Boom,"* he says.

It was Periwinkle who'd given Samuel his big break, Periwinkle who had plucked Samuel out of obscurity and given him an enormous book contract. Samuel had been in college then, and Periwinkle was visiting campuses all over the country looking for authors to sign for a new imprint that featured the work of young prodigies. He recruited Samuel after having read only one short story. Then he placed that story in one of the big magazines. Then offered a book contract that paid Samuel an exorbitant amount of money. All Samuel had to do was write the book.

Which of course he never did. That was a decade ago. This is the first conversation he's had with his publisher in years.

"So how's the book business?" Samuel says.

"The book business. Hah. That's funny. I'm not really in the book business anymore. Not in the traditional sense." He fishes a business card from his briefcase. *Guy Periwinkle: Interest Maker*—no logo, no contact information.

"I'm in the manufacturing business now," Periwinkle says. "I build things."

"But not books."

"Books. Sure. But mostly I build interest. Attention. Allure. A book is just packaging, just a container. This is what I've realized. The mistake people in the book business make is they think their job is to build good containers. Saying you're in the book business is like a winemaker saying he's in the bottle business. What we're actually building is *interest*. A book is simply one shape that interest can take when we scale and leverage it."

Above them, the Packer Attacker video has come to the point where security guards are rushing toward Samuel's mother, about to tackle her. Samuel turns away.

"I'm more like into multimodal cross-platform synergy," Periwinkle says. "My company was swallowed long ago by another publisher, which was swallowed in turn by a bigger one, and so on, like those Darwin fish stickers you see on car bumpers. Now we're owned by a multinational conglomerate with interests in trade book publishing, cable television, radio broadcasting, music recording, media distribution, film production, political consulting, image management, publicity, advertising, magazines, printing, and rights. Plus shipping, I think? Somewhere in there?"

"That sounds complicated."

"Imagine me as the calm center around which all our media operations tornado."

Periwinkle looks at the television above them and watches the Packer Attacker video replayed for the dozenth time. In a small window on the left side of the screen, the show's conservative anchor is saying something, who knows what.

"Hey!" Periwinkle shouts at a barista. "Could you turn this up?"

Seconds later the television is unmuted. They hear the anchor ask whether the Packer attack is an isolated incident or a sign of things to come.

"Oh, definitely a sign of things to come," says one of the guests. "This is what liberals do when they're trapped in a corner. They attack."

"It's really not all that different from, say, Germany in the late thirties," says another guest. "It's like, you know, first they came for the patriots, and I did not speak out."

"Right!" says the anchor. "If we don't speak out, nobody's going to be left when they come for *us*. We have to stop this now."

Heads nod all around. Cut to commercial.

"Oh, man," says Periwinkle, shaking his head and smiling. "The Packer Attacker. That's a woman I'd like to know better. That's a story I'd love to tell."

Samuel sips his drink and says nothing. The tea steeped for too long and has gone a little bitter.

Periwinkle checks his watch and glances at the gate, where people have begun to hover—not quite in line but poised to dart into one, should a line form.

"How's work?" Periwinkle says. "You still teaching?"

"For now."

"At that . . . place?"

"Yes, same school."

"What do you make, like thirty grand? Let me give you some advice. Can I give you some advice?"

"Okay."

"Get out of the country, dude."

"Sorry?"

"Seriously. Find yourself a nice third-world developing nation and go make a killing."

"I could do that?"

"Yes, absolutely. My brother does that. Teaches high-school math and coaches soccer in Jakarta. Before that, Hong Kong. Before that, Abu Dhabi. Private schools. Kids are mostly the children of government and business elite. He makes two hundred grand a year plus housing plus a car plus a driver. You get a car and a chauffeur at that school of yours?"

"No."

"I swear to god anyone with half an education who stays in America to teach is suffering some kind of psychosis. In China, Indonesia, the Philippines, the Middle East they're desperate for people like you. You could have your pick. In America you're underpaid and overworked and insulted by politicians and unappreciated by students. There, you'd be a goddamn hero. That's advice, me to you."

"Thanks."

"You should take it too. Because I have bad news, buddy."

"You do."

Big sigh, big clownish frown as Periwinkle nods his head. "I'm sorry, but we're gonna have to cancel your contract. That's what I came here to tell you. You promised us a book."

"And I'm working on it."

"We paid you a fairly large advance for a book, and you have not delivered said book."

"I hit a snag. A little writer's block. It's coming along."

"We are invoking the nondelivery clause in our contract, whereby the publisher may demand reimbursement for any advance payments if the product is never provided. In other words? You're gonna have to pay us back. I wanted to tell you in person."

"In person. At a coffee shop. At the airport."

"Of course, in the event you cannot pay us back, we'll have to sue you. My company will be filing papers next week with the New York State Supreme Court."

"But the book's coming along. I'm writing again."

"And that's excellent news for you! Because we relinquish all rights on any material related to said book, so you can do whatever you want with it. And we wish you the very best of luck with that."

"How much are you suing me for?"

"The amount of the advance, plus interest, plus legal fees. The upside here is that we're not taking a loss on you, which cannot be said for many of our other recent investments. So don't feel too bad for us. You still have the money, yes?"

"No. Of course not. I bought a house."

"How much do you owe on the house?"

"Three hundred grand."

"And how much is the house now worth?"

"Like, eighty?"

"Hah! Only in America, am I right?"

"Look. I'm sorry it's taken so long. I'll finish the book soon. I promise."

"How do I say this delicately? We actually don't want the book anymore. We signed that contract in a different world."

"How is it different?"

"Primarily, you're not famous anymore. We needed to strike while the iron was hot. Your iron, my friend, is ice cold. But also the country has moved on. Your quaint story about childhood love was appropriate pre-9/11, but now? Now it's a little quiet for the times, a little incongruous. And—no offense?—there's nothing terribly interesting about you."

"Thanks."

"Don't take that the wrong way. It's a one-in-a-million person who can sustain the kind of interest I specialize in."

"I can't possibly afford to pay that money back."

"It's an easy fix, dude. Foreclose on the house, hide your assets, declare bankruptcy, move to Jakarta."

The intercom crackles: First-class passengers to Los Angeles can now begin boarding. Periwinkle smoothes his suit. "That's me," he says. He slugs the rest of his coffee and stands up. "Listen, I wish things were different. I really do. I wish we didn't have to do this. If only there was something you could offer, something of interest?"

Samuel knows he has one thing yet to give, one thing of value. It's the only thing he has for Periwinkle. It is, right now, the only interesting thing about him.

"What if I told you I had a new book," Samuel says. "A different book."

"Then I would say we had another complaint in our civil suit against you. That when you were contracted to write a book for us, you were secretly working on a book for someone else."

"I haven't been working on it at all. Haven't written a word."

"Then in what way is it a 'book'?"

"It's not. It's more like a pitch. Do you want to hear the pitch?"

"Sure. Fire away."

"It's sort of a celebrity tell-all."

"Okay. Who's the celebrity?"

"The Packer Attacker."

"Yeah, right. We sent a scout. She's not talking. It's a dead end."

"What if I told you that she was my mother?"

7

SO THIS IS THE PLAN. They agree to it at the airport. Samuel will fulfill his contract with the publisher by writing a book about his mother—a biography, an exposé, a tell-all.

"A sordid tale of sex and violence," Periwinkle says, "written by the son she abandoned? Hell yeah, I could sell that."

The book will describe Faye Andresen's sleazy past in the protest movement, her time as a prostitute, how she abandoned her family and went into hiding and only came out to terrorize Governor Packer.

"We'd have to get the book out before the election, for obvious marketing reasons," Periwinkle says. "And Packer will have to come off as an American hero. A kind of folksy messiah. You okay with that?"

"Fine."

"We have those pages finished already, actually."

"What do you mean finished?" Samuel says.

"The Packer stuff. Ghostwritten. Done. About a hundred pages of it."

"How is that possible?"

"You know how a lot of obituaries are written before the subjects actually die? Same principle. We've been working on a bio, just waiting for an angle. So we had it in the hopper. Half your book is ready to go, in other words. The other half is the mother material. She is of course cast as the villain here. You understand that, right?"

"I do."

"And you can write it? You have no problems portraying her this way? Morally? Ethically?"

"I will savage her intimately, publicly. That's the deal. I get it."

And it will not be hard, Samuel imagines, to do this to the woman who left without a word, without warning, who left him alone to survive a motherless childhood. It's as if two decades' worth of resentment and pain has, for the first time, found an outlet.

So Samuel calls his mother's lawyer and says he's changed his mind. He says he'd be happy to write a letter to the judge in support of her case and would like to have an interview to gather key information. The lawyer gives him his mother's address in Chicago and sets up a meeting for the very next day, and Samuel is sleepless and jumpy and overstimulated all night as he imagines seeing his mother for the first time since she disappeared so long ago. It seems unfair that it's been twenty years since he's seen her and now he has only one day to prepare.

How many times has he imagined it? How many fantasies of reunion has he entertained? And in the many thousands, the millions of them, what happens every time is that he proves to his mother that he is successful and smart. He is important and grown-up and mature. Sophisticated and happy. He shows her how extraordinary his life is, how inconsequential her absence from it has been. He shows her how much he *does not need her.*

In his fantasies of reunion, his mother always begs his forgiveness and he does not cry. That's how it goes every time.

But how would he make this happen? In real life? Samuel has no idea. He googles it. He spends most of the night on online support boards for children of estranged parents, websites heavy in their use of capital letters and boldface type and animated GIFs of smiley faces and frowny faces and teddy bears and angels. As he reads through these sites, the thing that surprises Samuel most is the essential sameness of everyone's problems: the intense feelings of shame and embarrassment and responsibility felt by the abandoned child; the feelings of both adoration and loathing for the missing parent; loneliness coupled with a self-defeating desire for reclusiveness. And so on. It's like looking into a mirror. All his private weaknesses come publicly back at him, and Samuel feels ashamed about this. Seeing others express exactly what's in his own heart makes him think he's unoriginal and ordinary and not the astounding man he needs to be to prove to his mother she shouldn't have left him.

It's nearly three o'clock in the morning when he realizes he's been staring at the same animated GIF for five full minutes—a teddy bear giving something called a "virtual hug" where the bear repeatedly opens and closes its arms in a never-ending loop that's supposed to be read as an embrace but looks to Samuel more like a deliberate and sarcastic clap, like the bear is mocking him.

He abandons the computer and sleeps fitfully for a few hours before he wakes at dawn and showers and drinks about a whole pot of coffee and gets into his car to make the drive into Chicago.

Despite its proximity, Samuel rarely goes into Chicago these days, and now he remembers why: The closer he gets to the city, the more the highway feels malicious and warlike—wild zigzagging drivers cutting people off, tailgating, honking horns, flashing their lights, all their private traumas now publicly enlarged. Samuel travels with the crush of traffic in a slow sluggish mass of hate. He feels that low-level constant anxiety about not being able to get over into the turn lane when his exit is near. There's that thing where drivers next to him speed up when they see his turn signal, to eliminate the space he intended to occupy. There is no place less communal in America—no place less cooperative and brotherly, no place with fewer feelings of shared sacrifice—than a rush-hour freeway in Chicago. And there is no better test of this than watching what happens when there is a hundred-car line in the far-right lane, which there is when Samuel reaches his exit. How people bypass the line and dive into any available cranny in front, skipping all the drivers patiently waiting, all of whom are now enraged at this because they each have to wait incrementally longer, but also a bigger and deeper rage that the asshole didn't wait his turn like everyone else, that he didn't suffer like they suffer, and then also a tertiary inner rage that they are suckers who wait in lines.

So they yell and gesture obscenely and hover inches from the bumper in front of them. They do not provide any gaps for cutters. They do not make way for anyone. Samuel's doing it too, and he feels if he allows just one cutter in front of him, he will let down all who wait behind. And so with each movement of the line he guns the gas so that any space is closed. And they lurch toward the exit this way until, at one point when he is checking his mirror for possible cutters and a space opens up in front of him and he is sure this fucking BMW coming up fast on the left is going to cut in front, Samuel is a little too careless with the accelerator and leaps forward and lightly taps the car in front of him.

A taxi. The driver vaults out and screams "Fuck you! Fuck you! Fuck you!" pointing at Samuel as if to specially emphasize that it is him—and no one else—who needs to be fucked.

"Sorry!" Samuel says, holding up his hands.

The line stopping now produces a wail from the cars behind them, a squall of horns, shouts of anguish and disgust. The cutters see their opportunity and swerve in front of the stopped taxi. The cabbie comes right up to Samuel's closed window and says, "I will fucking fuck you up, you fucking fuck!"

And then the cabbie spits.

Actually physically leans back as if to get a good running start at it, then propels forward a mucusy glob that splats terribly onto Samuel's window and sticks there, doesn't even dribble down but lands and sticks like pasta on a wall, this spatter all yellowish and bubbly with flecks of chewed food and awful spots of blood in it, like one of those maybe-embryos you might find in a raw egg. And satisfied with his creation, the cabbie hustles back to his car and drives away.

For the rest of the drive to his mother's South Loop neighborhood, this splash of phlegm and snot is with Samuel like another passenger. It feels like he's driving with an assassin he doesn't want to make eye contact with. He can see it peripherally as a hazy whitish uneven penumbra as he exits the highway and proceeds down a narrow street whose gutters are dotted by the bags and cups of fast-food restaurants, past a bus station and a desolate weedy lot where it appears a high-rise was intended and abandoned immediately after its foundation was laid, over a bridge that spans the great braid of train tracks that once serviced this area's mass of slaughterhouses, just south of downtown Chicago, still in plain view of what was once the tallest building in the world, here in what was once the busiest meatpacking district in the world, to his mother's address in what turns out to be an old warehouse building near the train tracks with a giant sign on top saying LOFTS AVAILABLE, throughout all of this roughly a quarter of Samuel's attention remains focused on the gooey slop still sticking to his window. He has become amazed at how it doesn't budge, like an epoxy made to repair broken plastic things. He is moved by the feats the human body is capable of. He's nervous about this neighborhood. There is literally *nobody* on the sidewalk.

He parks, double-checks the address. At the building's front door there is a buzzer. Right there, written on slip of yellowed paper in ink now faded to a light pink, is his mother's name: Faye Andresen.

He presses the buzzer, which makes no noise whatsoever and makes him think, along with the age of the contraption and the rust and the wires jutting out, that it's broken. The way his mother's button sticks for a moment before finally giving way to the pressure of his finger with an audible *tick* makes him think the button has not been pressed in a very long time.

It strikes him that his mother has been here all along, all these years. Her name has been out here on this slip of paper, washed by the sun, for anyone to see. This does not seem allowable. It seems to Samuel that after she left, she should have ceased to exist.

The door, with a heavy magnetic-sounding click, opens.

He enters. The inside of the building, past the entryway and vestibule with its bank of mailboxes, seems incomplete. Tile floors that abruptly give way to subfloor. White walls that don't seem painted but rather merely primed. He climbs the three flights of stairs. He finds the door— a bare wooden door, unpainted, unfinished, like something you'd see at a hardware store. He doesn't know what he expected, but he definitely did not expect this blank nothingness. This anonymous door.

He knocks. He hears a voice inside, his mother's voice: "It's open," she says.

He pushes the door forward. He can see from the hall that the apartment is bright with sunlight. Bare white walls. A familiar smell he cannot place.

He hesitates. He cannot immediately bring himself to walk through this door and back into his mother's life. After a moment, she speaks up again, from somewhere inside. "It's okay," she says. "Don't be scared."

And it nearly breaks him, hearing that. He sees her now in a rush of memory, lingering over his bed in the bleary morning and he's eleven years old and she is about to leave and never come back.

Those words burn him straight through. They reach across the decades and summon up that timid boy he once was. *Don't be scared.* It was the last thing she'd ever said to him.

PART TWO

GHOSTS OF THE OLD COUNTRY

Late Summer 1988

1

SAMUEL WAS CRYING in his bedroom, quietly, so his mother wouldn't hear. This was a small cry, just tiptoeing on the edge of actual crying, maybe a light whimpering along with the normal halted breathing and squished face. This was a Category 1 cry: a small, concealable, satisfying, purgative cry, usually only a welling of the eyes but lacking actual tears. A Category 2 cry was more of an emotional cry, triggered by feelings of embarrassment or shame or disappointment. This was why a Category 1 cry could be vaulted to a Category 2 simply by the presence of someone else: He felt embarrassed about crying, about being a crybaby, and this fact created a new kind of crying—that wet-faced, whimpering, snotty crying that's not yet a full-throated Category 3, which involved larger raindrop-size tears and bouts of sniveling and convulsive breathing and a reflexive need to find a private hiding place immediately. A Category 4 was a weeping sobbing fit, whereas Category 5 was just unthinkable. His counselor at school had encouraged him to think of his crying in these terms, using categories like they do for hurricanes.

So that day he felt he needed to cry. He told his mother he was going to his room to read, which was not unusual. He spent most of his time alone in his room, reading the Choose Your Own Adventure books he bought from the bookmobile at school. He liked how the books looked on the shelves, all together like that, homogenous, with their white-and-red spines and titles like *Lost on the Amazon, Journey to Stonehenge, Planet of the Dragons.* He liked the books' forking paths, and when he came to a particularly difficult decision, he would hold the page with his thumb and read ahead, verifying that it was an acceptable choice. The books had a clarity and symmetry to them that he found mostly absent in the real world. Sometimes he liked to imagine his life was a Choose Your Own Adventure book, and that a happy story was just a matter of making the right choices. This seemed to give a structure to the sloppy and unpredictable world he found in most other contexts terrifying.

So he told his mother he was reading, but really he was having a nice little Category 1. He wasn't sure why he was crying, just that something about being at home made him want to hide.

The house, he thought, had lately become unbearable.

The way the house seemed to trap everything inside it—the heat of the day, the smell of their own bodies. They were caught in a late-summer heat wave, and everything in Illinois was melting. Everything was burning up. The air was a thick glue. Candles sagged where they stood. Flowers could not be supported by their stems. Everything wilted. Everything drooped.

It was August 1988. In the years to follow, Samuel would look back on this month as the final month he had a mother. By the end of August, she'll have disappeared. But he didn't know that yet. All he knew was that he needed to cry for certain abstract reasons: It was hot, he was worried, his mother was acting weird.

So he went to his room. He was crying mostly to get it out of the way.

Only she heard him. In the extreme quiet, she could hear her son crying upstairs. She opened his door and said "Honey, are you okay?" and immediately he cried harder.

She knew in these moments not to say anything about the elevation in his crying or react to it in any way because acknowledging it just fed the crying in a terrible feedback loop that sometimes ended—on those days when he cried over and over again and she couldn't help but let her exasperation show through—with a wet blubbering hyperventilating kid-size mess. So she said, as soothingly as possible, "I'm hungry. Are you hungry? Let's go out, you and me," which seemed to calm him enough to get his clothes changed and get him into the car with only minor, post-crying hiccups to deal with. That is, until they got to the restaurant and she saw they were having a "Buy Two Get One Free" deal on hamburgers and she said "Oh good. I'll get you a hamburger. You want a hamburger, right?" and Samuel, who all along had his heart set on chicken nuggets with that mustardy dipping sauce, worried that he'd disappoint her if he didn't go along with this new plan. So he nodded okay and stayed in the hot car while his mother fetched the burgers, and he tried to convince himself that he wanted a burger all along, but the more he thought about it, the more the burger seemed revolting—the stale bun and sour pickles and those uniformly cut maggot-size onions. Even before she returned with the burgers he was feeling a little sick and throw-uppy at the thought of having to eat one. And driving home he was trying to contain the crying that was almost certainly coming when his mother noticed his wet, sniveling nose and said "Sweetie? Is something wrong?" and all he managed to say was "I don't want a burger!" before he was lost inside a crushing Category 3.

Faye said nothing. She turned the car around while he buried his face in the hot fabric of the passenger seat and wept.

Back home, they ate in silence. Samuel sat with his mother in the hot kitchen, slumped in his chair and chewing the last of his chicken pieces. The windows were open in hopes for a breeze that did not come. Fans blew hot air from here to there. They watched a housefly buzz overhead, spinning circles near the ceiling. It was the only sign of life in the room, this insect. It bumped into the wall, then the window screen, then suddenly, unprovoked, directly above their heads, it fell. It dropped dead right out of the air and landed on the kitchen table heavy as a marble.

They looked at the small black corpse between them and then at each other. *Did that really happen?* Samuel's face was panicked. He was on the verge of crying again. He needed a distraction. The mother needed to intervene.

"Let's go for a walk," Faye said. "Fill your wagon. Bring nine of your favorite toys."

"What?" he said, his huge frightened eyes already slick and liquided.

"Trust me. Do it."

"Okay," he said, and this proved an effective diversion for about fifteen minutes. It felt to Faye like this was her primary duty as a mother: to create diversions. Samuel would begin to cry and she would head it off. Why nine toys? Because Samuel was a meticulous and organized and anal sort of kid who did things like, for example, keep a Top Ten Toys shoe box under his bed. Mostly in the way of *Star Wars* action figures and Hot Wheels. He revised it occasionally, substituting one thing for another. But it was always there. At any given moment, he knew exactly what his ten favorite toys were.

So she asked him to pick nine toys because she was mildly curious: What would he abandon?

Samuel did not wonder why he was doing this. Why nine toys? And why were they bringing them outside? No, he had been given a task and he was going to complete it. He thought little of arbitrary rules.

That he was so easily tricked made her sad.

Faye yearned for him to be a little smarter. A little less easily duped. She hoped sometimes he would talk back more. She wanted him to have more fight, wanted him to be a sturdier thing. But he wasn't. He heard a rule and he followed it. Bureaucratic little robot. She watched him count his toys, trying to decide between two versions of the same action figure—one Luke Skywalker with binoculars, and one Luke Skywalker with a lightsaber—and she thought she should be *proud* of him. Proud that he was such a mindful boy, such a sweet boy. But his sweetness came at a price, which was that he was delicate. He cried so easily. He was so stupidly fragile. He was like the skin of a grape. In response, she was sometimes too hard on him. She did not like how he went through life so scared of everything. She did not like to see her own failures reflected back at her so clearly.

"I'm done, Momma," he said, and she counted eight toys in his wagon—he had left behind *both* Luke Skywalkers, it turned out. But only eight toys, not nine. He hadn't followed her one simple instruction. And now she didn't know what she wanted of him. She was angry when he blindly obeyed, but now also angry that he didn't obey better. She felt unhinged.

"Let's go," she said.

Outside it was unimaginably still and sticky. No movement except the heat ripples coming off roofs and asphalt. They walked down the wide street that curved through their particular subdivision and branched occasionally into stubby cul-de-sacs. Ahead of them, the neighborhood was all crunchy yellow grass and garage doors and houses following identical plans: front door set way back, garage door pushed way forward, as if the house were trying to hide behind it.

Those smooth beige faceless garage doors—they seemed to capture something essential about the place, something about the suburbs' loneliness, she thought. A big front porch brings you out into the world, but a garage door shuts you off from it.

How had she ended up here, of all places?

Her husband, that's how. Henry had moved them to the house on Oakdale Lane, in this little city of Streamwood, one of Chicago's many indistinct suburbs. This after a string of small two-bedroom apartments in various Midwestern agro-industrial outposts as Henry climbed the corporate ladder in his chosen field: prepackaged frozen meals. When they landed in Streamwood, Henry insisted it was their final move, scoring as he had a job good enough to stay for: associate vice president of R&D, Frozen Foods Division. The day they moved in, Faye said, "I guess this is it," then turned to Samuel. "I guess this is where you're going to be from."

Streamwood, she thought now. *No streams, no woods.*

"The thing about garage doors . . . ," she said, and she turned around to find Samuel staring at the asphalt in front of him, concentrating hard on something. He hadn't heard her.

"Never mind," she said.

Samuel pulled the wagon, and its plastic wheels clacked on the street. Sometimes a pebble would lodge under one of the wheels and the wagon would stop moving and the jolt would almost knock him down. He felt, whenever this happened, like he was disappointing his mother. So he watched for any kind of debris and kicked away stones and pieces of mulch and bark, and when he kicked he was careful not to kick very hard for fear his shoe would get stubbed in a sidewalk crack and he'd go tumbling forward, tripping on nothing, just walking wrong, which he worried would also disappoint his mother. He was trying to keep up with her—since she might be disappointed if he fell behind and she had to wait for him—but he couldn't go so fast that one of his eight toys might topple out of the wagon, which would be a clumsy thing she definitely would be disappointed by. So he had to achieve exactly the right pace to keep up with his mother but then slow down on the parts of the street that were cracked and uneven, and watch for debris and kick debris away without tripping, and if he could do all of this successfully then it might be a better day. He might salvage the day. He might be less of a disappointment. He might erase what happened earlier, which is that he was a giant stupid crybaby, again.

He felt bad about this now. He felt that he certainly could have eaten the burger, that he just psyched himself out, and if he would have given it a chance he was sure the burger would have been a perfectly acceptable dinner. He felt guilty about the whole thing. The way his mother turned the car around and fetched him chicken nuggets seemed to him now so heroic and good. Good in a way he never could be. He felt selfish. The way his crying let him get whatever he wanted even though that was not his intention at all. And he was trying to figure out a way to tell his mother that if it were up to him he'd never cry again and she'd never have to spend hours calming him down or pandering to his inconsiderate and thoughtless needs.

He wanted to say this. He was getting the words right in his head. His mother, meanwhile, was looking at the trees. One of the neighbor's front-yard oaks. Like everything else, it was drooping and desiccated and sad, its branches listing to the ground. Leaves not really green but a scorched amber. There was no sound at all. No wind chimes, no birds, dogs were not barking, children were not laughing. His mother looked up at this tree. Samuel stopped and looked too.

She said, "Do you see it?"

Samuel didn't know what he was supposed to be seeing. "The tree?" he said.

"Up near the top branch. See?" She pointed. "All the way up. That leaf."

He followed her finger and saw a single leaf that did not look quite like the others. It was green, thick, it stood straight up and it was flopping around like a fish, twisting as if there were a swirling wind. It was the only leaf on the tree that was doing this. The rest hung quietly in the dead air. There was no wind on the block, and yet this leaf was a maniac.

"Do you know what that is?" she said. "It's a ghost."

"It is?" he said.

"That leaf is haunted."

"A leaf can be haunted?"

"Anything can be haunted. A ghost can live in a leaf as well as any-where else."

He watched the leaf spin around as if it were attached to a kite.

"Why is it doing that?" he said.

"That's the spirit of a person," she said. "My father told me about this. One of his old stories. From Norway, from when he was a kid. It's some-one not good enough to go to heaven but not bad enough to go to hell. He's in between."

Samuel had not considered this a possibility.

"He's restless," she said. "He wants to move on. Maybe he was a good person who did one really bad thing. Or maybe he did lots of bad things but felt very sorry about them. Maybe he didn't want to do bad things, but he couldn't stop himself."

And at this, once again, Samuel cried. He felt his face crumple. The tears came so unstoppably quickly. Because he knew he did bad things over and over and over. Faye noticed and closed her eyes and rubbed her fingers hard at her temples and covered her face with her hand. He could tell this was about as much as she could tolerate today, how she'd met the limits of her patience, how the crying about bad things was itself another bad thing.

"Sweetheart," she said, "why are you crying?"

He still wanted to tell her that what he desired more than anything else in the world was to stop crying. But he couldn't say it. All he managed to do was to spit out something incoherent through the tears and mucus: "I don't want to be a leaf!"

"Why on earth would you think that?" she said.

She took his hand and pulled him home and the only sound on the whole block was the clacking of the wagon wheels and his whimpering. She took him to his room and told him to put his toys away.

"And I told you to bring nine toys," she said. "You brought eight. Next time try to pay more attention." And the disappointment in her voice made him cry even harder, so hard that he couldn't talk, and thus he couldn't tell her that he put eight toys in the wagon because the ninth toy was the wagon itself.

2

SAMUEL'S FATHER INSISTED that Sunday evenings be devoted to "family time," and they'd have a mandatory dinner together, all of them sitting around the table while Henry tried valiantly to make conversation. They'd eat some of the packaged meals from his special office freezer, where the experimental and test-market foods were kept. These were usually more daring, more exotic—mango instead of baked apples, sweet potatoes instead of regular potatoes, sweet-and-sour pork instead of pork chops, or things that would not at first glance seem ideal for freezing: lobster rolls, say, or grilled cheese, or tuna melts.

"You know the interesting thing about frozen meals," Henry said, "is that they weren't popular until Swanson decided to call them 'TV dinners.' Frozen meals had been around for a decade when they changed the name to TV dinner and *boom,* sales exploded."

"Mm-hm," Faye said as she stared straight down into her chicken cordon bleu.

"It's like people needed permission to eat in front of the television, you know? It's like everyone *wanted* to eat in front of the TV already, but they were waiting for someone to endorse it."

"That's super fascinating," Faye said in a tone that made him shut right up.

Then more silence before Henry asked what the family wanted to do tonight, and Faye suggesting he just go watch TV, and Henry asking if she wanted to join him, and Faye saying no, she had dishes to put away and cleaning to do and "you should go on ahead," and Henry asking if she needed his help with the cleaning, and Faye saying no, he'd just get in the way, and Henry suggesting that maybe she should relax and he'd do the cleanup tonight, and Faye getting frustrated and standing up and saying "You don't even know where anything goes," and Henry looking at her hard and seeming like he was on the verge of saying something but then ultimately not saying it.

Samuel thought how his father married to his mother was like a spoon married to a garbage disposal.

"May I be excused?" Samuel said.

Henry looked at him, wounded. "It's family night," he said.

"You're excused," Faye said, and Samuel leaped off the chair and scurried outside. He felt that familiar desire to go hide. He felt this way whenever the tension in the house seemed to gather up inside him. He hid in the woods, a tiny patch of woods that grew along a sad creek that ran behind their subdivision. A few short trees sprouting out of the mud. A pond that was at best waist-deep. A creek that collected all the subdivision's runoff so the water had this colorful oily film after it rained. It was really pathetic, these woods, as far as nature goes. But the trees were thick enough to conceal him. When he was down here, he was invisible.

If anyone asked him what he was doing, he'd say "Playing," which didn't quite capture it. Could it really be called *playing* when he only sat there in the grass and mud, and hid in the leaves, and threw helicopter seeds into the air and watched them spin to the ground?

It was Samuel's intention to come down to the creek and hide for a couple of hours, at least until bedtime. And he was searching for a spot, a convenient depression in the ground that would give him maximum coverage. A spot where, if he put a few dead branches over him, a few leaves, he would be hidden. And he was collecting the twigs and branches he'd use to cover himself, and he was beneath this one particular oak tree digging among the dead leaves and acorns on the ground, when something cracked above him. A snapping of branches, a creaking of the tree, and he looked up in time to see someone jump down from the tree and land hard on the ground behind him. A boy, no older than Samuel, who stood up and stared fiercely at him with eyes sharp and green and almost feline. He was not larger than Samuel, nor taller, nor in any way physically special except in the certain intangible way he filled up space. His body had a *presence*. He stepped closer. His face was thin and angular and smeared, on his cheeks and forehead, with blood.

Samuel dropped his twigs. He wanted to run. He told himself to run. The boy moved closer, and from behind his back he now produced a knife, a heavy silver butcher's knife, the kind Samuel had seen his mother use when chopping things with bones.

Samuel began to cry.

Just stood there crying, rooted to the ground, waiting for whatever his fate was, succumbing to it. He vaulted right into a Category 3 slobbering wet helpless mess. He could feel his face constrict and his eyes bug out as if his skin were being stretched from behind. And the other boy stood directly before him now and Samuel could see the blood from close up, could see how it was still wet and shining in the sunlight and one drop dribbled down the boy's cheek and under his chin and down his neck and under his shirt and Samuel didn't even wonder where the blood came from so much as simply wail at the horrible fact of its presence. The boy had short reddish hair, eyes that seemed impenetrable and dead, freckles, something like an athlete's sense of bodily control and self-possession and fluidity of movement as he slowly brought the knife over his head in the universal language for psychopathic murderous stabbing.

"This is what we call a successful ambush," the kid said. "If we were at war, you'd be dead right now."

And the cry Samuel let out summoned all his misery and channeled it in one wail, a great sad scream for help.

"Holy shit," the kid said. "You are ugly when you're crying." He lowered the knife. "It's all right. Look. Just kidding?"

But Samuel could not stop. The hysteria kept rolling over him.

"It's okay," the kid said. "No problem. You don't have to talk."

Samuel wiped his arm across his nose and came away with a long slick streak.

"Come with me," the kid said. "I want to show you something."

He led Samuel to the creek and then along the bank for several yards until he came to a place near the pond where a tree had tipped over, leaving a large depression between the roots and the earth.

"Look," the kid said. He pointed to a spot where he'd smoothed out all the mud into a makeshift bowl. And inside the bowl were several animals: a few frogs, a snake, a fish.

"You see them?" he said. Samuel nodded. The snake, he could see now, was missing its head. The frogs had been slit open at the belly or stabbed in the back. There must have been eight or nine of them, all dead save for one, whose legs kicked, bicycling in the air. The fish were beheaded at the gills. They all rested in a bloody slime that gathered at the bottom of the bowl.

"I'm thinking about blow-torching them," the kid said. "You know, with insect spray and a lighter?"

He pantomimed this: flicking the lighter, holding the spray up to it.

"Sit down," he said. Samuel did as he was told, and the boy reached two fingers into the blood.

"We're gonna have to toughen you up," he said. He smeared the blood on Samuel's face—two streaks under his eyes and one on his forehead.

"There," he said. "Now you're initiated." He stabbed the knife into the mud so it stood straight up. "Now you're really alive."

3

THE SUN WAS SETTING, the day's heat lifting, mosquitoes buzzing forth in squadrons from the woods as two boys emerged from the tree line, muddy and wet. They'd been walking across terrain Samuel had never seen before, taking him away from his own neighborhood and into this other one: Venetian Village, it was called. The boys' faces were shiny and moist from where they'd used pond water to clean off the smears of animal blood. Though they were the same height, and the same age, and roughly the same build—which is to say short and eleven years old and tightly skinny, like ropes pulled to maximum tolerances—it was obvious to anyone seeing them that one of the boys was in charge. His name was Bishop Fall—he was the tree leaper, the ambusher, the animal killer. He was explaining to Samuel how he would someday be a five-star general in the United States Army.

"Duty, honor, country," he said. "Taking the fight to the enemy. That's my motto."

"What fight?" said Samuel, who was looking around at the houses of Venetian Village, houses larger than any he had ever seen.

"Whatever fight there is," Bishop said. *"Hooah."*

He was going to join the army as an officer after military college, then become a major, then a colonel, then finally, someday, a five-star general.

"A five-star general has a higher security clearance than the president," Bishop said. "I'm going to know all the secrets."

"Will you tell me?" Samuel said.

"No. They're classified."

"But I won't tell anyone."

"National security. Sorry."

"Please?"

"No way."

Samuel nodded. "You're going to be good at this."

It turned out that Bishop would be joining Samuel in the sixth-grade class at the local public elementary school, having been recently expelled from his private school, Blessed Heart Academy, for, he said, "not taking any shit," by which he meant listening to AC/DC on his Walkman and telling one of the nuns to "fuck off" and getting into fights with anyone who was willing, even high schoolers, even priests.

Blessed Heart Academy was a Catholic K–12 prep school that was really the only local option if you wanted your kids to go to one of the elite East Coast universities. All of the parents of Venetian Village sent their children there. Samuel had never been in Venetian Village before, but sometimes on his longer bike rides he passed the front gate, which was copper and ten feet tall. The homes here were large Roman-style villas with flat roofs of terra-cotta tile, circular driveways curving around dramatic fountains. Houses were separated from each other by a distance at least as great as a soccer field. A swimming pool in every backyard. Exotic sports cars in the driveways, or golf carts, or both. Samuel imagined who could possibly live here: television stars, professional baseball players. But Bishop said it was mostly "boring office people."

"That guy," Bishop said, pointing to one of the villas, "owns an insurance company. And that one," he said, pointing to another, "he runs a bank or something."

Venetian Village had nineteen single-family units, each of them a standardized three stories with six bedrooms, four full baths, three powder rooms, marble kitchen countertops, 500-bottle wine cellar, private interior elevator, tornado-grade impact glass, exercise room, four-car garage, all of them an identical 5,295 square feet that, due to a specially treated glue used in construction, smelled lightly of cinnamon. The exact sameness of the houses was actually a selling point for families worried about not having the nicest house on the block. Realtors often said that in Venetian Village you didn't have to "keep up with the Joneses," even though every family who lived in Venetian Village had been "the Joneses" in whatever neighborhood they'd come from. And hierarchies quietly emerged in other ways. Various backyard additions of gazebos or screened-in two-story lanais or even a lit Har-Tru clay-surfaced tennis court. Each house was built from exactly the same mold but was uniquely accessorized.

A backyard saltwater hot tub, for example, behind one of the villas that Bishop stopped in front of.

"This is where the headmaster of Blessed Heart lives," Bishop said. "He's a fat fuck."

He made a show of grabbing his crotch and flipping his middle finger at the house, then grabbed a small rock that lay in the gutter.

"Watch this," he said, and he flung the rock toward the headmaster's house. It seemed to happen before either of them could even think about it. Suddenly this rock was in the air, and they watched it fly and everything seemed to slow down for a moment as both boys realized that the rock was definitely going to hit the house and there was nothing they could do about this fact. The rock flew through the red-orange sky and it was only a matter of gravity now, and time. The rock arced downward and narrowly missed the forest-green Jaguar in the headmaster's driveway, striking the aluminum garage just beyond the Jaguar with a percussive, reverberative *thunk*. The boys looked at each other in elation and terror, the sound of rock on garage door seeming to them the loudest thing in the world.

"Holy shit!" said Bishop, and both of them, as if moved by the natural impulses of hunted animals, ran.

They ran down Via Veneto, the neighborhood's lone street, which followed roughly the same curvature as a path that deer had made when this place was still a nature preserve, a path that ran between the small manmade pond to the north and a large drainage ditch to the south, these two bodies of water being enough to sustain a modest deer population even through the Illinois winter, a herd whose offspring still lingered in Venetian Village and terrorized various carefully tended flowering plants and gardens. The deer were so annoying that the residents of Venetian Village paid quarterly fees to a deer exterminator who left salt licks laced with poison on posts high enough for adult deer to reach (but, importantly, too high for any of the neighborhood's twenty-five-pound-and-under dogs to accidentally ingest). The poison was not immediate but rather bioaccumulated in the deer's body, so that when the animal's death instincts kicked in, it tended to wander far away from its herd and die, conveniently, somewhere else. And so along with the standardized gondolier-themed mailboxes and front-yard water features, Venetian Village's other major repeating architectural items were posts with salt licks on them and signs saying DANGER. POISON. KEEP AWAY in a very tactful and elegant serif typeface that could also be found on the Venetian Village official stationery.

The neighborhood should never have existed but for a loophole that was exploited by three Chicago investors. Before Venetian Village, there was the Milkweed Nature Preserve, named after the plant that grew in great abundance here and drew huge numbers of monarch butterflies in the summer. The city was looking for a private organization—preferably nonprofit and/or charitable—to tend the preserve and its various paths and general health and biodiversity. The covenants the city drafted stated that the buyer of the land could not develop the land, nor could the buyer sell the land to anyone who would develop it. But the agreement said nothing about whom *that* buyer (i.e., the second one) could sell the land to. So one of the business partners bought the land, then sold it to another of the partners, who quickly sold it to the third partner, who immediately formed an LLC with the other two guys and went to work knocking down the forest. They installed a thick copper fence around what was once the Milkweed Nature Preserve, and advertised to high-end Sotheby's-style clients, one of their catchphrases being: "The intersection of luxury and nature."

One of the three founding partners still lived in Venetian Village, a commodities trader with offices at both the Chicago Stock Exchange and Wall Street. His name was Gerald Fall. He was Bishop's father.

Gerald Fall, the only person on the block, save for the two boys themselves, who saw the stone strike the headmaster's house, who watched as Bishop and Samuel ran down the soft slope of the road toward the low end of Via Veneto's terminating cul-de-sac, where he was standing in the driveway, the door of his black BMW open, his right foot already in the car, his left foot still on the driveway he'd had expensively done in high-gloss cobblestone. He was leaving when he spotted his son throw the rock at the headmaster's house. The boys did not see him there until they were upon the driveway themselves, where they squeaked to a halt on the polished stone, the sound like basketball players on a gym floor. Bishop and his father considered each other for a moment.

"The headmaster's sick," the father said. "Why are you bothering him?"

"Sorry," said Bishop.

"He's very ill. He's a sick man."

"I know."

"What if he's sleeping and you just ruined it?"

"I'll be sure to apologize."

"You do that."

"Where are you going?" Bishop asked.

"The airport. I'll be at the New York apartment for a while."

"Again?"

"Don't bother your sister while I'm gone." He looked at the boys' feet, wet and dirty from the woods. "And don't track mud in the house."

With that, Bishop's father dove fully into his car and shut the door hard and the engine purred to life and the BMW circled out of the driveway, its tires making this noise on the smooth stones like something screaming.

Inside, the Fall household had a formality that made Samuel not want to touch anything: bright white stone floors, chandeliers with crystal things hanging off of them, flowers in tall and thin and easily tippable glass vases, framed abstract artwork on the walls lit by recessed bulbs, a thick wooden display hutch with about two dozen snow globes inside it, the tops of tables buffed to a mirrorlike clarity, kitchen counters of white marble similarly shined, each room and hallway defined by a wide arch set atop Corinthian columns that were so intricately detailed at the top they looked like muskets that had backfired and been torn apart.

"This way," Bishop said. He led them to a room that could only be called the "TV room" for the big-screen television that Samuel felt dwarfed by. It was taller than he was, and wider than his own wingspan. Below the television were strewn various cords and wires for video-game consoles stacked clumsily in a small cabinet. Game cartridges lay haphazardly about them like spent artillery shells.

"Do you like *Metroid* or *Castlevania* or *Super Mario*?" Bishop said.

"I don't know."

"I can save the princess in *Super Mario* without even dying. I've also beaten *Mega Man, Double Dragon,* and *Kid Icarus.*"

"It doesn't matter what we play."

"Yeah, that's true. They're all pretty much the same game. Same basic premise: Go right."

He reached into the cabinet and produced an Atari all tangled in its own cords.

"I actually prefer the classics," he said. "Games made before all the clichés were established. *Galaga. Donkey Kong.* Or *Joust* is one of my favorites, even though it's weird."

"I've never played it."

"Yeah, it's pretty weird. Ostriches and stuff. Pterodactyls. There's also *Centipede*. And *Pac-Man*. You've played *Pac-Man,* right?"

"Yes!"

"Pretty fucking amazing, isn't it? Here's one." Bishop grabbed a cartridge called *Missile Command* and jammed it into the Atari. "You watch me first, then you'll know how to play."

The point of *Missile Command* was to protect six cities from a ceaseless hail of ICBMs. When a missile landed on one of the six cities, it did so with an ugly plosive noise and a little splash that was probably supposed to be a mushroom cloud but looked more like a small pebble or frog breaking the surface of a still pond. The game's sound track was mostly an eight-bit digital conversion of an air-raid horn. Bishop positioned his targeting reticule out in front of the incoming missiles and pressed his button and a small trace of light shot up from the ground and slowly climbed to the targeted spot, where it collided with a falling nuke. Bishop didn't even lose a city until around level nine. Samuel lost track of levels eventually, so by the time the sky was packed with missile trails falling fast and thick, he had no idea how many boards had been conquered. Bishop's face through all of this was utterly calm and fishlike and blank.

"Want to see me do it again?" Bishop said as the screen flashed GAME OVER.

"Did you win?"

"What do you mean, *win*?"

"Did you save all the cities?"

"You can't save all the cities."

"So what's the point?"

"Annihilation is inevitable. The point is delaying it."

"So people can escape?"

"Sure. Whatever."

"Do it again."

And so Bishop was onto level six or seven in his second game, and Samuel was watching Bishop's face instead of the game—how his face was so focused and undisturbed, even while missiles crashed down around his cities, even while his hands jerked the controller this way and that—when, from outside the room, Samuel heard something else, something new.

It was music. Clean and clear and not at all like the scratchy and digitized sounds currently coming out of the television. Musical scales, a solo string instrument going up and down a scale.

"What's that?"

"That's my sister," Bishop said. "Bethany. She's practicing."

"Practicing what?"

"Violin. She's going to be a world-famous violinist. She's really outstandingly good."

"I'll say!" Samuel blurted out maybe too enthusiastically, a bit out of proportion to the actual conversation. But he wanted Bishop to like him. He was trying to be agreeable. Bishop gave him a brief and curious look before staring forward again, blankly, onward to levels ten, eleven, while the music outside changed from a basic scale to real actual music, a soaring and densely noted solo that Samuel could not believe was coming from a person and not the radio.

"That's really your sister?"

"Yep."

"I want to see," Samuel said.

"Wait. Watch this," Bishop said as he annihilated two nukes at the same time with one shot.

"Just for one second," Samuel said.

"But I haven't even lost a city yet. This could the highest scoring game of *Missile Command* ever. You could be watching something historic."

"I'll be right back."

"Fine," Bishop said. "Your loss."

And Samuel left to find the source of the music. He followed the sounds through the main vaulted hallway, through the gleaming kitchen and to the back of the house, to an office where he slowly wrapped his nose around the frame of the door and peeked inside and saw, for the first time, Bishop's sister.

They were twins.

Bethany had Bishop's face, the same check-mark eyebrows, the same quiet intensity. She looked like an elven princess on the cover of a Choose Your Own Adventure novel: immortally young and beautiful and wise. The sharp angles of her cheeks and nose fit her better than they did Bishop. Whereas Bishop looked angry, she looked stately, statuesque. Her long and thick auburn hair, thin eyebrows crinkled in concentration, long neck and delicate arms and erect posture and the careful way she sat in a skirt, a kind of propriety and elegance and ladylike maturity that just killed Samuel. He loved the way she moved with her violin, the way the whole apparatus of her head and neck and torso seemed to glide with the movements of her bow. This was in sharp contrast to the kids in his school's orchestra, who forced sound out of their instruments mechanically and abusively. Her playing was so effortless.

He didn't know it then, but this would become his template for beauty for the rest of his life. Any girl he ever met from now on would be compared, in his head, to this girl.

She finished on a long note where she did that amazing thing where the bow kept moving back and forth and yet there was no break at all, just a prolonged, liquid sound. And she opened her eyes and looked directly at him, and they stared at each other for a terrifying moment until she brought the violin down into her lap and said, "Hi there."

Samuel had never felt such uncomfortable longings before. This was the first time his body tingled like this: Cold sweat gummed up his armpits, his mouth suddenly seemed too small, his tongue all of a sudden huge and arid, a panicky sensation in his lungs as if he'd been holding his breath for too long, all of these things coalesced in his body as a kind of hyperawareness, a strange magnetic pull toward the object of his fancy that departed significantly from the way he tried to ignore or hide from most people.

The girl waited for him to say something, her hands in her lap, resting on her violin, her ankles crossed, those penetrating green eyes—

"I'm Bishop's friend," Samuel finally said. "I'm here with Bishop."

"Okay."

"Your brother?"

She smiled. "Yes, I know."

"I heard you practicing. What are you practicing for?"

She looked at him quizzically for a moment. "To get the notes under my fingers," she said. "I have a concert coming up. What did you think?"

"It was beautiful."

She nodded and seemed to consider this. "The double-stops in the third movement are really hard to play in tune," she said.

"Uh-huh."

"And the arpeggios on the third page are rough. Plus I have to play in tenths, which is weird."

"Yes."

"I feel like I'm falling all over it, that third movement. Stumbling the whole way."

"It didn't sound like that."

"It's like I'm a bird stapled to a chair."

"Right," Samuel said. He was not comfortable with this topic *at all*.

"I need to relax," she said. "Especially in the second movement. There are these long melodic lines in the second movement, and if you play them with too much gusto it ruins the musicality of the whole piece. You have to be calm and serene, which is the last thing your body wants when you're playing a solo."

"Maybe you can, I don't know, breathe?" Samuel said, because that's what his mother told him during his uncontrollable Category 4s: *Just breathe.*

"You know what works?" she said. "I imagine my bow is a knife." She held it up, the bow, and pointed it at him with false menace. "And then I imagine the violin is a stick of butter. Then I pretend I'm drawing the knife *through* the butter. It should feel like that."

Samuel just nodded, helpless.

"How do you know my brother?" she said.

"He jumped out of a tree and scared me."

"Oh," she said, as if this made perfect sense. "He's playing *Missile Command* right now, isn't he?"

"How'd you know that?"

"He's my brother. I can *feel* it."

"Really?"

She held his stare for a moment, then giggled. "No. I can hear it."

"Hear what?"

"The game. Listen. Can't you hear it?"

"I don't hear anything."

"You have to concentrate. Just listen. Close your eyes and listen."

And so he did, and he began to hear the various sounds of the house separate themselves, break from one buzzy collective hum into individual details: the air conditioner working somewhere within the walls, the whoosh of air through vents, the wind outside brushing against the house, the refrigerator and freezer, and Samuel recognized these things and pushed them out of the way and felt his concentration extend back into the house and snake from room to room until, all at once, there it was, popping out of the silence, the faint and muffled air-raid sirens, missile explosions, the *pew-pew* sounds of rockets fired.

"I hear it," he said. But when he opened his eyes Bethany was no longer looking at him. She had her face turned away, toward the big window that looked out onto the backyard and the forest beyond. Samuel followed her stare and saw, outside, through the twilight, at the tree line, maybe fifty feet away, a large adult deer. Light brown and spotted. Big black animal eyes. And as it moved, it hobbled and staggered, fell down and recovered and got up again and kept going, swaying and bucking.

"What's wrong with it?" Samuel said.

"It's eaten the salt."

The deer's front legs gave out again, and it pushed itself along on its belly. Then it recovered momentarily, only to twist and crane its neck so that it could move only in circles. Its eyes were wide and panicked. A pink foam dripped from its nose.

"This happens all the time," Bethany said.

The deer turned toward the forest and made its way into the trees. They watched it go, tumbling forward, until they could no longer see it through the foliage. Then all was quiet, except for the faint sounds from the other end of the house: bombs dropping out of the sky and flattening whole cities.

4

AS THE SCHOOL YEAR BEGAN, this new thing started happening: Samuel would be sitting in class and taking faithful and meticulous notes about whatever Miss Bowles was teaching that moment—American history, multiplication, grammar—and sincerely thinking about the material and really trying to understand it and worrying that Miss Bowles could at any moment call on him and ask him pop-quiz questions about the material she'd just covered, which she often did, mocking those kids who answered incorrectly, suggesting for the next hour or so that perhaps they belonged in fifth grade rather than sixth, and Samuel paying attention closely and carefully and absolutely not letting his mind wander and not thinking about girls or doing anything regarding girls and yet this thing happened. It began as a kind of warmth, a tingle, like that feeling when someone is about to tickle you, that terrible anticipation. Then a sudden awareness of a body part that up until now was obscured, was among all those feelings that happened beneath what he paid attention to: the fabric on his shoulders, the fit of his socks, what his elbow was at any moment touching. Most of the time the body fades away. But lately, for no reason, more frequently than Samuel would like, his prick had become assertive. In class, at his desk, it would announce itself. It pushed against his jeans and then against the unforgiving metal underside of the school's one-size-fits-all desk. And the problem here was that all this rising and swelling and pressing was mortifying, but also, in a purely physical way, it was *really* pleasant. He wanted it to go away, but then again, he also didn't.

Did Miss Bowles know? Could she see it? That daily some of her boys went starry-eyed and glassy as their nervous systems took them somewhere else? If she did, she didn't say anything. And she never called on any of the boys in such a state and demand they stand while giving their answers. This seemed, for Miss Bowles, unusually merciful.

Samuel looked at the clock: Ten minutes till recess. His pants felt too tight. He felt wedged into his seat. Then his mind flashed involuntarily with visions of girls, his mental inventory of images accidentally caught here and there: cleavage seen when a woman at the mall bent over; a snip of leg and crotch and inner thigh glimpsed as girls in class sat down; and now a new vision, Bethany, in her room, sitting up straight, knees together, in a light cotton dress, violin at her chin, looking at him, those green catlike eyes.

When the bell rang for recess he acted like there was something important in his desk that he couldn't find. After everyone left the classroom, he stood up and maneuvered himself in such a way that, for anyone watching, would have looked like someone slowly hula-hooping without a Hula-Hoop.

The kids marched to the playground, marched with purpose and slow resolve even though they were by now surging with the energy that accumulates in an eleven-year-old body sitting rigidly still for hours under Miss Bowles's imperious gaze. They marched in total silence, single file on the far-right side of the corridor past all the signs the faculty had helpfully taped to the white concrete walls, one or two of which promoted some kind of LEARNING IS FUN! message, while the rest attempted strict behavior management: KEEP HANDS AND FEET TO YOURSELF; QUIET VOICES ONLY; WALK, DON'T RUN; WAIT YOUR TURN; USE POLITE LANGUAGE; DON'T USE MORE TOILET PAPER THAN YOU NEED; EAT BEFORE TALKING; USE TABLE MANNERS; RESPECT PERSONAL SPACE; RAISE YOUR HAND; DO NOT SPEAK UNLESS CALLED ON; STAY IN LINE; APOLOGIZE WHEN NEEDED; FOLLOW DIRECTIONS; USE SOAP APPROPRIATELY.

To most of the students, the education they received at school was only an incidental thing. To them, the overwhelming point of school was to learn how to behave in school. How to contort themselves to the school's rigid rules. Take, for example, bathroom breaks. No subject was more highly managed than the students' various excreta. Getting a bathroom pass was an elaborate ritual whereby Miss Bowles would—if you asked *really* nicely and convinced her that it was, indeed, an emergency and not some ploy to get out of class to smoke cigarettes or drink alcohol or do drugs—fill out this bathroom pass about the length of the Constitution. She'd write down your name and the time of your departure (down to the very second) and, horrifyingly, the nature of your visit (i.e., number one or number two), and then she'd ask you to read the hall pass aloud, which listed your "Rights and Restrictions," primarily among them that you could leave class for no more than two minutes and that while gone you assented to walk only on the right side of the corridor and go directly to the nearest bathroom and not say a word to anyone and not run in the halls and not be disruptive whatsoever and do nothing illegal while in the bathroom. Then you had to sign the hall pass and wait while Miss Bowles explained to you that you had signed a contract and there were severe penalties for people who broke contracts. Most of the time the kids would listen to her wide-eyed and panicked and doing that uncomfortable pee dance because they were already on the clock and the more Miss Bowles talked about contract law the more of their precious two minutes she cut into, such that when they finally got to the hall they had maybe ninety seconds to get to the bathroom and do their business and get back to class, all without running, which was impossible.

Plus you were only allowed two bathroom passes per *week*.

Then there was the rule about the water fountain: after students returned from recess they could only drink from the water fountain for *three seconds each*—this was probably meant to teach them about cooperation and selflessness—but of course the kids were panting and exhausted after a frenzied recess letting off all their stored-up angst, and there was a heat wave, and they were rarely allowed bathroom breaks, so the only water these sweaty and sunburned and overheated kids got all day came at the water fountain for these three seconds. This was a perverse double whammy for the students, because if they ran off their energy at recess, they would be parched and exhausted for the rest of the day, whereas if they didn't run around during recess, they'd feel so hyperactive in the late afternoon that they'd almost certainly get in some behavior-related trouble. So mostly the students played hard at recess, then gulped as much water as they could during their tiny three-second interval. And by the end of the day they were desolate, dehydrated lumps, which was actually how Miss Bowles preferred it.

So she stood over them and loudly counted out their time and each kid popped up at three, their chins dripping, not even close to enough water on this hot and humid and terrible Midwest day.

"This is bullshit," Bishop said to Samuel as they waited in line. "Watch this."

And when it was Bishop's turn he leaned over the fountain, pressed the button, and drank while making direct eye contact with Miss Bowles, who said, "One. Two. *Three.*" Then when Bishop did not stop drinking, she said "Three" again, more pointedly, then when Bishop still did not stop she said, "You're done now. Next!" And then it became clear that Bishop was not going to stop drinking until he was good and ready, and it appeared to most of the kids in line that Bishop wasn't even drinking anymore so much as letting the water run coolly over his lips, still looking directly at Miss Bowles as she finally realized this wasn't a matter of the new kid not knowing the rules but rather a direct challenge to her authority. And she responded to the confrontation by gathering herself into a rigid hands-on-hips, chin-jutting-out kind of posture and her voice dropped an octave as she said, "Bishop. You will stop drinking. *Now.*"

He stared at her with this bored, lifeless expression that was just so incredible and daring, and the kids in line were already bug-eyed and giggling dementedly because Bishop was about two seconds away from a paddling. Anyone who so blatantly disregarded the rules got paddled.

The paddle was famous.

It hung on the office wall of their principal, the school's chief disciplinarian, the unfortunately named Laurence Large, a short and oddly-shaped man who carried his weight almost entirely from the waist up—his legs were skinny and frail while his upper body ballooned. He looked like an egg standing on toothpicks. One wondered how his ankles and shinbones didn't snap. His paddle was made from a single three-inch-thick slab of wood, was about as wide as two pieces of notebook paper put together, and had about a dozen small holes drilled into it. For aerodynamics, the kids hypothesized. So he could swing it faster.

His paddlings were legendary for their force, for the technique required to generate enough power to, for example, shatter Brand Beaumonde's glasses, which was a historical fact that lived on as oral history among the members of the sixth-grade class, that Large struck Beaumonde's ass so hard the shock wave traveled up through the poor boy's body and cracked his high-prescription lenses. Comparisons were made to professional tennis players uncoiling 140-mph serves, how Large could transfer his weight in such a way to deliver a devastating—and athletically unlikely—blow. Sure, occasionally a parent might complain about the principal's retrograde punishment system, but since a paddling was the ultimate misbehavior prevention and deterrent, it was, for the most part, pretty rare. Certainly not frequent enough to spur any PTO campaigns. The absolute fact of assured backside annihilation was enough to keep even the rowdiest children in a more or less calm and low-decibel and narcotized fearful stupor for the whole of the school day. (That they went into spasms of wild hyperactivity as soon as they got home was something parents sometimes grumbled about to teachers, who quietly nodded their heads and thought: *Not my problem.*)

Every teacher had a unique point at which rebelliousness would no longer be tolerated. For Miss Bowles, that moment came after twelve seconds. For twelve seconds Bishop was at the water fountain. For twelve seconds he stared at Miss Bowles as she demanded he move along until finally she yanked Bishop by his shirt, physically grabbed him near the neck and with a stitch-tearing noise pulled him momentarily up off the ground before marching him toward the terrifying office of Principal Large.

What typically happened when a kid came back from a paddling is that somewhere between ten and twenty minutes after being sent away there would be a knock on the classroom door and Miss Bowles would open it and there would be Principal Large with his big hand on the back of some crimson-faced, snotty, sniveling kid. The faces of the recently paddled were always the same: wet and grim, eyes rubbed red, runny-nosed, defeated. There was no more rebellion in them, no more bravado. Even the loudest, most attention-seeking boys looked in this moment like they wanted to curl up under their desks and die. Then Large would say "I think this one is ready to rejoin the class" and Miss Bowles would say "I hope he's learned his lesson," and even students as young as eleven were sophisticated enough to know that this bit of dialogue was all theater, that the adults were not talking to each other but rather to the whole lot of them, the easily grasped subtext being: *Don't step out of line or you're next.* The kid would then be allowed to return to his seat, where his secondary punishment would begin, since his ass would be throbbing and bright red and tender as an open wound all over, and so sitting on the school's hard plastic chairs brought a sharp pain that felt, they said, like being paddled *again.* And so the kid would sit there in misery and cry and Miss Bowles would say "I'm sorry, I didn't hear you. Do you have something to add to our discussion?" and the kid would shake his head *no* in this pathetic, broken, miserable way and the whole class knew that Miss Bowles wanted to draw everyone's attention to his crying as a way to shame him more. In public. In front of his friends. There was a ruthlessness in Miss Bowles that the genderless blue sweaters she wore just barely contained.

That day they were all waiting for Bishop to return. They were excited. They were eager to accept him, after this initiation. Now he'd know what they'd been through. He was one of them. So they waited, ready to welcome Bishop back and forgive him for crying. Ten minutes passed, then fifteen, and finally right at the eighteen-minute mark came the inevitable knock on the door. And Miss Bowles made a big show of saying "Who could that be?" before putting the chalk onto the blackboard tray and striding to the door and opening it. And there they were, Bishop and Principal Large, and she was shocked, and the whole class was shocked, to see that not only was Bishop not crying, but he was also visibly smiling. He looked *happy*. Large's hand was not on Bishop's back. In fact, the principal was an odd two to three feet away from Bishop, as if the boy had some contagious disease. Miss Bowles stared at Principal Large for a moment, and Large did not stick to his usual script about Bishop being ready to rejoin the class, but only said, in a kind of distant way that soldiers sometimes talk about war: "Here. Take him."

And Bishop walked to his desk and every kid in the class watched him go and sit down, jumping into his seat and landing hard on his butt and looking up fiercely as if to challenge anyone to try to hurt him.

It was a moment that lived in the heart of every sixth grader who saw it. One of their own had taken the worst of the adult world and come out victorious. Nobody ever fucked with Bishop Fall after that.

5

SAMUEL'S MOTHER told him about the Nix. Another of her father's ghosts. The scariest one. The Nix, she said, was a spirit of the water who flew up and down the coastline looking for children, especially adventurous children out walking alone. When it found one, the Nix would appear to the child as a large white horse. Unsaddled, but friendly and tame. It bowed down as low as a horse was able, so the kid could leap onto it.

At first the children were afraid, but, ultimately, how could they refuse? Their very own horse! They jumped on and when it stood up again they were eight feet off the ground and they were delighted—nothing this big had ever minded them before. They became bold. They would kick at the horse to go faster, and so it broke into a light trot, and the more the kids loved it, the faster the horse would go.

Then they wanted other people to see them.

They wanted their friends to stare with envy at this brand-new horse. *Their* horse.

It always went like this. The kids who were victims of the Nix always felt, at first, fear. Then luck. Then possession. Then pride. Then terror. They'd kick at the horse to go faster until it was in a full gallop, the kids hanging on to its neck. It was the best thing that had ever happened to them. They'd never felt so important, so full of pleasure. And only at this point—at the pinnacle of speed and joy, when they felt most in control of the horse, when they felt the most ownership of it, when they most wanted to be celebrated for it and thus felt the most vanity and arrogance and pride—would the horse veer off the road that led to town and gallop toward the cliffs overlooking the sea. It ran full bore toward that great drop into the violent churning water below. And the kids screamed and yanked back on the horse's mane and cried and wailed but nothing mattered. The horse leaped off the cliff and dropped. The children clung to its neck even as they fell, and if they weren't bashed to death on the rocks, they drowned in the frigid water.

This was a story Faye had heard from her father. All her ghost stories came from Grandpa Frank, who was a tall and thin and intensely withdrawn man with a perplexing accent. Most people found him intimidating in his silence, but Samuel always thought it was a relief. Whenever they visited him in Iowa on those rare Thanksgivings or Christmases, the family would sit around the table eating and not saying a word. It was hard to have a conversation when it was met only with a nod of his head, a dismissive "Hm." Mostly they ate their turkey until Grandpa Frank was finished eating and left to watch television in the other room.

The only time Grandpa Frank was ever really animated was when he told them stories of the old country—old myths, old legends, old tales about ghosts he'd heard growing up where he'd grown up, in far-north Norway, in a little fishing village in the arctic that he left when he was eighteen. When he told Faye about the Nix, he said the moral was: *Don't trust things that are too good to be true.* But then she grew up and came to a new conclusion, which she told Samuel in the month before leaving the family. She told him the same story but added her own moral: "The things you love the most will one day hurt you the worst."

Samuel didn't understand.

"The Nix doesn't appear as a horse anymore," she said. They were in the kitchen hoping for a break in the heat wave that now seemed endless, sitting there reading with the refrigerator door wide open and a fan blowing the cold air onto them, drinking ice water, glasses sweating wet circles on the table. "The Nix used to appear as a horse," she said, "but that was in the old days."

"What does it look like now?"

"It's different for everyone. But it usually appears as a person. Usually it's someone you think you love."

Samuel still did not understand.

"People love each other for many reasons, not all of them good," she said. "They love each other because it's easy. Or because they're used to it. Or because they've given up. Or because they're scared. People can be a Nix for each other."

She sipped her water, then pressed the cold glass to her forehead. She closed her eyes. It was a long, tedious Saturday afternoon. Henry had gone into the office after another one of their fights, this one on the issue of dirty dishes. Their late-seventies-era avocado-colored dishwasher had finally stopped working this week, and not once had Henry volunteered to clean the growing pile of plates and bowls and cookware and glasses that had overrun the sink and much of the counter. Samuel suspected his mother was intentionally letting the pile get out of hand—maybe even contributing to it more than usual, using several pots for a meal that probably required only one—as a kind of test. Would Henry notice? Would he help? That he did neither of these things was something she extrapolated great meaning from.

"It's like home ec class all over again," she told him when the pile finally became unbearable.

"What are you talking about?" Henry said.

"Just like in high school. You go have fun while I cook and clean. Nothing's changed. In twenty years, absolutely nothing has changed."

Henry washed all the dishes, then claimed urgent weekend duties at the office, leaving Faye and Samuel alone, together, again. They sat in the kitchen and read from their respective books. Incomprehensible poetry for her. Choose Your Own Adventure for him.

"I knew a girl named Margaret in high school," Faye said. "Margaret was a very bright and witty girl. And in school she fell in love with a boy named Jules. A handsome boy who could do anything. Everyone was jealous of her. But it turns out Jules was her Nix."

"Why? What happened?"

She set her glass in the puddle it had made on the wood. "He disappeared," she said. "She got stranded, never left town. I hear she's still there, working as a cashier at her dad's pharmacy."

"Why did he do that?"

"That's what a Nix does."

"She couldn't tell?"

"It's difficult to see. But a good rule to remember is that anyone you fall in love with before you're an adult is probably a Nix."

"Anyone?"

"Probably anyone."

"When did you meet Dad?"

"In school," she said. "We were seventeen."

Faye stared into the yellow haze of the day. The refrigerator chugged and hummed and clicked and all at once, with a brief final electrical zap, it quit. And the light went out. And the countertop digital clock radio died. And Faye looked around and said, "We blew a fuse." Which meant of course that Samuel had to flip the breaker, because the breaker box was in the basement and his mother refused to go into the basement.

The flashlight was heavy and solid in his hand, its aluminum handle dimpled, its big round rubberized face an appropriate size for striking something violently in a pinch. His mother didn't go into the basement because the basement was where the house spirit lived. At least that was the story, another one from his grandfather: house spirits that inhabit basements and haunt you your entire life. His mother said she'd encountered one as a child and gotten spooked. She never liked basements after that.

But she insisted that her house spirit appeared only to her, only she was haunted, and Samuel was perfectly safe. He could go into the basement unharmed.

He began to cry. A soft and light whimper, because either there was a cruel ghost living in the basement watching him at this very moment or his mother was a little crazy. He shuffled his feet along the concrete floor and kept his attention narrowly focused on the beam of light in front of him. He tried to be blind to everything but that circle of light. And when he finally did see the fuse box on the other side of the room, he shut his eyes and walked as straight as he could. He shuffled forward and stuck the flashlight out in front of him and continued in this manner until he felt the flashlight's face bump into the wall. He opened his eyes. There was the fuse box. He threw the breaker and the basement lights came alive. He looked behind him and saw nothing. Nothing but the ordinary basement junk. He stayed a moment to collect himself, to stop crying. He sat on the floor. It was so much cooler down here.

IN THOSE FIRST FEW WEEKS of the school year, Bishop and Samuel fell into an easy alliance. Bishop would do whatever he wanted, and Samuel would follow. These were simple roles for the both of them. They never even discussed or acknowledged it, but fell into their positions like coins falling into their slots in a vending machine.

They'd meet in the woods for war games near the pond. Bishop always had a scenario ready for their games. They fought Charlie in Vietnam, the Nazis in World War II, the Confederacy in the Civil War, the British in the Revolutionary War, the Indians in the French and Indian War. And with the exception of their one confused attempt to play War of 1812, the wars always had a clear objective, and they were always the good guys, and their enemies were always bad, and the two of them always won.

Or if they weren't playing war, they'd play video games at Bishop's house, which was Samuel's preference because then he might run into Bethany, whom he loved. Though he probably wouldn't have called it "love" just yet. It was rather a state of heightened attention and agitation that manifested itself physically as a smaller vocal dynamic range (he had a tendency to shut down and become penitent in her presence even though he did not mean to or want to) and an intense desire to touch her clothes, between his thumb and forefinger, lightly. Bishop's sister exhilarated him and terrified him. But she usually ignored them. Bethany seemed unaware of her influence. She practiced her scales, listened to music, closed her door. She traveled to various music festivals and competitions, where she won solo violin ribbons and trophies that eventually went up on her bedroom wall, along with her various posters of Andrew Lloyd Webber musicals and a small collection of those porcelain masks representing comedy and tragedy. Dried flowers too, from her many recitals, when afterward she was given big bouquets of roses that she carefully dried and then affixed to her wall, above her bed, an efflorescence of pastel greens and pinks that exactly matched her bedspread and curtains and wallpaper color scheme. It was such a girl's room.

Samuel knew this bedroom because he had, two or three times, spied on it from a safe position outside, in the woods. He left his house right after sunset, under a deepening violet sky, came down to the creek, and made his muddy way through the woods, behind the houses of Venetian Village, past the gardens where roses and violets were closing up for the night, behind the odorous dog kennels and greenhouses that smelled of sulfur and phosphorous, behind the house of the headmaster of Blessed Heart Academy, who could sometimes be found this time of night relaxing in his custom-built outdoor saltwater Jacuzzi, and Samuel would move cautiously and slowly and watch out not to step on twigs or piles of dead leaves while he kept one eye on the headmaster, who from this distance looked like an indistinct white blobby thing, the many parts of him—belly and chin and underarms—notable only for their heavy sag. And on around the block, through the woods, down to the street's stubby end, where Samuel took a position among the tree roots behind the Fall house, perhaps ten feet from where the lawn met the forest, dressed entirely in black, with a black hood pulled down to within an inch of the ground so that the only bits of body that he showed the world were his eyes.

And there he watched.

The yellow-orange glow of lights, shadows of people as they migrated through the house. And when Bethany appeared within the frame of her bedroom window, a bolt of anxiety cracked in his belly. He pressed into the ground harder. She wore a thin cotton dress, which is what she always wore, always a little classier than anyone else, like she was returning from a fancy restaurant or church. The way the dress lightly swung as she walked, and then the way it so softly came to rest against her body when she stopped moving, gliding back down to her skin, like watching feathers fall elegantly through the air. Samuel could drown in that fabric, happily.

All he wanted was to see her. Just a confirmation that she did, in fact, exist. That's all he needed, and, upon seeing her, he would soon leave, long before she changed clothes and he could be accused of doing something dishonorable. Just this one thing—seeing Bethany and sharing this quiet, private moment with her—could calm him, get him through another week. That she attended Blessed Heart and not the public school, that she spent so much time in her room and so much time traveling, struck Samuel as unfair and unjust. The girls the other boys loved were always present, right there in front of them in class, right there next to them in the cafeteria. That Bethany was so inaccessible meant, to Samuel, in his head, that he was justified in occasionally spying on her. He was owed.

Then one day he was at their house when she walked right into the TV room while Bishop played Nintendo and collapsed into the same extra-large beanbag chair Samuel was at that moment sitting in. She sat in such a way that a small portion of her shoulder pressed against a small portion of his shoulder. And suddenly he felt that all the meaning in the world was concentrated in those few square inches.

"I'm bored," she said. She wore a yellow sundress. Samuel could smell her shampoo, rich with honey and lemon and vanilla. He held himself still, afraid that if he moved she might leave.

"Want a turn?" Bishop said, shoving the controller toward her.

"No."

"Want to play hide-and-seek?"

"No."

"Kick the can? Red rover?"

"How could we play red rover?"

"Just throwing out ideas here. Brainstorming. Spitballing."

"I don't want to play red rover."

"Hopscotch? Tiddlywinks?"

"Now you're being stupid."

Samuel felt his shoulder sweating where Bethany's shoulder pressed into him. He was so rigid it hurt.

"Or those weird games girls play," Bishop said, "where they fold up pieces of paper to find out who you're going to marry and how many babies you'll have."

"I do not want to do that."

"Don't you want to know how many babies you'll have? Eleven babies. That's my guess."

"Shut up."

"We could play dare."

"I don't want to play dare."

"What's dare?" Samuel said.

"It's truth or dare without the bullshit," Bishop said.

"I want to go somewhere," Bethany said. "For absolutely no reason. I want to go somewhere just for the point of being there and not here."

"The park?" Bishop said. "The beach? Egypt?"

"For no other reason than to be at a place for no reason."

"Oh," Bishop said, "you want to go to the mall."

"Yes," she said. "The mall. Yes I do."

"I'm going to the mall!" Samuel said.

"Our parents won't take us to the mall," Bethany said. "They say it's cheap and vulgar."

"I wouldn't be caught dead wearing those clothes," Bishop said, puffing his chest out and doing his best impression of his father.

"I'm going to the mall tomorrow," Samuel said. "With my mom. We have to buy a new dishwasher. I'll get you something. What do you want?"

Bethany thought about it. She looked toward the ceiling and tapped her finger on her cheekbone and thought about it hard and long before saying, "Surprise me."

And all that night and into the following day, Samuel thought about what he could buy for Bethany. What gift would capture everything he needed to let her know? The gift needed to distill his feelings for her, give her in one small package a quick potent shot of his love and commitment and total helpless devotion.

So he knew the gift's parameters, but he could not see the gift itself. Somewhere in the mall's million billion shelves, the perfect gift almost certainly waited for him. But what was it?

In the car, Samuel was quiet and his mother was agitated. She always got like this on their trips to the mall. She loathed the mall, and so her critiques of what she called "suburban mall culture" grew severe and brutal whenever she actually had to go there.

They navigated out of the subdivision, onto the wider arterial road that looked like any arterial road in any American suburb: a franchise hall of mirrors. This is what you get in the suburbs, his mother said, the satisfaction of small desires. The getting of things you didn't even know you wanted. An even larger grocery store. A fourth lane. A bigger, better parking lot. A new sandwich shop or video-rental store. A McDonald's slightly closer than the other McDonald's. A McDonald's next door to a

Burger King, across the street from a Hardee's, in the same lot as a Steak 'n Shake and a Bonanza and a Ponderosa all-you-can-eat smorgasbord thing. What you get, in other words, is *choice*.

Or, rather, the *illusion* of choice, she said, all these restaurants offering substantially the same menu, some slight variation on potatoes and beef. Like at the grocery store, when she stood in the pasta aisle looking at the eighteen different brands of spaghetti. She couldn't understand. "Why do we need eighteen spaghettis?" she said. Samuel shrugged. "Exactly," she said. Why did we need twenty different coffees? Why did we need so many shampoos? It was easy to forget when looking at the chaos of the cereal aisle that all these hundreds of options were actually one option.

At the mall—the tremendous, bright, vast, air-conditioned cathedral of a mall—they were looking at dishwashers, but Faye was distracted by various other home appliances: something that made it easier to store leftover food; something that made it easier to grind it up; something that prevented food from sticking to the pan; something that made it easier to freeze food; something that made it easier to warm it up again. When she looked at each item she clucked a surprised *Huh!* and inspected it, turned it over in her hand, read the box, and said, "I wonder who thought of this?" She was wary around these things, suspicious that someone else had created a need in her or had identified a need she didn't know she had. In the home-and-garden section it was a self-propelled lawn mower that got her attention, bright and macho-big and fantastically shiny red. "I never even thought I'd have a lawn," she said, "and yet I suddenly want this very badly. Is that wrong?"

"No, it's not wrong," she said later, in one of the mall's other kitchen stores, picking up the conversation as if she'd never stopped talking. "There's nothing wrong with it at all. But, I don't know. I feel like . . ." She paused, held some white plastic object in her hand, stared at it, some device that achieved perfectly julienned vegetables. "Doesn't it seem absurd? That I can just *buy* this?"

"I don't know."

"Is this really me?" she said, staring at the thing cupped in her hand. "The real me? Is this who I've become?"

"Can I have some money?" Samuel said.

"For what?"

Samuel shrugged.

"Don't just buy something to buy it. For the point of buying something."

"I won't."

"You don't *have* to buy something, is my point. Nobody really needs any of this stuff."

She reached into her purse and produced a ten-dollar bill. "Meet me back here in an hour."

He gripped the money in his hand and marched off into the mall's blazing white light. The place was unknowably large. It was like a big, breathing animal. The sound of a child or children somewhere distant yelling or crying became part of the omnidirectional din: Samuel had no idea where it was coming from, where the child was, whether the child was happy or sad. It was simply a disconnected audio fact. It was inconceivable that there were not enough stores at the mall, but someone decided there needed to be even more, thus the small stand-alone kiosks that occupied the middle of every thoroughfare, selling specialized and sometimes gimmicky merchandise: little toy helicopters that the salesman demonstrated by flying them over the crowd's worried heads; key chains with your name laser-engraved onto them; special hair-curler things Samuel couldn't begin to understand; sausages in gift boxes; blocks of glass that appeared to have 3-D holograms inside; a special girdle that made you look thinner than you really were; hats embroidered with personalized messages while you waited; T-shirts laser-printed with your own photographs. With its hundreds of stores and booths, the mall seemed to make a simple promise: that here you would find everything you needed. Even seemingly esoteric things could be found here. Teeth whitening, for example, seemed like an unlikely mall purchase. Or Swedish massage. Or a piano. And yet you could find them all here. The mall's overwhelmingness was meant to replace your imagination. Forget trying to dream up your desires; the mall had already dreamed them up for you.

Trying to find the perfect gift in the mall was like reading a Choose Your Own Adventure book when the choices were absent. He had to guess which page to turn to. The happy ending was out there somewhere, hidden.

Samuel walked by the candle store and breathed one or two lungfuls of its cinnamon odor. The nail salon gave him a momentary toxic headache. The candy store's plastic bins of jawbreakers called to him, but he resisted. The mall's music mixed with the music coming from each of the stores, the effect being like a car going into and out of radio coverage. Songs faded in, faded out. Earlier they were playing something happily Motown. Now they were playing "The Twist." Chubby Checker. One of his mother's least-favorite songs—a fact Samuel didn't know how he knew. And he was considering the music and listening to the music coming out of the stores and he actually saw the music store across the food court before the idea finally struck, and he couldn't believe it had taken him this long to come to it.

Music.

Bethany was a *musician*. He ran to the store and felt embarrassed that in all this time he'd been asking himself what *he* could give *her* without asking himself what she might actually *want*. And this felt egotistical and selfish and definitely something he'd have to work on personally some other time, when he didn't have to find the perfect gift in like ten minutes.

So he ran into the store and was briefly disheartened when he saw that all the popular cassette tapes were around twelve dollars and thus outside his budget. But this despair did not last long because at the back of the store he spotted a bin labeled "Classical Music" and, below that, "Half Off," which felt like providence. The cassettes here were six bucks and one of them—he was sure of it—was the perfect gift.

But as Samuel rifled through the clacking, disordered chaos of the clearance bin, he encountered a fundamental problem: He didn't know any of this music. He didn't know what Bethany would like, what she already owned. He didn't even know what was *good*. Some of the names were familiar—Beethoven, Mozart—but most were not. Some were unpronounceably foreign. And he was about to go with one of the famous names he'd heard before—Stravinsky, though he couldn't remember why he knew it—when he decided that if he'd heard of Stravinsky, then Bethany almost assuredly already owned every Stravinsky recording and was probably by now bored with them, and so he resolved to find something more modern, interesting, new, something that advertised his fascinating tastes and showed how he was different and independent and didn't follow the herd like everyone else. So he picked out the ten most interesting-looking covers. Nothing with the portrait of the composer, nothing with an old painting or a photograph of a stuffy-looking orchestra, nothing with a conductor holding a baton. He went for the conceptual stuff: splashy colors, abstract geometric shapes, psychedelic spirals.

He brought them to the counter and piled them in front of the cashier and asked, "Which of these would no one ever buy?"

The cashier, a sensitive-looking thirtysomething assistant-manager guy with a ponytail, did not act like this was an odd question but rather looked through the cassettes dutifully and then, with an air of authority that made Samuel trust him, picked one and shook it and said, "This one. No one ever buys this one."

Samuel put down his ten dollars and the cashier wrapped the cassette in a bag.

"This is really modern stuff," the cashier said. "Really out there."

"Good," Samuel said.

"It's the same piece recorded ten different times. Like, really weird stuff. You like this?"

"Very much."

"Okay," he said. He gave him his change and Samuel still had about four bucks left. He ran to the candy store. The perfect gift swung wildly in its bag and battered the back of his legs and his mouth puckered in anticipation of the jawbreaker he was going to buy and his head bounced to the mall's music and his eyes fluttered with daydreams where he made the right choice every time and all his adventures had the very best and happiest endings.

7

BISHOP FALL WAS A BULLY, but not an obvious bully. He did not prey on the weak. He left them alone, the skinny boys, the awkward girls. He wanted nothing easy. It was the strong and confident and self-possessed and powerful who drew his attention.

During the school year's first pep rally, Bishop took an interest in Andy Berg, resident champion of all things brutal, only member of the sixth-grade class to achieve dark growths of leg and underarm hair, local terrorizer of the small and shrill. It was the gym teacher who first started calling him "Iceberg." Or, sometimes, just "the Berg." Because of his size (colossal), speed (slow), and the way he moved (unstoppably). The Berg was your typical grade-school bully: vastly bigger and stronger than anyone else in class, and transparently externalizing some raging inner demons about his stunted mental abilities, which were the only things stunted about him. The rest of his body was on some kind of genetic sprint to adulthood. He was now, in sixth grade, taller than the female teachers. Heavier, too. His body was not one of those destined for athletic greatness. He was simply going to be *thick*. A torso shaped like a beer keg. Arms like beef flanks.

The pep rally began as it usually did, with grades one through six sitting in the bleachers of the odd-smelling rubber-floored gymnasium, watching assistant principal Terry Fluster (who, by the way, was dressed as a six-foot-tall red-and-white eagle, the school's mascot) lead them through a series of cheers, beginning, as always, with: *Eagles! Don't do drugs!*

Then Principal Large shushed them and gave his typical inaugural spiel about his expectations for behavior and his zero-tolerance, no-shit-taking teaching philosophy, during which the students stopped paying attention and stared narcoleptically at their shoes, save for the first graders, who were hearing this for the first time and were, naturally, terrified.

The pep rally concluded with Mr. Fluster's usual: *Let's go, Eagles! Let's go, Eagles!*

And the students yelled and clapped along with him at a level that was roughly one-quarter of the assistant principal's enthusiasm, still loud enough to mask Andy Berg's individual cheer, which was audible only to the several people standing around him, Samuel and Bishop included: *Kim's a faggot! Kim's a faggot!*

Directed of course at poor Kim Wigley, standing two paces to the Berg's left, by all accounts the easiest boy to make fun of in the entire sixth-grade class, one of those kids suffering through every prepubescent disaster there was: thick snowy dandruff, aggressive braces, chronic impetigo, extreme nearsightedness, severe allergies to nuts and pollen, destabilizing ear infections, facial eczema, bimonthly pinkeye, warts, asthma, even an occurrence of head lice in the second grade that no one ever let him forget. Plus he was all of about forty pounds soaking wet. Plus he had a girl's first name.

In these moments, Samuel knew the "right" thing to do would be to defend Kim and stop the bullying and stand up to the giant Andy Berg because *bullies back down when they encounter resistance* according to the brochures they were given in health class once a year. This was, everyone knew, a big fat lie. Because last year Brand Beaumonde actually did stand up to the Berg for the constant scorn directed toward Brand's bulletproof-thick eyeglasses, stood up to him right in the middle of the lunchroom and said "Shut up your big mouth you big jerk!" in a spasm of nervous agitation. And the Berg did indeed back down and left him alone the rest of the school day and everyone who witnessed it was jubilant because maybe they were safe now and maybe the pamphlets were right and this great sense of optimism pervaded the school and Brand was a minor hero until the Berg found him on his way home that day and beat him up so savagely that the police actually got involved and interviewed Brand's friends who, by now, had learned an important lesson: to keep their fucking mouths shut. Bullies do not back down.

The big rumor about the Berg this year—one propagated by the Berg himself—was that he was, by all accounts, the first member of the sixth-grade class to have sex. With a girl. With, he said, a former babysitter who, quote, *can't get enough of my dick*. This of course was unverifiable. Either the high-school girl in question or her interest in the Berg's anatomy, unverifiable but also unchallenged. Nobody in the locker room within earshot of the Berg's boasting was willing to risk personal injury by stating the obvious: There was no way a high-school girl would be interested in a sixth grader unless she was mentally disturbed, wicked ugly, or emotionally broken. Or all three of these things. There was just no way.

And yet.

There was something in the way the Berg spoke about sex that made the boys wonder. It was the specificity of the details. The exact and totally unglamorous particulars. That's what gave the boys pause, kept them up at night wondering and sometimes falling into private rages that maybe he was telling the truth, maybe he really was banging a high schooler, and if this was true it was the only proof they needed that the world was unjust and that God did not exist. Or if God did exist, God must hate them, for nobody in the school deserved sex less than Andy fucking Berg. Every gym class they endured it, how he had to smoke one of his dad's cigars to cover the smell of pussy, how he wasn't getting laid this week because the girl was on the rag, how one time when he blew his load, the condom he was wearing exploded because he was *just that horny*. These visions gave the boys nightmares, these and the larger tragedy that the repellent Andy Berg was having robust sex while most of them had only very recently had "the talk" with their parents and the whole idea of sex with a girl still seemed terrifying and gross.

It might have been the way the Berg taunted Kim at the pep rally that prompted Bishop to act. He would have thought it was too easy, too obvious—the way Kim didn't fight back, how his passive and slumped-over body revealed his hundred percent acceptance of the hierarchies at work here. Kim stood there reflexively prepared to be bullied. The shooting-fish-in-a-barrel nature of this probably outraged Bishop's odd sense of justice, his soldier's desire to protect the weak and innocent via disproportionate violence.

As all the students filed out of the gymnasium, Bishop tapped the Berg on the shoulder. "I heard a rumor about you," he said.

The Berg looked down at him, annoyed. "Yeah? What."

"That you've had sex."

"You better fucking believe it."

"It's true, then, the rumor."

"I get so much pussy you don't even know how much."

Samuel trailed carefully behind them. He was not usually comfortable being this close to the Berg, but with Bishop between them he felt safe. Bishop's personality tended to direct all attention to him. It was as if Bishop blocked Samuel from view.

"Okay," Bishop said, "I have something for you."

"What."

"It's something for people who are a little more mature. Such as yourself."

"What is it."

"I don't want to say right now. Someone might hear. And this is very juicy, really illegal stuff we're talking about."

"What the fuck are you saying?"

Bishop rolled his eyes and looked around as if to check if anyone was eavesdropping before leaning closer to the Berg and beckoning him with his fingers to lean down so that his giant head wasn't so far away and Bishop whispered, "Pornography."

"No *way*!"

"Quiet down."

"You've got porn?"

"A massive stash."

"Seriously?"

"I've been trying to decide who here is grown-up enough to see it."

"Rad!" the Berg said, roused. Because for kids his age, for kids hitting adolescence in the eighties, in those days before the internet, before the web made pornography easily accessible and therefore banal, for this last generation of boys for whom porn was primarily a *physical object,* possessing pornography was like having a superpower. One that made you immediately legitimate and popular among the other boys. This happened roughly once per semester, some obscure boy locating his father's collection of dirty magazines and suddenly finding himself elevated socially for as long as he didn't get in trouble, which might take a day to several months, depending on the constitution of the boy. The ones who were transparently desperate and begging for attention and craving to be liked tended to steal the whole pile in exchange for a one-time flash of celebrity, bright stars who burned out in a day when their fathers noticed the disappearance of all their pornography and put two and two together. Other boys, the ones with more impulse control and less desperation for approval, were more judicious in their porn approaches. They might remove only one magazine from the pile, say the second or third from the bottom, an edition that had presumably been perused, enjoyed, digested, and abandoned. They brought that one magazine to school and let everyone look through it before replacing it in the pile a week or two later, then removing another edition from near the bottom, and then repeating the pattern. These boys maintained a consistent popularity for, sometimes, months before a teacher noticed a group of boys sitting still in a huddle on the playground and came to investigate, because when grade-school boys weren't running around like spazzes it meant something was definitely wrong.

It was always temporary, in other words, the boys' access to porn. Which was why it so piqued the Berg's interest.

"Where is it?" he said.

"Most of these kids would freak out," Bishop said. "They wouldn't understand what they're looking at."

"Let me see it."

"You, on the other hand. I think you could handle it."

"Damn right."

"Okay, meet me after school. After everyone's left the building. At the stairwell behind the cafeteria, by the loading dock. I'll show you where I hide it."

The Berg agreed, then pushed his way out of the gymnasium. Samuel tapped Bishop on the shoulder.

"What are you doing?" he said.

Bishop smiled. "I'm taking the fight to the enemy."

Later that day, after the final bell, after the buses had come and gone and the building had emptied, Bishop and Samuel waited behind the school, that part of the school not visible from the road, all concrete and asphalt. It had the look of a regional high-volume shipping facility, industrial and mechanical and automated and apocalyptic. There were massive air-conditioning units whose fans spun inside aluminum shells crusted and emblackened with sooty exhaust, roaring like a squadron of attack helicopters readying for, but never quite managing, takeoff. There were scraps of paper and cardboard blown by the wind into corners and crevices. There was the industrial trash compactor: solid metal, the size of a dump truck, painted that forest-green color typical of waste-disposal vehicles, covered all over with a scum of sticky trash residue.

Just next to the loading dock was a stairwell that led down to a base-ment door nobody ever used. Nobody even knew where it led. The stair-well was enclosed on one side by the concrete wall of the loading dock, on the other by tall unclimbable vertical bars. There was also a gate at the top of the stairs. This stairwell was a riddle for anyone who both-ered thinking about it long enough. The bars obviously communicated a desire to keep people out, except that even if the gate were locked it would be a simple matter to leap down into the stairwell from the loading dock above it. But the basement door at the bottom of the stairs was one of those that opened only from the inside and didn't even have an exterior handle. So the only real function of the gate was to trap people in, which seemed at least architecturally odd and at most an extreme hazard in the event of fire. Anyway, the amount of dirt and dead leaves and thrown-away plastic wrappers and cigarette butts in the stairwell indicated that it hadn't been used in years.

They waited for the Berg here, Samuel feeling scared and nervous about this whole thing, about what Bishop planned to do, which was to lock Andy Berg in the stairwell and leave him there all night.

"I really don't think we should be doing this," he told Bishop, who was at the bottom of the stairwell hiding a black plastic bag he had produced from his backpack, burying it under the leaves and dirt and debris.

"Relax," he said. "It'll be fine."

"But what if it isn't?" said Samuel, who was right on the cusp of a Cat-egory 2 just thinking about the ways Andy Berg could get them back for what seemed like a pretty stupid trick.

"Let's just go right now," Samuel said, "before he gets here. No harm done."

"I need you to do your job. What's your job?"

Samuel frowned and touched the bulky metal padlock he was cur-rently hiding in his pocket. "When he gets to the bottom of the steps, close the gate."

"*Quietly* close the gate," Bishop said.

"Right. So he doesn't notice."

"I'll give you the signal and you'll close the gate."

"What's the signal?"

"I'll give you a look pregnant with meaning."

"A what?"

"A real bug-eyed look. You'll know it when you see it."

"Okay."

"And after the gate is closed?"

"I lock it," Samuel said.

"That's the essential part of the mission."

"I know."

"The very most important part."

"If I lock it, then he can't get out and beat us up."

"You have to think like a soldier here. You have to be focused on your part of the operation."

"Okay."

"I didn't hear you?"

Samuel kicked at the ground. "I said *hooah*."

"That's better."

It was warm and wetly humid, the shadows lengthening and the light a deep orange. Storm clouds gathered on the horizon, those great Midwestern clouds like floating avalanches, which meant an evening of thundershowers and heat lightning. The wind blew roughly through the trees. A tang of electricity and ozone in the air. Bishop finished arranging the bag at the bottom of the stairs. Samuel practiced closing the gate without making it squeak. Eventually they climbed up onto the loading dock and waited, Bishop checking and rechecking the contents of his backpack, Samuel fingering the ridges of the heavy padlock in his pocket.

"Hey, Bish?"

"Yeah."

"What happened in the principal's office?"

"What do you mean?"

"When you went for a paddling. What happened in there?"

Bishop stopped fussing with his backpack for a moment. He looked at Samuel, then away, off into the distance. He assumed a certain manner Samuel had begun to recognize, where his body seemed coiled and tightened and his eyes turned to slits and his eyebrows wrinkled into check marks. A posture of defiance, a look Samuel had seen before: with the principal, and Miss Bowles, and Mr. Fall, and when Bishop threw that rock at the headmaster's house. It was a fierceness and hardness usually foreign to eleven-year-olds.

But it dissolved just as quickly, as Andy Berg rounded the corner of the building, lumbering in his big stupid way, shuffling along, dragging his toes like his feet were too far away from his tiny brain, as if his body were too large for his nervous system to handle.

"He's here," Bishop said. "Get ready."

The Berg wore his usual uniform of black sweatpants, generic white sneakers, and a T-shirt with something juvenilely funny written on it, this time "Where's the Beef?" He was the only male in the class not made fun of for wearing imitation off-brand shoes. His giant size and proclivity to violence gave him a free pass, fashion-wise. The only acknowledgment he made to current tastes was the rattail he grew, a hairstyle that was en vogue with roughly a quarter of the boys in the class. A proper rattail was achieved when a boy cut his hair short but left a spot in the very middle of the back of his head to grow wildly away. The Berg had so far achieved a frizzy black curly rope that extended several inches down his neck and back. He approached the loading dock, where the two boys sat, elevated, slightly above him, cross-legged.

"You came," Bishop said.

"Let's see it, fag."

"First tell me you're not going to freak out."

"Shut the fuck up."

"A lot of kids freak out. They're not mature enough. This is hard-core stuff."

"I can handle it."

"Oh can you?" Bishop said. His tone was playful and sarcastic. That tone where you can't decide if he's having fun with you or insulting you. That tone that makes you feel like you're one or two steps behind him. The understanding of this registered on the Berg's face—he hesitated, unsure of himself. He was not accustomed to kids showing any kind of spirit or spine.

"Okay, let's say you can handle it," Bishop continued. "Let's say you're not going to freak out. Nothing you haven't seen before, am I right?"

The Berg nodded.

"Because you see it all the time, right? That high schooler you're banging?"

"What about her?"

"I'm wondering why you're so eager right now when you have a girl whenever you want her. Why do you need the porn?"

"I don't need it."

"And yet here you are."

"You don't even have it. You're lying."

"Makes me think maybe there's something you're not telling us. Maybe the girl's ugly. Maybe she doesn't exist."

"Fuck you. Are you gonna show me this shit or not?"

"Okay, I'll let you see one picture. And if you don't freak out, I'll let you see the rest."

Bishop rummaged in his backpack for a moment before pulling out a page from a magazine, folded several times, one ragged edge where it had been torn free. He handed it—carefully, slowly—to the Berg, who snatched it, annoyed at Bishop's manner, his theatricality. The Berg unfolded it, and even before it was fully undone his eyes seemed to open wider, his lips very slightly parted, and his face melted from its usual barbaric severity to a kind of giddiness.

"Whoa," he said. "Oh yes."

Samuel could not see the image that delighted the Berg so much. He could only see the back of the page, which appeared to be an advertisement for some kind of brown liquor.

"That is *awesome,*" the Berg said. He looked like a puppy staring at your food.

"It's good," Bishop said, "but I wouldn't call it *awesome.* Actually it's pretty par for the course. Even a little droll, if you ask me."

"Where'd you get it?"

"Irrelevant. Would you like to see more?"

"Fuck yeah."

"And you're not going to tell anyone?"

"Where is it?"

"You need to promise. You won't tell."

"Fine, I promise."

"Say it with feeling."

"Just show me."

Bishop raised his hands in an I-give-up gesture, then pointed at the stairwell below him. "Down there," he said. "I keep them down there, hidden in the dirt, bottom of the stairs."

The Berg dropped the page he was looking at and opened the gate to the stairwell and rushed down. Bishop looked at Samuel and nodded: *the signal.*

Samuel leaped off the loading dock down to the spot where the Berg had been standing. He walked over to the gate and very slowly shut it, just as they had practiced. He could see the Berg at the bottom of the stairs, his long horrible rattail, the fat expanse of his back as he huddled down and swept away the dirt and leaves and discovered the plastic bag that Bishop had planted there.

"In here? In the bag?" the Berg said.

"Yep. That's it."

When the gate shut, it did so with a small and trivial *click*. Samuel slipped the heavy padlock between the bars and closed it. The snap made by the lock's internal metal mechanism felt substantial and satisfying. It felt final. Irrevocable. *They had done it.* There was no going back.

A few feet away, fluttering in the wind, was the page Bishop had given the Berg. It spun in the eddies the breeze made around the loading dock, folding over itself at the creases made when it was pressed into eighths. Samuel grabbed it. Opened it. And the immediate impression the photo gave, before all its shapes resolved themselves into recognizable human forms, the dominant textural feature, the thing that seemed to define the photo and would later be pretty much the only thing Samuel remembered about it, was *hair.* Loads of dark, curly hair. Around the girl's head, a jet-black cascade that looked physically heavy and difficult to bear, hair in tight curls that reached all the way down to the dirt she sat on, the flesh of her butt smooshing out beneath her like bread dough, one arm behind her and supporting herself with her elbow in the dirt, the other hand reaching down to her crotch, opening herself up with two fingers in a gesture that looked like an upside-down peace sign, revealing this plump and mysterious bright-red spot amid another outbreak of dark black hair, hair that was thick and curly where it almost reached her belly button, but became wispy inside her pimpled thighs, where the hair resembled the desolate attempts teenagers make at mustaches and beards, hair that kept creeping down beneath her to the spot where she contacted the ground, where she sat in some anonymous tropical forest scene, Samuel seeing this and trying to gather all of it simultaneously and trying to make sense of it and trying to enjoy it the way Andy Berg seemed to enjoy it but achieving only this abstract sense of curiosity combined with maybe a mild revulsion or horror that the adult world seemed be a terrible, appalling place.

He folded the page into small squares. He was trying to forcibly forget what he'd just seen when, from the bottom of the stairwell, the Berg suddenly boomed: "What the *fuck*?"

And at that moment a bright white flash popped. Bishop held a Polaroid camera, and it buzzed and clicked and ejected a white square of film.

"What the fuck!" the Berg said again. Samuel climbed the ladder onto the loading dock and ran to the edge where Bishop stood overlooking the Berg and flapping the photo and laughing. The Berg had several pictures around him, presumably having upended the bag and let them all flutter out. And almost all of them, Samuel could see now, were close-ups of large, erect penises. Adult penises. Adult and very manly and horribly engorged and darkly empurpled and some of them dribbling and wet. Penises, some of them from glossy magazines, some actual real Polaroid pictures, whitely lit, softly focused, close-up anonymous disembodied cocks emerging from shadows or from beneath the folds of someone's sagging belly flesh.

"What the fuck!" Andy Berg could not seem to find any other words but these. "What in the fuck?"

"See? I knew it," Bishop said. "You're freaking out."

"What the fuck is this?"

"You're not quite mature enough."

"I'm going to fucking kill you."

"You're not quite there yet, developmentally speaking."

The Berg took the stairs two at a time. He was so big and he moved so destructively that it seemed impossible to contain him. Had they really trusted a stupid little padlock to keep them safe? Samuel imagined it snapping in half. He imagined the Berg erupting out of his cage like an insane circus animal. Samuel took a step back and stood behind Bishop, put a hand on Bishop's shoulder. The Berg ran to the top of the stairs and reached his arm forward to push open the gate. Only the gate did not budge. And the force of the Berg's huge momentum met the solid metal gate, and the only givable thing between them—the Berg's arm—gave.

His wrist bent back and his shoulder torqued wildly with this crunching, snapping sound, this horrible liquid pop. And the Berg bounced backward and landed hard on the stairs and slid down a few of them until he came to rest near the bottom, clutching his arm, moaning, crying. The gate vibrated against the lock.

"Oh my god," the Berg wailed. *"My arm!"*

"Let's go," Samuel said.

"Wait," Bishop said. "One more thing."

He walked along the edge of the loading dock until he was just above the Berg, roughly six feet over him.

"See, what I'm going to do now," Bishop said over the Berg's feeble crying, "is I'm going to take a leak, and you're not going to do anything about it. And you're not going to fuck with anybody ever again. Because I've got this photo." Bishop waved the Polaroid at him. "You should see it. There you are with all that faggot porn. You want this photo to show up in every locker in school? Taped under every desk? Slipped into every single textbook?"

The Berg looked at him and, for a moment, the actual sixth-grade mind that was trapped in his giant adult body broke through, and he looked astonished and hurt and pathetic and sad. Like an animal stunned in disbelief at having just been kicked.

"No," he spat out through the crying.

"Then I expect you'll start behaving," Bishop said. "No more picking on Kim. No more picking on anyone."

Bishop undid his belt and unzipped his pants and pulled down his underwear and released a long strong jet of urine right at Andy Berg, who wailed and turned around to hide from it and screamed. He curled up while Bishop splattered onto his back and shirt and rattail.

Then the two boys gathered their things and left. They didn't speak at all until they parted ways, at the spot where Bishop cut through the woods to Venetian Village and Samuel continued the other way to his own home. Bishop rapped him lightly on the arm and said "Be all you can be, soldier," then dashed away.

That night, the heat wave finally broke. Samuel sat at his bedroom window and watched the thunderstorm drench the whole outside world. The trees in the backyard whipped violently and the sky flashed with lightning. He imagined Andy Berg out in the storm, still trapped, soaking wet. He imagined him shivering and cold and injured and alone.

In the morning, the air had that chilly first feeling of autumn. Andy Berg was not in school. The rumor was that he hadn't come home last night. The police were called. Parents and neighbors went out looking. He was finally located in the morning, wet and sick, in the stairwell behind the school. Now he was in the hospital. Nobody mentioned anything about the Polaroids.

Samuel guessed the Berg had caught a cold, maybe the flu, from the rain. But Bishop had another theory. "He'd have to get rid of the porn, right?" he said at recess that day. "I mean, he wouldn't want to be found with those pictures."

"Yeah," Samuel said. "But how?"

They sat on the swings not swinging, watching a game of tag under way across the playground, a game that included Kim Wigley, which was rare, as Kim tended to avoid recess, or really any public space with a high Berg-bullying potential. Now he played in unself-conscious joy and delight.

"The Berg's in the hospital now," Bishop said. "Probably poisoned, I think."

"Poisoned how?"

"He ate them. The photos. That's how he got rid of them."

Samuel tried to imagine eating a Polaroid picture. Chewing that hard plastic. Swallowing those sharp, heavy corners.

"He ate them?" he said.

"Absolutely."

Across the playground, Kim glanced at them and offered Bishop a feeble wave. Bishop waved back. Then he laughed and said "Hooah" and ran over to join the game, actually almost skipped over there, barely even touching the ground as he went.

8

THE BLESSED HEART ACADEMY HEADMASTER could be seen lately taking short, plodding walks along Venetian Village's lone street, usually around sunset, shuffling his great heft carefully and gingerly, as if his legs could, at any moment, shatter. The cane he walked with was a recent acquisition, and the headmaster seemed to enjoy how regal it made him look. It was actually pretty incredible how his stooped body and painful-looking limp could be improved so much by the simple addition of a cane. Now he seemed *nobly impaired.* Like a war hero. The cane's shaft was made of oak and stained to a rich ebony. A pearl handle was attached to the top by a pewter collar etched with patterns of fleur-de-lis. Neighbors were relieved at the addition of the cane because it made the headmaster's pain not quite so visibly obvious, and so they did not feel required to ask him how he felt, and thus they did not have to endure yet another conversation about the Sickness. This was a topic that had frankly run itself dry in the last six months. The headmaster had by now told all his neighbors about the Sickness, the mysterious affliction that no doctor could diagnose and no medicine could cure. The symptoms were well-known up and down the block: tightness in his chest; shallow breathing; profuse sweating; uncontrollable salivation; abdominal cramps; blurry vision; fatigue; lethargy; general allover weakness; headache; dizziness; loss of appetite; slow heartbeat; and an odd involuntary twitching and rippling of the muscles just under his skin that he would horribly show to neighbors if it flared up while they were talking. The spells came either in the middle of the day or in the middle of the night, lasting roughly four to six hours before magically ceasing on their own. He was shockingly candid and personal about the details of his condition. He spoke in that manner of people experiencing catastrophic illness, how the illness eclipsed previous gentlemanly notions of modesty and privacy. He told people how confusing it was, priority-wise, when he needed to vomit and diarrhea *at the same time.* The neighbors nodded and smiled tightly and tried not to betray how awful this was to listen to, because their children—and indeed all the children of Venetian Village—attended Blessed Heart Academy, and it was widely known that the headmaster could pull some serious strings. One phone call from him to the dean of admissions at Princeton or Yale or Harvard or Stanford could improve a child's chances by about a thousand percent. Everyone knew this, so they suffered the headmaster's long and vivid descriptions of medical procedures and bodily effluence because they thought of it as a kind of investment in their child's education and future. So yes, they knew about his many trips to various expensive specialists, allergists, oncologists, gastroenterologists, cardiologists, his MRIs and CT scans and unpleasant organ biopsies. He made the same joke every time about how the best money he'd spent so far was on his cane. (It was, as canes go, breathtakingly beautiful, the neighbors had to agree.) He maintained that the best medicine was being active and outdoors, thus his evening walks and twice-daily soaks—once in the morning, once at night—in his backyard saltwater hot tub, which he said was one of the few joys left in his life.

Some of the less charitable neighbors insisted privately that the reason for his evening walks wasn't health but the opportunity to complain for an hour like the goddamn sympathy-seeking tyrant he really was. They would not tell this to anyone else, maybe a spouse but *that's it,* because they knew how selfish and insensitive and callous it sounded, that the headmaster was genuinely sick with a mysterious illness that caused a terrific amount of pain and mental anguish, and yet they were the ones who felt like victims, they were the ones who felt aggrieved, because they were forced to listen to it. And sometimes on these nights they felt under siege, attending to the headmaster for sixty tedious minutes before getting rid of him and retiring to their entertainment rooms to try to squeeze some enjoyment out of what was left of the evening. They turned on the television and saw some news story about another goddamn humanitarian crisis, another goddamn civil war in some godforsaken place, and saw images of wounded people or starving children and felt a bright, bitter anger *at the children* for invading and ruining the only moments of relaxation and "me time" the neighbors had all day. The neighbors would get a little indignant here, about how their own lives were hard too, and yet nobody heard them complaining about it. Everyone had problems—why couldn't they just quietly deal with them? On their own? With a bit of self-respect? Why did they have to get everyone else involved? It's not like the neighbors could *do* anything. It's not like civil wars were *their fault*.

Of course, they would never say this out loud. And the headmaster never suspected they thought this. But some of his most proximate neighbors had taken to leaving the lights off and sitting around in the dusky darkness until they saw him pass by. Others arranged early dinners out at restaurants at prime headmaster-walking times. Certain homes down the block had perfected a system of total avoidance, which was why the headmaster sometimes made it all the way to the end of the cul-de-sac and knocked on the Fall household door and asked to come in for some coffee, which was what happened the first time Samuel was allowed to spend the night at Bishop's house.

His first sleepover. Samuel's dad drove him and was plainly stunned when they pulled up to Venetian Village's large front copper gates.

"Your friend lives *here?*" he said. Samuel nodded.

The security guard at the gate asked to see Henry's license, asked him to fill out a form, sign a waiver, and explain the nature of his visit.

"We're not going to the White House," he told the guard. It was not a joke. There was venom in his voice.

"Do you have any collateral?" the guard asked.

"What?"

"You have not been preapproved, so I'll need some collateral. To insure against damages or violations."

"What do you think I'm going to do?"

"It's policy. Do you have a credit card?"

"I'm not going to give you my credit card."

"It's only temporary. Like I said, for collateral purposes."

"I'm just dropping off my son."

"You're leaving your son? Okay, that will do."

"For what?"

"For collateral."

The guard actually followed them in a golf cart, and Henry delivered Samuel to the Fall house with a brief hug, said "Be good" and "Call me if you need me," and then glared pure hatred at the security guard as he got back into his car. Samuel watched as both his father and the golf cart disappeared up Via Veneto. He held his backpack, which contained some overnight clothes and, at the bottom, the cassette tape he'd bought at the mall for Bethany.

Tonight he would give her the present.

They were all there—Bishop, Bethany, their parents—they were all waiting, in the same room, which Samuel had never seen before, all of them inhabiting the same space at the same time. And another person too, at the piano, Samuel recognized him: the headmaster. The same headmaster who had expelled Bishop from Blessed Heart Academy now sat taking up all the space on the bench in front of the family's Bösendorfer baby grand.

"Hi there," Samuel said, to nobody in particular, to the aggregate mass of them.

"So you're the friend from the new school?" the headmaster said.

Samuel nodded.

"It's good to see he's fitting in," the headmaster said. This remark was made about Bishop, but it was made to Bishop's father. Bishop sat in an upholstered antique wooden chair and looked small. It was as if the headmaster's large presence had colonized the room. He was one of those men whose body exactly matched his disposition. His voice was big. His body was big. He sat *bigly,* his legs far apart and his chest puffed out.

Bishop inhabited the farthest seat from the headmaster, arms crossed, feet under him, a tight little angry ball. He leaned so far back in his chair it seemed he wanted to physically dissolve into it. Bethany sat nearer the piano, perfectly upright, as she always did, on the edge of her chair, ankles crossed, hands in her lap.

"Back to it!" the headmaster said. He swiveled to face the piano and placed a hand on the keys. "Now don't cheat."

Bethany turned her head away from the piano and looked directly at Samuel. His chest seized, her stare carried such voltage. He fought the urge to look away.

The headmaster pounded a single note on the piano, a strong, dark, low note that Samuel could feel in his body.

"That's an A," Bethany said.

"Correct!" the headmaster said. "Again."

Another note, this time near the top of the keyboard, a delicate *plink*.

"That's C," Bethany said. She still stared at Samuel, expressionless.

"Right again!" the headmaster said. "Let's make it more challenging."

He hit three keys at once, and what came out was dissonant and ugly. It sounded like what an infant might do bashing the piano incoherently. Bethany's stare seemed to disengage for a moment—it was as if her consciousness receded, the way her eyes went glassy and remote. But then she came back and said, "B flat, C, C sharp."

"That's amazing!" the headmaster said, clapping.

"Can I go?" Bishop said.

"I'm sorry?" his father said. "What was that?"

"Can I go?" Bishop said.

"Maybe if you learn to ask correctly."

And here Bishop finally raised his head and met his father's eyes. They held each other's gaze like that for an uncomfortable few seconds. "May I please be excused?" Bishop said.

"Yes you may."

In the game room it was clear Bishop did not want to talk. He jammed *Missile Command* into the Atari. He sat stone-faced and quiet while he shot rockets out of the air. Then Bishop grew agitated and said "Fuck this, let's watch a movie," and he started a film they'd seen several times before, about a group of teenagers who defend their town from a surprise Russian invasion. They were about twenty minutes into the movie when Bethany opened the door and slipped in.

"He's gone," she said.

"Good."

Samuel could not believe how much his stomach flopped whenever he saw her up close. Even now, when he felt seriously conflicted about his presence here, when Bishop transparently wanted to be alone and Samuel didn't know what to do with himself and had been wondering if he should call his father and go back home, even through all this Samuel felt elated when Bethany entered the room. It was as if she erased every lesser thing. Samuel had to bat away his impulses to touch her, to muss up her hair or punch her in the arm or flick her earlobe or any of the other juvenile maneuvers boys do to terrorize the girls they love, maneuvers that were really meant to bring them into physical contact the only way they knew how: brutally, like little barbarians. But Samuel knew enough to know this was not a good long-term strategy, so he sat there heavy and still on his usual beanbag chair and hoped Bethany would sit next to him.

"He's an asshole," Bishop said. "A fat fucking asshole."

"I know," Bethany said.

"Why do they let him in the house?"

"Because he's the headmaster. But also? Because he's sick."

"That's ironic."

"He wouldn't be out walking around if he weren't sick."

"If there's a word for that, it's *ironic*."

"You're not listening," Bethany said. "You wouldn't see him if he *weren't sick*."

Bishop sat up and frowned at his sister. "Just what are you trying to say?"

Bethany stood there with her hands behind her back, chewing or biting the inside of her cheek the way she did when she was concentrating real hard. Her hair was pulled into a ponytail. Her eyes were so fiercely green. She was wearing a yellow sundress that gradually turned white at the bottom.

"I'm pointing out a fact," Bethany said. "If he weren't sick, he wouldn't go for these walks, and then you wouldn't have to see him."

"I don't think I like where this is going."

"What are you guys talking about?" Samuel said.

"Nothing," they said in twin-like unison.

The three of them watched the rest of the movie in an edgy silence, watched as the American teens successfully fought off the Russian aggressors, and the triumphant ending of the movie was not nearly as triumphant as it usually felt because the room was overflowing with some weird tension and unspoken conflict, and it felt to Samuel like he was back home having dinner with his parents while they were going through one of their *moments,* and when the movie finished the kids were told to get ready for bed, and so they washed up and brushed their teeth and changed into their pajamas and Samuel was led to the guest bedroom. And just before they were told to turn off their lights, Bethany softly knocked on the door and poked her head in his room and said, "Good night."

"Good night," he said.

She looked at him and lingered there a moment like she had something else to say.

"What were you doing?" Samuel said. "Earlier. With the piano."

"Oh, that," she said. "Parlor tricks."

"You were performing?"

"Sort of. I can hear things. People think it's special. My parents like to show it off."

"What things?"

"Notes, pitches, vibrations."

"From the piano?"

"From everything. The piano is easiest because all the sounds have names. But really from everything."

"What do you mean, from everything?"

"Every sound is actually many sounds put together," she said. "Triads and harmonics. Tones and overtones."

"I don't get it."

"A knock on the wall. A tap on a glass bottle. Birdsong. Tires on the street. The phone ringing. The dishwasher running. There's music in everything."

"You hear music from all that?"

"Our phone is a little sharp," she said. "It's awful, every time it rings."

Samuel tapped on the wall, listening. "I only hear a thud."

"There's a lot more than a thud. Listen. Try to separate the sounds." She knocked sharply on the doorframe. "There's the sound made by the wood, but the wood is not a constant density, so it makes a few different pitches, very close together." She knocked again. "Then there's the sound of the glue, the surrounding wall, the hum of the air inside the wall."

"You hear all that?"

"It's there. You add it up and it sounds like a thud. It's a very brown noise. Like if you melted all the colors in the crayon box, this is the sound you'd get."

"I don't hear any of that."

"It's harder to hear out in the world. A piano is tempered. A house is not."

"That's amazing."

"Mostly it's annoying."

"Why?"

"Well, take birds. There's this one bird, the tanager, that makes this sound like *chip che-ri che-ri che-ri*. Okay? It's a summer bird."

"Okay."

"But I don't really hear the *che-ri*. What I hear is a third and a fifth, in A-flat major."

"I don't know what that means."

"It's a C gliding into an E flat, which is exactly what happens in this one Schubert solo, and also in a Berlioz symphony, and also in a Mozart concerto. So the bird starts singing and it ignites all these phrases in my head."

"I wish I had that."

"No. It's terrible. It's all crashing around in there."

"But you have music in your brain. Mostly what I have is worry."

She smiled. "I just want to be able to sleep in the morning," she said. "But there's this tanager right outside my window. I wish I could turn him off. Or turn my head off. One of the two."

"I have something for you," Samuel said. "A present."

"You do?"

"Something from the mall."

"The mall?" she said, confused. But her face brightened as she registered the connection. "Oh! The mall! *Right.*"

Samuel rummaged through his backpack and produced the cassette. It was shiny, still wrapped in tight plastic. It struck him now that it was such a small thing—about the size and weight of a deck of playing cards. Too small, he thought, to be as meaningful as he needed it to be. He was seized with panic about this, and so he handed it to her quickly, jammed it at her fast and hard, so he wouldn't chicken out. "Here's this," he said.

"What is it?"

"It's for you."

She took the cassette in her hand.

"It's from the mall," he said.

In the daydreams he'd been having, Bethany would, at this moment, smile brightly and wrap her arms around him and express her disbelief and wonderment that he'd chosen such an *exactly perfect gift,* how he must understand her on a deep level and really get what's going on in her head and have a similarly interesting and artistically fulfilling inner life himself. But the expression now forming on Bethany's face was not that. The creases around her eyes and on her forehead—it was like how people squint when they're trying to understand someone with a thick and frustrating accent.

"Do you know what this is?" she said.

"It's really modern stuff," he said, repeating the cashier at the mall. "It's really out there."

"I can't believe they made a recording of this," she said.

"They made ten recordings!" he said. "It's the same piece recorded ten times."

Bethany started laughing now. And it was a laugh that made him understand that, for reasons he was not aware of, he was an idiot. There was an essential bit of information he was missing.

"What's so funny?" he said.

"This piece," she said, "it's sort of a joke."

"What do you mean?"

"It's all, well, it's all *silence*," she said. "The entire thing is just . . . silence."

He stared at her, not really comprehending this.

"There are no notes in the score," she said. "It was actually performed once. The pianist sat at the piano and did nothing."

"How could he do nothing?"

"He just sat there counting the beats. And then he was done. That was the piece. I can't believe they made a recording."

"Ten recordings."

"It was sort of a put-on. It's very famous."

"So this whole cassette," he said, "is blank?"

"I guess that's part of the joke."

"Shit."

"No, it's great," she said, clutching the tape against her chest. "Thank you. Really. It's quite thoughtful."

Quite thoughtful. Samuel kept thinking about the way she said this, long after she'd left and he'd turned out the lights and covered his whole body and head with blankets and curled up and lightly cried. How quickly his daydreams had given way to this merciless reality. He thought bitterly about his expectations for the night, and how everything had gone so very wrong. Bishop didn't want him here. Bethany was indifferent. The gift was a failure. This was the price of hope, he realized, this shattering disappointment.

He must have fallen asleep like that, because he woke up hours later, under the covers, curled, hot and sweaty, in the darkness, as Bishop shook him and said, "Wake up. Let's go."

Samuel followed him groggily. Bishop told him to put on his shoes, told him to climb out the first-floor TV-room window. Samuel did all this in a half-awake stupor.

"Follow me," Bishop said when they were outside, and they walked up Via Veneto's gentle slope in the total darkness and silence of the night. It must have been two in the morning. Maybe three. Samuel wasn't sure. There was such an odd stillness at this time—no sound, no wind, there was barely even *weather*. The only noises were the occasional click of a sprinkler head turning on, and the low groan of the headmaster's hot tub. Automated, mechanical noises. Bishop walked with purpose, maybe even arrogance. This was a different walk than when they played war games in the woods, and Bishop hid behind trees and dove between bushes. Now he walked in plain view, right down the middle of the road.

"You'll need these," he said, and handed Samuel a pair of blue plastic gloves, the kind people use for gardening. The fit was loose—they must have been Bishop's mother's. The gloves came up to Samuel's elbows, and each finger had an inch or so of floating empty space.

"Over here," Bishop said, and he led them to a spot near the headmaster's house where the lush, thick lawn met the wild forest. There stood a metal post, about as tall as the boys themselves, on top of which was a block of white salt, its surface smooth and spotted with brown specks. On top of the salt block was a copper disk. Bishop reached for the disk and pulled at it, trying to twist it off.

"Help me with this," he said, and they yanked at the cap until it finally budged. Up close like this, breathing hard, Samuel could smell the feral animal scent coming from the contraption, but also something else, something like sulfur, that rotten-egg smell, coming from the salt itself. At this range, he could read the sign affixed halfway up the post: DANGER. POISON. KEEP AWAY.

"This is what kills the deer, isn't it?" Samuel said.

"Grab your side."

They slid the block off the post. It was surprisingly heavy and dense. They carried it toward the headmaster's house.

"I don't think I want to do this," Samuel said.

"We're almost there."

They walked slowly, the big gray block between them, around the headmaster's pool and up the two steps to the hot tub, which was steaming, gently circulating, a small light at the bottom shining blue.

"In there," Bishop said, pointing his chin at the hot tub.

"I don't think I want to."

"On three," he said, and they heaved forward, then back, once, twice, three times, and then let go. They tossed the block into the water, where it was swallowed with a splash, followed by a low thud as it landed at the bottom of the tub.

"Good job," Bishop said. They watched the block come to rest down there, its image distorted by the shimmering water. "That'll dissolve by morning," Bishop said. "No one will know."

"I want to go home," Samuel said.

"Come on," Bishop said, and taking him by the arm, they walked back down the street. When they reached the house, Bishop opened the TV-room window, then stopped.

"You want to know what happened in the principal's office?" Bishop said. "Why I didn't get spanked?"

Samuel was holding back tears, wiping his runny nose with the sleeve of his pajamas.

"It was actually really easy," Bishop said. "The thing you have to understand is that everyone is afraid of something. As soon as you know what someone fears most, you can make them do whatever you want."

"What did you do?"

"So he had his paddle, right? And he told me to bend over the table, right? So I took off my pants."

"You did what?"

"I unbuckled my belt and took off my pants and my underwear and everything. I was naked from the waist down and then I said, 'Here's my ass. You want it?'"

Samuel stared at him. "Why would you do that?"

"I asked him if he liked my ass and wanted to touch it."

"I don't understand why you would do that."

"He got pretty weird then."

"Yeah."

"He stared at me for a long time and then told me to put my clothes back on. Then he took me back to class. That was it. Easy!"

"How did you even think to do that?"

"Anyway," Bishop said. "Thanks for your help tonight." He climbed through the window. Samuel followed and padded through the dark house, returning to the guest bedroom, getting into bed, then getting out again and finding a bathroom and washing his hands three, four, five times. He could not decide if the burning sensation in his fingers was from the poison or if it was in his mind.

9

THE INVITATION APPEARED in the mailbox, in a square envelope of heavy, cream-colored paper. Samuel's name was written on the front in very precise girl handwriting.

"What's this?" Faye said. "Birthday invite?"

He looked at the envelope and then at his mother.

"Pizza party?" she said. "At the roller rink?"

"Stop it."

"Who's it from?"

"I don't know."

"Maybe you should open it."

Inside was an invitation printed on expensive card stock. It shimmered, as if flecks of silver had been added to the pulp. The writing looked like it was pressed in gold leaf, a swirling, swooping cursive that said:

> *Please join us at the Blessed Heart Academy Cathedral*
> *as Bethany Fall performs*
> *the Bruch Violin Concerto no. 1*

Samuel had never been invited to anything in this manner: lavishly. At school, the invitations to birthday parties were generic, slipshod affairs, cheap thin cards with animals on them, or balloons. This invitation felt actually physically *heavy.* He handed it to his mother.

"Can we go?" he said.

She studied the invitation and frowned. "Who's this Bethany?"

"A friend."

"From school?"

"Sort of."

"And you know her well enough to get invited to this?"

"Can we go? Please?"

"Do you even like classical music?"

"Yes."

"Since when?"

"Since I don't know."

"That's not an answer."

"Mom."

"The Bruch Violin Concerto? Do you even know what that is?"

"Mom."

"I'm just saying. Are you sure you can appreciate it?"

"It's a very difficult piece and she's been practicing for months."

"And you know this how?"

Samuel then made an angry, abstract sound meant to convey his frustration and unwillingness to further discuss the matter of the girl, which came out something like *"Gaarrgh!"*

"Fine," she said with a satisfied little grin. "We'll go."

The night of the concert she told him to dress nice. "Imagine it's Easter," she said. So he put on the fanciest things in his closet: a stiff and itchy white shirt; a black necktie bound noose-tight; black slacks that popped with static electricity when he moved; a shiny pair of dress shoes that he shoehorned himself into, so granite-hard they removed a layer of skin on his heel. He wondered why adults felt they needed to be at their most uncomfortable for their most cherished events.

The Blessed Heart Academy Cathedral was already buzzing when they arrived, people in suits and flowery dresses filing into the large arched doorway, the sounds of musicians practicing audible even from the parking lot. The cathedral was built to mimic the great churches of Europe, at about one-third scale.

Inside, a wide central aisle was flanked on both sides by pews made of heavy and thick and ornately carved wood, polished and shining wetly. Beyond the pews were stone columns with torches attached about fifteen feet above the crowd, each lit with glowing fires. Parents chatted with other parents, the men giving soft platonic kisses to the cheeks of women. Samuel watched them, these small pecks, and realized the men weren't really kissing the women but instead miming a kissing action into the area around their necks. Samuel wondered if the women were disappointed about this—they'd been expecting a kiss and all they got was air.

They took their seats, studied the program. Bethany would not go on until the second half. The first half was all smaller works—minor chamber pieces and quick solos. It was clear Bethany's piece was the showstopper. The big finale. Samuel's feet bounced nervously on the soft, carpeted floor.

The lights dimmed and the musicians stopped their chaotic warm-ups and everyone took their seats and after a lengthy pause there came a sturdy note out of the woodwinds, then everyone else following it, tuning to that note, anchoring themselves to that spot, and something seemed to catch in his mother's throat. She inhaled sharply, then put her hand on her chest.

"I used to do that," she said.

"Do what?"

"The tuning note. I was the oboe. That used to be me."

"You played music? When?"

"*Shh.*"

And there it was, another secret his mother had kept. Her life was a fog to him; whatever happened before he came along was all mysterious, locked behind ambiguous shrugs and half answers and vague abstractions and aphorisms—"You're too young," she'd say. Or "You wouldn't understand." Or the particularly infuriating "I'll tell you someday, when you're older." But occasionally some secret would crack free. So his mother was once a musician. He added it to the mental inventory: *Things that Mom is.* She's a musician. What else? What other things didn't he know about her? She had acres of secrets, it was obvious. He always felt there was something she wasn't saying, something behind her bland partial attention. She often had that disassociated quality, like she was focusing on you with maybe one-third of herself, the rest devoted to whatever things she kept locked inside her head.

The biggest secret had slipped years earlier, when Samuel was young enough to be asking his parents ridiculous questions. (Have you ever been in a volcano? Have you ever seen an angel?) Or asking because he was still naïve enough to believe in stupendous things. (Can you breathe underwater? Can *all* reindeer fly?) Or asking because he was fishing for attention and praise. (How much do you love me? Am I the best child in the world?) Or asking because he wanted to be reassured of his place in the world. (Will you be my mom forever? Have you been married to anyone besides Dad?) Except when he asked this last question his mother straightened up and looked at him all tall and solemn and serious and said: "Actually . . ."

She never finished that sentence. He waited for her, but she stopped and thought about it and got that distant, bleak look on her face. "Actually *what*?" he said.

"Nothing," she said. "Never mind."

"You've been married before?"

"No."

"Then what were you going to say?"

"Nothing."

So Samuel asked his father: "Was Mom ever married to anyone else?"

"What?"

"I think she might have been married to someone else."

"No, she wasn't. *Jesus*. What are you talking about?"

Something had happened to her, Samuel was sure of it. Some profound thing that even now, years later, occupied her attention. It washed over her sometimes and she'd disengage from the world.

Meanwhile, there was a concert happening. High-school boys and girls playing important senior-year recitals, five- to ten-minute pieces that were right in the strike zone of each student's ability. Loud clapping after every performance. Pleasant, easy, tonal music, mostly Mozart.

Then it was intermission. People stood and made their way elsewhere: outside, to smoke, or to a nearby buffet table, for cheese.

"How long did you play music?" Samuel asked.

His mother studied the program. She acted like she didn't hear him. "This girl, your friend, how old is she?"

"My age," he said. "She's in my grade."

"And she's playing with these high schoolers?"

He nodded his head. "She's really good." And he felt this surge of pride just then, as if being in love with Bethany meant something important about *him*. As if he were rewarded for her accomplishments. He would never be a musical genius, but he could be a person a musical genius loved. Such were the spoils of love, he realized, that her success was also, by some odd refraction, his.

"Dad's really good too," Samuel added.

She looked at him, puzzled. "What are you talking about?"

"Nothing. It's just, you know, he's really good. At his job."

"That's an odd thing to say."

"It's true. He's *very* good."

She stared at him a moment, mystified.

"Did you know," she said, looking down at the program again, "that the composer of this piece never made any money from it?"

"Which piece?"

"The piece your friend is going to play. The guy who wrote it, Max Bruch, he never earned a penny."

"Why not?"

"He was cheated. It was around World War I, and he was bankrupt, so he gave it to a couple of Americans who were supposed to send him the money, but they never did. The score disappeared for a long time, then ended up in the vault of J. P. Morgan."

"Who's that?"

"A banker. Industrialist. Financier."

"A really rich guy."

"Yes. From a long time ago."

"He liked music?"

"He liked *things,*" she said. "It's a classic story. The robber baron gets more stuff, the artist dies with nothing."

"He didn't die with nothing," Samuel said.

"He was broke. He didn't even have the score."

"He had his memory of it."

"His memory?"

"Yeah. He could still remember it. That's something."

"I'd rather have the money."

"Why?"

"Because when all you have is the memory of a thing," she said, "all you can think about is how the thing is gone."

"I don't think that's true."

"You're young."

The lights dimmed again, and people around them took their seats, and the buzz of small talk quieted, and everything went dark and silent and the whole cathedral seemed to distill itself into one small circle of light at the front of the altar—a spotlight illuminating an empty bit of floor.

"Here we go," his mother whispered.

Everyone waited. It was agony. Five seconds, ten seconds. It was taking too long! Samuel wondered if someone had forgotten to tell Bethany she was on. Or if she'd left her violin at home. But then he heard the click of a door somewhere in front of him. Then footsteps, soft shoes on the hard floor. And finally there she was, Bethany, gliding into the light.

She wore a slim green dress and her hair had been done up and she looked, for the first time, tiny. Around all these adults and high schoolers, way up in front, it was as if Samuel's normal scale was thrown off. Bethany now looked like a child. And he was worried for her. This was too much to ask, all this.

The audience politely clapped. Then Bethany put her violin under her chin. She stretched her neck and shoulders. And without a word, the orchestra began to play.

It started with a low thrum, like thunder very far away, a faint drumming from beyond the light. Samuel could feel it in his torso and fingertips. He was sweating. Bethany didn't even have her music! She would do this from memory! What if she forgot? What if she blanked? He realized now how terrifying music is, how inevitable—the drums would keep driving forward, whether or not Bethany knew her part. And now, softly, the woodwinds came in—nothing dramatic, but three simple notes, each lower than the last, repeated. It wasn't a melody; more like a *preparation*. Like they were readying the sanctuary for sound. Like these three notes performed the ritual necessary to be in the presence of music. It wasn't the music yet but rather its leading edge.

Then Bethany straightened herself and placed her bow at the proper angle and it was clear something was about to happen. She was ready, the audience was ready. The woodwinds held a single long hovering note that gradually faded away, that sounded like taffy stretched to nothingness. And just as that note disappeared, just as it was swallowed by the darkness, a new note leaped from Bethany. It grew stronger and louder and then she was the only one speaking in that huge hall.

There was nothing more lonely than that sound.

Like all the heartbreak in someone's long life gathered and distilled. It began low and moaned higher, slowly, a couple of steps up, a few steps back, and so on, like a dancer, whirling its way to the top of the scale, more quickly now, to announce, at the very peak, a kind of forsakenness, a desolation. The way Bethany bent that last note as she climbed into it—it sounded like a cry, like somebody crying. An old familiar noise, and Samuel felt himself falling into the note, gradually folding himself around it. And just when he thought she'd reached the top, another note came, even higher, a wisp of music, the barest edge of the bow meeting the thinnest string, just the finest sound: clean, noble, soft, a slight quiver from Bethany's rolling finger, like the note itself were alive and pulsing. Alive, but dying, it seemed now, as the note diminished and decayed. And it didn't sound like Bethany's playing softened but rather like she was moving quickly away from them. Like she was being stolen. And wherever she went, they could not follow. She was a ghost passing into another realm.

Then the orchestra answered back, a full and deep barrel of sound, like they needed all the numbers they could muster to match this one tiny girl in her little green dress.

The concert passed in a kind of blur after that. Occasionally Samuel would be newly amazed by one of Bethany's maneuvers: how she could play on two strings at once and make them both sound good; how she could play so many hundreds of notes perfectly from memory; how fast her fingers moved. It was inhuman, what she could do. By the middle of the second movement, Samuel had concluded there was no way he deserved her.

The audience went mad. They stood and cheered and gave Bethany bouquets of roses so large they impeded her balance. She carried them in both arms and was barely visible behind them, waving and curtseying.

"Everyone loves a prodigy," his mother said, herself also standing and clapping. "Prodigies get us off the hook for living ordinary lives. We can tell ourselves we're not special because we weren't born with it, which is a great excuse."

"She's been practicing nonstop for months."

"My dad always told me I was nothing special," she said. "I guess I proved him right."

Samuel stopped clapping and looked at his mother.

She rolled her eyes and patted him on the head. "Never mind. Forget I said that. Do you want to say hi to your friend?"

"No."

"Why not?"

"She's busy."

And indeed she was busy: surrounded by well-wishers, friends, family, her parents, various musicians congratulating her.

"You should at least tell her she did a good job," Faye said. "Thank her for the invitation. It's polite."

"Plenty of people are telling her good job," Samuel said. "Can we go?"

His mother shrugged. "Okay. If that's what you want."

And they were on their way out of the hall, and they were moving slowly with the surge of people also leaving, Samuel brushing against hips and sport coats, when from behind him he heard his name. Bethany was calling his name. He turned and found her wrestling through the crowd to catch up to him, and when she finally did she leaned into him, her cheek to his, and he thought he was supposed to give her one of those fake-kiss things he saw all the adult men doing, until she brought her lips all the way to his ear and whispered, "Come over tonight. Sneak out."

"Okay," he said. That warmth on his face. He would have agreed to do anything she asked.

"There's something I have to show you."

"What is it?"

"The cassette you gave me? It's not just silence. *There's something else.*"

She pulled away. She no longer looked, as she had onstage, small. She had regained her normal Bethany proportions: elegant, sophisticated, womanly. She held his stare and smiled.

"You have to hear it," she said. Then she dashed away, back to her parents and her throng of giddy admirers.

His mother looked at him suspiciously, but he ignored her. He walked right past her, out of the church and into the night, limping slightly in his rock-hard shoes.

That night he lay in bed waiting for the sounds of the house to disappear—his mother rattling around in the kitchen, his father watching television downstairs, then eventually the *whoosh* of his parents' door opening as his mother went to bed. Then the television turning off with an electric *chunk*. The sound of water running, a toilet flushing. Then nothing. Waiting another twenty minutes to be sure, then opening his door, twisting and untwisting the knob slowly and tightly to avoid unwanted metallic clicks, walking lightly down the hall, stepping over the squeaky part of the hallway floor that Samuel could avoid even in total darkness, then down the stairs, placing his feet as close to the wall as he could, where there was less creaking danger, then taking a full ten minutes to open the front door—a small pull, a small *tic,* then silence, then another: *tic*—the door opening in fractions of an inch until the gap was finally wide enough to pass through.

And finally, once liberated, running! In the clean air, running down the block, toward the creek, into the woods that separated Venetian Village from everything else. His foot clomps and breathing were the only sounds in the whole big world, and when he felt afraid—of getting caught, of dangerous forest animals, of mad ax murderers, kidnappers, trolls, ghosts—he steeled his mind with the memory of Bethany's warm, wet breath on his ear.

Her bedroom was dark when he arrived, her window closed. Samuel sat outside for several long minutes panting and sweating and watching, reassuring himself that all relevant parents were asleep and that no neighbors would see him creep through the backyard, which, when he finally did, he did so quickly, running on the tips of his shoes to avoid all ground sounds, then crouching below Bethany's window and lightly tapping it with the pad of his index finger until, from out of the darkness, she appeared.

He could see only bits of her in the murky nighttime light: the angle of her nose, a toss of hair, collarbone, eye socket. She was a collection of parts floating in ink. She opened the window and he climbed in, rolling over the frame and wincing where the metal bit into his chest.

"Be *quiet,*" said someone who was not Bethany, who was elsewhere in the darkness. It was Bishop, Samuel realized after a moment of disequilibrium. Bishop was here, in the room, and Samuel was both disheartened and grateful for this. Because he didn't know what he would do if he were alone with Bethany, but also he knew he wanted to do it, whatever it was. To be alone with her—he wanted it very badly.

"Hi, Bish," Samuel said.

"We're playing a game," Bishop said. "It's called Listen to Silence Until You're Bored out of Your Mind."

"Shut up," Bethany said.

"It's called Be Put to Sleep by Cassette-Tape Static."

"It's not static."

"It's all static."

"It's not *only* static," she said. "There's something else."

"Says you."

Samuel could not see them—the darkness in here was total. They were more like impressions in space, lighter shapes against the blackness. He tried to place himself in the geography of her room, constructing a map from memory: the bed, the dresser, the flowers on the wall. There were glow-in-the-dark stars dotting the ceiling, Samuel noticed, suddenly, for the first time. Then the sounds of fabric and footsteps and the bed's quick squeak as Bethany probably sat down on it, near where Bishop seemed to be, near the cassette player, which she often listened to at night, alone, playing and rewinding and playing again the same few moments from some symphony, which Samuel knew because of all his spying.

"Come up here," Bethany said. "You have to be close." So he got up on the bed and moved slowly toward them and felt around clumsily and grabbed something cold and bony that was definitely a leg belonging to one of them, he didn't know which.

"Listen," she said. "Very closely."

A click of the tape player, Bethany leaning back into the bed, the fabric folding around her, then static as that brief dead space at the beginning of the tape ended and the recording actually began.

"See?" Bishop said. "Nothing."

"Wait for it."

The sound was distant and muffled, like when a faucet is turned on somewhere in the house and there's that rushing sound from hidden, far-off pipes.

"There," Bethany said. "Do you hear it?"

Samuel shook his head, then realized she couldn't see the gesture. "No," he said.

"There it is," she said. "Listen. It's *under* the sound. You have to listen below it."

"You are making no sense," Bishop said.

"Ignore what you can hear and listen to the other stuff."

"Listen to what?"

"To *them*," she said. "The people, the audience, the room. You can hear them."

Samuel strained to listen. He cocked his head toward the stereo and squinted—as if that would help—trying to pick out any kind of organized sound within the static: talking, coughing, breathing.

"I don't hear anything," Bishop said.

"You're not concentrating."

"Oh right. That's the problem."

"You have to focus."

"Fine. I will now attempt to focus."

They all listened to the hiss coming out of the speakers, Samuel feeling disappointed in himself that he also had not yet heard anything.

Bishop said, "This is me totally focused."

"Will you shut up?"

"I have never been so focused as I am at this moment."

"Please. Shut. Up."

"Concentrate, you must," he said. "Feel the force, you must."

"You can go away, you know. Like, leave?"

"Happily," Bishop said, scrambling away and leaping off the bed. "You two enjoy your nothing."

The bedroom door opened and closed and they were alone, Samuel and Bethany, alone together, finally, terribly. He sat rock-still.

"Now listen," she said.

"Okay."

He pointed his face in the direction of the noise and leaned in. The static was not a high-pitched trebly noise but a deeper kind. It was like a microphone had been suspended above an empty stadium—the silence had a fullness to it, a roundness. It was a substantial quiet. It wasn't just the sound of an empty room but rather like someone had gone to great lengths to manufacture nothingness. It had a created quality to it. It felt *made*.

"There they are," Bethany whispered. "Listen."

"The people?"

"They're like ghosts in a graveyard," she said. "You can't hear them the normal way."

"Describe it."

"They sound worried. And confused. They think they're being tricked."

"You can hear all that?"

"Sure. It's the stiffness of the sound. It's like those really short, tight strings at the top of the piano. The ones that don't vibrate. The white sounds. That's what these people sound like. They're like ice."

Samuel tried to listen for something like that, some high-pitched buzz inside the droning, persistent static.

"But it changes," she said. "Listen for the change."

He kept listening, but all he could hear was how the sound sounded like other sounds: escaping air from a bicycle tire, the whir of a small fan, water running behind a closed door. He heard nothing original. Only his own mental library bouncing back at him.

"There," she said. "The sound gets warmer. Do you hear it? Warmer and fuller. The sound gets bigger and blooms. They are beginning to understand."

"Understand what?"

"Maybe they're not being tricked. Maybe they're not being mocked. Maybe they're not outsiders. They're beginning to get it. That maybe they're part of something. They're beginning to realize they haven't come here to listen to music. They're beginning to realize that *they are the music*. They are themselves what they've come here to find. The thought is exhilarating to them. Can you hear it?"

"Yes," Samuel lied. "They're happy."

"They *are* happy."

And Samuel felt himself believing he really could hear this. The same kind of voluntary self-hallucination he felt when he convinced himself, at night, in bed, that there were intruders in the house, or ghosts, and every sound the house made validated this delusion. Or on those days he couldn't bear to go to school and told himself he was sick until he really became sick, felt actually physically ill, and he would wonder how the nausea could be real if he created it in his mind. It was like that, this thing he was hearing. The sound of static really did get warmer the more he thought about it; it really did become a happy static. The sound seemed to broaden in his mind, open up, and burn.

Was this her secret, he wondered. That she simply *wanted* to hear what no one else could?

"I can hear it now," he said. "You just have to chase it."

"Yes," she said. "That's exactly right."

He felt her hand grasp his shoulder and squeeze, then felt her move closer to him, felt the vibrations and swells in the mattress, the slight creaks of the bed frame as she swiveled around and came into him. She was close. He could hear her breathing, smell her toothpastey breath. But more than that he could *feel* her nearby, how she seemed to displace the air, had some kind of electricity around her, how you can sense the close-ness of another body, the presence of some kind of magnetism, her heart-beat throttled up, all this coming at him as an impression in space, a map his mind made, an intuition, and then finally as actual solid matter, the flesh of her face now close enough to comprehend.

They were, he realized, going to kiss.

Or, rather, she was going to kiss him. *This was going to happen.* All he had to do was not screw it up. But in that moment, in those few seconds between realizing she was going to kiss him and the actual kiss, there seemed to be so many ways to screw it up. He felt the pressing and unex-pected need to clear his throat. And scratch the back of his neck, at that spot where his neck joined to the shoulder, which always itched when he was nervous. And he did not want to move into the kiss, as it was dark and he could accidentally knock teeth with Bethany. But then in his desire to avoid knocking teeth he felt himself maybe leaning back and overcompensating and he worried that Bethany might mistake his lean-ing away from her as a desire *not* to kiss and she might stop. And then there was the matter of breathing. As in: Do it? His first impulse was to hold his breath, but then he realized if she approached slowly enough or if they kissed long enough, he would eventually run out of air and be forced to breathe mid-kiss and expel his lungs in a big poof right into her face or mouth. All of these thoughts happening roughly simulta-neously in that brief moment before the kiss, Samuel's most rudimentary actions, his body's most automatic functions—sitting straight, being still, breathing—now turned *crazily difficult* by the prospect of the kiss, which is why when the kiss actually did successfully commence, it felt like a miracle.

Mostly what Samuel felt during the kiss was relief that the kiss was happening. And also that Bethany's lips felt dry and chapped. This odd detail. That Bethany had chapped lips. It surprised him. In his imagina-tion of her, Bethany seemed elevated beyond stupid earthly concerns. She did not seem to be the kind of girl whose lips ever chapped.

On the way home that night, he was surprised that everything looked exactly the same as it did before, with absolutely no signs that the world had fundamentally, radically changed.

10

THE FIRST BOOK Samuel ever wrote was a Choose Your Own Adventure story called *The Castle of No Return*. It was twelve pages long. He illustrated it himself. Its premise: You are a brave knight fighting your way through a haunted castle to save a beautiful princess. Pretty standard fare, he knew. He was sure he'd read something similar in one of the many Choose Your Own Adventure books that filled his bedroom shelves. He really had tried to come up with a better, more original story. He sat cross-legged on his floor and stared at the books before him and eventually decided they represented the full range of human possibility, the entire narrative spectrum. There were no other stories that could be told. Every idea that came to him was either imitative or stupid. And his book *could not be stupid.* The stakes were too high. Every kid was writing a book in an all-class contest where the winning author would have the book read aloud by the teacher.

So *The Castle of No Return* was derivative. So be it. He hoped his classmates would not be tired of the old tropes just yet. He hoped they would be comforted by the familiarity of the tale like they were comforted by the old toys and blankets they sometimes hid in their backpacks.

The next problem was plot. He knew Choose Your Own Adventure books forked this way or that, then forked again, and then again, and that each story was in the end a unified narrative whole—many stories in one. But his first draft of *The Castle of No Return* resembled more of a straight line with six short dead ends, with choices that would cause little debate or consternation: Do you want to go left or do you want to go right? (If you go left *you die!*)

He hoped his classmates would forgive these shortcomings—the plagiarized setting, the lack of multiple cohesive plots—if he could find really interesting and creative and entertaining ways to die. Which he did. Samuel had a talent, it turned out, for killing his characters interestingly. In one possible ending involving a trapdoor and a bottomless pit, Samuel wrote: "You are falling, and you fall forever, and even after you close this book and eat dinner and go to bed tonight and wake up tomorrow, you will still be falling"—which just totally blew his mind. And he used the ghost stories his mother told him, all those old Norwegian stories that terrified him. He wrote about a white horse that appeared suddenly, offering a ride, and if the reader decided to mount the horse, terrible death quickly followed. In another ending, the reader becomes a ghost trapped inside of a leaf, too bad to go to heaven, too good to go to hell.

He typed up the pages on his mother's old typewriter, leaving room for illustrations, which he did in crayon and pen. He bound the book in cardboard and blue fabric and, using a ruler to achieve perfectly straight lines, he wrote "The Castle of No Return" on the cover.

And maybe it was the illustrations. Maybe it was the excellent blue binding. Or maybe—he left room in his mind for this possibility— maybe it was the writing itself, the creative deaths, the unity of his vision, that instead of "Prologue" he used the word "Prolegomenon," which he found in a thesaurus and which he thought sounded awesome. He could not say for sure what swayed Miss Bowles, but swayed she was. He won. *The Castle of No Return* was read to the whole class and he sat at his desk trying not to burst.

It was the best thing he'd done in his life.

So when his mother came into his bedroom one morning and woke him and asked him, weirdly, "What do you want to be when you grow up?," he still glowed with his literary victory, and so he said, quite sure of himself, "Novelist."

The light outside was weakly blue. His eyes were still heavy and hazy.

"A novelist?" she said, smiling.

He nodded. Yes, a novelist. He had decided sometime in the night, as he relived his great success. How his classmates roared with pleasure when the princess was saved. Their gratitude, their love. Watching them navigate his story—surprised in the places he meant to surprise them, fooled in the places he meant to fool them—he felt like a god who knew all the answers to the big questions peering down at the mortals who did not. This was a feeling that could sustain him, that could fill him up. Being a novelist, he decided, would make people like him.

"Well," said his mother, "then you should be a novelist."

"Okay," he said, bleary and half awake, still not quite comprehending how deeply strange this was, his mother fully dressed, carrying a suitcase, coming in here at dawn asking about his plans, his future plans, when she had never once asked about this before. But Samuel accepted it and went along with it, like how one accepts the premise of a strange dream whose strangeness only clarifies after it's over.

"You write your books," she said. "I'll read them."

"Okay." He wanted to show his mother *The Castle of No Return*. He'd show her his drawing of the white horse. He'd show her that thing about the bottomless pit.

"I want to tell you something," she said. And she was oddly formal about this, as if she'd privately practiced it many times. "I'm going away for a while. And I want you to be good while I'm gone."

"Where are you going?"

"I have to find someone," she said. "Someone I knew a long time ago."

"A friend?"

"I suppose," she said. She put a cold palm on his cheek. "But you don't have to worry about that. You don't have to worry about anything. You don't have to be so scared anymore. That's what I wanted to tell you. Don't be scared. Can you do that for me?"

"Is your friend missing?"

"Not really. We've just been apart for a long time."

"Why?"

"Sometimes," she said, and she paused, and she looked away from him, and her face crumpled.

"Mom?" he said.

"Sometimes you take a wrong turn," she said. "Sometimes you get lost."

Samuel started to cry. He did not know why he was crying. He tried to stop it.

She gathered him in her arms and said "You're so sensitive" and rocked him and he pressed into her soft skin until his whimpering ceased and he wiped his nose.

"Why do you have to go *now*?" Samuel said.

"It's just time, honey."

"But why?"

"I don't know how to explain it," she said. She stared at the ceiling with this hopeless look on her face, then seemed to gather herself. "Have I ever told you about the ghost that looks like a rock?" she said.

"No."

"My father told me about it. He said you could find it on beaches sometimes back home. It looks like a normal rock, like a little stone covered with green fuzz."

"How can you tell it's a ghost?"

"You can't, unless you take it out to sea. If anyone takes it onto the ocean, it'll get heavier the farther you travel from shore. And if you're really far, the ghost will get so heavy it'll sink your ship. They called it a *drowning stone*."

"Why would it do that?"

"I don't know. Maybe it's angry. Maybe something bad happened to it. The point is, it gets too big for you to carry anymore. And the longer you try to carry it, the bigger and heavier it gets. Sometimes it can get inside you and it gets bigger and bigger until it's too much. You can't fight it anymore. You just . . . sink." She stood up. "Do you understand?"

"I think so," he said, nodding.

"You will," she said. "I know you will. Just remember what I told you."

"Don't be scared anymore."

"That's right." She leaned over and kissed him on the forehead, held him close to her and seemed to breathe him in. "Now go back to sleep," she said. "It'll all be okay. Just remember: Don't be scared."

He heard her footsteps disappear down the hall. Heard her wrestling with the suitcase down the stairs. He heard the car start, the garage door open and close. He heard her drive away.

And Samuel tried to obey his mother. He tried to fall back asleep and not feel scared. But this unbearable panic rose up in him and so he got out of bed and ran to his parents' room and found his father still sleeping, curled with his back to the room.

"Dad," Samuel said, shaking him. "Wake up."

Henry squinted at his son. "What do you want?" he said in a sleepy whisper. "What time is it?"

"Mom's gone," Samuel said.

Henry lifted a heavy head. "Huh?"

"Mom's gone."

His father looked at the empty side of the bed. "Where'd she go?"

"I don't know. She drove away."

"She *drove*?"

Samuel nodded.

"Okay," Henry said, and he rubbed his eyes. "Go downstairs. I'll be there in a minute."

"She's gone," Samuel said.

"I got it. Please go downstairs."

And Samuel waited in the kitchen for his father until he heard a crash from his parents' bedroom. He ran upstairs and opened the door and saw his father standing straight and rigid with the reddest face Samuel had ever seen. Faye's closet door was open, some of her clothes strewn on the floor.

But it wasn't the clothes Samuel would remember best, nor the crash, nor the broken pieces of a small vase that had been hurled at the wall, apparently with great force. What he would remember clearly, even decades later, was that color on his father's face: a deep crimson, and not just in the cheeks but all over—neck and forehead and down into his chest. A dangerous-looking color.

"She's gone," he said. "And her stuff, it's all gone. Where did all her stuff go?"

"I saw her leaving with a suitcase," Samuel said.

"Go to school," his father said, not looking at him.

"But—"

"Don't argue."

"But—"

"Just go!"

Samuel didn't know what it meant, that his mother was "gone."

Gone where? Gone how far? When would she come back?

During the journey to school, Samuel felt himself far away from his surroundings, like he was looking at the world through binoculars turned backward—standing at the bus stop, getting on the bus, sitting and looking out the window and not really hearing any of the kids around him, focusing on a water spot on the window glass, the passing landscape beyond all blurry and whizzing indistinctly by. Samuel felt a gathering sense of dread, and narrowing his attention to something very small, like a water spot, seemed to keep the dread, for the moment, at bay. He just needed to get to school. He just needed to talk to Bishop, to tell Bishop what had happened. Bishop, he had decided, would keep him afloat. Bishop would know what to do.

Only Bishop wasn't at school. Not at his locker. Not at his desk.

Gone.

Bishop was gone.

That word again: What did it mean? To be gone? Everyone was disappearing. Samuel sat in his chair examining the wood of his desk and didn't even notice when Miss Bowles called his name, then again, then a third time, didn't even notice the class nervously laughing at him, nor Miss Bowles walking up the row toward him, did not even notice when she stood directly above him waiting while the class chittered behind her. It wasn't until she touched him, physically contacted his shoulder with her hand, that he flinched and broke away from what had become a really absorbing exercise in tracing wood grain with his eyes. And he wasn't even mortified when Miss Bowles said "Good of you to come back to us" in her mocking way, to the class's laughter. He didn't even feel embarrassed. It was as if his misery overwhelmed everything else—all his normal worries were buried. Gone.

Example: At recess, he left. He simply marched away. He walked toward the most distant swing set and then walked on. He just didn't stop. It had never occurred to him before that he could not stop. Everyone stopped. But in the face of his mother's goneness, all the world's normal rules fell away. If she could leave, why couldn't he? So he did. He walked away and was surprised how easy it was. He walked along the sidewalk, didn't even attempt to run or hide. He walked in plain view and nobody stopped him. Nobody said a word. He floated away. It was a whole new reality. Maybe, he thought, his mother also found it this easy. To go. What kept people where they were, in their normal orbits? Nothing, he realized for the first time. There was nothing to stop anyone from, on any given day, vanishing.

He kept going. For hours he kept going, staring down at the sidewalk, thinking *Step on a crack, break your mother's back,* repeating this until he finally reached the copper front gates of Venetian Village, then slipping between the bars and not even looking at the security window, just walking right on through, and if the guard saw him he didn't say anything, and Samuel briefly wondered if in the middle of everything he hadn't in fact turned invisible, such was the oddness of this total lack of reaction from the world, his breaking all the rules and the world completely not noticing. And he was thinking about this and walking Via Veneto's smooth asphalt and cresting the neighborhood's gentle hill when he looked down at the street's terminating cul-de-sac and saw, in front of Bishop's house, two police cars.

Samuel stopped walking. His immediate fear was that the police were looking for *him*. And in some way this was a relief. And a comfort. Because it meant that his disappearance mattered. He played the scene out in his head, the phone call from the school to his father, his father frantic with worry, calling the police, who would ask where Samuel might go, and his father telling them *Bishop's house!* because his father knew about Bishop, had dropped him off here, and would remember this because he was a good and caring father who would not one day just leave.

Samuel felt devastated by this. What had he done to his father? The agony he must have caused. His father waiting at home, alone now, both his wife and son disappearing *on the same day*. And Samuel walked toward Bishop's house, walked with haste: He would turn himself in, be driven home, be reunited with his father, who must have been sick with worry by now. It was, he knew, the right thing to do.

And he got as far as the headmaster's house before noticing something that stopped him again. Around the small post that once contained the block of poisoned salt was a line of thin, bright yellow ribbon. It was wrapped around four small stakes in the ground, making a square containing the empty post. The ribbon had words on it, and even though it had been twisted and so some of the words were upside down and backward, the message was easy to comprehend: POLICE LINE DO NOT CROSS.

Samuel glanced at the headmaster's hot tub and saw more of the ribbon there too, surrounding the entire pool and deck area. And the scene in his head changed: The police were looking for him, but not because he'd ditched school.

So he ran. Into the forest. Down to the stream. Splashed along its banks and breathed in the damp leafy rot and ran in the wet sand, water bubbling up and squishing out of the ground wherever his shoes landed. The sun was blocked by the trees above him, the woods taking on that misty bluish color of midday shade. And he saw Bishop exactly where he expected him to be: in the large oak tree by the pond, up on the sturdy first branch, hiding, mostly obscured except for his feet, which Samuel saw only because he was looking for them. Bishop climbed down out of the tree, landing on the ground with a flutter of the surrounding leaves just as Samuel arrived.

"Hey, Bish," he said.

"Hey."

They eyed each other a moment, not knowing what to say.

"Shouldn't you be in school?" Bishop said.

"I left."

Bishop nodded.

"I just came from your house," Samuel said. "The police were there."

"I know."

"What do they want?"

"No idea."

"Is it about the headmaster?"

"Maybe."

"The hot tub?"

"Could be."

"What's going to happen to us?"

Bishop smiled. "So many questions," he said. "Let's swim."

He yanked off his shoes without untying them, pulled off his tube socks and threw them, inside out, on the ground. His belt buckle jingled as he undid it, then he pulled off his jeans and shirt and jumped toward the water trying as best he could to avoid sharp rocks and twigs, all flailing skinny legs and arms and underpants, which were gray-green camouflage briefs, about two sizes too big. When he made it to the pond he jumped off a tree stump and cannonballed in, broke the surface with a loud *Whoop,* then came back up and said "Let's go, soldier!"

Samuel followed him, but carefully: Untying his shoes and putting them where they wouldn't get wet. Pulling off his socks and stuffing them inside the shoes. Taking off and folding his jeans and shirt and placing them gently on top of the shoes. He was deliberate about this. He always was. When he reached the pond he didn't jump in but rather waded, wincing as the cold grasped first his ankles, then knees, then waist, then the water reached his underwear and the chill spread.

"It's easier if you jump in all at once," Bishop said.

"I know," Samuel said, "but I can't."

When finally the water reached his neck and the pain subsided, Bishop said, "Good. Okay. Here's the scenario." And he outlined the premise of the game they were to play. The year would be 1836. The place would be the Mexican borderlands. The epoch was the Texas Revolution. They were to be scouts in Davy Crockett's army, spying on the enemy, caught behind Mexican lines. They had important information concerning the size of Santa Anna's army, and now they needed to get it back to Crockett. The fate of the Alamo hung in the balance.

"But enemies are everywhere," Bishop said, "and rations are low."

His knowledge of American wars was thorough, impressive, and frightening. When he played war, he played it immersively. How many times had they killed each other around this pond? Hundreds of deaths, thousands of bullets, bullets sprayed along with the white spittle ejected from their mouths as they made the bullet sounds, the machine gun's *tch-tch-tch-tch*. Ducking behind trees, yelling, "I got you!" The pond had become sacred to them, the grounds hallowed, the water holy. They felt a kind of formality here, like the feeling one has entering a cemetery, this being the site of their own many imaginary deaths.

"Someone's coming," Bishop said, pointing. "Mexican troops. If they catch us, they will torture us for information."

"But we won't tell," Samuel said.

"No we won't."

"Because of our training."

"That's right." Bishop had always insisted that members of the U.S. military underwent advanced and mysterious training that allowed them to resist, among other things, pain, fear, booby traps, and drowning. Samuel had wondered how anyone could be trained not to drown. Bishop said it was classified.

"Hide," Bishop said. Then he dropped below the water. Samuel looked upstream to where he'd been pointing but saw nothing. He tried to imagine enemy troops advancing on their position, tried to call up the usual fear he felt during these games, tried to see the bad guys, which up until now was always very easy. To see them, the bad guys, whatever bad guys they were fighting that day—Soviet spies, the Vietcong, the redcoats, storm troopers—all they'd have to do was say it aloud and they were there, before them. Their imaginations melted into the real world. This was usually so simple that Samuel had never thought about it before, not until this moment, when it stopped working. He saw nothing, felt nothing.

Bishop popped out of the water to find Samuel staring at the trees.

"Hello? Soldier?" he said. "We're gonna get caught?"

"It's not working," Samuel said.

"What's not working?"

"My brain."

"What's wrong?" Bishop said.

His mind felt overwhelmed. All he could see was his mother, her absence. She was like a fog that obscured everything. He was not even able to pretend.

"My mom is gone," he said, and even as he said it, he felt the crying come, the familiar throat constriction, the way his chin tightened and balled up like a rotten apple. Sometimes he hated himself so much.

"What do you mean, gone?" Bishop said.

"I don't know."

"She left?"

Samuel nodded.

"Is she coming back?"

He shrugged. He didn't want to talk. Another word would make the crying start.

"So there's a chance she *won't* come back?" Bishop said.

Samuel nodded again.

"You know what?" he said. "You're *lucky*. Seriously. I wish *my* parents would leave. You might not understand it now, but your mother's done you a favor."

Samuel looked at him helplessly. "How?" His throat felt like a hose with a knot in it.

"Because you get to be a man now," Bishop said. "You're free."

Samuel did not respond. Just hung his head. Below him, he dug his bare feet into and out of the mud. This seemed to help.

"You don't need your parents," Bishop said. "You may not realize it now, but you don't need anybody. This is an opportunity. This is your chance to become a different person, a new and better person."

Samuel found a small, smooth stone on the bottom of the pond. He picked it up with his toes, then let it go.

"It's like you're going through training," Bishop said. "Difficult training that will eventually make you stronger."

"I'm not a soldier," Samuel said. "This isn't a game."

"Sure it is," Bishop said. "Everything is a game. And you have to decide whether you're going to win or lose."

"This is stupid." Samuel made his way out of the pond, back to the tree where he'd organized his clothes. He sat down in the dirt and brought his knees up to his chest and wrapped his arms around his legs and rocked slowly back and forth. At some point the crying had started. His nose was now running, his face squished, his lungs spasming.

Bishop followed him out. "Right now, I'd say you're losing."

"Shut up."

"You have a losing quality about you at this moment."

Bishop stood above him, closely, his dripping underpants sagging ridiculously between his legs. He tugged them up.

"You know what you need to do," Bishop said. "You need to replace her."

"That's impossible."

"Not with another mother. With another *woman*."

"Whatever."

"You need to find a woman."

"For what?"

"For what." Bishop laughed. "A woman to, you know, to take advantage of. To take liberties with."

"I don't want that."

"There are plenty who will let you."

"That won't help."

"Sure it will." He took a step closer, leaned down, and touched Samuel's cheek with the palm of his hand. It was cold and damp, but also tender, soft. "You've never been with a girl, right?"

Samuel looked up at him, still hugging his own legs. He was beginning to shiver. "Have you?" he said.

Bishop laughed again. "I've done all sorts of things."

"Like what?"

Bishop stood silent a moment, then withdrew his hand. He walked over to the tree and leaned against it, pulling up his soggy underpants. "There are lots of girls at school. You should ask one out."

"That's not going to help."

"There's got to be someone, right? Who are you in love with?"

"Nobody."

"That's not true. Tell me. There's somebody. I already know who it is."

"You do not."

"I do too. You might as well say it." Bishop took a few steps toward Samuel and put his hands on his hips, one leg out, a pose that was conqueror-triumphant. "It's Bethany, isn't it?" he said. "You're in love with my sister."

"No I'm not!" Samuel said. But he knew as he said it that it wasn't convincing. He said it with too much urgency, too loudly, too much protest. He was not a good liar.

"You're in love with her," Bishop said. "You want to fuck her. I can tell these things."

"You're wrong."

"It's okay. Listen. You have my permission."

Samuel stood up. "I should go home," he said.

"Seriously, ask her out."

"My dad is probably wondering where I am."

"Don't go," Bishop said. He clutched Samuel's shoulders, to stop him. "Please stay."

"Why?"

"There's something you need to see."

"I should go."

"It'll only take a second."

"What is it?"

"Close your eyes."

"How can you show me something if I'm closing my eyes?"

"Trust me."

Samuel blew a long loud breath meant to convey his impatience at all this. He closed his eyes. He felt Bishop let go of his shoulders. He heard the sounds of Bishop moving in front of him, a footfall, then another, something wet splatting on the ground.

"When you open your eyes," Bishop said, "only open them a tiny bit. Like a squint."

"Fine."

"No more than a squint. Okay? Do it."

He opened his eyes, only a fraction. At first there was nothing but indistinct smudges of light, the abstract brightness of the day. A blur of Bishop before him, a round pink blob. Samuel opened his eyes a little wider. Bishop stood there, a few feet away. He was, Samuel could now tell, naked. His underwear lay wetly at his feet. And Samuel's gaze drifted to his crotch. This was involuntary. It happened all the time, in locker rooms, at urinals—any opportunity to compare his own body with the bodies of other boys: Who was bigger? Who was smaller? These questions seemed enormously important. So he looked. But where Bishop's prick should have been, Samuel saw *nothing*. Bishop was leaning forward, canted at the waist. His legs were slightly bent at the knees in a sort of half bow or curtsy. He had hidden his prick, Samuel could now see. He'd tucked it between his legs so that all Samuel saw was a smooth, soft nothingness.

"This is what she looks like," Bishop said. "My sister."

"What are you doing?"

"We're twins. This is what she looks like."

Samuel stared at Bishop's body, his skinny torso, ribs showing through the skin, but rigid also, tense and solid. He stared at that triangle of skin between his legs.

"You can pretend I'm her," Bishop said. He stepped toward Samuel and pressed his cheek to Samuel's and whispered into his ear, "Just pretend." Samuel felt Bishop's hands on his waist, then felt them gently pulling down his underwear, felt the wet fabric plop against his feet, felt the tiny wobble of his own prick, withered by the cold.

"Pretend I'm Bethany."

Then Bishop turned around and all Samuel could see was the small pale sweep of his shoulders and back. Bishop took both Samuel's hands and guided them to his hips. He leaned forward, pressed himself against Samuel, who was having that feeling again, of dislocation, detachment, like at the bus stop this morning, as if he were seeing everything from a great distance. It looked absurd. It wasn't even him, he thought, down there. Only an odd combination of parts that had never before been put together.

"Are you pretending?" Bishop said. "Is it working?"

Samuel didn't answer. He was far away. Bishop pressed harder against him, then released, then again, finding a slow rhythm. Samuel felt like a statue, incapable of doing anything but holding this pose.

"Pretend I'm her," Bishop said. "Make it happen. In your mind."

Bishop pressed into him and Samuel felt that surge that happened so often in class, at his desk, that cascade of tension, that explosive nervous twitching warmth, then looking down, seeing himself rising and swelling, knowing that he should not be rising and swelling but doing it anyway, unstoppably, and how this seemed to clarify things, how it answered something important—about him, about what had happened to him this day—and being absolutely convinced suddenly that everyone knew what he was doing right now. His mother and father, his teachers, Bethany, the police. Samuel was sure this was true, and it would remain with him for years, the event of his mother's departure locked in his mind with this moment in the woods, with Bishop, bonded in this way, pulsing against each other, Samuel not exactly liking it but not hating it either, thinking the whole time that his mother knew exactly what he was doing and she disapproved.

It was, he decided, the reason she had gone.

| PART THREE |

ENEMY, OBSTACLE, PUZZLE, TRAP

Late Summer 2011

1

SAMUEL STOOD at the threshold of his mother's apartment, his hand on the slightly ajar front door, readying himself to open it but not yet feeling able to. "Don't be scared," his mother had said. It had been more than twenty years since she last uttered those words to him, and ever since that morning he'd felt haunted by her, always imagining that she was around, spying on him from a distance. He'd check the windows at odd moments and scan crowds for her face. He lived his life wondering what he looked like from the outside, to his mother, who might be watching.

But she never was watching. And it took a long time for Samuel to remove her from his thoughts.

She had been a quiet sleeping memory until this moment, and he tried to calm himself and center himself by repeating some of the advice he'd found last night as he scanned those websites: Start fresh. Don't insult each other. Maintain boundaries. Go slowly. Have a support network. And the number one thing, the big primary commandment: Be prepared for your parent to be radically different from the person you remember.

And it was true. She *was* different. Samuel walked into her apartment finally and found her sitting at a large wooden table near the kitchen, waiting for him like a receptionist. There were three glasses of water on the table. And a briefcase. There were three chairs. She sat looking at him—not smiling, not having any reaction at all to his presence, just simply waiting, her hands in her lap. The long brown mane of her hair had been replaced by a short cut of military severity, turned to such a silver that it looked like a bathing cap. Her skin was wrinkled in that way common to people who have lost weight—under her arms, around her mouth, near her eyes. He was not expecting these wrinkles, and realized that in his imagination he had not been picturing his mother aging. He had to remind himself that she was, by now, sixty-one years old. She wore a simple black tank top that revealed the bony knobs of her shoulders and her thin upper arms. He worried suddenly that she hadn't been eating, then felt surprised to feel this way, worried.

"Come in," she said.

There wasn't any other sound. His mother's apartment had a penetrating silence rarely found in the city. She stared at him. He stared back. He did not sit down. There was something unbearable about being too close to her right now. She opened her mouth as if to say something but then did not say it. His mind emptied completely.

A noise came from another room just then: a toilet flushing, a faucet turned on and off. Then the bathroom door opened and out stepped a man in a white button-down shirt and a brown tie and brown slacks that were not exactly the same shades of brown. When he saw Samuel, he said "Professor Anderson sir!" and offered a damp hand for shaking. "I'm Simon Rogers," the man said, "of Rogers and Rogers? Your mother's attorney? We spoke on the phone."

Samuel looked at him for a moment, confused. The lawyer smiled pleasantly. He was a thin and short man with unusually broad shoulders. His brown hair was clipped close and arranged into the unartful and inevitable M-shape of early-onset male-pattern baldness. Samuel said, "We need a lawyer for this?"

"I'm afraid that was my idea," he said. "I insist on being present any time my client is being deposed. It's part of my service."

"This isn't a deposition," Samuel said.

"Not from *your* point of view. But of course you're not the one being deposed."

The lawyer clapped his hands together and moseyed to the table. He snapped open his briefcase and produced a small microphone, which he placed at the table's center. That his shirt fit his big shoulders but hung broadly on the rest of him made him look, Samuel realized, like a kid dressing in his dad's stuff.

"My role here," the lawyer said, "is to protect my client's interests—legal, fiduciary, emotional."

"You're the one who asked me to come," Samuel said.

"Indeed, sir! And the important thing to remember is that we're all on the same team. You agreed to write a letter to the judge explaining why your mother deserves lenience. My job is to help with said letter and make sure you are not here under, shall we say, false pretenses?"

"Unbelievable," Samuel said, but he wasn't sure what was more unbelievable: that the lawyer suspected Samuel of deceit, or that the lawyer was right. Because Samuel had no intention of writing any letter to a judge. He had come today to satisfy his contract with Periwinkle, to gather dirt on his mother so that he could, eventually, malign her publicly for money.

"The purpose of today's inquiry," the lawyer said, "is primarily to understand your mother's actions regarding her brave protest against the former governor of Wyoming. And, secondarily, to explicate why she's a great person. Everything else, sir, is outside our strict scope of interest. Would you like some water? Juice?"

Faye remained sitting and silent, not participating but still taking up all the space in Samuel's mind. He felt wary of her like he'd feel wary of a buried land mine he knew the approximate, but not exact, location of.

"Shall we sit?" the lawyer said, and together they joined Faye at the table, a rectangular table made of weathered wooden planks that probably had seen another life as a fence or barn. Three water glasses sat sweating onto cork coasters. The lawyer sat and adjusted his tie, which was mahogany-colored, as opposed to his more cocoa pants. He placed both his hands on his briefcase and smiled. Faye kept staring in her neutral, detached, indifferent way. She looked as austere and unfussy and bleak as the apartment itself—a single long space with a bank of windows facing north toward the tall buildings of downtown Chicago. The walls were white and bare. There was no television. There was no computer. The furniture was simple and restrained. Samuel noted the total lack of things that needed to be plugged in. It was as though she had ejected all unnecessary things from her life.

Samuel sat across from her and nodded like he might nod to a stranger on the street: slight downward tilt of the chin.

"Thank you for coming," she said.

Another nod.

"How have you been?" she asked.

He did not answer her immediately, but instead glared at her with an expression he hoped projected steely resolve and coldness. "Fine," he finally said. "Just fine."

"Good," she said. "And your father?"

"He's *great*."

"Well okay then!" the lawyer said. "Now that we've gotten that out of the way." He laughed nervously. "Why don't we go ahead and begin?" Small beads of sweat were now manifesting on his forehead. He picked involuntarily at his shirt, which was not exactly white, but that gray-white of something that's been washed many times, with definite yellow discoloring at the armpits.

"Now, Professor Anderson, sir, this would be an ideal moment to ask your question regarding our primary interest today." The lawyer reached across the table and pressed a button on the microphone that sat between Samuel and his mother. A small diode on the microphone glowed a placid blue.

"And what question would that be?" Samuel said.

"Regarding your mother's heroic protest against tyranny, sir."

"Right." Samuel looked at her. Up close like this, he found it difficult to reconcile this new person with the woman he used to know. She seemed to have lost all the softness of her former self—her long soft hair and soft arms and soft skin. A new, harder body had replaced all that. Samuel could see the outline of her jaw muscles just below the skin. The ripple her collarbone made across her chest. The swell of her biceps. Her arms were like ropes that ships use to dock with.

"Okay, fine," Samuel said. "Why did you do it? Why did you throw rocks at Governor Packer?"

His mother looked at the lawyer, who popped open his briefcase and fished out a single sheet of paper, dense with text on one side, which he handed to Faye and which she read verbatim.

"Regarding my actions toward Republican presidential candidate and former Wyoming governor Sheldon Packer, hereinafter referred to simply as 'the governor,'" she said, and she cleared her throat, "I do hereby attest, maintain, swear, certify, and solemnly affirm that my throwing gravel in the direction of the governor should in no way be construed as an attempt to hurt, assault, injure, batter, maim, cripple, deform, mangle, or otherwise create a reasonable apprehension of an imminent harmful or offensive contact with the governor nor anyone the gravel may have had inadvertent physical exposure with, nor was it my intention to inflict emotional distress, pain, suffering, misery, anguish, or trauma to anyone who witnessed or was otherwise affected by my purely political and symbolic actions. My actions were a necessary and essential and knee-jerk response to the governor's fascist politics and therefore, having no alterna-

tive with regards to the time, place, or manner of my response, not voli-
tional, the governor's extreme right-wing, pro-gun, pro-war, pro-violence
rhetoric having put me under unusual and substantial duress to such a
degree as to constitute a reasonable belief on my behalf of bodily harm
to my person. I also believed that the governor's relentless and fetishis-
tic law-and-order pro-violence stance *implied consent* to engage in violent
roughhousing-type behavior in much the same way people who engage
in sadomasochism for sexual gratification consent to being struck without criminal or civil liability. I chose gravel as the vehicle of my symbolic
protest because my unathletic and crime-free background in which I was
never trained in a ball-throwing sport meant that the danger posed by
my casting tiny stones represented de minimis harm and therefore the
gravel was definitely not a dangerous, deadly, or aggravated weapon that
I in no way used to purposely, knowingly, negligently, menacingly, reck-
lessly, or with indifference to the value of human life cause bodily injury.
My purpose instead was solely, entirely, wholly, and altogether in every
respect political, to communicate a political speech act that was neither
inciting nor provocative nor offensive nor presenting clear danger, a symbolic speech similar to protestors legally exercising their free speech rights
by desecrating the flag or mutilating a draft card, et cetera."

Faye laid the paper on the table, carefully and deliberately, like it was
something fragile.

"Excellent!" said the lawyer. His face had grown red, a subtle but
noticeable change from his previous pallor, which Samuel would describe
as plastic-baby creamy yellow. Blobs of sweat now clung to his forehead,
like the way paint on exterior walls can bubble on a very hot day. "Now
that we're all clear on that front, let's take a little break." The lawyer
switched off the microphone. "Excuse me," he said, and headed to the
bathroom.

"He does that," Faye said, watching him go. "He apparently needs to
use the bathroom every five to ten minutes. That's just his deal."

"What the hell was that all about?" Samuel said.

"I'm guessing he goes to the bathroom to towel off the sweat. He's a
very moist man. But he also does something in there involving quite a lot
of toilet paper, I'm not sure what."

"Seriously," Samuel said, grabbing the paper and looking at it, "I have
no idea what any of this means."

"He also has the tiniest feet. Have you noticed?"

"Faye, *listen*," he said, and they both flinched at the use of her name. It was the first time he'd ever done that. "What is going on?"

"Okay. Fine. Here's what I understand. My case is a seriously complicated one. Many charges of assault and several other charges of battery. Aggravated. First degree. I guess I scared a bunch of people in the park—those are the assaults—but the rocks only struck a few of them—those are the batteries. Plus also charges of, let's see"—she ticked these off on her fingers one by one—"disturbing the peace, public lewdness, disorderly conduct, resisting arrest. The prosecutor is being unusually aggressive, egged on by the judge, we believe."

"Judge Charles Brown."

"That's him! The sentence for aggravated battery, by the way, is somewhere in between three hundred hours of community service and twenty-five years in prison."

"That's a pretty wide range."

"The judge has a lot of discretion in sentencing. So you know that letter you're writing to him?"

"Yeah."

"It better be pretty damn good."

A whoosh of plumbing now, and the bathroom door opened and the lawyer returned, smiling, wiping his hands on his pants. Faye was right: He had the smallest feet Samuel had ever seen on an adult male.

"Fantastic!" the lawyer said. "This is going really well." How could he keep steady with those broad shoulders and those tiny feet? He was like a pyramid balancing upside down.

The lawyer sat and drummed his fingers on his briefcase. "On to part two!" he said. He turned on the microphone. "Our new subject, sir, is why your mother is an excellent human being with regards to why she shouldn't go to prison for upward of twenty years."

"That's not really a possibility, right?"

"I believe not, sir, but I'd like to cover all my bases, obviously. Now, would you like to hear about your mother's charitable giving?"

"I'm sort of more interested in what she's been up to these last couple decades."

"The public schools, sir. She's doing some really excellent work in the public schools. Plus poetry? A real advocate for the arts, let me tell you."

"This part is going to be tricky for me," Samuel said. "This whole 'excellent human being' part, no offense."

"And why is that, sir?"

"Well, what am I going to tell the judge? That she's a great person? A wonderful mother?"

The lawyer smiled. "That's right. Exactly that."

"I don't think that's something I could truthfully say."

"And why not?"

Samuel looked from the lawyer to his mother and back again. "Seriously?"

The lawyer nodded, still smiling.

"My mother abandoned me when I was eleven!"

"Yes, sir, and as you can probably imagine it's best that as little of that information about that part of her life reach the public as possible."

"She abandoned me without any warning."

"Perhaps, sir, for our purposes, sir, you shouldn't think of it as your mother *abandoned* you. Instead, perhaps think of it as she gave you up for adoption slightly later than usual."

The lawyer opened his briefcase and produced a pamphlet. "Your mother actually did a lot more legwork than most birth mothers do," he said, "in terms of looking into prospective adoptee families and ensuring her child landed in a positive environment and such. From a certain standpoint, I'd say her diligence in this matter could be considered above and beyond."

He handed Samuel the pamphlet. The cover was bright pink with pictures of smiling multicultural families and the words *So You're Adopted!* at the top in bubbly type.

"I wasn't adopted," Samuel said.

"Not *literally,* sir."

The lawyer was sweating again, a shiny film on his skin like what you might find on the ground on a dewy morning. A smear of liquid had now also appeared under his armpit and down his sleeve. It looked like his shirt was being swallowed slowly by a jellyfish.

Samuel looked at his mother, who gave him a sort of shrug like *What are you going to do?* Behind her, out the bank of windows looking north, was the great gray face of the Sears Tower, hazy in the smoggy distance. It used to be the tallest building in the world, but it no longer was. It wasn't even in the top five. Come to think of it, it wasn't even called the Sears Tower anymore.

"It's quiet in here," Samuel said.

His mother frowned. "What?"

"No traffic noise, no people noise. It's very isolated."

"Oh. They were renovating the building when the housing market collapsed," she said. "They had only done a couple of units when they just left it, unfinished."

"So you're the only one in the building?"

"There's a married couple two floors up. Bohemian artist types. We mostly ignore each other."

"Sounds lonely."

She studied his face for a moment. "It suits me," she said.

"You know, I'd done a pretty good job forgetting about you," Samuel said. "Until these recent events."

"Is that so?"

"Yeah. I'd say you were pretty much forgotten, until this week."

She smiled and looked at the tabletop in front of her—a sort of inward smile that suggested some private thought now occurring to her. She swept the table with her palms, as if she were cleaning it.

"What we think of as *forgetting* really isn't," she said. "Not strictly speaking. We never actually *forget* things. We only lose the path back to them."

"What are you talking about?"

"I read this thing recently," she said. "There was this study about how memory works. This team of physiologists, molecular biologists, neurologists, they were trying to figure out where we keep our memories. I think it was in *Nature*. Or *Neuron*. Or *JAMA*."

"A little light reading?"

"I have many interests. Anyway, what they discovered is that our memories are tangible, physical things. Like, you can actually *see* the cell where each memory is stored. The way it works is, first, you have a perfectly pristine, untouched cell. Then that cell is zapped and gets all deformed and mangled. And that mutilation is, itself, the memory. It never really goes away."

"Fascinating," Samuel said.

"I'm pretty sure it was in *Nature*, now that I think about it."

"You're serious?" Samuel said. "I'm baring my soul here and you're talking about a study you read about?"

"I liked the metaphor," Faye said. "And besides, you weren't baring your soul. Not even close, not yet."

The lawyer cleared his throat. "Perhaps we should return to our topic?" he said. "Professor Anderson, sir? If you'd like to begin your direct examination?"

Samuel stood up. He paced one way, then another. There was a single small bookcase along the wall, and this is where he went. He could feel his mother's eyes boring into his back as he inspected the shelves: mostly poetry, a large collection of Allen Ginsberg. Samuel realized that what he was really looking for was a copy of the famous magazine his story was published in. He realized this when he felt disappointed not to see it.

He spun around. "Here's what I'd like to know."

"Sir?" the lawyer said. "You're out of microphone range?"

"I'd like to know what you've been doing these twenty years. And where you went when you left us."

"That, sir, is probably outside the scope of our inquiry."

"And all this business about you in the sixties. Getting arrested. What they're saying about you on TV—"

"You want to know if it's all true," Faye said.

"Yes."

"Was I a radical? Was I in the protest movement?"

"Yes."

"Was I arrested for prostitution?"

"Yes. There's about a month of 1968 unaccounted for. I had always thought you were in Iowa, at home, with Grandpa Frank, waiting for Dad to come back from the army. But you weren't."

"No."

"You were in Chicago."

"For a very short time, yes. Then I left."

"I want to know what happened."

"Hah-hah!" the lawyer said, and did a little drumroll on his briefcase. "I think we've traveled slightly far afield, yes? Now perhaps we could get back to our subject?"

"But you have other questions, right?" Faye said. "Even bigger questions?"

"We could get to those. In time," Samuel said.

"Why wait? Let's get it all out in the open right now. Go on and ask me. There's only one real question."

"We could begin with the photograph. The photo taken of you at that protest, in 1968."

"But that's not why you're here. Ask your real question. The thing you came here to find out."

"I came here to write a letter to the judge."

"You did not. Go ahead. Ask your question."

"It's not relevant."

"Just ask. Do it."

"It's not important. It's nothing—"

"I'd agree with that!" the lawyer cut in. "Immaterial."

"Shut up, Simon," Faye said, then leveled her eyes at Samuel. "This question is everything. It's why you're here. Now why don't you stop lying and ask it."

"Okay. Fine. I want to know. Why did you leave me?"

And Samuel could feel the cry coming almost as soon as he said it: *Why did you leave me?* The question that had tormented his adolescence. He used to tell people she was dead. When they would ask about his mother, it was easier to say she'd died. Because when he told them the truth, they'd wonder why she left and where she'd gone and he didn't know. Then they'd look at him funny, like it was his fault. Why did she leave him? It was the question that kept him awake night after night until he learned to swallow it and deny it. But asking the question now let it break back out—the shame and loneliness and self-pity washed over the question so that he was barely able to pronounce the last word before his throat tightened and he could feel himself on the verge of crying.

They considered each other for a moment, Samuel and his mother, before the lawyer leaned across the table and whispered something into her ear. Then her defiance seemed to fizzle. She looked into her lap.

"Perhaps we should return to our topic?" the lawyer said.

"I think I deserve some answers," Samuel said.

"Perhaps we could get back to the subject of your letter, sir?"

"I'm not expecting to be best friends," Samuel said. "But answering a few questions? Is that too much to ask?"

Faye crossed her arms and seemed to curl into herself. The lawyer stared at Samuel and waited. The sweat blobs on his forehead had grown thick and bulbous. At any moment, they could rain down into his eyes.

"The thing about that article in *Nature*?" Faye said. "The one about memory? What really struck me was how our memories are sewn into the meat of the brain. Everything we know about our past is literally *etched into us.*"

"Okay," Samuel said. "What's your point?"

She closed her eyes and rubbed her temples, a gesture of impatience and irritation that Samuel recognized from his childhood.

"Isn't it obvious?" she said. "Every memory is really a scar."

The lawyer slapped the top of his briefcase and said, "Okay! I think we're done here!"

"You haven't answered any of my questions," Samuel said. "Why did you leave me? What happened to you in Chicago? Why did you keep it secret? What have you been doing all these years?"

And Faye looked at him then, and all the hardness in her body dissolved. She gave him that same look she'd given him the morning she disappeared, her face full of grief.

"I'm sorry," she said. "I can't."

"I need this," Samuel said. "You don't even understand how much. I *need* to know."

"I've given you all I can."

"But you haven't told me *anything*. Please, why did you go?"

"I can't," she said. "It's private."

"Private? Seriously?"

Faye nodded and looked at the tabletop. "It's private," she said again.

Samuel crossed his arms. "You goad me into asking this question and then you say it's private? Fuck you."

Then the lawyer was gathering his things, turning off the microphone, sweat dropping onto his shirt collar. "Thank you so much, Professor Anderson, for all your efforts," he said.

"I didn't think you could get any lower, Faye, but *congratulations*," Samuel said, standing up. "Really, you're like a virtuoso. A maestro of being awful."

"We'll be in touch!" the lawyer said. He ushered Samuel toward the front door, pushed him from behind with a warm, wet hand. "We will be in contact to touch base about how we can move forward." He opened the door and walked Samuel through it. Liquid BBs hung on to the skin of his forehead. The area under his armpit was now a soggy mess, as if he'd spilled a movie-theater-size drink there. "We're very excited to read your letter to Judge Brown," he said. "And good day!"

He closed the door behind Samuel and locked it.

All the way out of the building, and for the whole long ride back through Chicago and into the suburbs, Samuel felt like he was going to crumble. He remembered the advice from those websites: *Have a support network.* He needed to talk to someone. But who? Not his father, clearly. Not anyone from work. The only people he regularly communicated with were his *Elfscape* friends. So, once home, he logged on. He was greeted by the usual barrage of *Hey Dodger!* and *Good to see ya!* He asked a question in guild chat: *Any of you Chicago folks want to meet up tonight? I feel like going out.*

Which was met with an embarrassed silence. Samuel understood he'd crossed a boundary. He'd asked to meet *in real life,* a request usually made only by creeps and stalkers. He was about to apologize and tell them all to forget it when Pwnage, their brilliant leader, the guild's *Elfscape* savant, finally, mercifully, wrote back.

Sure. I know a place.

2

LAURA POTTSDAM SAT in the frightening office of the university dean, explaining exactly what had transpired between herself and Samuel. "He told me I didn't have a learning disability," Laura said. "He told me I just wasn't very smart."

"Oh my goodness," the dean said, looking stricken. Her office shelves were filled mostly with books about the Black Death, her walls decorated with old-looking illustrations of people suffering from boils or lesions or being piled into wheelbarrows, dead. Laura had not thought any wall art was more insufferable than her roommate's giant weight-loss calendar, but the dean's apparent interest in the history of open sores proved her totally wrong.

"Samuel really said, out loud, that you weren't smart?"

"It was a pretty big blow to my self-esteem."

"Yes, I'd imagine."

"I am an elite college student with a perfect GPA. He can't tell me I'm not smart."

"I think you're *very* smart, Laura."

"Thank you."

"And you should know I take this very seriously."

"I might also mention that Professor Anderson sometimes curses in class. It's really distracting and offensive."

"Okay, here's what we can do," the dean said. "Why don't you rewrite your *Hamlet* paper for a new grade. Meanwhile, I'll smooth things over with Professor Anderson. Does that sound like a plan?"

"Yes, that sounds like a great plan."

"And if there's anything else I need to know, please call me directly."

"Okay," Laura said, and she walked out of the administration building feeling the bright, buoyant warmth that accompanies victory.

It was a feeling that lasted only briefly, only until she cracked open her Shakespeare and sat on her dorm-room floor looking forlornly at all those words and realized she was right back where she started: trying to complete yet another worthless assignment for yet another worthless class, Intro to Lit, one of five classes she was enrolled in this semester, all of which were, in her opinion, bullshit. Just totally stupid time sucks that had nothing to do with real life, was what she thought about college classes, so far. And by "real life" she meant the tasks she'd be asked to perform upon graduation with a bachelor's degree in business, tasks she couldn't even really guess at now since she hadn't taken any advanced communication and marketing classes and hadn't held an internship or "real job" ever, unless you counted her high-school gig working part-time at the concession stand at a second-run movie theater, where she learned several important lessons about workplace etiquette from a thirty-two-year-old assistant manager who liked staying after hours to smoke weed and play strip poker with the pretty teenage girls he always hired, which required of her a careful social negotiation to continue having access to the weed without doing anything so retrograde she couldn't show her face at work the next day. But even if this was the only quote-unquote *work experience* she'd ever had, she was still pretty sure her inevitably successful future career in marketing and communications would not require the stupid shit she was currently learning in college.

Like *Hamlet*. She was trying to read *Hamlet,* trying to form a thought for an essay she had to rewrite about *Hamlet*. But the thing that was more interesting to her right now was a fistful of paper clips that she tossed lightly into the air and then watched as they bounced and scattered all over the linoleum of her dorm-room floor. This was more fun than reading *Hamlet*. Because even though every paper clip was shaped exactly like every other paper clip, they bounced in chaotic, random, unduplicatable ways. Why didn't they bounce exactly the same? Why didn't they all land in the same place? Plus there was that delicious *click-chhh* sound when they all hit the floor and slid. She had lofted the paper clips into the air roughly fifteen to twenty times in the last few minutes—a pretty transparent *Hamlet*-reading stalling maneuver, she had to admit—when her phone dinged. A new message!

Heeeeeeeeeeeey honey

From Jason. And she could tell by the several iterations of the letter *e* that he was feeling that very special urgent way tonight. Boyfriends were so transparent sometimes.

Hey! :-D

The reason college was so stupid was due to learning things she would never need in life, ever. Like knowledge of Greek statuary, for example, such as she was memorizing for the Intro to Humanities class that was required of every student and that the university offered online. This was such a dumb waste of time because she was sure when she interviewed for her first real job they would not show her flash cards of statues and ask "What myth does this represent?," which was what she had to do in the timed two-minute weekly quizzes the class required and that were such a total joke—

Her phone chirped. It was an update on iFeel, the excellent new app that was the social media darling du jour among the college set. Laura's friends were all on it, and used it obsessively, and would abandon it as soon as it was discovered by the late-adopters, meaning old people.

Laura looked at her phone. *iFeel happy tonight!!!* one of her friends had posted. It was Brittany, who had so far survived the several purges Laura had made to her Alert List.

The phone asked: *Do you want to Ignore, Respond, or Autocare?*

Laura selected Autocare. Placed the phone back on the floor, on the paper clips.

What had she been thinking about? Right, the art quizzes, which were a total joke because all she had to do was scroll through the quiz taking screen-grabs along the way and then unplug her modem, which the test interpreted as a "crash" or "network failure" (i.e., not her fault), thus allowing her to take the quiz again. So she looked up all the answers and plugged in the modem and aced the quiz and didn't have to think about Greek statuary for another week.

Then there was biology, which pretty much made Laura gag just thinking about it. Because she was pretty sure the first week of her powerful marketing and communications job that she would someday have would not require her to identify the chemical chain reaction that converted a photon of light to photosynthesized sugar, such as she was currently memorizing in her Intro to Biology class that she was stupidly forced to take in order to satisfy a science requirement *even though hello? she wasn't going to be a scientist?* Plus the professor was so dry and boring and the lectures so unbearable—

Her phone dinged again. A message from Brittany: *Thanx girl!!* Responding to whatever message iFeel selected to Autocare with, obviously. And because Laura was in the middle of studying and trying really hard to read *Hamlet* she decided not to engage and instead sent back the universal glyph signifying the end of a conversation:

:)

Anyway the biology lectures were so unbearable she'd begun paying her roommate twenty bucks a week to record herself reading aloud from the important parts of the textbook so Laura could listen to the recording during the biweekly chapter tests, when she sat inconspicuously next to the wall about halfway down in the three-hundred-person lecture hall and slipped one small earbud into the wall-side ear and leaned against the wall and listened to her roommate reading the chapter while scanning the test for keywords, vaguely impressed by her own multitasking skills and her ability to pass the test without ever studying once.

"You're not using this to cheat, are you?" her roommate asked a few weeks into the operation.

"No. It's so I can study. At the gym," Laura said.

"Because cheating is wrong."

"I know."

"And I've never seen you exercise."

"I do exercise."

"I'm at the gym all the time and I've never seen you there."

"Well, rats' eggs on you!" Laura said, which was something her mother always said instead of cursing. Something else her mother always said is *Don't let anyone EVER bully you or make you feel bad about yourself,* and at that moment her roommate was making her feel very bad indeed, which was why instead of apologizing Laura said, "Listen, feeb, if you haven't seen me at the gym it's 'cuz some of us don't need to be there as long as you do," because her roommate was, let's face it, objectively morbidly (almost fascinatingly) obese. She had legs like sacks of potatoes. For real.

The word "feeb" was something she made up on the spot and felt pretty proud of, actually, how sometimes a nickname can capture a person's essence like that.

Her phone dinged.

Whatcha doin 2nite?

Jason again, probing. He was never as obvious as when he wanted to sext.

Homework :'(

The only class Laura was taking this semester that related in any way to her future was her one business class, macroeconomics, which was so abstractly mathematical and had basically nothing to do with the "human element" of business, which was really why she was going into this field at all, because she liked people and she was good with people and she maintained a huge cavalry of online contacts who texted her and messaged her several times daily through the many social media sites she kept a presence on, which made her phone ding all day, repeatedly, the sound like a spoon lightly tapped against a crystal goblet, these pure high singing notes that made her feel bolts of Pavlovian happiness.

And that was why she was a business major.

But macroeconomics was so stupid and boring and unnecessary for her future career that she did not feel at all bad collaborating with a boy from her orientation group, a graphic design major and Photoshop artist who could, for example, scan the label of a Lipton Green Tea bottle, erase the ingredients list (a surprisingly long and sciencey thing for something that claimed to be "tea"), and replace the ingredients with an answer key to the test—all the formulas and concepts they were supposed to have memorized—matching exactly the original Lipton typeface and color so that there was no way the teacher would ever know she had all the test answers in front of her except by reading the ingredients list on her Lipton Green Tea. Fat chance, in other words. This boy was quasi-repaid with hugs that were maybe a little too tight and too close, as well as bi-semester visits to his dorm room downstairs when she "forgot" the key to her own room while going for a shower and so had nothing to do but crash at his place wearing only her favorite tiny towel.

Did Laura feel bad about all this cheating? She did not. That the school made it so easy to cheat meant, for her, that they tacitly approved of it, and moreover it was actually the school's fault for making her cheat by (a) giving her so many opportunities, and (b) making her take so many bullshit courses.

Example: *Hamlet.* Trying to read stupid *Hamlet* again—

Her phone chirped. Another iFeel update. It was Vanessa: *iFeel scared about all this terrible economic news!!!* Which was exactly the kind of boring update that got you taken right off the Alert List. Laura selected Ignore. One strike against Vanessa.

Anyway trying to read *Hamlet* and identify "logical fallacies" in Hamlet's course of action, which was *such bullshit* because she knew for a fact that when she interviewed for executive vice president of communications and marketing for a major corporation they would not ask her about *Hamlet.* They would not ask her about logical fallacies. She had tried to read *Hamlet* but it kept getting all gummed up in her brain:

> *How weary, stale, flat, and unprofitable,*
> *Seem to me all the uses of this world!*
> *Fie on't! ah fie!*

What the fuck is that?

Who talks like that? And who said this was great literature? Because mostly from what she could tell in the few places where Shakespeare actually wrote in English was that Hamlet's just stupid and depressed, which she was like if you're sad and depressed and cheesed about something it's probably your own dumb fault and why did she have to sit here and listen to you wallow in it? Plus there was the matter of her phone, which chimed and squawked and dinged roughly ten times per soliloquy and made her feel mentally encumbered trying to read stupid *Hamlet* knowing there was an update just sitting there waiting for her. It was a chiming sound for a text message but a birdlike chirping sound whenever her closest seventy-five friends updated their iFeel status, was how she'd programmed the phone. At first, she set it to alert her when any of her iFeel friends posted anything, but she quickly realized this was untenable given her thousand-plus friend roll, making the phone look something like a stock ticker and sound like an Audubon sanctuary. So she culled the Alert List to a more manageable seventy-five, though this list was a fluid, ever-changing one as she spent at least a couple of hours weekly reevaluating it and swapping some people out for others on the bubble using an intuitive sort of regression analysis based on several metrics, including the interestingness and frequency of the friend's recent posts, the number of hilarious pictures recently uploaded and tagged, the presence of anything political-ish in the friend's status stream (political statements usually caused bickering, so anyone chronically guilty was ejected from the top seventy-five), and finally the friend's ability to find and link to worthwhile internet videos, since finding, in any consistent manner, good internet videos was a skill like panning for gold, she thought, and so it was important to keep in one's top list a couple of these people who could spot cool videos and memes before they went viral, which made her feel good vis-à-vis her place in the culture, seeing these things a day or a week before everyone else in the world. It made her feel like she was on the leading edge of everything. It was approximately the same feeling she had walking around the mall and seeing how every clothing store reflected exactly what she wanted right back at her. The photographs, poster-size, life-size, some even blown up bigger than that, showed attractive young girls just like her, in groups of attractive and racially kind of diverse friends that looked just like her friends, having fun in outdoor settings that she and her friends would totally go to if there were anything like that around here. And the feeling she had when she saw these images was that *she was wanted*. Everyone wanted her to like them. Everyone wanted to give her exactly what she desired. She never felt as secure as she did in dressing rooms rejecting clothes for not being good enough for her, breathing in the deep, gluey smell of the mall.

Her phone dinged. Jason again.

Ur at home?

Yep all alone feeb's at the gym :-)

Only now there was this dumb English professor who seemed set on not giving her what she wanted. Who actually seemed intent on failing her. Not even her learning disability had persuaded him, to her dismay. The paperwork for this disability was on file at the Office of Adaptive Services. It was official, this learning disability, because of a particularly brilliant plan that was hatched at the beginning of the year, when her new plump roommate, who was on several medications for her truly severe ADHD problems, let slip how many legally mandated accommodations she was entitled to, including someone to take notes for her, extra time for quizzes and tests, extended deadlines, excused absences, and so on. In other words, complete freedom from the scrutiny of her professors that— even better!—was *legally binding* under the Americans with Disabilities Act. All Laura needed to do was answer a questionnaire in such a way as to trigger a certain diagnosis. Simple. She went down to the Office of Adaptive Services. The questionnaire was composed of twenty-five statements she had to either agree or disagree with. She figured it would be pretty obvious what she needed to lie about, but once she started the questionnaire she was troubled by how true some of the statements were, such as: *I have trouble remembering things I just read.* Yes, she did! That was true almost every time she was asked to read an actual printed book. Or: *I find myself daydreaming when I'm supposed to be paying attention.* Which was something that happened to her literally dozens of times per class. She started feeling queasy that there might be something actually wrong with her until she got deeper into the questionnaire:

> *The thought of homework makes me feel panicked and stressed.*
> *I have trouble making friends.*
> *The stress of school sometimes gives me unbearable headaches and/or*
>   *indigestion.*

None of these things were a hundred percent true, and this made her feel more or less normal again, such that when she was diagnosed with severe learning disabilities she felt really good about herself, like when she interviewed for that movie theater job and got it immediately, that same sense of accomplishment. She did not feel guilty about playing the learning disability card, since she had answered several of the statements on the questionnaire honestly, making her roughly ten percent learning disabled, plus her classes were so boring and stupid and impossible to pay attention to that she added another forty-five percent to that as a kind of de facto environmental learning block, making her fifty-five percent learning disabled, which she then rounded up.

She tossed a handful of paper clips approximately three feet into the air and watched as they began spiraling away from each other as they flew. She thought if she could practice this enough she could achieve perfect paper-clip symmetry. She could toss them in such a way that they'd go up and down as a single aggregate lump.

The paper clips sprinkled themselves across the floor. Hamlet said,

> O, that this too too solid flesh would melt
> Thaw and resolve itself into a dew!

This was such a waste of time.

She had one move left, one more bullet in the chamber. She dialed the dean's number.

"Professor Anderson is not creating ideal conditions for my education," she said once she had the dean on the line. "I don't feel like his classroom is a good place to learn."

"I see," the dean said. "I see. Could you explain why?"

"I do not feel I can express my individual viewpoint."

"And why is that, specifically?"

"I feel like Professor Anderson does not value my unique perspective."

"Well, maybe we should have a meeting with him then."

"It is not a safe space."

"I'm sorry, what?" the dean said. Laura could almost hear the woman sitting up straighter in her chair.

Safe space. It was the current buzzword on campus. She wasn't even entirely sure what it meant, but she knew it tended to tweak the ears of university administrators.

"His classroom does not feel safe," Laura said. "It is not a safe space."

"Oh my."

"Feels abusive, actually."

"Oh my."

"I'm not saying he *is* abusive or has quote-unquote *abused me*," Laura said. "I'm saying it is my perception that in his classroom I am fearful of encountering abuse."

"I see. I see."

"I cannot emotionally deal with writing my *Hamlet* paper, and the reason is because he has not created a safe space in which I feel okay expressing my actual true self to him."

"Oh, of course."

"Writing a paper for Professor Anderson triggers negative feelings of stress and vulnerability. It feels oppressive. If I write a paper using my own words he'll give me a bad grade and I'll feel bad about myself. Do you think I should have to feel bad about myself in order to get a degree?"

"No, not necessarily," the dean said.

"Me neither. I would hate to have to reveal this situation to the student newspaper," Laura said. "Or post about it on my blog. Or to my thousand friends on iFeel."

Which was pretty much checkmate for this particular conversation. The dean said she would be looking into the matter, and in the meantime why didn't Laura forget about the essay for now and keep quiet until they could all come to a nice resolution.

Victory. Another assignment completed. She closed *Hamlet* and tossed the book in the corner. She shut down her laptop. Her phone dinged. Jason again, finally asking for what he'd wanted this whole time:

Send me a pic I miss you!!!

Naughty or nice? ;-)

Naughty!!!

Haha lol }:-)

She stripped off her clothes and, holding a camera at arm's length, posed in several of the smoky ways she'd absorbed from two decades of looking at *Cosmo* and Victoria's Secret catalogs and internet pornography. She took about a dozen pictures of herself from slightly different angles and with slightly different pouts: smoky-sexy, smoky-amused, smoky-ironic, smoky-smirky, and so on.

Afterward, she could not decide which one of them to send to Jason, because they were all so great.

PWNAGE SUGGESTED they meet at a bar called Jezebels.
Samuel wrote:

That sounds like a strip club.

Ya it does lol

Is it?

No … but sort of

It was in another of Chicago's suburbs, one that had ballooned in the mid-sixties in the first great migration out of the city. Now it was gently dying. All the people who had fled a generation before were moving back in, heading to the high-rises of Chicago's newly gentrified downtown. White flight had given way to white infill, and now these first-generation suburbs—with their modest homes, their quaint malls—just seemed *old*. People were leaving, and as they left, home values declined, driving still more out in an unstoppable cascade. Schools closed. Shops were shuttered. Streetlights broken. Potholes left unfixed and widened. The giant shells of big-box retailers sat empty and anonymous but for old logos still legible in dirt outline.

Jezebels was situated in a strip mall between a liquor store and a place where you could rent to own tires. Its big front windows were covered with sheets of black plastic tinting that undulated where air bubbles were trapped and never smoothed out. Inside, the place had all the makings of a strip club: an elevated stage, a metal pole, purplish lights. But no strippers. The only thing to watch was the televisions, about two dozen of them arranged such that no matter where you sat, you always had an adequate sight line to at least four. The TVs were tuned to various niche cable channels specializing in sports or music videos or game shows or food. The largest television, which hovered above the stage and seemed to be bolted directly onto the stripper pole, was showing a nineties movie about strippers.

The place was mostly empty. A handful of guys sat at the bar looking at their phones. A larger party in the back, six people at a booth, currently quiet. Samuel didn't see anyone matching Pwnage's description (*I'll be the blond guy in a black shirt,* is how he'd described himself), so he sat at a table and waited. A TV above the bar was tuned to a music channel where Molly Miller was being interviewed. Tonight was the premiere of her new video: "The song's about, you know, being yourself?" said Molly. "It's like what the song says. 'You have got to represent.' Just be true to who you are. Just, like, don't change."

"Yo Dodger!" said a man near the door. He was indeed wearing a black shirt, but his hair wasn't so much blond as it was white with maybe a kind of jaundice-yellow discoloring at the tips. His face was pale and pocked and of an ambiguous age: He was either a fifty-year-old or a thirty-year-old who'd had a hard life. He wore jeans that were a few inches too short, a long-sleeve shirt that was maybe two sizes too tight. Clothes purchased for a younger and smaller self.

They shook hands. "Pwnage," he said. "That's my name."

"I'm Samuel."

"No you're not," he said. "You're Dodger." He slapped Samuel on the back. "I feel like I already *know* you, man. We're war buddies."

It looked like he carried a bowling ball under his shirt, just above his belt. A skinny guy with a big guy's belly. His eyes were protuberant and red. His skin had the texture of cold wax.

A waitress came, and Pwnage asked for a beer and something called the "Double-D Nachos, extra super loaded."

"Interesting place," Samuel said after the waitress had gone.

"It's the only bar within walking distance of my house," Pwnage said. "I like to walk. For the exercise. I'm starting a new diet soon. It's called the Pleisto Diet. Heard of it?"

"Nope."

"It's the one where you eat like they did in the Pleistocene. Specifically, the Tarantian epoch, during the last ice age."

"How do we know what they ate in the Pleistocene?"

"Because science. You eat like a caveman, minus the mastodons. Plus it's gluten-free? The key is tricking your body into thinking you've gone back in time, before the invention of agriculture."

"I don't understand why you'd want to do that."

"There's a feeling that civilization was a mistake, is why. That we screwed up along the way, took a wrong turn. Now, because of it, we're fat."

His body had a noticeable tilt to one side, his right side. His mouse hand seemed dominant. His left arm seemed to lag a few moments behind the rest of him, like it was permanently asleep.

"I'm assuming nachos weren't on the menu during the Pleistocene," Samuel said.

"See, what's important right now for me is to be frugal. I'm saving up. Do you know how expensive that organic health food stuff is? A sandwich is seventy-nine cents at the gas station but like *ten bucks* at the farmer's market. Do you know how cheap, on a per-calorie basis, nachos are? Not to mention the Go-Go Taquitos or Pancake and Sausage To-Go Sticks or other foods that have no organic equivalent that I get for free at the 7-Eleven down the street."

"How do you get them for free?"

"Well, if you know they can be cooked a maximum of twelve hours before they have to be thrown away for FDA-mandated public-health reasons, and if you arrive at the 7-Eleven a few minutes before the appointed food-rotation hour, then you can fill a plastic bag with not only a dozen or more taquitos and pancake sticks but also more conventional hot dogs, bratwurst, corn dogs, and bean burritos and such."

"Wow. You have a whole system."

"Of course, eating these food items is not what I might describe as *pleasant,* since they're tough and scorched and moistureless from their all-day cooking on high-temperature rollers. Sometimes biting through a burrito's thick tortilla casing can feel like chewing through your own toe calluses."

"That's an image that's going to linger."

"But it's cheap, you know? And given my current level of income, which is, frankly, minimal since I lost my job, and also my unemployment checks are due to run out in like three months or so, right about the time I'll be seeing real results, waistline-wise, of the new diet. And if I have to start eating bad cheap food then because the money is gone, well, it would be a momentum-stopping blow, I just know it. So I have to make the diet financially viable and sustainable long-term, which is why it's important to not eat healthy right now in order to save up for the time I will be eating healthy. Get it?"

"I think so."

"Every week I eat cheap shitty things, like nachos, is a week I can tick like seventy bucks to the other side of my mental ledger as cash 'saved' for my new life. This plan is going very well so far."

There seemed to be a not-rightness about him, a sense of disorder and exotic illness. His features were off in a way Samuel could not immediately put his finger on, like he suffered from some long-eradicated disease—scurvy, maybe.

Their drinks came. "Cheers," said Pwnage. "Welcome to Jezebels."

"This place," Samuel said. "Seems like there's a story here."

"Used to be it was a strip club," Pwnage said. "Then the strippers stopped coming because the mayor banned alcohol at strip clubs, then banned lap dances at strip clubs, then banned strip clubs."

"So now it's more of a bar with a strip-club theme?"

"That's right. He was a strict disciplinarian, the mayor. Elected in a last-ditch fit of anger when the city started going downhill."

"You've been coming here a long time?"

"Not when it was a strip club," Pwnage said, and he held up his hand to show Samuel his wedding ring. "She doesn't really support strip clubs, my wife. Because of the patriarchy and stuff."

"That's sound."

"How strip clubs are degrading to feminists and all that. Oh, hey, I love this song."

He was talking about Molly Miller's new single, the video to which had now begun on roughly one-third of the televisions in the bar: Molly singing in an abandoned drive-in movie theater where scores of good-looking young people had parked their cars, their late-sixties or early-seventies American muscle cars—Cameros, Mustangs, Challengers—in what was one example of the odd dislocation and ambiguity Samuel felt watching this video and processing its many props. The abandoned state of the drive-in spoke to a present-day setting, while the automobiles were forty years old and the mic Molly sang into was one of those chunky metal things that radio people used in the thirties. Meanwhile, her wardrobe appeared to be a hip, ironic nod to eighties fashion, most obviously in the form of large white plastic sunglasses and skinny jeans. It was a large ever-shifting referential stew of anachronistic symbols with no logical connection between them except their high cool quotient.

"So why did you want to meet?" Pwnage said, returning to his normal sitting position, his feet tucked beneath him.

"No reason," Samuel said. "Just wanted to hang out."

"We could have done that in *Elfscape*."

"I suppose."

"Actually, come to think of it, this is the first time I've hung out with someone *not* in *Elfscape* in a very long time."

"Yeah," Samuel said, and he considered this for a moment, and felt a little unsettled that this was also true for him. "Do you think it's possible that we play *Elfscape* too much?"

"No. But yeah, maybe."

"I mean, think about all the hours we spend on *Elfscape,* all the *cumulative hours*. And not only the hours spent playing but also the hours reading about playing and watching videos of other people playing and talking and strategizing and getting on discussion boards and such. It's so much *time*. Without *Elfscape* we could all be, I don't know, leading meaningful lives. Out in the real world."

The nachos came in what looked like a lasagna pan. A corn-chip mound covered in ground beef and bacon and sausage and steak and onions and jalapeños and probably a couple of full pints of cheese, this bright orange cheese that looked thick and shiny and plastic.

Pwnage dove into the dish, then said, between bites, nacho shrapnel clinging to his lips, "I find *Elfscape* way more meaningful than the real world."

"Seriously?"

"Absolutely. Because, listen, what I do in *Elfscape* matters. Like, the things I do affect the larger system. They change the world. You cannot say this about real life."

"Sometimes you can."

"Rarely. Most of the time you can't. Most of the time there's nothing you can do to affect the world. Like, okay, almost all my friends in *Elfscape* work retail in real life. They sell televisions or pants. They work in a mall. My last job was at a copy shop. Explain to me how that's going to change the larger system."

"I don't think I can accept that a game is more meaningful than the real world."

"When I lost my job, they told me it was because of the recession. They couldn't afford so many employees. Even though that same year the CEO of the company got a salary that was literally eight hundred times bigger than mine. In the face of something like that, I'd say sinking into *Elfscape* is a pretty sane response. We're fulfilling our basic human psychological need to feel meaningful and significant."

The nachos were lifted to Pwnage's mouth still tethered to the plate by strings of orange slime. He scooped up as much cheese and meat as each chip could maximally accommodate. He wouldn't even finish chewing the last bite before taking the next one. It was like he had some kind of conveyor-belt system going on in there.

"If only the real world operated like *Elfscape,*" Pwnage said, chewing. "If only marriages worked that way. Like every time I did something right I earned man points until I was a grand-master level-hundred husband. Or when I was a jackass to Lisa I'd lose points and the closer I was to zero the closer I'd be to divorce. It would also be helpful if these events came with associated sound effects. Like that sound when Pac-Man shrivels up and dies. Or when you bid too high on *The Price Is Right.* That chorus of failure."

"Lisa's your wife?"

"Mm-hm," Pwnage said. "We're separated. But actually more accurately we're divorced. For the time being." He looked at his wedding ring, then up at the video, watching its swirl of disassociated images: Molly in a classroom; Molly cheering at a high-school football game; Molly at a bowling alley; Molly at a high-school dance; Molly in a grassy field having a picnic with a cute boy. The producers had obviously targeted the teen and tween demographic, and were blatantly rolling around in their idiom as dogs do on rotten food.

"When Lisa and I were married," Pwnage said, "I thought everything was great. Then one day she said she was no longer satisfied with our relationship and boom, divorce papers. She just left one day, no warning."

Pwnage scratched at a spot on his arm so heavily scratched-at that he'd left a threadbare spot on his shirtsleeve.

"That would never happen in a video game," he said. "Being surprised like that. In a game, there's immediate feedback. In a game, there would be a sound effect and a graphic of me losing man points whenever I did whatever I did to make her want to divorce me. Then I could have apologized right away and never done it again."

Over his shoulder, Molly Miller sang to the dancing, cheering throngs. She was not supported onstage by a band or even a boom box and appeared to be singing a cappella. But her fans danced and jumped all out of proportion to someone singing a cappella, implying that actual music was coming from somewhere off camera in the non-diegetic fashion that has become de rigueur in pop music videos. Just go with it.

Pwnage said, "A game will always tell you how to win. Real life does not do this. I feel like I've lost at life and have no idea why."

"Yeah."

"I mean, I screwed up with the only girl I've ever loved."

"Me too," Samuel said. "Her name was Bethany."

"Yeah. And I don't have any career to speak of."

"Me too. I actually think there's a student who wants to get me fired."

"And I'm upside down on my mortgage."

"Me too."

"And I spend most of my time playing video games."

"Me too."

"Dude," Pwnage said, looking at Samuel with bulbous, bloodshot eyes. "You and I? We're, like, twins."

They watched Molly Miller's video in silence for a time, Pwnage eating, the both of them listening to the song, which was circling back to its chorus for like the fourth time now and so must have been approaching its end. Molly's lyrics hinted at something barely out of reach, something just beyond comprehension, mostly because of her use of the pronoun "it" with shifting, ambiguous antecedents:

> Don't hurt it. You gotta serve it.
> You gotta stuff it, kiss it.
> I want to get it.
> Push up on it. 'Cuz I'm gonna work it.
> You got it? Think about it.

Then, after each verse, Molly shouted and the whole crowd shouted the line that launched them into the chorus—"You have got to represent!"—

while throwing their fists into the air as if they were protesting something, who knows what.

"My mother abandoned me when I was a kid," Samuel said. "She did to me what Lisa did to you. One day, gone."

Pwnage nodded. "I see."

"Now I need something from her and I don't know how to get it."

"What do you need?"

"Her story. I'm writing a book about her, but she won't tell me anything. All I have is a photograph and a few sketchy notes. I know nothing about her."

Samuel had the photograph in his pocket—printed out on copy paper and folded up. He opened it and showed it to Pwnage.

"Hm," Pwnage said. "You're a writer?"

"Yeah. My publisher's going to sue me if I don't finish this book."

"You have a publisher? Really? I'm a writer too."

"No kidding."

"Yeah, I have this idea for a novel. I started it in high school. A police detective with psychic abilities on the trail of a serial killer."

"Sounds exciting."

"I have it all mapped out in my head. At the end—spoiler alert—there's an epic showdown when the trail finally leads to the detective's own ex-wife's daughter's boyfriend. I'll write it as soon as I find the time."

The skin of his cuticles, and the skin around his eyes, and the skin around his lips, and really the skin at all the intersections of his body had a deep and aching redness. A scarlet pain wherever one thing turned into another. Samuel imagined it hurt him to move, or blink, or breathe. Pink splotches on his scalp where tufts of white hair had fallen out. One eye seemed to open wider than the other.

"My mother is the Packer Attacker," Samuel said.

"The Packer what?"

"The woman who threw rocks at that politician."

"I have no idea what you're talking about."

"Yeah, I missed it too at first. I think it happened the same day as our raid. The one against the dragon."

"That was an epic win."

"Yeah."

"*Elfscape* can actually teach us a lot about living," Pwnage said. "Take this problem with your mother? Easy. You only need to ask yourself what kind of challenge she is."

"What do you mean?"

"In *Elfscape,* as in every video game, there are four kinds of challenges. Every challenge is a variant of these four. It's my philosophy."

Pwnage's hand hovered over the nacho rubble, searching for any chip that still retained its structural integrity, many of them having gone flaccid in the cheese-and-oil swamp that gathered on the bottom of the pan.

"Your philosophy came from video games?" Samuel said.

"I find this is also true in life. Any problem you face in a video game or in life is one of four things: an enemy, obstacle, puzzle, or trap. That's it. Everyone you meet in life is one of those four things."

"Okay."

"So you all you have to do is figure out which kind of challenge you're dealing with."

"And how do you do that?"

"Depends. Say they're an enemy? The only way to defeat an enemy is to kill them. If you killed your mother, would it solve your problem?"

"Definitely not."

"So not an enemy then. That's good! Maybe she's an obstacle? Obstacles are things you have to find your way around. If you avoided your mother, would it solve your problem?"

"No. She has something I need."

"Which is?"

"Her life story. I need to know what happened to her, in her past."

"Okay. And there's no other way to get this?"

"I don't think so."

"Aren't there historical documents?" Pwnage said. "Do you not have family? Can you not do an interview? Do writers not do research?"

"Well, my grandfather, on my mother's side. He's still alive."

"There you go."

"I haven't talked to him in years. He's in a nursing home. In Iowa."

"Mm-hm," Pwnage said. He was using a spoon to lap up the remaining nacho sludge.

"I should go talk to my grandfather, is your advice," Samuel said. "Go to Iowa and ask him about my mother."

"Yes. Figure out her story. Piece it together. It's the only way you'll solve your problem, if indeed it's an obstacle-type problem and not in fact a puzzle or a trap."

"How can you tell the difference?"

"You can't at first." He discarded the spoon. The nachos were, for the most part, entirely consumed. He dabbed his finger into a spot of cheese, then licked it clean.

"You have to be careful," Pwnage said, "with people who are puzzles and people who are traps. A puzzle can be solved but a trap cannot. Usually what happens is you think someone's a puzzle until you realize they're a trap. But by then it's too late. That's the trap."

4

HERE'S A MEMORY: Samuel is riding in the backseat on a summer trip to his parents' hometown in Iowa. Mom and Dad are up front, and he's avoiding the side with the sun, and he's staring out the window at the passing scenery, the terrifying traffic of Chicago and the brick-and-steel girth of the city giving way to the more predictable ebb of the prairie. The DeKalb Oasis is the last tendril of civilization before the surrounding farmland begins. Huge open sky that's all the more huge because there's nothing to interrupt it: no mountains, no hills, no topography at all, just flat green endlessness.

Then crossing the Mississippi River and Samuel trying to hold his breath for the whole span of that great concrete bridge, looking down and seeing the barges traveling south, and tugboats, pontoon boats, speedboats pulling inner tubes on which people—pink specks from this height—bounce. They exit the interstate and turn north and follow the river all the way home, to where his parents come from, where they grew up and became high-school sweethearts, is the story he'd been told. Up Highway 67, the river on his right, past the gas stations that advertise live bait, the American flags flying from VFWs and public parks and golf courses and churches and boats, the occasional John Deere tractor halfway on the shoulder, the occasional Harley riders who stick out their left hand to greet other Harley riders going the opposite direction, past the quarry where orange gravel gets kicked up by tires, past the speed limit signs rigidly enforced, and past other signs too, some torn back by buckshot—DEER NEXT TWO MILES, CAUTION PLANT ENTRANCE, THIS HIGH-WAY ADOPTED BY THE KIWANIS CLUB. Then the red-and-white stacks of the nitrogen plant coming into view, followed by the massive white vats of Eastern Iowa Propane, the behemoth ChemStar facility that regularly makes the whole town smell like burned breakfast cereal, the grain eleva-tor, the little townie businesses: Leon's Body Shop, Bruce's Beauty Hut and Firearm Repair, Sneaky Pete's Rare Finds Antiques, Schwingle's Pharmacy. Toolsheds in backyards built from aluminum siding. Second garages whose walls are all exposed Tyvek. Houses with three or four or maybe five operational and sometimes meticulously maintained and decked-out automobiles. Teens riding on mopeds, little orange flags whipping above their heads. Kids in bare fields riding four-wheelers and dirt bikes. Trucks towing boats. Everyone using their blinker.

The memory felt so specific because so little had changed. As Samuel took the drive again, to interview the grandfather he'd not seen in decades, he saw how everything was more or less the same. The Mississippi River valley still looked green and lush, despite being one of the most heavily chemicalized places in the country. The towns along the river still flew flags from almost every house. Ritualistic patriotism had not been dampened by two cruel decades of labor outsourcing and manufacturing shrink. Yes, the gravitational center of town had crept away from the quaint old downtown toward the big new Walmart, but nobody seemed to mind. The Walmart parking lot was bustling and full.

He saw all this as he drove around. He was, as Pwnage suggested, doing research. He was trying to breathe in the town, trying to feel what it would have been like to grow up here. His mother never spoke of it, and they rarely visited. Once every other summer, generally, when he was a kid.

But Samuel still received a trickle of information about the old hometown, and knew his grandfather was here, slowly wasting away from dementia and Parkinson's at a nursing home called Willow Glen, where Samuel had an appointment later in the day. Until then, he planned to explore, observe, do research.

First, he found his father's childhood home, a farm near the banks of the Mississippi. He found his mother's too, a quaint little bungalow with a big picture window in one of the upstairs rooms. He visited her high school, which looked like any generic high school anywhere. He took a few photographs. He visited the playground near his mother's house—the standard swing set, slide, monkey bars. He took a few photographs. He even visited the ChemStar facility where his grandfather had worked for many years, a factory so large it was impossible to take in all at once. Built along the river, surrounded by train tracks and power lines, it looked like an aircraft carrier had tumbled sideways out of the water. A mess of metal and tubing that kept going for miles, furnaces and chimneys, concrete bunker-looking buildings, steel holding tanks, round vats, smokestacks, pipes that all seemed to lead to a massive copper dome on the far north end of the factory, where if the light was shining properly it looked like a second, smaller sun rising from the ground. The atmosphere around the factory was sulfurous and overheated, a smell of exhaust, burned carbon, thin and difficult to breathe, like there wasn't quite enough air in the air. Samuel photographed all of it. The holding tanks and twisted pipes, the brick smokestacks breathing a white cumulus vapor that disintegrated into the sky. He could not fit the factory's whole apparatus into one frame, and so he walked down its length photographing panoramically. He hoped the photographs would shake loose something important, hoped that he could see some connection between the brutality of the ChemStar facility and his mother's family, who for so long were tied umbilically to it. He took dozens of pictures, then left for his appointment.

He was driving to the nursing home when Periwinkle called.

"Hey, buddy," said his publisher, his voice all echoey. "Just checking in."

"You sound far away. Where are you?"

"In New York, in my office. I have you on speakerphone. There are protestors outside my building right now. They're yelling and screaming. Can you hear them?"

"I can't," Samuel said.

"I can," Periwinkle said. "They're twenty stories down, but I can hear them."

"What are they yelling?"

"I cannot actually hear *them,* I should say. Their speeches or whatever? Mostly I hear the drumming. Whole rock operas of it. They are drumming in a circle. Loudly and daily. Reasons unclear."

"This must feel strange to you, being protested against."

"They're not protesting *me,* per se. Nor my company, specifically. More like the world that brought my company into being. Multinational. Globalization. Capitalism. The ninety-nine percent is, I believe, their catchphrase."

"Occupy Wall Street."

"That's the one. Pretty grandiose name, if you ask me. They are not occupying Wall Street so much as a small rectangle of concrete about a thousand feet away from it."

"I think the name is symbolic."

"It's a revolt against things they don't understand. Imagine our homi-nid ancestors protesting a drought? This is like that."

"A rain dance, you're saying, this protest."

"It's a primitive tribal response to godlike power, yes."

"How many people?"

"More every day. It started with a dozen. Now several dozen. They try to engage us in conversation as we go to work."

"You should try talking to them."

"I did once. This kid, maybe twenty-five years old. He was down by the drum circle, juggling. His hair was in white-boy dreads. He began every sentence with the word 'Well.' It was a tic he had. But he pronounced it like *wool*. I literally could not hear anything else he said."

"So not a true dialogue, then."

"Have you ever protested anything?"

"Once."

"How was it?"

"Unsuccessful."

"A drum circle. Jugglers. They're a living, breathing non sequitur in the middle of the financial district. But what they don't understand is that there is nothing capitalism loves so much as a non sequitur. This is what they need to learn. Capitalism gobbles up non sequiturs happily."

"By non sequitur you mean . . ."

"You know, the fashionable. The trendy. Every trend begins its life as a fallacy."

"That maybe explains Molly Miller's new video."

"You've seen it?"

"Real catchy," Samuel said. " 'You have got to represent.' What does that even mean?"

"You know, there used to be a difference between authentic music and sellout music. I'm talking about when I was young, in the sixties? Back then we knew there was a soullessness to the sellouts, and we wanted to be on the side of the artists. But now? Being a sellout is the authentic thing. When Molly Miller says 'I'm just being real,' what she means is that everyone wants money and fame and any artist who claims other-wise is lying. The only fundamental truth is greed, and the only question is who is up front about this. That's the *new authenticity*. Molly Miller can never be accused of selling out because selling out was her goal all along."

"The point of her song seems to be, like, *be rich, have fun.*"

"She's appealing to her audience's latent greed and telling them it's okay. Janis Joplin tried to inspire you to be a better person. Molly Miller tells you it's okay to be the horrible person you already are. I'm not making a judgment about this. It's just my job to know it."

"But what about the juggler?" Samuel said. "The guy down at the drum circle? He doesn't want to sell out."

"He's doing an impression of a protest he saw on TV once, many years ago. He has sold out, just to a different set of symbols."

"But not to greed, is what I'm saying."

"Are you old enough to remember Stormin' Norman Schwarzkopf? And Scud missiles? Yellow ribbons and the line in the sand and Arsenio Hall going *woof-woof-woof* for the troops?"

"Yes."

"There is nothing capitalism cannot gobble up. Non sequitur is its native language. Did you call me or did I call you?"

"You called."

"Right. Now I remember. I heard you met with your mother."

"I saw her, yes. I went to her apartment."

"You were in the same room with her. What did she say?"

"Not much."

"You were in the same room and you heroically overcame years of resentment and she opened up to you in a way she's never opened up to anyone before, spilling out a dramatic life story that ideally concludes after two hundred and fifty pages of easy reading, give or take."

"Not exactly."

"I know I'm asking you to process your feelings quickly. But we're on a schedule."

"It didn't seem like she wanted to talk. But I'm working on it. I'm doing some research. It might take some time."

"Some time. Right. You remember that big oil spill in the Gulf last year?"

"I do."

"People cared about that for, on average, thirty-six days. They've done studies on this."

"What do you mean 'cared'?"

"For the first month, people expressed mostly indignation and retarded anger. After about five weeks, the average response was 'Oh, right, I *forgot* about that.'"

"So you're suggesting we have a window here."

"A very small and shrinking window. That was the worst environmental disaster in North America ever. Compared to that, who cares about some lady who threw rocks at a guy most people acknowledge is sort of a douche bag?"

"But what do I do? What's my alternative?"

"Bankruptcy. Jakarta. I already explained this."

"I'll work fast. I'm actually in Iowa right now, collecting information."

"Iowa. I have no concept of what that looks like."

"Think abandoned factories. Farms up for auction. Cornfields with little signs advertising Monsanto. I'm driving past one right now."

"Delightful."

"Barges on the river. Hog lots. Hy-Vee."

"I'm sort of not listening to you anymore."

"I'm interviewing my grandfather today. Maybe he can tell me what really happened to my mom."

"How can I say this delicately? We're not all that interested in 'what really happened' to your mom. We're much more interested in getting all those people who go temporarily insane before a presidential election to open up their wallets."

"I'm at the nursing home now. Gotta go."

The place was an anonymous-looking structure that, from the outside, appeared to be an apartment building—plastic siding, curtains over the windows, the ambiguous name: Willow Glen. Samuel walked through the front doors and smelled the aggressive, claustrophobic odor of institutionalized medicine: bleach, soap, carpet cleaner, the underlying omnipresent sweet tang of urine. At the front desk, there was a form for all guests to sign and state the reason for their visit. Next to his name, Samuel wrote "Research." His plan was to talk to his grandfather until he got some answers. Hopefully his grandfather would, indeed, talk. Frank Andresen had always been such a quiet man. He had an inward, disinterested manner, spoke with a perplexing accent, often smelled of gasoline, and seemed a little out of reach. Everyone knew he'd emigrated from Norway, but he never said why. "To find a better life" was as much as he'd reveal. Really the only specific thing he'd ever say about his life back there was that their family farm was a beautiful thing to behold: a big salmon-red house with a view of the water, there in the northernmost city in the world. It was the only time he seemed happy, talking about that house.

A nurse led Samuel to a table in the empty cafeteria. She warned him that when Frank spoke, he rarely made much sense.

"The medicine he's on for the Parkinson's causes a bit of confusion," she said. "And the drugs for the depression cause drowsiness, lethargy. Between that and the dementia, you probably won't get much."

"He's depressed?" Samuel said.

The nurse frowned and held out her arms. "Look around."

Samuel sat, took his phone out to record the conversation and saw he had several new e-mails—from the dean, and the director of Student Affairs, the director of University Relations, also the Office of Adaptive Services, the Office of Inclusivity, Student Health, Academic Counseling, Student Psychological Services, the provost, the ombudsperson, all of them with the same subject line: *Urgent Student Matter.*

Samuel sank into his chair. Swiped the phone to make the e-mails disappear.

When the nurse wheeled his grandfather to the table, Samuel's first impression was that he was small. So much smaller than in Samuel's memory. He was unshaven, a spotty beard showing black and white and red, mouth agape and white dots of spit on his lips. He was thin. He wore a thin bathrobe the green of pistachio pudding. His gray hair was tangled from sleeping, sticking up like grass. He was looking at Samuel and he was waiting.

"It's good to see you again," Samuel said. "Do you know who I am?"

5

FRANK'S OLDEST MEMORIES were the sharpest. He remembered the boat especially. Fishing off the back of the boat those months the arctic would allow it. This memory was clear and vivid still: the guys in the warm cabin eating and drinking because the work was done and the nets were in and it was midnight in the summer when the sun didn't quite set but moved horizontally across the sky.

A red-orange twilight that lasted a whole month.

Everything was more dramatic in that light—the water, the waves, the distant rocky shore.

He was Fridtjof then, not Frank.

Still a teenager.

How he loved it, Norway, the arctic, the water cold enough to stop your heart.

He fished at the end of the day for sport, not money. What he loved was the struggle. Because when you're catching those boiling schools of blackfish in those great big nets, you don't feel the struggle like you do when it's just you and the fish connected by a thin white line.

Life was uncomplicated then.

Here is what he loved: the way it felt setting the hook with that snap of his wrist; the feeling of the fish plunging to the bottom, all power and muscle and mystery; resting the rod on his hip and pulling so hard it'd leave a bruise; how he couldn't see the fish until it shimmered just below the surface; then that moment when it finally emerged.

The world had that quality now.

This was what life was like.

Like a fish pulled from wine-dark water.

Faces seemed to issue forth from nowhere. He opened his eyes and there was someone new. Right now, a young man, fake shitty grin, a bit of fear around his eyes. A face that wanted to be recognized.

Frank didn't always recognize the faces but he recognized their *need*.

The young man was speaking, asking questions. Like the doctors did. There were always new ones coming and going. New doctors, new nurses.

Same flowcharts.

A flowchart for every bruise. A flowchart for every bed-wetting. If he seemed confused, there was a flowchart. Cognition tests, problem solving, safety awareness. They measured body mobility, balance, pain threshold, skin integrity, comprehension of single words, phrases, commands. They rated all this on scales of one to five. They asked him to roll, sit up, lie back down, go to the toilet.

They checked the toilet to see if he made it in the bowl.

They measured his swallowing. There was a whole flowchart for swallowing. On a scale of one to five, they rated his chewing, how he worked chewed food around in his mouth, how well his swallow reflex triggered, whether he drooled or spilled. They asked him questions to see if he was able to speak while eating. They checked for food pocketed in his cheek.

Stuck their fingers right in there and checked.

Made him feel hooked. Like he was the fish now. He was the one diving into darkness.

"It's good to see you again," said this young man in front of him. "Do you know who I am?"

He had a face that reminded Frank of something important.

It was like a screwed-up look, like what a poisonous secret does to your face, the pain that lives just below the skin and twists it.

Frank was getting worse at most things but better at some. And he was definitely better at this: reading people. He could never do this before. All his life, people were such a mystery. His wife, her family. Even Faye, his own daughter. But now? It was like something had been reshaped within him, like how a reindeer's eyes change color: blue eyes in winter, gold in summer.

This is what it felt like to Frank.

Like he could see a different spectrum now.

What did he see in this young man? The same look he saw on Clyde Thompson's face beginning in 1965.

He worked with Clyde at the ChemStar factory. Clyde's daughter had thick golden-blond hair. She grew it down to the small of her back, straight and long like they used to back then. She complained that it was too heavy but Clyde wouldn't allow her to cut it because he loved her hair so much.

Then one day in 1965 she got the hair caught in the band saw at school and she died. Took her whole scalp right off.

Clyde asked for a couple days off work and then came back like nothing happened.

Just kept soldiering on.

This Frank remembered very well.

People said how brave he was. Everyone agreed. Like the more Clyde could dodge the pain, the more heroic he was.

This was a formula for living a life full of secrets.

Frank knew this now. People constantly hid. It was a sickness maybe worse than the Parkinson's.

Frank had so many secrets, so many things he never told anyone.

The look on Clyde's face and the look on this young man's face were the same. How that frown gets etched on there.

Same with Johnny Carlton, whose son fell off a tractor and was crushed under the tire. And Denny Wisor's son was shot in Vietnam. And Elmer Mason's daughter and granddaughter died at the same time during childbirth. And Pete Olsen's son died when he tipped a motorcycle on a gravel road and it landed on him and broke a rib and punctured a lung, which filled with blood and made him drown right there on the road near a babbling brook in the middle of summer.

None of them said anything about it ever again.

They must have died shrunken, miserable men.

"I'd like to talk to you about my mother," the man said. "Your daughter?"

And now Frank is Fridtjof again and he's back at that farm in Hammerfest, a salmon-red house that overlooked the ocean, a great big spruce tree in the front yard, a pasture, sheep, a horse, a fire kept going all the way through the arctic's long winter night: He's home.

It's 1940 and he's eighteen years old. He's twenty feet above the water. He's the spotter. He has the sharpest eyes on the ship. He's on the tallest mast looking for fish and telling the guys in the rowboats to take the nets this way, that way.

Whole schools churn into the bay and he intercepts them.

But this is not the memory where he's looking for fish. This is the one where he's looking at home. That salmon-red house with the pasture, the garden, the little path leading down to the dock.

It's the last time he'll see it.

His eyes are stinging from the wind as he watches from the crow's nest as they sail away from Hammerfest and the salmon-red house gets smaller and smaller until it's just a dot of color on the shore and then the shore is just a dot on all that water and then it's nothing at all—it's nothing but the lonely cold fact of the blue-black ocean everywhere around them forever, and the salmon-red house becomes a dot in his mind that grows larger and more terrible the farther away he sails.

"I need to know what happened to Faye," said the young man in front of him, who seemed to appear out of the murk. "When she went to college? In Chicago?"

He was looking at Frank with that face people gave him when they didn't understand what he was talking about. That face they thought looked like patience but actually looked like they were quietly shitting pinecones.

Frank must have been saying something.

Speaking these days was like speaking in dreams. Sometimes it felt like his tongue was too large for words. Or he'd forgotten English and the words came out a jumble of disconnected Norwegian sounds. Other times whole sentences shot out unstoppably. Sometimes he had whole conversations and didn't even know it.

This probably had something to do with the meds.

One guy in here stopped taking his meds. Just stopped swallowing them. Refused. A real slow suicide, that one. They tried restraining him and forcing down the medicine, but he resisted.

Frank admired his dedication.

The nurses did not.

The nurses in Willow Glen didn't try to prevent death. But they did try to guide you to *die in the right way*. Because if you died from something you weren't supposed to die from, families became suspicious.

The nurses here were kind. They meant well. Or at least they did at first, when they were new. It was the institution that was the problem. All the rules. The nurses were human, but the rules were not.

Those PBS nature documentaries they showed in the common room said all life aimed toward reproduction.

At Willow Glen, all life aimed toward avoiding litigation.

Everything was charted. If a nurse fed him dinner but forgot to write it down, then in court, technically, she did not feed him dinner.

So they came in with these stacks of paper. They spent more time looking at the paper than looking at the people.

One time he hit his head on the bed frame and got a black eye. The nurse came in with her charts and said to Frank, "Which eye is injured?"

All the nurse had to do was take one look at him to answer that question. But her nose was in the charts. She cared more about documenting the injury than the injury itself.

They recorded everything. Physician progress reports. Dietitian records. Weight-loss charts. Monthly nurse summaries. Food-service logs. Tube-feeding sheets. Medication histories.

Photographs.

They made him stand naked and shivering and they took photographs. This happened roughly once a week.

Checking for evidence of falls. Or bedsores. Bruises of any kind. Evidence of abuse, infections, dehydration, malnutrition.

For court cases, if needed later, in their defense.

"Do you want me to ask them to stop taking photographs?" the young man said.

What were they talking about? He'd lost the thread again. He looked around him: He was in the cafeteria. It was empty. The young man smiled his uncomfortable smile. Smiled like those high-school kids who came in here once or twice a year.

There was this one girl, Frank forgot her name. Maybe Taylor? Or Tyler? He asked her, "Why do you high-school kids come in here?" And she said, "Colleges think it looks good if you've done some charity work."

Two or three times they'd come, then disappeared.

He asked this Taylor or Tyler why all the students only showed up twice and then never came back, and she said, "If you do it twice, that's good enough to put on your college application."

She said this with no shame. Like she was such a good girl doing the absolute minimum to get what she wanted.

She asked him about his life. He said there's not much to tell. She said what did you do? He said he worked at the ChemStar factory. She said what did the factory make? He said it made a compound that when jellied and lit on fire would literally melt the skin off of a hundred thousand men, women, and children in Vietnam. And then she realized she'd made a big mistake coming here and asking him that.

"I was wondering about Faye," the young man said. "Your daughter Faye? You remember her?"

Faye was so much more hardworking than these high-school shits ever were. Faye worked hard because she was *driven*. There was something inside that pushed her. Something big and deadly and serious.

"Faye never told me she went to Chicago. Why did she go to Chicago?"

And now it's 1968 and he's in the kitchen with Faye under a pale light and he's kicking her out of the house.

He is so angry with her.

He'd tried so hard to live in that town unnoticed. And she made it impossible.

Leave and never come back, is what he's telling her.

"What did she do?"

She got herself knocked up. In high school. She let that boy Henry get her pregnant. Wasn't even married yet. And everybody knew about it.

Which was the thing that enraged him most, how everyone knew. All at once. Like she advertised it in the local mailer. He never figured out how that happened. But he was more mad that everyone knew than about her getting knocked up.

That was before he picked up the dementia and stopped caring about things like this.

After that, she had to go to college. She was an outcast. She left for Chicago.

"But she didn't stay long, right? In Chicago?"

Came back a month later. Something happened to her there she never talked about. Frank didn't know what. She told people college was too hard. But he knew that was a lie.

Faye came back and married Henry. They moved away. Left town.

She never really liked him, Henry. Poor guy. He never knew what hit him. There was a word for this in Norwegian: *gift,* which could mean either "marriage" or "poison," and that probably seemed about right to Henry.

After Faye left, Frank became like Clyde Thompson after his daughter died: kept a straight face in public and nobody asked him about Faye and eventually it was like she'd never even existed.

No reminders at all, except for the boxes in the basement.

Homework assignments. Diaries. Letters. Those reports from the school counselor. About Faye's *issues*. Her panic attacks. Nervous fits. Making up stories for attention. It was all documented. It was here, at Willow Glen. In storage. In the basement. Many years' worth. Frank kept everything.

He hadn't seen her now in so long. She'd disappeared, which of course Frank deserved.

Pretty soon, he hoped, he wouldn't remember her at all.

His mind was falling away.

Soon he would be only Fridtjof again, blessedly. He'd remember only Norway. He'd remember only his expansive youth in the northernmost city in the world. The fires they kept going all through the winter. The gray midnight sky of summer. The green swirls of the northern lights. The splashing schools of blackfish he could spot from a mile away. And maybe if he were lucky the walls of his memory would enclose only this one moment, fishing from the back of the boat, pulling up some grand thing from the depths.

If he were lucky.

If not, he'd be stuck with the other memory. The terrible memory. He would watch himself watching that salmon-red house. Watch it shrinking in the distance. Feel himself growing older as it faded. He would live it out over and over again, his mistake, his disgrace. That would be his punishment, this waking nightmare: sailing away from his home, into the darkening night, and judgment.

SAMUEL HAD NEVER HEARD Grandpa Frank talk so much. It was a constant bewildering monologue with occasional moments of clarity, moments when Samuel managed to seize a few critical details: that his mother had gotten pregnant and left for Chicago in shame, and that all the records from Faye's childhood were stored here, in boxes, at Willow Glen.

About the boxes, Samuel asked the nurse, who led him down into the basement, a long concrete tunnel with chain-link cages. A zoo of forgotten things. Samuel found his family's heirlooms under a skin of dust: old tables and chairs and china hutches, old clocks no longer running, boxes stacked like crumbling pyramids, dark puddles on the dirty bare floor, the light a hazy green mist of overhead fluorescents, the sour smells of mold and damp cardboard. Amid all this he found several large boxes marked "Faye," all of them heavy with paper: school projects, notes from teachers, medical records, diaries, old photographs, love letters from Henry. As he skimmed through them, a new version of his mother took shape—not the distant woman from his childhood but a shy and hopeful girl. The real person he'd always longed to know.

He lugged the boxes to his car and called his father.

"It's a great day for frozen food," his father said. "This is Henry Anderson. How can I help you?"

"It's me," Samuel said. "We have to talk."

"Well, I would love to interface with you one-on-one," he said in that polite, artificial, high-pitched lilt he used whenever he was at work. "I'd be happy to discuss this at your earliest convenience."

"Stop talking like that."

"Can I tell you about an upcoming webinar you might be interested in?"

"Is your boss, like, standing over your shoulder right now?"

"That's an affirmative."

"Okay, then just listen. I want you to know that I figured something out about Mom."

"I think that's outside my area of expertise, but I'd be happy to send you to someone who could help you with that."

"Please stop talking that way."

"Yes, I understand. Thank you *so much* for bringing this up."

"I know that Mom went to Chicago. And I know why."

"I think we should put in some face time on this. Shall I schedule an appointment?"

"She left Iowa because you got her pregnant. And her dad kicked her out. She had to leave town. I know this now."

There was a pause on the other end of the line. Samuel waited. "Dad?" he said.

"That's not true," his father said, now much more quietly, and in his normal voice.

"It is true. I talked to Grandpa Frank. He told me all about it."

"*He* told you?"

"Yes."

"Where are you?"

"Iowa."

"That man hasn't spoken ten words to me since your mother left."

"He's sick now. He's on some pretty heavy-hitting medication. One of the side effects is loss of inhibition. I don't think he knows what he's saying."

"Good lord."

"You need to tell me the truth. Starting now."

"First of all, Frank is wrong. It was all a dumb misunderstanding. Your mother wasn't pregnant. Not before you."

"But Frank said—"

"I know why he'd think that. And he believes it's true. But I'm telling you that's not what happened."

"Then what happened?"

"Are you sure you want to hear about this?"

"I need to."

"There are things you might not want to know. Children don't have to know *everything* about their parents."

"This is important."

"Please come home."

"You'll tell me?"

"Yes."

"No more lying? The whole story?"

"Fine."

"No matter how embarrassing it might be to you?"

"Yes. Just come home."

On his drive back, Samuel tried to imagine himself in his mother's shoes, making that first trip to Chicago, going to college, her future all precarious and full of mystery. He felt like they were both going through this at the same time. A new world was about to open up. Everything was about to change. He almost felt like she was there with him.

It was odd, but he had never felt closer to her than he did at that moment.

| PART FOUR |

THE HOUSE SPIRIT

Spring 1968

1

FAYE HEARS THE CRACK of metal and knows work is being done. Metal is moved and dropped, battered and bent; metal collides with metal and sings. She cannot see the ChemStar factory but she can see its glow, the coppery light beyond the backyard oaks. She pretends sometimes it's not a factory over there but an army. An ancient army—the light from torches, the noise from brutal weapons at forge. This is what it sounds like to her, like war.

She thought maybe tonight—because of what happened, what is on television at this very moment—the works would go quiet. But no; ChemStar, even on this night, roars. She sits in the backyard and listens. She stares into the thick gloom. Her father is over there right now, working the night shift. She hopes he's not watching the news, hopes he's keeping his focus and concentration. For the ChemStar factory is a deadly place. She toured it once and was horrified at the masks and gloves and thorough safety demonstration, the emergency fountain for the washing of eyes, the way her breathing seemed interrupted, how her scalp itched. She's heard stories of men spending months in the hospital after some stupid ChemStar mistake. Whenever she drives past the factory she sees that logo with the interlocking C and S, and the sign: CHEMSTAR—MAKING OUR DREAMS COME TRUE. Not even her uncles will work there. They prefer the steelworks, the nitrogen plant, the fertilizer plant, the corn plant, or they cross the river to Illinois to take shifts making Scotch tape. Not the tape itself but the glue that makes it sticky. In big vats of milky foam, stirred and shipped out in oil drums. How it appears on Scotch tape, no longer liquid but rather perfectly adhesive, is a mystery. How it appears on shelves, packaged so pleasingly, sent to every store in America—that's another factory's job, another set of thick, itinerant men. No wonder her uncles never talk about what they *make*. Such is the way of commerce. Such is the way of this strange little river town. There's something always eluding her. She can see the pieces but not the whole.

It is April, four months before her first college classes begin, and she sits in her backyard, and inside the house the television howls its news: Martin Luther King has been killed in Memphis. Chicago is a rage tonight—of rioters, looters, arsonists. Pittsburgh, too. And Detroit, Newark. Mayhem in San Francisco. Fires three blocks from the White House.

Faye had watched until she could no longer bear it, then came out here, into the backyard and the wide-open night and the sounds of Chem-Star rumbling somewhere distant and loud, the whistles and cranes and crankshafts, the cascade of metal as a train abruptly lurches forward, how commerce keeps buzzing, even tonight. All these men who won't know a thing about the riots, she wonders why they're still working. Who needs chemicals this much? A factory is a terrifying, relentless thing.

She hears the patio door open, and footsteps—Faye's mother, coming with another update.

"It's anarchy," she says, exasperated. She's been glued to Cronkite all night long. "They're tearing up *their own neighborhood*."

The Chicago police have, apparently, sealed off the ghetto. Molotov cocktails are hurled into liquor stores. Snipers on the tops of buildings. Cars smashed on the street. Traffic lights wrenched down and twisted like tree branches. Bricks thrown through windows.

"What good will it do?" her mom says. "All this destruction? With everybody seeing on TV? Do these rioters really think this is going to make anyone sympathetic to their cause?"

Martin Luther King was shot in the neck while standing on his hotel balcony—every reporter and anchor on TV describes this exactly the same way, using the same words. Words that nobody's ever thought about have popped out of ordinary language and become incantations. *Lorraine Motel. Remington rifle. Mulberry Street.* (And how could the shot have been fired across something as wonderful-sounding as Mulberry Street?) Police are on the lookout. Massive manhunt. Early thirties, slender build. White male. The man in room five.

"Probably just an excuse for these people to do whatever they want," her mom says. "Running around with their shirts off looting stores like: Hey, let's get a new stereo without having to pay for it."

Faye knows her mom's interest in the rioters is an incidental thing. Mostly what she's out here to do is convince Faye not to go to college in Chicago. The riot has simply given her a delicious new angle. She wants Faye to stay home and go to the nice little two-year school the next town over, and she reminds Faye of this every chance she gets, a more or less constant needling attack that began when Faye was accepted, a few months ago, to Chicago Circle.

"Listen," her mom says, "I'm all for civil rights, but you can't be some kind of animal destroying innocent people's private property."

Chicago Circle is the catchy name for the brand-new university in downtown Chicago: the University of Illinois at Chicago Circle. The promotional brochures that came with Faye's acceptance letter spoke of Circle as *the UCLA of the Midwest.* It was the world's first *thoroughly modern campus,* the brochures said, built in just the last few years, conceptually groundbreaking, a campus unlike any other: created as a single vast system using the most fashionable principles of social design and engineering; buildings constructed from the most indestructible materials; a raised walkway, one story up, to get you from building to building with a bird's-eye view, a kind of *pedestrian expressway in the sky;* innovative architecture that included field theory mathematics, which as far as Faye could tell involved overlaying squares on top of each other and rotating each square slightly to achieve a many-angled, multifaceted design that looked, from above, like a honeycomb. This was an advance at least as important as the flying buttress or the geodesic dome, the brochure said, and it was all part of the school's overriding mission: to build the *Campus of the Future.*

Faye had applied to the school in secret.

"If these people weren't so destructive and angry," her mom says, "I think regular people would be more likely to support them. Why don't they go out and organize voters? Propose some solutions instead of just smashing everything?"

Faye looks out across the backyard to ChemStar's distant glow. Her father would be working now, probably ignoring the news of the world. The one time he spoke on the matter of college was when Faye showed him Circle's acceptance letter and brochure. He was the first person she told. After a brief private celebration in her bedroom, she came to him in the living room, where he was reading the newspaper in his easy chair. She handed him the documents. He looked at her and then at the papers. Read through them silently, slowly accommodating this new information. Faye was ready to burst. She waited for him to praise this extraordinary thing she'd done. But when he finished reading, he simply handed back the papers and said, "Don't be ridiculous, Faye." Then he opened the newspaper and gave it a shake to snap out the wrinkles. "And don't tell anyone," he said. "They'll think you're bragging."

"It's chaos in the streets!" her mom says. She's getting really roiled now. Sometimes lately it's like she's a top capable of spinning herself. "I don't even know what they're fighting for! These people. What do they want?"

"Probably, for starters, less murder," Faye says. "That's just a guess."

Her mom gives her a long, measured look. "When John Kennedy was shot *we* didn't riot."

Faye laughs. "Yeah, because those things are exactly equivalent."

"What's gotten into *you* tonight?"

"Nothing, Mom. Sorry."

"I'm worried about you."

"Don't be."

"I'm worried about you going to Chicago," she says, finally coming around to her point. "It's just—it's so far away. And so big. And so full of, you know, this *urban element*."

By which she means Negroes.

"I don't want to scare you," she says, "but think about it. One night you're coming home from class and they snatch you and take you into a dark alley and rape you and shove a gun in your mouth so hard you can't even pray to God."

"Okay!" Faye says, and she stands up. "Thanks, Mom. Great talking to you."

"Plus, what if you have an episode while you're away? What are you going to do if I'm not around?"

"I'm leaving now."

"Where are you going?"

"Out."

"Faye."

"Nowhere, Mom. I just need to take a drive. Clear my head."

Which is a lie. She's going to Henry's, of course. Good, gentle Henry. She will go to him tonight, before her mom can scare her even more with tales of violence and rape. She takes the car and drives out of her little neighborhood, a parcel of small bungalows called Vista Hills (but this is

Iowa, and that name has always confused her, the Vista Hills sign showing a wide panorama atop mountains that nowhere in this state actually exist). Then out onto the main boulevard, past the Dairy-Sweet Good-Food, the Dollar General, Schwingle's Pharmacy. She drives past the Quik Mart station, across the street from the Spotless Touchless, past the gray water tower that some of the old folks call the *green tower* because it was green many years ago, before the sun bleached it, and Faye wonders if she should pity those who live so narrowly inside their memories. Then past the VFW and the restaurant named Restaurant with its sign that never changes: ALL YOU CAN EAT WALLEYE. FRIDAY, SATURDAY, AND WEDNESDAY.

She turns onto the highway and sees in the distance, through a clearing in the trees, what she playfully calls *the lighthouse:* It's really a tower at the nitrogen plant where gas is vented and burned, where one can see, at night, a blue flame. So it looks like a lighthouse, sure, but it's also a joke about geography: Iowa, after all, is landlocked for a billion miles. This is the way to Henry's. She drives the empty streets, the night like any other night except for what's on TV. The catastrophe on the news means people won't notice her—they won't be on their porches, in open garages, won't say: *There goes Faye. I wonder where she's heading.* Faye is aware of the attention, the neighborly curiosity, the unyielding abstract gaze of the town, the way everything sort of shifted when word got out about Circle. People at church who previously had no outward opinion of Faye whatsoever suddenly began saying things that felt hostile and passive-aggressive: "I suppose you'll forget about us when you're off in the big city," or "I guess you won't be coming back to our boring little town," or "I imagine when you're a big shot you won't have time for little old me," and so on. Things that seemed to have an ugly edge to them, like: *You think you're better than us?*

The answer being, in fact, *Yes.*

On her desk back home is a letter from Circle—so official-looking with its logo and heavy paper—informing her of her scholarship. The first girl from her high school to win a college scholarship. The first girl *ever.* How could she not feel better than everyone else? Being better than everyone else *was the whole point!*

Faye knows it is wrong to think this, for these thoughts are not humble; they are arrogant and vain and choked with pride, that most hazy of sins. *Everyone proud of heart is an abomination,* the pastor said one Sunday, and Faye in the pew nearly crying because she did not know how to be good. It seemed so hard to be good, and yet the punishments were so vast. "If you're a sinner," the pastor said, "not only will you be punished but your kids will be punished, and their kids will be punished, to the third and fourth generation."

She hopes the pastor doesn't find out she visited Henry without permission.

Or that she was so sneaky about it. That she drove without headlights while approaching his family's farm. That she parked the car at a distance and walked the rest of the way. That she crouched on the gravel road, let her eyes adjust to the dark, watched for the dogs, spied on the house. That there was some sly maneuver to get his attention without stirring his parents: tossing pebbles at his window. Teenagers have their ways.

The town knows about them, of course. The town knows about *everyone*. And they approve. They wink at Faye and ask her questions about weddings. "Won't be long now," they say. It seems obvious they would prefer she marry than go to college.

Henry is kind, quiet, well-mannered. His family's farm is large and well-run, respectable. A good Lutheran, a hard worker, his body is built like cement. She feels his muscles tense when she touches him, that nervous boy voltage that gathers up and breaks him. She doesn't love him, or rather she doesn't *know* if she loves him, or maybe she *loves* him but she's not *in love* with him. She hates these distinctions, these tiny matters of vocabulary that, unfortunately, matter so much. "Let's go for a walk," Henry says. His farm is bordered on one side by the nitrogen plant, on the other by the Mississippi River. They walk in that direction, to the riverbank. He does not seem surprised to see her. He takes her hand.

"Have you been watching the news?" he says.

"Yes."

His hand is rough and calloused, especially on the palm, above each knuckle, where Henry's body connects with the various implements important to farm labor: shovel, spade, hoe, broom, the long and finicky stick shift of the John Deere tractor. Even a baseball bat would cause such marks, if it were used as he uses it, to kill the abundant sparrows that nest in the corn crib. It's too small in there for buckshot, he explained to her once. It could ricochet. You could lose an eye. So you have to go in with a baseball bat and take the birds out of the air. She asked him never to tell that story again.

"Are you still going to Chicago?" he asks.

"I don't know," she says.

The ground grows spongier the closer they are to the river. She can hear the *whoosh* of each small wave. Behind them the lighthouse burns a bright azure blue, like a splinter of daytime that got stuck here through the night.

"I don't want you to go," Henry says.

"I don't want to talk about it."

When they're holding hands, he'll often rub his fingers on the soft skin between her thumb and index finger, or on the even softer skin of her wrist. Faye wonders if he does it because otherwise he can't feel anything. Not beneath so many layers of thick, dead skin. It's the friction that tells him his fingers are where he thinks they are, and Faye worries what will happen when he begins reaching for other things, for new things. She's waiting for it—it's inescapable—waiting for him to make a move beneath her clothes. Will they hurt, those hard, impenetrable hands of his?

"If you go to Chicago," Henry says, "I don't know what I'll do."

"You'll be fine."

"I won't," he says, and he squeezes her hand hard and stops walking and turns to her, theatrically—seriously and profoundly—like there's something of great weight he must tell her. Henry always has had a bit of the melodramatic in him. Teenage boys are like that sometimes, the emotions they feel blown so tremendously out of proportion.

"Faye," he says, "I've made a decision."

"Okay."

"I have decided"—and here he pauses, makes sure she's listening with appropriate attentiveness, feels assured that she is and so continues—"if you go to Chicago, I'm joining the army."

And here she laughs—a little bark she tries to hold back but cannot.

"I'm serious!" he says.

"Henry, please."

"I've decided."

"Don't be stupid."

"The army is honorable," he says. "That's an *honorable* thing."

"But why on earth would you do that?"

"I'll be lonely if I don't. It's the only way I could forget you."

"Forget me? Henry, it's college. I'm not dying. I'll come back."

"You'll be so far away."

"You could visit."

"And you'll meet other boys."

"Other boys. Is that what this is about?"

"If you go to Chicago, I'm joining the army."

"But I don't *want* you to join the army."

"And I don't want you to go to Chicago." He crosses his arms. "My mind is made up."

"They could send you to Vietnam."

"Yeah."

"Henry, you could die."

"If I did, I guess it'd be your fault."

"That's not fair."

"Stay here and be with me," he says.

"That is *not* fair."

"Stay here where it's safe."

She feels the injustice of this, and she's angry about it, but she also feels, strangely, relief. The riots, the looting, all the horrible things on television tonight, and her mother, and the town: If she stays here with Henry, they need no longer terrorize her. Things would be so much easier if she stayed, so much cleaner.

Why did she come here? She regrets it now. She regrets summoning Henry under the pale blue flame of the lighthouse. She hasn't told him, but there's another reason she calls that thing a lighthouse. It's because a lighthouse is two-faced, and this is how she feels each time she visits. A lighthouse is both an invitation and a warning. A lighthouse says *Welcome home.* But next to that, right after that, it also says *Danger.*

2

IT'S A SATURDAY NIGHT late in April 1968—the night of Faye's senior prom. Henry picks her up at six o'clock with a rose and a corsage. His hands fumble as he pins the flowers to her gown. He pulls on the fabric near her chest as if he were pantomiming, right there before her parents, all the awkward gestures of teenage groping. Yet her mother takes photographs, says *Smile*. And Faye guesses this corsage business was invented by parents—very protective parents wanting to ensure that their daughters' suitors were not too familiar with the garments and breasts of women. Clumsiness is probably the best thing here—it signals little danger of bastard children. And Henry is a man inept with flowers. He cannot get the corsage pinned correctly. He grazes the needle across her skin and leaves a thin red line on her breastbone. It reminds her of the horizontal bar in the letter A.

"It's my scarlet letter!" she says, laughing.

"What?" Henry says.

"My scarlet dash, actually."

Everything is easier when they dance. She takes to the floor and does the Twist. She does the Madison. She does the Mashed Potato and the Jerk and the Watusi. Faye's teenage years have been consistently buoyed by new dance crazes that appear every few weeks on the Top 40. The Monkey. The Dog. The Locomotion. Songs and dances that enact a perfect circle—the song tells you everything you need to know about the dance, and the dance gives reason for the song. When Marvin Gaye sang "Hitch Hike," she knew exactly what to do. When Jackie Lee sang "The Duck," Faye could do it even before she saw it on TV.

So here she is, staring at the floor, doing the Duck in a blue charmeuse prom dress—lift the left leg, then the right leg, then flap your arms, then repeat. That's what goes for dancing these days. Every prom and homecoming and Valentine's Day dance is like this, the deejay playing a song that tells you precisely what to do. The big new thing this year is Archie

Bell and the Drells singing "Tighten Up"—shuffle to your left, then shuffle to your right. "Tighten it up now, everything will be outta sight." Somewhere nearby Henry is dancing too, but Faye doesn't notice. These are dances meant to be done alone. When you do the Freddie, the Chicken, the Twist, even on a crowded dance floor, you do them by yourself. They aren't allowed to touch each other and so they dance alone. They perform the dances that fit exactly what their chaperones want of them. They are told how to dance and they respond like proper bureaucrats, is what Faye thinks now as she watches all her classmates. They are happy, satisfied, soon-to-be-graduates, pro-authoritarian, their parents support the war, they have color televisions. When Chubby Checker says, "Take me by my little hand and go like this," he is telling her generation how to respond to what is happening to them—the war, the draft, the sexual prohibitions—he is telling them to obey.

But then at the end of the night, the deejay announces he has time for one more song—"This one's very special," he says—and so Faye and Henry and the other students move slowly back to the dance floor, feet tired from all the shuffling and twisting, and the deejay puts on a new record and Faye hears the needle catch, the scratch before it falls into the groove, the static, and then comes *this song*.

It doesn't even sound like music at first; more like some crude primeval screeching, the dense noise of strings all playing dissonant and muddy—a violin maybe, and some freakish guitar repeatedly striking the same chord—the slow, monotonous beat of a bass drum, the insistent reverb, the singer not actually singing but chanting. Faye can't make out the words, can't identify a chorus, can find no beat to dance to. A dreadful sexy moaning, that's what it is. A phrase pops out: "Whiplash girlchild in the dark." What does that even mean? Around her, the students move with the music, move as sluggishly and languidly as the music itself: They stagger toward each other, touch each other, grab each other by the waist and squeeze their bodies together. It is the slowest dance Faye has ever seen. She looks at Henry, who stands there worried and helpless while around him dancers wiggle like giant worms. How do they know what to do? The song gives no instructions. Faye loves it. She grabs Henry by the back of the neck and pulls him into her. Their bodies slap together. He stands there bewildered as Faye lifts her arms over her head and closes her eyes and turns her face to the ceiling and sways.

The chaperones, meanwhile, are wary. They don't know what is happening but they are sure it's *wrong*. They force the deejay to stop the song and the dancers groan. They walk back to their tables.

"What were you doing out there?" Henry asks.

"Dancing," Faye says.

"What dance is it? What's it called?"

"Nothing. It's not called anything. It's just, you know, it's just *dancing*."

Afterward, Henry takes her to the park, a quiet neighborhood park near her house, unlit, private, one of the few places in this small town to be alone. She expects this. Henry is a boy who believes in romantic gestures. He pays for candlelit dinners and buys candy in heart-shaped boxes. He shows up at her house smiling like a jack-o'-lantern handing her fat bunches of lilies and irises. He leaves roses in her car. (That the roses shrivel in the heat and die, she never tells him.) Henry doesn't know the meaning of the flowers, the differences between red roses and white, between a lily and an iris. This is a language he does not speak. He does not know how to love Faye creatively, and so he does what everyone else in high school does: candles and chocolates and flowers. He treats love like a balloon, like it is all a very simple matter of accumulation, just adding more air. And so the flowers keep coming. And the dinners. And the love poems that appear in her locker from time to time, typewritten, unsigned—

> *I love you with all my love*
> *more than the stars above*

"Did you get my poem?" he'll ask, and she'll say "Yes, thank you," and smile and look at the ground and cross her feet and hope he doesn't ask if she liked it. Because she never likes it. How could she like it when in her free time she's reading Walt Whitman and Robert Frost and Allen Ginsberg? How ugly Henry seems compared to Allen Ginsberg! How simple and stupid, how quaint and provincial. She knows Henry wants to impress her and woo her, but the more of these poems she reads, the more she feels tranquilized, like her mind is sinking slowly into sand.

> *When you are away*
> *I have the worst day*
> *Because I can't hold you*
> *I feel real sad too*

She can't bring herself to criticize him. She'll only nod and say, "I got the poem. Thank you," and Henry will make that face—that grinning self-satisfied face, that triumphant face, that big stupid muffin face—which makes her so angry she wants to tell him cruel things:

That it would be a better poem if he wrote it in meter.

Or if he owned a dictionary.

Or if he knew more multisyllabic words.

(And how awful of her to even *think* that!)

No, he is a nice enough boy, a good enough boy. Good-hearted, big-hearted. He is kind. Gentle. Everyone says she should marry him.

"Faye," he says as they sit on the merry-go-round, "I think we've come a long way, you know, in our relationship." And she nods but does not know exactly what he means. He has certainly given her lots of flowers and poems and dinners and chocolates, but he's never told her a secret. She feels she knows nothing about him, nothing more than what everyone else knows: Henry, whose family owns the farm by the nitrogen plant, who wants to be a veterinarian, the football team's mediocre tight end, the baseball team's backup third baseman, the basketball team's third-string forward, who on weekends fishes on the Mississippi and plays with his dogs, who sits quiet in class and needs her tutoring for algebra—Faye knows his résumé but not his secrets. He never tells her anything important. He never explains why, for example, when he kisses her he doesn't act like a boy should, doesn't try the things boys are supposed to try. She's heard the stories—famous in high school—of boys who will do *anything* if you let them. Who will go *all the way* if you let them. And anywhere! In the backseats of cars or on the baseball field at night, in dirt or grass or mud or whatever cheap and lucky spot they find themselves when they find a girl who doesn't say no. And the girls who let them, who invite it, who aren't going steady, their reputations are massacred with that one whispered syllable: *slut*. The fastest word in the language. It moves through school like a plague. One has to be careful.

So she's been waiting for Henry to try it—paw at her belt, stick his hands somewhere private—so she can protest and defend her chastity and he can try again next time, try harder and better, and she can protest more until finally, after enough protesting, after enough of saying no, she will have demonstrated that she is virtuous and chaste and good, not easy, not a slut. And then finally she can say yes. She is waiting for this, the whole ritual, but instead Henry only kisses her, smashes his face against hers and stops. It goes like this every time. They sit together at night on the riverbank or in the park and listen to the sound of motorcycles on the highway, the squeaks of the swing set, and Faye picks at the rust on the merry-go-round and waits. And nothing has ever happened, not until tonight, this night after the prom, when Henry is so full of ceremony it seems he's memorized his lines.

"Faye, I think we've come a long way. And you're very important to me and special. And it would make me feel honored and happy and really happy . . ." He stutters, stops, he is nervous, and she nods and touches his arm lightly with her fingertips.

"I mean," he says, "it would make me feel honored and happy and really *lucky* if you, you know, to school, from now on," and he pauses, gathers his courage, "if you can, please, wear my jacket. And my ring."

And he exhales greatly, spent from the effort, relieved. He can't even look at her now. He stares at his feet and twists his shoelaces tightly around his fingers.

She finds him adorable in this moment, in his embarrassment and fear, in how much power she has over him. She says yes. Of course she says yes. And when they stand up to leave, they kiss. And the kiss feels different this time, feels like it is a greater and more powerful thing, a kiss with *meaning.* They both must know they've crossed a boundary: the class ring is a harbinger, everyone knows that. An engagement ring almost always follows, and these symbols make their coupling official and sanctioned and certified and good. Whatever a girl might do in the backseat of a car, she is protected if she wears the boy's decorations. These things insulate her. They guard her. She is immune from insult. A girl is not a slut if she has a ring.

And Henry must sense it too, that they now have permission to do as they want, because he pulls Faye closer, kisses her harder, presses his body tightly to hers. She feels something then, some blunt and rigid thing pressing into her belly. It's him, of course, Henry. He is pushing up through his thin gray slacks. He is shaking a little and kissing her and he is hard as stone. It surprises her, how solid a boy can be. Like a broom handle! It's all she can think about. She is aware she is still kissing him but she is doing it automatically—all her attention is on these few square inches, that obscene pressure. She thinks she can feel his pulse *through it* and she starts sweating, grabbing him tighter to tell him it is all okay. He runs his hands over her back and makes little squeaking sounds; he is jittery, jumpy; he is waiting for her. It is her turn to do something. His was an opening gambit, pressing himself so obviously into her. It is a negotiation. Now it is her move.

She decides to be bold, to do what she'd insinuated during that final dance at the prom. With one hand she pulls on the waistband of his slacks, pulls hard enough that there is enough space for her other hand. Henry twitches then, and his body goes tense, and everything about him stops moving for a split second. Then it all happens so fast. She drives her hand down as he leaps back. Her fingers begin to grasp him—she feels him for the smallest moment, and knows that he is warm and solid but also soft and delicately fleshy—and she has just begun to understand this when he jumps back and turns slightly away from her and yells, "What are you *doing?*"

"I'm, I don't know—"

"You can't *do* that!"

"I'm sorry, Henry, I'm—"

"*God,* Faye!" And he turns from her then and adjusts his pants, jams his hands in his pockets and walks away. He paces from one side of the swing set to the other. She watches him. It's hard to believe that his face can go so cold so quickly.

"Henry?" she says. She wants him to look at her, but he doesn't. "Henry, I'm sorry."

"Forget it," he says. He digs his foot into the sand, wiggles his shoe until it's buried, then does it again, getting his nice black dress loafers all dirty.

She sits again on the merry-go-round. "Come back," she says.

"I don't want to talk about it, Faye."

He is an even-keeled boy, mild and modest; he must have frightened himself, reacting the way he did. And now he is trying to make it go away, to erase what happened. Faye sits on the merry-go-round and says, "It's okay, Henry."

"No, it's not," he says, his back to her, hands pocketed, shoulders hunched up. He is a closed fist, all tense and curled in on himself. "It's just . . . You can't *do* that."

"Okay."

"It's not right," he says, and she considers this. Picks off red flakes of rust and listens to his feet crunching the sand as he paces and she stares at his back and finally says: "Why?"

"You shouldn't want to. It's not what a girl like you is supposed to want."

"A girl like me?"

"Never mind."

"What does that mean?"

"Nothing."

"Tell me."

"Forget it."

And then Henry is gone. He sits on the merry-go-round and shuts everything off, becomes a silent, cold lump. He crosses his arms and stares out into the night. He is punishing her. And it makes her furious, makes her begin trembling. She can feel a nausea beginning in her gut, an agitation in her chest—her heart beating, the little hairs on her neck standing up. She can feel something coming, a familiar wave of sweat and dizziness. She is lightheaded suddenly, and hot and tingly and a little outside herself, as if she is floating above the merry-go-round, looking down, watching the buzzing of her own body. Can Henry see it? The wrecking ball is on its way—the sobbing and choking, the shakes. This has happened before.

"Take me home," she whispers through clenched teeth.

Who knows if he understands what is happening, but Henry looks at her then and seems to soften. "Listen, Faye—"

"Take me home now."

"I'm sorry Faye, I shouldn't have—"

"*Now,* Henry."

So he takes her home, and for the whole terrible ride they don't speak. Faye squeezes the leather seats and tries to fight off the feeling she is dying. When he stops in front of her house, she feels like a ghost, flying away from him without making a sound.

Faye's mother knows right away. "You're having an attack," she says, and Faye nods, wide-eyed, panicky. Her mother takes her to her room and undresses her and puts her in bed and gives her something to drink, dabs a cold washcloth on her forehead and says "It's okay, it's all okay" in her quiet and sweet and hushed motherly voice. Faye holds her knees to her chest and sobs and gulps for air while her mother runs her fingers through her hair and whispers "You're not dying, you're not going to die" as she has all through Faye's childhood. And they stay that way until finally the episode passes. Faye calms down. She begins breathing again.

"Don't tell Dad," she says.

Her mother nods. "What if this happens in Chicago, Faye? What will you do?"

Her mother squeezes her hand and leaves to fetch another washcloth. And Faye thinks about Henry then. She thinks, almost gladly: *Now we have a secret.*

3

FAYE DID NOT ALWAYS SUFFER SO. She was once a normally social, normally functioning kid. Then one day something happened to change all that.

It was the day she learned about the house spirit.

It was 1958, a late-summer barbecue, light fading purpley in the west, mosquitoes and lightning bugs, kids playing tag or watching the bug zapper do its frightening business, men and women outside smoking and drinking and leaning against fence posts or each other, and Faye's father grilling food for a few neighbors, a few guys from work.

This was all his wife's idea.

Because Frank Andresen had a reputation: He was a little intimidating, a little standoffish. There was the matter of his accent, sure, that he was a foreigner. But more than that was his manner—melancholy, stoic, inward. The neighbors would see Frank outside gardening and ask how he was doing and he wouldn't say a word, just simply wave with this expression on his face like he had a broken rib he wasn't telling them about. Eventually they stopped asking.

His wife insisted: We will invite people over, we will let them get to know you, we will have fun.

So here they were, all these neighbor guys in his backyard, having a conversation about some sports team Frank knew nothing about. He could only listen and stand on the conversation's periphery, because even after eighteen years in the States there were still some words that eluded him, and many of them were sports-related. He listened and tried to have the correct reactions at the appropriate moments and, thus distracted, he let the hot dogs burn.

He motioned to Faye, who was playing tag with two neighbor boys, and when she came to him he said, "Go inside and fetch some hot dogs." Then he leaned over her and whispered: "From downstairs."

By which he meant the bomb shelter.

The immaculately cleaned, brilliantly lit, fully stocked bomb shelter that he spent the previous three summers building. He had constructed it at night—only at night, so the neighbors wouldn't see. He would leave and come back with a truck full of supplies. One night it was two thousand nails. Another it was eleven bags of concrete. He had this kit that showed him how to do it. He would pour the concrete into plastic molds that Faye loved touching because while the concrete was hardening it was also hot. Only once did Faye's mother ask him about it, early on, asked him why on earth he was building a bomb shelter in their basement. He stared at her with these horrible hollow eyes and gave her this face like *Don't make me say it out loud.* Then he went back to the truck.

Faye said yes, she would fetch the hot dogs, and when her father's back was turned she ran to the two neighbor boys and, because she was eight years old and desperate to be liked, she said, "You want to see something?" To which the answer was of course *yes.* And so with the two boys Faye entered the house and took them downstairs. Her father had dug up the basement's stone floor so that the shelter looked like a submarine surfacing right out of the ground. A rectangular concrete box with steel-reinforced walls that could withstand their own house collapsing on top of it. A small door with a padlock—the combination being Faye's birth date—that Faye opened and took the four steps down into the structure and flipped on the lights. The effect here was like a single aisle from the grocery store had been magically transported into their basement: the brilliant white fluorescents, the cans of food that lined the walls. The boys gasped.

"What is this?" one of them said.

"Our bomb shelter."

"Wow."

Shelves crowded with cardboard boxes and wooden crates and mason jars and cans all turned identically label-out: tomatoes, beans, dehydrated milk. Ten-gallon jugs of water, dozens of them, stacked in a pyramid near the door. Radios, bunk beds, oxygen tanks, batteries, boxes of cornflakes stockpiled in the corner, a television with a cord that disappeared into the wall. A hand crank on the wall labeled AIR INTAKE. The boys looked around astonished. They pointed to a locked wooden cabinet with a frosted glass cover and asked what was in there.

"Guns," Faye said.

"Do you have the key?"

"No."

"Too bad."

Upstairs, the boys were delirious. They could not contain their excitement.

"Dad!" they said, running crazily into the backyard. "Dad! Do you know what they have in the basement? A bomb shelter!"

And Frank looked at Faye so hard that she couldn't bear to meet his eyes.

"A bomb shelter?" said one of the fathers. "No kidding?"

"Not really," Frank said. "Just supply closet. Like a wine cellar."

"No it isn't," said one of the boys. "It's huge! And it's concrete and full of food and guns."

"Is that so?"

"Can we build one?" said the other boy.

"You get one of those kits?" said the father. "Or did you do it yourself?"

Frank seemed to consider whether he wanted to engage this question, then softened a bit and stared at the ground.

"Bought the plans," he said, "then built it myself."

"How big is it?"

"Thirty by twelve."

"So that fits, what, how many people?"

"Six."

"Great! Russians drop the bomb, we'll know where to go."

"Funny," Frank said. His back was turned now. He placed the new hot dogs on the grill, moving them around with long metal tongs.

"I'll bring the beer," the father said. "Hear that, kids? We're all saved."

"Sorry," said Frank, "no."

"We'll bunk it up for a few weeks. Be like we're in the service again."

"No can do."

"Aw, c'mon. What are you going to do, turn us away?"

"I'm all full."

"It'll fit six. You said so yourself. I only count three of you."

"No telling how long we'll be down there."

"Are you serious?"

"I am."

"You're pulling my leg. You'd let us in, right? I mean, if there really was a bomb. You'd let us in."

"Listen to me," Frank said. He put down the tongs and turned around and put his hands on his hips. "If anyone comes near that door, I will shoot them. You understand? I will shoot them in the head."

And everyone was quiet. Faye heard nothing but the air hissing out of the sizzling meat.

"Okay, jeez," the father said. "I was joking, Frank. Settle down."

And he took his beer and went into the house. And Faye and everyone else followed, leaving Frank out there alone. She watched him that night from a dark upstairs window as he stood over the grill and silently let the meat blacken and burn again.

This would be an enduring memory of her father, an image that captured something important about the man: alone and angry and hunched over with his arms on the table like he was praying to it.

He stayed out there the rest of the evening. Faye was put to bed. Her mom gave her a bath and tucked her in and filled her glass with water. It was always there, that glass, in case she got thirsty in the night. A short, wide tumbler, adult-size with a thick base. She liked to hold it on hot summer evenings, wrap her hands around it and feel its solidity and heaviness. She liked to press it against her cheek and feel its smooth crystalline coldness. And this was what she was doing, holding the glass to her face, when, after a brief and gentle knock, after the door swung slowly and silently open, her father appeared in her bedroom.

"I have something for you," he said. He reached into his pocket and pulled out a small glass figurine: an old man, white beard, sitting with his legs around a bowl of porridge, wooden spoon in his hand, wrinkly face full of satisfaction.

"It's very old," he said.

He handed it to Faye and she studied it, ran her fingers over it. It was hollow and thin and brittle, the colors yellowed, about the size of a small teacup. The figure looked like a smaller, thinner Santa Claus, though with a very different attitude: Whereas Santa always seemed so animated and cheerful, this thing seemed nasty. It was the ugly smirk on his face, maybe, and the way he held the bowl so guardedly, like a dog tensing over food.

"What is it?" Faye asked, and her father said it was a house spirit, a ghost that usually hid in basements, back in old Norway, in a time more enchanted than this one, it seemed to Faye, a time when everything in the world must have been paranormal: spirits of the air, sea, hills, wilderness, house. You had to look for ghosts everywhere back then. Anything in the world might have been another thing incognito. A leaf, a horse, a stone. You could not take them literally, the things of the world. You always had to find the real truth the first truth concealed.

"Did you have one in your basement?" Faye asked. "On the farm?"

Her father brightened as he thought of it. He always brightened at the thought of the old house. He was a serious man who only seemed to cheer up when describing that place: a wide salmon-red three-story wooden house on the edge of town, a view of the ocean out back, a long pier where he fished on quiet afternoons, a field in the front bounded by spruce trees, a pen for the few goats and sheep they owned, and a horse. A house at the top of the world, he said, in Hammerfest, Norway. Talking about it always seemed to restore him.

"Yes," he said, "even that house was haunted."

"Do you wish you still lived there?"

"Yes, sometimes," he said. "It was haunted, but not in a bad way."

He explained that house spirits weren't evil. They were sometimes even kind, would take care of the farm, help with the crops, brush the horse's hair. They kept to themselves and got angry if you didn't bring them cream porridge on Thursday nights. With loads of butter. They weren't friendly ghosts, but they weren't cruel either. They did what they pleased. They were selfish ghosts.

"And this is what they looked like?" Faye said, turning the figurine around in her palm.

"Most of the time they're invisible," Frank said. "You can only see them if they want you to see them. So you don't see them very much."

"What's it really called?" she said.

"A *nisse*," he said, and she nodded. She loved the weird names her father gave his ghosts: *nisse, nix, gangferd, draug.* Faye understood that these were old words, European words. Her father used these words sometimes, sometimes accidentally, when he was excited or angry. He once showed her a book full of these words, incomprehensible. It was a Bible, he said, and on the first page was a family tree. There was her name, he pointed out: *Faye.* And her parents' names, and names above them too, names she'd never heard before, strange names with strange marks. The paper was thin and fragile and yellow, the black ink faded to lavender and blue. All of these people, she was told, stayed behind, while Fridtjof Andresen changed his name to Frank and came bravely to America.

"Do you think we have a *nisse* here?" Faye asked.

"You never know," her father said. "Sometimes they'll follow you around your whole life."

"Are they nice?"

"Now and then. They're temperamental. You mustn't *ever* insult them."

"I wouldn't insult them," she said.

"You could do it accidentally."

"How?"

"When you take your bath, do you splash water on the floor?"

She considered it and admitted yes, she did do that.

"If you spill any water, you must clean it up quickly. So the water doesn't seep into the basement and drip on your *nisse*. That would be a big insult."

"What would happen?"

"He would get angry."

"Then what would happen?"

"I'll tell you a story," he said. And this was the story he told her:

At a farm near Hammerfest, many years ago, there was a beautiful little girl named Freya (and Faye smiled at this, at the proximity of the beautiful girl's name to her own). One Thursday night, Freya's father told her to take cream porridge to the *nisse*. And the little girl was planning to obey her father, but on her way to the basement she grew very hungry. Her mother had made a special batch of porridge that night, with brown sugar and cinnamon and raisins and even thin slices of mutton on top. Freya thought it was a pity to waste all that good food on a ghost. So once she was in the basement and hidden from view, she ate it herself. She licked it from the bowl, then drank the drippings. And scarcely had she finished wiping her chin clean when the *nisse* rushed out and grabbed her and started to dance. She tried to break free but the grip of the *nisse* was strong. He crushed her into him and sang "From the *nisse* did you steal! So dance now until you reel!" and she screamed and screamed, but the *nisse* pressed her face into his wiry beard so nobody heard. He twirled her around and galloped from one end of the basement to the other. He was too fast. She couldn't keep up. She kept falling and tripping, but the *nisse* pulled her up again and yanked her arms and tore her clothes, and he did this until finally she lay on the ground, in bloody rags, gasping for breath. In the morning, when they found her, she was pale and sick and nearly dead. She was bedridden for months, and even after she was well enough to walk, her father never asked her to take food to the *nisse* again.

"I'm sorry I took those boys to the basement," Faye said after he finished the story.

"Go to sleep," her father said.

"Someday I want to see your home," Faye said. "The farm in Hammerfest, with the salmon-red house. I'll go visit."

"No," he said, and when he looked at her he looked tired, maybe sad, like when he was standing outside, over those dying coals, alone. "You'll never see that house."

That night she couldn't sleep. She was kept awake for hours by every squeak—every little crack, every rustle of wind and she thought there was an intruder or an apparition. The lights outside shined through tossing leaves and phantomed hideous forms on her wall: burglars, wolves, the devil. She felt hot and fevered and tried to cool herself down with the bedside glass of water, pressing it to her forehead and chest. She sipped the water and thought about her father's story, about the house spirit: *Sometimes they'll follow you around your whole life.* It was a horrifying thought, this beast downstairs, watching them, speaking gibberish.

She looked at the floor as if she could see through it, down to the basement where the ghost was prowling, greedily waiting. She tipped the glass and poured out the water. She felt a bolt of panic as she watched what she was doing, watched the water puddle, a dark brown blot on the light brown carpet. She imagined the water as it seeped into the floor, dripped down through cracks in the wood, over metal slats and across nails and glue and slunk its way beneath her, picking up dust and dirt as it washed into the basement and coldly fell on whatever angry thing was down there, lurking in the darkness.

At some point in the night—this is the truth—they found Faye in the basement.

In some dead hour of the morning, they heard a scream. They found her downstairs. She was shaking and shivering, her head rattling on the concrete floor. Her parents didn't know how she got there. She couldn't talk, couldn't see, her eyes rolled blindly into her head. At the hospital she eventually calmed down, and the doctors said she had a nervous fever, a nervous disposition, a case of hysteria, which is to say they had no diagnosis at all. Rest in bed, they said. Drink milk. Don't get too excited.

Faye didn't remember a thing, but she knew what happened. She knew absolutely what happened. She had insulted the ghost, and the ghost had come for her. The ghost had followed her father all the way from the old country, and now it was haunting her. This was the moment that would forever divide her childhood, which would set her on a path that made everything that came after—the seizures, the disaster of Chicago, her failure at motherhood and marriage—feel inescapable.

Every life has a moment like this, a trauma that breaks you into brand-new pieces. This was hers.

THE PINKEST CLASSROOM in Faye's high school. The most ruffled and doilied. The cleanest, brightest. The most elaborate, with ovens and sewing stations, refrigerators, banks of saucepans and stockpots. By far the most aromatic, that warm chocolately air spilling into the hallway during their two-week unit on cake-making. The home economics classroom—electric, full of light, cleaning products bright and chemical, sharp knives, soup cans, blazing silver-white skillets made of aluminum, modern appliances of the atomic age. Not once has Faye seen a boy here, not even poking his head in for cupcakes or waffles. The boys stay away, their reasons cruel: "I'd *never* eat something *you* made!" they tell the girls, making choking sounds and grabbing their necks and wheezing and dying to howls of laughter. But really the boys are nervous about the posters.

Word has reached them about the posters.

Tacked onto the pink walls, posters of women looking lonely and ashamed, advertising products whose existence the boys deny—douches, pads, absorbent powders and carbolic sprays. Faye sits in her cushioned seat, arms crossed, shoulders hunched, reading them in quiet disgust.

Unfortunately, the trickiest deodorant problem a girl has isn't under her pretty little arms, says a poster for a can of something called Pristeen. *The odor problem that men don't have,* says one for Bidette Towelettes. A woman sitting alone in her bedroom, headline above her in bold black letters: *There's something every husband expects from his wife.* Or a mother talking to her daughter: *Now that you're married, I can tell you. There's a womanly offense greater than bad breath or body odor,* and the daughter—beautiful, young, face all eager and happy, as if they were talking about movies or memories and not antiseptic germicides—says, *It's so much easier to hear it from you, Mom!*

What a terrible thing, this world of married women. Faye imagines that funk from the kitchen sink when the water sits too long, or how the dishrags reek of something like gasoline when they're crumpled and wet. The secret, envenomed married life—naked, moist, unperfumed—hiding away one's stink. Women in despair as their husbands hurry madly out the door. *Why does she spend evenings alone? She keeps her home immaculate, and looks as pretty as she can, but she neglects that one essential . . . personal feminine hygiene.* That's an ad for Lysol brand disinfectant, and Faye's mother has never mentioned *any* of this. Faye is afraid to look through her mother's bathroom, afraid of what she'll find. The pink-and-white bottles and boxes with such awful names, they sound like what the boys study in chemistry class: Zonite, Koromex, Sterizol, Kotex. Words that sound vaguely scientific and smart and modern, but words that don't really exist. Faye knows. She's looked them up. There is no dictionary definition for Koromex, nor for any of the others. Words like empty balloons, all those useless *K*s and *X*s and *Z*s.

A poster from their Kinney beauty consultant about controlling perspiration. A poster from Cover Girl about hiding blemishes. Another showing girdles and padded bras. No wonder the boys are afraid. The girls are afraid. *Deodorizes so thoroughly you know you're the woman your husband wants you to be.* Their home ec teacher is on a crusade, stamping out all manner of bacteria and uncleanliness, making the girls tidy, sweet-smelling, preventing them from becoming, as she says, "dirty cheap people." She doesn't call the course "home ec." She calls it "cotillion."

Their teacher, Mrs. Olga Schwingle, the wife of the local pharmacist, tries to teach these small-town girls manners and etiquette. She shows them how to be proper ladies, how to take up the habits necessary to join the faraway sophisticated world. To brush their hair each night one hundred times. To brush their teeth fifty times up and down. To chew each bite at least thirty-four times. To stand up straight, don't lean, don't hunch, make eye contact, smile when being spoken to. When she says "cotillion" she pronounces it with a French affect: *co-ti-YO.*

"We must rinse that farm off you!" Mrs. Schwingle says, even to the girls who do not live on farms. "What we need is some elegance." And she'll put on a record—chamber music or a waltz—and say, "You girls are so lucky to have me here."

She teaches them things their mothers know nothing about. What kinds of glasses to serve wine in, or scotch. The difference between a dinner fork and a salad fork. Where all these things belong in a proper place setting. Which direction the blade of the knife should face. How to sit without putting your elbows on the table. How to approach a table, how to leave one. How to gracefully accept a compliment. How to sit when a man pushes the seat in behind you. How to make a good cup of coffee. How to serve it properly. How to set out sugar cubes in adorable little pyramids on fragile-looking painted china the likes of which Faye has never seen in her own home.

Mrs. Schwingle teaches them how to host a dinner party, how to cook for a dinner party, how to make pleasing conversation with dinner guests, how to create the sophisticated dishes she insists the wives on the East Coast are right now making, mostly involving some kind of gelatin, some kind of lettuce trim, some kind of food-within-another-food conceit. Shrimp salad in an avocado ring mold. Pineapple in lime gelatin served with cream cheese. Cabbage suspended in jellied bouillon. Peaches split and filled with blueberries. Canned pear halves covered in shredded yellow cheese. Pineapple boats filled with cocktail sauce. Olive pimento mousse. Chicken salad molded into white warheads. Tuna squares. Lemon salmon towers. Ham-wrapped cantaloupe balls.

These are the new and fabulous dishes that ladies of culture are serving. America has fallen in love with these foods: modern, exciting, unnatural.

Mrs. Schwingle has been to New York City. She has been to Chicago's Gold Coast. She goes all the way to Dubuque to get her hair done, and when she isn't buying clothes from the catalogs of East Coast retailers, she shops the boutiques of Des Moines or Joliet or Peoria. When the weather is pleasant she announces "What a wonderful day" and throws open the classroom shutters so dramatically that Faye expects to see cheerful animated birds flying in from outside. She tells them to enjoy the breeze and the scent of lilacs. "They're in bloom, you know." They go collect the flowers and place them around the class in small vases. "A lady's house will always have such touches."

Today she begins class with her usual exhortation regarding marriage.

"When I was in college becoming a certified professional secretary," she says, standing powerfully erect, her hands clasped in front of her, "I decided to take classes in biology and chemistry. All my teachers wondered why I would do that. Why go to all that trouble? Why not more typing?"

She laughs and shakes her head like someone patiently tolerating a fool.

"I had a plan," she says. "I knew since I was a girl that I wanted to marry *someone in the medical field.* I knew I needed to expand my mind so that I could attract someone in the medical field. If all I could talk about was typing and filing, who in the medical field would be interested in me?"

She looks at the girls solemnly and profoundly like she is delivering some awful adult truth.

"Nobody," Mrs. Schwingle says. "That's the answer. *Nobody.* And when I met Harold, I knew my science electives really paid off."

She smoothes her dress.

"What I'm trying to say is, set big goals. You do not have to settle for marrying a farmer or plumber. You might not be able to marry someone in the medical field, like me, but someone in the accounting field is not out of the question for any of you young ladies. Or perhaps business, banking, or finance. Figure out the kind of man you want to marry, and arrange your life to make it happen."

She asks the girls to think about the kind of husband they want. I want a man who can take me on trips to Acapulco, they say. I want a man who can buy me a convertible. I want a man who is a boss, so I never have to worry about impressing the boss when he drops in because I'm married to him! Mrs. Schwingle teaches them to dream in these terms. You can have a life that includes cruises in the Mediterranean, she says, or you can have a life of bass fishing on the Mississippi.

"It's your choice, girls. But if you want a better life, you've got to work for it. Do you think your husband will want to talk about stenography?" The girls gravely shake their heads no.

"Faye, this is especially important for you," she says. "Chicago will be full of sophisticated men."

Faye feels the collective gaze of the class land on her, and she sinks into her chair.

They move on to the day's primary lesson: toilets. As in, where are the germs? (They are everywhere.) And how is it cleaned? (Thoroughly, with bleach and ammonia, on our hands and knees.) In groups of five they practice toilet-scrubbing in the bathroom. Faye waits her turn with the other girls, who stare out the classroom windows at the boys, who are currently in gym class.

Today it's baseball, the boys fielding grounders at shortstop—the thud of the bat, the ball skipping over the dirt as they charge and scoop it up and snap it to first base with that gratifying *thwack*. This is pleasing to watch. The boys—who act so aloof and nonchalant in real life, who try to be so cool in class, sitting slumped in their chairs, defiant—they perk up like puppies on the baseball field, their movements exaggerated and eager: Charge. Stop. Catch. Pivot. Throw.

Henry is out there with them. He's not quite quick enough for short-stop, a bit of a lumberer, but he tries nonetheless. He slaps his fist into his mitt, shouts encouraging things. The boys know the girls watch them during practice. They know, and they like it.

Faye sits on a stool at one of the cooking stations, her elbows on the dark brown metal stovetop. Beneath her is a generation of culinary disasters—burned tomato sauces, burned pancake batters, roasted eggs and puddings, fossils now on the burners, black and carbonized. An old scorching that not even their teacher's most penetrating potions can remedy. Faye runs her hand across the char, feels the roughness on her fingertips. She watches the boys. Watches the girls watch the boys. Watches, for example, Margaret Schwingle—the teacher's daughter, with her fair, slightly plump face, expensive wool sweater, nylons, shiny black shoes, blond hair extravagantly curled—and the assembly that clings to Margaret, her disciples, who all wear the same silver clique bands on their fingers, who help arrange Margaret's hairdo in the morning, fetch her Cokes and candy in the cafeteria, and spread hateful rumors about her enemies. Faye and Margaret don't talk, not since elementary school. They're not unfriendly; Faye has simply receded from her view. Faye has always been intimidated by Margaret and usually avoids making eye contact. She knows the Schwingles are wealthy, that their huge house sits on a bluff overlooking the river. Margaret is wearing a boy's class ring around her neck, another on her right hand. On her left hand, a gold promise ring. (This on a girl who yawns during English-class discussions on *symbolism*.) Margaret's quasi-fiancé—her steady since freshman year—is one of those impossible, intolerable boys who's a star at everything: baseball, football, track and field. He pins his medals to his school jacket, then gives his jacket to Margaret, who walks around school clinking like a wind chime. His name is Jules, and Margaret has stripped him of all his tokens. She's remarkably proud of him. She's watching him right now, in fact, while he waits his turn on the baseball diamond. Meanwhile, she makes fun of the other boys, the clumsy ones, the ones who are not Jules.

"Oops!" she says when a ball squirts under a glove and into the outfield. "You forgot something!" The few friends around her laugh. "It's behind you, fella!" She's speaking loud enough for the rest of the room to hear her but quiet enough that they're not part of the conversation. This is a typical Margaret pose: extroverted, yet also exclusive.

"A little faster next time, big boy!" she says when poor John Novotny—overweight, thickish ankles, a bumbling hippopotamus among the faster boys—doesn't reach a ground ball to his right. "Really. Why is he even out there?" she says. Or when it's Pauly Mellick's turn—little Pauly Mellick, all of maybe five feet tall and a hundred pounds—she says, "Noodles! Go, Noodles!" because of how his arms look. She preys on the fat, the skinny, the short. She preys on the weak. *She's a carnivore,* Faye thinks. *A fangy wolf pup.*

Then it's Henry's turn. All the girls are waiting, watching, *Margaret* is watching, they all see him: Henry smacking his glove with his fist and getting into an approximation of an infielder's crouch. Faye suddenly feels very protective of him. She senses that the class wants to be entertained, wants to hear more of Margaret's intoxicating cruelty, like they're *rooting* for Henry to fail. Faye can do nothing but watch and hope. And when she looks at Margaret again, she finds Margaret is looking *right back at her,* and Faye's stomach does a loop, she blushes, her eyes grow wide, she feels somehow that she's already lost at whatever kind of showdown this is, and Margaret's cold scrutiny makes the hierarchy very clear: Margaret can say whatever she wants right now, and Faye cannot stop her.

So they're all watching Henry as the coach hits the ball. It bounces across the dirt field and Henry bounds to his left to retrieve it and Faye is angry. Not at Margaret but at *Henry.* Angry at his imminent public failure, that he put her in this position, in this stupid rivalry with *Margaret Schwingle.* Angry that she feels responsible for him, accountable for his weaknesses as if they were her own. He seems to be waddling like a toddler, and Faye *hates* him right now. She's attended enough weddings to know that essential line from the liturgy: *And the two shall become one.* Everyone seems to think this is really romantic, but Faye has always been appalled by the thought. And this moment, right now, this is why. It's like taking all your fallibility and doubling down.

But this is Henry's moment. He's running to fetch a baseball.

And wouldn't you know it, he does so flawlessly. Snares the ball, plants his feet, and throws directly and precisely and quickly to first base. Perfect. The archetype of ground-ball fielding technique. And the coach claps and the boys clap and Margaret says nothing at all.

Soon it's their turn in the toilets, and Faye sits on the tile floor feeling miserable. Though the moment passed without incident, Faye was *ready* for an encounter with Margaret, and her body still registers that tenseness. She's one big exposed nerve right now, her insides still squawking. She had been so ready for a fight that it seems as if she actually *had* the fight. And it does not help that Margaret is here with her, in the bathroom, is sitting in the neighboring toilet stall. Faye can feel her presence almost like an oven.

The toilet in front of her is spotless and white and shiny and smells like bleach—the work of home ec girls in here moments before. The teacher paces behind them explaining the perils of an unclean toilet: scabies, salmonella, gonorrhea, various resident microorganisms.

"There is no such thing as a too-clean toilet," she says. She hands them new scrubbing brushes. They crouch on the floor—some of them sit— and they wash the bowl, jostling the water, foaming the water. They scour and cleanse and rinse.

"Remember the handle," Mrs. Schwingle says. "The handle might be the dirtiest of all."

The teacher shows them how much bleach to use, how to contort their arms to most effectively clean under the lip of the bowl. She tells the girls how to keep their inevitable future children healthy, how to stop colds from spreading by keeping a clean bathroom, how to prevent toilet germs from infecting the rest of the house.

"Germs," she says, "can be propelled into the air when the toilet is flushed. So when you flush, close the cover and step away."

Faye is scrubbing when, from the next stall over, Margaret speaks. "He looked cute out there," she says.

And Faye doesn't know who she's talking to, finds it unlikely that Margaret would be talking to her, so she keeps scrubbing.

"Hello?" Margaret says, and she knocks lightly on the wall. "Anybody home?"

"What? Yes?" Faye says.

"Hello?"

"Are you talking to me?"

"Um, yeah?" Then Margaret's face appears beneath the john wall—she's leaning over, she's almost upside down, her huge blond curls hang comically off the top of her head.

"I was telling you," she says, "that he looked cute out there."

"Who?"

"Henry. *Duh.*"

"Oh, right, sorry."

"I saw you watching him. You must have thought he looked cute."

"Of course," Faye says. "Yes. That's what I was thinking."

Margaret looks at Faye's necklace, on which she's wearing Henry's ring. His big opal-stoned class ring. She says, "Are you going to put that ring on your left hand?"

"I don't know."

"If you two were really serious, you'd wear it on your left hand. Or he could get another ring. And then you'd have one for your neck and one for your left hand. That's what Jules did."

"Yes, right."

"Jules and I are *very* serious."

Faye nods.

"We'll be married soon. He has a lot of prospects."

Faye keeps nodding.

"A lot."

Their teacher notices the chattering and walks over, hands on hips, saying, "Margaret, why aren't you cleaning?," and Margaret gives Faye this look—conspiratorial, like *We're in this together,* that sort of look—and disappears behind the wall.

"I'm cleaning it mentally, Mom," Margaret says. "I'm visualizing it. I'll remember it better that way."

"Perhaps if you were as focused as Faye here, you'd be going to the big city too."

"Sorry, Mom."

"Your husband," Mrs. Schwingle says, louder now, talking to the whole group, "will expect a certain level of household cleanliness," and Faye thinks about the posters on the classroom walls, husbands with their big demands, husbands in hats and coats storming out the door when their wives can't meet basic womanly requirements, husbands in advertisements on television or in magazines—for coffee, how he'll expect you to make a fine pot for his boss; or for cigarettes, how he'll want you to be hip and sophisticated; for the Maidenform bra, how he'll expect you to have a womanly figure—and it seems to Faye that this *husband* creature is the most particular and demanding species in human history. Where does he come from? How do the boys on the baseball field—goofballs, clowns, clumsy as chickens, unsure of themselves, idiots at love—ever become *that*?

The girls are excused. They return to the classroom to summon the next wave. They sit back at their desks and look, in boredom, outside. The boys are still at it—some are dirtier now, having found reasons to dive or slide. And Jules is up, that gladiator of a boy with a sugar-cookie face. Margaret says, "Go honey! Go baby!," though he can't hear her. Margaret's exaltation is for the girls in the class, so they'll watch. And the grounder comes in at Jules and he moves for it, moves so fluidly and easily, his feet so fast and sure, not slipping in the dirt like the other boys, as though he moves on some other, more tactile earth. And he plants himself in front of the ball, arriving in the correct spot with so much time to spare, relaxed and effortless. The baseball bounces toward his glove and—maybe it hits a rock or a pebble, maybe it strikes an odd indentation in the dirt, who knows—the ball suddenly shoots upward, unexpectedly and crazily, bounces up fast and strikes Jules square in the throat.

He drops to the ground, kicking.

And the girls in the home economics classroom find this hilarious. They giggle, they laugh, and Margaret turns to them and yells, "Shut up!" She looks so hurt at this moment. So ashamed. She looks like the women in the posters, their husbands abandoning them: frightened, damaged, rejected. That feeling of being unfairly and cruelly judged. Margaret looks like that, and Faye wishes she could take Margaret's vulnerability and embarrassment and bottle it, like deodorant. Like cans of germicidal spray. She'd give it to wives everywhere. She'd shoot it at grooms on wedding days. She'd throw bombs of it, like napalm, off the roof and onto the baseball diamond.

Then the boys, too, could know how it feels.

5

FAYE SITS ALONE, outside, after school, a book in her lap, her back pressed against the school's warm, gritty wall, listening through the wall to musicians idly playing: a trumpet runs up a scale to its highest, loudest peak; a xylophone is plinked on its smallest bars; a trombone makes that splatty-fart noise only a trombone is capable of. The students of the school orchestra seem to be on a break right now, fooling around between numbers, and so Faye waits and reads. The book is a thin collection of poems by Allen Ginsberg, and she's reading the one about sunflowers again, for maybe the hundredth time, each time becoming more convinced that the poem is about her. Well, not *really*. She knows the poem is really about Ginsberg sitting in the Berkeley hills, staring out at the water, feeling depressed. But the more she reads it, the more she sees herself in it. When Ginsberg writes about the "gnarled steel roots of trees of machinery," he might as well be describing the ChemStar plant. The "oily water on the river" could easily be the Mississippi. And the sunflower field he describes could just as well be this Iowa cornfield in front of her, separated from the school by a rickety barbed-wire fence, the field recently tilled and planted, a rippled blanket of black, wet, slippery earth. By the time school resumes in the fall the field will be busy with big-shouldered plants, spine-straight, corn-armored, and ready, finally, to be hacked down, to crumple weakly where they're chopped at the knees. Faye sits and waits for the orchestra to begin playing again and thinks about this—harvest—and how it always makes her sad, how the cornfields in November look like battlegrounds, the chopped-down plants blanched and bonelike, cornstalks like femurs half buried and poking sharply out of the ground. After that, the chilly approach of another Iowa winter—the late-autumn snow dusting, the first November frost, the desolate January tundra this place becomes. Faye imagines what a Chicago winter would be like, and she imagines it would be better, and warmer, heated by all that traffic and movement and concrete and electricity, by all those hot human bodies.

Through the wall she hears someone squawking on a reed, and she smiles at that noise, the memory of that noise. She had been a musician once—one of the woodwinds, one of those who crowed her reeds. It's one of the things she gave up after the panic attacks began.

That's what the doctors called them—*panic attacks*—which didn't seem accurate to Faye. It didn't feel like she was panicking; it felt more like she was being forcibly and methodically deactivated all over. Like a wall of televisions being turned off one by one—how the images on each TV shrank to pinholes before disappearing altogether. It felt like that, the narrowing of her vision when an attack began, how she could only really take in and focus on one small thing, a dot in the wider field, usually her shoes.

At first it seemed to happen only when she displeased her father, when she did something—like taking those boys to the bomb shelter—that angered him. But then later the attacks struck in moments when she *might* displease him, when she had the *opportunity* to fail in front of him, even if she had not yet failed.

Example: the concert.

She had joined the school orchestra after listening to a compelling recording of *Peter and the Wolf*. She had wanted to play the violin, maybe the cello, but the school had openings only in the woodwinds. They gave her an oboe—dull black, the color rubbed off in places, the keys once silver but now a flat brown, one long, deep scratch running down its entire length. Learning the oboe was a calamity of honks and squawks, missed notes, her pinkie fingers sliding off the keys because they couldn't yet move independently of the rest of her hand. Yet she liked it. She liked that the oboe gave the tuning note at the beginning of rehearsal. She liked the constancy of that, the hard solid A she delivered that anchored the whole group. She liked the severe posture needed to play it, sitting up straight, holding it in front of her, elbows at right angles. She even enjoyed the rehearsals. The camaraderie. Everyone working toward a common goal. The general feeling of high artistry. The magnificent sound they could make together.

For their first concert, each musician would have a very small solo. She practiced hers for months, until the notes were inside her, until she could play her solo perfectly without even looking at the music. The night of the performance, she was all dressed up and she looked into the audience and saw her mother, who waved, and her father, who was reading the program. And there was something about his concentration, something about the humorless way he studied the program, the way he scrutinized it, that just terrified Faye.

A thought popped into her head: *What if I screw up?*

It was something she had never before considered. And suddenly whatever magic she summoned when she practiced could not be summoned now. She could not clear her mind, could not let go as she had let go in rehearsal. Her palms moistened and her fingers grew cold. By intermission she had a headache, a stomachache, dark patches of sweat under her arms. She felt the urgent need to pee, but once in the bathroom she found that she couldn't. Then during the concert's second half, she began to feel dizzy, her chest was tight. When the conductor pointed his baton to cue her solo, Faye couldn't play. The air stopped in her throat. What she squeezed out was a small cry, a short and helpless wheeze. Now all the faces turned. Everyone was looking. She heard music coming from elsewhere, but it sounded far away, like being underwater. The light in the auditorium seemed to dim. She stared at her shoes. She tumbled out of her chair. She blacked out.

The doctors said nothing was wrong.

"Nothing medically," they quickly added. They made her breathe into a brown paper bag and diagnosed her with a "chronic nervous condition." Her father looked at her, mortified and stricken. "Why did you do that?" he said. "The whole town was watching!" Which ignited her nerves all over again, his disappointment about her panic attack combined with her anxiety about not having another one in front of him.

Then she began having panic attacks even in situations that had nothing to do with her father, in moments that seemed otherwise innocent and even-keeled and calm. She would be having a normal conversation and suddenly this toxic thought would, for no reason, appear: *What if I screw up?*

And whatever blithe thing Faye had been saying the moment before was suddenly elevated to catastrophic proportions: Was she being stupid, insensitive, dim-witted, boring? The conversation became a horrible test she could easily fail. She felt a sense of doom combined with those bodily fight-or-flight mechanisms—headaches, chills, blushing, sweating, hyperventilating, hairs standing on end—which made everything worse because the only thing more painful than a panic attack was someone else seeing it.

Moments when she failed in front of other people, or moments when she felt the *potential* to fail in front of people—these could trigger an attack. Not *every* time, but sometimes. Frequent enough that she had adopted a certain self-protective behavior: She became a person who never screwed up.

A person who *never failed at anything.*

It was easy: The more afraid Faye felt on the inside, the more perfect she was on the outside. She blunted any possible criticism by being beyond reproach. She remained in people's good graces by being exactly who they wanted her to be. She aced every test. She won every academic award the school offered. When the teacher assigned a chapter from a book, Faye went ahead and read the whole book. Then read every book written by that author that was available at the town library. There was not a subject in which she did not excel. She was a model student, a model citizen, went to church, volunteered. Everyone said she had a good head on her shoulders. She was easily likable, a great listener, never demanding or critical. She was always smiling and nodding, always agreeable. It was difficult to dislike her, for there was nothing to dislike—she was accommodating, docile, self-effacing, compliant, easy to get along with. Her outward personality had no hard edges to bump into. Everyone agreed that she was *really nice.* To her teachers, Faye was the achiever, the quiet genius in the back of the room. They gushed about her at conferences, noting especially her discipline and drive.

It was, Faye knew, all an elaborate mental game. She knew that way down deep she was a phony, just your average normal girl. If it seemed like she had abilities that no one else did, it was only because she worked harder, she thought, and all it would take for the rest of the world to see the real Faye, the true Faye, was *one failure.* So she never failed. And the distance between the *real Faye* and the *fake Faye,* in her mind, kept widening, like a ship leaving the dock and slowly losing sight of home.

This was not without cost.

The flip side of being a person who never fails at anything is that you never do anything you could fail at. You never do anything risky. There's a certain essential lack of *courage* among people who seem to be good at everything. Faye, for example, gave up the oboe. It goes without saying that she never played sports. Theater was an obvious no. She declined almost all invitations to parties, socials, mixers, afternoons at the river, nights drinking around a bonfire in somebody's backyard. She has to admit that now, as a result, she really has no close personal friends at all.

Applying to Circle was the first risky thing she'd done in living memory. And then dancing the way she danced at the prom. And going after Henry the way she did at the playground. Risky. And now she felt punished for it. How the town resented her, and how Henry had shamed her—such was the price for asserting herself.

What had changed? What had inspired this new boldness? It was a line from this very poem, actually, the Ginsberg sunflower poem, a line that seemed written exactly for her, a quick jolt that seemed to slap her awake. It summed up exactly how she felt about her life even before she knew she felt it:

Poor dead flower? when did you forget you were a flower?

When had she forgotten that she was capable of bold things? When had she forgotten that bold things bubbled constantly inside her? She flips to the back of the book and studies the author photo once again. There he is, this dashing young man, fresh-faced, his short hair lightly tousled, clean-shaven, wearing a baggy white shirt, tucked in, and round tortoiseshell glasses that look like Faye's glasses. He's standing on a rooftop somewhere in New York—behind him, the antennas of the city, and beyond those, the hazy shapes of skyscrapers.

When Faye discovered that Ginsberg would be a visiting professor at Circle this coming year, she applied to the school immediately.

She leans back against the brick wall. What would it be like to be in his presence, this man of such abundance? She worries about what she'd do in his class: freak out, probably. Have a panic attack right there on the spot. She would be like the desolate narrator of the sunflower poem: *Unholy battered old thing.*

But the orchestra is coming back now.

The musicians are assembling, and Faye can hear them warming up. She listens to the cacophony. She feels it through her spine where she leans against the wall. And as she turns to press her cheek against the warm brick, she sees movement at the far end of the building: *Someone has just rounded the corner.* A girl. Light blue cotton sweater, intricately styled blond hair. It is, Faye sees, Margaret Schwingle. She's reaching into her purse, pulling out a cigarette, lighting it, blowing out that first drag with a delicate little *phoo*. She has not yet seen Faye, but she will, it's only a matter of time, and Faye does not want to be caught doing what she's doing. Slowly, so as not to disturb the bushes around her, Faye reaches into her bag and replaces the Ginsberg collection with the first book she feels: *The Rise of the American Nation,* their history textbook. On the cover is a bronze statue of Thomas Jefferson surrounded by a monochrome of bright teal. She does this so that when Margaret finally notices her, which she quickly does, and walks over to her and says "What are you doing?" Faye can respond "Homework."

"Oh," says Margaret, and this makes sense to her, since everyone knows Faye to be a studious, hardworking, brainy, scholarship-getting girl. And thus Faye does not have to explain her deeper motives, that she's here reading questionable poetry and pretending to be an oboist.

"What homework?" says Margaret.

"History."

"Jeez, Faye. *Boring.*"

"Yeah, it really is," Faye says, though she does not find history boring at all.

"It's all so boring," Margaret says. "School is so boring."

"It's terrible," Faye says, but she worries that she sounds insincere. Because of course she loves school. Or maybe more accurately she loves that she's good at school.

"I cannot wait to be finished," says Margaret. "I want to be done."

"Yeah," Faye says. "It won't be long." And this fact, the quickly coming end of the semester, has lately been filling her with dread. Because she loves the clarity that school brings: the single-minded purpose, the obvious expectations, how everyone knows you're a good person if you study hard and score well on exams. The rest of your life, however, is not judged in this manner.

"Do you read here a lot?" Margaret asks. "Behind the building?"

"Sometimes."

Margaret stares out at the black cornfield before them and seems to consider this. She puffs lightly on her cigarette. Faye follows her lead, stares blankly ahead and tries to act aloof.

"You know," says Margaret, "I always knew I was a special kid. I always knew I had certain talents. That everyone liked me."

Faye nods, to agree, maybe, or to show she's listening, interested.

"And I knew I'd grow up to be a special woman. I always knew that."

"Uh-huh."

"I was a special child and I'd grow up to be a special person."

"You are," Faye says.

"Thanks. I'd be a special woman who would marry a special man and we'd have these great children. You know? I always thought that was going to be true. This was my destiny. Life was going to be comfortable. It was going to be great."

"It will be," Faye says. "All those things."

"Yeah. I guess," Margaret says. She smothers her cigarette in the soil. "But I don't know what I want to do. With my life."

"Me neither," says Faye.

"Really? You?"

"Yeah. I have no idea."

"I thought you were going to college."

"Maybe. Probably not. My mom doesn't want me to. Neither does Henry."

"Oh," says Margaret. "Oh, I see."

"Maybe I'll put it off a year or two. Wait for things to calm down."

"That might be smart."

"I might stay here a while longer."

"I don't know what I want," says Margaret. "I guess I want Jules?"

"Of course."

"Jules is great, I guess. I mean, he's really really great."

"He's *so* great."

"He is, isn't he?"

"Yes!"

"Okay," she says. "Okay, thanks." And she stands, brushes off the dirt, and looks at Faye. "Hey, look, I'm sorry for being weird."

"It's fine," Faye says.

"Please don't tell anyone."

"I won't."

"I don't think other people would understand."

"I won't tell anyone."

And Margaret nods and begins to leave when suddenly she stops, turns back to Faye. "Would you like to come over this weekend?"

"Come over where?"

"My house, dummy. Come have dinner with us."

"Your house?"

"Saturday night. It's my father's birthday. We're having a surprise party for him. I want you to come!"

"Me?"

"Yeah. If you're going to stay in town after graduation, don't you think we should be friends?"

"Oh, okay, sure," says Faye. "Sure. That'd be swell."

"Great!" says Margaret. "Don't tell anyone. It's a surprise." She smiles and struts away, rounds the corner, and disappears.

Faye leans back against the wall again and realizes the orchestra is going full tilt. She hadn't noticed. A big torso of sound, a big crescendo. She is overcome by Margaret's invitation. What a victory. What a *shock*. She listens to the orchestra and feels vast. She finds that music muffled through a wall makes her more aware of the physicality of it, that when she can't hear the music exactly she can still sense it, the vibrations, like waves. That buzz. The wall she presses her face to makes it a different kind of experience. No longer music but a crossing over of the senses. She is aware of the friction needed for music, the striking and stroking of string, wood, leather. Near the end of the piece, especially. When, louder, she can *feel* the bigger notes. Not abstract, but a quaking, like a touch. And the feeling moves down her throat, a great pulse of noise now, a banging inside. It hums her.

Beyond everything else, she loves this: how swiftly things can strike her—music, people, life—how quickly they can surprise her, all of a sudden, like a punch.

6

SOMETIMES SPRING SEEMS to happen all at once. Trees bloom, the first green shoots curl out of rain-muddy cornfields, things are renewing, beginning, and for certain members of the graduating class, this is a time of hope and optimism: Commencement approaches, and the girls—those with steady boyfriends, those who daydream about weddings and gardens and toddlers—begin talking about soul mates, how they can feel it, destiny, the ineluctable hand of fate, how they *just know*. Soft adoring eyes and a quiver in their pulse—Faye feels sorry for them, then sometimes sorry for herself. She seems to lack some essential *romance* in her life. To Faye it all seems so arbitrary, love. All happenstance. As easily one thing as another, as easily one man as another.

Take Henry.

Why, of all men, Henry?

The two of them sit on the riverbank one night throwing stones into the water, picking at the sand, nervously attempting wit and conversation, and this is what she's thinking: Why am I here *with him*?

Simple. Because Peggy Watson started a dumb rumor last autumn.

Peggy had come galloping to Faye after home ec all smiles and high drama. "I know a secret," she said, then teased Faye the rest of the day, slipping her a note in trigonometry: *I know something you don't know.*

"It's a good one," she said at lunch. "Grade-A juicy. Something to write home about."

"Tell me."

"It's better if you wait," she said. "Till after school. You'll want to be sitting down."

Peggy Watson, vague friend since the third grade, house down the street, same bus ride home, the closest thing Faye has to a "best friend." When they were children they played this game where they used all the crayons in the box and whole pads of paper to write "I Love You" in different colors, scripts, and designs. It was Peggy's idea. She couldn't stop. It never got old for her. Peggy's favorite was a picture of a heart with *I Love You* written in a circle around it. "A circle, so no beginning and no end," she said. "Get it? It keeps going? Forever!"

After school that day Peggy was ecstatic, exhilarated with big rumors and alarming news: "There's a boy who likes you!"

"No there's not," Faye said.

"There is. Most definitely. I have it on good authority."

"Who told you?"

"Lips are sealed," Peggy said. "I swore up and down."

"Who's the boy?"

"He's a boy in our class."

"Which one?"

"Guess!"

"I am not guessing."

"Do it! Guess!"

"Tell me."

But Faye didn't really want to know. She didn't want the hassle. She was single, kept to herself, perfectly happy with that tableau. Why couldn't people just leave her alone?

"Okay," Peggy said. "Fine. No guessing. No games. I'll blurt it all out. Hope you're ready."

"I am," Faye said, and she waited, and Peggy waited, savoring it, staring at Faye, full of mischief, and Faye suffered through the big theatrical pause until she could no longer bear it. "Damn it, Peggy!"

"Okay, okay," she said. "It's Henry! Henry Anderson! He likes you!"

Henry. Faye didn't know what she was expecting, but she was not expecting that. Henry? She'd never even considered him before. He was barely a presence in her thoughts.

"Henry," Faye said.

"Yes," Peggy said. "Henry. It's destiny. You two are *destined.* You wouldn't even have to change your last name!"

"I would too! Andresen, Anderson, they're different."

"Still," Peggy said, "he's pretty cute."

Faye went home and locked herself in her room. Seriously considered, for the first time, having a boyfriend. Sat on her bed. Didn't sleep much. Cried a little. Decided by the next morning that, strangely, she actually cared for Henry a great deal. Had convinced herself that she'd always liked his looks. His sturdy linebacker physique. His quiet manner. Maybe she'd liked him all this time. At school he seemed different now—more pink, alive, handsome. What she didn't know was that Peggy had done the same thing to him. Harassed him all day with hints about a certain girl who liked him. Revealed later that it was Faye. He came to school that day and saw Faye and couldn't understand why he'd never noticed how beautiful she was. How elegant and simple. What fierce eyes hid behind those big round glasses.

They began dating shortly thereafter.

Love is like this, Faye thinks now. We love people because they love us. It's narcissistic. It's best to be perfectly clear about this and not let abstractions like *fate* and *destiny* muddle the issue. Peggy, after all, could have picked any boy in the school.

This is what's racing through her mind tonight on the riverbank, where Henry has brought her so he can, she believes, apologize. He's been timid ever since that night at the playground. The incident after the prom. They talk about it, but obliquely. They don't say anything specific. "I'm sorry about . . . you know," he says, and she feels bad for him, the way he slumps over when addressing the subject. He's been irritatingly contrite and penitent. Carrying her book bag home, walking a step behind her, head down, buying more flowers and candy. Sometimes, in fits of self-pity, he'll say things like "God I'm so stupid!" Or he'll ask her to go to the movies and before she can accept he'll say something like "If you still want be my girl, that is."

It's all arbitrary. Had Faye attended a different school. Had her parents moved away. Had Peggy been sick that day. Had she chosen a different boy. And on and on. A thousand permutations, a million possibilities, and almost all of them kept Faye from sitting here in the sand with Henry.

He is a cauldron of nerves tonight, clenching and unclenching his hands, picking at the dirt, throwing rocks into the water. She sips a Coca-Cola out of the bottle and waits. He had planned it this far, getting Faye alone, here, on the riverbank. Now he doesn't know what to do. He wobbles back and forth in the sand, swats at something in front of his face, sits there hard and tense like a nervous horse. It irritates her, his torment. She drinks her Coke.

The river smells of fish tonight—a damp and funky stench like spoiled milk and ammonia—and Faye thinks about this one time she was out with her father on his boat. He was showing her how to fish. This was important to him. He had grown up a fisherman. When he was a kid, that was his job. But she had no taste for it. She couldn't even hook the worm without crying—how it coiled around her finger and brown goo came spurting out as she pierced the skin.

Henry reminds her of that worm right now: ready to pop.

They stare at the river, and the blue flame of the nitrogen plant, the moon, the light breaking on the water and scattering. A bottle bobs ten yards out. A bug whizzes by her face. Waves come ashore in their rhythmic way, and the longer they sit here in silence the more it seems to Faye like the river is *breathing*—how it contracts and expands, rushes in and rushes out, water caressing rocks as it pulls away.

Finally Henry turns to her and speaks. "Hey, listen, I want to ask you something."

"Okay."

"But . . . I don't know if I can," he says. "If I can ask you this."

"Why not?" she says. And she looks at him, sees him and realizes she hasn't done that—actually *looked* at him—in how long? All night? She's been avoiding his eyes, embarrassed for him, hating him a little, and now she finds him grim and scowling.

"I want to . . . ," he says, but stops. He never finishes the sentence. Instead, he leans quickly into Faye and kisses her.

Kisses her *hard*.

Like he did that night at the playground, and it surprises her—the sudden taste of him, his warmth pressing into her, the oily smell of his hands now clutching her face. It's shocking, his forcefulness, pushing his mouth to hers, driving his tongue past her lips. He's kissing like it's *combat*. She falls back into the sand and he pushes himself onto her, over her, still seizing her face, kissing wildly. He isn't rough, exactly. But commanding. Her first impulse is to shrink away. He squeezes her, crushes his body into hers. Their front teeth knock together but he keeps going. She's never felt Henry so strongly and savagely *male*. She can't move under his weight, and now she feels other of her body's demands—her skin is cold, her belly full of cola, she needs to burp. Needs to wiggle out and run.

And just at that moment he stops, draws back a few inches, and looks at her. Henry, she sees now, is in agony. His face is screwed up in knots.

He's staring at her with big pleading desperate eyes. He's waiting for her to protest. Waiting for her to say *No*. And she's about to, but she catches herself. And this will be the moment, later on in the night, after everything's over, after Henry has driven her home, as she stays awake till dawn thinking about it, the thing that will confuse her most is this precise moment: when she had the chance to flee, but she did not.

She does not say *No*. She does not say anything at all. She simply meets Henry's gaze. Maybe—though she's not entirely sure of it—maybe she even nods: *Yes*.

And so Henry goes back at it, vigor renewed. Kissing her, tonguing her ear, biting her neck. He drives his hand down, between them, and she hears the undoings of various mechanisms—belt and buckle, zipper.

"Close your eyes," he says.

"Henry."

"Please. Close your eyes. Pretend you're asleep."

She looks at him again, his face inches away, eyes closed. He's consumed by something, some unutterable need. "Please," he says, and he takes her hand and guides it down. Faye pulls against him, weakly resisting until he says "Please" again and tugs harder and she lets her hand go limp, lets him do what he wants. He draws himself out of his slacks and guides her hand the rest of the way, between the folds of his pants, under his briefs. When she touches him, he leaps.

"Keep your eyes closed," he says.

And she does. She feels him move against her, feels him slide across her fingers. It's an abstract feeling, removed from the world of actual things. He's pressing his face to her neck and pumping his hips and, she realizes, he's crying, soft little whimpers, warm tears puddling where he's bearing into her.

"I'm sorry," he says.

And Faye feels like she should be mortified but mostly she feels pity. She feels bad for Henry, his despair and his guilt, the crude needs wrecking him, the hopeless way he's gone about it tonight. And so she pulls him closer and grips him tighter and suddenly, with a great shudder and a splash of warmth, it's all over.

Henry collapses, groans, falls into her, and cries.

"I'm sorry," he keeps saying.

His body is curled up against her, and in her hand, he's quickly shrink-

ing away. "I'm so sorry," he says. She tells him it's okay. Strokes his hair slowly, holds him as the sobs ripple through his body.

This cannot be what people mean when they talk about *fate* and *romance* and *destiny*. No, these things are ornaments, Faye decides, decorations hiding this one bleak fact: that Henry's master tonight was not love but rather catharsis, plain old animal release.

He whimpers into her chest. Her hand is sticky and cold. *True love,* she thinks. And she almost laughs.

7

THERE ARE TWO CONDITIONS, Margaret says, for dinner at the Schwingles. First, pick up a package at the pharmacy. And second, tell no one.

"What's in the package?" Faye says.

"Sweets," Margaret says. "Chocolates and stuff. Bonbons. My dad doesn't want me to have that kind of food. He says I need to watch my figure."

"You don't need to watch your figure."

"That's what I said! Don't you think that's unfair?"

"That is *so* unfair."

"Thank you," she says. She smoothes her skirt, a gesture that seems inherited from her mother. "So when you pick it up, can you pretend it's yours?"

"Sure. Of course."

"Thank you. I already paid for it. I placed the order in your name, so I wouldn't get yelled at."

"I understand," Faye says.

"The dinner is going to be a surprise for my dad. So when you see him at the pharmacy, tell him you're going on a date that night. With Henry. To throw him off the track."

"Okay, I will."

"Better yet, tell *everyone* you're going on a date that night."

"Everyone?"

"Yeah. Don't tell anyone you're coming over."

"All right."

"If people know you're coming over, my dad could find out and he'd suspect something. I know you wouldn't want to ruin the surprise."

"Of course not."

"If you tell anyone it will definitely get back to my dad. He's *very* well-connected. You haven't told anyone yet, have you?"

"No."

"Okay, good. Good. Just remember. Pick up the package at the pharmacy. And say you're going on a date with Henry."

The party would be unforgettable. Margaret has promised balloons, streamers, her mother's famous salmon aspic, a cake with three different layers, homemade vanilla ice cream, maybe afterward they would even take the convertible out for a nighttime joyride along the river. Faye feels so special to be singled out for the occasion.

"Thank you for inviting me," she tells Margaret, to which Margaret gently touches her shoulder and says, "I wouldn't have it any other way."

On the evening of the party, Faye is in her bedroom trying to decide between two versions of the same dress, a smart little summer dress—one green, one yellow. Both were purchased for special occasions that Faye can no longer remember. Probably church-related. She looks into the mirror and holds one up in front of her, then the other.

On her bed, spread out over the blankets and pillows, is paperwork from Chicago Circle. Documents and forms that will, once delivered, officially hold her seat in the freshman class of 1968. She'll need to put them in the mail within the next week to meet the deadline. She's already filled them out, in ink, in her neatest handwriting. Each night she's been spreading out the materials like this, the brochures and pamphlets, hoping something will speak to her, hoping to see something that will finally convince her to go or stay.

Each time she feels near a decision, some worry compels her in the opposite direction. She'll read another Ginsberg poem and think, *I'm going to Chicago.* She'll look at the brochures and read about the space-age campus and imagine being in a place where the students are roundly smart and serious and wouldn't look at her all funny when she aces another algebra test, and she'll think, *I'm definitely going to Chicago.* But then she'll imagine how everyone in town would react if she went, or, worse, if she came back, which is just about the most mortifying thing in the world, if she can't cut it at Circle and has to come back, then the whole town would be gossiping about her and rolling their collective eyes. She pictures this and thinks, *I'm staying in Iowa.*

And so it goes, this awful pendulum.

But she can make one decision, at least: the yellow dress. Yellow feels like the more celebratory color, she thinks, the more birthday-appropriate.

Downstairs she finds her mother watching the news. A story about student protesters, again. Another night, another university overrun. Students pack themselves into hallways and won't leave. They invade the office of the president and provost. They sleep there, right where people work.

She watches it on television, Faye's mother, gaping at the weird happenings in the world. On the couch she sits and stares, each night, at Walter Cronkite. The events lately have seemed otherworldly—sit-ins, riots, assassinations.

"The vast majority of college students are not militant," explains the reporter. He interviews a girl with pretty hair and a soft wool sweater who tells him how much all the other students disagree with the extremists. "We just want to go to class and get good grades and support our boys overseas," she says, smiling.

Cut to a shot, wide angle, of a hallway filled with students: bearded, long-haired, unkempt, shouting slogans, playing music.

"Good lord," says Faye's mother. "Look at them. They're like hoboes."

"I'm going out," Faye says.

"They probably started as nice boys," says her mother. "They probably took up with the wrong crowd."

"I have a date tonight."

Her mother looks at her finally. "Well. You look very nice."

"I'll be back by ten."

She passes through the kitchen, where her father is twisting off the top of the percolator. He's brewing coffee and fixing a sandwich in preparation for his ChemStar shift tonight.

"Bye, Dad," she says, and he gives her a quick wave. He's wearing his uniform, his gray jumpsuit with the ChemStar logo on the front, the interlocking C and S on the chest. She used to joke with him that if he removed the C he'd look like Superman. But they haven't joked like that in a long time.

She's opening the outside door when he stops her. "Faye," he says.

"Yeah?"

"The guys at the factory are asking about you."

Faye pauses in the doorway, one foot in the house and one foot out. She looks back at her dad. "They are? Why?"

"They're wondering about your scholarship," he says as the percolator's top clatters off. "They're asking when you're leaving for college."

"Oh."

"I thought we agreed not to tell anyone."

They stand there in silence for a moment, her father scooping spoonfuls of coffee grounds, Faye gripping the doorknob.

"It's not something you have to be ashamed of," she says. "Me getting into college, and getting a scholarship. That's not—what did you call it? Bragging?"

He stops fussing with the percolator then, and looks at her and smiles his tight smile. Puts his hands in his pockets.

"Faye," he says.

"That's just—I don't know what that is. *Doing a good job.* It's not bragging."

"Doing a good job. Right. Does everybody get this scholarship?"

"No, of course not."

"So you're special then. You're singled out."

"I had to work hard, get good grades."

"You had to be better than everyone else."

"Yes, I did."

"That's pride, Faye. Nobody is better than anyone else. Nobody is special."

"It's not pride, it's . . . reality. *I* got the best grades, *I* scored the highest marks. Me. It's an objective fact."

"Do you remember the story I told you about the house spirit? The *nisse?*"

"Yes."

"And the little girl who ate the *nisse's* meal?"

"I remember."

"She wasn't punished because she stole his food, Faye. She was punished because she thought she deserved it."

"You don't think I deserve to go to college?"

He chuckles and looks at the ceiling and shakes his head. "You know, most fathers have it easy. They teach their daughters to value hard work and a day's wage. Chase off the wrong boys and buy an encyclopedia set. But you? You complain if a book is a *poor translation.*"

"What's your point?"

"Everyone already thinks you're a big shot. You don't have to go to Chicago to prove it."

"That's *not* why I want to go."

"Trust me, Faye. It's a bad idea, leaving home. You should stay where you belong."

"You did it. You left Norway and moved here."

"So I know what I'm talking about."

"Do you think it was a mistake? Do you wish you'd stayed back there?"

"You don't understand anything."

"I *earned* this."

"What do you suppose is going to happen, Faye? Do you really believe that because you work hard the world is going to be kind to you? You think the world owes you something? Because the world isn't going to give you a damn thing." He turns around to attend to his coffee. "It doesn't matter how many straight-A report cards you have, or where you go to college. The world is cruel."

Faye is still angry about this as she drives to the pharmacy. Angry at her father's cynicism. Angry that what always earned her the most praise—being a good student—is now the thing that makes her a target. She feels double-crossed by this, betrayed by some implicit promise made to her long ago.

And she thinks maybe it's providence that she'll be seeing Mrs. Schwingle tonight. Because if there's anyone in this entire town who would not accuse Faye of being pretentious, it is Mrs. Schwingle, who brags about her world travels and worships whatever new thing the elegant ladies of the East Coast are doing. Certainly Mrs. Schwingle, of all people, could sympathize.

Faye arrives at the pharmacy and walks up to the counter, where she finds Harold Schwingle standing with a clipboard counting aspirin jars.

"Hi, Dr. Schwingle," she says.

He considers her sternly and coldly for what seems like an oddly long moment. He is tall and wide, his hair cut high and tight with military precision.

"I'm here to pick up my package," Faye says.

"Yes, I suppose you are." He leaves and remains somewhere in the back room for what seems like far too long. Over the tinny speakers a brass band plays a waltz. The automated air freshener releases a small *poosh* and a few seconds later there's the cloying, perfumey odor of synthesized lilacs. There is nobody else in the pharmacy. The overhead lights flicker and buzz. On the counter, buttons for Richard Nixon's presidential campaign stare woodenly back at her.

When Dr. Schwingle returns he's carrying a dark brown paper bag, stapled shut. He drops it—and not particularly gently—on his side of the counter, too far away for Faye to comfortably reach it.

"Is this for you?" he says.

"Yes, sir."

"Will you swear to that, Faye? You're not buying this for someone else, are you?"

"Oh, no sir, it's for me."

"You can tell me if it's for someone else. Be honest."

"Cross my heart, Dr. Schwingle. This is mine."

And he breathes in a dramatic way that reads as exasperation, maybe disappointment.

"You're a good girl, Faye. What happened?"

"I'm sorry?"

"Faye," he says, "I know what this is. And I think you should reconsider."

"Reconsider?"

"Yes. I'm going to sell this to you because it's my duty. But it's also my duty, my moral duty, to tell you I think it's a mistake."

"That's very nice of you but—"

"A *big* mistake."

She was not prepared for the intensity of this conversation. "I'm sorry," she says, though she doesn't know what she's apologizing for.

"I always thought you were so responsible," he says. "Does Henry know?"

"Of course," she says. "I have a date with him tonight."

"Do you?"

"Yes," she says, as instructed. "We're going out tonight."

"Has he proposed to you?"

"What?"

"If he were a gentleman he would have proposed to you by now."

And Faye feels defensive under his criticism. What comes out sounds hollow. "All in good time?"

"You really need to think about what you're doing, Faye."

"Okay. Thanks very much," she says, and she leans over the counter and closes her fist around the brown paper bag with a loud, poignant crunch. She doesn't know what's happening here, but she wants it to be over. "Goodbye."

She drives quickly to the Schwingle house, a grand thing that sits on a rocky bluff overlooking the Mississippi River, a rare point of elevation in the otherwise gentle rolling flatness of the prairie. Faye drives up through the trees to the house, which she finds unexpectedly dark. The lights are off and everything is silent. Faye panics. Did she get the date wrong? Were they meeting somewhere else first? She's considering driving back home and calling Margaret when the front door opens and out she walks, Margaret Schwingle, in sweatpants and a baggy T-shirt, hair disheveled in a way Faye has never seen before, scooped to one side like she's been sleeping on it.

"Do you have the package?" she asks.

"Yes." Faye gives her the crinkly brown bag.

"Thanks."

"Margaret? Is everything okay?"

"I'm sorry," she says. "We can't have dinner tonight."

"Okay."

"You have to go home now."

"Are you sure you're all right?"

Margaret is staring at her feet, not looking at Faye. "I'm really sorry. For everything."

"I don't understand."

"Listen," she says, and now she looks at Faye for the first time. She stands up straight and points her chin out, trying to look tough. "Nobody saw you come here tonight."

"I know."

"Remember that. You can't prove you were here."

Then Margaret nods to Faye and spins on her heel and leaves, locking the door behind her.

8

IN 1968, in Faye's small Iowa river town, the girls of the graduating class knew—though they never spoke of it—dozens of ways to get rid of unplanned, unwanted, unborn children. Some of these methods were almost always unsuccessful; some were nothing more than old wives' tales; some required advanced medical training; some were too horrible to think about.

The most attractive were of course those that could be done innocently, without any special chemical or apparatus. Long-distance bicycling. Jumping from a great height. Alternating hot and cold baths. Placing a candle on the abdomen and letting it burn all the way down. Standing on one's head. Falling down stairs. Punching oneself repeatedly in the belly.

When these failed—and they almost always did fail—the girls moved on to new techniques, remedies that wouldn't arouse suspicion. Simple, over-the-counter things. Douching with Coca-Cola, for example. Or Lysol. Or iodide. Ingesting incredibly high quantities of vitamin C. Or iron tablets. Filling the uterus with saline solution, or a mixture of water and Kirkman Borax Soap. Eating uterine stimulants like julep. Or croton oil. Calomel. Senna. Rhubarb. Magnesium sulfate. Herbs that initiated or increased menstrual flow, such as parsley. Or chamomile. Ginger.

Quinine was also effective, according to many grandmothers.

And brewer's yeast. Mugwort. Castor oil. Lye.

Then there were those other methods, those things that none but the most desperate would ever consider. Bicycle pump. Vacuum cleaner. Knitting needle. Umbrella rib. Goose quill. Cathartic tube. Turpentine. Kerosene. Bleach.

None but the most desperate, the most alone and unconnected, those who had no friends with medical access who might procure certain behind-the-counter items. Methergine. Synthetic estrogens. Pituitary extract. Abortifacient ergot preparations. Strychnine. Suppositories known in some quarters as Black Beauties. Glycerin applied via catheter. Ergotrate, which makes the uterus stiffen and contract. Certain medicines used by cow breeders to regulate animal cycles—difficult to acquire, polysyllabic: dinoprostone, misoprostol, gemeprost, methotrexate.

What was in that paper bag? Almost certainly not small chocolate bonbon things, Faye decides as she drives home, rounds the corner into Vista Hills, regrets that she did not open the bag. Why didn't she open it?

Because it was *stapled,* she thinks.

Because you're a *coward,* another part of her thinks.

She has an abstract feeling of panic and distress right now. How strangely Margaret had acted tonight. Dr. Schwingle too. A feeling like there's something she's missing, some essential fact whose revelation she dreads. The air is misty, the sky not raining so much as lightly spitting, a humidity like when the girls boil things in home ec. Once, one of the girls forgot her pot and left it there to burn all day and the water boiled out and the pot got scorched and red-hot and its plastic handle melted and then outright burned. It set off all the alarms.

Tonight has that same quality to it. Like there's something very close and dangerous and alarming that Faye has not yet noticed.

She's sure of this when she arrives home. Only one light is on in the house—the kitchen light. There's something wrong with that one lonely light. From outside it looks almost green, like the color of cabbage once you cut way down deep into it.

Her parents are there, in the kitchen, waiting for her. Her mother cannot look at her. Her father says, "What have you *done?*"

"What do you mean?"

He says they got a phone call from Harold Schwingle, who said Faye had been in the store tonight to pick up a package. What kind of package? *Well, let me tell you,* said Dr. Schwingle, *I've been in this business long enough to know that any girl buying the things Faye bought tonight is only trying to do one thing.*

"What?" Faye asks.

"Why didn't you tell us?" says her mother.

"Tell you *what?*"

"That you're knocked up," says her father.

"What?"

"I cannot believe you let that idiot farmer boy shame you like this," he says. "And shame *us,* Faye."

"But he didn't! There's been a mistake."

The phone had been ringing all night. Calls from the Petersons. And the Watsons. And the Carltons. And the Wisors. And the Krolls. All of them saying, *You should know, Frank, what I heard about your daughter.*

How on earth did everyone know this? How does the whole town already know?

"But it's *not true,*" Faye says.

And she wants to explain to them about the birthday party that never happened, and about Margaret's strange behavior tonight. She wants to explain what she immediately understands is the truth: that Margaret is pregnant and needs certain drugs without her father knowing, so she used Faye to get them. She wants to say all this but she can't, first because her father is now in a blind rage about how she's *ruined her reputation* and how *she can't show her face here ever again* and how *god will punish her* for what she wants to do to *her own child*—yelling more words at her right now than he's spoken to her in the last year—and also because she feels an attack coming on. Coming on strong now because she's having trouble breathing and she's sweating and her field of vision is beginning to narrow. Soon it will be like looking at the world through a pinhole. And she's fighting off the feeling that this is the Big One, the really big seizure that finally kills her; she's fighting the sense that these are the last breaths she will ever take.

"Help me," she tries to say, but it comes out a whisper, inaudible above her father, who's now telling her how many years he's worked to gain a good reputation in this town and how she's ruined it all in one night, how he's never going to forgive her for what she's done to him.

For how much she's hurt him.

And she thinks: Hang on.

She thinks: Hurt *him*?

Because even though she's not pregnant, if she were pregnant, wouldn't *she* be the one needing comfort? Wouldn't *she* be the one the neighbors were talking about? How is this about *him*? And she feels suddenly defiant, suddenly uninterested in defending herself anymore. And when her father reaches the end of his lecture and says "What do you have to say for yourself?," she stands up as vertically and nobly as she can manage and says: "I'm leaving."

Her mother looks at her now for the first time.

"I'm going to Chicago," Faye says.

Her father stares hard at her for a moment. He seems like a twisted version of himself, the expression on his face like when he was building that bomb shelter in the basement, that same determination, that same dread.

She remembers once he had come up from the basement, his clothes powdered gray from whatever construction was happening down there that night, and Faye had just taken a bath and she was so happy to see him that she broke free from the mass of towels her mother used to dry her and she bolted out the door, happy, bright, bounding like a rubber ball. She was wiry, sinewy, she had just bathed, she was nude, she was eight. Her dad stood in this very kitchen and she burst in and did a cartwheel, that's how happy she was. A *cartwheel,* oh lord, imagine it now, at the cartwheel's middle, spread open like some giant tropical plant. What a thing for her father to see. He frowned and said "I think this is inappropriate. Why don't you put on some clothes," and she ran to her room not quite knowing what she'd done wrong. Inappropriate *for whom,* she wondered as she stood naked looking at the neighborhood through her big picture window upstairs. She didn't know why her father had sent her here, why she was inappropriate, and she looked out her window and perhaps thought about her body for the first time. Or maybe she thought for the first time of her body as a thing *separate from her.* And who cares if she imagined a boy walking by and spotting her? Who cares if this image would continue to interest her for reasons that would never be entirely clear? From that moment, there was no other purpose to Faye's big picture window than to imagine what she looked like through it.

That was many years ago. Faye and her father never talked about this. Time heals many things because it sets us on trajectories that make the past seem impossible.

And now Faye is back in the kitchen, and she's waiting for her father to say something, and it's like the space that opened between them that day has reached its apogee. They are two bodies orbiting each other, connected by the thinnest tether. They will either drift back together now or fling themselves forever apart.

"Did you hear me?" Faye asks. "I said I'm going to Chicago."

And now Frank Andresen finally speaks, and when he does there is just nothing in his voice, no emotion, no feeling. He's dislodged himself from the moment.

"Damn right you are," he says, and he turns away from her. "Leave and never come back."

| PART FIVE |

A BODY FOR EACH OF US

Summer 2011

"HELLO? Hello?"

"Yes? Hello?"

"Hello? Samuel? Can you hear me?"

"Barely. Where are you?"

"It's me, Periwinkle! Are you there?"

"What's that noise?"

"I'm in a parade!"

"Why are you calling me from a parade?"

"I'm not really in the parade! More like walking directly behind it! I'm calling about your e-mail! I read your e-mail!"

"Is there a tuba right next to your head?"

"What?"

"That noise!"

"So I wanted to call and say I read the—" Sudden silence on the line, a muffled indistinct digital gibberish, signal coming into and out of strength, a robotic garble, the sound all compressed and Dopplerized. Then: "—is what we expected, more or less. Can you do that for me?"

"I missed literally everything you said."

"What?"

"You're cutting out! I can't hear you!"

"It's Periwinkle, goddammit!"

"I know that. Where are you?"

"Disney World!"

"It sounds like you're in the middle of a marching band."

"One second!"

Seashell-like whooshing sounds, friction noises as a thumb or the wind passes over the microphone, abstract musical whooping, then a diminishment, as if Periwinkle were suddenly encased in a thick lead box.

"How's that? Can you hear me?"

"Yes, thank you."

"Cell coverage seems bad at the moment. Bandwidth problems, I'm guessing."

"Why are you at Disney World?"

"For Molly Miller. We're promoting her new video. Cross-promo'd with the reissue of a classic Disney animated film, now digitally remastered and in 3-D. I think it might be *Bambi*? All the parents are filming the parade with their phones and texting their friends. I think it's jamming the cell towers. Have you ever been to Disney World?"

"No."

"I've never seen a place so utterly committed to dead technology. Animatronics *everywhere*. Automatons with their wooden parts clacking together. I guess it's quaint?"

"Is the parade over?"

"No, I ducked into a store. Ye Olde Soda Shoppe, it says. I'm in this facsimile of Main Street USA. This charming little street that multinationals like Disney helped annihilate in the real world. Nobody here seems to mind the irony, though."

"I am having trouble imagining you enjoying things like roller coasters. Or children."

"Every ride, it's the same conceit: agonizingly slow boat trip through robot wonderland. Like that ride It's a Small World, which by the way is just a horror of narcotized puppets doing the same rote tasks over and over in what I'm sure Disney totally did not intend to be an accurate and prescient vision of third world labor."

"I believe that ride is supposed to be about international unity and global peace."

"Uh-huh. The Norway ride at Epcot was like floating through a life-size pamphlet for the oil and natural gas industries. And there's this one ride called the Carousel of Progress. Heard of it?"

"No."

"Originally made for the 1964 World's Fair. Animatronic theater. A guy and his family. The first act is in 1904 and the guy marvels at all the recent inventions: gas lamps, irons, washing cranks. The amazing stereoscope. The incredible gramophone. You get the idea? The wife says it now only takes her five hours to do the laundry and we all laugh."

"They think they have it easy, but we know better."

"Right. Between each act they sing this terrible song that is so catchy in a uniquely Disney way."

"Sing it."

"No. But the chorus goes like 'It's a great big beautiful tomor-roooooow.'"

"Okay, don't sing it."

"Song about unending progress. Been stuck in my head nonstop and I think at this point I'd lobotomize myself to remove it. Anyway, they move on to the twenties in the second act. The age of electricity. Sewing machines. Toasters. Waffle irons. Icebox. Fan. Radio. Third act is in the forties. There's a dishwasher now. And a big refrigerator. You see where this is going."

"Technology keeps making everyone's life better and easier. Unstoppable forward movement."

"Yeah. What an adorable mid-sixties conceit that was, eh? *Everything is going to improve.* Hah. I swear to god, me being at Disney World is like Darwin being at Galápagos. And by the way, the employees of the soda fountain have been smiling at me like maniacs this entire time. There must be a rule, a smiling-at-the-customer rule. Even when I'm on the phone and"—*yelling now*—"OBVIOUSLY NOT INTERESTED IN A CREAM SODA!"

"You said you read my e-mail? I didn't hear anything you said after that."

"They are smiling like drunk children. Like gnomes on Ecstasy. It must take an enormous act of willpower to do that every day. And yes, I did read your e-mail, your description of the mother-in-high-school material. Read it on the plane."

"And?"

"I couldn't help but notice that there's very little information about throwing fucking rocks at Governor fucking Packer."

"I'm getting to that."

"Zero information, in fact. Absolutely fucking nothing, would be my rough estimate."

"That comes later. I have to set it up."

"Set it up. How many hundreds of pages will that take, exactly?"

"I'm going where the story is."

"You agreed to deliver a book that told your mother's story while also ripping her to shreds, rhetorically."

"Yes, I know."

"It's the 'ripping her to shreds' part I'm worried about right now.

Because *Son of Packer Attacker Defends His Mom* might be persuasive in a few quarters, but *Packer Attacker Gets Eviscerated by Own Flesh and Blood* has serious appeal."

"I'm trying to tell the truth."

"Plus it's a little coming-of-agey."

"You didn't like it much, did you."

"Slipped into some familiar coming-of-age conventions, is all I'm saying. Also what's the big message here? What's the life lesson?"

"What do you mean?"

"It's no secret that most memoirs are really self-help books in disguise. So what's your book going to help people do better? What is it going to teach?"

"I have not thought about that for even one second."

"How about, for your life lesson: *Vote Republican.*"

"No. That is not at all what I'm writing about. Not in the same galaxy."

"Listen to Mister Artist Guy all of a sudden. Look. In today's market, most readers want books with accessible, linear narratives that rely on big concepts and easy life lessons. The life lessons in your mother's story are, to put it kindly, *diffused.*"

"What's the big life lesson in Molly Miller's book?"

"Simple: *Life Is Great!*"

"Well, that's pretty easy for her to say. Born into money. Prep schools on the Upper East Side. Billionaire at twenty-two."

"You'd be amazed at the facts people are willing to set aside to believe that life is, indeed, great."

"Life is hardly great."

"And this is why we need Molly Miller. The country is falling apart around us. This is plain even to the pay-no-attention-at-all crowd, even to the low-information undecided-voter segment. It's all crumbling right in front of our eyes. People lose their jobs, their pensions disappear overnight, they keep getting those quarterly statements showing their retirement funds are worth ten percent less for the sixth quarter in a row, and their houses are worth half what they paid for them, and their bosses can't get a loan to make payroll, and Washington is a circus, and they have homes full of interesting technology and they look at their smartphones and wonder 'How could a world that produces something as amazing as this be such a shitty world?' This is what they wonder. We've done studies on this. What was my point?"

"About Molly Miller, life being great."

"Here's how desperate people are for good news. *Rolling Stone* wanted an interview with Molly. But because they were reporting on her writing and not her music, they said they wanted it more 'real.' A more real interview, to reflect the more real memoir, I guess? Setting aside for a moment that the memoir itself was focus-grouped and ghostwritten? And that the 'more real' *Rolling Stone* interview would be staged from the get-go? What they wanted wasn't reality, per se, but a simulation that felt closer to reality than their usual simulations. But whatever. We brainstormed and spitballed and one of our junior publicists, this recent Yale grad who is going places let me tell you, he has this dazzling idea. He says let's have them watch her make pasta at home. Brilliant, right?"

"I'm guessing there's a special reason it was pasta."

"It focus-tests better than meat. Steak and chicken have too much baggage these days. Was it free-range? Antibiotic-free? Cruelty-free? Organic? Kosher? Did the farmer wear silken gloves to caress it to sleep every night while singing gentle lullabies? You can't order a fucking hamburger anymore without embracing some kind of political platform. Pasta is still pretty neutral, unobjectionable. And of course we'd never show anyone what she really actually eats."

"Why? What does she eat?"

"Steamed cabbage and mushroom broth, mostly. A reporter sees that and it becomes a different kind of story altogether. How the poor teen idol is starving herself to death. Then we get dragged into the whole body-image debate, which no one ever scored any mass public points arguing either side of, ever."

"I don't think I really want to read about Molly Miller making pasta."

"In the face of national calamity and utter annihilation of their personal prospects, people generally go in one of two directions. We have reams of paper showing this. They either get righteously indignant and hyperaware, in which case they'll usually begin posting libertarian screeds on iFeel or something, or they'll sink into a somewhat comfortable ignorance, in which case Molly Miller warming up marinara *out of a jar* is pleasantly and weirdly diverting."

"You're making it sound like a public service."

"There is no creature more arrogant than a self-righteous libertarian on the web, am I right? Those folks are just *intolerable.* And yes, it *is* a public service. You want to know my secret hope for your book?"

"Sure."

"That it's the one to replace Molly's on the best-seller list. You know why?"

"I find that wildly improbable."

"Because there are very few products that appeal to those two groups of people: the angry *and* the ignorant. Very few products can make that jump."

"But my mom's story—"

"We've tested this. Your mom has *huge crossover appeal.* This is rare and usually unpredictable, the thing that pops out of culture and becomes universal. Everyone sees what they want to see in your mom, everyone gets to be offended in their own special way. Your mother's story allows people of any political stripe to say 'Shame on you,' which is just delicious these days. It's no secret that the great American pastime is no longer baseball. Now it's sanctimony."

"I'll be sure to work on that."

"Remember, less empathy, more carnage. That's advice, me to you. And by the way? Those ghostwriters we used for Molly's book? They're available. I have them on retainer, should you need assistance writing your book."

"No thank you."

"They are seriously professional and discreet."

"I can write the book myself."

"I'm sure you would *like* to write the book yourself, but your record is not what I might call promising, book-finishing-wise."

"This time is different."

"I'm not judging you, simply pointing out certain historical facts. Speaking of which? All these years, I have never asked: Why couldn't you finish your first book?"

"It's not that I *couldn't* finish it—"

"I'm curious. What happened? Did I not send enough letters of encouragement and praise? Did you lose your inspiration? Did your ambition buckle under the weight of expectations? Were you—what do they call it—*blocked?*"

"None of those things, really. I just made a few bad decisions."

"A few bad decisions. That's how people explain a hangover."

"There were some poor choices made, on my part."

"That is a pretty blithe way of explaining your total failure to become a famous writer."

"You know, I'd always wanted to be a famous writer. I thought being a famous writer would help me solve certain problems. And then suddenly I was a famous writer and the problems weren't solved at all."

"Certain problems?"

"Let's just say there was a girl involved."

"Oh lord, I'm sorry I asked."

"A girl I very much wanted to make a big impression on."

"Let me guess. You became a writer to impress a girl. And then you didn't get the girl."

"Yes."

"This happens, not surprisingly, all the time."

"I keep thinking I could have gotten it right. I could have gotten the girl. I just needed to do things a little differently. I just needed to make some better choices."

YOU CAN GET THE GIRL!

A Choose Your Own Adventure Story

This is no ordinary story. In this story, the outcome depends on the decisions you make. Think carefully about your choices, as they will affect how the story ends.

You are a timid and shy and hopeless young man who for some reason wants to be a novelist.

A really important one. Like a really big deal. Award-winning, even. You think that the way to fix the problem of your life is to become a famous author. But how?

Turns out, it's easy. You don't know it, but you already have all the qualities you will need. Everything is already in motion.

First, and this is essential: *You feel hopelessly, irredeemably unloved.*

You feel abandoned and unappreciated by the people in your life.

Especially women.

Especially your mother.

Your mother and a certain girl you become obsessed with in childhood, a girl who makes you feel all woozy and manic and fuzzy-headed and disconsolate. Her name is Bethany, and she does to you roughly what fire does to a log.

Her family moves to the East Coast shortly after your mother abandons you. These events are not related, but they feel connected in your head, the great pivot point of your life, that month in early autumn when your childhood cracks in two. When she leaves, Bethany promises she will write, and she does: Every year, once a year, on your birthday, you get a letter from Bethany. And you read it and write back immediately, write like a maniac until three o'clock in the morning, draft after failed draft, trying to achieve exactly the perfect letter to send back to her. Then for a month afterward your mailbox-checking is obsessive-compulsive. But nothing comes, not for another year, when on your birthday another letter from Bethany arrives, full of updates. She is living in D.C. now. She is still playing the violin. She is taking lessons from all the best people. They say she has great promise. Her brother is going to a military boarding school. He loves it. Her father spends most of his time in their Manhattan apartment now. The trees are blooming. Bishop says hi. School is nice.

And you are despondent about the neutral and cold tone of the letter until you reach the end, where she's signed it:

> *Love you,*
> *Bethany*

She does not sign it "With love" or "All my love" or any of the things one can say without really meaning them. Bethany writes "Love you," and these two words sustain you for a whole year. Because why would she say "Love you" unless she really loves you? Why wouldn't she use one of those sign-offs everyone else uses? *All best. Be well. Yours sincerely.*

No, she says "Love you."

But of course there is the problem of the letter itself, which is so impersonal and safe and harmless and devoid of romance or love. How to explain this dissonance?

You decide that her parents are reading the letters.

They are monitoring her communication with you. Because even though you were never formally implicated in any of it, you were best friends with Bethany's brother during a time when Bishop was doing some pretty fucked-up shit to the headmaster of his school. And so her parents probably do not approve of you, nor of their daughter's love for you. Thus, the only place she can sneak that message past the censors is in the valediction, where she writes, crucially, "Love you."

When you write back, you assume the letter will be inspected. So you tell Bethany about the bland details of your life while also trying to hint at your enormous love for her. You imagine she can sense your love at the edges of the letter, hovering ghostlike over the words, barely beyond her parents' comprehension. And of course at the end of the letter you sign it "Love you too" just to show her that you got the message—the *real* message—of her letter. And this is how the two of you communicate, like spies during wartime, sending a single meaningful fact obscured in a cloud of banality.

Then you wait a year for another letter.

And in the meantime you count the days until you both graduate high school and go to college and, no longer under her parents' scrutiny, she will be free to express her real, true, deep feelings. And during this time you entertain fantasies of attending the same college she does and becoming campus sweethearts and how awesome it would be to attend parties with Bethany on your arm, how much instant credibility you'd have being the guy dating the violin prodigy, the beautiful violin prodigy (no, gorgeous, actually, *stunning,* and you know this because she occasionally sends a new picture of herself and her brother in the annual letter, where on the back of the picture she writes "Miss you! B&B" and you put the photo on your nightstand and during the first week with the new photo you barely sleep because you wake up hourly having these weird nightmares where the photo is blowing away or disintegrating or someone is sneaking into your bedroom to steal the photo or something). And you seriously believe you'll be attending the same college all the way up until Bethany gets into Juilliard, and you tell your father you want to go to Juilliard, and your father raises an eyebrow and says "Yeah, okay" in a really dismissive manner that you don't understand until you find a brochure for Juilliard at your high-school guidance office and discover that Juilliard is pretty much only for people in music, theater, and dance. Plus tuition is like ten times your father's stated budget.

So, shit.

You revise the plan and tell your father you are not going to Juilliard but instead somewhere in New York City.

"Maybe Columbia," you say, because that campus looked very close to Juilliard on the map of New York you found in the high-school library. "Or NYU?"

Henry, who at that moment is testing the consistency of a

new-concept "quiche" frozen dinner by swishing the eggy liquid batter around in his mouth and making notes on a fifteen-step flowchart, stops for a moment, swallows, looks at you, and says, "Too dangerous."

"Oh come on."

"New York City is the murder capital of the world. No way."

"It's not dangerous. Or if it is, at least the campus isn't dangerous. I'll stay on campus."

"Listen. How do I say this? You live on Oakdale Lane. There isn't a single Oakdale Lane in New York City. It is nothing at all like this. You will be eaten alive."

"There are lanes in New York," you say. "I'll be fine."

"You're not catching my symbolism. See? This is exactly my point. There are people from the *Street*. And, other side of the spectrum? There are people like us, from *Lanes*."

"Stop it, Dad."

"Besides," he says, returning to his quiche, "it's way too expensive. We can afford public, in-state. That's it."

Which is where you end up, and where you discover this thing called *e-mail*, which all the students use now, and in your next letter from Bethany she gives you her e-mail address and you send her an e-mail and after that the paper letters stop forever. The upside here is that you and Bethany can write each other much more often, even weekly now. E-mail is so immediate. This seems great until about a month in, when you realize the downside is the lack of any physical object, any actual thing that Bethany has touched, which in your teenage years often soothed you, holding the thick paper she used, covered with her neat cursive—Bethany was a thousand miles away but this thing could fill in for her. You could close your eyes and hold the letter and almost feel her touches on the paper, her fingers running across each page, her tongue licking the envelope. It was an act of imagination and faith, a Christlike transubstantiation, this thing becoming, for a moment, in your mind, a body. Her body. Which is why after the e-mails start and you write each other all the time, you feel more lonely than ever. Her physical embodiment has disappeared.

As has the "Love you."

At college, at Juilliard, the "Love you" at the end of her corre-spondence switches quickly to "Love ya," which stings. "Love ya" seems to be what happens to real love when its formality and dig-nity are amputated.

The other problem is that despite the fact that Bethany is no longer under her parents' rule, her letters do not substantially change. The best way to describe their tone is *informational*. Like a guide on a campus tour. Given the chance to finally express her true feelings, Bethany falls back into the familiar patterns, giv-ing updates, sharing news. It is like, after nine years of writing this way, she has written herself into a rut. It is so familiar it becomes the only way she can converse. And no matter how much news you get—that some classes are easy (like Ear Training) and some classes are hard (like Diatonic Harmony), that the cellist in her chamber group is really talented, that dorm food is bad, that her roommate is a percussionist from California who gives herself regular migraines from cymbal practice—there is a quality to this information that seems to lack warmth or humanity. It lacks inti-macy. It is romanceless.

And then Bethany starts telling you about boys. Flirty boys. Brash boys at parties who make her laugh so hard she spills her drink. Boys, usually brass players, usually trombonists, who ask her out on dates. Further, she says yes. Further, the dates are *fun*. And you boil inside your skin that you've been pining for this woman for nine years and suddenly these guys, these *strang-ers*, have more success with her in one night than you've had your whole life. It's unjust. You deserve better, after what you've been through. This is about the time that "Love you" turns to "Love ya," which then turns to "Love," which eventually becomes "xoxo," and by then you realize that something fundamental has shifted in the nature of your relationship. Somewhere along the way, you missed your chance.

This is, incidentally, an essential step in becoming a famous writer. This failure. It gives you a rich inner life, fantasizing about all the ways you might not have screwed it up, and all the ways to win Bethany back. Top of the list: Beat the trombone boys. Method: Writing deep and pseudo-intellectual and artsy and important literary fiction. Because you are not a person who can make Bethany laugh until she spills her drink. You cannot compete with the trombone boys on this front. Because you always become deadly serious and formal when you think about her or write to her. It's like a religious response, becoming solemn and official in the face of that which could annihilate you. When it comes to Bethany, you are utterly without humor.

And so you write humorless stories about Big Social Issues and you congratulate yourself because the funny trombone boys wouldn't touch Big Social Issues with a ten-foot pole. ("Ten-foot pole" being a cliché that the trombone boys would use unthinkingly but you, as an artist who does all things originally, would not.) You believe that the point of being a writer is to show Bethany how much more unique and special you are than the same-feeling, same-doing masses. You believe that becoming a writer is the life equivalent of wearing the most creative and interesting Halloween costume at the party. When you decide to become a writer—this is in your early twenties, when you do that really important-seeming thing where you go to grad school to study "Writing, Creative"—you throw yourself into the lifestyle: You go to artsy readings; hang out in coffee shops; wear black; build a whole dark melancholic wardrobe that might best be described as postapocalyptic/postholocaust; drink alcohol, often late into the night; buy journals, leather-bound; pens, heavy and metal, never ballpoint, never clicky; and cigarettes, first the normal kind, the brands that everyone buys at the gas station, then fancy European numbers that come in long flat boxes that you can find only at special tobacco stores and head shops. The cigarettes give you something to do when you are out in public and feel like you're being examined and appraised and judged. They serve the same function the smartphone will in about fifteen years: a kind of social shield, something to pull out of your pocket and fiddle with when you feel awkward about yourself. Which you feel pretty much all the time, and for which you blame your mother.

You never write about this, of course. You typically avoid all introspection. There are things inside you that you prefer to ignore. There is a molten mass of anguish and self-pity way deep inside you and you keep it pressed down there by never looking at it or acknowledging it. When you write, you don't write about yourself. Instead, you write dark and heavy and violent stories that get you the reputation that maybe you have secrets. Maybe some really brutal shit went down in your past. You write a story about an abusive alcoholic plastic surgeon who gets drunk every night and rapes his teenage daughter in unimaginably cruel ways, a horror that continues through most of her high-school years until one day the girl comes up with a plan to murder dad by slipping huge amounts of botulinum toxin pilfered from his Botox stores into the maraschino cherry supply, so that after several old-fashioneds the father is reduced to total paralysis, whereby the daughter invites this brutal gay psychopath she met under shadowy circumstances to rape the father repeatedly while the father is totally conscious to experience all of it, and then after getting his proper comeuppance he is killed when the daughter cuts off his genitalia and allows him to bleed to death slowly over a period of seven days down in the basement where no one can hear him scream.

In other words, you write stories that have *nothing to do with your life or really anything you know anything about.*

And while you write these stories, all you care about is what Bethany will think reading them. The stories are really just a large ongoing performance that has a single goal: To get Bethany to feel certain things about you. To make her believe you are talented, artsy, brilliant, deep. To make her love you again.

The paradox here is that you never show her any of these stories.

Because even though you hang out with the writing crowd and take the writing classes and dress like a writer and smoke like a writer, ultimately you have to recognize that your writing *isn't very good.* It earns a lukewarm reception in classes, unenthusiastic feedback from teachers, loads of anonymous form rejections from the editors you query. The worst is when a teacher asks in an unusually intense office-hours visit, "Why do you want to be a writer?"

The subtext here being, of course, maybe you shouldn't.

"I've always wanted to be a writer" is your pat response. An answer that is not altogether true. You didn't *always* want to be a writer but rather wanted to be a writer ever since your mother abandoned you, at age eleven, and because life before that feels like an altogether different person's life, it might as well have been *always*. You were, essentially, reborn on that day.

This is not something you tell your teacher. This is something you carry on the inside, in a cavity filled with every true thing about you so that there is nothing true left on the outside. The morning your mother disappeared, especially, is stuffed way down deep, your mother asking you what you wanted to be when you grew up. And you said a novelist, and she smiled and kissed your forehead and said she'd be reading whatever you wrote. And so becoming a writer was the only communication you'd have with your mother, a one-way communication, like prayer. And you thought if you wrote something really great that she'd read it and, by some strange calculus, it would prove to her that she should never have left.

Problem is, you can't write anything near this level of quality. Not even close. Despite all the training, there is an elusive element missing.

"Truth," suggests your teacher in the end-of-year meeting, when you are called into the office because you have one more story to write before graduation and so your teacher wants to impress upon you in a last-ditch way that you absolutely have to "write something that's true."

"But I write fiction," you say.

"I don't care what you call it," the teacher says. "Just write something true."

So you write about one of the only true things that ever happened to you. A story about a pair of twins living in the Chicago suburbs. The sister is a violin prodigy. The brother is a troublemaker. They sit tensely at the dinner table under the imperious gaze of their stockbroker father, then are released into the night where they have adventures, among them the slow poisoning of the Jacuzzi belonging to their neighbor, the headmaster of their elite private school. The manner of poisoning is simple: pesticide overdose. But the explanation? Why does the brother want to poison the headmaster? What has the headmaster done to deserve it?

This one is easy to answer, but difficult to write.

It all clicked a few years ago. You finally connected the dots you were unable to connect when you were eleven. Why Bishop seemed to know things beyond his years. Sexual things. Like at the pond that final afternoon together when he pressed himself into you in exactly the correct position for sex—how did he know that? How did he know to do that? How did he know to seduce the principal to avoid a paddling? Where did he get all that pornography, all those creepy Polaroids? Why was he acting out? Becoming a bully? Getting expelled from school? Killing small animals? Poisoning the headmaster?

The moment you grasped this and suddenly understood it you were in high school, walking to school one morning, and you weren't even thinking about Bishop or the headmaster or any of it when suddenly it came to you all at once, like in a vision, like your mind had been putting it together all this time beneath the surface: Bishop was being abused. Molested. Of course he was. And the headmaster was doing it.

And the guilt washed over you so hard you staggered. You sat down right in someone's front yard, dizzy, dumbfounded, astonished, and missed the first three periods of school. You felt like you'd broken open right there on the lawn.

Why hadn't you seen it? You'd been so wrapped up in your little dramas—your crush on Bethany, buying her a gift at the mall, which at the time seemed like the biggest problem in the world—so wrapped up that you didn't see this tragedy happening right in front of you. It was an immense failure of perception and empathy.

Which is maybe why you decide finally to write about it. In your story about the twins, you describe how the brother is being abused by the headmaster. You don't tiptoe around it; you don't evade it. You write it the way you think it happened. You write it true.

Your classmates are, predictably, bored with it. They are by this time weary of you and your subject matter. Yet another child-abuse story, they say. Seen it before. Move on. But your teacher is unusually enthusiastic. He says there is a different quality to this story, a measure of humanity and generosity and warmth and *feeling* that was missing from your earlier efforts. Then, during another private chat, the teacher mentions that a bigwig New York publishing guy named Periwinkle has been asking around, trying to find new young talent, and could he, the teacher, send him this story?

This is the final step in becoming a famous writer. This is the final step in fulfilling the ambition you've had since your mother walked out: impressing her from afar, winning her approval and praise. And this is the last thing you need to do to get Bethany to notice you again, to see the very special qualities that the trombone boys can't compete with, to get her to love you the way you should be loved.

All you have to do is say yes.

To say yes, go to the next page . . .

You say yes. You don't even think about the long-term consequences of this. You don't once consider how Bethany or Bishop might feel about this violation of their privacy. You are so blinded by your desire to impress and dazzle and awe the people who left you that you say yes. Yes, absolutely.

So the teacher sends the story to Periwinkle, and things happen pretty fast after that. Periwinkle phones the next day. He tells you that you're an important new voice in American letters, and he wants you for a new imprint featuring only the work of young geniuses.

"We don't have a name for the press yet, but we're thinking of calling it The Next Voice," Periwinkle says, "or maybe Next, or maybe even Lime, which many of the consultants seem really fond of, weirdly."

Periwinkle hires a few ghostwriters to smooth out the story—"Totally normal," he says, "everyone does it"—then works to get it placed in one of the huge taste-maker magazines, where you are declared one of the five best writers under twenty-five in America. Periwinkle then leverages that publicity to finagle a ridiculous contract for a book that hasn't even been written yet. This gets into the papers along with all of the other good news of early 2001: the information superhighway, the New Economy, the nation's engine humming powerfully forward.

Congratulations.

You are now a famous writer.

But two things keep you from enjoying this. The first is that there is no word from your mother. Instead, there is just a wretched silence. There is no evidence she has even seen the story.

The second is that Bethany—who absolutely *does* see the story—stops writing. No e-mails, no letters, no explanation. You write her wondering if something is wrong. Then you assume there is definitely something wrong and you ask to talk about it. Then you assume that the thing that's wrong is that you completely stole her brother's story and profited immensely from it, and so you try to justify this move as a writer's prerogative while also apologizing for not clearing it with her first. None of these letters are answered, and eventually you understand that the story you hoped would win Bethany back has, perversely, killed any chance you may have had with her.

You don't hear from Bethany for years, during which time you do no writing whatsoever, despite monthly encouraging phone calls from Periwinkle, who is eager to see a manuscript. But there is no manuscript to see. You wake up every morning intending to write but you don't, ultimately, write. You can't really say what exactly you spend your days doing, except that it is not writing. The months fly by, filled with not-writing. You buy a big new house with all your advance money and you do not write in it. You use your bit of fame to snag a teaching job at a local college, where you teach students about literature but make no literature yourself. It's not that you're "blocked," exactly. It's simply that your reason to write, your primary motivation, has melted away.

Bethany does eventually send another e-mail. On the afternoon of September 11, 2001, an e-mail that she sends to about a hundred people that says, simply, "I'm safe."

Then in the early spring of 2004, on a day that is otherwise completely insignificant, you see in your in-box a message from Bethany Fall and you read the first paragraph about how she has something very important to tell you and your heart is popping because the thing she needs to confess, you decide, has to be her deep lifelong enduring love for you.

But that's not it at all. You realize this when you come to the next paragraph, which begins with a sentence that cracks you open all over again: "Bishop," she writes, "is dead."

It happened last October. In Iraq. He was standing next to a bomb when it detonated. She's sorry she didn't tell you sooner.

You write back begging for details. Turns out after Bishop graduated military prep school he went to college at the Virginia Military Institute, and after he graduated he enlisted in the army as a normal soldier. Nobody could figure it out. All his education and training entitled him to a commission and officer's rank, which he refused. He seemed to enjoy refusing it, seemed to enjoy taking the more difficult, less glamorous path. By this time, he and Bethany weren't really talking. They'd been growing distant for a while. For years they had only seen each other at rare holidays. He enlisted in 1999 and spent two uneventful years in Germany before September 11, after which he was deployed to Afghanistan for a time, then Iraq. They'd hear from him only a couple of times a year, in short e-mails that read like business memos. Bethany was becoming a seriously successful violin soloist, and in her letters to Bishop she'd tell him all the things that were happening to her—all the venues she played, the conductors she worked with—but she never heard back. Not for another six months, when she'd get a quick impersonal e-mail with his new coordinates and his typically formal sign-off: *Respectfully, Pfc Bishop Fall, United States Army.*

Then he died.

You spend a long time feeling miserable about this, feeling in some way that your brief friendship with Bishop was a test you failed. Here was a person who needed help, and you did not help him, and now it was too late. And you write a letter to Bethany expressing this misery because she is the only person who would understand it, and it's probably the only letter you've ever sent her that is utterly without guile, without subterfuge or ulterior motive, the first time you aren't self-consciously trying to get her to like you and instead just sincerely expressing a true emotion, which is that you feel sad. And this letter begins a thawing in your relationship with Bethany. She writes back and says she too is sad. And you both have this in common, this sadness, and you grieve together and the months go by and your letters begin to move on to other subjects and your grief seems to lift and then one day Bethany signs her letter—for the first time in years—"With love." And all your guile and obsession ignites again. You think: *I might still have a chance!* All your love and neediness comes back, especially when she writes one day in the first week of August 2004 and *invites you to New York.* She asks you to come at the end of the month. There will be a march, she says, through the streets of Manhattan. The idea is a silent vigil honoring soldiers who've died in Iraq. It will happen during the Republican National Convention, which will be under way at Madison Square Garden. She wants to know if you'll come march with her. You can stay at her place.

And suddenly your nights are sleepless and agitated as you

fantasize about seeing Bethany again and you worry about not screwing up what is obviously your very last chance to capture her heart. It's like you are living the plot of the Choose Your Own Adventure books you loved as a child, and it's up to you to make the right choices. This is all you can think about until the very day you leave: In New York, if you do everything right, if you choose correctly, you can get the girl.

To go to New York, go to the next page . . .

You drive from Chicago to New York, stopping once in Ohio for fuel, again in Pennsylvania for sleep, checking into a shabby hotel you're too amped up to actually sleep in. Next day, well before dawn, you drive the rest of the way and stash your car in a parking garage in Queens and take the subway into the city. You walk up the stairs from the subway station into the mid-morning light and crowds of downtown Manhattan. Bethany lives on one of the upper floors of the building at 55 Liberty Street, a few blocks from the World Trade Center site, which is where you are right now, at this moment, in 2004. Where the towers once stood is now a well-cleared and poignant hole in the ground.

You walk its perimeter, past street vendors selling falafel or candied nuts, guys hawking purses and watches laid out on blankets on the ground, conspiracy theorists handing you pamphlets about 9/11 being an inside job or seeing the face of Satan in the smoke of Tower Two, tourists on tiptoe craning their necks to see above the fence and holding their cameras aloft and checking the picture, then doing it again. You walk past all this, past the department store on the other side of the street where European tourists taking advantage of the weak dollar and surging euro load their bags with jeans and jackets, past a coffee shop with a sign that says NO FREE BATHROOMS, down Liberty Street where a mom tugging her two children asks "Which way to 9/11?," until you're there, Liberty and Nassau, Bethany's apartment.

You know all about this building. You'd looked it up before coming. Built in 1909 as the "tallest small building in the world" (due to narrow lot size), with a foundation going five stories down, unnecessarily deep for a building that size, but the architects of 1909 didn't yet understand skyscraper construction, so they overdid it. Was built next door to the New York Chamber of Commerce, which has since been converted into the New York office of the Central Bank of China. Just across Nassau Street from the ass-end of the Federal Reserve Bank. Teddy Roosevelt's law office was among the first tenants.

You walk through the front doors, past a wrought-iron gate, and into the golden lobby, tiled floor-to-ceiling with polished cream-colored stone slabs pressed so close together you can't see the seams. The whole place feels airtight. You approach the guard desk and tell the man sitting there you are here to see Bethany Fall.

"Name?" he says. You tell him. He picks up a phone and dials. He stares at you while he waits. His eyelids look heavy from sleeplessness or boredom. It seems to take a long time for someone to pick up, long enough that the guard's stare becomes uncomfortable and so you break eye contact and pretend to look around the lobby, admiring its austere tidiness. You notice the total lack of bare lightbulbs, as every light source has been cleverly hidden inside recesses and alcoves, making the space seem less like it's lit and more like it's being thoroughly glowed upon.

"Miss Fall?" the guard finally says. "Got a Samuel Anderson to see you?"

The guard keeps staring. He has no expression whatsoever.

"Okay." He hangs up and does some motion under the desk—turns a key, flips a switch—something that makes the elevator doors open.

"Thanks," you say, but the guard is staring at his computer, ignoring you.

To go up to Bethany's apartment, go to the next page . . .

On the way up to Bethany's apartment, you wonder how long you can reasonably wait in the hall before she'll think you've gotten lost. You're feeling like you need a minute to compose yourself. You're having that hollowed-out nervous feeling like all your insides have fallen into your feet. You try to convince yourself that it's foolish to feel this way, foolish to feel so nervous over Bethany. After all, you only really knew her for three months. *When you were eleven years old.* Silly. Almost comical. How could someone like this have any sway over you? Of all the people in your life, why does this one matter so much? This is what you tell yourself, which does very little to calm the riot in your belly.

The elevator stops. The doors slide open. You had been expecting a hallway or corridor, like at a hotel, but instead the elevator opens directly into a blazingly sunlit apartment.

Of course. She owns the whole floor.

And walking toward you right now is someone who is definitely not Bethany. A man, about your age—late twenties, maybe early thirties. Pressed white shirt. Skinny black tie. Perfectly rigid posture and down-his-nose gaze. He's wearing an expensive-looking watch. You consider each other a moment, and you're about to say you have the wrong apartment when he says, "You must be the writer." And there's something about the way he inflects the word *writer* that carries an edge, like he doesn't believe writer is a real profession and so he says it like someone might say, "You must be the psychic."

"Yeah, that's me," you say. "I'm sorry, I'm looking for—"

And at that moment, behind him, just past his shoulder, she appears.

"Bethany."

For a moment it's as if you had forgotten what she looked like, as if all those photos she packed in her letters never existed, as if you had never scoured the internet finding all manner of publicity portraits, concert photos, after-party candids with Bethany standing next to some wealthy donor smiling and hugging—it's as if all you have is that memory of her practicing the violin in her room when she thought she was alone and you were peeking around the corner and you were a child and you were in love. And how much she resembles that vision here in her apartment, that same self-contained, self-possessed, easy confidence—so formal, even now, as she strides toward you and embraces you with a platonic hug and kisses your cheek in the way she's kissed the cheeks of a thousand friends, fans, well-wishers, where it's less a kiss than the suggestion of one in the atmosphere around your ear, and how she says "Samuel, I'd like to introduce you to Peter Atchison, my fiancé," as if there's nothing at all odd about that. *Her fiancé?*

Peter shakes your hand. "Pleasure," he says.

Then Bethany gives you a tour while your heart plummets and you feel like the stupidest man on earth. You do your best to listen, to act like you're really interested in hearing about the apartment, which is windowed on all sides so you can see the construction equipment over the World Trade Center site to the west, and Wall Street to the south.

"This is my father's apartment," she says, "but he doesn't come here anymore. Not since he retired."

She spins on her heel and smiles at you.

"Did you know that Teddy Roosevelt used to work here?"

You pretend not to know this fact.

"He was a banker at the beginning of his career," she says. "Like Peter."

"Hah!" Peter says. He slaps you on the back. "Talk about great expectations, eh?"

"Peter worked with my father," Bethany says.

"Worked *for* your father," he says. Bethany waves him off.

"Peter is really very brilliant at finance."

"Am not."

"Are too!" she says. "He discovered that a certain number, a formula, or algorithm, or something—anyway, it was this thing people were using and he realized it was wrong. Honey, you explain it."

"I don't want to bore our guest."

"But it's *interesting*."

"Do you really want to know about this?"

You absolutely do not want to know about this. You nod.

"Well, I won't go too much into it," he says, "but it's about the C-Ratio. You heard of it?"

You are not sure if he meant *C* or *see* or *sea*. You say, "Remind me."

"Basically it's a number investors use to predict volatility in the precious metal markets."

"Peter realized it was wrong," Bethany says.

"Under certain circumstances. Under very specific circumstances, the C-Ratio stops being a useful predictor. It lags behind the market. It's like . . . how do I describe it? It's like believing the thermometer is the thing that's making it hot."

"Isn't that brilliant?" Bethany says.

"And so while everyone was betting with the C-Ratio, I bet against it. And the rest is history."

"Isn't that *so brilliant*?"

They're both looking at you now, waiting.

"Brilliant," you say.

Bethany smiles at her fiancé. The diamond on her finger might best be described as *protuberant*. The gold band seems to lift the diamond up like a baseball fan who has just caught a foul ball.

Throughout all this banter you've found yourself barely looking at Bethany. You're focusing instead on Peter, because you don't want to be caught staring at Bethany, by Peter. Looking at him and ignoring her is your way of telling him you're not here to steal his woman, is something you realize you're doing after you've been doing it already for several minutes. Plus every time you look at Bethany you're jolted by surprise, how none of those photos prepared you for the actual person. Like how photographs of famous paintings always lack some essential beauty that's startling when you encounter the painting in real life.

And Bethany is really, terribly beautiful. The catlike features of her childhood have resolved themselves sharply now. Eyebrows like check marks. Stern jaw and liquid neck. Eyes green and cool. Black dress that manages to be both conservative and open-backed. Necklace and earring and shoe combo that is the very definition of *well put together*.

"Too early for a drink?" Peter says.

"I'd love one!" you say, maybe too enthusiastically. You're finding the more attracted you are to this man's fiancée, the more ingratiating you become toward him. "Thanks!"

He explains that he's pouring you something special—"It's not every day that an old pen pal comes to visit!" he says—a whiskey they bought on a recent trip to Scotland, a bottle that won certain awards, that a certain magazine gave its only perfect score in history, that nobody can even buy anywhere but at the distillery itself, where the technique and recipe is a guarded secret passed through like ten generations—all the while Bethany is beaming at him like a proud parent—and he hands you a tumbler with an inch-deep pool of straw-colored liquid and explains something about the way it clings to the side of the glass and something about the patterns it makes as it swirls and how you can tell something about the quality of the scotch that way, and also something about the opacity too, and he has you lift up the glass to watch how the light filters through it and the view you get, unexpectedly, is the wobbly lines of cranes over the World Trade Center hole as seen through the liquid's curvy distortion.

"Beautiful, isn't it?" Peter says.

"Sure is."

"Drink it. Tell me how it tastes."

"Sorry?"

"I'd like to hear a writer describe it," he says. "Because you're so good with words."

You try to figure out if he's being sarcastic, but cannot. You taste the scotch. And what can you say? It tastes like scotch. It has a very *scotchlike* quality. You search your memory for words that are used to describe scotch. You come up with *peaty*, a word you don't really know the definition of. The only word that pops into your head as accurate and defensible is *strong*.

"It tastes strong," you say, and Peter laughs.

"Strong?" he says, then laughs again, harder. He looks at Bethany and says, "He called it strong. Hah! I'll be damned. Strong."

The rest of the morning goes something like this. Bethany regaling you with factoids, Peter finding reasons to expound lavishly on some exquisite purchased thing: the coffee they buy, for example, the rarest in the world, coffee that has actually been eaten and excreted by a kind of catlike Sumatran mammal that has a gift for selecting only the best coffee beans to eat, plus the digestion process aids the flavor when the beans are roasted, Peter insists. Or his socks, sewn by hand by the same Italian seamstress who makes the pope's socks. Or the sheets on the bed in the guest room with their four-digit thread counts that make Egyptian cotton feel like sandpaper in comparison.

"Most people go through life not paying attention to the small details," Peter says, his arm around Bethany, leg kicked up on the coffee table, the three of you sitting on the leather sectional sofas that take up the center of the astoundingly sunlit apartment. "But I can't imagine going through life that way. You know? I mean, what's the difference between your average violin player and Bethany here? It's the small details. I think that's why she and I understand each other so well."

He gives her a squeeze. "That's right!" she says, smiling at him.

"So many people live their life so fast and never slow down and enjoy themselves and be thankful. You know what I believe? I believe you should live in each season as it passes. Breathe the air. Drink the drink. Taste the fruit. You know who said that? Thoreau said that. I read *Walden* in college. I realized, yeah, live life, you know? Be in the world. Anyway"—he checks his watch—"I gotta go. Meeting in D.C. in a couple of hours, then London. You hippies have fun at your protest. Don't overthrow the government while I'm gone."

They give each other brisk kisses before Peter Atchison throws on a suit jacket and rushes out the door and Bethany looks at you in this, the first moment you are alone together. And before you can ask *What do you mean pen pal?* she says "I guess we should get going! I'll call the driver!" in this manic way that blunts any thought of actual conversation. And you hope to have a real one-on-one, heart-to-heart kind of experience with her maybe in the car on the way to the protest, but when you climb into the back of the Cadillac Escalade and get under way Bethany spends most of the time making small talk with the driver, an older and intensely wrinkled man named Tony, who is Greek, you learn, and whose three daughters and eight grandchildren are all doing fine, just fine, you learn, after Bethany insists he go through them all one by one giving little updates for each of them: where they are, what they're doing, how it's all going, etc. This takes you roughly to Thirty-Fourth Street, whereby the Tony conversation naturally runs its course as Tony runs out of progeny to talk about, and there occurs a blip of silence before Bethany turns on the Escalade's overhead television screen and turns it to a news channel already very deep into its daily coverage of the Republican National Convention and associated protests, and she says "Can you believe what they're saying about us?" and spends the rest of the trip either complaining about the news or typing messages on her cell phone.

The news is, it's true, dismaying. Reporters saying you and your ilk are all marginal protest types. Coming out of the woodwork. Malcontents. Provocateurs. Clouds of marijuana. Playing footage from Chicago, 1968: some kid throwing a brick at a hotel window. Then speculating on the protest's effects on heartland swing voters. Their opinion? Heartland swing voters will find it all rather distasteful. "Your average Ohio voter is not going to respond to this," says one guy who's not the anchor and not a reporter but rather some middle-type person: the opinion-haver. "Especially if it gets violent," he continues. "If what happened in Chicago in '68 happens here, you can bet it will once again help the Republicans."

All this time Bethany clicks at her device, her violin fingers whirring over the tiny keypad, the little sound it makes like listening to a tap dancer through earmuffs, so engrossed in this she doesn't notice you staring at her—or doesn't *acknowledge* it, anyway, your staring—looking at her profile and then looking at the knot on her neck where her violin sits while she plays, a gnarled cauliflower callus there, the only not-smooth part of her, discolored dark brown spots amid the pale white scar tissue, this ugly thing barnacled onto her, the effect of a lifetime's musicianship, and it reminds you of something your mother once said, not long before she left. She said, *The things you love the most will one day hurt you the worst.* And as you reach your destination—the meadow in Central Park that serves as the staging ground for today's march—and as Bethany slaps her BlackBerry into her purse and leaps out of the vehicle, and as you realize there is just no way you're going to get the intimate-type moment with her that you wanted and your heart sinks and all you really want now is to leave New York and hide for like a decade, you understand that your mother was right: The things we love the most are the most disfiguring. Such is our greed for them.

To follow Bethany into the park, go to the next page . . .

The coffins are finished and waiting for you.

In the great bowl of the Sheep Meadow, there they are, about a thousand of them, maybe more, set out in a grid in the scruff of the long and tufted lawn.

"What is this?" you say, looking at the whole disquieting scene, all those hundreds of coffins with American flags draped over them, and people walking between them, many of them taking pictures, or talking on their cell phones, or playing hacky sack.

"Our march," Bethany says, like there's nothing at all weird about this.

"This isn't quite what I was expecting," you say.

She shrugs. She pushes past you and into the crowd, into the park, toward the coffins.

And the downright oddity of seeing normal park behavior around all these coffins. A man walking his dogs seems inappropriate here, even unseemly—how the dogs pull toward a coffin to sniff it and everyone watching is preemptively horrified because *is he going to let them pee on it?* Turns out he is not. The dogs lose interest and do their business elsewhere. A woman with a bullhorn in some official organizing capacity is asking everyone to remember that these aren't just coffins, they're bodies. To think of them as bodies. Bodies of real soldiers who really died in Iraq so please have a little respect. Murmurs that this message is a not-so-subtle dig at those who came too festively costumed: a troupe in colonial garb dressed as the Founding Fathers with plaster-of-paris heads about twelve times the size of real heads; or a team of women dressed in flamboyant red, white, and blue wearing giant strap-on dildos in the shape of intercontinental ballistic missiles; or lots of George Bush Halloween masks with drawn-on Hitler mustaches. The coffins all have American flags on top of them so that they look like the coffins you see on TV coming out of the backs of planes bringing dead soldiers to that one air force base in Delaware. The woman with the bullhorn says everyone can have a body, but if you want a specific body, come talk to her, she has a spreadsheet. People were instructed to wear black for the day and

many of them have followed this instruction. Somewhere someone is playing drums. Along Eighth Avenue, brightly logoed news
vans are parked with rooftop transceivers extended into the sky
like a line of lodgepole pines. Popular signage today includes STOP
BUSH and ARREST BUSH and various puns on the word "bush" that
involve gardening or genitalia. Two girls out sunbathing in biki-
nis are not successfully convinced to join the cause. Guys are
walking through the crowd selling bottles of water, selling various anti-GOP buttons and bumper stickers and T-shirts and mugs
and baby onesies and hats and visors and illustrated children's
books identifying monsters that hide under kids' beds as Republicans. Someone is definitely smoking marijuana or has just smoked
marijuana nearby. SMITE BUSH FOR HE IS AN ABOMINATION UPON THE
EARTH among the oddly evangelical signs that make folks in this
particular crowd a little uncomfortable. A man dressed as Uncle
Sam walking on stilts, for some reason. Hacky sack is kicked an
average of three times before plopping on the ground. FREE LEONARD
PELTIER.

"There's a body for each of us!" says the woman on the bullhorn,
and people are finding their bodies now, lifting coffins. A body for
the guy dressed as Castro, and the guy dressed as Che, and the guy
with the sign that says LENNON LIVES! A body for the LGBTQ delega-
tion with T-shirts that say "Lick Bush." For each of a busload of
Young Democrats of Greater Philadelphia, a body. A body for every
sign-waving member of Jews for Peace. A body for the plumbers of
UA Local No. 1. For members of the CUNY Muslim Student Association. For the several women who came today in matching pink
prom dresses, questions ("Why?") and a body. A body for the skater
kid. The Rasta man. The priest. The 9/11 widow, especially for her.
For the one-armed army vet in camo fatigues: a spot up front, a
body. And for you and Bethany, a body in row thirty, according to
the bullhorned woman's spreadsheet, where, sure enough, you find
a coffin with a sticker on the side that says "Bishop Fall." Bethany does not seem to have any reaction to this except to touch it,
lightly, as if for luck. She looks at you as she does this and offers a
small, sad smile, and this might be the first true moment you've
shared since you arrived.

And it's over just that quickly. All of you lifting your bodies now. In teams of two or three or four you raise them up. The sun is luminous and the grass is green and the daisies are abloom and the colossal field is dotted with black coffins. A thousand rectangular black wooden coffins.

They alight onto shoulders. You begin your march. You are all pallbearers.

It's thirty or so blocks to the Republican National Convention, and in Central Park the coffins are on the move. The chanting begins. The woman on the bullhorn shouts instructions. The marchers surge out like magma, past the baseball fields, onto the avenue, past the skyscraper with its silver world-conquering globe. They are wearing black and they are baking in the sun but they are bright with excitement. They are shouting, cheering. They roll out of Central Park, into Columbus Circle, and they are promptly stopped. The police stand there ready—roadblocks, riot gear, pepper spray, tear gas—a display of force to dampen the protest's vigor before it begins. The crowd halts, looks down the channel of Eighth Avenue, the perfectly geometric view to downtown, the wall of buildings on both sides like a sea parting. The police have reduced the street's four lanes to two. The crowd waits. They look up at the obelisk in the middle of the circle, the statue of Columbus on top, dressed in flowing robes like a high-school graduate. The usual northbound traffic on Eighth Avenue is shut down today, and all the signs that face the protestors say DO NOT ENTER and WRONG WAY. To many of them, this seems to epitomize something important.

If the cops attack, do not resist is the message from the protest's organizers, the bullhorned woman at the front of the crowd. If a cop wants to put you in handcuffs, let him. If he wants to put you in a police car, ambulance, paddy wagon—no resistance whatsoever. If the cops come at us with clubs and stun guns, do not resist or panic or fight or run. This can't be a riot. The message here is calm, level-headed, always be aware of cameras. This is a protest, not a circus. They have rubber bullets and they hurt like a motherfucker. Think Gandhi, peace, love, Zen-like tranquillity. Please do not get pepper-sprayed. Please do not take off your clothes. Remember, somber. We're carrying coffins, for god's sake. This is our message. Stay on message.

You hold the coffin where the feet would be. Bethany is in front of you, holding the symbolic head. You try not to think of it in these terms: feet, head. You are holding a plywood coffin: empty, hollow. Ahead of you, somewhere, the enormous assembly is oozing slowly southward. Where you stand is the doldrums, coffins bobbing above a lake of stiffening arms. You are full of conflict here, full of competing impulses. You're holding Bishop's coffin and it feels awful. It ignites all your appalling guilt, the guilt you felt for not saving Bishop when you were young. And the guilt you now feel for trying to woo Bethany at what is essentially her own brother's funeral. *Oh my god you are such an asshole.* It's as if you can feel your desire physically crawl up into you and die. Until, that is, you look at Bethany again, her bare back, the sweat on her shoulders, the strands of hair that cling to her neck, the angles of muscle and bone, the nakedness of her spine. She's reading the sticker they affixed to the coffin: *Pfc Bishop Fall was killed in Iraq on October 22, 2003. He was a graduate of the Virginia Military Institute. He grew up in Streamwood, Illinois.*

"Doesn't really capture him," she says, but not to you. Not to anyone really. It's as if a passing thought had been vocalized by accident.

Still, you answer her. "No," you say, "it doesn't."

"No."

"They should have mentioned how good he was at *Missile Command.*"

A small laugh, maybe, from Bethany here? You can't be sure; her back is still turned. You keep going: "And how all the kids in school loved him and admired him and were terrified of him. And the teachers too. How he always managed to get what he wanted. How he was the center of attention without even trying. You wanted to do anything he asked you to do. You wanted to please him, even though you didn't know why. It was that personality of his. It was so big."

Bethany is nodding. She's looking at the ground.

"Some people," you say, "go through life like a pebble falling into a pond. They barely make a splash. Bishop tore through life. We were all in his wake."

Bethany doesn't look at you, but she says "That's true," then stands up straighter. You suspect, but cannot verify, that she is looking away from you because, right now, she is crying, and she doesn't want you to see.

The procession begins again, the coffins are moving, and the protestors start to chant. The leaders, bullhorned, and the thousands behind them, singing, raising their voices and fists in fiery unison: *Hey! Hey! Ho! Ho!*

But that's where the chant breaks down as the throngs are unsure what to say, then all the voices coming back together for the verse's final line: *Has got to go!*

What has got to go? It is cacophony. You hear many things. Some people shout *Republicans*. Others, *war*. Others, *George Bush. Dick Cheney. Halliburton. Racism, sexism, homophobia.* Some people seem to have come from entirely different protests, are roaring against Israel (oppressing Palestinians), or China (oppressing Falun Gong), or third world labor, or the World Bank, or NAFTA, or GATT.

Hey! Hey! Ho! Ho!

[incomprehensible gibberish]

Has got to go!

Nobody knows the words to use today. They are committed only to their individual furies.

That is, until they reach a certain spot near Fiftieth Street, where along their route a group of counter-protestors have arranged themselves to protest the protestors, which provides a clarity of purpose for all involved. The counter-protestors howl loudly and wave their homemade signs. The signs run the rhetorical spectrum from transparent simple sincerity (VOTE BUSH) to clever irony (COMMUNISTS FOR KERRY!), from verbal expansiveness (WAR NEVER SOLVED ANYTHING—EXCEPT FOR ENDING SLAVERY, NAZISM, FASCISM, AND THE HOLOCAUST) to verbal concision (image of NYC skyline overlaid with mushroom cloud), from invocations of patriotism (SUPPORT OUR TROOPS) to invocations of religion (GOD IS A REPUBLICAN). This is also the spot, not accidentally, where the news stations have chosen to set up their cameras, and so the entire event—the march from Central Park to Madison Square Garden—will be represented tonight on television by a quick clip where half the frame is taken up by protestors and the other half by counter-protestors, all of them behaving badly. They yell non sequiturs at each other, one side calling the other side "Traitors!" and that side retorting "Who would Jesus bomb?" The whole thing will just look very ugly.

This will be the protest's most exciting encounter. The attack by the police that worried everyone will never come. The protestors will stay within their narrow Free Speech Zone. The cops will bemusedly watch them.

Oddly, when this becomes clear, some of the protestors' vigor seems to vanish. As the march ebbs its way slowly on, you begin seeing coffins abandoned on the street—soldiers downed on the battlefield for a second time. Maybe it's too hot. Maybe it's too much to ask, carrying these boxes for this long. Bethany continues to silently proceed, block after quiet block. By now you've memorized the contours of her back, the outline of her shoulder blades, the small field of freckles at the base of her neck. She has a little curl to her long brown hair, a quick twist at the tips. She wears ballet flats that reveal small shoe-related cuts on her heels. She doesn't speak, doesn't chant—she simply moves forward in that extraordinarily upright and proper way of hers. She doesn't even switch the hand she's using to carry the coffin, which you've been doing every couple of blocks as one hand gets sore and cramped. The coffin's burden does not seem to physically affect her—not the plywood's rough edges, nor the weight, which did not at first seem all that demanding but after carrying the thing a few hours begins to feel considerable. The tendons in your hands lock up, the muscles of your forearms burn, a knot twists itself into the flesh behind your rib cage—all for this, this thin and empty box. Not heavy, exactly, but given enough time, any weight can become too much to bear.

And finally this, the end of the march. Those who have carried their coffins from Central Park now deposit them at the foot of Madison Square Garden, where the Republicans are holding their nominating convention. The symbolism here is easy to parse: The

Republicans are responsible for the war; they should also be responsible for the war dead. And there is something upsetting about the way the coffins pile up. One hundred coffins cover the avenue. Two hundred coffins begin to look like a wall. Then it gets too tall and the marchers begin heaving the coffins up to places they cannot themselves reach and the coffins are stacked atop one another like children's blocks, balancing perilously, sliding off the pile and landing at oblique angles. The whole thing begins to look like an impromptu roadblock that you associate with *Les Misérables*. By the time they get to about five hundred coffins the scene has a mass-grave quality that's downright disturbing, no matter how hawkish one might be. The marchers add their coffins to the pile and then offer some choice words to the Republicans, shaking their fists and yelling in the direction of the giant ovoid arena just beyond the line that demarcates the end of their march as per the permit recently approved by city hall, a line that is recognizable for the massive security buildup—steel fencing and armored trucks and riot police standing elbow to elbow—in case you forget where your Free Speech Zone ends.

When you and Bethany add your coffin to the pile, you do so gently. No throwing. No yelling. You place it quietly on the ground and then listen to the commotion around you for a moment, the many thousands who showed up today, a good turnout for a protest, but a number that is dwarfed by the audience watching you on television right now, on a certain cable news outlet that's using the live feed from the end of the march as B-roll footage to play in a box on the left side of the screen next to a few smaller boxes on the right side of the screen where pundits' heads debate whether the protest you've just finished will backfire on you or be merely useless, whether you are a traitor or merely giving comfort to the enemy, and underneath your image is a bright yellow headline that reads LIBERALS USE SOLDIER DEATHS FOR POLITICAL GAIN. The protest turns out to be a great triumph for this particular news show, as it will notch its highest post–September 11 ratings today, clocking in at 1.6 million viewers, which is itself dwarfed by the 18 million households that will tune in for tonight's network broadcast of a reality singing show, but it's a pretty good score for basic cable nonetheless, and will allow them to bump their ad rates next quarter by a tenth of a percent.

Meanwhile, Bethany looks at you for the first time in hours. She says, "Let's go home."

To go home with Bethany, go to the next page . . .

This might not seem like a Choose Your Own Adventure story yet, because you haven't made a choice.

You've been with Bethany for an entire day—you listened to her intolerable fiancé and allowed her to drive you to the protest and followed her into the park and all the way through Manhattan and now she hails a cab and you follow her into it and you ride silently south back to her extravagant apartment and you have not made a single significant decision. You're not choosing your own adventure; the adventure has been chosen for you. Even the decision to come to New York in the first place wasn't really a decision so much as a reflexive and impulsive *yes*. How could it be a "decision" when you never considered saying no? The yes was there already, waiting for you, inevitable, the sum of all those years of pining and hoping and obsessing. You never even decided your life would be this way—it's simply the way life has become. You've been carved out by the things that have happened to you. Like how the canyon can't tell the river which way to shape it. It just allows itself to be cut.

But perhaps there's *one* choice you're making, which is the constant minute-by-minute low-level tacit choice to act more or less normally and not exclaim in a fit of passion "What the fuck is wrong with you?" or "Don't marry Peter Atchison!" or "I still love you!" Maybe bolder and more romantic men would do this, but to you it seems impossible. It goes against your nature. You've never been able to assert yourself like that. Your greatest dream has always been to fade from view completely, become invisible. You long ago learned to tuck away your biggest emotions because those are the things that trigger the crying, and there is nothing worse than that, the blubbering, in public, in front of people.

So you don't try to shake Bethany out of this quiet and distant and infuriating stupor she's in, you don't proclaim your love for her, and you're not even really aware that this is a choice. You're like the ancient cave painter drawing 2-D animals before the invention of three-point perspective: You are incapable of working in anything but your narrow dimensions.

You will, eventually, have to make a choice. You're approaching the choice—you've been getting closer to it ever since Bethany touched the coffin with her brother's name on it and the manic person she'd been since you arrived shriveled and she became silent and introspective and very, very far away. So far away that when you return to her palatial apartment and she disappears into her bedroom, you assume she's gone to sleep. Instead, she reappears a few minutes later having changed from one dress into another, from black to yellow, a thin smart summery thing. She has an envelope in her hand, which she places on the kitchen counter. She turns on a few lights and pulls a bottle of wine from the special wine fridge and says, "Drink?"

You agree. Outside, the financial district glows through the night, whole office buildings lit and empty.

"Peter works at that one," Bethany says, pointing. You nod. You have nothing to say about that.

"He really is very highly regarded," she says. "My dad can't stop gushing about him."

She pauses. Looks into her wineglass. You sip your drink. "I'm sorry I didn't tell you I was engaged," she says.

"It's not really my business," you say.

"That's what I told myself too." She looks at you again with those green eyes of hers. "But that's not entirely true. You and I, we're . . . complicated."

"I don't know what you and I are," you say, and she smiles, leans back on the kitchen counter, and breathes a big dramatic sigh.

"They say when one twin dies the other twin can feel it."

"I've heard that."

"It's not true," she says, and takes a big gulp of wine. "I didn't feel anything. He'd been dead a few days when we found out and I didn't feel a thing. Even after, even long after, even at the funeral, I didn't feel what everyone thought I should feel. I don't know. I guess we'd drifted apart."

"I'd always meant to write him, but I never did."

"He changed. He went to military school and became a different person. Stopped calling, stopped writing, stopped coming home at holidays. He disappeared. He'd been in Iraq for three months before any of us even knew he was there."

"He was probably happy to escape your father. But I'm surprised he wanted to escape you."

"We disappeared from each other. I don't know who started it, but for a while it was easier pretending the other didn't exist. I'd always resented how he used people and how much he got away with. He'd always resented my talent and the way adults gushed over it. Everyone thought I was the special one and he was the screwup. Last time we saw each other was at his graduation from college. We shook hands."

"But he adored you. That's what I remember."

"Something came between us."

"What?"

Bethany looks at the ceiling and tightens her lips and searches for the right words.

"He was being, well, you know. Being abused."

"Oh."

She walks over to one of the floor-to-ceiling windows and stares out, her back to you. Beyond her, the radiance of downtown Manhattan, quiet this time of night, like embers smoldering after the fire's gone out.

"Was it the headmaster?" you ask.

Bethany nods. "Bishop wondered why he was targeted and I wasn't. Then he started getting mean with me. Implying that I was *happy* about it. Like it was a competition between us and I was winning. Every time I had any kind of success he reminded me that life was so easy for me because I didn't have to deal with the things he had to deal with. Which was of course true, but he used it as a way to minimize me." She turns around to look at you. "Does this make any sense? It probably sounds horribly selfish."

"It's not selfish."

"It is selfish. And I was mostly able to forget about it. He went to military school and we drifted apart and I felt relieved. For years, I ignored it. Like it never happened. Until one day—"

She lowers her face, gives you this look, and suddenly you understand.

"You ignored it," you say, "until the day my story was published."

"Yes."

"I'm sorry about that."

"Reading your story was like realizing a terrible dream wasn't a dream."

"I'm really sorry about that. I should have asked your permission."

"And I thought, my god, you only knew us for a few months. And if *you* understood so clearly what was going on, how awful am I? For ignoring it?"

"I only understood it much, much later. I didn't know at the time."

"But *I* knew at the time. And I did nothing. I told no one. And I was angry at you for dredging it all up again."

"That's understandable."

"It was easier to be angry at you than to feel guilty, so I was mad at you for years."

"And then?"

"And then Bishop died. And I just felt numb." She looks down at her wineglass, traces its edge with her fingertip. "It's like when you're at the dentist and they give you some really serious painkillers. You feel fine, but you're pretty sure underneath it all you still hurt. The hurt is simply not registering. That's how life has felt."

"All this time?"

"Yes. It's made music pretty weird. After concerts people tell me how moved they were by my playing. But to me it's just notes. Whatever emotion they hear is in the music, not me. It's only a recipe. That's how it feels."

"And what about Peter?"

Bethany laughs and holds up her hand so the both of you can take a good long look at the diamond, sparkling in kitchen's recessed lights, those million tiny rainbows inside.

"It's pretty, isn't it?"

"It's big," you say.

"When he proposed, I didn't feel happy about it. Or sad about it. I guess if I had to describe how I felt I'd say it was the sensation of having one's interest piqued. His proposal felt *really interesting*."

"That's not exactly poetry, is it."

"I think he proposed to snap me out of my funk. But it backfired. And the funk became more terrifying because it does not seem like something I am able to snap out of. Now Peter's pretending it doesn't exist, and spending a lot of time away. Hence London."

Bethany refills her wineglass. Outside, the moon has risen over the jagged sweep of Brooklyn. Blinking lights in single file across the sky are aircraft descending into JFK from points south. In the kitchen there's a very small framed drawing of a bull that might be an actual Picasso.

"Are you still mad at me?" you say.

"No, I'm not mad at you," she says. "I'm not anything at you."

"Okay."

"Did you know that Bishop never even read that story of yours? I never told him about it. I was furious at you on his behalf, but he never read it. Isn't that funny?"

You feel relieved by this. That Bishop never knew that his secret was not a secret to you. That he had his privacy, at least, till the end.

Bethany grabs the wine bottle by the neck and walks into the living room and plunks herself down on the couch, doesn't even turn on a lamp or anything, just plunks herself down in the semi-darkness so that you can't really see the plunking so much as you hear the crackling of the expensive leather (alligator, you guess) as Bethany comes to rest on top of it. You sit across from her on the very same couch you were sitting on earlier today listening to a hyper Bethany and Peter simulate a happy relationship. The only light in the apartment comes from the two little spots in the kitchen, and the glow of the surrounding skyscraper windows—not nearly enough to see by. When Bethany talks, her voice seems to come out of the void. She asks you about Chicago. About your job. What your job is like. If you enjoy it. Where you live. What your home looks like. What you do for fun. And you answer all her small-talk questions and while you're talking she pours herself another glass of wine, and then another, swallowing the wine with the occasional audible gulp while saying "uh-huh" at the key moments in your stories. You tell her the job is fine except for the students, who are unmotivated; and the administrators, who are ruthless; and the location, which is suburban-drab; and come to think of it you don't really like your job at all. You tell her you live in a house with a backyard that you never use and pay someone else to mow. Sometimes kids run through your backyard playing various games and you are fine with that and you see that as your contribution to community civics. Otherwise, you do not know your neighbors. You're trying to write a book for which you've already been paid, which presents certain motivation problems. When she asks what the book is about, you say, "I don't know. Family?"

By the time Bethany opens the second bottle of wine you get the sense she's trying to gear herself up for something that requires courage and that the wine is helping her do this. She begins reminiscing, talking about old times, when you were kids: playing video games or playing in the woods.

"Do you remember the last time you came to my house?" she says. And of course you do. It was the night you kissed her. The last moment of real joy you felt before your mother left. But you don't tell Bethany that part. You just say, "Yes."

"My first kiss," she says.

"Mine too."

"The room was dark, like this one," she says. "I couldn't really see you. I could only feel you very close to me. Do you remember?"

"I remember," you say.

Bethany stands—the couch announces it, the popping of the leather, the little suction sound releasing—and she comes over to you and sits next to you and she takes the glass from your hand and sets it on the floor and she's very close now, one of her knees pressing into yours, and you're beginning to understand about the lights and the wine.

"Like this?" she says, drawing her face to yours, smiling.

"It was darker than this."

"We could close our eyes."

"We could," you say. But you don't.

"You were about this far away," she says, your cheeks almost touching now. You can feel the heat of her, the lavender smell of her hair. "I didn't know what to do," she says. "I pressed my lips out and hoped it was right."

"It was right," you say.

"Good," she says, and she lingers there a moment, and you're afraid to do anything or say anything or move or breathe, feeling like this whole moment is made of air and could scatter at the smallest agitation. Your lips are only a few inches from hers, but you do not lean in. The space between you is something she must resolve herself. Then Bethany says in a whisper, "I don't want to marry Peter."

"You don't have to."

"Can you help me not marry Peter?"

To help her not marry Peter, go to the next page . . .

And so you finally kiss her, and when you do you feel a great cascade of relief deep inside break through, and all your obsessing and pining and worrying and regret, and all the ways you've been haunted by this woman, and all the torture and self-loathing that you had failed to make her love you, they all seem to shatter on the ground. It feels like you've been holding up a wall of glass all this time and only now you realize it's okay to let it fall. And fall it does, and it's almost percussive the way it tumbles and breaks around you—you try not to flinch as Bethany kisses you, as she pulls at you with her hands and you have this powerful sense memory of kissing her when you were a child, how you were surprised that her lips were dry, that you didn't know what to do except smash your face into hers, back when kissing was not a signpost along the way but rather the destination itself. But now you are both older and you've had all the relevant experiences and each of you knows exactly what to do with another body—which is to say you know that kissing is a kind of communication sometimes, and what you're telling each other right now is that you both very much want *more.* And so you press into her and slide your hands around her waist and curl your fingers into the slight fabric of her dress and she tugs you closer by the collar and still you're kissing—deeply, wildly, devouring each other—and you're aware of your awareness of this, how you seem able to concentrate on everything and feel everything all at once: Your hands and her skin and your mouth and her mouth and her fingers and her breathing and the way her body responds to yours— these things don't feel like separate sensations but rather like layers of a single greater sensation, that drift of consciousness that can happen when you're entwined with another and it's all going very well and it's almost as if you know exactly what the other person wants and can feel her emotions as they shudder through her body as if they're shuddering through your own, like your bodies have momentarily ceased to have edges and have become things without boundaries.

This is how it feels, this expansiveness, which is why it's such a shock when Bethany jolts up and away from you and grabs your hands to stop their progress and says, "Wait."

"What?" you say. "What's wrong?"

"Just . . . I'm sorry." And she pulls away from you and fully disengages and curls up on the other side of the couch.

"What is it?" you say.

Bethany shakes her head and looks at you with these sad, terrible eyes.

"I can't," she says, and inside you feel something you might call a *plummeting*.

"We could go slower," you say. "We can just slow down a little. It's okay."

"This isn't fair to you," she says.

"I don't mind," you say, and you hope you don't betray all the desperation you're feeling because you know if you come this close and still fail with this girl it will break you. You will not come back from this one. "We don't have to have sex," you say. "We can, I don't know, take it easy?"

"The sex isn't the problem," she says, and laughs. "The sex I can do. I *want* to do that. But I don't know if you want to. Or will want to."

"I want to."

"But there's something you don't know."

Bethany stands and smooths her clothes, a gesture meant to signal calm levelheaded dignity, a very serious break from the theatrics on the couch.

"There's a letter for you," she says. "On the kitchen counter. It's from Bishop."

"He wrote a letter? To me?"

"We got it from the army, a few months after he died. He wrote it in case something happened."

"Did you get one?"

"No. Yours was the only one he wrote."

Bethany turns now and walks slowly to her bedroom. She's moving in that careful way of hers again—perfectly straight, perfectly upright, all movements composed and purposive. When she pulls open her bedroom door, she stops halfway and turns to look at you over her shoulder.

"Listen," she says, "I looked at the letter. I'm sorry, but I did. I don't know what it means, and you don't have to tell me, but I want you to know I read it."

"Okay."

"I'm going to be in here," she says, nodding toward the bedroom. "After you've read it, if you want to come in, that's fine. But if you want to leave"—she pauses a moment, turns around, drops her head, seems to look at the floor—"I'll understand."

She withdraws into the dark bedroom, the door closing behind her with a soft click.

To read the letter, go to the next page . . .

Private First Class Bishop Fall sits in the belly of a Bradley Fighting Vehicle, his chin on his chest, asleep. His is the second vehicle in a small convoy—three Bradleys, three Humvees, a supply truck—driving single file to a village they don't know the name of. All they know is that insurgents have recently kidnapped the mayor of this village and beheaded him on TV. It strikes the soldiers in the convoy as bizarre that the executions are televised, and also that they're done in this particular manner: beheading. It feels like a kind of death from another era, a viciousness called up from the dark ages.

Three Bradleys and three Humvees can carry approximately forty soldiers. The supply truck carries two more, plus water and gasoline and ammo and many hundreds of boxes of MREs. Each MRE—or Meals Ready to Eat—has a densely syllabic ingredient list that makes many of the soldiers claim that, behind beheaders and IEDs, MREs are the biggest threat to their physical health out here. A popular game is to guess whether a certain chemical is found in an MRE or a bomb. Potassium sorbate? (MRE.) Disodium pyrophosphate? (MRE.) Ammonium nitrate? (Bomb.) Potassium nitrate? (Both.) It's a game they might play during meals when they're feeling complexly cynical, but not when they're traveling via Bradley to a village an hour away. When they're on the road like this, mostly what they do is sleep. They've been pulling twenty-hour shifts lately, so an hour in the armored belly of a Bradley is a little slice of what goes for heaven around here. Because it's totally dark and it's the safest place to be when they're outside the wire and—because a Bradley at top speed sounds like a flimsy wooden roller coaster going Mach 2—they're wearing earplugs, so it all feels real nice and cocooned. Everyone loves it. Everyone except this one guy Chucky, whose real name no one even remembers because he was nicknamed Chucky a long time ago for his tendency to vomit while riding in the back of a Bradley. It's due to his motion sickness. So they nicknamed him "Up Chuck," which was soon shortened to "Chuck," which inevitably became "Chucky."

Chucky is nineteen years old, short-haired, spindly muscled, fifteen pounds lighter now than he was at home, often forgets to brush his teeth. He comes from some kind of rural place no one has strong opinions about (maybe Nevada? Nebraska?). He's a kid with very deep convictions that are unburdened by facts or history. Example: One time he overheard someone calling this whole operation in the Gulf "George Bush's war," and Chucky got all puffed up about it and said Bush was doing the best he could with the mess Bill Clinton left. And that started this whole fight about who actually declared war and whose idea it was to invade Iraq, and everyone was trying to convince Chucky that Clinton didn't start the war and all Chucky did was shake his head and say "Guys, I'm pretty sure you're wrong about this" like he felt sorry for them. Bishop pressed him and insisted that it didn't matter if he was pro-Bush or pro-Clinton or whatever, that who started the war was a simple neutral objective fact. And Chucky said he thought Bishop needed to "support our C and C" and Bishop blinked at that and asked "What's a C and C?" and Chucky said "Commander and chief." So this started a whole new argument where Bishop told him it's not commander *and* chief, it's commander *in* chief, and Chucky looked at him with an expression like he knew they were pulling a prank on him and he was determined not to fall for it.

Anyway, they don't talk politics much. None of them do. It's sort of beside the point.

One time Chucky tried to get them to open the portals in the Bradley so that during the trip he could watch the horizon and keep his bearings, which he said would help with the dizziness and vomiting. But that argument went nowhere because if the portals came off then it wouldn't be dark inside the Bradley and they couldn't sleep, and also because the portals are covered with armor, and no one wants to sacrifice any armor at all given the number of mines and bombs and snipers they'd encountered thus far. Chucky pointed out that the Bradley was equipped with several M231 assault rifles that are expressly designed to fit through the portals (they are basically M16s without the front sighting assembly, which is too tall to fit inside the portal, and a much shorter stock, because the inside of a Bradley is pretty narrow) and Chucky asked didn't the mere existence of the M231 imply that they should have the external portals open so they could shoot through them? Bishop said he was impressed with Chucky's logic, even if it was transparently self-serving. Anyway, the commander of the Bradley, whose name is actually Bradley but whose nickname is "Baby Daddy" for the several families back home he joined the army to get away from, decided that the armor would stay. He said, "If you have protection you'd be a fool not to use it," which was pretty funny coming from him.

So one would think with the vomiting and the brittle knowledge of world events and the constant whining about the closed firing portals that Chucky would be a prime candidate for pariah status. Given how many times they have to go somewhere in the back of a Bradley, Chucky should be very unpopular indeed. But that's not how it works. Chucky is roundly loved and adored and has been ever since this one midnight raid on a suspected enemy compound when his night-vision goggles broke, and instead of falling back like any of them would have done he kept on opening doors and clearing rooms with a goddamn flashlight. Which in an operation like that might as well have been a giant neon sign that said *Shoot Me!* Seriously, the courage of this kid is off the charts. He once told Bishop that the only thing worse than being shot at is when the people shooting run away. And Bishop really thought that Chucky would prefer the enemy stand still while trying to kill him rather than not try to kill him at all. So everyone loves Chucky. And it's clear they do because they keep calling him Chucky, which is a nickname that maybe to an outsider sounds cruel for the way it ribs someone for his greatest personal flaw, but what it actually does is acknowledge that they accept this person and love this person *despite* that flaw. It's a very male way of expressing unconditional love. All of this goes unsaid, naturally.

Plus there is the thing about the girl. Chucky's primary conversational topic: Julie Winterberry. Everyone likes hearing about her. Hands down the most beautiful girl in Chucky's whole high school, the girl who won every relevant queen-type prize a girl could win, who ran the table four years in a row, a face that launched a thousand erections, a girl whose beauty didn't cause the usual nervous sniggering among the teenage boys but rather an almost physical pain that biting the inside of one's cheek was sometimes an effective cure for. The boys were despondent if she did not look at them, shattered if she did. Chucky has a photo, a senior portrait, that he passes around and everyone has to agree that he is not exaggerating. *Julie Winterberry.* He says it with church-like reverence. The thing about Julie Winterberry is that Chucky had always been so intimidated by her beauty that he'd never spoken to her. She didn't even know his name. Then they graduated high school and he went to basic training, where he had the most punishing drill sergeant in the history of the U.S. Armed Forces, after which he figured if he could overcome that asshole, he could talk to Julie Winterberry. She didn't seem like much of a challenge anymore, not after basic. So in those few weeks he was home before deployment he asked her on a date. And she said yes. And now they're in love. She even sends him dirty pictures of herself that everyone begs Chucky to show that he will not show. People are literally on their hands and knees, begging.

What everyone likes about the story is the part where he finally asks out the girl. Because the way Chucky tells it, it's not like he had to *work up the courage* to do it. It's more like it no longer required courage to do. Or maybe he discovered that he had plenty of courage all along, inside him, ready to be used, and everyone likes imagining that. They hope the same thing has happened to them, too, because they are occasionally terrified out of their minds over here, and they hope when the time comes for them to be brave, they will be brave. And it's nice to think that they have this well of courage inside that can get them through the impossible things ahead.

If a kid like Chucky could land a girl like Julie Winterberry, surely they can make it through one lousy war.

They ask him to tell about it especially when they're on clean-up, which is just about the biggest injustice of this war, that soldiers sometimes have to clean up the remains of suicide bombers. Imagine hunting around for body parts with a burlap bag oozing slop that looks like the inside of a pumpkin. And the road is baking in the sun and so the random pieces of flesh aren't only sitting there but actually literally *cooking*. That smell: blood and meat and cordite. When they're doing this, they ask Chucky to tell them about Julie Winterberry. It passes the time.

Eventually Baby Daddy struck a deal with Chucky that he could ride up top next to the gunner. Of course this is against regulations because a person standing where Chucky stands interferes with the movement of the M242. But Baby Daddy was willing to go against regulations in this one instance because it's better than having to smell Chucky's puke every time. So Chucky gets to ride up top where he can watch the horizon in that way he needs to do to avoid motion sickness, with the tacit agreement that if any shit goes down he needs to drop into the cargo area pronto. Which he'd have no problem doing because no one wants to be near the M242 when it's firing. That thing can tear up an SUV like it's tissue paper. The bullets are as long as Chucky's forearm.

They were told to expect an hour's travel to the village with the recently murdered mayor. Bishop sits in the back of the Bradley with his helmet over his eyes and his earplugs pushed practically into his brain. Blessed silence. Sixty sweet minutes of nothingness. Bishop doesn't even dream over here. One of the many surprises of war is how it has turned him into a sleeping savant. If he's told he has twenty minutes for a nap, he will use all twenty minutes. He can tell the difference between sleeping two hours and sleeping two and a half. He can feel the contours of consciousness over here that he never felt back home. Back home, life was like driving a road at sixty miles per hour, every little bump and texture flattened into an indistinguishable buzz. War is like stopping and feeling the road with his bare fingers. A person's awareness expands like that. War makes the present moment slow. He feels his mind and body in ways he never knew were possible.

Which is why Bishop knows for sure when the Bradley comes to a halt and he wakes up that they are not yet at their destination: that was a thirty-minute nap. He can tell by the way his eyes feel, or maybe more accurately the way the space just behind his eyes feels, a certain kind of pressure there.

"How long have we been driving?" he asks Chucky.

"How long you think?" he says. They like to test each other this way.

"Thirty minutes?"

"Thirty-two."

Bishop smiles. He climbs up top, blinks at the mighty desert sunlight, looks around.

"Suspicious thing in the road," Chucky says. "Up ahead. Possible IED. You gotta see this. You'll never believe it."

He hands Bishop the binoculars and Bishop searches the dusty and cracked asphalt in front of them until he sees it: a soup can in the center of the road. Standing straight up. Its label pointing right at the convoy. That familiar red logo.

"Is that—"

"Yep," Chucky says.

"A Campbell's soup can?"

"Affirmative."

"Campbell's tomato soup?"

"All the way out here. I shit you not."

"That's not a bomb," Bishop says. "That's modern art."

Chucky gives him a queer look.

"It's a Warhol," Bishop explains. "It looks like a Warhol."

"What the fuck is a war hall?" Chucky says.

"Never mind."

What happens when they see something that might be an IED is they call in the explosive ordnance disposal techs and then wait around, glad that disarming bombs is not their job. And of course the EODs are like thirty minutes away and so everyone's on edge waiting and smoking and Chucky staring out into the distance suddenly says to Bishop, "I'll bet I can hit that camel with your rifle."

So everyone turns to see what camel he's pointing at and they see this haggard lonely thing way off in the distance without anything around it, this weak-looking straggler all alone in the desert about a quarter mile away all wavy-looking from the heat radiating off the sand. Bishop is interested; Chucky is not known for his precision with a rifle. "What are we betting?" he says.

"Whoever loses," says Chucky, who's clearly thought this part through because he's right there with an answer, "has to stand in the Port-a-John for an hour."

Cries of disgust from the surrounding eavesdroppers. This is a proper bet. Everyone knows the only thing hotter than the sun in the desert is a Port-a-John in the sun in the desert. How the desert heat gets trapped inside the thick plastic walls and brings the collective excrement of the whole company practically to boiling. People swear a pork chop could be braised in there, not that anyone ever would. Most people hold their breath and get out as quickly as they can. There are stories of people becoming dehydrated only because they had a particularly long shit.

Bishop thinks about this. "An hour?" he says. "You have things to do, Chucky. I wouldn't want to take you away from jerking off for a whole hour. How about five minutes?"

But Chucky's not having it, because everyone knows that Bishop has been through sniper training, and one of the things snipers learn is to hold their breath a long time, maybe even upward of five minutes. Those are the stories, anyway.

"An hour," Chucky says. "That's the deal."

So Bishop makes a show about thinking it over, but everyone knows he'll take the bet. He can't turn down a bet like that. And eventually he says "Fine" and everyone cheers and he hands Chucky the M24 and says, "Doesn't matter. You're never gonna hit it." And Chucky gets into this kneeling position that looks exactly like the little green army men that kids play with—a posture that is decidedly *not* the textbook way to fire the M24 and which makes Bishop smile and shake his head—and the onlookers, who include the Bradley's full complement and now even the guys from the supply truck behind them, start hollering and offering advice both genuine and not.

"Whaddya say there, Chucky? About four hundred meters?"

"I'd say three ninety."

"More like three seventy-five."

"Wind at about five knots?"

"Ten knots!"

"Ain't no wind, jackass."

"Make sure you account for the heat coming up off the ground!"

"Yeah, it'll make the bullet rise."

"That true?"

"That's not true."

"Stop fucking with him."

"Shoot it, Chucky! You got this!"

And so on, Chucky just ignoring it all. He settles into position and holds his breath and everyone waits for the shot—even Baby Daddy, who as commander of the Bradley unit is supposed to be above all this and detached but really privately savors the idea of Chucky's chutzpah landing him in a Port-a-John for an hour (Baby Daddy is in a war because of his shenanigans, so he loves when anyone else gets their comeuppance too). And the seconds tick by and everyone gets quiet expecting Chucky to shoot and they can't decide if they should be looking at the camel or at Chucky, and he wiggles and lets his air out and sucks back in again and Bishop laughs and says, "The more you think about it, the worse you're gonna miss."

"Shut up!" says Chucky, and then—frankly faster than anyone expected after the shut up thing—Chucky fires. And everyone looks at the camel in time to see a small mist of blood poof up where the bullet glances off its left hind quarter.

"Yes!" Chucky said, his arms up. "I hit him!"

Everyone cheers and looks at Bishop, who is now sentenced to sixty ungodly merciless minutes in the shit oven. Except that Bishop is shaking his head saying, "No, no, no. You didn't hit him."

"What do you mean?" Chucky says. "I did too hit him."

"Look," Bishop says, pointing at the camel, who is understandably surprised and upset and confused and is now terrified and running, weirdly, right at the convoy. Bishop says, "That doesn't look like a dead camel to me."

"The bet wasn't to *kill* the camel," Chucky says. "The bet was to hit it."

"What do you think *hit* means?" Bishop says.

"I shot it, with a bullet. That's what it means, end of story."

"Do you know what I'd be if all my hits were glancing shots off the ass? Demoted, that's what."

"You're trying to get out of losing."

"Didn't lose," Bishop says. "You tell a sniper you're gonna hit something, that something better be dead. Otherwise you didn't hit it."

The camel, meanwhile, is now full-out charging the convoy, and some of the assembled spectators laugh at the idiocy of the thing, running *toward* the people who shot it. Kind of the opposite of an insurgent, someone says. Big dumb stupid animal. And Chucky and Bishop keep arguing about who won the bet and defending their own interpretation of what the verb "to hit" really means— Chucky taking a strictly literal approach against Bishop's, which is more context-driven—when the camel, which is now maybe a hundred yards off, suddenly veers to its right and begins moving more or less directly at the Campbell's soup can.

Baby Daddy is the first to recognize this.

"Hey!" he says, pointing at it. "Whoa! Stop it! Kill it! Kill it now!"

"Kill what?"

"The fucking camel!"

"Why?"

"Look!"

And they see the camel running at the soup can, which is right now also being approached by the EODs in their massive and almost comically large armor, and the soldiers who understand what is happening take out their sidearms and shoot at the camel. And they can see where their bullets strike the thing harmlessly, shaving off the outermost layer of fur and hide. All the gunshots really do is terrify the thing more, and it increases speed and runs with these huge bulging eyes and a foam dripping from its mouth and people start yelling "Duck!" or "Run!" at the EODs, who have no idea what is happening, not having been part of the whole camel-shooting thing in the first place. And the camel keeps going and it's clear its path is going to take it right over the soup can and everyone now finds whatever cover they can find and they close their eyes and shield their heads and wait.

It takes a few moments to realize nothing is going to happen.

The first soldiers who pop their heads up see the camel tearing ass away from them, the empty soup can bouncing harmlessly behind it, end over end.

They watch the camel half gallop, half stagger into the immense desert horizon, overtaken eventually by the shimmers coming off the sand. The EODs have removed their helmets and are walking back toward the company, cursing loudly. Bishop stands next to Chucky, watching the camel race away.

"Fuck, man," Chucky says.

"It's okay."

"That was too close."

"It wasn't your fault. You didn't mean to."

"It's like everything slowed down. I was just like—*ffft*," he says, and he puts his palms up by his eyes indicating a total narrowing and tunneling of his vision. "I mean, I was in it."

"In what?"

"The war hall," Chucky says. "I get it now. That was it."

And they think that's the end of the story—a bizarre one to tell back home, one of those surreal moments that present themselves during war. But just as everyone is getting comfortable back in their positions and the convoy begins to rumble forward and they've been driving maybe thirty seconds, suddenly from inside the Bradley Bishop feels a jolt and a wave of heat and hears that crack-boom sound of something in front of them exploding. It's that sound—in the desert they can hear it for miles—the worst sound of the war, the sound that will later make them all flinch even when they've been home for years whenever a balloon pops or fireworks explode, because it will remind them of this, the sound of a mine or IED, the sound of violent gruesome random death.

And now comes the panic and the screaming and Bishop pushes his way up to the turret and stands next to Chucky and sees how the Bradley in front of them is on fire, this tar-black smoke rolling out of it as one by one soldiers climb out bleeding and dazed. The front of the Bradley seems to have been cracked in half right at the spot where the driver would have been sitting. One soldier is being carried away by two others, his leg attached by only bare red ribbons at the knee, swinging like a fish on a line. Baby Daddy is already calling for helicopters.

"The soup can," Bishop says, "must have been a decoy. So we let our guard down." And he turns to Chucky and knows right away by

Chucky's look of terror and panic that something is wrong. Chucky holds his hands over his belly, clutching the wound. Bishop pulls the hands back and doesn't see anything.

"There's nothing here, Chuck."

"I felt it. I felt something go in." He is already turning pale. Bishop sits him in the belly of the Bradley and pops open his jacket to reveal the body armor underneath and still sees nothing.

"Look. You're all armored up. You're fine."

"Trust me, it's there."

And so he pulls off the armor with Chucky moaning and peels off his undershirt and there it is, exactly where he said it would be, a few inches above his belly button, a dime-size spot of blood. Bishop wipes it away and sees the small cut underneath—maybe the size of a large splinter—and laughs.

"Jesus, Chucky, you're all worked up about *this*?"

"Is it bad?"

"You dumb motherfucker."

"It's not bad?"

"It's tiny. You're fine. You're an asshole."

"I don't know, man. There's something wrong."

"There's nothing wrong. Shut the fuck up."

"It feels like there's something very not right here."

So Bishop stays with him insisting everything is okay and suggesting he stop being such a pussy while Chucky keeps saying that something doesn't feel right, and they stay like that until they hear the thumping of the helicopters, at which point Chucky says, very quietly, "Hey Bishop, listen, I have something to tell you."

"Okay."

"You know about my girlfriend? Julie Winterberry?"

"Yeah."

"She's not my girlfriend. I made that up. She doesn't even know who I am. I only talked to her once. I asked her for her picture. It was the last day of school. Everyone was trading pictures."

"Oh man, you're going to be sorry you said that."

"Listen, I made it up because every day I think about not talking to her."

"This is good info. This might be new-nickname worthy."

"I regret it so much, not talking to her."

"Seriously, you are never going to hear the end of this."

"Listen. If I don't make it—"

"You will be taking shit for this literally nonstop forever."

"If I don't make it, I want you to find Julie and tell her how I really feel. I want her to know."

"Seriously, it will last the rest of your life. I will call you when you are eighty years old and make fun of you about Julie Winterberry."

"Just promise."

"Fine. I promise."

Chucky nods and closes his eyes until the medics come and take him on a stretcher and into the helicopter and they all disappear into the dull-copper sky. Then the rest of the convoy continues its loud, slow journey.

What happens that night is that Chucky dies.

A piece of shrapnel only about half an inch long and as thin as the straw on a juice box had clipped the artery feeding his liver, and by the time doctors figured it out he'd lost too much blood and was in full-blown acute liver failure. Baby Daddy is the one to tell them, the next day, right before going out in sector.

"Now forget about it," he says when it becomes clear the news is going to interfere with their concentration on the upcoming patrol. "If the army wanted us to have emotions, they would have issued us some."

And it's a quiet and subdued and uneventful evening, and the whole time Bishop feels angry. Angry at Chucky's senseless death and the fuckers who planted that bomb, but also angry at Chucky, at Chucky's cowardice, that he could never say what he needed to say to Julie Winterberry, that a man who could rush into dark rooms where people with machine guns wanted to kill him was unable to talk to a stupid girl. These two kinds of courage seem so different they ought to have separate words.

That night, he can't sleep. He broods. His anger has twisted so that he is no longer angry at Chucky but rather angry at himself. Because he and Chucky are no different. Because Bishop has terrible things inside him that he cannot bring himself to tell anyone. The great evil secret of his life—sometimes it feels so big it's like he needs a new inner organ to contain it. The secret sits inside him and devours him. It devours time and grows stronger as time passes, so that now when he thinks of it he cannot separate the event itself from his later revulsion of it.

What happened with the headmaster.

The man whom everyone revered and loved. The headmaster. Bishop loved him too, and when, in fifth grade, he picked Bishop for tutoring, for extra weekend lessons that absolutely had to be kept secret because the other boys would be jealous, it made ten-year-old Bishop feel so special and wanted. Picked out of the crowd. Admired and loved. And how he shudders at it now, years later, that he was so easily tricked, that he never questioned the headmaster, not even when he told Bishop that their lessons would be about *what to do with girls*, because all the boys were terrified of girls and didn't know what to do with girls, and Bishop felt really lucky he had someone to show him. It started with photographs from magazines, men and women both, together, separate, nude. Then Polaroid pictures, then the headmaster suggesting they take Polaroids of each other. Bishop remembers only fragments, images, moments. The headmaster gently helped Bishop out of his clothes and still Bishop did not think this was wrong. He did everything willingly. He let the headmaster touch him, first with his hands, then with his mouth, afterward telling Bishop how wonderful and handsome and special he was. The headmaster saying, after a few months of this, *Now you try it on me*. The headmaster disrobing. The first time Bishop saw him, red and swollen and strongly persuasive. Bishop trying to do on the headmaster what the headmaster had done on him, and doing so awkwardly, clumsily. The headmaster getting frustrated and angry for the first time when Bishop's teeth accidentally got involved, grabbing Bishop by the back of the head and thrusting and saying *No, like this* and later apologizing at the tears that arrived when Bishop's gag reflex engaged. Bishop feeling like this was his fault. That he would practice and do it better next time. Then doing no better next time, nor the next time. One day the headmaster stopping him halfway through and turning him around and leaning over him and saying, *We'll have to do this the way adults do it. You're an adult, right?* And Bishop nodding his head because he didn't want to be bad at this anymore, didn't want the headmaster to be angry anymore, so when the headmaster positioned himself behind Bishop and pushed himself in, Bishop endured it.

The horror of it now, these images cascading back to Bishop—so many years later and ten thousand miles away, in a desert, in a war. Bishop thinking how even this secret has another secret, a deeper and more devastating layer, the thing that made him sure he was evil and broken, which is that while the headmaster was doing what he was doing, Bishop liked it.

He looked forward to it.

He *wanted* it.

And not only because of how it made him feel wanted and special and unique and picked out of the crowd, but also because what the headmaster did to him, especially at first, *felt good.* It jolted his body in a way nothing else did. A way that he loved while it was happening and missed when it stopped, the headmaster abruptly canceling their lessons in the spring. And Bishop felt rejected and abandoned and realized all at once sometime in early April that the headmaster had taken up with a new boy—Bishop could tell by the looks they shared in the hallway, and how the new boy had recently turned sullen and quiet. And this made Bishop furious. He began acting out in school, talking back to the nuns, getting into fights. When he was finally expelled he was sitting with his parents in the headmaster's office and the headmaster said *I'm very sorry it came to this* and there were so many layers of meaning to this that Bishop just laughed.

He began poisoning the headmaster's hot tub the next week.

And this is the part that horrifies him most now. How he tried to get back at the headmaster like a jilted girlfriend. How he would have stopped behaving badly if the headmaster had only taken him back, invited him in. It's horrifying because he can't tell himself now that he was an innocent victim. He feels more like an accomplice in his own perversion. It was an evil that happened—and he *wanted* it to happen.

The full consequence of this didn't reveal itself until later, in adolescence, at military school, where the worst thing in the world was to be a queer or faggot, and if anyone called another boy a queer or faggot or gaywad or homo he would routinely want to fight, and the way the boys showed everyone else they weren't queers or faggots was to make fun of others for being huge queers and faggots, and to do so loudly. This became Bishop's calling card. He was especially ruthless to his roommate sophomore year, a slightly effeminate boy named Brandon. Whenever Brandon walked into the communal shower Bishop would say something like, "Careful boys, don't drop your soap." Or before going to bed, he'd ask, "Do I have to put duct tape over my asshole tonight or can you behave yourself?" Things like that, the typical late-eighties jock-type harassment. Nicknames included "Ass Pirate" and "Daisy." As in "Eyes forward, Daisy" when they were standing next to each other at the urinals. Brandon eventually left the school, which was a relief to Bishop, who had developed powerful longings for Brandon that had become almost physically painful. How he watched as Brandon undressed, watched him in class hovering intently and dutifully over his notes, chewing on a pencil.

But that was so many years ago, and in all this time he's never told anyone. And he suddenly jolts up in his bed on this, the day that Chucky has died, and he decides he needs to write a letter. Because Chucky was killed with so many secrets still inside him that his dying wish was to let them out, and Bishop does not want to feel the same when his time comes. He wants to have more courage than that.

He decides he'll write to everyone in his life. He'll write his sister, apologizing for becoming so distant, explaining that he detached because he was damaged—because the headmaster must have flipped some switch inside him and now he felt so much rage, at the headmaster for doing this to him, and at himself for being so awful and perverted and deviant and unfixably broken. He was trying to protect her, he would tell Bethany; he didn't want to break her, too.

And he'll write his parents, and Brandon. He'll track down Brandon and ask his forgiveness. Even mighty Andy Berg, whom he never saw again after trapping the poor kid in a stairwell and pissing on him. Even the Berg needs a letter. He'll do one every night until all his secrets are laid bare. He fetches some army stationery, sits in the barren and concrete-walled break room lit fluorescently green. He'll write to Samuel first, he decides. Because he knows exactly what he wants to say and it will be a short letter and already it's very deep into the night and he has to be awake again in a few hours, so he begins, and in a flare of inspiration and focus he finishes the letter in under five minutes. And he folds it up and places it inside an official U.S. Army envelope and licks it closed and writes Samuel's full obnoxiously hyphenated name on the outside and places it in his locker with all his other personal effects. He feels good about it, about getting that off his chest and out into the world, and he feels good about his new project, about letting go of the things that have been bundled up inside him all these years. He feels like he's actually looking forward to writing the letters to his sister and his parents and the various friends he's abandoned along the way, and he falls asleep feeling really good about these letters, not knowing that they will never be written, because tomorrow he will be out on patrol and he'll be thinking about Julie Winterberry (who obviously also needs a letter) when a trash can will explode a few feet away from him, remote-detonated by someone watching from a second-story window way down the street, someone who doesn't really see Bishop but rather sees only his uniform, who has stopped recognizing anyone wearing that uniform as anything remotely human, who if he could have heard what was going through Bishop's head at that moment as Bishop tried to mentally compose a letter to a beautiful girl back home about a dead friend who loved her would have never exploded that bomb. But of course we can't ever do this, hear these things. So the bomb exploded.

And the force of the bomb propelled Bishop into the air where for a moment everything was quiet and cold and the feeling of being inside the bomb's blast was like being inside one of his mother's snow globes, everything around him moving as though through thick liquid, hanging there, suspended, in its way beautiful, before the bomb shattered everything inside him and all his senses went dark and Bishop's body—no longer containing in any meaningful way Bishop himself—crashed into the street many meters away, and for the second time that week someone died while thinking about Julie Winterberry, who was ten thousand miles away at that moment and probably wishing that something exciting would finally happen to her.

The army collected his things and sent them to his parents, who found the letter addressed to Samuel Andresen-Anderson and remembered that was the strange name of their daughter's childhood pen pal, and so they gave the letter to Bethany, and she struggled many months before deciding she would finally give the letter to you.

And so this is how the letter traveled from a classified village somewhere in Iraq to this kitchen counter in downtown Manhattan, where it looks spotlighted by one of the kitchen's overhead recessed lights. You pick it up. It's almost weightless—a single page inside, which you remove. He's only written a few paragraphs. You sense that your big decision is approaching. It's a decision that will shape you and go on shaping you for years. You read the letter.

Dear Samuel,

The human body is so fragile. It's ruined by the smallest things. You can put twenty bullets into a camel and it will just keep coming for you, but half an inch of shrapnel is enough to kill us plain little people. Our bodies are the thin knife's edge separating us from oblivion. I am beginning to accept this.

If you're reading this, then something has happened to me and so I have a favor to ask. You and I did a terrible thing together that morning by the pond. The day your mother left, the day the police came. I'm sure you remember. What we did that morning, to each other, is terrible and unforgivable. I was corrupted, and I corrupted you too. And this corruption, I've discovered, does not go away. It stays with you and poisons you. It's with you for life. I'm sorry, but it's true.

I know you love Bethany. I love her too. She is good in a way I have never been good. She's not broken the way we are. I'd ask you to keep it this way.

This is my dying wish. The only thing I ask of you. For her sake, for my sake, please, stay away from my sister.

And so you've arrived. It's finally the moment to make your choice. To your right is the door to the bedroom, where Bethany waits for you. To your left, the elevator door and the whole great empty world.

It's time. Make a decision. Which door do you choose?

| PART SIX |

INVASIVE SPECIES

Late Summer 2011

1

PWNAGE OPENED THE REFRIGERATOR DOOR, then closed the refrigerator door. He stood in his kitchen trying really hard to remember the reason he came in here, but he couldn't come up with it. He checked his e-mail. He tried logging on to *World of Elfscape* but could not; it was Tuesday. He thought about going outside to the mailbox to get the mail but did not end up going outside because the mail might not have been delivered yet and he didn't want to make two trips. He looked across his front lawn at the mailbox, trying to judge whether there was mail in it by staring. He closed the door. He felt like something needed his attention in the kitchen but did not know what. He opened the refrigerator and looked at every item in the fridge, hoping one of them would serve as a kind of trigger for the thing he was supposed to remember about the kitchen. He saw the jars of pickles and plastic squeeze bottles of ketchup and mayonnaise and a bag of flaxseed he bought once in a moment of diet optimism but had not yet opened. There were five eggplants on the bottom shelf, clearly mushening from the inside, slowly collapsing in on themselves, five little purple pillows with small pools of biscuit-colored juice gathering under them. In the produce drawer, his various greens were brown and wilted. So were the cobs of corn on the top shelf, which were a sickly ecru, every kernel having lost its ripe, yellow puffiness and shriveled into roughly the shape of a diseased human molar. He closed the refrigerator door.

What happened on Tuesdays was that the *World of Elfscape* game servers were taken offline for most of the morning and sometimes part of the afternoon for regular maintenance and bug fixes and whatever genius-level technical things were required of computers that otherwise ran twenty-four hours a day and hosted ten million game players simultaneously with almost no network lag using some of the most ruthlessly secure encryption on the planet, servers so fast and efficient and mighty that they put to shame the machines now being used by the space program, or in nuclear missile silos, or in voting booths, for example. How a country that made *World of Elfscape* servers could not make a functional electronic voting machine was a question often posed on Election Day Tuesdays on the *Elfscape* message boards, while the gaming community patiently waited for the servers to come back online and, sometimes, also voted.

Some of these Tuesdays, though, were very special and particularly agonizing Tuesdays known as "Patch Days," when the engineers added some kind of game update so that the next time players logged on there would be *new things to do*—new quests, achievements, monsters, treasure. Such patches were necessary to keep the game fresh and interesting, but of course Patch Days had the longest game downtime because of the elaborate things being done to the game's servers and coding. It was not unheard of for the servers to be down all morning and all afternoon and sometimes, to the dismay of the game community, into the early evening. And this was happening today. The game was being patched. It was Patch Day.

And not knowing exactly when the servers would come back online made Pwnage feel stressed out, which was a bit of a paradox because the ostensible reason he played *Elfscape* was because it so effectively relieved his stress. It was where he turned when he felt too encumbered by the wearying details of his life. It all began about a year ago, just after Lisa left, one day when he felt the stress coming on particularly strong and none of the DVDs seemed very good and nothing was on TV and nothing in his online movie queue seemed interesting and all the console games he owned had been beaten and discarded and he felt this weird panicky sensation like when you're at a good restaurant but nothing seems appetizing, or like when you're first starting to come down with a cold or flu and not even water tastes good, that kind of all-encompassing negative darkness where the whole world seems boring and tedious and you feel this global weariness, and he was sitting in his living room in the gathering darkness of an evening just after daylight saving time ended so it was unusually gray at a depressingly early time of day, and he was sitting there realizing he was about to have a direct frontal head-on collision with the stress, that if he did not find a diversion quickly he was definitely going to get worked up to a degree that would spell certain trouble for his blood pressure and general circulatory system health, and what he usually did when this happened was to go to the electronics store and buy something, this time about a dozen video games, one of which was *World of Elfscape.* And since beginning with an Elf warrior named Pwnage he had advanced to play a whole stable of alternate characters with names like Pwnopoly and Pwnalicious and Pwner and EdgarAllanPwn, and he made a name for himself as a fearsome gladiatorial opponent and a very strong and capable raid leader, directing a large group of players in a fight against a computer-controlled enemy in what he came to regard as being a conductor in a battle-symphony-ballet type of thing, and he rather quickly got extraordinarily good at this—since being good required all manner of research, watching online videos of relevant battles and reading the forums and sifting through the numbers of the theory-crafting websites to see which stat was most useful during certain fights, such that he had slightly different gear-and-weapon combos for every fight in the game, each of them designed to mathematically maximize his death-dealing ability for that particular engagement, because he believed if he was going to do something he was going to do it *right,* he would give *one hundred and ten percent,* a work ethic he liked to think would soon help him with his kitchen renovation and novel-writing and new-diet plans, but which so far seemed to apply only in the area of video games. He created more characters and more accounts that he would play simultaneously on several computers, each of these new accounts requiring the purchase of a new computer, new game DVD, expansion pack, and monthly subscription fee, which meant that whenever he felt the need to create another character (usually because all his other characters were at the very highest level and were as good as they could possibly be and he was getting bored with dominating the game so thoroughly and the boredom would set off his stress alarms and so something had to be done immediately), it was such a massive capital outlay that he felt absolutely beholden to play the game even more, even if he was dimly aware of the irony here, that the stress of his deplorable financial situation created the need for all of these electronic stress relievers, the expense of which created more of the very same stress he was trying to avoid in the first place, which made it seem like his current level of electronic distraction was now failing and so he sought out newer and ever-more expensive distractions, thereby magnifying the stress-and-guilt cycle, a bit of a consumerist psychological trap that he frequently noted among Lisa's customers at the Lancôme counter, whose purchases of makeup only reinforced the central unattainable beauty illusion that drove them to buy makeup in the first place, but for some reason he could not spot in himself.

He checked the *Elfscape* servers. Still down.

It was like waiting out an airline delay, he thought, that urgency one felt at the airport, knowing people who love you are waiting at another airport, and the only thing keeping you from them is some intractable failure of technology. It felt like that, these Patch Days: Whenever he logged on after hours of delay, it felt like he'd gone home. It was hard to ignore this feeling. It was hard not to feel conflicted about it. It was a little troubling that when he thought about the vistas of *Elfscape*—the animated, digitally rendered rolling hills and misty forests and mountaintops and such—they struck him with the force of real memory. That he had a nostalgia and fondness for these places that outpaced the fondness he had for the real places in his life—this was complicated for him. Because he knew in some way the game was all false and illusory and the places he "remembered" didn't really exist except as digital code stored on his computer's hard drive. But then he thought about this time he climbed to the top of a mountain on the northern edge of *Elfscape*'s western continent and watched the moon rise over the horizon, watched the moonlight sparkle off the snow, and he thought it was beautiful, and he thought about how people talked about feeling transported by works of art, standing in front of paintings feeling hopelessly persuaded by their beauty, and he decided there was really no difference between their experience and his experience. Sure, the mountain wasn't real, the moonlight wasn't real, but the beauty? And his memory of it? *That* was real.

And so Patch Days were a unique horror because he was cut off from his source of wonder and beauty and surprise and was forced, sometimes for a whole day, to confront his normal everyday analog existence. And all week he'd been thinking about how to occupy his Tuesday so that the intolerable gap between waking up and logging on was more tolerable. Things to do that would make the time go by more quickly. He started a list on his smartphone, a "Patch Day To-Do List," so that he could record any thought he might have during the week regarding ways to make Patch Day more pleasant and endurable. The list contained, so far, three items:

1. Buy health food
2. Help Dodger
3. Discover great literature

That last item had been on his to-do list every week for six months, ever since he saw a sign at a nearby mega bookstore that said DISCOVER GREAT LITERATURE! and he'd put it on the list. He told the phone to repeat it, to put it on every weekly list thereafter, because he'd always wanted to be a reader, and he thought the whole curled-up-snugly-all-afternoon-with-a-cup-of-tea-and-a-good-book thing was a really excellent image to project about oneself online. Plus if Lisa ever happened to secretly check his phone's to-do list in a moment of curiosity or obsessional divorce regret, he was pretty sure she would approve of "Discover great literature" and maybe realize he was really changing as a person and want to take him back.

However, in six months he had discovered no literature whatsoever, great or otherwise. And every time he thought about discovering great literature, the effort made him feel tired, spent, boggy-headed.

So then there was item number one: Buy health food.

He had tried this already. Last week, he had finally entered the organic grocery store after having cased it from the street for several days watching people going in and out and quietly judging them for their yuppie elitist privileged lifestyle and their skinny hipster clothes and electric cars. It seemed necessary for him to construct an elaborate mental bulwark like this before even entering the organic grocery store because the more he sat in his car outside the store judging the customers the more he was convinced they were judging him too. That he wasn't hip enough, or fit enough, or rich enough to shop there. In his mind he was the protagonist of every story, the center of everyone's appalling attention; he was on display and out of place; the store was a panopticon of sneering, abusive judgment. He carried on long imaginary dialogues with the idealistic cashiers who were the gatekeepers between the food and the exits, explaining to them how he wasn't shopping there because it was the trendy thing to do but rather because it was coldly absolutely medically necessary according to the rules of his radical new diet plan. And whereas the other customers were there only out of fidelity to some hip movement—like the organic movement or the Slow Food movement or the locavore movement or whatever—he was there because he *needed* to be there, making him actually a *more authentic shopper* than they were, even if he did not per se fit the image of the typical customer according to the store's elaborate branding campaign. And so after several dozens of these practice dialogues he felt prepared and strong-willed enough to enter the grocery store, where he crept around and very quietly purchased the exact organic replicas of what he usually bought at the 7-Eleven down the street: canned soups, canned meat products, white bread, energy bars, frozen and reheatable pizza and dinner things.

And when he was unloading his cart at the checkout he felt a brief surge of belongingness that nobody had challenged his presence there or really even looked at him twice. That is, until the cashier—this cute girl with hip square glasses who was probably a grad student in ecology or social justice or something like that—looked at his boxed and frozen and canned food items and said "Looks like you're stocking up for a hurricane!" and then laughed lightly as if to say *Just kidding!* before bwooping the stuff over the laser scanner. And he smiled and halfheartedly chuckled but could not shake for the rest of the day the feeling of having been judged harshly by the cashier, who was not so subtly telling him his food purchases were unfit for consumption except in the most dire circumstances, such as apocalypse.

Point taken. On his next visit he bought only fresh things. Fruits, vegetables, meats wrapped in wax paper. Only things perishable, easily spoilable, and even though he had no earthly idea how to prepare the food, he felt healthier just buying it, just having it nearby, having people see him with it, like being on a date with someone extraordinarily attractive, how you want to go to public places with that person, he felt the same about his cart full of shiny eggplants and corn and various green growing things: arugula, broccoli, Swiss chard. It was so beautiful. And when he presented his food to this same cute cashier at the front of the store he felt like a child giving his mother a card he made at school.

"Did you bring a bag?" she said.

He stared at her, not fully comprehending the question. A bag for what?

"No," he said.

"Oh," she said, disappointed. "We encourage all our customers to bring reusable bags. You know, to save paper?"

"Okay."

"Plus you get a rebate," she said. "For every bag you bring, you get a rebate."

He nodded. He was no longer looking at her. He was instead looking at the cash register's video screen. He was pretending to very carefully analyze the price of each food item to ensure he wasn't overcharged. The cashier must have sensed his unease and his feeling of having been scolded (again) and so tried to diffuse the situation with a change of subject: "Whaddya gonna do with all this eggplant?"

But this did not diffuse the situation at all because the only answer he was capable of giving was the true one: "I don't know." And then when the cashier girl seemed sort of disappointed by this answer he added: "Maybe, like, a soup?"

This was so fucking unbearable. He couldn't even shop correctly.

He went home and found a website that sold reusable grocery bags, some outfit that used the proceeds from all their bag sales to do something good in some rain forest somewhere. More important, this outfit's logo was printed prominently on both sides of the bag so that when he gave the bags to the cashier she would see the logo and be impressed by it, since not only was he being a good environmentalist customer by bringing his own bags but the bags themselves also did good environmental things, making him *twice as pro-nature* as any of the other shoppers in the store.

He had the bags shipped, next day air. He went back to the store. He bought perishable fresh foods again, but only one of each kind—no overbuying one item and drawing attention to it, à la eggplant. He got in the line of the cute cashier girl with the square black glasses. She said "Hi," but it was a generic greeting. She did not remember their connection. She scanned and tallied his groceries. She said "Did you bring a bag?" and he said, casually, like it was no big deal and totally something he did all the time, "Oh sure, I brought a bag."

"Do you want to keep the rebate," she said, "or donate it?"

"Do what?"

"You get a rebate for bringing a bag."

"I know that."

"Would you like to donate it to one of our fifteen approved charities?"

And here he reflexively said "No," but it wasn't because he was stingy

...idn't genuinely want a charity to have his rebate. It was because ...knew he would have no idea how to choose among the fifteen charities, probably never having heard of any of them. So he declined because that seemed the smoothest, least embarrassing way to proceed and be done with the social encounter that, to be honest, had eaten up a lot of his spare brainpower all week, envisioning it, preparing for it.

"Oh," said the cashier, surprised, "okay, well, fine," with a kind of upturned lip and sarcastic eyebrow flare that conveyed something along the lines of *Aren't we being an asshole today?*

She continued swiping his food across the scanner and weighing his fruits and vegetables in what he interpreted as a cold and mechanical manner. Her fingers flew over the register buttons quickly and expertly. She was so comfortable here, so at home. She did not feel one bit of anxiety about her lifestyle or opinions. She so easily judged and dismissed him. And he felt something inside him sort of break, something curdled and sour, a fury he felt all the way to his liver. And he raised the empty cloth reusable grocery bag over his head. And he held it that way for a moment, maybe waiting for someone to say something. But no one did. No one paid an ounce of attention to him. And this seemed like the worst insult of all, that he was standing in this theatrical pose of violence and passion and no one cared.

So he threw it. The bag. He threw it point-blank, right at the cashier's feet.

And as he threw it, he made a war cry of wild anger—or at least he'd meant to. What actually came out was a garbled and low kind of gruff animal noise. He *gruntled.*

The bag struck the cashier sidelong in the hip region and she let out a sharp surprised cry and jumped backward as the bag crumpled and fell loosely to the floor. She stared at him with her mouth open and he stepped toward her and leaned over the cash register and opened his arms wide as a condor and yelled, "You know what?"

He did not know why he was opening his arms this way. He realized he didn't have anything on tap, mentally, with which to follow that question. The store had suddenly gone terribly quiet, the usual register-area beeping noises having stopped at the cashier's first shriek. He looked around him. He saw faces aghast—mostly women's—staring at him scornful and outraged. He backed slowly away from the cashier. He felt he needed to say something to the crowd, to explain the offense that provoked him, to justify his outburst, to communicate his innocence and righteousness and virtue.

What came out was: "You have got to *represent*!"

He didn't know why he said that. He remembered hearing it in that pop song recently. That Molly Miller song. He liked the sound of it, when he heard it in that song. He thought it was edgy and hip. But as soon as he said it out loud he realized he had no idea what it meant. He quickly left. Jammed his hands into his pockets and speed-walked out the door. He vowed never to return. That store, that cashier—you could never be good enough for them. There was no pleasing those people.

So item number one—Buy health food—that was a nonstarter.

There was still one thing he could check off his list on this Patch Day: Help Dodger. And to be honest this seemed like the most attractive option anyway, helping his guild mate, his brand-new friend, his *irlfriend,* was the term used among some *Elfscape* players, IRL being the community's popular acronym for "in real life," a place they talked about as if it were another country, far away. And he wanted to pretend the primary reason he found this option most appealing was because of some altruistic impulse to *help friends in need.* And that impulse might have been in there somewhere, part of the stew, but if he really thought about it he'd say the real reason was that his new friend was a writer. Dodger had a book contract, a publisher, access to the deeply mysterious book world that Pwnage needed because Pwnage was a writer too. And while he had been talking with his new friend that night at Jezebels he had trouble focusing completely because as soon as he discovered his new friend was a writer he kept thinking about his psychic-detective serial-killer novel, which he was sure was a million-dollar book. He'd begun the story in high school, in his junior-year creative writing class. He wrote the first five pages the night before it was due. The teacher had written that he'd done a "great job" and that he'd "captured the voice of the detective effectively" and in the margins during a certain scene where the detective had a vision of the killer stabbing a girl in the heart the teacher wrote "Scary!" and this confirmed that Pwnage could do very special things. He could ignite a real emotional response with something he wrote hastily in one night. It was a gift. You had it or you didn't.

Helping his new irlfriend, he decided, would give him the motivation

do everything he needed to do, because Dodger would then
him a favor, which he could cash in to find a publisher and receive
his *huge book contract,* which would not only dig him out of the hole he
was in mortgage-wise, and not only allow him the budget to buy actual
organic health food and renovate the kitchen, but would also convince
Lisa to come back, knowing as he did that one of her main complaints
about him was his "lack of initiative and drive," which she had spelled
out with painful clarity in the Irreconcilable Differences portion of the
paperwork that made their divorce agreement official.

So Dodger needed information about his mom, and his mom wasn't
talking. He needed information about her past, but the only concrete
things they had were a woefully incomplete arrest report and a photograph taken in 1968 of his mother at a protest. There was a girl sitting
near her in the photo who maybe seemed part of her group—the one
with the aviator shades—and Pwnage wondered if she was still alive.
Maybe she was, and maybe she still lived in Chicago, or maybe she had
friends still living in Chicago—all he needed were names. He texted
the photograph to Axman, a level-ninety elf warrior in the guild who
IRL was a high-school senior who was really good at writing code but
terrible at playing sports (unfortunately the only thing his father cared
about). Axman's programming specialty was something he called "social
bombing" where he was able to get his message almost simultaneously on
every blog comment thread and wiki page and community network and
message board on the internet. This was almost certainly worth a lot of
money to someone, this software, yet Axman had only used it so far to
exact revenge on the jocks who picked on him at school, photoshopping
their faces into explicit scenes from gay pornography, usually, and then
spamming the resulting real-looking image to half a billion people. It
was still in beta, Axman said of his application. He said he still needed
to figure out how to monetize it, though Pwnage suspected he was just
waiting to turn eighteen and move out of the house so he didn't have to
share his millions with his asshole dad.

So anyway, Pwnage sent Axman the photograph along with a quick
note: "Spam the Chicago boards. I want to know who this woman is."

And Pwnage sat back and felt really excellent about this. And even
though it took him maybe a minute or two tops, he felt mentally exhausted
by the effort: coming up with the plan, executing the plan. He felt spent,

done for the day, stressed out. He tried logging on to *Elfscape,* but the servers were still down.

He looked out the front window at the mailbox. He sat down in a chair to decide what to do next, then stood and sat in a different chair, because the other one was sort of uncomfortable. He stood again and walked to the center of the room and played a quick little game in his mind where he tried to stand in the room's exact middle, perfectly equidistant from all four walls. He abandoned this game before he got to the point where he felt like getting out the tape measure to verify his accuracy. He thought about watching a movie, but he'd seen them all before, his entire collection, many times. He thought about buying and downloading some new movies, but the effort of looking seemed like it would make him feel tired. He walked to the back of the house, then to the front, hoping something in the house would trigger a thought. There was something in the kitchen he needed to do, he was sure of it. He could feel the memory of it dancing beyond his grasp. He opened the oven, then closed it. Opened the dishwasher, then closed it. He opened the refrigerator, certain there was something in here that would remind him of the thing he was supposed to remember about the goddamn kitchen.

2

THE THING IS? Is that Laura Pottsdam had the feeling she was feeling a brand-new emotion. Like something she'd never felt before. Which was totally weird! She sat alone in her messy dorm room and fiddled with her iFeel app and waited for Larry to arrive and felt, for the first time, this new thing: *doubt*.

Doubt about many things.

Doubt right now about the iFeel app itself, which would not let her express her doubt, "Doubt" not being one of the fifty standard emotions available on iFeel. The app was letting her down. For the very first time, iFeel didn't know how she felt.

iFeel Horrible, she wrote, then decided no, she did not feel that way. That wasn't quite accurate. "Horrible" was what she felt after she hurt her mother's feelings again, or after she ate. She did not feel "Horrible" now. She deleted it.

iFeel Lost, she wrote, but that sounded stupid and cheesy and definitely not a Laura thing to say. People who were "Lost" were people with *no direction in life,* and she had direction in life, Laura did: Successful future vice president of communications and marketing, hello? Successful business major? Elite college student? She deleted "Lost."

iFeel Upset was wrong too, due to not seeming important enough. Delete.

The thing about iFeel was that she could broadcast how she felt at any given moment to her huge network of friends, and then their apps could auto-respond to her feelings with whatever message was appropriate given the emotion she expressed. And Laura usually loved this, how she could post *iFeel Sad* and within seconds her phone lit up with encouragement and support and pick-me-ups that made her feel actually less sad. She could select an emotion from the fifty standard emotion choices and post a little explanatory note or photo or both, then watch the support roll in.

But now, for the first time, the fifty standard emotion choices seemed, to Laura, limited. For the first time, she did not seem to feel any of the standard emotions, and this was really surprising to her because she'd always thought fifty choices were sort of a lot. And indeed there were some emotions she had never expressed feeling. She had not once ever written *iFeel Helpless,* even though "Helpless" was right there among the fifty standard emotions. She had never written *iFeel Guilty* or *iFeel Ashamed.* She had never written *iFeel Old,* obviously. She wasn't quite "Sad," nor was she "Miserable." It was more that she felt a kind of doubt that what she was thinking and feeling and doing wasn't exactly, totally right. And this was really uncomfortable because it contradicted the primary message of her life—that everything she did was correct and praiseworthy and whatever she wanted she should have because she deserved it, which was the more or less constant message from her mother, whom Laura called after the meeting with her Intro to Lit professor: "He thinks I cheated! He thinks I plagiarized a paper!"

"Did you?" her mother asked.

"No!" Laura said. Then, after a long pause: "Actually, yes. I did cheat."

"Well, I'm sure you had a good reason for it."

"I had an *excellent* reason for it," she said. Her mother had always done this, supplied her with good excuses. Once when she was fifteen and she came home at three in the morning obviously drunk and maybe also a little stoned, dropped off by three very loud, very much older boys who had recently either graduated high school or dropped out of it, the hair on the back of her head tangled and disheveled from what had obviously been vigorous friction against the backseat upholstery of a car, in a state so near comatose that when her mother said "Where have you been?" she could not think of anything to say and just stood there and dumbly wobbled, *even then* her mother had bailed her out.

"Are you sick?" she asked Laura, who, taking the bait, nodded her head. "You're sick, aren't you. You're coming down with something. You were probably taking a nap and lost track of time, right?"

"Yes," Laura said. "I don't feel well." Which of course required her to play hooky the next day to keep up the lie, claiming an unbearable cold-and-flulike illness, which was not too much of a stretch given the top-shelf hangover she woke up with.

The weirdest thing about these interactions was how much her mother seemed to believe them.

only that she was covering for her daughter; she seemed to
ly hallucinating about her. "You're a strong woman and I'm
of you," she'd tell Laura afterward. Or: "You can have anything
you want." Or: "Don't let anyone get in your way." Or: "I gave up my
career for you and so your success *literally means everything in the world
to me.*" Or whatever.

But now Laura also felt doubt, which was not one of the fifty allowable emotions according to iFeel, which itself made her doubt that it was
doubt she was feeling, a kind of mind-bending paradox she tried not to
spend too much mental time with.

She could not fail her Intro to Lit course. That much was clear. There
were too many things at stake—internships, summer jobs, grade point
average, a besmirched permanent record. No, that could not happen,
and she felt mistreated and wronged by her professor, who was willing to effectively *take away her future* because of one stupid assignment,
which seemed to her a response all out of proportion to the crime she'd
committed.

But, okay, even *this* she doubted, because if it didn't matter if she
cheated on any single assignment, then by extension it would be okay
if she cheated on *every* assignment. Which struck her as at least a little
weird because the agreement she'd reached with herself in high school
when all the cheating started was that it was okay to cheat on every
assignment now as long as sometime in the future she stopped cheating
and began doing the actual work, as soon as the assignments started to
matter. Which had not yet happened. In four years of high school and one
year of college, she had not done anything that registered even remotely
as *mattering.* So she cheated. On everything. And lied about it. All the
time. And did not feel one ounce of regret.

Not until today. What was screwing with her head today was this:
What if she made it all the way through college never having done any
actual college work? When she got her first very powerful publicity and
marketing job, would she know what to do? It struck her that she did
not even fully comprehend what was involved in the word "marketing,"
despite a low-level innate ability to recognize when someone else had
done it well, to her.

But every time she thought about maybe paying attention in her classes
and doing the work herself and really studying for tests and writing her
own papers, the fear that grabbed her was this: What if she couldn't do it?

What if she wasn't good enough? Or smart enough? What if she failed? She worried that the Laura unaided by deception and duplicity was not the elite college student both she and her mother assumed her to be.

For her mother, this knowledge would be crippling. Her mother—who since the divorce signed all her e-mails to Laura with *You are my only joy*—she could never handle Laura's failure. It would be like a nullification of her whole life's project.

So Laura had to do this, press forward with her plan, however risky, for her mother's sake. For both their sakes. There was no room for doubt.

Because the thing is? Is that now the stakes were even higher. Her phone call to the dean had effectively relieved her of any *Hamlet*-related suffering, but it had caused an unexpected problem, which was that the dean was now going to extraordinary lengths to show how sensitive the university was to Laura's hurt feelings. The dean was organizing a Mediation and Conflict Resolution Conference, which, as far as Laura could tell, was a two-day summit where she and Professor Anderson would sit across from each other at a table while several third-party peacemaker coaches would help them *engage in, manage, cope with, and productively resolve their differences in a safe and respectful environment.*

Which sounded like just about the worst thing in the world.

Laura knew it would be difficult to maintain her fabrications over two days of intense scrutiny. She knew she had to prevent this meeting at all costs, but she felt doubt and maybe even a bit of guilt and remorse about the only solution she'd so far devised.

There was a knock at the door. That, finally, would be Larry.

"One second!" she yelled.

She pulled off her shorts and tank top, yanked off her bra and underwear, and fetched the towel from her closet. It was the thinnest, smallest towel she owned. It was probably not even a proper bath towel because it did not wrap fully around her but rather revealed a long dagger of flesh all the way up her side. And the towel wasn't a standard width either, since the bottom came down only to that soft fleshy ticklish part where her legs met her torso. Any sudden movement and all would be revealed, in other words. It was white, threadbare from many washings, almost see-through in places. She had laundered it many times to achieve exactly this look. She used it roughly the same way a magician used a watch: to hypnotize.

She opened the door.

e said, and Larry's eyes darted south the moment he saw
mprehended her and her fantastically small towel. "I'm not
sorry," she said. "I was just about to shower."

e walked in and closed the door behind him. Larry Broxton, wearing his usual outfit: shiny silver basketball shorts, black T-shirt, big flip-
flops. It was not that Larry didn't own any other clothes—he did, she'd
seen his closet, filled with nice-looking button-downs that were surely
mother-supplied. It was just that this was the outfit he always chose, picking it up off the floor every morning and sniffing it and putting it on
again. She wondered how long before he'd get sick of this one outfit, but
it had been a month now and she hadn't seen him change yet. Boys can be
obsessively focused in their desires, she'd noticed. The things they liked
they tended to repeat again and again and again.

"You needed something?" Larry said. Guys were often so eager to do
what she wanted, especially when she wore the Towel. Larry sat on her
bed. She stood in front of him, so that her body was directly at his eye
level. If she drew the towel up an inch or two, he could probably see her
perfectly manicured pubic everything.

"Just a little favor," she said.

She had met Larry in her Intro to Lit course. She'd noticed him early
on and wondered if he was trying to grow a beard or simply forgetting
to shave. She'd seen him on campus. She knew he always wore the same
outfit and drove a really big black Humvee. He never spoke to anyone
until one day after class he asked if she wanted to come to a party at his
frat. A theme party. They were roasting a pig on a spit. Grilling hamburgers they called Brontosaurus Burgers. Making something called
Jurassic Juice. They called it the Slutty Cavegirls party.

Which was just so totally offensive! Because it's a party at a frat. *Obviously* she would dress slutty. They didn't have to tell her to do that. Did
they think she was stupid?

But okay, she went. Leather toga, no undies, whatever, and drank
Jurassic Juice until it tasted good, and talked to Larry, who used the word
circumspect in a sentence, which was impressive. They talked about what
was the worst thing about college. "The classes," Laura had said. "The
parking spaces are too small," Larry had said. And Laura felt that familiar intoxicated grabby allover need where all she wanted was to press herself up against him tightly. But she wasn't yet so drunk that she was going

to ho it up in front of all these people. She invited Larry back to her dorm room, where she gave him a blow job and he totally came in her mouth *without even asking,* which she personally found rude, but whatever.

She didn't know what *circumspect* meant, but sometimes you have to give a guy some credit. That's a good word.

"Do you still have your job?" Laura said, by which she meant his fantastic work-study position at the campus computer support center, where Larry spent most of his three-hour shift watching internet videos, occasionally helping some poor professor who didn't know how to hook up a printer.

"Yes," he said.

"Oh good," she said, and she stepped toward him, lightly touching her leg to his.

The weirdest thing that had happened when she seduced Larry in her dorm room that first time was that at the moment he orgasmed, she felt some odd lump of something suddenly enter her mouth, something soft but definitely, surprisingly, solid. She spit it into her hand and found what appeared to be a partially digested piece of Brontosaurus Burger. Which she assumed came out of Larry, and thus she concluded he had the unique ability to ejaculate his dinner out his penis, which was gross. After that, she requested that Larry do his deposits elsewhere.

"So at your job," Laura said, "you can remotely log in to any computer on campus, right?"

"Yeah."

"*Perfect.* There's a computer that needs to be investigated."

Larry frowned. "Whose computer?"

"Professor Anderson's."

"Oh, man. For real?"

She stroked his hay-colored hair with one hand. "Definitely. He's hiding something. Something *bad.*"

Laura had not considered another possibility: that men in fact did not have the biological capability to ejaculate the contents of their stomach, but rather that the bit of Brontosaurus Burger had been in Laura's mouth from the beginning, before the blow job even started, stuck there in the pit where a wisdom tooth used to be, and it was simply Larry's orgasmic bucking that jimmied it loose. In other words, a coincidence, if an unfortunate one. Afterward, she told Larry he was no longer welcome to come in her mouth, and he enthusiastically suggested other places to do his business. Her face, breasts, and butt were the expected targets. Expected because they had both ingested so many hours of internet pornography that they were simply acting out scenes that had become normalized, even banal. That Larry wanted to finish every sex act by splashing onto some part of her seemed like the customary way sex should end, raised as they were on porn's ejaculatory clichés. But then Larry expanded the target zone: He wanted to come on her feet, her back, in her hair, on the bridge of her nose, he wanted her to wear glasses so he could come on her glasses, on her elbows, on that thin part of her wrists. He was remarkably specific! She had no opinion about this, that Larry seemed to have a mental checklist of body parts he wanted to ejaculate onto. No opinion except that occasionally this made her feel like the sexual equivalent of a bingo card.

"What's Professor Anderson hiding?" Larry said. "What's on his computer?"

"Something embarrassing. Maybe even criminal."

"Seriously?"

"Definitely," Laura said, and she was maybe about eighty percent sure this was true. Because who didn't have something embarrassing on their computer? A dubious downloaded image, something questionable in the browser history. The odds were in her favor.

"I'm only supposed to log in to someone's computer if they ask me for help," Larry said. "I can't go snooping around."

"You can say you were doing routine maintenance."

She took another step toward him so that she emerged from behind the towel. She couldn't be sure what was going on down there, focused as she was on Larry, but judging by his expression—the way he stared at her—she figured she was now mostly exposed from the waist down.

"Think about it," Laura said. "If you find something that proves he's not fit to be a teacher, you'd be a hero. *My* hero."

Larry stared at her.

"Will you do this for me?" she said.

"I'll get in trouble," he said.

"You won't, I promise," she said, taking his head with the other hand, letting go of the towel, which dropped softly to the floor.

She always loved this moment, the change that came over men when they recognized what was about to happen, how fast they clicked over to a new kind of intensity and focus. Larry was already grabbing at her.

"Okay," he said. "I'll do it."

She smiled. At that moment, he would have agreed to anything.

It was never this moment that Laura had a problem with, the moment of seduction. The problem was *afterward*. Men tended to drift away from her in a few weeks. They could not be counted on. She'd had three different guys, for example, all friends-with-benefits type guys, come out as bi-a-sexual soon after their encounters, meaning, they said, that they were no longer attracted to either gender, equally.

Which she was like, what are the odds?

After Larry had finished and left her dorm room and she had wiped the slimy traces of him off her shinbones (which was a first), she returned to iFeel, hoping that maybe she'd have more clarity now, maybe she'd be able to figure out what to say, what she felt. But no luck. Her emotions seemed as foreign as ever.

She decided to activate the auto-correct function on iFeel, a really excellent little piece of software that took whatever emotion you thought you were feeling and compared it to the millions of entries collected in the iFeel database and, in a crowd-surfing, data-mining sort of way, extrapolated which of the fifty standard emotions you were actually feeling. Laura clicked a link, a text field opened up, and she began typing:

iFeel like i dont deserve 2 fail my class just b/c i cheated on some dumb assignment but also i know i prolly shouldnt be cheating so much in all of my classes b/c someday ill have to go out & get a job & have knowledge in my field or whatever ~('•~•)~ but at this point i actually HAVE TO cheat b/c ive cheated so much in the past that i usually have no idea whats going on in any of my classes (☉﹏☉) so if i stopped cheating i would get really bad grades & maybe even fail out of school so it seems 2 me if im going 2 fail either way i might as well cheat & get the grades i need 2 become the powerful business professional my mother so desperately wants me 2B. so i have to prevent this meeting with the professor & ive thought about it alot & ive realized that the university wont require the professor to come to this meeting if the professor is NOT AN EMPLOYEE OF THE UNIVERSITY \(^.^)/ so maybe the way forward is to totally discredit the professor & get him fired & ruin

his life which makes me feel a little guilty & also angry that the school
has boxed me in this way & essentially forced me 2 do something i will
feel sort of remorseful about later all b/c i plagiarized one stupid paper
¯_(☉ᴖ☉)_/¯

She pressed Enter and the iFeel app processed this for a moment before
the auto-correct displayed the answer:

Do you mean "Bad"?

Sure, that must be what she meant. She posted it right away: *iFeel Bad*.
And seconds later the text messages poured in.

cheer up grl! :)

don't feel bad ur gr8!!

luv ya!

ur the best!!!!

And so on, dozens of them, from friends and admirers, boyfriends
and lovers, colleagues and acquaintances. And while they did not know
the reason she felt bad, it was surprisingly easy to pretend they did, that
they knew about the plan, and so each message had the effect of steeling
her resolve. This is what she had to do. She thought about her future, her
mother, everything that was at stake. And she knew she was right. She
would go through with the plan. The professor had it coming. He was
asking for it. He wouldn't know what hit him.

3

THEY MET at one of the chain restaurants near Henry's suburban office park, the kind of place erected right off the highway, on a terrifyingly busy one-way access road. The route here tended to confuse one's GPS device or map app, as it required a series of awkward and counterintuitive U-turns to navigate the various viaducts and on-ramps and cloverleafs made necessary by the nearby fourteen-lane expressway.

Inside, the music was happy Top 40 sing-along stuff, the floors industrially carpeted and, within the orbits of children in high chairs, chummed with food globs and milk slicks and crayons and damp little twisted flecks of napkin. Families stood in the front vestibule awaiting their tables, staring at the round plastic puck the hostess gave them, a device that contained some kind of inner motor-and-light apparatus that would blink and agitate when their table was free.

Henry and Samuel sat in a booth holding menus—large, laminated menus, dynamically colored and complexly subdivided, roughly the size of the Ten Commandments in that one movie about the Ten Commandments. The food was pretty standard chain-restaurant fare: burgers, steaks, sandwiches, salads, a list of inventive appetizers with names involving whimsical adjectives, e.g., *sizzlin'*. What allegedly set this particular restaurant chain apart from others was that it did something weird with an onion—cut it and fried it in such a way that the onion unfurled itself and resembled, on the plate, a kind of desiccated, many-fingered claw. There was a Rewards Club one could join to earn points for the eating of such things.

Their table was cluttered with the several appetizers Henry had already purchased with his company's credit card. They were here doing "field research," as Henry called it. They sampled the menu and discussed which items had frozen-meal potential: golden fried cheddar bites, yes; seared ahi tuna, probably not.

Henry noted all this on his laptop. They were digging into a plate of miso-glazed chicken skewers when Henry finally asked about the topic he was eager to discuss but trying hard to seem indifferent about.

"Oh, by the way, how's it going with your mother?" he said in this dismissive way while sawing at a chicken chunk with a fork.

"Not great," Samuel said. "Today I spent the whole afternoon at the UIC library, going through the archive, looking at everything they had from 1968. Yearbooks. Newspapers. Hoping to find something about Mom."

"And?"

"Zilch."

"Well, she wasn't in college very long," Henry said. "Maybe a month? I'm not surprised you can't find anything."

"I don't know what else to do."

"When you saw her, at her apartment, did she seem, I don't know, happy?"

"Not really. More like quiet and guarded. With a hint of hopeless resignation."

"That sounds familiar."

"Maybe I should go see her again," Samuel said. "Drop by sometime when her lawyer's not there."

"That is a terrible idea," Henry said.

"Why?"

"For one? She doesn't deserve it. She has given you nothing but problems all your life. And two? The crime. It's way too dangerous."

"Oh, c'mon."

"Seriously! What's the address again?"

Samuel told him and watched as his father typed this into his laptop. "It says here," Henry said, staring at his screen, "there've been sixty-one crimes in that neighborhood."

"Dad."

"Sixty-one! In the last month alone. Simple assault. Simple battery. Forcible entry. Vandalism. Motor vehicle theft. Burglary. Another simple assault. Criminal trespass. Theft. Another simple assault. On the sidewalk, for Pete's sake."

"I've been there already. It's fine."

"On the sidewalk *in the middle of the day*. Broad daylight! Guy just hits you with a crowbar and takes your wallet and leaves you for dead."

"I'm sure that won't happen."

"That *did* happen. That happened yesterday."

"I mean, it won't happen to me."

"Attempted theft. Here's a weapons violation. Found person, which I think is a goddamn kidnapping."

"Dad, listen—"

"Simple assault on the bus. Aggravated battery."

"Okay, fine. I'll be careful. Whatever you want."

"Whatever I want? Great. Then don't go. Don't go at all. Stay home."

"Dad."

"Let her fend for herself. Let her rot."

"But I need her."

"You do not."

"It's not like we're going to start spending Christmases together. I only need her story. I'm going to be sued by my publisher if I don't figure it out."

"This is a very bad idea."

"You know what my alternative is? Declaring bankruptcy and moving to Jakarta. That's my choice."

"Why Jakarta?"

"It's just an example. The point is, I need to get Mom talking."

Henry shrugged and chewed his chicken and made notes on his laptop. "You see the Cubs game last night?" he said, still staring at his screen.

"I've been a little distracted lately," Samuel said.

"Hm," Henry said, nodding. "Good game."

This was how they usually related to each other—through sports. It was the topic they fled to whenever conversation lulled or became dangerously personal or sad. After Faye left, Samuel and his father rarely talked about her. They grieved independent of each other. Mostly what they talked about were the Cubs. After she left, both of them found within themselves a sudden and surprisingly powerful and devotional all-consuming love for the Chicago Cubs. Down came the framed reproductions of incomprehensible works of modern art from Samuel's bedroom walls, down came the nonsensical poetry broadsides hung there by his mother, and up went posters of Ryne Sandberg and Andre Dawson and Cubs pennants. Broadcasts on WGN weekday afternoons, Samuel literally praying to God—on his knees on the couch looking up to the ceiling—praying and crossing his fingers while actually making deals with God in exchange for one home run, one late-inning victory, one winning season.

Occasionally they took trips into Chicago for Cubs games—always during the day, always preceded by an elaborate ritual where Henry packed the car with enough supplies to get them through any roadside catastrophe. He packed extra jugs of water for drinking or radiator malfunction. Spare tire, sometimes two. Flares, emergency hand-crank CB radio. Walking maps of Wrigleyville on which he'd written notes from previous trips: where he'd found parking spots, where he'd encountered beggars or drug dealers. Particularly rough-seeming neighborhoods he etched out completely. He brought a fake wallet in case of mugging.

When they crossed the boundary into Chicago and the traffic congealed around them and the neighborhoods started to change, he said "Doors locked?" and Samuel jiggled the handle and said "Check!"

"Eyes peeled?"

"Check!"

And together they remained vigilant and watchful for crime until returning home again.

Henry had never worried like this before. But after Faye disappeared, he became preoccupied with disasters and muggings. The loss of his wife had convinced him that even more loss was imminent and near.

"I wonder what happened to her," Samuel said, "in Chicago, in college. What made her leave so quickly?"

"No idea. She never talked about it."

"Didn't you ask?"

"I was so happy she came back I didn't want to jinx it. Don't look a gift horse in the mouth, you know? I let the matter drop. I thought I was being very modern and compassionate."

"I have to find out what happened to her."

"Hey, I need your opinion. We're launching a new line. Which logo do you prefer?"

Henry slid two glossy pieces of paper across the table. One said *FARM FRESH FROZENS,* the other, *FARM FRESH FREEZNS.*

"I'm glad you're so concerned about your son's well-being," Samuel said.

"Seriously. Which do you like better?"

"I'm glad my personal crisis is so very important to you."

"Stop being dramatic. Pick a logo."

Samuel studied them for a moment. "I guess I'd vote *FROZENS*? When in doubt, spell words correctly."

"That's what I said! But the advertising folks said *FREEZNS* made the product seem funner. That's the word they actually used. *Funner.*"

"Of course I'd also argue that *FROZENS* isn't a proper word either," Samuel said. "More like a word that is not a noun conscripted to dress like one."

"My son the English professor."

"Which I guess there's some precedent for. Take the tuna *melt*. Or the corn *pop*."

"The advertising folks do that kind of thing all the time. They tell me that thirty years ago you could get away with saying something simple and declarative: *Tastes Great! Be Happy!* But consumers these days are way more sophisticated, so you have to get tricky with the language. *Taste the Great! Find Your Happy!*"

"I have a question," Samuel said. "How can something be both farm fresh *and* frozen?"

"That's something that way fewer people stop and think about than you would expect."

"Once it's frozen isn't it, by definition, no longer farm fresh?"

"It's a trigger word. When they want to advertise to hipster foodies, they use *farm fresh*. Or maybe *artisanal*. Or *local*. For millennials, they use *vintage*. For women, they use *skinny*. And don't even get me started on the quote-unquote *farm* where all this farm-fresh stuff comes from. I'm from Iowa. I know farms. That place is not a farm."

Samuel's phone dinged with a new text message. He made a reflexive move to his pocket, then stopped and folded his hands on the table. He and Henry stared at each other for a moment.

"You gonna get that?" Henry said.

"No," Samuel said. "We're talking."

"Mighty big of you."

"We're talking about your work."

"Not really *talking*. More like you're listening to me complain about it, again."

"How much longer till retirement?"

"Oh, too long. But I'm counting the days. And when I finally do leave, no one will be happier than those advertising folks. You should have seen the fuss I made about spelling jalapeño poppers with a Z. Or mozzarella sticks with an X. *Popperz. Stix.* No thank you."

Samuel remembered how happy his father was the day he got this job and moved the family to Streamwood—their final exodus from crowded apartment buildings to the expansively grassy and well-spaced houses of Oakdale Lane. For the first time they had a yard, a lawn. Henry wanted to get a dog. They had a washer and dryer *inside the house.* No more walking to the laundromat on Sunday afternoons. No more carrying groceries five blocks. No more random car vandalism. No more listening to the couple fighting in the apartment upstairs or the baby wailing from below. Henry was ecstatic. But Faye seemed a little lost. Maybe there'd been a struggle between them—she'd wanted to live in a city, he'd wanted to move to the suburbs. Who knows how such things are resolved; there are other, more interesting lives that parents keep hidden from their children. Samuel only knew that his mother had lost the struggle, and she sneered at all the symbols of her defeat—their big tan garage door, their patio deck, their bourgeois barbecue grill, their long secluded block brimming with happy, safe, bechildrened white people.

Henry must have thought he had it all figured out—a good job, a family, a nice house in the suburbs. It was everything he'd always wanted, and so it was a terrible and maybe even shattering blow when it all fell apart, first when his wife abandoned him, then when his job did too. That would have been in 2003—after more than twenty years working there, when Henry was maybe eighteen months from a comfortable early retirement, close enough that he was already making plans to travel and take up new hobbies—when his company filed for bankruptcy. This even though the company had issued to its employees an "All is well" memo not two days before declaring bankruptcy, this memo saying that rumors of bankruptcy were overblown and to hold on to your stock or even buy more, since it was so undervalued at that moment, which Henry did, though it was later revealed the CEO was at that very moment secretly dumping all his shares. Henry's retirement was tied up completely in the now worthless company stock, and when the company came out of bankruptcy and issued new stock, they offered it only to the board of directors and big-time Wall Street investors. So Henry was left with nothing. The nest egg he'd spent so long amassing evaporated in a single day.

That day, as the realization settled over him that his retirement would have to be pushed back ten or maybe even fifteen years, Henry had the same bewildered look he'd had the day that Faye disappeared. He had once again been betrayed by the very thing that was supposed to keep him safe.

Now he just seemed cynical and wary. The kind of person who no longer believed in anyone's promises.

"The average American eats six frozen meals a month," Henry said. "My job is to get that to seven. That's what I'm tirelessly working for, sometimes even on weekends."

"Doesn't sound like your heart's really in it."

"The problem is that nobody in the office takes the long view. They're all focused on the next quarterly statement, the next earnings report. They haven't seen what I've seen."

"Which is?"

"That whenever we identify some new market niche, all we do, in the long run, is dismantle it. This is like our guiding principle, our original philosophy. In the 1950s, Swanson saw that families ate meals together and wanted to get into that market. So they invented the TV dinner. Which made families realize they didn't have to eat meals together. Selling the family dinner made the family dinner go extinct. And we've been pulverizing the market ever since."

Samuel's phone dinged again, another new text message.

"For Christ's sake," Henry said. "You young people and your phones. Just look at it."

"Sorry," Samuel said as he checked the message. It was from Pwnage. It said: *OMG FOUND WOMAN IN PHOTO!!!!*

"Sorry, one second," Samuel said to his father while typing a reply.

what woman? what photo?

photo of ur mom from the 60s!! I found woman in that pic!!

for real??

come to jezebels right now I'll tell u everything!!!

"It's like I'm at work trying to have a conversation with one of our interns," Henry said. "Your head's in two places at once. Not paying quality attention to anything. I don't care if that makes me sound old."

"Sorry, Dad, I gotta run."

"You can't sit down for ten minutes without interruption. Always so busy."

"Thanks for dinner. I'll call you soon."

And Samuel raced south to the suburb where Pwnage lived and parked under the purple lights of Jezebels and hurried inside, where he found his *Elfscape* buddy at the bar, watching TV, a popular food channel show about extreme eating.

"You found the woman in the photo?" Samuel said as he sat down.

"Yes. Her name is Alice, and she lives in Indiana, way out in the boonies."

He gave Samuel a photograph—pulled from the internet and printed on copy paper: a woman at the beach on a sunny day, smiling at the camera, wearing hiking boots and cargo pants and a big green floppy hat and a T-shirt that said "Happy Camper."

"This is really her?" Samuel said.

"Definitely. She was sitting behind your mom when that photo was taken at the protest in 1968. She told me herself."

"Amazing," Samuel said.

"Best part? She and your mom were *neighbors*. Like, in the dorm, at school."

"And she'll talk to me?"

"I already set it up. She's expecting you tomorrow."

Pwnage gave him the printout of a short e-mail correspondence, as well as Alice's address and a map to her house.

"How did you find her?"

"I had some time on Patch Day. No big whoop."

He looked again at the TV. "Oh, check it out! Do you really think he'll be able to eat that whole thing? I vote yes."

He was talking about the TV show's host, a man known for his ability to eat ridiculous quantities of food without passing out or vomiting. His name was famously etched onto Hall of Fame plaques in dozens of American restaurants where he overcame some food object: a 72-ounce porterhouse steak, an XXL pizza burger, a burrito weighing more than most newborn babies. His face was puffy in the way of someone who, all over his body, had a quarter-inch of extra muchness.

Right now the host gave colorful commentary as a chef in what appeared to be a greasy-spoon diner prepared hash browns on a large discolored griddle—a potato mound he shaped into a square roughly the size of a chess board. On top of the hash browns the chef piled two handfuls of crumbled sausage, four handfuls of chopped bacon, ground beef, several diced onions, and what appeared to be shredded white cheddar or mozzarella or Monterey Jack cheese, so much cheese that the meats were now obscured totally under a white melty mess. In the upper right-hand corner of the screen it said: *9/11 Remembered*.

"I owe you, man," Samuel said. "Thank you so much. You need something? Just ask."

"You're very welcome."

"Seriously. Is there anything I can do for you?"

"No. It's okay."

"Well, if there is, please tell me."

The chef splatted six spatula-size balls of sour cream atop the white cheesy layer and spread them over the big brick of food. He rolled the entire apparatus into a log, the fried-potato side facing out, cut it in half, and lifted the two halves onto a white serving platter, where they stood vertically. They broke apart in places and oozed steam and thick creamy fatty liquid. The dish was called the Twin Towers Gut Buster. The host sat in the restaurant's dining area surrounded by patrons excited to be on television. In front of him were the golden potato-meat logs. He asked for a moment of silence. Everyone bowed their heads. Close-up on the Gut Buster, leaking its white slime. Then the crowd, perhaps cued by someone off camera, started yelling "Eat! Eat! Eat! Eat!" as the host picked up a knife and fork and sliced into the Gut Buster's outer fried crust and scooped up some of its inner drippy mash and guided it into his mouth. He chewed and looked into the camera plaintively and said, "That is *heavy*." The crowd laughed. "Bro, I don't think I'm gonna *make it*." Cut to commercial.

"Actually?" Pwnage said. "Yes. There is one thing you could do for me."

"Name it."

"I have this book," Pwnage said. "Well, more like a book idea. A mystery thriller novel?"

"The psychic detective story. I remember."

"Yeah. I always intended to write that book, but I had to push back the writing because there were all these tasks that needed to be completed before I could begin—you know, my readers would expect me to understand how police operate and how the justice system actually works, and so I would need to shadow a real detective for a while, which means I would need to find a detective and explain how I'm a writer working on a novel about police work and I need a few nights on the job to get the *flavor* of real police lingo and procedure. That type of thing."

"Sure."

"You know, research."

"Yes."

"But then, okay, I worry that any detective I send my letter to probably won't believe the 'writer' claim since I've never published anything ever, a fact that the detective would almost certainly deduce because detectives *know how to find things*. So before I can contact a detective I'll have to publish a few short stories in a few literary journals and maybe win a few little awards to corroborate the 'writer' claim, after which the detective would be more apt to allow me on duty."

"I suppose."

"Not to mention all the books about ESP and other paranormal psychic phenomena that I'd need to read to achieve the proper verisimilitude. In fact, there are so many things I need to finish before the writing can even *begin* that I'm having trouble finding motivation."

"Are you trying to ask me something specific?"

"If I had a publisher for my book already lined up, then the detective I contacted would automatically believe that I'm a writer, plus it would give me an incentive to actually *start writing*. Plus there's the advance money, of course, which could fund renovations I plan to make to my kitchen."

"So you want me to show your book to my publisher?"

"Yeah, if it's not too much trouble."

"No problem. Done."

Pwnage smiled and slapped Samuel on the back and turned again to watch the guy on TV, who was now halfway through eating the Gut Buster, having completely devoured one of the twin logs, the other having lost its internal structural integrity and loosened into a cone of slimy potato rubble. The host looked wearily into the camera with the expression of a staggered and exhausted boxer trying to remain conscious. The chef said he'd created the Twin Towers Gut Buster a few years back in order to "never forget." The host started in on the other log. His fork moved slowly. It visibly shook. A concerned onlooker offered him a glass of water, which he refused. He swallowed the next bite. He looked like he hated himself.

Samuel stared at the photograph of Alice. He wondered how the fierce-looking protestor of 1968 could become *this* person, who apparently wore cargo pants and ironic T-shirts and tromped along beaches looking perfectly happy and at ease. How could two people who seemed so different inhabit the same body?

"Did you talk to Alice?" Samuel said.

"Yep."

"What did she seem like? What was your impression of her?"

"She seemed very interested in mustard."

"Mustard?"

"Yep."

"Is that slang?"

"No. I mean that literally," Pwnage said. "She's super interested in mustard."

"I don't understand."

"Neither did I."

The man on TV, meanwhile, was down to his last few bites. He was exhausted and miserable. His forehead rested on the table and his arms splayed out and if it weren't for his heavy breathing and visible sweating it would seem like he was dead. The crowd was ecstatic that he'd almost consumed the entire dish. The chef said no one had ever been this close before. The crowd chanted "USA! USA!" as the host held the final bite, trembling, on his fork, aloft.

4

ALICE KNELT on the soft, spongy ground of the forest behind her house. She clutched a small tuft of mustard plant and pulled—not too hard, and not straight up, but rather gently and twistingly, a torsion that freed the roots from the sandy soil without breaking them. This was what she did most days. She roamed the woods of the Indiana dunes, absolving them of their mustard.

Samuel stood about twenty paces away, watching her. He was on the narrow gravel path that cut through the woods and connected Alice's cabin with her distant garage. The path was maybe a quarter-mile long, up and down a hill. His cresting the hill had set her dogs to barking.

"The problem," Alice said, "is the seeds. Garlic mustard seeds can linger for years."

It was a one-woman crusade she waged in the dunes along Lake Michigan's southern shore. This certain exotic mustard had found its way into Indiana forests from its native home in Europe, then proceeded to annihilate the local flowers, shrubs, trees. If she weren't here to beat it back, the stuff would take over in just a few summers.

Yesterday she'd been reading one of the Chicago-area invasive-species online discussion boards that she moderates, her job being to tell people when they were posting in the wrong area and move their misplaced threads to different discussion boards. She kept everything nice and tidy; she engaged in a sort of pruning that mimicked in a digital way what she did most days in these woods, ripping out things that didn't belong. And since most websites were bombarded with an unthinkable amount of spam—mostly advertisements for male enhancement pills or pornography or who knows what because it's in Cyrillic—even the smallest and most niche sites needed a moderator to vigorously patrol the boards and delete unwanted posts and ads and spam or else the whole thing choked with senseless data. Most of Alice's time not spent with mustard or her dogs or her partner was spent like this, beating back the advancing chaos, trying to achieve Enlightenment order in the face of twenty-first-century madness.

She was at her laptop looking in on her invasive-species discussion forum and saw that someone named Axman had posted a thread titled "Do you know the woman IN THIS PHOTO?" Which seemed definitely like spam because of its unnecessary use of all-caps words, and because it certainly did not have anything to do with that specific board's ostensible topic, which was "Honeysuckle (Amur, Morrow's, Bell's, Standish, and Tartarian)." So she was about to move the post to the Odds 'n' Ends forum and scold Axman for putting it in the wrong place when she clicked on the image in question and saw, incredibly, *herself*.

A photo taken in 1968, at the big protest in Chicago that year. There she was, in her old sunglasses, in her army fatigues, staring at the camera. *Goddamn* she was such a badass. She was in the park, in a field of student revelry. Thousands of protestors. Behind her were flags and signs and outlines of old Chicago buildings on the horizon. Faye sitting in front of her. She could hardly believe what she was seeing.

She contacted Axman, who sent her to a strange guy named Pwnage, who sent her to Samuel, who came to visit the very next day.

He stood several paces away from her, far from this patch of leafy shrub that to the uninitiated looked in no way special but was, in fact, garlic mustard. Each twig on a garlic mustard plant contained dozens of seeds, which wedged in shoe soles and inside socks and on the cuffs of jeans and were then spread by walking. Samuel was not allowed anywhere near it. Alice wore large plastic boots up to her knees that seemed appropriate for swamps or bogs. She carried black plastic bags that she carefully wrapped around each mustard plant to catch the seeds that dropped as she jostled it out of the ground. Every plant had hundreds of seeds, and not one of them could be allowed to escape. The way she held these bags when they were full of mustard plants—carefully, and at a small distance away from her—looked like how one might carry a bag that contained the body of a dead cat.

"How did you get involved with this?" Samuel asked. "With mustard, I mean."

"When I moved out here," she said, "it was killing all the native plants." Alice's cabin overlooked a small dune at the edge of Lake Michigan, the closest thing you could get to a beach house in Indiana. She bought the house for next to nothing in 1986, back when the lake was at a record height. The water was a few feet from the porch. If the lake had kept rising, the house would have been washed away.

"Buying the house was a gamble," Alice said, "but an educated one."

"Based on what?"

"Climate change," she said. "Hotter, drier summers. More droughts, less rain. Less ice in the winter, more evaporation. If the climate scientists were right, the lake would have to recede. So I found myself rooting for global warming."

"That must have felt, I don't know, complicated?"

"Every time I was stuck in traffic I imagined the carbon from all the cars filling the air and saving my house. It was perverse."

Eventually the lake did recede. Now she had a nice big beach where the water used to be. She'd purchased the place for ten grand. It was now worth millions.

"I moved out here with my partner," she said. "It was the eighties. We were sick of lying about our relationship. We were fed up telling our neighbors we were *roommates,* that she was my *good friend.* We wanted our privacy."

"Where's your partner now?"

"She's away on business this week. It's just me and the dogs. Three of them, rescue dogs. They are not allowed in the woods since their paws would pick up mustard seeds."

"Of course."

Alice's white hair was pulled back in a ponytail. She wore blue jeans under her giant rubber waders. A simple, clean white T-shirt. She had that naturalist's lack of attention to outward appearances, an indifference toward things like cosmetics and grooming that read not as apathy but rather as transcendence.

"How's your mother?" Alice said.

"Indicted."

"But other than that?"

"Other than that, I have no idea. She won't talk to me."

Alice thought about that quiet young girl she used to know, and she regretted that Faye never overcame what tortured her. But such was the way with people—they loved the things that made them miserable. She'd seen it so many times among her movement friends, after the movement splintered and grew ugly and dangerous. They were miserable all the time, and the misery seemed to feed them and nourish them. Not the misery itself but its familiarity, its constancy.

"I wish I could help," Alice said. "But I don't think I have much for you."

"I'm trying to understand what happened," Samuel said. "My mother kept everything about Chicago a secret. You're the first person I've met who knew her there."

"I wonder why she never talked about it."

"I was hoping you could tell me. Something happened to her there. Something important."

Of course he was right, but Alice wouldn't say so.

"What's to tell?" she said, trying to act aloof. "She went to school for a month, then left. College wasn't for her. It's a pretty common story."

"Then why would she keep it a secret?"

"Maybe she was embarrassed."

"No, there's more to it than that."

"She was a troubled soul when I knew her," Alice said. "Small-town girl. Smart, but also a little clueless. Quiet. She read a lot. Ambitious and driven in a way that probably meant she had big-time daddy issues."

"What do you mean?"

"I'll bet she had a dad who was always disappointed in her, you know? So her anxiety about being disappointing to her father was swapped out for a drive to be special to everyone. Psychoanalysts would call this *replacement*. The child learns what is wanted of her. Am I right about that?"

"Maybe."

"At any rate, she left Chicago right after the protests. I never even got to say goodbye. Just all of a sudden, gone."

"Yeah, she's pretty good at that."

"Where did you get the photo?"

"It was on the news."

"I don't watch the news."

"Do you remember who took it?" he said.

"That whole week is a big blur. Everything kind of merges with everything else. I can't really remember one day from the next. Anyway, no, I don't remember who took it."

"In the photo it looks like she's leaning against someone."

"That would probably have been Sebastian."

"Who's Sebastian?"

"He was the editor of an underground newspaper. The *Chicago Free Voice*. Your mother was attracted to him, and he was attracted to anyone who paid attention to him. It wasn't a good match."

"What happened to him?"

"No idea. That was a long time ago. I left the movement in 1968, right after that protest. Afterward, I didn't keep track of anyone."

The mustard plants Alice pulled were about a foot tall, with green heart-shaped leaves and small white flowers. To the untrained eye they looked like any other ground shrub, not at all out of the ordinary. The problem was that they grew so quickly they stole sunlight from other ground plants, including young trees. They also had no natural predators—the local deer population ate everything but the mustard, leaving it free to colonize. It also produced a chemical that killed off bacteria in the soil that other plants needed for growth. A perfect botanical terror, in other words.

"Was my mother in the movement?" Samuel said. "Was she, like, a radical hippie or something?"

"I was a radical hippie," Alice said. "Your mother definitely was not. She was a normal kid. She was dragged into it against her will."

Alice remembered her young, idealistic self, how she refused to own any possessions, refused to lock her door or carry money, crazy behavior she wouldn't even consider now. What her younger self worried about were the hang-ups that came with possessions—the territoriality, the worry, the potential for loss, the way the world looked when you owned precious things: like one big threat always ready to take your stuff. And yes, Alice had purchased this home in the Indiana dunes, she filled it with her stuff, she put locks on all the doors, she built a wall of sandbags to contain the advance of the lake, she cleaned and sanded and painted, brought in exterminators and contractors and took down walls and erected new ones, and slowly this home came into being, bubbling up out of itself like Venus from the sea. And yes, it was true that all her former radical energies now poured into things like selecting the perfect pendant lamps, or achieving the ideal kitchen work flow, or constructing excellent built-in bookcases, or finding the most calming master bedroom color palette that ideally involved the same blue the lake took on when she looked out her window certain winter mornings, when the surface of the water was a slushy, shimmering mass that appeared—depending on the paint sample she used—like "glacier blue" or "liquid blue" or "blue-bell" or a really lovely gray-blue called "soar." And yes, occasionally she felt bolts of raw guilt and regret that these were the hang-ups that inter-ested her, not the peace and justice and equality movements she intended to devote her life to when she was twenty.

She'd decided that about eighty percent of what you believe about yourself when you're twenty turns out to be wrong. The problem is you don't know what your small true part is until much later.

"Who dragged her into it?" Samuel said.

"Nobody," Alice said. "Everybody. The events of the time. She got swept up. It was all terribly exciting, you see."

For Alice, the small true part of her was that she wanted something that deserved her faith and devotion. When she was young, she saw fami-lies retreat into their homes and ignore the greater problems of the world and she hated them: bourgeois cogs in the machine, unthinking sheeplike masses, selfish bastards who couldn't see beyond their own property lines. Their souls, she thought, must have been small and shrunken things.

But then she grew up and bought a house and found a lover and got some dogs and stewarded her land and tried to fill her home with love and life and she realized her earlier error: that these things did not make you small. In fact, these things seemed to enlarge her. That by choos-ing a few very private concerns and pouring herself into them, she had never felt so expanded. That, paradoxically, narrowing her concerns had made her *more* capable of love and generosity and empathy and, yes, even peace and justice. It was the difference between loving something out of duty—because the movement required it of you—and loving something you actually loved. Love—real, genuine, unasked-for love—made room for more of itself, it turned out. Love, when freely given, duplicates and multiplies.

Still, she could not help feeling stung when old movement friends said she had "sold out." That was the worst of all charges because, of course, it was true. But how could she explain that not all sellouts are the same? That it wasn't money she was selling out to? That sometimes on the other side of selling out there's a compassion she'd never felt in her revolutionary days? She could not explain this to them, nor would they hear it. They still held to all the old principles: drugs, sex, resistance. Even as drugs began killing them one by one, and even as sex became dangerous, still this is where they turned for some kind of answer. They never saw how their resistance had begun to look comical. They were beaten by the cops and the public cheered. They thought they were changing the world and what they did was help get Nixon elected. They found Vietnam intolerable, but their answer was to become intolerable themselves.

The only thing less popular than the war in those days was the antiwar movement.

This truth was obvious, though none of them saw it, convinced as they were of their own righteousness.

She managed not to think about this too much, these ligatures to the past. For the most part she thought about her dogs, and mustard. Except when something popped up to remind her of her former life, like, for example, the son of Faye Andresen, coming to the dunes and asking questions.

"Were you close," he said, "with my mother? Were you friendly?"

"I suppose," she said. "We didn't know each other very well."

He nodded. He seemed disappointed by this. He was hoping for more. But what could Alice say? That Faye had indeed been on her mind all these years? That Faye's memory was a small but constant and needling companion? For that was the truth. She'd promised to look out for Faye, but things got out of hand, and she failed. She never knew what happened to her. She never saw her again.

There is no greater ache than this: guilt and regret in equal measure. She'd tried to bury it, along with all the other mistakes of her youth, out here in the dunes. And she would not dig these stories up now, even for this man who so plainly needed them. The subject of his mother seemed like a splinter he could not remove. She grabbed a small bunch of mustard and pulled—not too hard, and with a gentle spin to get the roots up. She had long ago perfected this technique. For a long quiet moment they stayed like this, the only sounds being mustard plants tearing free from the earth, and the whoosh of the nearby lake, and a certain bird whose call sounded like *uh-uh, uh-uh, uh-uh.*

"Even if you figure it all out," Alice said, "what good will it do?"

"What do you mean?"

"Even if you know your mom's story, it's not going to change anything. The past is the past."

"I guess I hope it'll explain something. About all the things she's done. Plus she's in trouble and maybe I can help. There's this judge who seems intent on putting her in jail. It's like he came out of retirement just to torment her. The *Honorable* Charlie Brown my ass."

Alice perked up at that, lifted her gaze from the mustard. She placed her half-full trash bag on the ground. She removed her gloves, her specialized rubber gloves that mustard seeds did not stick to. She walked over to where Samuel stood, taking the big awkward steps made necessary by her wading boots.

"That's his name?" she said. "Charlie Brown?"

"Hilarious, right?"

"Oh, god," she said, sitting down right there in the grass. "Oh, no."

"What?" Samuel said. "What's wrong?"

"Listen to me," Alice said. "You have to get your mother out of here."

"What do you mean?"

"She needs to leave."

"Now I'm sure there's something you're not telling me."

"I used to know him," she said. "The judge."

"Okay. And?"

"We were all sort of intertwined—in Chicago, in college—me and the judge and your mom."

"That's information you maybe should have led with."

"You have to get your mom out of town, like immediately."

"Tell me why."

"Maybe even get her out of the country."

"Help my mom flee the country. That's your advice."

"I wasn't entirely honest about why I moved out here, to Indiana. The real reason was because of him. When I heard he was back in Chicago, I moved away. I was afraid of him."

Samuel sat down with her in the grass and they stared at each other a moment, shell-shocked.

"What did he do to you?" he asked.

"Your mom is in trouble," Alice said. "The judge will never yield. He's ruthless and dangerous. You have to take her away. Do you hear me?"

"I don't understand. What's his grudge against her?"

She sighed and looked at the ground. "He's like the most dangerous species of American there is: heterosexual white male who didn't get what he wanted."

"You need to tell me *exactly* what happened," Samuel said.

About three feet past her left knee, she noticed a small and heretofore unseen patch of garlic mustard—first-year shoots, a smattering of clover hiding under the grass. It wouldn't go to seed until next summer, but when it did it would race up above the surrounding plants and kill them all.

"I've never told this story," she said. "Not to anyone."

"What happened in 1968?" Samuel said. "Please tell me."

Alice nodded. She ran her hands along the grass and the thin blades tickled her palms. She made a mental note to come prune this spot tomorrow. The problem with mustard is that you can't just chop it down. The seeds can last for years. It will always come back. You have to cut it out completely. You have to cut it out by the roots.

| PART SEVEN |

CIRCLE

Late Summer 1968

1

HER OWN ROOM. Her own key and mailbox. Her own books. Everything was hers but the bathroom. Faye hadn't considered this. The dorm's clinical foul-smelling community bathroom. Stale water, dirty floors, sinks strewn with hair, trash cans thick with tissues and tampons and balled-up brown paper towels. A smell like slow decay that reminded her of a forest. Faye imagined, beneath the floor, earthworms and mushrooms. How the bathroom bore the evidence of so much appalling use—soap slivers now fused to their trays, fossils. The one toilet that's always plugged. The slime on the walls like a brain where the memory of each girl's cleaning lived. She thought if you looked deep enough into the floor you could find there, embalmed in the pink tiles, the whole history of the world: bacteria, fungus, nematodes, trilobites. A dormitory was a hopeless idea. Whoever thought of encasing two hundred girls in a concrete box? The narrow rooms, shared bath, massive cafeteria—the comparison to prison was unavoidable. It was a dark and creepy bunker, their dorm. From the outside its concrete skeleton looked like some martyr's flayed chest—all you could see were the ribs. All the buildings on Circle's campus looked this way: inside out, exposed. Sometimes walking to class she ran her fingers along the walls where the concrete resembled acne and she felt embarrassed for the buildings, how an eccentric designer had taken their guts and put them on view. A perfect metaphor, she thought, for dormitory living.

Take this bathroom, where all the girls' private fluids commingled. The big open shower with sour puddles of water like gray jelly. A vegetable smell. Faye wore sandals. And if her neighbors were awake they would know it was Faye walking down the hall by the *flop flop flop*. But they weren't awake. It was six o'clock in the morning. Faye had the bathroom to herself. She could shower alone. She preferred it this way.

Because she didn't want to be here with the other girls, her neighbors, who gathered nightly in their small rooms and giggled, got high, talked about the protest, the police, the pipes they passed to smoke with, the medicines they expanded their minds with, the electric songs they screeched along with: "Looks like everybody in this whole round world / They're down on me!" they cried to the record player like it bled from them. Faye heard their wails through her wall, a litany to a terrible god. It seemed disallowable that these girls could really be her neighbors. Freaky beatniks, psychedelic revolutionaries who needed to learn to clean up after themselves in the bathroom, was Faye's opinion, looking at a glob of tissue near the wall, now mostly liquefied. She took off her robe and turned on the spray and waited for the water to warm.

Every night the girls laughed and Faye listened. She wondered what made the girls able to sing so unself-consciously. Faye didn't talk to them and looked at the floor when they passed by. They chewed on their pencils in class and complained about the teacher, how he only taught the *old straight shit*. Plato, they said, Ovid, Dante—dead men assholes with nothing to say to today's youth.

That's how they said it—*today's youth*—as if college students these days were a brand-new species totally disconnected from the past and from the culture that spawned them. And as far as Faye could tell, the rest of the culture pretty much agreed. Older adults complained about them endlessly on CBS News's nightly examinations of the "Generation Gap."

Faye stepped into the warm water and let it soak her. One hole in the shower nozzle was clogged and sprayed out thinner and harder than the rest—she felt it like a razor on her chest.

In these first days of college, Faye mostly kept to herself. Each night she sat alone and did her homework, underlining key passages, writing notes in the margins, and next door she heard these girls laughing. The college brochures had said nothing about this—Circle was supposed to be known for its expectation of excellence, its academic rigor, its modern campus. None of this turned out to be exactly true. The campus especially was just an inhuman concrete horror: concrete buildings and concrete walkways and concrete walls that made the place about as comfortable and inviting as a parking lot. No grass anywhere. Concrete edifices scarred and ribbed to evoke the look of corduroy, perhaps, or the inside of a whale. Concrete bitten off in places to expose raw and rusted rebar. The same basic architectural patterns endlessly repeating in a faceless grid. No windows wider than a few inches. Bulky buildings that seemed to hang over the students carnivorously.

It was the kind of place that would be the only place to survive an atom bomb.

The campus was impossible to navigate, as every building looked like every other building and so directions were confused and meaningless. The elevated second-story pedestrian walkway that covered the entire campus and sounded so cool in the brochures—*a pedestrian expressway in the sky*—was in reality maybe the most horrible thing about Circle. It was advertised as a place for students to come together for community and friendship, but what usually happened is you were up on the walkway and saw a friend down below and you yelled and waved but had no easy way to actually talk. Faye noticed this daily, friends waving and then sadly abandoning each other. Plus the walkway was never the shortest path from anywhere to anywhere, and the places to get on and off were spaced such that the length of your walk doubled if you wanted to use it, and the midday August sun had a tendency to cook the concrete expanse to the heat of a pancake griddle. So most of the students used the sidewalks below, the whole student body trying to shoulder their way through narrow corridors made crowded and claustrophobic by the big concrete posts needed to hold up the walkway, all of it dark and shadowy because the walkway blocked the sun.

A rumor that the Circle campus had been designed by the Pentagon to instill terror and despair among students could not be entirely dismissed.

Faye had been promised a campus fit for the space age, but what she got was a place where every building's surface evoked the gravel roads from back home. She'd been promised a hardworking and studious student body, and what she got instead were these neighbors next door, these girls less interested in academics, more interested in how to score dope, how to sneak into bars, get free drinks, how to screw, and they talked about this endlessly, one of their two favorite topics, the other being the protest. The upcoming protest of the Democratic National Convention, now only a few weeks away. A great battle would happen in Chicago, it was becoming clear, the year's apotheosis. The girls talked excitedly about their plans: an all-female march right down Lake Shore Drive, a protest in the form of music and love, four days of revolution, orgies in the park, the perfect silvery human voice in song, we'll touch the honky young,

394 | THE NIX

bring down the amphitheater show, shove a great spike in America's eye, we'll take back the streets, and all those people watching on TV? We're gonna anti-America them, man. *With all that energy, we'll stop the war.*

Faye felt far away from such concerns. She soaped herself, her chest and arms and legs, thickly. The lather made her feel like a ghost or mummy or some other generally white and scary thing. The water in Chicago was different from the water at home, and no matter how much she rinsed, the soap never came entirely off. A thin varnish lingered on her skin. How easily and smoothly her hands glided over her hips and legs and thighs. She closed her eyes. Thought of Henry.

His hands on her body as they lay on the riverbank her last night in Iowa. They were cold and hard, those hands, and when he reached under her shirt and pressed them to her belly it was like they were stones from the bottom of the riverbed. She gasped. He stopped. She didn't want him to stop, but she couldn't tell him without sounding unladylike. And he hated when she was unladylike. He gave her an envelope that night with instructions not to open it until she got to college. Inside was a letter. She had been fearing another poem, but what she found was a little couplet that knocked her over: *come home / marry me.* Meanwhile, he'd joined the army, just as he said he would. He had promised to go to Vietnam but had gotten only as far as Nebraska. He did riot-control exercises in preparation for whatever civil disorder was inevitably next. He practiced sticking his bayonet into dummies filled with sand and dressed like hippies. He practiced using tear gas. He practiced phalanxing. They would be seeing each other again at Thanksgiving, and Faye dreaded it. Because she had no answer to his proposal. She had read his letter once and hidden it like contraband. But she did look forward to meeting again on the riverbank, when they were alone, and he could try touching her again. She had found herself thinking about it these desolate mornings in the shower. Pretending her hands were someone else's. Maybe Henry's. Maybe more accurately the hands of some abstract man—in her imagination she could not see him but instead felt his presence, a solid masculine warmth pressing into her. She thought about this as she felt the soap on her body, the slippery water, the smell of the shampoo as she rubbed it into her hair. She turned around to wash it out and opened her eyes and saw, across the room, standing at the sink, watching her right now, a girl.

"Excuse me!" Faye yelped, for it was one of *those girls*—Alice was her

name. Faye's neighbor. Long-haired, mean-looking Alice, silver-framed sunglasses settled halfway down her nose so at this moment she stared over them directly and curiously and terribly at Faye.

"Excuse you for what?" Alice said.

Faye shut off the water and wrapped herself in her robe.

"Man," Alice said, smiling, "you are too much."

She was the craziest of them all, this Alice. Green camo jacket and black boots, wild brunette Buddha girl seen in the cafeteria sitting cross-legged on a table chanting gibberish. Faye had heard stories about Alice—how she hitchhiked to Hyde Park on weekend nights, met boys, scored drugs, entered strange bedrooms and emerged more complicated.

"You're so quiet all the time," Alice said. "Always alone in your room. What do you do in there?"

"I don't know. I read."

"You read. What do you read?"

"Lots of things."

"You read your homework?"

"I guess."

"You read what your teachers tell you. Get good grades."

Faye saw her up close now, her eyes bloodshot, hair tangled, clothes wrinkled and reeking, that funky cocktail of tobacco, pot, and perspiration. Faye understood now that Alice had not yet slept. Six in the morning and Alice had just returned from whatever free-love odyssey these girls chased at night.

"I read poetry," Faye said.

"Yeah? What kind?"

"All kinds."

"Okay. Say me a poem."

"Huh?"

"Say me a poem. Recite one. Should be easy if you read so much. Come on."

There was a splotch on Alice's cheek that Faye had never noticed before—a trace of red and purple gathered just beneath the surface. A bruise.

"Are you okay?" Faye said. "Your face."

"I'm fine. Great. What's it to you?"

"Did someone hit you?"

"How about you mind your own business."

"Fine," Faye said. "Never mind. I gotta go."

"You're not very friendly," Alice said. "Are you down on us or something?"

Those lyrics again. "Down on Me." They played that damn song every night. "Everybody in this whole round world!" They sang it four or five off-key times in a row. "They're down on me!" As if the girls needed them—all these other people in the world—needed them to be down and thus give a reason for singing.

"No, I'm not down on you," Faye said. "I'm just not going to apologize to you."

"Apologize for what?"

"For doing my homework. Being good at school. I'm sick of feeling bad about it. Good day."

Faye left the bathroom, flop-flopped back to her room, put on her clothes, and felt so full of poison and abstract anger that she sat on her bed and held her knees and rocked. She had a headache. She pulled her hair back and put on her big round glasses that looked to her suddenly like some elaborate Venetian disguise. She frowned into the mirror. She was gathering her books into her backpack when Alice knocked on the door.

"I'm sorry," Alice said. "That wasn't in the spirit of sisterhood. Please accept my apology."

"Forget it," Faye said.

"Let me make it up to you. I'll take you out tonight. There's a meeting. I want you to come."

"I don't think that's necessary."

"It's sort of a secret. Don't tell anyone."

"Really, it's okay."

"I'll be here at eight," Alice said. "See you then."

Faye closed the door and sat on her bed. She wondered what Alice had seen her doing, back there in the shower, when Fay had been thinking about Henry: his hands on her. What a treacherous thing a body was, how it so blatantly acted out the mind's secrets.

Henry's letter was hidden in her bedside table, in the bottom drawer, way in the back. She had tucked it inside a book. *Paradise Lost*.

2

THEY ASSEMBLED in the office of the *Chicago Free Voice,* a small, irreg-
ularly printed handbill that called itself "the newspaper of the street."
Into a dark alley, through an unmarked door, up a narrow set of stairs,
Alice led Faye to a room with a sign at the entrance that read: TONIGHT!
WOMEN'S SEXUALITY AND SELF-DEFENSE.

Alice tapped the sign with her finger and said, "Two sides of the same
coin, eh?"

She had not made any effort to hide the bruise on her cheek.

The meeting had already begun when they arrived. The room,
crowded with maybe two dozen women, smelled of tar and kerosene,
old paper and dust. A warm mist of ink and glue and spirits hung in the
air. Odors drifted in and out of perception—shoe polish, linseed oil, turpentine. The sting of solvents and oil reminded Faye of the garages and
toolsheds of Iowa, where her uncles spent long afternoons fiddling with
cars that hadn't been driven in decades—hot rods bought cheap at auc-
tions and slowly restored, part by part, year by year, whenever the uncles
could find time and motivation. But whereas her uncles decorated their
garages with sports logos and pinup girls, this office had a Vietcong flag
on the largest wall, the smaller nooks covered with broadsides of past *Free
Voice* editions: CHICAGO IS A CONCENTRATION CAMP said one headline; IT IS
THE YEAR OF THE STUDENT said another; FIGHT THE PIGS IN THE STREET and
so on. A fine dark soot coated the walls and floor, a sheath of carbon that
turned the light in the room to a gray-green smog. Faye's skin felt clammy
and covered with grit. Her sneakers quickly stained.

The women sat in a circle—some on folding chairs, some leaning
against the wall. White girls and black girls all wearing sunglasses and
army jackets and combat boots. Faye sat down behind Alice and listened
to the woman presently talking.

"You slap him," she said, a finger pointed into the air, "you bite him, you scream as loud as you can and when you do you scream *fire*. You break his kneecaps. Box his ears to pop his eardrums. Stiffen your fingers and jab his eyes out. *Be creative*. Ram his nose into his brain. Your keys and knitting needles can be weapons if held tightly. Find a nearby rock and bash his head in. If you know kung fu, use your kung fu. It goes without saying that you should be kneeing him in the groin repeatedly"— and women in the circle nodded, clapped, encouraged the speaker with *oh yeahs* and *right ons*—"knee him in the groin and yell, *You are not a man!* Break his will. Men attack you because they think they can. Knee him in the groin and yell, *You cannot do this!* Don't rely on other men to help you. Every man in his heart wants you to be raped. *Because it confirms your need for his protection.* Armchair rapists, that's what they are." And Alice shouted "Hell yeah!" and other women whooped and Faye didn't know how to compose herself. She felt stiff and nervous, and she looked around at the women and tried to enact their casually bad posture while the speaker wrapped it up: "Since men have their potency and masculinity vicariously confirmed through rape, they will never do anything to stop it. *Unless we force them to.* So I say we take a stand. No more husbands. No more weddings. No more children. Not until rape is extinguished. Once and for all. *A total reproductive boycott!* We will grind civilization to a halt." And to this the woman got great applause, the others standing and patting her on the back, and Faye was about to join the ovation when from a far dark corner of the room came a loud gnashing of metal. Everyone turned to look, and that's when Faye saw him for the first time.

His name was Sebastian. He wore a white apron covered in pitch, smudged gray where he'd rubbed his hands, his shaggy bowl of black hair flopping in front of his eyes as he looked back sheepishly at the group and said, "Sorry!" He stood behind a machine that seemed built like a train—all black cast metal, shining with oil, silver spindles and toothy gears. The machine hummed and vibrated, the occasional *tock* of metal falling down chutes somewhere in its innards, like pennies dropped onto a table. The man—he was young, olive-skinned, a hangdog look—pulled a sheet of paper from the machine and Faye realized the contraption was a printing press, the sheet a copy of the *Free Voice*. Alice called out to him: "Hey, Sebastian! What's cooking?"

"Tomorrow's edition," he said, smiling, turning the paper to the light.

"What's in it?"

"Letters to the editor. I had a stockpile."

"Are they good?"

"They'll blow your mind," he said, loading more paper onto the bed of the machine. "Sorry. Act normal. I'm not even here."

And so everyone turned back and the meeting began again, but Faye kept watching Sebastian. How he fiddled with knobs and cranks, how he lowered the head of the machine to smash ink onto the paper, how he pressed his lips together in concentration, how the collar on his white shirt had been stained a deep, dark green, and she was thinking about how he looked like some beautifully sloppy mad scientist and how she felt connected to him in the way outsiders feel a certain kinship with each other when she heard someone in the group say something about *orgasms*. Faye turned to see who was speaking—tall woman, blond hair like a waterfall down to her back, a string of beads around her neck, a bright red shirt with a deep neckline. She was leaning forward and asking about orgasms. Can you have them only in one position? Faye could not believe she'd said such a thing with a boy in the room. Behind them, his machine punched at paper, throbbing like a heartbeat. Someone suggested that you could have orgasms in two and perhaps as many as three positions. Someone else said the orgasm was a fiction. It was invented by doctors to make us feel ashamed. Ashamed of what? That we don't have them like boys do. People nodded at this. They moved on.

It was suggested you could orgasm on weed, and sometimes acid, but almost never on heroin. Someone said sex on the natch was best anyway. One woman's boyfriend couldn't have sex unless he was drunk. Another woman's boyfriend had recently asked her to douche. There was a boyfriend who, after sex, spent an hour cleaning the bedroom with a mop and germicide. There was another boyfriend who named his dick Mr. Rumpy-Pumpy. Another only wanted blow jobs until marriage.

"Free love!" someone said, and everyone laughed.

Because despite what the newspapers said, it was not the time of free love. It was the time of free-love *writing,* when free love was widely condemned, rarely practiced, and terrifically marketed. Photos of topless women dancing in public in Berkeley were greatly criticized and distributed. News of the oral-sex scandal at Yale reached every bedroom in the country. Everyone had heard of the Barnard girl who was living with a boy she wasn't even married to. The imagination was seized by the pelvic regions of university girls—stories of once-chaste daughters turned to deviants in only one semester. Magazine articles condemned masturbation, the FBI warned against clitoral orgasm, and Congress investigated the dangers of fellatio. Never before had the authorities been so remarkably *explicit*. Mothers were taught the warning signs of sex addiction, kids were counseled against criminal and soul-destroying pleasure. Police flew helicopters over beaches to catch bare-breasted women. *Life* magazine said slutty girls had penis envy and were turning real men into pansies. *The New York Times* said excessive fornication caused girls to go psychotic. Good middle-class kids were becoming queers, dopers, dropouts, beatniks. It was true. Heard it on Cronkite. Politicians vowed to get tough. They blamed the pill, permissive liberal parents, the climbing divorce rate, raunchy movies, go-go clubs, atheism. People shook their heads, appalled at youth run amuck, and then set out looking for more tawdry stories, found them, and read every word.

The barometer for the health of the country seemed to be what middle-aged men thought about the behavior of college girls.

But for the girls, it was not the time of free love. It was the time of awkward love, embarrassed and nervous and ignorant love. This is what nobody reported, how free-love girls gathered in these dark rooms and *worried*. They'd read all the stories, and believed them, and thus thought they were doing something wrong. "I want to be hip, but I don't want my boyfriend fucking all these other women," said many, many girls who found that free love was still tangled up in all the old arguments— jealousy, envy, power. It was a sexual bait and switch, the free-love trip not quite measuring up to its hype.

"If I don't want to have sex with someone, does that mean I'm a prude?" said one of the women at the meeting.

"If I don't want to strip at a protest, am I a prude?" said another.

"Men think you're a hip chick if you take your shirt off at rallies."

"All those nude girls in Berkeley holding flowers."

"They sell lots of papers."

"Posing with psychedelic paint on their tits."

"What kind of freedom is that?"

"They're just doing it to be popular."

"They're not free."

"They're doing it for men."

"Why else would they do it?"

"There's no other reason to do it."

"Maybe they like it," said a new voice, a small voice, and everyone looked to see where it had come from: the girl with the funny round glasses who had been unnaturally quiet up to this point. Faye's face flushed red and she looked at the floor.

Alice turned around and stared at her. "What do they like about it?" she asked.

Faye shrugged. She'd shocked herself by saying anything, much less *that*. She wanted to take it back immediately, reach out and stuff it into her stupid mouth. *Maybe they like it,* oh lord, oh god, the girls looked at her and waited. She had the feeling of being a wounded bird in a room full of cats.

Alice cocked her head and said, "Do *you* like it?"

"Sometimes. I don't know. No."

She had forgotten herself. She had been caught up in the moment—all this talk of sex, all the girls so excited, and she imagined herself at home standing in front of her big picture window imagining some dark stranger walking by and seeing her, when this thing erupted, it just came out. *Maybe they like it.*

"You like putting on a show for men?" Alice asked. "Parading your tits so they'll like you?"

"That's not what I meant."

"What's your name?" someone asked.

"Faye," she said, and the girls waited. They watched her. She wanted more than anything to run out of the room, but that would draw so much more attention. She sat in a tight ball, trying to think of something to say, and that's when Sebastian stepped out from the shadows and saved her.

"I'm sorry to interrupt," he said, "but I have an announcement."

And as he talked the group mercifully forgot about Faye. She sat there boiling and listening to Sebastian—he was talking about the upcoming protest, how the city hadn't given them a permit to occupy the park but they were going to do it anyway. "Make sure to tell your friends," he said. "Bring everybody. We're gonna have a hundred thousand people or more. We're gonna change the world. We're gonna end the war. Nobody will go to work. Nobody will go to school. We're gonna shut the city down. Music and dancing at every red light. The pigs can't stop us."

And at the mention of the pigs, the pigs themselves laughed.

For they were listening.

They were packed into a small office several miles south called the "war room" in the basement of the International Amphitheater, where the detectives listened through static to Sebastian's exhortations, the girls' inane chatter. They wrote on legal pads and remarked on the stupidity of college kids, how they were so trusting. The office of the *Chicago Free Voice* had been bugged for how long now? How many months? The kids didn't have a clue.

Outside the amphitheater were the slaughterhouses—the famous stockyards of Chicago, where the police heard the screams of animals, the last wails of cattle and hogs. Some of the cops, interested, peered over fences and saw carcasses torn off the ground by hooks and trolleys, pulled to death, dismembered, floors covered in entrails and shit, men hacking tirelessly at limbs and throats—it all seemed appropriate. The butchers' curved knives offered the police a kind of clarity, a kind of purity of intent that gave their jobs a helpful, if unspoken, guiding metaphor.

They listened and wrote down anything, any indictable threat, calls to violence, outside agitating, communist propaganda, and tonight they were given something special—a name, one never mentioned before, someone new: *Faye*.

They glanced over at the new guy, standing in the corner, legal pad in hand, recently promoted from beat cop to the Red Squad: Officer Charlie Brown. He nodded. He wrote it down.

The Red Squad was the Chicago PD's covert antiterrorist intelligence unit that was created in the 1920s to spy on union organizers, expanded in the 1940s to spy on communists, and concentrated now on threats to the domestic peace posed by radical leftists, mostly the students and the blacks. It was a glamorous job, and Brown was aware that some of the other officers, the older officers, were skeptical of him and his promotion: He was young, nervous as all hell, had a brief career that as yet lacked distinction—he had, so far, mostly busted screwed-up hippie kids for minor infractions. Loitering. Jaywalking. Curfew. The vague statute against public lewdness. His goal as a beat cop was to become such an annoyance they simply gave up, the hippies, gave up and moved along to some other precinct or, better, some other city. Then Chicago wouldn't have to deal with what was roundly agreed to be the worst generation ever. Easily the worst, even though it was his generation too. He wasn't much older than the kids he busted. But the uniform made him *feel* older, the uniform and crew cut and wife and child and preference for quiet things like bars without too much music where the only thing you heard was the murmur of conversation and the occasional sharp thwack of billiard balls. And church. Going to church and seeing the other beat cops there: It was a brotherhood. They were Catholic guys, neighborhood guys. You slapped them on the back when you saw them. They were good guys, they drank but not too much, they were kind to their wives, fixed up their houses, built things, played poker, paid their mortgages. Their wives knew each other, their kids played together. They'd been living on the block since forever. Their fathers had lived here, grandfathers too. They were Irish, Poles, Germans, Czechs, Swedes, but now thoroughly *Chicagoans.* They had city pensions that made them a good catch for the neighborhood ladies looking to settle down. They loved each other, loved the city, loved America, and not in an abstract way like kids asked to pledge allegiance but way down to their core—because they were *happy,* they were doing it, living, being successful, working hard, raising kids, sending kids to goddamn school. They had watched their own fathers raise them and, like most boys, they worried about measuring up. But here they were, doing it, and they thanked God and America and the city of Chicago for it. They hadn't asked for much, but what they'd asked for, they'd gotten.

It was hard not to feel personal about all this. When some new bad element moved into the neighborhood, it was hard not to take it personally. It *was* personal. Officer Brown's own grandfather had moved to this neighborhood as a very young man. He was Czeslaw Bronikowski until he reached Ellis Island, where he was given the name Charles Brown, a name then bestowed on the family's firstborn sons each generation since. And even though Officer Brown could have done without the teasing this name prompted when kids began reading that goddamn comic strip circa first grade, still he loved it—it was a good name, an *American* name, a consolidation of his family's past and its future.

It was a name that fit in.

So when some out-of-town doper, some punk peacenik, some longhaired hippie freak sat on the sidewalk all day scaring the daylights out of the old ladies, it was, indeed, personal. Why couldn't they just fit in? With the Negroes it was at least reasonable. If the blacks didn't particularly appreciate America, well, he could wrap his head around that one. But these kids, these middle-class white kids with their anti-America slogans—what gave them the right?

And so his job was simple: Target and annoy the bad elements in the city as far as the law allowed. As far as he could go without risking his pension or publicly embarrassing the city or the mayor. And yeah, sometimes somebody appeared on TV, usually some East Coast idiot with no idea what the fuck he was talking about, who said the cops in Chicago were harsh or brutal or obstructing people's First Amendment rights. But nobody paid much attention to that. There was a saying: Chicago problems, Chicago solutions.

For example, if a beatnik was walking through his precinct at two o'clock in the morning, it was a pretty easy matter to bust him for curfew violation. It was well known that most of these types did not carry any form of identification, so when they said "The curfew doesn't apply to me, pig," he could say "Prove it," and they absolutely could not. Simple. So they spent an uncomfortable few hours in a holding pen while the message sunk in: You are not welcome here.

And that had been an acceptable job for Officer Brown—he was aware of his own talents and limitations, he was not ambitious. He was content as a beat cop until, almost by accident, he got to know and earn the trust of a certain hippie leader, and when he told his bosses that he had "made contact with a leading student radical" and now had "access to the underground's inner sanctum" and asked to be assigned to the Red Squad—specifically the division investigating anti-American activity at Chicago Circle—they reluctantly agreed. (Nobody else on the force had been able to infiltrate Circle—those college kids could sniff out a fake *easy*.)

The Red Squad wiretapped rooms and telephones. They took covert photos. They tried to be as generally disruptive as they could be to the antiwar fringe. He saw it as a simple amplification of what he did on the street—annoying and detaining hippies—only now it was done in secret, using tactics that pushed the boundaries of what was, at face value, legal. For example, they raided the office of Students for a Democratic Society, stole files, broke typewriters, and spray-painted "Black Power" on the walls to throw the kids off. That seemed a bit questionable, yes, but the way he thought about it was that the only change between his old job and his new one was the method. The moral calculus, he figured, was the same.

Chicago problems, Chicago solutions.

And now he had been given the gift of a new name to investigate, some new fringe element recently arrived at Circle. He wrote the name down in his notebook. Put a star next to it. He would get to know this Faye very soon.

3

FAYE, OUTDOORS, in the grass, back leaning against a building, in the shade of a small campus tree, gently placed the newspaper on her lap. She smoothed its crinkles. She bent the corners where they'd begun to curl. The paper did not feel like ordinary newsprint—stiffer, thicker, almost waxy. Ink smeared off the page and onto her fingertips. She wiped her hands on the grass. She looked at the masthead—*Editor in Chief: Sebastian*—and she smiled. There was something both brazen and triumphant about Sebastian using only his first name. He had achieved enough renown that he was publicly mononymous, like Plato or Voltaire or Stendhal or Twiggy.

She opened the paper. It was the edition Sebastian had been printing last night, full of letters to the editor. She began to read.

> *Dear Chicago Free Voice,*
> *Do you like hiding from the pigs and those other people that stare at us put us down? Because of our clothes and hair? I mean I used to but I don't anymore I talk to them. Get them to like me and become friends and then tell them I smoke grass. And if they like you they might smoke it with you sometime and listen. You will help add one more of us to our ever growing number I think 50 percent of the USA is doing it and Narcotics Officers think we're all mental patients haw haw.*

It was hot today, and bright, and buggy: The gnats dove into her face, black dots between her eyes and the page, as if the punctuation marks were fleeing. She shooed them away. She was alone, nobody around; she'd found a quiet little spot on the northeast part of campus, a patch of grass separated from the sidewalk by a small hedge, back behind the brand-new Behavioral Sciences Building, which was roundly the most loathed building on the entire Circle campus. This was the one all the brochures talked about, designed according to the geometric principles of field theory, a new architecture meant to break the old architecture's "tyranny of the square," the brochures had said. A modern architecture that abandoned the square in favor of an overlapping matrix of octagons inscribed by circles.

Why this was better, philosophically, than a square, the brochures never explained. But Faye could guess: A square was old, traditional, antique, and therefore bad. It seemed to Faye that the worst thing on this campus, for both the students and the buildings, was to be *square*.

So the Behavioral Sciences Building was modern, many angled, which in practice made the place a bewildering mess. The interconnected honey-combs made no intuitive sense, hallways jagged and serpentine so you couldn't walk ten feet without having to make some kind of navigational choice. Faye's poetry class met here, and simply finding the correct class-room was an ordeal that taxed both her patience and her sense of spatial awareness. Certain stairs led into literally nothing, just a wall or a locked door, while other stairs led down to tiny landings where several other staircases intersected, all of them identical-looking. What seemed like a dead end actually opened into an entirely new area she never would have predicted was there. The third floor was visible from the second floor, with no obvious way to get up to it. That everything was built in circles and oblique angles pretty much guaranteed anyone would get lost, and indeed all who encountered this building for the first time had the same baffled expression, trying to navigate a place where concepts like "left" and "right" had little meaning.

It seemed less a place where students would study the behavioral sciences and more a place where behavioral scientists would study the students, to see how long the students could endure this nonsensical environment before going completely berserk.

So mostly the students avoided it, if they could, which made it a good place for Faye to be alone and read.

Do you people out there think you're crazy? I mean you're part of those 50 percenters right? I mean you all smoke grass don't you? I do. And I work hard or almost as hard as anyone else at the post office. And all my fellow workers know I turn on I mean they're always

asking me if some box of tea smells like grass. Today I found one that
did and most of them wanted to smell it. Then we wrapped it up and
delivered it. That person who got it might have gotten it by now. He
might be enjoying his package. He might be reading my rap. Hello
friend.

Movement in the distance distracted her, and she looked up, worried.
Because if any of her teachers saw her reading the *Chicago Free Voice,* if any
of the college officials who administrated her scholarship saw her reading the pro-narcotic, pro-Vietcong, antiestablishment "Newspaper of the
Street" . . . Well, they would think certain unfortunate things about her.

So her head popped out of reading at the first peripheral sight of the
approaching figure, walking down the sidewalk on the other side of
the hedge. And she gathered at a glance that he was no teacher, no admin-
istrator. His hair was too big for that. *Moppy* was the word going around,
but his hair had gone well beyond moppy and into a kind of efflorescence.
Wild growth. She watched him come, her head bent into the newspaper
so it wouldn't look like she was staring, and as he approached his features
clarified and she realized she knew him. He was the boy from last night.
At the meeting. Sebastian.

She pushed her hair back and wiped the sweat off her forehead. She
lifted the newspaper to conceal her face. Pressed her back into the wall
and felt thankful that the building had so many overhangs and corners.
Maybe he'd walk by.

I'd rather smoke a joint with a pig than keep on running from him I
mean wouldn't you? I mean wouldn't you like it if everybody did? No
fights no wars! Just a bunch of happy people. Wild thought or is it?

Her head buried in the newspaper—she recognized this as a somewhat pathetic, ostrichlike maneuver. She could hear Sebastian's footsteps
in the grass. Her face felt ten degrees warmer. She felt the sweat on her
temples and smeared it off with her fingers. She squeezed the newspaper
and held it close.

How would you people, my people, like to all, and I mean ALL, get
together? I mean at least 10 million people well maybe 9 million. I'd

sure like to shake all you good people's hands out there. All we need is someplace to have a huge Turn On Festival and let them know how many of us there really are!

The footsteps stopped. Then started again and came closer. He was walking toward her now, and Faye breathed and wiped the moisture from her forehead and waited. He approached—maybe ten feet away, maybe five. The paper blocked her, but she sensed him there. It would be absurd to pretend otherwise. She lowered the paper and saw him smiling.

"Hello, Faye!" he said. He bounced over and sat down beside her.

"Sebastian," she said, and she nodded and smiled her most genuine-feeling smile.

He looked handsome. Professional, even. He seemed pleased she'd remembered his name. The mad-scientist lab coat was gone. Now he was in a proper jacket—neutral beige, corduroy—and a plain white shirt, thin navy blue tie, brown slacks. He looked presentable, acceptable, except maybe the hair—too long, too disheveled, too big—but good-boy material nonetheless, one that could be, in his current state, maybe even furnished to parents.

"Your newspaper is quite good," Faye said, already working out how to be maximally likable in this moment, how to ingratiate herself to him: be supportive, be full of praise. "That letter from the man at the post office? I really think he has a point. It's quite interesting."

"Oh, lord, can you imagine that guy organizing a festival? Ten million people? Yeah, right."

"I don't think he really wants to organize a festival," Faye said. "I think he wants to know he's not alone. He just seems lonely to me."

Sebastian gave her a look of mock surprise—cocked his head and raised an eyebrow and smiled.

"I thought he was nuts," he said.

"No. He's looking for people he can be himself around. Aren't we all?"

"Huh," Sebastian said, and stared at her for a moment. "You're different, aren't you."

"I don't know what you mean." She wiped the sweat off her forehead.

"You're sincere," Sebastian said.

"I am?"

"Quiet, but sincere. You don't talk much, but when you talk you say what you mean. Most people I know talk constantly but never say anything true."

"Thanks?"

"Also you have ink all over your face."

"What?"

"Ink," he said. "All over."

She looked at her fingertips, blackened by the newspaper, and put it together. "Oh no," she said. She reached into her backpack for her cosmetics. She flipped open the compact, looked into the mirror, and saw what had happened: dark black streaks across her forehead, cheeks, temples, exactly where her fingers wiped away the sweat. And this was the kind of moment that could wreck her whole day, the kind of moment that would usually summon the tightness, the panic: doing something foolish in front of a stranger.

But something else happened instead, something surprising. Faye did not have an episode. Instead, she laughed.

"I look like a Dalmatian!" she said, and *she laughed*. She didn't know why she was laughing.

"It's my fault," Sebastian said. He handed her a handkerchief. "I should use better ink."

She rubbed away the smudges. "Yes," she said. "It is your fault."

"Walk with me," he said, and he helped her up and they left the shade of the tree, Faye's face now clean and bright. "You're fun," he said.

She felt weightless, happy, a little flirty even. It was the first time in her life anyone had ever described her as *fun*. She said, "You have a good memory, mister."

"I do?"

"You remembered my name," she said.

"Oh, well, you made an impression. That thing you said at the meeting."

"I wasn't thinking. I just blurted it out."

"You were right, though. It was an important point."

"It was not."

"You were suggesting that sometimes what people want sexually is in conflict with what they want politically, which made everyone uncomfortable. Plus that group tends to pounce on shy people. It looked like you were in trouble."

"I'm not shy," she said, "it's just . . ." And she stopped to find the right word, the correct and comprehensible way to say it, then skipped the explanation altogether. "Thanks for speaking up," she said. "I appreciate it."

"It's no problem," Sebastian said. "I saw your *maarr*."

"My what?"

"Your *maarr*."

"What is a *maarr*?"

"I learned about it in Tibet," he said, "visiting this sect of monks, one of the oldest Buddhist groups on earth, met them while I was abroad. I wanted to meet them because they've solved the problem of human empathy."

"I didn't know that was a problem needing to be solved."

"Oh sure. The problem is, we can never really feel it. Empathy. Most people think empathy is like understanding someone else or relating to them. But it's more than that. Real empathy is the actual corporeal *feeling* of someone else's emotions, so that it's experienced not only in the brain but also in the body, the body vibrating like a tuning fork to the sadness and suffering of another, as in, for example, you cry at the funerals of people you never even knew, you feel actual physical hunger when you see a starving child, you get vertigo when you watch an acrobat. And so forth."

Sebastian glanced at Faye to see if she was interested. "Go on," she said.

"Okay. Well, if we follow this to its conclusion, then empathy becomes like a haunting, a condition that is impossible since we all have separate egos, we've attained individuation, we can never really *be* another person, and that's the great empathy problem: that we can approach it but cannot realize it."

"Like the speed of light."

"Exactly! Nature has certain boundaries—perfect human empathy being one of them—that will always be slightly beyond our reach. But the monks have solved the problem this way: the *maarr*."

Faye listened in wonder. That a boy was saying such things. To her. Nobody had ever spoken to her this way. She wanted to wrap her arms around him and cry.

"Think of the *maarr* as the seat of emotions," Sebastian said, "held deeply inside your body, somewhere near the stomach—all desire, all yearning, all feelings of love and compassion and lust, all of one's secret wants and needs are held in the *maarr*."

Faye placed her palm on her belly.

"Yeah," Sebastian said, smiling. "Right there. To 'see' someone's *maarr* means recognizing someone else's desire—without asking, without being told—and acting on it. That last part is essential: The 'seeing' is not complete until one *does something about it*. So a man only 'sees' a woman's desires when he fulfills them without being asked to do so. A woman 'sees' a hungry man's *maarr* when, unprompted, she gives him food."

"Okay," Faye said, "I get it."

"It's this *active* sense of empathy that I love so much, the sense that one must do more than quietly relate to another human. One must also *make something happen*."

"Empathy is achieved only by deed," Faye said.

"Yes. So at the meeting, when I saw the group begin to criticize you, I turned their attention away, and in this way I saw your *maarr*."

And Faye was about to thank him when they came to a clearing and, ahead of her, she saw people, heard chanting. She'd been hearing some slight noise during their walk, as they moseyed counterclockwise around the Behavioral Sciences Building, taking the zigzagging route necessary on a campus that had few direct paths from anywhere to anywhere. It had grown louder as Sebastian told his story of empathy and monks and seeing her *maarr*.

"What's that sound?" she said.

"Oh, that's the demonstration."

"What demonstration?"

"You don't know? There are posters up everywhere."

"I guess I didn't notice."

"It's the ChemStar protest," he said, and they emerged into the courtyard of the monolithic University Hall, the tallest, most intimidating building on campus, by far. Whereas most of Circle's buildings were squat three-story things, University Hall was a thirty-story monster. It was visible from everywhere, looming over the trees, fatter at the top than at the bottom—anonymous, boxy, tyrannical. It looked like a beige concrete exoskeleton had been scaffolded around a slightly smaller, slightly browner building. Like every other campus structure, this one had narrow windows too small to fit a body through. Except, that is, for the top floor. The only windows on the entire campus that looked big enough to jump through were located suspiciously, almost invitingly, on the campus's highest point—the top floor of University Hall—and this fact struck some of the more cynical students as malevolent and sinister.

Here dozens of students were on the march: Bearded, long-haired, angry, they shouted at the building, shouted at the people inside the building—administrators, bureaucrats, the university president—holding signs that showed the ChemStar logo dripping with blood, that ChemStar logo Faye knew so well. It was stitched brightly on the uniform her father wore to work, right there on the chest, the logo's interlocking C and S.

"What's wrong with ChemStar?" she said.

"They make napalm," Sebastian said. "They kill women and children."

"They do not!"

"It's true," Sebastian said. "And the university buys their cleaning products, which is why we're protesting."

"They make napalm?" she said. Her father never mentioned this. In fact, he never talked about work at all, never said what he did there.

"It's a benzene and polystyrene compound," Sebastian explained, "that, when jellified and mixed with gasoline, becomes a sticky, highly flammable syrup that's used to burn the skin off the Vietcong."

"I know what napalm is," Faye said. "I just didn't know ChemStar made it."

That Faye's childhood and education were funded by paychecks from ChemStar was something she could not bear to tell Sebastian now, or ever.

Sebastian, meanwhile, watched the protest. He did not seem to notice her anxiety. (He had stopped seeing her *maarr*.) Rather, he watched the two journalists on the periphery of the mob—a writer and a photographer. The writer wasn't writing anything, and the photographer wasn't shooting.

"Not enough people showed up," he said. "It won't get in the newspaper."

The crowd was maybe three dozen strong, and loud, and walking in a circle holding signs and chanting "Murderers, murderers."

"A few years ago," Sebastian said, "a dozen picketing people would get you a few inches on page six. But now, after so many protests, the criteria have changed. Each new protest makes the next protest more usual. It's the great flaw of journalism: The more something happens, the less newsworthy it is. We have to follow the same trajectory as the stock market—sustained and unstoppable growth."

Faye nodded. She was thinking about the ChemStar billboard back home: MAKING OUR DREAMS COME TRUE.

"I guess there's one way to make sure it gets into the paper," Sebastian said.

"What's that?"

"Someone has to be arrested. Works every time." He turned to her. "It's been very nice talking to you, Faye," he said.

"Thank you," she said, distractedly, for she was still thinking about her father, about the way he smelled when he came home from work: like gasoline and something else, some heavy and suffocating smell, like car exhaust, hot asphalt.

"I hope to see you again soon," Sebastian said. And then he took off running toward the crowd.

Startled, Faye cried "Wait!" but he kept going, sprinting toward a police car parked near the mob. He bounded onto its hood, leaped onto the roof, and raised both fists into the air. The students cheered wildly. The photographer began shooting. Sebastian jumped up and down, denting the top of the car, then turned and looked at Faye. He smiled at her, and held her gaze until the police reached him, which they did quickly, and wrestled him down and put him in handcuffs and took him away.

4

WHEN SEBASTIAN LANDED on the police car, he landed hard. On his jaw. The police were brutal. Faye imagined him in jail right now, a lump of bruise. He would need someone to rub ice on that jaw, maybe change a bandage, massage a sore back. Faye wondered if he had someone who could do that for him, someone special. She found herself hoping he did not.

Her schoolwork was spread out across her bed. She was reading Plato. *The Republic.* The dialogues. She had finished the required reading, had swallowed everything about Plato's allegorical cave, the allegorical people living in the allegorical cave and seeing only shadows of the real world and believing the shadows *were* the real world. Plato's basic point being that our map of reality and actual reality sometimes do not match.

She had finished the homework and was reading the only chapter in the whole book the professor had not assigned, which seemed curious. But now, halfway through reading it, Faye understood. In this chapter, Socrates was teaching a bunch of old men how to attract very young boys. For sex.

What was his advice? Never praise the boy, Socrates said. Do not attempt romance, do not sweep him off his feet. When you praise a beautiful boy, he said, the boy is filled with such a high opinion of himself that he becomes more difficult to catch. You are a hunter who shoos your prey away. The person who calls an attractive person attractive only becomes more ugly. Better not to praise him at all. Better, maybe, to be a little mean.

Faye wondered if that was true. She knew every time Henry called her beautiful she tended to think he was more pathetic. She hated this about herself, but maybe Socrates was right. Maybe desire was best left unspoken. She didn't know. Sometimes Faye wished she lived another life parallel to this one, a life exactly the same but for the choices she made.

In this other life, she wouldn't have to worry so much. She could say any-thing, do anything, kiss boys and not worry about her reputation, watch movies with abandon, stop obsessing about tests or homework, shower with the other girls, wear far-out clothes and sit at the hippie table for kicks. In this other more interesting life, Faye would live consequence-free, and it seemed beautiful and lovely and, as soon as she thought about it objectively for ten seconds, ridiculous. Totally beyond her reach.

Which was why today's great success—her pleasant and honest embarrassment with Sebastian—was such a breakthrough. That she'd embarrassed herself in front of a boy and laughed about it. That she had smeared ink all over her face and didn't react with horror, did not yet feel horror, was not obsessing over it right now, was not disgusted by it, was not replaying it, reliving it again and again. She needed to know more about Sebastian, she decided. She didn't know what she'd say, but she needed to know more. And she knew where to go.

Alice lived next door, in a corner suite by the fire exit, a spot that had become a haven for far-out students, mostly women, mostly of the kind Faye had encountered at the meeting, who stayed up late screaming to the record player and smoking grass. When Faye peeked into the room (the door was almost always open), several faces swiveled to look at her, none of them Alice's. They suggested she might be found at People's Law, where Alice held an unpaid position keeping the books.

"What's People's Law?" Faye asked, and the girls looked at each other and smirked. Faye realized she'd embarrassed herself, that the question revealed she was square. This happened to her all the time.

"They help people arrested for protesting," one of the girls explained.

"Help them get out of jail," another added.

"Oh," Faye said. "Would they be able to help Sebastian?"

They smiled again. The same way. Some new conspiracy. Another bit of the world obvious to everyone but Faye.

"No," said one of the girls. "He has his own methods. You don't have to worry about Sebastian. He gets arrested, he's back out in an hour. No one knows how he does it."

"He's a magician," another of the girls added.

They gave her the address of People's Law, which turned out to be a hardware store crammed into the first floor of a creaky and hot two-story apartment building, a building that might have seen a previous exis-tence as a resplendent Victorian home but had since been cut up into this live/work retail puzzle. Faye looked for some kind of sign or door, but only found shelves crammed with your typical hardware things: nails, hammers, hoses. She wondered if the girls had given her the wrong address, if they were putting her on. The wooden floor squeaked, and she felt how it rippled and sloped down toward the heaviest shelves. She was about to leave when the proprietor, a tall and thin white-haired man, asked if he could help her find anything.

"I'm looking for People's Law?" she said.

He looked at her for an uncomfortable moment, seemed to inspect her. "You?" he said at last.

"Yes. Is it here?"

He told her it was in the basement of the building, accessible through a door out back, via the alley. So Faye found herself tapping on a wooden door with a simple "PL" painted on it in an alley that was empty save for about half a dozen dumpsters cooking in the sun.

The woman who answered—probably no older than Faye herself— said she hadn't seen Alice that day but suggested Faye could find her at a place called Freedom House. And thus Faye had to endure the whole ritual again, the admission that she did not in fact know what Freedom House was, the awkward look, the embarrassment at not knowing something everyone else knew, the explanation from the girl telling her that Freedom House was a shelter for runaway girls and that Faye was forbidden to give the location to any man *ever*.

So this is how Faye discovered Alice in an otherwise unremarkable three-story brick building, in an unmarked top-floor apartment, accessible only if you knew the secret knock (which by the way was Morse code for SOS), in a spartan living room decorated mostly with mismatched and obviously secondhand or donated furniture made more inviting and homey by various crocheted and knitted things, where Alice was sitting on the couch, her legs up on the edge of a coffee table, reading *Playboy* magazine.

"Why are you reading *Playboy* magazine?" Faye asked.

Alice gave her that impatient, withering stare that announced exactly how little she cared about stupid questions.

"For the articles," she said.

The thing that made Alice so frightening was that she did not seem to care if she was liked. She did not seem to spend any mental energy accommodating other people, accounting for their wishes, expectations, desires, their basic need for decorum and manners and etiquette. And Faye's opinion was that everyone should want to be liked—not out of vanity but because wanting to be liked provided an essential social lubricant. In a world without a vengeful god, the desire to be liked and to fit in was the only check on human behavior, it seemed to Faye, who wasn't sure if she believed in a vengeful god but knew for a fact that Alice and her cronies were atheists to the bone. They could be as rude as they cared to be and not worry about retribution in the afterlife. It was disarming. Like being in the same room with a large and unpredictable dog—that constant latent fear of it.

Alice sighed heavily like this was going to be a huge mental burden, this talking. It was almost as if Alice *expected* Faye to waste her time, and it was up to Faye to prove otherwise.

"Look at this woman," Alice said. She kicked her feet to the floor and laid the magazine on the coffee table and opened it to the centerfold. The photo, vertically oriented, took up three full pages. And once Faye got over the initial shock, that first somersault in her belly when she found herself looking at something she was sure she wasn't allowed to see, the first thing she thought, tilting her head so she could see better, was that the young woman in the photo looked cold. Physically cold. She was standing in a swimming pool, her back turned at a slight angle to the camera, twisting at the waist so that her torso was in profile. She was standing in perfectly turquoise water and hugging a child's inflatable swimming pool toy—a blow-up swan—hugging it around its long neck, pressing it against her cheek as if she might find warmth there. Of course she was nude. The skin of her butt and lower back appeared rough and coarse, a crocodile skin from the goose bumps popping up all over. Beads of water dribbled off her butt and upper thigh where she had dipped a few inches into the water, but no farther.

"What am I looking at here?" Faye said.

"Pornography."

"Yes, but why?"

"I think she's very pretty, this one."

The centerfold girl. Miss August, it said in the corner. Her pink body was mottled a slight maroon in places where she was cold or where the blood showed under her skin. Water streaked down her back, a few drops clung to her arm, not enough to look like she'd really been swimming—maybe the photographer had spritzed her, for effect.

"There's an ease to her," Alice said, "a quiet charm. I'll bet she's capable, powerful even. Problem is she has no idea what she can do."

"But you like her looks."

"She's beautiful."

"I read somewhere that you shouldn't compliment people's looks," Faye said. "It diminishes you."

Alice frowned. "Says who?"

"Socrates. Via Plato."

"You know," Alice said, "you're way strange sometimes."

"Sorry."

"You don't have to apologize for it."

Miss August was not quite smiling. Rather, she had that mechanically forced smile of someone who's very cold being told to smile. Her face was summer-freckled. Two drops of water hung from her right breast. If they fell, they would land on her bare belly. Faye could feel it, that chill.

"Porn is a problem for the whole project of enlightenment," Alice said. "If otherwise rational, educated, literate, moral, and ethical men still need to look at this, then how far have we really come? The conservative wants to get rid of pornography by banning it. But the liberal wants to get rid of it too, by making people so enlightened they no longer want it. Repression versus education. The cop and the teacher. Both have the same goal—prudishness—but use different tools."

"All my uncles subscribe," Faye said, pointing to the magazine. "They leave it out in the open. They put it on the coffee table."

"They say the sexual revolution is not really about sex but about shame."

"This girl does not appear to be ashamed," said Faye.

"This girl does not appear to be anything. It's not her shame we're talking about, it's ours."

"You feel ashamed?"

"By *ours* I mean the general we, the abstract we."

"Oh."

"The capital *V* Viewer. Capital *L* Looker. Not us in particular, you or I."

"*I* feel ashamed," Faye said. "A little, I guess. I don't want to, but I do."

"And why is that?"

"I don't want anyone to know I've seen this. They might think I'm weird."

"Define 'weird.'"

"That I was looking at girls. They might think I like girls."

"And you're worried about what they think?"

"Of course I am."

"That's not real shame. You think it's shame, but it's not."

"What is it?"

"Fear."

"Okay."

"Self-hatred. Alienation. Loneliness."

"Those are just words."

There was also the odd fact of it, the magazine, sitting there between them, its objectness. The creases in the photo, the undulations of the pages, the way the gloss of the magazine reflected the light, the curling paper's sensitivity to humid air. One of the staples holding the magazine together erupted out of Miss August's arm, as if she'd been struck by shrapnel. The windows in the apartment were open, a small electric fan whirred nearby, and the centerfold pages bounced and shimmied in the shifting air, animating it—it looked like Miss August was moving, twitching, trying to hold still in the cold water but not able to.

"The men in the movement say this shit all the time," said Alice. "Like if you don't want to fuck them they wonder why you have such big hang-ups. If you won't take off your shirt, they tell you not to be so ashamed of yourself. Like if you don't let them feel your tits you're not a legitimate part of the movement."

"Does Sebastian do that?"

Alice stopped and squinted at her. "Why do you want to know about Sebastian?"

"No reason. I'm curious, is all."

"Curious."

"He seems to be, you know, interesting."

"Interesting how?"

"We had a nice afternoon together. Today. On the lawn."

"Oh, lord."

"What?"

"You dig him."

"Do not."

"You're thinking about him."

"He seems interesting. That's all."

"Do you want to ball him?"

"I would not phrase it like that."

"You want to fuck him. But you want to make sure he's worthy first. That's why you came here today. To ask about Sebastian."

"We simply had a pleasant conversation and then he was arrested at the ChemStar protest and now I'm worried about him. I'm worried about my friend."

Alice leaned forward, put her elbows on her knees. "Don't you have a boyfriend back home?"

"I don't see how that's relevant."

"But you do, right? Girls like you always do. Where is he right now? Is he waiting for you?"

"He's in the army."

"Oh, wow!" Alice said, clapping her hands together. "Oh, that's rich! Your boyfriend's going to Vietnam and you want to screw a war protestor."

"Never mind."

"And not just any war protestor. *The* war protestor." Alice clapped, a mocking applause.

"Be quiet," Faye said.

"Sebastian's got a Vietcong flag *on his wall*. He gives money to the National Liberation Front. You know that, right?"

"This is none of your business."

"Your boyfriend is going to get shot. And Sebastian will have supplied the bullets. This is who you choose."

Faye stood up. "I'm going to leave now."

"You might as well pull the trigger yourself," Alice said. "That's low."

Faye turned her back to Alice and marched out of the apartment, her hands balled up in fists, her arms straight and rigid.

"Now this is it," Alice called after her. "Shame. *Real* shame. This is how it feels, girly."

The last thing Faye saw as she slammed the door shut was Alice kicking her feet back up on the coffee table and flipping the pages of *Playboy* magazine.

5

NO CAB FARE, no train tokens. Alice believed in freedom, free movement, being free—here, at five o'clock in the morning, walking in the purple and cool and damp light of Chicago. The sun was beginning to show over Lake Michigan and the faces of buildings glowed weakly pink. Certain delis were opening, and shopkeepers hosed off the sidewalks, where batches of newspapers tossed from trucks landed in heaps like sacks of grain. She looked at one and saw the headline—NIXON NOMINATED BY GOP—and she spat. She inhaled the early-morning scent of the city, its waking breath, asphalt and engine oil. The shopkeepers ignored her. They saw her clothes—her big green military jacket and leather boots, her ripped-up skintight jeans—and they saw her black rumpled hair, her unimpressed eyes leveled over silver sunglasses, and they assumed correctly she was not a paying customer. She carried no cash. She did not warrant being courteous to. She liked the transparency of these interactions, the lack of bullshit between herself and the world.

She didn't carry a purse because if she carried a purse she might be tempted to put keys in the purse, and if she had keys she might be tempted to lock her door, and if she began locking her door she might be tempted to buy things that needed locking up: clothes purchased at actual stores rather than hand-sewn or shoplifted—that's where it would begin—then shoes, dresses, jewelry, stockpiles of collectible doodads, then still more stuff, a television, small at first, then a bigger one, then another, one for each room, and magazines, cookbooks, pots and pans, framed pictures on the walls, a vacuum cleaner, an ironing board, clothes worth ironing, rugs worth vacuuming, and shelves and shelves and shelves, a bigger place, an apartment, a house, a garage, a car, locks on the car, locks on the doors, multiple locks and bars on the windows that would finally turn the house more fully into the jail it had long ago become. It would be a fundamental change in her stance toward the world: from inviting the world in to keeping the world out.

Tonight was one of those nights that would not have happened if she carried a purse, or keys, or money, or hang-ups regarding easy necking with motley strangers. She went looking for free kicks and found them so quickly, so easily: two men downtown who invited her up to their dirty apartment, where they drank whiskey and played Sun Ra records and she danced with them and swayed her hips and, after one of the men passed out, gave gentle kisses to the other until the weed was gone. The music was not hummable, was not really even danceable, but was excellent to kiss to. And it was fun until the guy unbuttoned his pants and said, "Would you do something with your mouth?" That the guy couldn't even ask for it correctly, couldn't even name the thing he wanted, was, she thought, pathetic. He seemed surprised when she said so. "I thought you were *liberated,*" he said, by which he meant that she should indulge all his various wants and like it.

Such were the expectations of the New Left.

She still felt the pot in her body, in her legs, the way her legs felt like stilts, harder and thinner and longer than normal sober legs. Step after westward step, through downtown and back to Circle, Alice walked a clownish walk that made her love her body, for she could feel her body working, could feel its various wonderful parts.

She was testing her legs when the cop saw her. She was hopscotching past an alley where his car was hidden and he called out to her: "Hey, honey, where ya going?"

She stopped. Turned to the voice. It was him. The pig with the ridiculous name: Officer Charlie Brown.

"What you been up to, honey," he said, "out so late?"

He was large as an avalanche, a big pumpkin-faced enforcer of petty laws—panhandling, littering, jaywalking, curfew. The cops had lately been stopping them for minor infractions, stopping and searching them, looking for anything contraband, anything arrestable. Most of the pigs were idiots, but this one was different. This one was interesting.

"Come here," he said. He leaned on the hood of his police cruiser. One hand on his nightstick. It was dark. The alley was a cave.

"I asked you a question," he said. "Whatcha doing?"

She walked to him and stopped just out of arm's reach, stared up at him, at the great imposing mountain of him. His uniform was a light blue, almost baby blue, and short-sleeved, too small for him. His chest was shaped like a keg and strained against the buttons. He had a light blond mustache that you couldn't really see unless you were up this close. His badge was a five-pointed silver star directly over his heart.

"Nothing," she said. "Just going home."

"Going home?"

"Yes."

"At five in the morning? Just walking home? Not doing anything illegal?"

Alice smiled. He was obeying the script she'd given him. One of the few things she admired about Officer Brown was his persistence.

She said, "Fuck off, pig."

He lunged for her then, grabbed her neck and brought her to him, to his face, pressed his nose into her scalp and sniffed loudly right above her ear.

"You smell like weed," he said.

"So what?"

"So I'm gonna have to search you now."

"You need a warrant for that," she said, and he laughed a laugh that was admittedly pretty fake-sounding, but she appreciated it, that he was trying. He spun her around and pinned her arm behind her back and walked her deeper into the alley, then forced her over the trunk of his cruiser. They'd been through this once before, only a couple of nights ago, and had gotten this far, bending her over the car, before Brown broke character. He had shoved her onto the car a little too forcefully—to be honest, she had let him shove her, had gone slack at the key moment—and when her cheek met the metal she was momentarily dazed, which is exactly what she wanted, a brief escape from her head.

But it had scared him, her face hitting the car like that. She bruised almost immediately. "Little piggy!" he had cried, and she admonished him for using their safe word, had to explain to him that their safe word was reserved for *her only* and it didn't even make sense for him to use it. And he shrugged and looked at her penitently and promised to be better next time.

Here is what Alice had asked of Officer Brown: She wanted him to find her some random night when she didn't expect it and act like he didn't know her and certainly not act like they'd been carrying on a summer-long affair, just act like she was another hippie freak and he was another brutal cop and he'd take her into a dark alley and bend her over the trunk of his police cruiser and rip off her clothes and have his way with her. That is what she wanted.

Officer Brown was deeply perturbed at this request. He wondered why on earth she would want that. Why not have some more normal backseat sex? And she gave him the only answer that mattered: Because she had already tried normal backseat sex, but had yet to try this.

Her face against the car now, and Brown's hand pressing hard against her neck—it seemed like he was going to go through with it this time, and she was not exactly enjoying it, but more like hoping she would enjoy it very soon, if he kept it going.

Officer Brown, meanwhile, was terrified.

Terrified of hurting her, but also terrified of *not* hurting her, or not hurting her in the correct way, not being good enough for her, terrified that if he wasn't good enough at the weird kinky things she wanted from him that she'd up and leave him. That was the biggest terror of them all, that Alice would lose interest and go.

This was what it was like for him, every time. The more of these encounters Officer Brown had with Alice, the more afraid and paranoid he became about losing her. He knew this about himself. He could feel it happening, but he could not stop it. After each new encounter, the thought of no longer encountering her became more devastating and impossible to bear.

This is what he called them, privately, to himself, in his head: encounters.

Because the word sounded passive and almost accidental. You "encounter" a stranger in an alley. You "encounter" a bear in the woods. It sounded like it happened by chance and certainly not in the elaborately premeditated way the encounters actually occurred. The word *encounter* was a word that did not sound like he was aggressively on-purpose cheating on his wife, which of course he was doing. Willingly. And often.

When he thought about his wife discovering his secret, he was ashamed. When he imagined what it would be like admitting to his wife what he'd been doing and how he'd been doing it in such a well-thought-out, behind-your-back way, he felt full of shame and disgust, yes, but also a kind of recrimination and justifiable anger and a sense that he was beyond reproach and driven into Alice's arms by a wife who, since the birth of their daughter, had changed.

Changed drastically and fundamentally. It began when his wife started calling him "Daddy," and so he called her "Mommy," and he thought it was a joke, a game between them, trying to get used to these new roles, like the way she called him "Husband" all through their honeymoon. It seemed so suddenly formal and exotic and strange. "Would you join me for dinner, my dearest husband?" she would ask each night for a week after they were married, and they would fall giggling onto the bed feeling much too young and immature for names like Husband and Wife. And so he figured in the hospital in the days after his daughter was born and they called each other Mommy and Daddy that it was similarly comic and temporary.

Only that was five years ago and she was still calling him Daddy. And he was still calling her Mommy. She never explicitly asked to go by that name, but rather slowly stopped responding to other names. It was weird. He'd call to her from the other room: "Honey?" Nothing. "Sweetie?" Nothing. "Mommy?" And she'd appear, as if that was the only word she could still hear. He found it creepy she'd refer to him as Daddy, but this remained, for the most part, unsaid, except for furtive suggestions here and there: "You don't have to call me that if you don't want to," he'd say, to which she'd respond, "But I want to."

Plus there was also the matter of sex, which was not happening, at all, sex between them, a fact he chalked up to the family's now regular sleeping arrangement, which involved their daughter sleeping with them, between them, in their bed. He did not remember agreeing to this. It simply happened. And he suspected it wasn't even for his daughter's benefit, this arrangement, but for Mommy's. That Mommy liked sleeping this way because in the morning their daughter would climb on Mommy and kiss her all over and tell her she was pretty. He got the feeling that Mommy did not want to live without this daily ceremony.

She had in fact *trained their daughter to do this*.

Not on purpose, not at first. But Mommy had definitely actively ritualized this behavior, which began innocently enough, their daughter waking up one morning and saying all puffy-eyed and bleary, "You're pretty, Mommy." It was cute. Mommy hugged her and said thank you. Innocent. But then a few mornings later Mommy asked "Do you still think I'm pretty?," and the daughter responded enthusiastically "Yes!" That wasn't weird enough to say anything about—just enough to note, quietly, in his head. Then again a few mornings after that, when Mommy asked the daughter "What do we say to Mommy in the morning?," and the daughter said, reasonably, "Good morning?" And Mommy said no and this quizzing went on until the poor kid got it right: "You're so pretty!"

That was kind of weird.

Weirder still the next week when Mommy *actively punished* the daughter for not saying she was pretty, withholding the pancakes and cartoons that were their Saturday-morning tradition and instead directing the daughter to clean her room. And when the daughter asked through her disappointed tears why this was happening and Mommy said "You didn't tell me I was pretty this morning," he thought it was very weird indeed.

(It goes without saying that when he told his wife she was pretty, she rolled her eyes and pointed out some new part of her that had lately become wrinkled or fat.)

He began working the night shift. To avoid the cascade of kisses and hollow compliments that had now become the normal and habituated way each day began. He slept during the day, the whole bed to himself. At night, he was on patrol, which is how he encountered Alice.

She was exactly like the rest, at first, memorable only because of the sunglasses she wore in the middle of the night. He found her out walking and asked her to produce identification. Predictably, she could not. So he cuffed her and pressed her against his car and searched her for drugs, which about one in three of these types usually carried, stupidly, right in their pockets.

But she carried nothing—no drugs, no money, no makeup, no keys. Homeless, he guessed. He took her to the lockup, dropped her off, and promptly forgot about her.

She was at the exact same spot the next night.

At exactly the same time. Dressed exactly the same: green military jacket, sunglasses worn most of the way down her nose. She wasn't walking this time, just standing there on the sidewalk like she was waiting for him.

He pulled up and asked, "What are you doing?"

"Breaking curfew," she said. She glared at him, stood stiff and straight, a pose of abstract anger and resistance.

"You want to go through this again?" he said.

"Do what you're gonna do, pig."

So again he cuffed her, pressed her against the car. Again she was carrying nothing. All the way to the lockup she stared at him. Most people slumped against the door, defeated, almost like they were trying to hide. Not this girl. It unnerved him, her stare.

The next night he saw her again, at the same spot, the same time. She stood leaning against the wall of a brick building, one knee up, hands in her pockets.

"Hey there," he said.

"Hey, pig."

"Breaking curfew again?"

"Among other things."

He felt a little afraid of her. He was not accustomed to people reacting this way. The freaks and hippies were unbearable, of course, but they could be trusted to act rationally. They did not want to go to jail. They did not want to be hassled. But this girl, she emitted a kind of danger, a flirtatiousness and fierceness that he found alien and unpredictable. Maybe even thrilling.

"You gonna cuff me?" she said.

"Are you causing trouble?"

"I could. If that's what it took."

The next night was his night off, but he found someone to trade shifts. She was there again, same spot. He drove past her once, then again. She followed him with her eyes. She was openly laughing at him by the third time around the block.

The first time they screwed it was in the backseat of his police cruiser. Alice was at her usual spot, at the usual time. She'd simply pointed at the alley and told him to park the car there. He did. It was dark, the car almost completely hidden. She told him to get in the backseat. He did. He was not used to taking orders from girls, from hippie street freaks especially. He felt briefly resistant to the whole thing, but that evaporated as soon as she got into the backseat with him and closed the door and removed his belt, which fell loudly to the floor, holding as it was his radio and nightstick and gun. A great thud and clatter on the floorboards. And

Alice didn't even try to kiss him. She didn't seem to want to, though he kissed her—it seemed gentlemanly, to kiss her, to stroke her face with his fingers, a gesture that he hoped conveyed thoughtfulness and human affection, that he wanted more than simply what was in her pants, except that what was in her pants was mostly what he wanted, at that moment very much so. She yanked at his slacks and all thoughts of his wife and the guys back at the station and the superintendent and the mayor and the slim chance of somebody walking by and seeing them, they were all obliterated.

They didn't have sex "together" so much as Alice had vigorous sex with him while he lay there also participating.

Afterward, exiting the car, she turned and smiled her sly smile and said, "See you around, pig." And for the rest of his shift he obsessed over what she meant by that. *See you around.* Not "See you next time." Not "See you tomorrow." Not even "See you later." She'd said *See you around,* which was the least forward-thinking, most noncommittal thing she could have said.

Each encounter followed roughly the same basic emotional pattern: massive relief that Alice had returned, followed by ceaseless worry that she'd never come back.

And he needed her to come back. Desperately. Harrowingly. It felt like his chest and guts were held together by a single wooden clothespin that she could remove by simply not showing up. He imagined arriving at their usual spot and not finding her anymore and feeling his insides burst like a water balloon. The rejection would be terminal. He knew it. This led him to a morally questionable but, in his mind, totally necessary employment request: He asked to be assigned to the Red Squad.

After which his full-time job became to *spy on Alice,* which was really excellent because he could both keep track of where she was at all times and, even better, have a somewhat-plausible excuse if anyone found out about them. He wasn't having an affair; he was *undercover.*

He bugged her room. He photographed her going into and out of various known subversive meeting places. And he felt more free when he screwed her. That is, until she asked him to do things to her that he found more than a little weird.

"Fuck me while I'm handcuffed," she'd said that first time their love-making changed from standard-issue backseat sex to something kinkier.

He asked her why on earth she would ever want something like that and she gave him that withering, crushing, sarcastic face he hated so much. "Because I've never tried it in handcuffs," she said.

But he hadn't thought that was a very good reason. He could think of a million things he had never tried and had no interest in.

"Do you like balling me?" she'd asked.

He paused. He hated this, all this talking about himself and his feelings. One advantage to his wife's post-child metamorphosis was that she had stopped asking personal questions completely. It occurred to him that he hadn't had to express his feelings verbally in years.

Yes, he'd told her. He liked making love to her, and she laughed at that—the quaintness of a phrase like "making love." He blushed.

"And did you ever think that you'd enjoy screwing a freaky beatnik like me?" she said.

"No."

She shrugged, as if to say, *Clearly I am right.* She raised her hands to him, presented her wrists, which he reluctantly handcuffed.

The next time she asked for the handcuffs again.

"And try to be a little rougher," she'd said.

He asked her to be more specific.

"I don't know," she said. "Just don't be so gentle."

"I'm not entirely clear what that means in practice."

"Smash my face into the car or something."

"Or something?"

And this is how it went every time: Alice asked for something new and weird, something that Brown had never done before and maybe had never even *considered* before, something that gave him the creeps and made him feel all sorts of dread that he wouldn't be able to bring himself to do it—or wouldn't be able to do it *to her standards*—and so Brown resisted it until eventually his fear of disappointing Alice or losing Alice overcame his shame and panic and he muscled through with whatever sexual act she wanted, self-conscious the entire time, not exactly enjoying it but knowing the alternative was much, much worse.

"You got anything to show me?" he said now, pressing Alice's belly into the car and pressing himself against her back.

"No."

"Anything in those jeans? Best to admit it."

"Honest, no."

"We'll see about that."

She felt his hands in her pockets, front and back, turning them inside out, finding nothing but lint and old tobacco. He patted her legs, outside the thigh, then inside.

"See?" she said. "Nothing."

"Shut up."

"Let me go."

"Shut your mouth."

"You're a fuckin' pig," she said.

He pressed her face harder into the cold metal of the cruiser. "Say that again," he said. "I dare you."

"Fuckin' cockless pig," she said.

"Cockless," he said. "I'll show you cockless."

Then he leaned over her and whispered into her ear, in a tone about five octaves higher and full of tenderness and affection, "Am I doing this right?"

"Don't break character!" she scolded.

"Okay," he said, "fine." And she felt him pull at her jeans and yank them down. She felt the slight buckle of the metal where he forced her cheek against the trunk of the cruiser. Then the feeling of the morning air as he exposed her, brought her jeans all the way off and kicked her legs apart so she was spread out and easily enterable. Then entering her, pressing at her until he worked his way in, and she felt him inflate inside her, thicken and fatten, before he began pushing. Whining and pushing, light little puppy yelps each time he bucked. No rhythm to it. A chaotic and spastic pulse that ended quickly, after only a minute or two, with a final catastrophic jab.

Then the quick diminishment. His body softening, his hands becoming gentle. He released her and she stood up. He handed her the jeans he'd removed. He looked at the ground sheepishly. She smiled and put her pants back on. They both sat down, behind the cruiser, leaning into each other and the bumper. At length he finally spoke.

"Too rough?" he said.

"No," she said. "It was fine."

"I was worried it was too rough."

"It was good."

"Because last time you said you wanted it rougher."

"I know," she said. She twisted her back, one way, then the other, felt the spot on her cheek where she'd met the trunk of the cruiser, the spot on her neck where his hand had been.

"Why you gotta walk alone all the time?" he said. "It's not safe."

"It's perfectly safe."

"There are dangerous people out here," he said, and he gathered her up in his big arms and squeezed her right where it hurt.

"Ouch."

"Oh, god," he said, releasing her. "I'm a moron."

"It's fine." She patted him on the arm. "I ought to get going." Alice stood up. She felt the dampness in her jeans turning chilly. She wanted to go home. She wanted a shower.

"Let me drive you," Brown said.

"No. People will see us."

"I'll drop you a couple blocks from the dorm."

"It's okay," she said.

"When will I see you again?"

"Yeah, about that. Next time I'd like to try something different," she said, and his heart leaped: *There would be a next time!*

"Next time," she said, "I'd like you to choke me."

Brown felt his butterflies disappear. "I'm sorry, what?"

"You don't have to *actually* choke me," she said. "How about you put your hand there and act like you're choking me."

"Act like it?"

"If you also wanted to squeeze a little, that would be fine too."

"Jesus!" he said. "I am *not* doing that."

She frowned. "What's your problem?"

"*My* problem? What's *your* problem? Did I hear you right? Choke you? That's going way too far. Why on earth would I do that?"

"We've been over this before. Because I've never tried it."

"No. That's not it. That's a reason to eat teriyaki. That's not a reason to goddamn *choke* you."

"It's all I have."

"If you want me to do this, you need to explain yourself."

It was the first time he'd really stood up to her, and he was immediately regretting it. He worried that she'd simply shrug her shoulders and leave. As with most dysfunctional couples, there was an imbalance between them regarding who needed the relationship more. It was an unspoken fact that she could leave at any moment with very little pain, whereas he would be devastated. A puddle of rejection. Because he knew *nothing like this would ever happen to him again for the rest of his life.* He would never again find a woman like Alice, and after she was gone he would return to the life she had revealed to be tedious and barren.

His response to Alice was really a response to the exigencies of monogamy and mortality.

Alice sat there thinking a moment, more reflective than he'd ever seen her. Part of her confidence was that she seemed to know exactly what she wanted to say at any given moment, so this pause felt unusual and out of character. She gathered herself up and looked at him above those dark sunglasses she always wore and breathed a heavy, somewhat exasperated sigh.

"Here's the thing," she said. "Normal sex with boys doesn't really interest me. The usual stuff, I mean. Most boys treat sex like it's a pinball game. Like it's a matter of whapping the same levers again and again and again. It's boring."

"I've never played pinball."

"You're missing the point. Okay, different analogy: Imagine everyone was eating this cake. And they told you how good the cake was. And when you tried the cake, it tasted, you know, like paper and cardboard. It was terrible. And yet all your friends loved it. How would you feel?"

"Disappointed, I guess."

"And crazy. Especially if they told you it *wasn't the cake's fault.* That the real problem was you. That you weren't eating it right. I know I'm stretching the metaphor pretty thin."

"So I'm a new piece of cake for you?"

"I just want to be made to feel something."

"Have you told your friends about me?"

"Hah. *No way.*"

"I embarrass you. You're ashamed of me."

"Listen, in real life, I'm an antiauthoritarian anarchist. And yet, there's this electric part of me that also wants to be dominated sexually by a cop. I prefer to go with it and not judge. But I don't think my friends would understand."

"All these things we're doing," he said, "the handcuffs, the rough stuff. Are they, you know, are they working?"

She smiled. She touched his cheek lightly, the most gentle touch she'd ever administered. "You're a good man, Charlie Brown."

"Don't say that. You know I hate that."

She kissed him on the top of his head. "Go fight crime."

She felt his eyes on her as she left. She felt his bruises on her neck and cheek. As she walked away, she felt a great cold glob of him sliding out.

IT WAS A WHISPER on campus, spread between one turned-on student and another. It was a secret not shared with the pro-war ROTC cadets, nor the fraternity jocks, nor the husband-seeking debutantes. Only the most committed, only the most sincere were allowed to hear it: On certain days, in a certain classroom, deep within the bewildering labyrinth of the Behavioral Sciences Building, for an hour at a time, the war was officially over.

Vietnam did not exist during this hour, in this class. Allen Ginsberg, the great poet newly arrived from the coast, led them, beginning each class with the same words: "The war is officially over." Then the students repeated the words, then repeated them again, in unison, and the fact of their voices harmonizing made the words more real. Ginsberg told them how language has power, how thought has power, how releasing these words into the universe could begin a cascade that would make the words facts.

"The war is officially over," Ginsberg said. "Say it until the meaning disappears and the words become pure physical things that erupt from the body because the names of gods used in a mantra are identical with the gods themselves. This is very important," he said, raising a finger into the air. "If you say 'Shiva' you are not calling for Shiva, you are *producing* Shiva, creator and preserver, destroyer and concealer, the war is officially over."

Faye watched him from the back of the room, where she sat, like everyone else, on the dusty linoleum floor—watched his swinging silver peace-sign necklace, his eyes blissfully closed behind horn-rimmed glasses, and all his hair, that scrum of black and tangled hair that had migrated from the now-smooth crown of his head down to his cheeks and jowls, a beard that shook as he shook, rocking and swaying during the prayer chanting like congregants did in the more exuberant churches, his whole body getting involved, his eyes closed, his legs crossed, he brought his own special rug to sit on.

"A body vibration like they do on the plains of Africa," said Ginsberg, who with a harmonium and finger cymbals played the music they notched their chants to. "Or the mountains of India, or any place absent television machines that do the vibrating for us. We have all forgotten how to do this except maybe Phil Ochs singing 'The War Is Over' for two whole hours once, a mantra more powerful than all the antennas of the Columbia Broadcasting System, than all the broadsides printed for the Democratic National Convention, than ten full years of political speech yakking."

The students sat cross-legged on the floor and rocked themselves to some private interior tempo. It looked like a room of spinning tops. The desks were shoved to the outer edges of the class. Someone's jacket hung over the window on the door, blocking the view into the room, in case of passing administrators or campus security or some of the less-hip professoriate.

Faye knew that the war-is-officially-over chant would eventually give way to "Hare Krishna, Hare Rama," and then they would end their hour together with the sacred vowel: "om." This was how each of their classes had gone so far, and Faye felt crushed that all she might learn from the great Allen Ginsberg was this: how to sway, how to chant, how to growl. This was the man who'd written poems that burned her right through, and sitting in her chair on the first day of class she was worried she'd be struck dumb in his presence. Then she saw him and wondered where the nice neat man from the author photo had gone. No more tweed jacket and combed hair—Ginsberg had fully embraced the counterculture's most obvious emblems, and at first Faye felt disappointed at the lack of creativity this implied. Now her feelings were closer to plain annoyance. She wanted to raise her hand and ask "Are we ever going to learn about, you know, *poetry?*" if it weren't such an obviously unwelcome question. For the students in this class didn't care about poetry—they cared about the war, and what they wanted to say about the war, and how they were going to stop the war. Primarily, they cared about the war protest at the upcoming Democratic National Convention, now only days away. It would be a mighty thing, they all agreed. Everyone was coming.

"If the police attack," Ginsberg said, "we must sit on the ground and say 'om' and show them what peace looks like."

The students rocked and hummed. A few opened their eyes and exchanged looks, a kind of telepathy zapping between them that said, *If the cops come, I'm not sitting, I'm fucking running.*

"It will take all the bravery you can muster," Ginsberg said, as if reading their thoughts. "But the only answer to violence is its opposite."

The students closed their eyes.

"This is how to do it," he said. "Let us practice. Do you feel it? Obviously it is a subjective experience, which is the only kind that matters. Anything objective is not really feelable."

Faye held straight As in her other courses. In economics, biology, classics—she'd yet to miss a question on the weekly quizzes. But poetry? It did not appear that Ginsberg intended to grade them. And while most of the students found this liberating, it roiled Faye's equilibrium. How was she supposed to act if she didn't know how she was being measured?

So she tried to be as committed as she could to the meditating while also feeling acutely self-conscious about what she looked like meditating. She tried to chant and rock in a fully committed, one hundred percent way, to feel what Ginsberg said she should feel, a deepening of her soul, a freeing of her mind. And yet every time she began the meditating in earnest, a small thorny idea popped into her head: that she was doing it wrong and everyone would notice. She feared she'd open her eyes and the class would be staring at her or laughing at her. And she tried to bat the thought away, but the longer she meditated the stronger it grew, until she couldn't even properly sit anymore because she was overwhelmed with anxiety and paranoia.

So she opened her eyes, realized that she was ridiculous, and then the whole process began again.

She vowed this time she would do it right. She would be in the moment without feeling inhibited and insecure. She would pretend she was totally alone.

Except that she was not totally alone.

Among the anonymous strangers in the room, about five paces to her left and up a couple of rows, sat Sebastian. It was the first time she'd seen him since his arrest a few days earlier, and now she was profoundly aware of his presence. She was waiting to see if he'd noticed her. Each time she opened her eyes, this is where they were drawn, to him. It did not appear that he'd seen her yet, or if he had seen her, it did not appear that he cared.

"How do you deepen your soul?" Ginsberg asked. "This is how: You feel your feelings truly, then repeat. You chant until the chanting is automatic and you feel what's been lying underneath all this time. By 'deepen your soul' I don't mean you add to it, like putting a room on a house. The house has always had that room. But this is the first time you've gone in it."

She imagined what would happen if Ginsberg wandered into one of her uncles' Iowa garages, with that big ridiculous beard and peace-sign necklace. They'd have a field day, her uncles.

And yet she was being persuaded, despite herself. Especially by his exhortation to calmness and quiet. "You have too much in your heads," he said. "It's too noisy in there." Which Faye had to admit was true for her almost all of the time, all day long, her constant prickling worry.

"When you chant, think only about the chanting, think only about your breath. *Live* in your breath."

And Faye tried, but if it wasn't worry that brought her out of the trance, it was the impulse to glance at Sebastian, to see what he was doing, if he was succeeding, if he was chanting, taking this stuff seriously. She wanted to stare at him. In this group overflowing with the counterculture's ugly flair—wiry beards, spit-flecked mustaches, sweat-stained headbands, torn jeans and jean jackets, dark sunglasses stupid-looking indoors, fucking berets, that smell of secondhand-store musk and tobacco—Sebastian was easily the good-lookingest guy in the room, Faye thought, objectively. Gentle hair carefully careless. Clean-shaven. That dab of infant cuteness. Toadstool head. The way he tightened his lips while concentrating. She gathered all of this and then closed her eyes and tried again at achieving perfect allover mental peace.

"Stop being so interested in yourselves," Ginsberg said. "If you're interested only in *you*, then you're stuck with you, and you're stuck with your own death. It's all you have."

And he tapped his finger cymbals and said "Ommmmm" and the students repeated it, "Ommmmm" they said, raggedly, discordantly, out of sync and tune.

"There is no you," Ginsberg said. "There is only the universe and beauty. Be the beauty of the universe and the beauty will get in your soul. It will grow and grow there, and take over, and when you die, you're *it*."

And Faye was beginning to visualize (as instructed) the all-white pristine light of total awareness, the peace-nirvana when (as instructed) the body is no longer producing sound or meaning but rather perfect bliss-sensation, when she felt the presence of someone nearby, very close, sitting down annoyingly within her personal-space bubble, breaking the spell, lifting her once again to the mundane level of flesh and worry. So she breathed a heavy, passive-aggressive sigh and wiggled her body hoping to broadcast that her mental flow was indeed broken. She tried again: the white light, peace, love, bliss. And the room was saying "Ommmmm" when she felt her new neighbor draw even closer to her, and she thought she could feel a presence in the area around her ear, and she heard his voice, a whisper, saying, "Have you achieved perfect beauty yet?"

It was Sebastian. The shock of this realization made her feel like she was, momentarily, filled with helium.

She swallowed hard. "You tell me," she said, and he snorted, a contained and muffled laugh. She'd made him laugh.

"I'd say yes," he whispered. "Perfect beauty. You've done it."

She felt a warmth spread across her face. She smiled. "How about you?" she said.

"There is no me," he said. "There is only the universe." He was mocking Ginsberg. And how relieved she felt. Yes, she thought, this was all very silly.

He drew closer, right up next to her ear. She could feel it, that electricity, on her cheek.

"Remember, you're perfectly calm and at peace," he whispered.

"Okay," she said.

"Nothing can disturb your perfect calmness."

"Yes," she said. And then she felt him, his tongue, lightly lick the very tip of her earlobe. It almost made her yelp right there in the middle of meditation.

Ginsberg said "Think of a moment of instantaneous perfect stillness," and Faye tried to compose herself by focusing on his voice. "Maybe in some meadow in the Catskills," he said, "when the trees came alive like a Van Gogh painting. Or listening to Wagner on the phonograph and the music became nightmarishly sexy and alive. Think of that moment."

Had she ever felt something like that? A transcendent moment, a perfect moment?

Yes, she thought, she had. Right now. This was that moment.

And she was in it.

WHAT USUALLY HAPPENED on Monday nights was that Alice sat alone in her room, reading. The girls who crowded in there with her most other nights and sang enthusiastically to the record player and smoked weed out of tall intimidating-looking hookah things were gone on Mondays, presumably recovering. And despite her public rhetoric, her general homework-is-a-tool-of-oppression stance, Alice used Monday nights to read. One of her many secrets was that she did her work, she was studious, she read books, whenever she was alone, consumed them with speed and vigor. And not the books you'd expect from a radical. They were textbooks. Books on accounting, quantitative analysis, statistics, risk management. Even the music coming out of the record player changed on these nights. It wasn't the screechy folk-rock that was typical the rest of the week. It was classical, soft and comforting, little piano sonatas and cello suites, soothing and unthreatening stuff. She had this whole other side to her, sitting on her bed unbelievably still for hours, the only movement being a page-flip once every forty-five seconds. She had a kind of serenity in these moments that Officer Brown loved while he sat and watched her from a dark hotel room two thousand meters away, watching Alice through the high-powered telescope requisitioned by the Red Squad unit, listening to the music and the crinkly page-turns on his radio tuned to the high-band frequency of the bug he'd planted in her room a few weeks ago on top of the small overhead lamp, replacing the bug he had previously planted under her bed, the sound quality of which was unacceptable, all muffled and echoey.

He was still new at this, espionage.

He had been watching her read for about an hour when there was a loud, sharp knock at the door—a moment of disequilibrium for Brown when he didn't know if it was a knock on his hotel-room door or Alice's dorm-room door. He froze. He listened. Felt relieved when Alice leaped from her bed and opened the door. "Oh, hello," she said.

"Can I come in?" said a new voice. A girl. A girl's voice.

"Sure. Thanks for coming," Alice said.

"I got your note," said the girl. Brown recognized her, the freshman from next door with the big round glasses: Faye Andresen.

"I wanted to tell you I'm sorry," Alice said, "for how I acted at Freedom House."

"It's okay."

"It's not okay. I keep doing this to you. I should stop. It is not in the spirit of sisterhood. I should not have shamed you like that. I'm very sorry."

"Thanks."

It was the first time Officer Brown had ever heard Alice apologize or sound remorseful in any way.

"If you want to screw Sebastian," she said, "that's your business."

"I didn't say I wanted to screw him," Faye said.

"If you want Sebastian to ball you, that is entirely up to you."

"I wouldn't really put it that way."

"If you want Sebastian to pump the ever-living daylights out of you—"

"Would you stop!"

They were both laughing now. Brown noted this in his journal: *Laughing.* Though he didn't know why or how this would be germane, later, whenever he came back to these notes. The Red Squad's surveillance training was maddeningly brief and vague.

"So about Sebastian," Alice said, "has he tried anything yet?"

"What do you mean 'tried anything'?"

"Made a move? Been extra especially affectionate lately?"

Faye looked at her a moment, doing some calculation in her head. "What did you do?"

"So that's a yes?"

"Did you tell him something?" Faye said. "What did you tell him?"

"I simply communicated to him your very special interest."

"Oh my god."

"Your singular fascination with him."

"Oh, no."

"Your special secret feelings."

"Yes, *secret.* That was *my secret.*"

"I accelerated the process. I thought I owed it to you. After being such a prude at Freedom House. Now we're even. You're welcome."

"How does this make us even? How is this a favor?"

Faye paced around the room. Alice sat cross-legged on the bed, enjoying herself.

"You were going to quietly suffer and pine," Alice said. "Admit it. You weren't going to tell him."

"You don't know that. I wouldn't have *pined*."

"He made a move. What was it?"

Faye stopped pacing and looked at Alice. She appeared to be chewing at the inside of her cheek. "He licked my ear during meditation practice."

"Sexy."

Brown noted this in his journal: *Licked ear*.

"And now," Faye said, "he wants me to come over. To his place. Thursday night."

"The night before the protest."

"Yes."

"How romantic."

"I guess."

"No. How *insanely* romantic. That's going to be the most important day of Sebastian's life. He's heading off to a dangerous protest and riot. He could be hurt, injured, killed. Who knows? And he wants to spend his last free evening with you."

"That's right."

"It's so, like, *Victor Hugo*."

Faye sat down at Alice's desk and stared at the floor. "I do have a boyfriend, you know. Back home. His name is Henry. He wants to marry me."

"Okay. And do you want to marry him?"

"Maybe. I don't know."

"That kind of indifference usually means no."

"It's not indifference. I just haven't made up my mind."

"Either you want to marry him more than anything in the world, or you say no. It's very simple."

"It's not simple," Faye said. "Not at all. You don't understand."

"So explain it to me."

"Okay, here's what it's like. Imagine you're feeling desperately thirsty. Like insanely thirsty. All you can think about is a big tall glass of water. Got it?"

"Got it."

"And you fantasize about this big tall glass of water, and the fantasy is really vivid in your head, but it does not actually quench your thirst."

"Because you can't drink the imaginary glass of water."

"Right. So you look around and see this murky, oily puddle of water and mud. It's not exactly the tall glass of water, but it does have the advantage of being wet. It's real, whereas the tall glass of water is not. And so you choose the oily mud puddle, even though it's not really what you'd prefer. And that's roughly why I'm with Henry."

"But Sebastian, though."

"He, I think, is the tall glass of water."

"Someone should really make a country-western song out of this."

"So I *really* don't want to mess it up with Sebastian. And I'm worried he's going to want to, you know, maybe"—Faye paused, searching for the right word—"be intimate?"

"You mean screw."

"Yes."

"Okay. So?"

"So, I was hoping . . ."

Brief moment of heavy silence. Faye stared at her hands; Alice stared at Faye. They were both sitting on the bed now, perfectly encircled and framed by Officer Brown's telescopic viewfinder.

"You want advice," Alice finally said.

"Yes."

"From me."

"Yes."

"About screwing."

"That's right."

"And you're assuming I'm an expert on this subject why?"

Brown smiled at this. She was such a tease, his hippie girl.

"Oh," Faye said, her face falling. "I didn't mean to imply—"

"Jesus, *lighten up.*"

"I'm sorry."

"That's your problem. You want advice? You have to relax."

"I'm not sure I know how to do that. Relax."

"Just, you know, relax. Just breathe."

"It's not that easy. I had some doctors try to show me certain breathing techniques once, but sometimes I get really nervous and I can't do it."

"You can't breathe?"

"Not correctly."

"What happens? Something is going on in your head? You try to relax and breathe but you can't do it. Why?"

"It's complicated."

"Tell me."

"Okay, well, when I start my breathing techniques the first thing I feel is shame. I feel ashamed right off the bat that I have to practice *breathing*. Like, you know, like I can't even do the simplest most fundamental thing right. Like it's one more thing I'm failing at."

"Okay," Alice said. "Go on."

"And then when I start to do the actual breathing I'll start worrying that I'm not doing it right, that maybe my breathing is flawed or something. That it's not perfect. That it's not the *ideal breathing technique,* which I don't even know what that is but I'm sure it exists and if I'm not doing it I feel like I'm failing. And not only failing at breathing but generally failing. Like I'm a *failure in life* if I can't do this correctly. And the more I think about how to breathe, the more difficult the breathing becomes, until I feel like, you know, I'm going to hyperventilate or pass out or something."

Brown wrote this down in his journal: *Hyperventilate.*

"And then I start thinking about if I *do* pass out then someone will find me and make a big fuss over it and I'll have to explain why I spontaneously passed out for no reason at all, which is a stupid thing to have to explain to someone, because they'll think they were being heroic, saving someone from a serious injury or heart emergency or something, and when they find out the only thing that's wrong with me is that I freaked myself out *breathing* they get, well, you know, disappointed. You can see it on their face. They're like: *Oh, that's it?* And then I start freaking out that I did not measure up to their expectations of a quality sick or injured person, that perversely my problems are *not bad enough* to justify their worry, which they are now full of resentment about. And even if none of this actually happens, I see it all play out in my mind, and I get so anxious about the possibility of it happening that it might as well have happened. I feel like I actually experience it, you know? It's like something doesn't have to happen for it to feel real. This probably all sounds insane to you."

"Keep going."

"Okay, well, let's say even if I'm able to achieve some feeling of peace and relaxation by miraculously doing the breathing techniques correctly, I'll enjoy feeling happy and relaxed for maybe ten seconds before I begin to worry about how long it's going to last, the good relaxed feeling. I worry that I won't be able to maintain it long enough."

"Long enough for what?"

"To, you know, be successful at it. To do it right. And every second I feel objectively happy is a second I'm closer to failing and returning again to being essentially myself. The metaphor I have in my mind of what this feels like is walking on a tightrope that has no ending and no beginning. The longer you stay up there, the more energy it takes not to fall. And eventually you begin to feel this melancholy and doom because no matter how good a tightrope walker you are, you will inevitably fall. It is only a matter of time. It is guaranteed. And so instead of enjoying the happy relaxed feeling while I'm having it, I feel this huge sense of dread about the moment I will no longer feel happy or relaxed. Which of course is the very thing that obliterates the happiness."

"Holy god."

"This is all going through my head more or less constantly. So when you say 'Just breathe,' I think it means something different to you than it does to me."

"I know what you need," Alice said. And she rolled across the bed and opened the bottom drawer of her nightstand and rummaged around what appeared to be several brown paper bags until finding the appropriate one and turning it over and shaking out what looked like two small red pills.

"From my personal inventory," she said, which Officer Brown considered writing down but ultimately did not write down; he never logged anything she did that might be indictable. "Alice's pharmacy," she said.

"What is it?"

"Something to make you relax."

"No, I don't think so."

"It's not dangerous. It simply quiets the head a bit, lowers the inhibitions."

"I don't need it."

"Yes, you do. You're like the Great Wall of Inhibitions."

"No thank you."

What were they, Brown wondered. The pills. Maybe psilocybin, mescaline, morning glory seeds? Maybe methedrine, DMT, STP, some kind of barbiturate?

"Listen," Alice said, "would you like to have a pleasant evening with Sebastian?"

"Yes, but—"

"And do you think you could do that in your current mental state?"

Faye paused a moment and thought this over. "I could produce the appropriate outward appearance of it. I think Sebastian would think I was having a great time."

"But really, on the inside?"

"Dread and panic that feels just barely bottled up."

"Yeah, you need these. If you have any interest in having a sincerely good time. Not for him but for *you*."

"What do they feel like?"

"Like a sunny day. Like you're strolling along on a sunny day without a care in the world."

"I have literally never felt like that."

"Side effects are they make your mouth gluey. Also weird dreams. Mild hallucinations, but that's really rare. You want to take them with food. Let's go."

Alice took Faye's hand and they left the room, presumably down to the cafeteria, which would be mostly empty this time of night. The only available food would be breakfast cereal, probably, or the refrigerated leftovers of that day's dinner. Meat loaf. Brown's research was narrow but exhaustive. He knew the routines of this dorm as well as he knew those at his own house, where his wife would be waking up in about six hours to a slathering of kisses and compliments from their child. He wondered how much of her was able to sincerely enjoy these compliments, knowing she got them by intimidation and blackmail. He guessed nine-tenths. Almost all of her. But that other bit, he thought, would be throbbing.

He hoped, down in the cafeteria right now, that the girls were talking about him. He hoped Alice would reveal her burgeoning relationship with this cop and how, despite herself, she was falling for him. One of the more depressing things about his nightly surveillance was realizing how little she talked about him or even seemed to think about him when they were not together. Actually never, it would be more accurate to say.

She *never* talked about him. Not once. Even after one of their encounters she'd usually come back and shower and if she did talk to anyone it was about mundane things: school, the protest, girl stuff. Lately the primary topic was the all-female march Alice was organizing for Friday—they planned to parade down Lake Shore Drive with no permit or anything, to stop traffic and walk as they pleased. Alice talked about this endlessly. Not once had she mentioned him. When he wasn't around it was like he didn't exist for her, which was painful because he thought about her *almost all the time*. When he shopped for clothes he wondered how to impress Alice. When he sat through daily Red Squad briefings he waited to hear anything that might involve her. When he watched the TV news with his wife, he imagined it was Alice there with him instead. He was a compass needle always pointed toward her.

He looked out past the dorm to the lights of the lakeshore, the vast gray expanse of Lake Michigan beyond them, a shimmering hot emptiness. The dots in the sky were planes coming into Midway, many of them now containing the advance teams for senators and ambassadors, various chairmen of boards, industry lobbyists, Democratic insiders, pollsters, judges, the vice president, whose itinerary was a secret the White House wouldn't share even with the police.

He sat on the bed and waited. He risked some light to read the newspaper, the entire front page of which was devoted to either the convention or the protest of the convention. He poured himself a whiskey from the small bar knowing the hotel would provide it gratis, just like all the city diners provided cops with free coffee. This job had its perks.

He must have fallen asleep there because he woke up to the sound of laughter. Girls laughing. His face rested on the crinkled newspaper, his mouth was sticky. He clicked off the small reading light and lumbered over to his position behind the telescope, moving lopsidedly, his arms swinging, his feet scraping along the carpeted floor. He sat and shook his head a few times and tried to blink the sleep away. He had to rub his eyes roughly before he could see anything through the telescope. His stomach felt sour and empty. These night shifts were killing him.

The girls had returned. They were both on the bed, facing each other. They were laughing at something. There were sleep crumbs in his eyes that he had to pick out. The image through the telescope was out of focus, weirdly, as if while he slept their two buildings had crept slowly apart. He fiddled with the knobs. The picture of the girls bounced and bobbed as he did this, triggering a very mild kind of motion sickness that reminded him of sitting in the backseat of a car trying to read.

"There's so much inside you," Alice said, recovered now from the laughing fit. She lightly stroked Faye's hair. "So much happiness."

Faye was still giggling, softly. "No there's not," she said, batting at Alice's hand. "This isn't real."

"You're wrong. This is *more* real. You should remember this. This is the real you."

"It doesn't feel like the real me."

"You're encountering your true self for the first time. It's bound to be foreign."

"I'm tired," Faye said.

"You should remember this feeling and find your way back when you're sober. This is a map for you. You're so happy right now. Why aren't you happy like this all the time?"

Faye stared at the ceiling. "Because I'm haunted," she said.

Alice laughed.

"I'm serious," Faye said. She sat up and hugged her knees. "There was a ghost that lived in our basement. A house spirit. I offended it. Now I'm haunted."

She turned to measure Alice's reaction.

"I've never told anyone that," Faye said. "You probably don't believe me."

"I'm just listening."

"The ghost came with my father from Norway. It used to be his ghost, but now it's mine."

"You should take it back."

"Back where?"

"Back where it came from. That's the way to get rid of a ghost. You take it back home."

"I'm really, really tired," Faye said.

"Okay, here, I'll help."

Faye spread herself drunkenly across the bed. Alice removed her glasses and set them carefully on the nightstand. She walked to the foot of the bed and unlaced Faye's sneakers and pulled at them lightly until they slipped off. Took off Faye's socks and balled them up and put them inside the shoes, which she arranged toes-out by the front door. She retrieved a thin blanket from under the bed and covered Faye with it, tucking the edges under her. She took off her own shoes and socks and pants and lay next to Faye, snuggled up against her, stroking her hair. It was the most gentle he'd ever seen Alice act. Certainly more gentle than she'd ever been with him. This was an entirely new side of her.

"D'you have a boyfriend?" Faye said. Her words were slurring together now—she was stoned or on the verge of sleep or both.

"I don't want to talk about boys," Alice said. "I want to talk about you."

"You're too cool t'have a boyfriend. You'd never do something as square as have a boyfriend."

Alice laughed. "I do," she said, and two thousand meters away Officer Brown let out an excited squeak. "Sort of. I have a gentleman friend I'm consistently intimate with, is how I'd describe him."

"Why not just say *boyfriend*?"

"I prefer not to name things," Alice said. "As soon as you name and explain and rationalize your desire, you lose it, you know? As soon as you try to pin down your desire, you're limited by it. I think it's better to be free and open. Act on any desire you feel, without thinking or judging."

"That sounds fun right now, but probably 'cuz of those red pills."

"Go with it," Alice said. "That's what I do. Like, for example, take this guy? My gentleman friend? I don't feel anything particularly special for him. I have no commitment to him. I'll use him until I no longer find him interesting. Simple as that."

And across the street Brown felt his insides plunge.

"I'm always on the lookout for someone who's more interesting," Alice said. "Maybe it's you?"

Faye grunted a kind of sleepy reply: "Mm-hm."

Alice reached over Faye and clicked off the light. "All your worries and secrets," she said. "I could do a number on you. You'd love it."

The bed squeaked as one or both of them stretched into it.

"You know you're beautiful?" Alice said into the darkness. "So beautiful and you don't even know it."

Officer Brown turned up the sound on the speakers. He got into bed and wrapped his arms around a pillow. He concentrated on her voice. He'd been having new and terrifying thoughts lately, daydreams of leaving his wife and convincing Alice to run away with him. They could start a new life in Milwaukee, say, or Cleveland, or Tucson, or wherever she wanted. Crazy new daydreams that left him feeling both guilty and exhilarated. At home his wife and daughter would be asleep in the same bed. They would be doing this for years to come.

"Please stay here," Alice said. "Everything will be fine."

Before Alice came along, Brown wasn't even aware he lacked an essential part of his life, not until he suddenly had it. And now that he had it, there was no way he was letting it go.

"Stay as long as you like," he heard Alice say, and he tried real hard to pretend she wasn't talking to Faye. "I'm not going anywhere. I'm going to stay right next to you."

He tried to pretend she was talking to him.

THE DAY BEFORE THE RIOTS, the weather turned.

The grip of Chicago's summer loosened and the air was springlike and agreeable. People got a good night's sleep for maybe the first time in weeks. In the very early dawn there appeared on the ground a thin, slick dew. The world was alive and lubricated. It felt hopeful, optimistic, and therefore disallowable as the city prepared for battle, as National Guard troops arrived by the thousands in green flatbed trucks, as police cleaned their gas masks and guns, as demonstrators practiced their evasion and self-defense techniques and assembled various projectiles to lob at cops. There was a feeling among them all that so great a conflict deserved a nastier day. Their hatred should ignite the air, they thought. Who could feel revolutionary when the sun shone so pleasantly on one's face? The city instead was full of desire. The day before the greatest, most spectacular, most violent protest of 1968, the city was saturated with *want*.

The Democratic delegates had arrived. They'd been police-escorted to the Conrad Hilton Hotel, where they assembled nervously inside the ground-floor Haymarket Bar and maybe had a little too much to drink and did things they wouldn't do under less extraordinary circumstances. Regret, they discovered, was a flexible and relative thing. Those who would not normally engage in exuberant public drunkenness or casual sex found this particular setting encouraged both. Chicago was about to explode. The presidency was on the line. Their own fine America was falling apart. In the face of calamity, a few small extramarital affairs seemed like background static, too quiet to register. The bartenders kept the bar open well past closing. The place was busy, and tips were good.

Outside, across Michigan Avenue, cops on horseback patrolled the park. Ostensibly, they were there to find troublemakers and saboteurs. What they found were couples in the bushes, under trees, on the beach, youths in various states of undress slithering over each other so ensconced they didn't even hear the horses' hooves approaching. They were necking (or more), doing unspeakable things right there in the dirt of Grant Park, in the sand off Lake Michigan. The cops told them to run along, and they did, the boys waddling uncomfortably away. And the cops might have found this funny if they didn't also suspect these very boys would be back tomorrow, yelling, fighting, throwing things, getting beaten by the cops' own hands. Tonight, it was carnal. Tomorrow, carnage.

Even Allen Ginsberg found a few moments' relief from the melancholy. He sat naked in the bed of the skinny twentysomething Greek busboy he'd discovered that afternoon, at the restaurant, where he met with the youth leaders as they conspired and planned. They wondered how many people would be showing up for the protest. Five thousand? Ten thousand? Fifty thousand? He told them a story.

"Two men went into a garden," he said. "The first man began to count the mango trees, and how many mangoes each tree bore, and what the approximate value of the whole orchard might be. The second man plucked some fruit and ate it. Now which, do you think, was the wiser of these two?"

The kids all looked at him, eyes as blank as lambs.

"Eat mangoes!" he said.

They didn't understand. The conversation moved along to the great crisis of the day, which is that the city had finally denied their applications to demonstrate downtown, to parade through the streets, to sleep in the park. Hordes of people were showing up tomorrow and they had nowhere to sleep but the park. Of course they were going to sleep there, of course they were going to demonstrate, and so they debated the likelihood of police intervention now that they lacked the proper permits and credentials. The likelihood, they decided, was a hundred percent. And Ginsberg tried to pay attention, but mostly what he noticed was how the busboy reminded him of a sailor he saw in Athens one night walking the old streets under the skeleton-white Acropolis and seeing this sailor plant his lips earnestly and tenderly on the lips of some young boy-whore, right there in the open, in the land of Socrates and Hercules and statuary everywhere all muscle-smooth and polished to solid cream. The busboy had that sailor's face, that same hint of debauch. He got the busboy's attention, got his name, got him up to his room, got him undressed: skinny boy with a huge cock. Isn't that always the way? Now curled afterward under the covers and reading to the boy from Keats. Tomorrow there would be war, but tonight there was Keats, there was the window open for the pleasant breeze, there was this boy, there was the way this boy gripped his hand, lightly squeezing like he was inspecting fruit. It was all too beautiful.

Faye, meanwhile, was scrubbing. She had purchased several teen magazines and something all of them recommended brides do before going *all the way* was to scrub vigorously and thoroughly and relentlessly with many different scrubbing media: soft cloths, porous sponges, emery boards, rough pumice. She spent most of her week's food budget on things to make her allover smooth and invitingly fragrant. She'd been thinking about the posters in her high-school home economics classroom, the first time in months. They were no less horrifying even at this distance, now that she was the one going *all the way*. Sebastian would be here soon, and Faye was still scrubbing, had yet to apply certain strong-smelling unguents she worried would sting, jellies that smelled so powerfully of roses and lilacs that they actually reminded her of a funeral home, the way funeral homes set out flower bouquets to overwhelm that chemical death smell that was always there, underneath. Faye purchased perfumes, deodorants, douches, salts she was supposed to bathe in, soaps she was supposed to scrub with, alcohols minty and prickly she was supposed to gargle with and spit. She was beginning to grasp that she'd underestimated the time it would take to pumice, scrub, clean, shampoo, never mind squirting and applying her new solvents and salves. Her bedroom floor was littered with dainty pink cardboard boxes. She would not have time to do everything before Sebastian arrived. She had yet to polish her nails, spray her hair into place, choose the right bra-and-sweater combo. These things were not negotiable, not at all skippable. She finished work on her left-foot calluses. She decided to triage pumicing the right foot. If Sebastian noticed calluses on one foot and not the other, hopefully he would keep it to himself. She vowed to keep her shoes on until the last possible moment. She hoped he wouldn't be paying attention to her feet by that time. Her stomach flopped when she thought about this, about actually *doing* this. She concentrated again on her brand-new beauty products, which helped to keep sex vaguely and safely abstract, a kind of marketing idea and not something her body would really do. On her date. Tonight.

She had three different colors of nail polish, each of them some varia-

tion on purple: there was "plum" and "eggplant" and the more conceptual purple called "cosmos," which was the one she eventually chose. She
painted her toenails and did that thing with the cotton balls between
each toe and walked around her dorm room on her heels. Hair curler
was warming up. Little glass jars of cream-colored powders she dabbed
on her face with a sponge. Cleaned out her ears with a Q-tip. Plucked a
few eyebrow hairs. Replaced her white underwear with black underwear.
Then changed back to white, and then back again. She opened the windows and smelled the city's cool air and, like everyone else, felt hopeful,
optimistic, sensually physical.

All over the city, people were doing this. And there might have been
a moment here, an opportunity that, if grasped, could have prevented
all that followed. If everyone involved took a deep breath of that fertile
springlike air and realized it was a *sign*. Then the mayor's office might
have given the demonstrators the permits they'd been for months request-
ing, and the demonstrators could have peacefully assembled and not
thrown anything or taunted anyone, and the police could have bemusedly
watched them from a great distance, and everyone could have said their
piece and gone home with no bruises or concussions or scrapes or nightmares or scars.

There might have been a moment, but then this happened:

He had just arrived in Chicago on a bus from Sioux Falls—twenty-
one years old, aimless drifter, probably in town for the protest but we'll
never know. Dressed in the ragtag fashion—old leather coat cracking at
the collar, beat-up and duct-taped duffel bag, brown shoes bearing the
scuffs of many miles, begrimed denim pants that bloomed outward at
the bottom in the manner currently favored by the youth. But it would
have been the hair that identified him to police as an enemy. Long and
tangled, reaching down past the collar of his leather coat. He brushed it
out of his eyes in a gesture that always struck the more militant conservatives as really girly-looking. Really feminine and faggoty. For some reason, this particular gesture caused them *so much rage*. He batted the hair
out of his eyes, pulled at it where it caught like Velcro to his mustache and
wiry beard. To the cops, he looked like any other local hippie. To them,
his long hair was the end to a kind of conversation.

But he wasn't local. He didn't have the local counterculture's predict-
ability. Say what you want about the Chicago left, at least they let them-

selves be arrested without too much fuss. They might call the cops some dirty names, but their general reaction to handcuffs was an annoying limpness, sometimes elevated to full-body flaccidity.

But this young man from Sioux Falls was of a different idiom. Something had happened to him along the way, something dark and real. Nobody knew why he was in Chicago. He was alone. Maybe he'd heard about the protest and wanted to be part of a movement that must have seemed very far away in Sioux Falls. One can imagine the loneliness he might have felt, looking the way he did in a place like South Dakota. Maybe he'd been hassled, taunted, bullied, beaten up. Maybe he'd had to defend himself against the police or Hell's Angels—those self-appointed defenders of love-it-or-leave-it culture—one too many times. Maybe he was exhausted by it.

The truth is that nobody knew what had happened to him that made him hide a six-shot revolver in the pocket of his worn leather jacket. Nobody knew why, when police stopped him, he pulled the gun from his jacket pocket and fired it.

He must not have known what was at that moment happening in Chicago. How the police were taking every idle threat seriously, how they were on edge, pulling double shifts, triple shifts. How the hippies threatened to give all of Chicago an acid trip by dumping LSD into the city's drinking water, and even though it would take five tons of LSD to pull this off, still there were cops posted at every pumping station of the municipal water supply. How the police were already patrolling the Conrad Hilton with bomb-sniffing dogs because the hippies had threatened to blow up the hotel that housed the vice president and all the delegates. There was word that the hippies were planning to pose as chauffeurs at the airport in order to kidnap delegates' wives and then get them stoned and have inappropriate relations with them, and so police were giving escorts directly from the runway. There were so many threats it was hard to respond to them all, so many scenarios, so many possibilities. How do you prevent the hippies, for example, from shaving their beards and cutting their hair and dressing straight and faking credentials to get into the International Amphitheater where they'd set off a bomb? How do you stop them from gathering en masse and turning over cars in the street, as they'd done in Oakland? How do you stop them from building barricades and taking over whole city blocks, as they'd done in Paris? How do you stop them from occupying a building, as they'd done in New York, and how do you extract them from the building in front of newsmen who knew that trumped-up claims of police brutality moved papers? It was the sad logic of antiterrorism that had them on edge: The police had to plan for everything, but the hippies only had to be successful *once*.

So they built a barbed-wire perimeter around the amphitheater and filled the inside with plainclothes cops looking for troublemakers, demanding the credentials of anyone who didn't seem in favor of the current administration. They sealed manhole covers. Got helicopters into the sky. Put snipers atop tall buildings. Prepped the tear gas. Brought in the National Guard. Requisitioned the heavy armor. They heard about Soviet tanks rolling through the streets of Prague that week, and a small, complicated part of them felt envy and admiration for the Russians. *Yes, that's how you fucking do it,* they thought. Overwhelming force.

But our man from Sioux Falls could not have known any of this.

Or else he might have thought twice about pulling a gun out of his pocket. When the cop car drove past as he walked this night, this clear clean moment when he could see all the stars hanging over Michigan Avenue, and the car stopped and those two pigs got out in their short-sleeved baby-blue shirts, walking toward him with all manner of gadgetry bouncing on their belts, and they said something vague about curfew violation and did he have any identification, had he known what was happening all over Chicago right at that moment, he might have found it preferable to spend a few nights in jail for possession of an unregistered and concealed handgun. But he'd come all the way to Chicago on that horrific thirty-hour bus ride, and maybe he'd been waiting for this protest all his life, maybe this was some kind of turning point for him, maybe the idea of missing the whole demonstration was too painful, maybe he hated the war that much, and maybe he didn't want to lose the gun, which might have been his only security, having spent a rough adolescence in the Dakotas, where he was different and alone. In his head, it went like this: He'd pull the gun out and fire a warning shot and while the cops ducked for cover he'd run down the nearest dark alley and get away. It was as easy as that. Maybe he'd even done this before. He was young, he could run, he'd been running all his life.

But as it turned out, the cops didn't duck for cover. They didn't give him the chance to get away. At the gun's first report, they unholstered their own revolvers and shot him. Four times in the chest.

Word got around pretty quickly, from the police to the Secret Service to the National Guard to the FBI: The hippies were armed. They were shooting. *This radically changed the stakes.* A day before the protest began, this was, they all agreed, a very bad omen.

The students asked around their ranks to see if anyone was expected from Sioux Falls. Who was he? What was he doing here? Spontaneous candlelight vigils popped up for this young man who might have been a brother to them. They sang "We Shall Overcome" and wondered privately about whether they'd die for their cause. His protest, they thought, was greater than all the riots that whole long year—greater in its privacy, its intimacy, its stakes. He broke their hearts, dying in Chicago the way he did, before anyone even knew his name.

And when Sebastian heard the news he was in the office of the *Chicago Free Voice* giving an interview to CBS and the phone rang and he was told that someone had been shot, a drifter in from South Dakota. And Sebastian's first impulse, the very first thing that rushed unwillingly into his brain, was how *great* the timing was. CBS News was right there. This was *gold.* And so he called up some outrage and announced to the journalists that "the pigs have murdered a protester in cold blood."

Boy did that get their attention.

He ratcheted up the rhetoric with each new telling. "One of our brothers has been shot for the crime of disagreeing with the president," he told the *Tribune.* "The police are killing as indiscriminately as the bombs in Vietnam," he told *The Washington Post.* "Chicago is becoming the western outpost of Stalingrad," he told *The New York Times.* He organized even more candlelight vigils and told the TV news crews and photographers where the vigils could be found, sending each outlet to a different gathering so that each of them thought they were the one getting the scoop. The only thing journalists liked more than getting a story right was getting it first.

This was his job, to add heat.

In the months before the protest, it was Sebastian who had printed those outrageous stories in the *Free Voice* about spiking the city's water supply with LSD, about abducting delegates' wives, about bombs going off at the amphitheater. That no such plans were ever actually considered was irrelevant. He had learned something important: What was printed *became the truth*. He vastly inflated the number of demonstrators expected in Chicago, then felt a surge of pride when the mayor mobilized the National Guard. The message was getting out. This is what he cared about: the message, the narrative. When he imagined it, he imagined an egg that he had to hold and protect and warm and coddle and nourish, one that grew to huge fairy-tale proportions if he did it right, glowing and floating above them all, a beacon.

It was only dawning on him now, on the night before the protest, the implications of all his work. Kids were coming to Chicago. They would be battered and beaten by the police. They would be *killed*. This was more or less inevitable. What had been up to this point all illusion and fantasy and hype, an exercise in the molding of public opinion, would tomorrow become manifest. It was a kind of birth, and he trembled at the thought of it. So here he was, alone, doing the last thing anyone would expect from brash, confident, fearless Sebastian: He was sitting on his bed in tears. Because he understood what was going to happen tomorrow, understood his odd role in it, knew that everything up to this point was done and unchangeable and set solid in the infuriating past.

He was a lighthouse of regret tonight. And so he was weeping. He needed to stop thinking about this. He remembered vaguely that he had a date. He splashed water on his face. He threw on a jacket. He looked at a mirror and said, *Pull yourself together.*

Which was exactly what a certain police officer was telling himself across town, sitting on the back bumper of his patrol car, parked in the usual dark alley, sitting next to Alice, who appeared to be breaking up with him. *Pull yourself together,* he thought.

Just like everyone else in the city, Officer Brown was hoping to get laid tonight. But when he met Alice, she did not get in the car and make any funky requests but rather sat heavily down on the trunk and said: "I think we should take a break."

"Take a break from what?" he said.

"From everything. All of it. You and me. Our affair."

"Can I ask why?"

"I want to try something new," Alice said.

Brown thought about this for a moment. "You mean you want to try *someone* new," he said.

"Well, yes," Alice said. "I've met someone, maybe. Someone interesting."

"So you're breaking up with me for this new person."

"Technically, to break up we would need something to break, a commitment to each other that, obviously, we do not have."

"But—"

"But yes."

Officer Brown nodded. He stared at a dog on the other side of the alley getting into the trash of a local diner. One of the city's many strays, a bit of the German shepherd in it but muddled and runted by a swirl of other breeds. It pulled out a black garbage bag from the tipped-over bin, yanked it with its teeth.

"So if it weren't for this new person, you wouldn't be breaking up with me?" he said.

"That's irrelevant, since there *is* a new person."

"Humor me. Go with it. If this new person didn't exist, you'd have no reason to end our affair."

"Okay. Sure. That's a fair assessment."

"I want you to know I think this is a mistake," he said.

She gave him that condescending look he couldn't stand, that look communicating how she was the interesting and far-out one and he was the one stuck in a bourgeois middle-class hole from which there was no escape.

"What can this new person give you that I can't?" he said.

"You don't understand."

"I can change. You want me to do something different? I can do that. We don't have to meet so often. We could meet every other week. Or once a month. Or you want me to be rougher? I can be rougher."

"This isn't what I want anymore."

"We'll keep it, you know, loose. Informal. You can be with this new person *and* me, right?"

"That's not going to work."

"Why? You haven't given me any good reasons."

"I no longer want to be with you. Isn't that a good reason?"

"No. Absolutely not nearly good enough. Because there's no explanation. Why don't you want to keep doing this? What did I do wrong?"

"Nothing. You did nothing wrong."

"Exactly. So you can't punish me like this."

"I'm not trying to punish you. I'm trying to be honest."

"Which is having the effect of punishing me. Which is not fair. I did everything you asked. Even the weird stuff. I did *everything,* so you can't just up and leave for no good reason."

"Will you please stop whining?" she said, and she jumped off the car and walked a few paces away. Her sudden movement caught the dog's attention; it tensed, evaluated her intentions, guarded his scraps. "Will you please be a man about this? We're done."

"All those things we did together, all those strange things. They made a promise. Even if you never said it out loud. And now you're breaking that promise."

"Go home to your wife."

"I love you."

"Oh, fuck."

"I do. I love you. This is me saying I love you."

"You don't love me. You're just afraid of being alone and bored."

"I've never met anyone like you. Please don't leave. I don't know what I'll do. I said I love you. Doesn't that mean something?"

"Would you please *please* stop it?"

To Alice, he seemed on the verge of something substantial: crying or violence. You could never be sure with men. Across the alley the dog seemed satisfied that she did not have designs on its food. It resumed eating the thrown-out burgers and cold limp french fries and coleslaws and tuna melts at a velocity both ferocious and probably vomit-inducing.

"Listen," she said, "you want a good reason? Here's the reason. I want to try something new. It's the same reason I started things with you. I want to try something I haven't tried before."

"Which is what, exactly?"

"Girls."

"Oh, give me a break."

"I want to try girls. I feel very motivated to do this."

"Oh my god," he said. "Please tell me you don't think you're all of a sudden a dyke now. Please tell me I haven't been screwing a dyke."

"Thanks very much for the good times. And I wish you all the best."

"It's not the neighbor girl, is it? What's her name. Faye, right?"

She stared at him, confused, and he laughed. "Don't tell me it's her," he said.

"How do you know about Faye?"

"She's the one you spent the night with. Monday night? Don't tell me you've fallen in love with *her.*"

Everything about Alice now seemed to steel and harden at this moment. Whatever softness she had, whatever openness she ever felt with him, all at once disappeared. Her jaw clenched, her fists balled.

"How the *fuck* do you know about that?" she said.

"Please tell me you're not leaving me for Faye Andresen," he said. "That's rich."

"You've been watching me, haven't you? You're a goddamn psychopath."

"You're no dyke. I can tell you that for sure. I'd know."

"We are done. I am *never* speaking to you again."

"That is not going to happen," he said.

"Watch me."

"You leave and I'll arrest you. I'll arrest Faye too. I'll make your lives hell. Both of you. That's a promise. You're stuck with me. This is over when *I say it's over.*"

"I'll tell all your cop buddies how much you liked screwing me. I'll tell your wife."

"I could have you fucking killed. Easy." He snapped his fingers. "Just like that."

"Goodbye."

She walked away from the squad car. Her back tingled in expectation of something—a chase, a nightstick, a bullet. She ignored the alarms inside her to turn around and see what he was doing. She heard her own heartbeat in her ears. Her hands were stuck in tight fists. She couldn't unclench them if she wanted to. The road was another twenty paces away when she heard it: the sharp pop of his pistol.

He'd fired his gun. A gun had been fired. Something had been shot.

She turned around, expecting to see his corpse on the ground, his brains on the wall. But there he was, staring down at the trash can behind the diner. And she gathered what had happened. He didn't shoot himself. He shot the dog.

She sprinted away. As fast as she could. And she was two blocks from the alley when his squad car screamed by. He passed her and sped west, in the general direction of the Circle campus, in the direction of the dorms, where Faye, cleaned, spritzed, floral-smelling, her makeup done, her fanciest clothes on, waited for Sebastian to arrive. Alice had given her two more of those red pills, and she'd taken them before her beauty routine. Now their warmth and optimism were spreading. Her excitement at this moment was unbearable. Lonely her whole life, expected to marry a man she didn't really love, waiting now for this guy who seemed like a fairy-tale prince. Sebastian seemed like a kind of answer to the question of her life. The nervousness had passed and now she was thrilled. Maybe it was the pills, but who cared? She imagined a life with Sebastian, a life of art and poetry, where they debated the merits of movements and writers—she'd defend Allen Ginsberg's early work; he, of course, would prefer the later—and they would listen to music and travel and read in bed and do all the things that working-class girls from Iowa never got to do. She fantasized about moving to Paris with Sebastian and then coming back home and showing Mrs. Schwingle who the real sophisticate was, showing her father how she was pretty damn special indeed.

It seemed like the beginning of the life she actually wanted.

So she was elated when her phone rang and it was the front desk downstairs saying she had a visitor. She left her room and flounced down the stairs to the ground-floor lobby, where she found that the visitor was not Sebastian. It was the police.

Imagine the look on her face at that moment.

When this big crew-cut cop put her in handcuffs. Led her out of the dorm in silence as everybody watched and she cried, "What did I do?" How could he bear it, her shattered heart? How could he shove her into the backseat of his squad car? How could this man call her a whore over and over for the entire ride downtown?

"Who are you?" she kept saying. He'd removed his badge and name tag. "There's been some mistake. I didn't do anything."

"You're a whore," he said. "You are a fucking whore."

How could he arrest her? How could he book her for prostitution? How could he actually go through with it? She tried to keep her face calm and defiant when they took her picture, but in the jail cell that night she felt an attack coming on so strong that she curled up in the corner and breathed and prayed she didn't die here. She prayed to get out. *Please,* she said to God, or the universe, or anyone, rocking and crying and spitting into the damp cold floor. *Please help me.*

PART EIGHT

SEARCH AND SEIZURE

Late Summer 2011

1

JUDGE CHARLES BROWN WOKE before dawn. Always before dawn. His wife slept in bed beside him. She would stay sleeping there another three hours or more. It had been this way since they were first married, when he was still a Chicago beat cop working the night shift. Their schedules rarely overlapped back then, and it stayed that way all these years—habituated, normalized. Recently he'd been thinking about it, for the first time in a long time.

He climbed out of bed and into his wheelchair and rolled over to the window. He looked out at the sky—dark navy blue, but gathering color. It must have been four o'clock, four fifteen, give or take. It was trash day, he saw. The bins were out on the street. And beyond the bins, parked at the curb, right in front of his house, there was a car.

Which was odd.

Nobody ever parked there. It couldn't be a neighbor. His neighbors were too far away. One of the reasons he bought here, in this particular subdivision, was its facsimile of private woodsy living. Across the street from his house was a small grove of sugar maples. The distant neighbors were hidden behind two rows of oak trees—one row on his side of the property divide, one on theirs.

He looked at the screen next to the bed where he'd installed the controls for the home's elaborate security system: no open doors, no broken windows, no movement. The feeds from his various video cameras showed nothing unusual.

Brown chalked it up to teenagers. Always a good scapegoat. Probably a boy secretly visiting a girl down the block. There was some passionate and quick deflowering happening somewhere in the neighborhood tonight. Fair enough.

He took the elevator to the first-floor kitchen. Pressed the button on the coffeemaker. Dutifully it bubbled and spurted, his wife having prepared it the night before. Their ritual. One of the few ways he knows he's really living with someone. They see each other so rarely. He's off to work before she wakes, and she's off to work before he comes home.

It's not that they avoid each other on purpose—it's just how things worked out.

When he quit the police and decided to go to law school—this was about forty years ago now—she took evening shifts at the hospital. They were raising a daughter then; it was the compromise they made so someone would always be home with her. But even after the daughter grew up and moved out, their schedules did not change. It had become comfortable. She'd leave a plate of something for him to eat. She'd fix up the coffeemaker at night because she knew he hated fiddling with the filter-and-grounds apparatus, which always struck him as too much to ask of a person at four o'clock in the morning. He was grateful she still performed these small kindnesses. On weekends, they saw each other more, provided he wasn't in his study all day poring over various documents, precedents, opinions, journals, law. Then they'd catch each other up on the independent and totally separate lives they were living in parallel to one another. They made vague promises about all the things they'd do together in retirement.

He rolled himself into the study, coffee in hand, and turned on the television. Another morning ritual, watching the news. He wanted to know everything that was everywhere happening before he went to work. At his age, people were looking for signs of decline, waiting for his inevitable diminishment. He remembered when he was a young prosecutor there were judges of a certain age who let themselves slide as they approached retirement. They stopped keeping up with the news, local politics, the enormous amounts of reading required of the job. They began acting like mad scientists—unpredictable megalomaniacs, supremely confident in their fading abilities, treating the courtroom as their own personal laboratory. He would not devolve into *that,* he vowed. He watched the news in the morning, got the newspaper delivered (even if that was a bit quaint these days, the actual physical newspaper).

But the news was talking about what the news was always talking about these days: the election. Election Day was still pretty distant, but you'd never know it judging from the news, from the way the news salivated over the primary race, the dozen or so candidates for president now practically taking up permanent residency on both the cable news channels and in Iowa, where the nation's first nominating vote would happen in roughly three months. Among them all, Sheldon "the Governor" Packer was out to an early lead according to various polls and surveys and pundits who debated whether the governor's popularity was a post-attack sympathy bubble that would soon burst. So far it seemed that Faye Andresen's attack was the best thing to happen to him.

This was what the nation had to look forward to for the next year. Twelve full months of stump speeches and gaffes and ads and attacks and stupidity, agonizing stupidity, bordering on immoral stupidity. It was as if every four years all news everywhere just lost perspective. And then billions of dollars would be spent to achieve what was already inevitable—that the whole election would come down to a handful of swing voters in Cuyahoga County, Ohio. The electoral math pretty much ordained this.

Democracy! Huzzah!

The two most popular words on TV to describe Packer's campaign appeared to be "buzz" and "momentum." At rallies Packer talked about how the recent attempt on his life had made him more resolute than ever. He said he wouldn't be cowed by liberal thugs. He played the chorus to "Break My Stride" at campaign events. He was awarded an honorary Purple Heart by the new governor of Wyoming. Cable news personalities said he was either "bravely continuing his campaign despite tremendous personal risk" or "callously milking this minor distraction for all it's worth." There did not seem to be any position between these two. The video of Faye Andresen throwing rocks at the governor was shown again and again. On one channel, they said it was evidence of a liberal conspiracy, pointing out people in the crowd who might have been aiding and abetting. On another channel, they said when the governor ducked and ran away from the thrown rocks he "did not seem presidential."

That the news could not mention Governor Packer without also mentioning Faye Andresen's trial made Judge Brown feel happy. Made him feel important and big. The governor was "still riding high in the polls after his brutal attack in Chicago," was how they said it. Of course, the reasons for this were simple—the attack made him more famous, and fame tends to attract more fame. Like wealth tends to build upon itself, so too fame, which is a kind of social wealth, a kind of conceptual abundance. One of the many benefits of taking the Faye Andresen case was that it made Judge Brown a little famous. Another was that it forestalled retirement for as long as it would take to adjudicate. At least a year, he guessed.

Those were not the primary reasons he took the case, but they were part of the decision, part of the tableau. The primary reason was of course that Faye Andresen deserved whatever cruelty came to her. What a gift, this case. Like an early retirement present, this chance at retribution, his righteous reward for so much suffering.

Good lord, *retirement.* What in the world would they do together, he and his wife, in retirement?

There were all the usual clichés: They should travel, their daughter told them. And, yes, maybe they would travel, to Paris or Honolulu or Bali or Brazil. Wherever. All places seemed equally horrible because the thing they never mentioned about traveling in your retirement is that in order for it to work you must, at the very least, be able to endure the person you're traveling with. And he imagined all that time together—on planes, in restaurants, in hotel rooms. They couldn't escape each other, he and his wife. The nice thing about their current arrangement was that they could always blame their isolation on work. That the reason they saw so little of each other was their very demanding schedules and not in fact their total mutual resentment of each other.

How easily a simple façade can become your life, can become the truth of your life.

He imagined them in Paris trying to talk to each other. She'd give small lectures on the country's innovative health care system; he'd give similar disquisitions on French jurisprudence. That would get them through one day, maybe two. Then they'd start making small talk about whatever was in front of them at that moment: the charming Parisian streets, the weather, the waiters, the daylight that clung on until well past ten. Museums would be a good choice because of the enforced silence. But then they'd be at a restaurant looking at menus and she'd say what looked good and he'd say what looked good and they'd stare at the plates of other diners and point out those that also looked good and express how they were perhaps changing their mind about what they intended to order and that whole inner debate one usually has when ordering food at a restaurant would be vocalized and performed for the express purpose of filling space, of jamming the silence so full of meaningless idle chitchat that they'd never get around to talking about the thing they never talked about but were always thinking: that if they had been born into a generation that found divorce more acceptable, they would have left each other *so long ago*. For decades they had avoided this subject. It was like they'd come to an agreement—they were who they were, they were born when they were born, they were taught that divorce was wrong, and they openly disapproved of other couples, younger couples, who divorced, while secretly feeling bolts of envy at these couples' ability to split and remarry and become happy again.

Where was all this piety getting them? Who was benefiting?

She'd never forgiven him for the lustfulness of his youth, for his early indiscretions. She'd never forgiven him but also never spoke of it, not after the accident that put him in the wheelchair, which was an effective solution. Yes, he'd been punished by God for his lust, and punished for decades by his wife, and now he was in the punishment business. It suited him. He'd learned from the best.

No, they would not travel. More likely they would sink into separate hobbies and try as best they could to reproduce in retirement exactly their working lives. They'd repair to separate floors of their giant house. It was an uncomfortable life, yes, a painful life. But it was a familiar life. And this made it less scary than whatever would happen if they finally acknowledged all this resentment and loathing and actually talked.

Sometimes what we avoid most is not pain but mystery.

He had finished a half pot of coffee when he heard the newspaper delivery truck drive by, and heard the newspaper land softly on his front driveway. He opened his front door and glided down the house's short front ramp, landing on the sidewalk and letting the momentum carry him into the driveway, where the newspaper lay wrapped in its rainproof orange plastic sleeve. That car, he noticed, was still there. A nondescript sedan that could have been made by anyone, foreign or domestic. A light tan color, mildly dented on the front bumper, otherwise completely inoffensive and anonymous, one of those cars you'd never even notice on the road, a car that salesmen pitched to families as "sensible." Teenager borrowed his daddy's ride, Brown thought. Better be moving along, as the rest of the neighborhood would soon be stirring. In less than an hour, joggers, dog walkers, they'd all be out and alert to the presence of strangers, especially a teenage boy wandering down the street postcoitally.

But as Judge Brown reached for the newspaper, something caught his attention, something in the trees: a slight movement. The sky was beginning to lighten, but the block was still dark, the trees beyond the car still black. He stared and searched for confirmation: Did something move over there? Was someone there right now, watching him? He looked for the shape of a person.

"I see you," he said, though he didn't see anything.

He rolled himself into the street, and as he did so a figure emerged from the tree line.

Brown stopped. He had enemies. Every judge did. What small-time dealer, what pimp, what crackhead was there across the street waiting for revenge? There were too many to count. He thought about his gun, his old revolver, sitting uselessly in the upstairs nightstand. He thought about calling out to his wife for help. He sat up as straight as he could. He exuded the most calm and intense and frightening expression he could currently produce.

"Can I help you?" he said.

The figure approached and moved into the light—a young man, perhaps mid-thirties, a face that seemed mortified and cowed, a look Brown recognized from his years in the criminal justice system: the embarrassed face of someone caught doing something wrong. This man was no crackhead out for revenge.

"You're Charles Brown, right?" the man said. His voice—young, a little shrill.

"I am," Brown said. "Is this your car?"

"Uh-huh."

"Were you hiding behind a tree?"

"I guess so."

"May I ask why?"

"I don't have a very good answer for that."

"Do your best."

"It was a spur-of-the-moment decision. I suppose I wanted to see you, to find out more about you. Frankly, it made way more sense in my head than it does now, as I attempt to explain it."

"Let's start over. Why are you spying on my house?"

"I'm here because of Faye Andresen."

"Oh," Brown said. "You a reporter?"

"Nope."

"Lawyer?"

"Let's just say I'm a concerned party."

"C'mon, man. I've already memorized your license plate number. I'm going to run it as soon as I get inside. No sense being coy."

"I wanted to talk to you about Faye Andresen's case."

"Usually that's done in the courtroom."

"I was wondering if maybe it's possible to, you know, drop all charges against her?"

Brown laughed. "Drop all charges. Right."

"And maybe just leave her alone?"

"That's funny. You're a funny guy."

"Because, here's the thing. Faye never did anything wrong," the man said.

"She threw rocks at a presidential candidate."

"No, not that. I mean back in '68. She didn't do anything wrong back then. To you."

Which gave Brown a moment's pause. He frowned and studied the man. "What do you think you know?"

"I know all about what happened between you and her," he said. "I know about Alice."

Brown's throat tightened at the thought of her. "You know Alice?" he said.

"I've spoken with her."

"Where is she?"

"Not going to tell you that."

Brown's jaw muscles tightened—he could feel it happen, that old tic of his, the way his face seemed to constrict and ossify whenever he thought about Alice and all that had happened back then, a habit that had caused him some pretty intense TMJ-related suffering now, in his old age. His memory of Alice had never faded—more like it became a reservoir for all his guilt and remorse and lust and anger, decades-deep. When that old photograph of her appeared on television recently, he had such a powerful and tactile sense memory of her body that he momentarily felt that gush of excitement he used to feel when he found her out walking the streets in the deadest part of the night.

"So I suppose you're here to blackmail me then, right?" Brown said. "I agree to back off Faye Andresen, and in exchange you don't release your information to the press. Am I close?"

"I actually hadn't considered that."

"Do you also want money?"

"I'm sort of embarrassingly bad at this," the man said. "You just right now came up with a way better plan than mine. I really came here only to spy on you."

"But now you're considering blackmail. Is that fair to say? You are threatening me with blackmail. You are threatening a judge."

"Wait. Hold on. Note that I said nothing of the sort. You are putting incriminating words in my mouth."

"What would you tell the press? How would you explain what happened? I would love to hear your story."

"Well, I guess I'd tell the truth? That you were having an affair with Alice, and Faye ruined it. And you've been waiting all these years to get your revenge. Which is why you took the case."

"Uh-huh. Good luck proving that."

"If I told everyone—and I'm not saying I *will* tell everyone, I'm saying *if*, this is a hypothetical, you understand—then you'd be embarrassed in public. You'd be tried and convicted in the press. You'd be taken off the case."

Brown smiled and rolled his eyes. "Look, I am a Cook County circuit judge. I have brunch regularly with the mayor. I was the Chicago Bar Association Man of the Year. I don't know who the fuck you are, but I'd guess from your shitty car that you're nobody's man of the year."

"What's your point?"

"If it's my word against yours, I feel pretty comfortable with those odds."

"But Faye didn't *do* anything to you. She shouldn't go to prison for something she didn't do."

"She ruined my life. She put me in this chair."

"She never even knew who you were."

"I warned Faye once—never let me catch you in Chicago. That's what I told her. I'm a man of my word. And now you have the gall to come here and tell *me* what to do with her? Let me explain what's going to happen. I'm going to do everything in my power to see she's convicted of high crimes. And I'm going to see her hang."

"That's insane!"

"It would be best if you didn't try to stop me."

"Or else what?"

"You know the penalties for threatening a judge?"

"But I never threatened you!"

"That's not what it'll look like. From the point of view of that security camera on my porch, it'll look like you hid in the trees—*very* suspicious—until I came out of my house, at which point you approached me in a threatening manner."

"You have a security camera?"

"I have *nine* security cameras."

And at that, the man walked to his car, got in, and turned the ignition. The car's engine thrummed quietly. Then with an electric buzz, the driver's window came down.

"Alice was right," the man said. "You're a psychopath."

"Just stay out of my way."

Then the car rolled off, and Brown watched as it reached the end of his street, turned, and zoomed lightlessly away.

2

FAYE SAT SLUMPED on her couch, watching television, her eyes glassy, her face expressionless. Behind her, Samuel paced the apartment, from the kitchen to the couch and back, watching her. She flipped channels, staying between one and five seconds on any given show. Commercials she jumped away from immediately. Any other program she gave roughly a single breath to impress her. Then *flip*. The small television sat on the mantel of the apartment's inoperative fireplace. Samuel could swear the TV wasn't there on his first visit.

Outside, the midmorning sun shone brightly off Lake Michigan. Through the open windows, Samuel could hear car horns, far off. The city's usual weekday roar. To the west, he could see the traffic on the Dan Ryan Expressway moving at its usual viscous creep. He'd come here directly from his unfortunate encounter with Judge Brown. Samuel decided he needed to warn his mother, to tell her what he now knew about the judge. He had buzzed her apartment, and then buzzed again, and then again, and was about to start throwing rocks at Faye's third-story windows when the front door finally clicked open. He came up and found his mother like this: quiet, distracted, a little befuddled.

Faye flipped to a reality show about a couple renovating their kitchen, which seemed to hold her attention.

"This is a show ostensibly about home improvement," she said, "but really it's about watching these two sweep away the ashes of their dead marriage."

The show seemed to cut between clips of the couple's inept DIY misadventures and interviews where they independently complained about the other. The husband—too eager with his sledgehammer—put a hole in a wall that he thought was slated for demolition but, turns out, wasn't. Cut to clip of the wife complaining about how he never listens and is constitutionally unable to take directions. Cut to clip of the husband examining the damage he's done to the wall and proclaiming with false authority: *It'll be fine, just calm down.*

"These two hate each other so much," Faye said. "They're using their kitchen like America used Vietnam."

"That TV you're watching," Samuel said, "it wasn't here the first time I visited. I'm pretty sure of it."

Faye didn't respond. She stared blankly forward. For a full minute. During which she watched a clip of the husband kicking a panel of drywall, which broke and flew across the room, and even though it landed a full ten feet from his wife, she yelled at him as if she were in mortal peril: *Hey? I'm standing here?* Then Faye blinked and shook her head like someone waking from a trance and looked at him and said, "Huh?"

"You seem stoned," Samuel said. "Are you high on something right now?"

She nodded. "I took some pills this morning."

"What pills?"

"Propranolol for blood pressure. Benzodiazepine for excitability. Aspirin. Something else that was originally developed to prevent premature ejaculation in men but is now used for anxiety and insomnia."

"You do that a lot?"

"Not a lot. You'd be amazed how many beneficial drugs were originally developed to treat sex problems in men. They practically drive the whole pharmaceutical industry. Thank god for male sexual dysfunction."

"Any reason you needed all that this morning?"

"Simon called. You remember Simon. My lawyer?"

"I remember."

"He had some news. Apparently the prosecution is expanding their case against me. They added a couple of new charges today. Domestic acts of terrorism. Making terrorist threats. That kind of thing."

"You're kidding."

She picked up a notepad stuck between the couch cushions and read: "Acts dangerous to human life that cause fear, terror, or intimidation, or attempt to influence the policy of a government through intimidation and coercion."

"That seems like a stretch."

"Judge Brown convinced the prosecutor to add the new charges. I guess he came in this morning super enthusiastic about putting me in prison for the rest of my life."

Samuel felt his insides sort of freeze. He knew exactly what spurred the judge's new zealotry but could not at this moment bear to tell his mom about it.

"So I'm rattled today," Faye said, "and anxious. Hence the pills."

"I understand."

"By the way? Simon tells me I should not be talking to you."

"I personally question that guy's legal aptitude, frankly."

"He suspects your motives."

"Well," Samuel said, looking at his shoes. "Thanks for letting me in."

"I'm surprised you wanted to see me. Especially after the last time you were here. Your meeting with Simon? That couldn't have been pleasant. I'm sorry."

Outside, Samuel could hear the squeals of a train coming to a halt, the doors shunting open, the ding-dong warning bell and the automated train voice saying, *Doors closing.* Samuel realized it was the first time she'd apologized to him for anything.

"Why did you come?" Faye said. "All unannounced and unexpected like this."

Samuel shrugged. "I don't know."

On television, the husband was being interviewed about how he sent his wife to a giant home-improvement store to fetch a tool that does not actually exist: a countertop caliper.

"These people can't repair their relationship," Faye said, "so they repair their relationship's largest metaphor."

"I need some air," Samuel said. "How about a walk?"

"Fine."

He went to her and extended his hand to help her up, and when she took it, when he felt her thin and cold fingers, he realized it was the first time they'd touched in years. The first physical contact between them since she'd kissed his forehead and pressed her face into his hair that morning she left, when he promised to write books and she promised to read them. He had not anticipated feeling anything about this, taking her hand, helping her up. But it made his heart clutch. He did not know he needed this.

"Yeah, my hand is cold," Faye said. "It's a side effect of the medication." She stood and shuffled off to find her shoes.

She seemed to wake up, and her mood seemed to lighten, when they left the apartment. It was a mild and pleasant late-summer day. The streets were for the most part deserted and quiet. They walked east, toward Lake Michigan. His mother explained how real estate in this particular neighborhood was exploding before the recession. This was part of the turn-of-the-century meatpacking and slaughterhouse district. It was abandoned for many years, until recently, when the warehouses had begun their transformation into trendy lofts. But the renovations stalled when the real estate market collapsed. Most developers pulled out. Improvements were abandoned halfway through, buildings stuck mid-transformation. A few of the taller buildings still had cranes standing idle above them. Faye said she used to watch them from her window as they brought up pallets of Sheetrock and concrete. There was a time when every building on the block had one of these cranes.

"Like fishermen over a tiny pond," she said. "That's what it looked like."

But most of the cranes had since been disassembled. Those that still stood hadn't moved in a couple of years. So the neighborhood remained empty, just on the brink of habitation.

She said she had moved here because rents were low and because she didn't have to deal with people. It was a real shock when the developers came, and she looked on in anger as they began putting names on buildings: The Embassy Club, The Haberdasher, The Wheelworks, The Landmark, The Gotham. She knew when a building got a fancy name, insufferable people soon followed. Young professionals. Dog walkers. Stroller pushers. Lawyers and their miserable lawyer wives. Restaurants that reproduced Italian trattorias and French bistros and Spanish tapas bars in a toned-down, safely mainstream way. Organic grocery stores and *fromageries* and fixed-gear bicycle shops. She saw her neighborhood turning into this, the city's newest hip yuppie enclave. She worried about her rent. She worried about having to talk to neighbors. When the housing market tanked and the developers all disappeared and the signs with the fancy names began crumbling in the snow, she cheered. She walked her empty streets alone, exultant, that hermit's special appetite for isolation and ownership. This abandoned block was *hers*. There was great pleasure in this.

She needed the rent to remain low, otherwise she couldn't afford to live doing what she did, which turned out to be reading poetry to children, and businesspeople, and patients recovering from surgery, and prison inmates. A one-person nonprofit charitable service. She'd been doing it for years.

"I thought I wanted to be a poet," she said. "When I was younger."

They had come to a neighborhood with more life: an arterial street, people walking, a few small bodegas. It was a place not yet gentrified, but Samuel could see gentrification's leading edge: a coffee shop advertising free Wi-Fi.

"Why didn't you?" he said. "Become a poet?"

"I tried," she said. "I wasn't very good."

She explained how she'd given up writing poetry but had not given up poetry itself. She started a nonprofit to bring poetry into schools and prisons. She decided if she couldn't write poetry she would do the next best thing.

"Those who can't do," she said, "administrate."

She survived on small grants from arts groups and the federal government, grants that always seemed precarious, always attacked by politicians, always in danger of evaporating. In the boom times before the recession, several area law firms and banks had hired her to provide "daily poetic inspiration" to their employees. She began doing poetry seminars at business conferences. She learned to speak the language of the mid-level executive, which mostly involved turning silly nouns into silly verbs: incentivize, maximize, dialogue, leverage. She prepared PowerPoints on *leveraging poetic inspiration to maximize customer communication*. Power-Points on *externalizing stress and reducing workplace violence risk factors through poetry*. The junior VPs who listened to her had no idea what she was talking about, but their bosses ate it up. This was back before the recession hit, when the big banks were still throwing money at anything.

"I charged them fifteen times what I charged the schools and they didn't even blink," she said. "Then I doubled that, and still they didn't notice. Which was crazy to me because it was all bullshit. I was making it up as I went along. I kept waiting for them to figure it out and they never did. They just kept hiring me."

That is, until the recession hit. After it became clear what was happening—how the global economy was more or less utterly fucked—the gigs went away fast, along with the junior VPs, who were mostly laid off, with no warning, on a Friday, by the very same bosses who only a year earlier wanted them to live a life full of beauty and poetry.

"By the way," she said. "I hid the television the first time you visited. You were right about that."

"You hid it. Why?"

"A house without a television makes a statement. I wanted to improve the Zen-like asceticism quotient. I was trying to make you think I was sophisticated. Sue me."

They kept walking. They were coming back to his mother's neighborhood now, the eastern boundary of which was a bridge spanning a knot of train tracks that cut through the city like a zipper. Enough tracks to keep all the old slaughterhouses in feed and animals, enough to keep the old foundries in slag, enough now to accommodate the millions of suburbanites taking commuter rail into and out of downtown. A wide causeway whose retaining walls had been thoroughly inscribed by graffiti, the various tags and retags of the city's adventurous youth, who must have jumped down from the bridge because the only other way into the causeway seemed to be a thick chain-link fence with razor wire at the top.

"I went to see the judge this morning," Samuel said.

"What judge?"

"*Your* judge. Judge Brown. I went to his house. I wanted to get a look at him."

"You were spying on a judge."

"I guess."

"And?"

"He can't walk. He's in a wheelchair. Does that mean anything to you?"

"No. Why? Should it?"

"I don't know. It's just . . . there it is. An unexpected fact. The judge is disabled."

There was an aspect of graffiti Samuel found romantic. Especially graffiti sprayed in dangerous locations. There was something romantic about a writer risking injury to put down words.

"What was your impression?" Faye said. "Of the judge?"

"He seemed angry and small. But the kind of small where he probably used to be big and slowly shrank. White guy. Pasty white. His skin was paper-thin, almost translucent."

Of course, it's not like the graffitists wrote anything important. Just their own names, over and over, bigger and louder and more colorful. Which come to think of it was the same strategy used by fast-food chains on billboards across the country. It was just self-promotion. It was simply more noise. They weren't writing because something desperately needed to be said. They were advertising their brand. All that sneaking around and risk-taking to produce something that only vomited back up the dominant aesthetic. It was depressing. Even subversion had been subverted.

"Did you talk to him?"

"I didn't mean to," Samuel said. "I was really only intending to watch. I was collecting information. It was purely a stakeout. But he saw me."

"And is it possible this conversation has anything to do with the new charges this morning?"

"I suppose that's possible."

"You suppose it's possible you got me charged with *domestic terrorism*. That's what you're saying?"

"Maybe."

They had reached her block. He could tell they were almost home by the buildings that looked stuck in some sci-fi time warp—their first floors from the future, their upper floors from the past. Crumbling and windowless buildings sitting atop gleaming new empty storefronts of modern-looking green-blue glass and slick white plastics typical of information age electronics. The city's usual pullulation had given way to her neighborhood's great round silence. An empty plastic grocery bag bounded down the street, pushed by the wind that came off the lake.

"There's something you need to know," Samuel said, "about the judge."

"Okay."

"He's the one who arrested you. In 1968."

"What are you talking about?"

"The cop who arrested you, the night before the protest. That was Charles Brown, the judge. Same guy. He arrested you even though you'd done nothing wrong."

"Oh my god," Faye said, looking at him and grabbing his arm.

"He said you put him in that wheelchair. He said it was your fault he's disabled."

"That's ridiculous. How do you know all this?"

"I tracked down Alice. You remember her? She was your neighbor? In college?"

"You talked to *her*?"

"She told me all about you, when you were at Circle."

"Why are you talking to these people?"

"Alice said you should leave the country. Right now."

They rounded a corner, came into view of her building, and saw a strange clump of activity up ahead: a large police van with big block letters on the side—SWAT—was parked next to Samuel's car, towering over it like a bear guarding dinner. Police were exiting Faye's building and leaping into the van's open rear door—they were dressed in black, militarily bulletproofed, helmeted, goggled, machine guns strapped tightly to their chests.

Samuel and his mother ducked back around the corner.

"What is going on?" Faye said.

Samuel shrugged. "Is there another way in?"

She nodded and he followed her down the block, into an empty alley, to a rusted red door next to several garbage bins. They were quiet as they ascended the stairs, quiet as they listened, from the stairwell, to the last of the police exit her building. They waited another ten minutes to be sure, then exited the stairwell and walked down the hall to her apartment's front door, which they found in pieces, lying at an angle on the floor, connected to the wall only by the bottom hinge, which was twisted and bent.

Inside her apartment, the furniture had been tipped over and torn apart. The cushions on the couch were in tatters. The bed mattress lay on the floor, a long rip down the middle where the stuffing had been yanked out, an incision from top to bottom as if it hadn't been searched but rather autopsied. Mattress fluff all over. Books that had been on the bookshelves were now scattered and bent. The kitchen cabinets were open, everything inside either knocked down or broken. The trash can overturned and dumped on the floor. Slivers of glass crunching under their shoes.

They were looking at each other, bewildered, when a noise came from the bathroom—a whoosh of water, a faucet turned on and off. Then the door opened and there emerged, wiping his hands on his tan slacks, Simon Rogers.

He saw them and smiled. "Well hello there!"

"Simon," Faye said, "what happened?"

"Oh," he said, with a wave of his hand, "the police were here."

3

TODAY WAS THE DAY he would quit *Elfscape.*

Today he would stop playing forever, is what Pwnage resolved yesterday, actually, when he sat down vowing to quit *Elfscape* but then found several matters that needed addressing in order to *settle his affairs,* as it were, before sending his excellently geared avatars into digital oblivion, primarily among these was saying goodbye to the dozens of guild mates who over time he'd come to think of very fondly and feel a responsibility and paternalistic affection for, rather like how a summer camp counselor might feel for the kids in his charge, and Pwnage knew that if he disappeared without saying goodbye they would feel a sharp and personal betrayal and a sense of loss without closure and a shock to their sense that the world was predictable and understandable and for the most part good and just and fair (a few of these guildies, incidentally, really were the age of summer camp kids, and he felt an especially strong impulse not to betray or wound them in any way), and so he decided pretty early on in the play session that began yesterday morning that he could not quit and delete his account until he'd personally privately chatted with and said goodbye to the many regular *Elfscape* players that he'd played with for roughly twelve hours a day for the last couple of years, which required him to write a heartfelt note of gratitude to each player and an explanation that he no longer had the time to play *World of Elfscape* since he was now turning his attention to a brand-new career, that of being a *famous detective mystery novelist,* and he explained to his colleagues that he would have a big-time New York publisher just as soon as he finished a first draft of his novel and so he needed to turn his efforts to book-writing in a full-on, hundred percent type of way, which meant giving up *Elfscape* because his normal *Elfscape* schedule interfered with writing—the daily quests especially, the hundreds of daily quests he completed every morning on all his various avatars in a punishing five-hour grind, after which he'd vow to skip the daily quests the next day and instead use that time to make some serious progress in his detective novel, figuring he could probably write about two pages an hour (which was a reasonable number according to various online novel-writing self-help websites) and thus about ten pages a day, and at this clip he could finish the detective novel in a month using only the time he usually spent on *Elfscape* dailies, and this feeling of determination and resolve would hold pretty strong until the following morning, when he would try to write his novel but instead find himself thinking about all the daily quests that were now unlocked and newly available again, and he'd make an agreement with himself that in order to get the quests off his mind and really be able to *focus* on the novel-writing he'd take a break and do the quests on his main character *only,* and if his various secondary characters could not ultimately have access to all the excellent rewards, well, so be it, that was the price he'd have to pay for becoming a famous mystery-thriller writer—but then after finishing the twenty quests on his main avatar he'd get that disconcerting mental fatigue that felt as if his brain had been kneaded like bread dough, squeezed and pressed and soft and certainly not in the state to produce great literature, and so he went ahead and did all the daily quests on all his alt characters too and five hours later he felt that same bitter disgust with himself he'd felt the day before, vowing again that the next day he would skip the daily quests and work on his novel *all day long,* a feeling that never seemed as powerful the following morning, when the cycle would repeat, until eventually he had to admit that the only way the novel was going to get written was if he quit the game completely and deleted all his characters in an apocalyptic move there was just no going back from, but of course not before saying goodbye to all the people who were friends with him, people who, when he told them he was quitting in order to spend more time with his book, usually responded at first with "NOOOOOOOOOOOOO!!!!!!!!!!" (which, if he was being honest, was delightful), followed by an expression of confidence that they knew the book would be a huge best-selling hit, and even though they didn't know anything about the novel or even Pwnage's real name, still he very much liked being told of his inevitable future success, which kept him sitting in his chair for many hours waiting on each of his *Elfscape* friends to log on one by one so that he could tell them the news and have a version of the same conversation he had already had about two dozen times, during which he'd been sitting in exactly the same position with one leg tucked under his body for so long that his leg skin was deeply imprinted with the lines of his faux-leather plastic chair, while meanwhile he was developing inside his leg what doctors would call a *deep vein thrombosis,* or in other words a blood clot, which was causing redness and swelling in the leg, as well as a slight ache and tenderness and warmth and pain that he might have felt had the leg not already gone way beyond the pins-and-needles stage and into complete and almost anesthetic numbness due to the prolonged compression it endured while he said goodbye to friends and explained his upcoming account deletion and often did one last quest or dungeon run with these friends for, as they said, "old time's sake," and he was surprised how nostalgic this made him feel (this by the way being one of the reasons he'd forgotten to move his legs or stand or stretch or in any way get the blood circulating in the lower trunk or anywhere but the thumbs and digits strictly necessary for effective video-game operation), nostalgic that his friends wanted to revisit scenes of former triumph with the same verve that some people really looked forward to their high-school reunions, and so with each friend he'd repeat some adventure they'd shared weeks or months ago, and this gave Pwnage the idea that he wanted to visit *all* of the spots on the immense *Elfscape* map that he was fond of or had some important memory about or were in any way significant to his development as a serious gamer, a kind of "farewell tour" of the places he'd come to know and adore, and which of course would take, seriously, like hours and hours (the game's developers made a lot of hay about the huge size and scale of their virtual world, saying that if the *Elfscape* world were real it would literally be about the size of the moon), and so he visited the Silverglade Forest (site of his avatar's first death, at level eight, due to lurking panthers) and the Caves of Jedenar (close scrape with a pack of demons) and the Shrine of Aellena (because of the awesome sound track that played while in the shrine) and the Wyrmmist Strand (where he encountered his first dragon) and the Gurubashy Ruins (where he murdered his first orc) and so on, just loving all these weird place-names, and he flew from spot to spot on his ultrafast flying gryphon, then remembered how interesting it was when he was new to the game and had not earned any flying or riding animals yet and had to walk through the countryside and really take it in and enjoy the way one ecosystem gave way to another and he longed for the simplicity and naïveté of those days and so he parked his gryphon on the northern tip of the world's largest continent and began walking south, first through the white snowy tundra of the Wintersaber Glaciers, over the Timberfrost Mountains and down into Frost-Thistle Gorge, happening upon only a few occasional charging wildebeests or polar bears, through caves controlled by a semi-sentient race of ice yeti he was friendly with, and on south, walking and occasionally taking screen grabs the way tourists take photographs, and seeing orc players who ran like hell from him because they knew his name and he had a badass reputation, and by this time the online message boards were lighting up with the news that the game's most dominant and elite player was retiring, and Pwnage kept getting all these private messages asking if it was true and pleading with him to change his mind, messages that were actually having the effect of *changing his mind* because he was suddenly aware that he was possibly way more popular and supported and loved as an *Elfscape* avatar than he ever would be as an in-real-life real human being, and this made him feel sad and sort of panicky, and he remembered the anxiety of this last Patch Day when he couldn't log on to *Elfscape* for almost an entire day and he walked circles around every room in his house and stared at the mailbox for hours, and so as he now walked south through the vast *Elfscape* terrain he felt a crushing and excessive stress and dread that if he went through with the whole quitting-video-games thing then *every* day would be like the last Patch Day, and the realization of this washed over him like a cold rain and he felt his willpower and commitment to the plan erode and he decided that the only way he'd ever be able to bring himself to really quit *Elfscape* was if his characters were no longer the elite and super-cool characters that earned everyone's love and support, and the only way that would happen was if he got rid of all the treasure he'd worked tirelessly for, the thinking here being that he might be *less* roundly loved and popular and elite and therefore *more* likely to quit if he didn't have all his epic loot, plus it would be so frustrating to go back to the bottom of the totem pole after being on top for so long, so annoying to earn all that loot back again, so pointless that he would prefer to quit, and so he announced to his guild mates that he was giving away all his possessions and if they came to find him on his long walk south he would give them something really cool and valuable, and soon he was followed by a pack of lesser players in a kind of parade—at this point, it's important to note, the deep thrombus in his leg had shaken free at the moment he reached his epiphany and announced the news to the guild and switched from sitting on one leg to sitting on the other leg, and the clot was now slowly making its way up his circulatory system, a small hard glob about the size of a marble pushing through his body that registered occasionally as a tightness and sometimes a shooting pain, which frankly did not separate itself from the biologic human noise Pwnage felt mostly all the time, pain stemming from near-constant exhaustion and immobility and surviving on a diet consisting mostly of caffeine and frozen microwavable processed food things, a condition that caused regular shooting pain all over his body and meant the shooting pain that was now caused by his newly mobile blood clot made no impression on him as anything out of the ordinary, since he felt some kind of stabbing pain *almost all the time* and anyway the stabbing was blunted by the fact that he rarely actually *remembered* the stabbing pain as his brain's frontal lobe and hippocampus had been severely atrophied from sleep deprivation, malnutrition, and exposure to computer screens at a volume that seems to be dangerous in a way scientists don't even understand yet, so that each time he felt the stabbing pain his overtired, morbidly taxed brain promptly ejected the information so that the next time he felt the shooting, stabbing, awful pain it was like he was feeling it for the first time, duly noting it and thinking that if it happened again he'd definitely seek some kind of help from some manner of health professional within probably the next week or so maybe—and as his friends all gathered around him he began giving away first his gold, the many coins of gold, silver, and copper that he'd looted from the dead bodies of slain orc players and gathered from treasure chests guarded by dragons and earned on the server's auction house, where he'd learned to manipulate the various raw-material exchanges and leverage his wealth into far greater wealth by exerting near-monopolistic control of the *Elfscape* supply chain, and he was aware that all this gold had real-world value, that some people sold their *Elfscape* gold on real-world auction sites to other *Elfscape* players for real American dollars, and he was aware that a Stanford economist had even invented a *WoE*-gold-to-dollar currency converter that, if correct, meant that he could sell his gold and make at least as much money as he did when he worked at that copy shop, a thing he would never do because *Elfscape* was *fun* and he knew from experience that jobs were not (except if he really thought about it he'd say his *Elfscape* game experience was not *one hundred percent fun,* since each day's playing began with five hours of the same rote daily quests completed over and over until they achieved the monotony typical of manual labor, which was of course not very fun but which unlocked rewards that would allow him to have fun later, when he used them, except when he finally earned the rewards the game's developers would by that time have issued a new patch that made available new rewards that were slightly, incrementally better than the old rewards, and so even as he earned these rewards he knew they were already devalued because better rewards were right there on the horizon, and if he thought about it really hard he'd say that most of his *Elfscape* game experience involved him preparing to have fun but never really having it, the fun, except in those raids when, working together with his guild, he took down some importantly evil enemy and won some cool loot, but even then it was only fun the first couple of times they succeeded, and after that it became just a repeatable exercise that no longer provided fun, per se, and which actually caused a great deal of stress and rage when the guild failed some week where they had succeeded the week before, and so most raid nights were less about having fun and more about anger avoidance, and so he concluded the fun must have been happening elsewhere, maybe not even in the discrete game moments themselves but in the general, abstract state of playingness, because when he was logged on to *Elfscape* he felt a deep sense of satisfaction and mastery and belonging that he felt nowhere in the real world, and this feeling might be what he would interpret as "fun"), all of which is to say that Pwnage had a vast fortune indeed, and when he began giving away his wealth in 1,000-gold-coin increments it still took many dozens of players coming to collect before the purse was depleted, which made Pwnage feel something like Robin Hood walking through the forest giving away fortunes to the needy, and when his fortune was gone he began giving away his gear, clicking randomly on people in the very large crowd around him and giving them his weapons, his longswords and broadswords, his cleavers, claymores, rapiers, daggers, dirks, sabers, sickles, scimitars, shivs, axes, cudgels, hatchets, hammers, tomahawks, maces, picks, staves, polearms, pikes, spears, halberds, and one mysterious weapon he didn't even remember obtaining called a *flammard,* and when he had no more weapons to give he gave away his body armor, the various pieces of chain mail and plate metal he'd won and plundered, the kick-ass pauldrons with the spikes all over them, the greaves covered in razor wire, the awesome helmet with bull's horns that made him look like the goddamn minotaur (already this bounty was becoming legendary, as several players were taking video footage of Pwnage's long walk south and posting it online with captions like "EPIC PLAYER GIVES AWAY ALL HIS LOOTZ!"), and at first Pwnage felt sharp pangs of regret giving away his stuff because he *loved his stuff* and also because he knew how much time and effort went into acquiring every item (the bull's-head helmet alone took like two months to win), but that feeling soon gave way to an unexpected sense of calm purpose and spiritual goodness and generosity and even warmth and peace (this might have been the exhaustion talking, as he'd been playing *Elfscape* at this point for thirty hours straight) as he shed all his possessions and he was followed now by his many admirers and he was feeling like he was maybe *inspiring* these people and should maybe say something important and wise and he wondered whether there was a Buddha story like this, or maybe it was Gandhi, or Jesus, a story about giving everything away and walking—this all sounded really familiar— and Pwnage eventually thought of this whole episode not as a last-ditch desperate effort to quit a game he did not seem to have the willpower to quit but rather as an altruistic and spiritual journey of renunciation, like he was doing something good and important, charity-wise, being a role model for all these people, and this feeling held pretty strongly and pleasantly until the crowd began to thin, which it did when it was clear he had no more loot to give away and people began to private-message him asking "Is that it? Is there any more?" and he realized they were not there to join him on his long metaphysical journey but instead they simply wanted cool new toys to play with, and Pwnage felt angry at their crass materialism until he remembered that this was the point of the whole giving-away-all-his-possessions maneuver in the first place, that he would be abandoned and therefore not tempted to continue playing *Elfscape* due to his drastically diminished popularity, but now that it had happened, now that he actually had been abandoned, now that he was walking through the big open country without weapons or armor or gold or friends, just an elf in a loincloth, pathetic-looking, weak, he still did not feel much like quitting, and so he kept walking south until he reached the bottom of the continent, a rocky plateau that looked out over the ocean, and he knew he'd reached the end of his journey and knew it was time to log off and delete his account and begin living his real-life life and writing his novel and becoming successful and winning Lisa back and starting his diet and doing the all-around radical change that was necessary to live the way he wanted to live, and even though he could no longer think of a single excuse to stay in the game, and even though there was literally nothing his avatar could do now in its state of total poverty and nakedness, still he could not log off, still he stared out at the digital ocean, still the thought of abandoning the game and returning to the real world filled him with dread, a dread more powerful than anything most normally functional human adults ever experience due to the serious problems of brain physiology and neural microstructure reorganization that had gone down inside his cranium during his addict-level *Elfscape* binges, which had, along with the inevitable physical tolls like weight gain and muscle waste and back fatigue and a semipermanent knot on the back of his rib cage that seemed correlated with repetitive right-handed mouse usage, also severely degenerated the tissue of his rostral anterior cingulate cortex, an area in the front of the brain that acts as a kind of recruiter engaging the other more rational brain areas to aid during conflicts (think of a very impulsive and distraught person calling more level-headed friends to get some perspective and objective advice) and is necessary for proper cognitive and impulse control, except in Pwnage this area had begun to shut down completely, like a house that took down all its Christmas lights, just deactivating, which was what happened in the brains of heroin-dependent individuals when presented with heroin: their anterior cingulate cortexes shut down and they got no decision-making input from the quote-unquote *smart* parts of their brains and their brains offered them *literally no help* with overcoming their most basic, primal, self-destructive impulses, impulses with which they needed the *most* help to overcome, which was precisely what was happening to Pwnage as he looked out at the sea: he functionally remembered the desire to quit *Elfscape,* but there was no part of his brain actively telling him to do so, plus there was the problem of decreased gray-matter volume in several clusters of the orbitofrontal cortex—responsible for goal orientation and motivation—this atrophy resulting in a brain that was aware of the existence of a goal but did not offer any aid achieving that goal, instead idly seeing the goal on the horizon and noting the goal the way Midwestern farmers note the weather

("Yep, rain's comin'"), which was another of *Elfscape*'s neurobiological traps, that the more he played *Elfscape* the more his brain was unable to compute any but the most short-term and proximate goals, which happened to be the goals of *Elfscape* itself—the way the game was designed to reward players every one or two hours with some cool new piece of loot or a new level gained or achievement accomplished, which was accompanied by a horn fanfare and fireworks animations—and becoming habituated to these kinds of insidious, small, near-future goals made any long-term goals that required substantial planning and discipline and mental fortitude (like writing a novel or starting a new diet) seem, for the brain, *literally unfathomable,* not to mention the problems happening deep inside his brain's internal capsule, posterior limb, the only part of Pwnage's brain to have strengthened during his massive, unyielding addiction to *Elfscape,* where the primary motor cortex sent its axons that controlled fine finger movements, and Pwnage had *excellent* fine finger agility, clicking with his right hand on his many-buttoned mouse and with his left hand a full 104-key Western keyboard, keeping a mental map of all of this so that he could press any one of these hundreds of keys and buttons in a split second without even looking at them, this behavior having changed the actual physical structure of his brain and greatly thickened the axons in the internal capsule, the problem here being that such giant finger-control fibers were never, in an evolutionary sense, strictly necessary (there's no equivalent in our human ancestry to a fifteen-button electronic gaming mouse), and so the area available within the capsule was limited and not very accommodating to unexpected growth, meaning that Pwnage's giant finger-related white matter was crowding out other essential brain tissues, primarily communication tracts between the frontal and subcortical brain regions, which governed executive decision-making and which, among other things, helped inhibit inappropriate behaviors, which may have explained Pwnage's actions at the organic health food store specifically and his actions over the last year more generally, his slow wasting away in front of his computer, his lack of sleep, his diet, his delusions of grandeur about becoming a famous author and winning Lisa back, the partial mini seizures he didn't even know were happening, the seizures caused either by sleep deprivation or flashing computer lights or severe nutrition-related chemical imbalances (or all three of those things together, probably) that presented physically as a loss of sensation in various limbs and the sudden need to pick at his own skin and seeing sparkly things at the edge of his vision, symptoms that Pwnage might have gotten a medical opinion about if his dorsolateral prefrontal cortex weren't completely shut down, this brain area being responsible for decision-making and emotion control and which went dormant in the brains of heavy multitaskers during what might be called "information overload," which in the event of dormancy the emotion centers of the brain took over executive control in the neural equivalent of giving the keys to a forklift to a six-year-old, and Pwnage's mind was overloaded indeed, as his computer screen was jammed with the various boxes of add-on software that gave him real-time and constantly in-flux feedback on his opponent's health, his own available moves, various countdown timers that let him know when other moves would be available again, the attacks that would at that moment inflict the highest damage mathematically possible, the status of each of his raid members, the full party's damage-per-second output, an overhead bird's-eye view of the fight's layout with principal actors color-coded depending on their roles in the fight, all of this happening in addition to the actual game also happening behind all the flashing and glowing boxes, and Pwnage monitored not only everything happening on this screen—which itself would be enough to drive your basic slow-living eighteenth-century peasant to near psychotic breaks—but since he usually played while "multiboxing" several characters at once, he monitored the events on six different computer screens simultaneously, such that he was ingesting way more information per second than all the air traffic controllers at O'Hare put together, making that very sensitive and logical brain part essentially wave the white flag and hide, allowing his emotion centers to easily shut down whatever was left of his logical, rational, disciplined mind, which meant, to put it simply, that the more *Elfscape* he played the more impossible it felt to stop playing *Elfscape,* and this went way beyond simply kicking a bad habit and into problems of brain morphology and a kind of fundamental neural disfigurement so complete that Pwnage's mind *literally would not allow him* to quit *Elfscape,* which was what he was realizing standing on the southern edge of the continent wondering what to do next and not coming up with anything and so just standing there, until finally one of his enemy-proximity alarms went off and the game's camera auto-flipped to reveal an orc player behind him spying from a great distance, and what he would usually do in this moment would be to charge the orc and slam it with his shield and then hack at it with his ax of unusual size until it was good and dead, and even though he currently had no shield or ax or really anything with which to attack the orc, he reflexively went to attack it—except that he couldn't, something was preventing it, he felt hazy and nauseous and light-headed and found he couldn't move his arms or, come to think of it, breathe (it should be mentioned here that the blood clot that had formed in his leg was by now a full-blown pulmonary embolism that was currently blocking blood flow to the lungs and which caused substantial chest pain whenever Pwnage breathed combined with a desperate desire to *breathe more,* Pwnage registering this mostly as a quick dimming of the light, almost as if the sun had gone down all at once, skipping twilight and plunging directly into nocturnal darkness), and when Pwnage did not attack the orc player, the orc player moved closer, gaining confidence, a step or two at a time, testing him, ready to run, until the orc was in melee range and Pwnage desperately wanted to attack it except that he couldn't move under the weight of what felt like an anvil on his chest, and when Pwnage did not move the orc player removed from his belt a small dagger and—after a brief moment where he was probably wondering if this was a good idea and not a put-on by the server's most famous elf warrior—the orc stabbed him, then stabbed him again, then again, and Pwnage's loinclothed elf stood there wobbling and taking it while alarms went off everywhere and his health bar dropped and he sat there watching in horror unable to move as the darkness closed in and his field of vision narrowed and he lost all control of his motor functions and his lips and fingertips turned blue and his elf warrior eventually, after so many wounds, dropped down dead, and Pwnage watched the orc dance on his own fallen corpse and the last thing he saw before the lights went off completely was a message from the orc-player saying *ZOMG I PWNED UR FACE ROFLOLOLO-LOLOLOL!!!!!!!!* and Pwnage resolved that he would earn all his treasure back and become twice as powerful as before just so he could hunt down this one fucking orc and kill him over and over and over, and he would start doing that as soon as he could move his legs and arms again, and breathe, and for that matter see, and even as all his systems were in a cascading and catastrophic failure his brain told him his number one priority right now was *killing this orc,* which he would never be able to do, because today was the day he was quitting *Elfscape,* and since his mind would not let him do it, his body had to do it for him.

4

SIMON ROGERS PACED through Faye's wrecked apartment, stepping carefully to avoid debris on the floor and explaining that there were certain laws that allowed *all this* (when he said "all this," he said it with a sweep of his arms, meaning the apartment's general desecration and ruin), certain statutes passed after 9/11 governing the searches of terrorist suspects, the allowable use of military force.

"Basically," he said, "the police can send a SWAT team whenever they want, and we have no way to stop it, prevent it, countermand it, or redress it."

Faye was in the kitchen, silent, stirring tea in her one unbroken mug.

"What were they looking for?" Samuel asked. He kicked at the remains of the television, which had been fractured by some kind of blunt force, its electronic guts scattered over the floor.

Simon shrugged. "It's procedure, sir. Since your mother is being charged with domestic terrorism, they're allowed to do this. So they did it."

"She's not a terrorist."

"Yes, but since she's being *charged* under a statute designed for sleeper-cell al-Qaeda agents, they have to treat her as if she might actually be one."

"This is so fucked up."

"The law was written at a time when folks were not that interested in the Fourth Amendment. Or the Fifth Amendment, for that matter. Or, actually, the Sixth." He chortled lightly to himself. "Or the *Eighth*."

"Don't they need some kind of specific *reason* to search the house?" Samuel said.

"They do, sir, but they keep it a secret."

"Don't they need a warrant?"

"Yes, but it's sealed."

"Who gives them permission?"

"Confidential, sir."

"And is there anyone watching over all of this? Anyone we can appeal to?"

"There is a sort of habeas process, but it's classified. National security reasons. Mostly, sir, we're meant to trust that the government has our best interests in mind. I should note that this kind of search isn't actually mandatory. It's at the court's discretion. They didn't *have* to do this. And I know for a fact the prosecutor didn't ask for it."

"So it was the judge."

"Technically, that is information withheld from the public. But yes. Judge Brown. We can infer that he ordered it himself."

Samuel looked at his mother, who was staring down into her tea. It did not appear that she was drinking the tea so much as intensely stirring it. The wooden spoon she used clunked softly against the sides of the mug.

"So what are we going to do?" Samuel said.

"I am prepared to mount a vigorous defense, sir, against these new charges. I believe I can persuade a jury that your mother is not a terrorist."

"On what grounds?"

"Primarily, that the recipient of the terrorist threat, Governor Packer, did not actually *feel terror*."

"You're going to summon Governor Packer."

"Yes. I'm betting he won't want to admit in pubic that he was terrified. Of your mom. Not during a presidential campaign."

"That's it? That's your defense?"

"I will also argue that your mother merely made a threatening *gesture* and did not convey her terroristic threat verbally, electronically, on television, or in writing, which for certain convoluted reasons is a mitigating factor. I'm hoping this will reduce her sentence from life to merely ten years, maximum security."

"That doesn't sound like a win to me."

"I have to admit that I'm more comfortable in free-speech law. Defenses against terrorism are not my, shall we say, cup of tea? Haha."

They looked at Faye, who continued to stare into her mug and had no reaction at all.

"Excuse me," said the lawyer, and he walked between mounds of ripped-open pillows and couch cushions and clothes still attached to their hangers, into the bathroom.

Samuel made his way to the kitchen, each footstep provoking a shriek of broken glass. Food was strewn over the countertops where police had upended the pantry—coffee grounds and cereals and oat bran and rice. The refrigerator was pulled from its place and unplugged, water now dribbling out of it and puddling on the floor. Faye held her mug, which appeared to be handmade from clay, to her chest.

"Mom?" Samuel said. He wondered what she was feeling right now, given the high-end anxiety meds she'd taken earlier that day. "Hello?" he said.

At the moment, she seemed numb to everything, oblivious. Even the way she stirred her tea was automatic and mechanical. He wondered if the shock of the police raid had put her in some kind of fugue.

"Mom, are you all right? Can you, like, hear me?"

"This wasn't supposed to happen," she said finally. "It wasn't supposed to be this way."

"Tell me you're okay."

She stirred her tea and stared into the mug. "I've been so stupid."

"*You've* been stupid? This is *my* fault," Samuel said. "I went to see the judge and I made everything worse. I'm really sorry."

"I've made such stupid decisions," Faye said, shaking her head, "one after the other."

"Listen. We should figure out a plan. Alice said we needed to get out of town. Maybe even out of the country."

"Yeah. I'm beginning to believe her."

"Just for a little while. If Brown is retiring soon, why not wait him out? Make sure he knows it will be *years* before a trial happens. Get rid of him, get another judge."

"Where would we go?" Faye said.

"I don't know. Canada. Europe. Jakarta."

"Actually, no," she said, and she put the mug on the counter. "We can't leave the country. I've been charged with *terrorism*. There's no way they'll let me on an airplane."

"Yes. Right."

"We'll have to trust Simon, I guess."

"Trust Simon. I *really* hope that's not our best option."

"What else can we do?"

"Alice said the judge will never back down. He really seriously wants to put you away forever. This is not a joke."

"It doesn't feel like a joke."

"He said he's in a wheelchair because of you. What did you do to him?"

"Nothing. I have no idea what he's talking about. Honest."

A rush of plumbing came from the bathroom then, and Simon emerged, little water specks dotting the arms of his sport coat.

"Professor Anderson, sir, I'm actually glad you're here. I've been meaning to talk to you. About your letter? The letter to the judge that you've been working on tirelessly, I assume?"

"Right. Yes. What about it?"

"Well, I wanted to personally thank you, sir, for all your efforts and all the time you've no doubt put into this already. But you should know that we will no longer be needing your services."

"My services. Sounds like you're firing me."

"Yes. The letter you're writing? That will no longer be necessary."

"But my mom is in pretty big trouble."

"Oh, yes, she most certainly is, sir."

"She needs my help."

"She definitely does need help from *somebody,* sir. But probably not from you. Not anymore."

"Why not?"

"How do I say this delicately? It's just that I've become convinced, sir, that you are not in a position to help her. Probably you'd make things worse. I'm referring of course to the scandal."

"What scandal?"

"At the university, sir. Dreadful."

"Simon, what the hell are you talking about?"

"Oh, you haven't seen yet? Oh, my. I'm so sorry, sir. Seems like I'm always the one to bring you bad news, eh? Haha. Perhaps if you checked your e-mail more often, or watched the local news?"

"*Simon.*"

"Of course, sir. Well, it looks like there's a brand-new student organization that's gaining some serious attention at your school. This organization's purpose, its singular raison d'être, if you will, seems to be getting you fired."

"Seriously?"

"They have their own website, which has been gleefully shared and circulated by your students, both current and former. You are now pretty much the textbook definition of what PR people call *toxic.* Hence our no longer needing you to vouch for your mother."

"Why do my students want me fired?"

"Perhaps it would be best to look at it yourself?"

Simon removed a laptop from his briefcase and called up the website: a new student organization called S.A.F.E.—or Students Against Faculty Extravagance—arguing that university professors were wasting taxpayer money. Their evidence? One Samuel Anderson, a professor of English, who, according to the website, *abused his office computer privileges:*

> *During routine maintenance, the Computer Support Center found logs showing Professor Anderson uses his computer to play "World of Elfscape" for a frankly shocking number of hours each week. This is a completely unacceptable use of university resources.*

There was also an associated letter-writing campaign that had gotten the attention of the dean, the press, and the governor's office. Now the whole matter was being sent to the university disciplinary committee for a full hearing.

"Oh, shit," Samuel said at the thought of explaining *Elfscape* to a committee of humorless gray-haired professors of philosophy and rhetoric and theology. It made him break out in an immediate sweat, justifying to his colleagues why he had a robust second life as an *elven thief.* Oh god.

The president of S.A.F.E. was quoted on the website as saying that students needed to be vigorous watchdogs of faculty who wasted their tuition dollars. The student's name was, of course, Laura Pottsdam.

"Fuck this," Samuel said, closing the laptop. He walked over to the expanse of windows on the apartment's north wall and looked out at the jagged city.

He remembered Periwinkle's ridiculous advice: that he should declare bankruptcy and move to Jakarta. That was actually sounding pretty good right about now. "I think it's time to leave," he said.

"Excuse me, sir?"

"It's time to get on a plane and leave," Samuel said. "Leave my job, and my life, and the whole country. Start fresh, somewhere else."

"You are, of course, free to do that, sir. But your mother needs to stay here and fight this within the strict confines of the law."

"I know."

"My various oaths bar me from telling anyone accused of a crime that they should flee the jurisdiction."

"Doesn't matter," Samuel said. "She can't leave anyway. She'd be on the no-fly list."

"Oh, no, sir. She wouldn't be on the list yet."

Samuel turned around. The lawyer was carefully tucking his laptop back into its special briefcase sleeve.

"Simon, what do you mean?"

"Well, the no-fly list is administered by the Terrorist Screening Center, or TSC, which, interestingly, is actually a part of the National Security Branch of the FBI, under the auspices of the Department of Defense. The no-fly list is not, as many people believe, controlled by the Transportation Security Administration, or TSA, which is part of the Department of Homeland Security. They are completely different departments!"

"Okay. So?"

"So to get onto the no-fly list, one's name has to be nominated by an approved government official from the Department of Justice, or Homeland Security, or Defense, or State, or the Postal Service, or certain private contractors, and since each of these agencies has different criteria and guidelines and rules and processes, not to mention different documents and forms that sometimes are incompatible with another administrative agency's equivalent documents and forms, the TSC has to filter through everything and evaluate it and standardize it. This is made infinitely more complicated by the fact that every agency and department uses its own special computer software, like, for example, the Circuit Court of Cook County uses a Windows operating system that's at least three iterations out of date, whereas the FBI and CIA are more Linux-based, I believe. And getting those two systems speaking to each other? *Hoo-boy.*"

"Simon, get back to your point."

"Of course, sir. What I'm saying is that the information on your mother's status as a terrorist must be processed by the Circuit Court of Cook County's First Municipal District, then passed along to the regional FBI office, then to the TSC, where it's evaluated and approved by the TSC's multiagency Operations Branch and Tactical Analysis Group, then that information needs to percolate over to the Department of Homeland Security, which then sends it along to the TSA in some manner that probably involves a fax machine, all this before the no-fly information is available to individual airport and security personnel."

"So my mom is not, in fact, on the no-fly list."

"She's not on the no-fly list *yet*. This whole process usually takes around forty-eight hours, start to finish. More if it's a Friday."

"So, hypothetically, if we wanted to leave the country, we could do so, as long as we did it today."

"That's right, sir. You have to remember we're dealing with huge bureaucracies staffed by people who are, for the most part, criminally underpaid."

Samuel glanced over at his mother, who looked back at him and, after a moment where she seemed to consider this, the gravity of this, gave him a little nod.

"Simon?" he said. "Thank you so much. You've been very, very helpful."

AT O'HARE INTERNATIONAL AIRPORT, terminal five, people waited
quietly in lines: lines to get their ticket, lines to drop off their luggage,
lines to get through security, all the lines running at such a laggard and
reluctant and frankly un-American pace that they forced everyone to fully
imbibe the terminal's deeply disorienting combination of melancholy
and chaos. The smell of car exhaust from all the taxis outside, and the
inside smells of meats that had been cooking all day at Gold Coast Dogs.
Easy-listening standards heavy on saxophone occupied the aural spaces
between security announcements. Televisions showing airport news that
was different from regular news in unknown ways. Samuel felt disappointed that a foreigner's first impression of America would be made
here, and what America was offering them was a McDonald's (whose
big message to the incoming throngs seemed to be that the McRib was
back) and a store specializing in gadgets of questionable necessity: HD
video pens, shiatsu massage chairs, wireless Bluetooth-activated reading lamps, heated foot spas, compression socks, automatic wine-bottle
openers, motorized barbecue-grill brushes, orthopedic dog couches, cat
thundershirts, weight-loss armbands, gray hair prevention pills, isomet-
ric meal replacement packs, liquid protein shots, television swivel stands,
hands-free blow-dryer holders, a bath towel that said "Face" on one end
and "Butt" on the other.

This is who we are.

Men's bathrooms that required you touch nothing but yourself. Automated dispensers that pooed little globs of generic pink soap onto your
hands. Sinks that did not run enough water to fully wash. The same
threat-level warning issued ad nauseam. The security mandates—empty
your pockets, remove your shoes, laptops out, gels and liquids in separate
bags—repeated so many times that eventually everyone stopped hearing them. All of this so reflexive and automatic and habituated and slow

that the travelers were a little zoned out and playing with their phones and just simply *enduring* this uniquely modern, first world ordeal that is not per se "difficult" but is definitely exhausting. Spiritually debilitating. Everyone feeling a small ache of regret, suspecting that, as a people, we could do better. But we don't. The line for a McRib was quiet and solemn and twenty people deep.

"I'm feeling a surge of pessimism about our plan," Faye said to Samuel as they stood in the security line. "I mean, do you think they're really going to let us through? Like, *Oh yes, Miss Fugitive from Justice, right this way.*"

"Would you keep it down?" Samuel said.

"I can feel the drugs wearing off. I can feel my anxiety bounding back to me like a lost dog."

"We are normal passengers taking a normal vacation abroad."

"A normal vacation to a country with very strict extradition laws, I sincerely hope."

"Don't worry. Remember what Simon said."

"I can literally feel my confidence in our plan disintegrating. It's like someone has taken our plan and applied a cheese grater. That's what it feels like."

"Please be quiet and please relax."

They had taken a cab to the airport and purchased one-way tickets on the next available international flight, a nonstop to London. Their boarding passes were issued without a problem. They checked their luggage, again without a problem. They waited in the security line. And when they finally handed their tickets and passports to the blue-uniformed TSA agent, whose job it was to visually inspect their photographs and run their tickets over a bar-code scanner and wait for the computer to make a pleasant sound and for the light to flash green, the computer did not, in fact, make the pleasant sound. The sound it made instead was the harsh *errrrrr* sound like the buzzer at the end of a basketball game, that sound indicating authority and finality. And in case anyone was confused over the sound's meaning, the light also turned red.

The security agent sat up straighter at this, surprised at the computer's negative judgment. A rare moment of drama in terminal five.

"Could you please wait over there," he said, pointing at an empty little holding pen whose boundaries were demarcated only by strips of dirty purple masking tape on the floor.

While they waited, the other travelers glanced at them once or twice, then were drawn back to their phones. A television above them showed the airport news network, currently a story about Governor Packer.

"They know about me," Faye whispered into Samuel's ear. "That I'm a fugitive. I'm on the run."

"You are neither of those things."

"Of course they know. This is the information age. They all have access to the same data. There's probably a room somewhere covered with TV screens monitoring us right now. It's in Langley, or Los Alamos."

"I doubt you'd register as that high a threat."

They watched the slow crawl of the line through the security checkpoint: people taking off their shoes and belts and standing in clear plastic tubes and putting their hands over their heads while gray metal arms circled their bodies, probing them.

"This is the post-9/11 world," Faye said. "The post-privacy world. The law knows where I am at all times. Of course they wouldn't let me fly."

"Relax. We don't know what's happening yet."

"And you. They'll arrest you as an accessory."

"Accessory to what? A vacation?"

"They'll never believe we're taking a vacation."

"Aiding and abetting a weekend trip abroad? Hardly criminal."

"We're being watched right now on a bank of televisions and computer screens. Probably in the basement of the Pentagon. A feed from every port in the world. Bundles of fiber-optic cables. Face-recognition software. Technology we don't even know exists. They are probably reading my lips at this exact moment. The FBI and CIA working in conjunction with local law enforcement. That's how they always say it on the news."

"This is not the news."

"This is not the news *yet*."

A man with a clipboard had by now begun talking in low tones with the security agent, glancing at them occasionally. He looked like he'd been pulled from a previous era—his hair cut into a severe and geometric flattop, a white short-sleeved shirt and thin black tie, square jaw, bright blue eyes—like he'd once been an *Apollo* astronaut but was now doing this. A badge hanging on his shirt pocket turned out to be, upon closer inspection, a laminated card with the image of a badge on it.

"He's talking about us," Faye said. "Something is about to happen."

"Just stay calm."

"Do you remember the story I told you about the Nix?"

"Which one was that?"

"The horse."

"Right, yeah. The white horse that picked up children, then drowned them."

"That's the one."

"Excellent story to tell a nine-year-old, by the way."

"Do you remember the moral?"

"That the things you love the most can hurt you the worst."

"Yes. That people can be a Nix to each other. Sometimes without even knowing it."

"What's your point?"

The man with the clipboard had begun walking in their direction.

"That's what I was to you," she said. "I was your Nix. You loved me most, and I was hurting you. You asked me once why I left you and your father. That's why."

"And you're telling me this *now*?"

"I wanted to get it in under the wire."

The man with the clipboard crossed the purple tape and cleared his throat.

"So it looks like we have sort of a problem here," he said in an unusually upbeat way, like one of those customer-service people you sometimes get on the phone who seem really into their jobs. He was not making eye contact with either of them, staring instead at whatever was on his clipboard. "It looks like, it turns out, you're on that no-fly list, there." He seemed uncomfortable having to say this, as if it were his fault.

"Yes, I'm sorry," Faye said. "I should have known."

"Oh, no, not you," the man said, looking surprised. "You're not on the list. He is."

"Me?" Samuel said.

"Yes, sir. That's what it says right here," tapping the clipboard. "Samuel Andresen-Anderson. Absolutely not allowed on an airplane."

"How am *I* on the no-fly list?"

"Well," he said, flipping through the pages as if he were reading them for the first time. "Were you recently in Iowa?"

"Yes."

"Did you visit the ChemStar factory while you were there?"

"I stopped by."

"Did you, um"—and here he lowered his voice, as if he were saying something obscene—"did you *take photographs* of the factory?"

"A couple, yeah."

"Well," he said, and shrugged as if the answer should have been obvious. "There you go."

"Why were you taking photographs of ChemStar?" Faye said.

"Yes," the man with the clipboard said. "Why *were* you?"

"I don't know. It's nostalgic."

"You were taking nostalgic pictures of a *factory*," the man said. He frowned. He was dubious. Not buying it. "Who does that?"

"My grandfather works there. Used to work there."

"That part is true," Faye said.

"That *part*? All of it is true. I was visiting my grandfather and took some pictures of all the old childhood places. The old house, the old park, and yes, the old factory. I think the better question here is why am I on the no-fly list for photographing a corn-processing plant?"

"Oh, well, those kinds of facilities have some pretty dangerous toxic chemicals. And it's right there on the Mississippi. Let's just say that your presence raised"—and here he put up two fingers to indicate air quotes—"homeland security concerns."

"I see."

He flipped to another page on his clipboard. "It says here that they saw you on their closed-circuit cameras, and you fled when security approached."

"Fled? I didn't flee. I *left*. I was done photographing. I never even saw security."

"That's exactly what I would say if I were fleeing," the man said to Faye, who nodded.

"I know," she said. "You're exactly right."

"Would you stop?" Samuel said. "So am I never going to fly again? Is that what this means?"

"It means you're not going to fly *today*. But you can take steps to remove yourself from the list. There's a website for that."

"A website."

"Or an 800 number, if you prefer," he said. "Then an average wait time of six to eight weeks. I'm afraid I'm going to have to escort you out of the airport now."

"And my mother?"

"Oh, she can do whatever she wants. She's not on the list."

"I see. Can you give us a second?"

"Oh sure!" the man said. Then he took one step beyond the purple tape and turned his back three-quarters to them and clasped his hands in front of him and began very slightly tilting back and forth like someone whistling and rocking to his own tune.

"Let's forget about it," Faye whispered. "Let's go home. The judge can do whatever he wants. It's not like I don't deserve it."

And Samuel thought about his mother going to jail, thought about his life returning to normal: losing his job, in debt, alone, passing through his days in a digital fog.

"You have to leave," he said. "I'll come find you, when I can."

"Don't be stupid," Faye said. "Do you know what the judge will do to you?"

"A lot less than what he'll do to you. You need to go."

She looked at him a moment, wondering whether to fight him.

"Don't argue," he said. "Just go."

"Fine," she said, "but we're not going to have one of those sappy parent-child moments, right? You're not going to cry, right?"

"I am not going to cry."

"Because I was never very good at dealing with that."

"Have a good flight."

"Wait," she said. She grabbed his arm. "This has to be a clean break. If we do this, we won't be able to contact each other for a while. Radio silence."

"I know."

"So I'm asking you, are you prepared to do that? Can you handle that?"

"You want permission?"

"Permission to leave you. Again. For the second time. Yes, that's what I want."

"Where will you go?"

"I don't know," Faye said. "I'll figure that out in London."

On the television above them, the airport news network came back from commercials and into a segment on the Packer for President campaign. It looked like Governor Packer was out to an early lead in Iowa, they said. Looks like the attack in Chicago really boosted his peripherals.

Faye and Samuel looked at each other.

"How did we get into this?" he said.

"It's my fault," she said. "I'm sorry."

"Go," he said. "You have my permission. Get out of here."

"Thank you," she said. She picked up her bag, looked at him for a moment, then dropped it back on the ground and leaned into Samuel and wrapped her arms around him and buried her face in his chest and squeezed. Samuel didn't know what to do, it was such an out-of-character gesture. She took one long hard breath, like someone about to plunge underwater, then quickly let go.

"Be good," she said, and patted him on the chest. She collected her suitcase and wandered back to the TSA agent, who let her through uneventfully. The man with the clipboard asked Samuel if he was ready to leave. And Samuel watched his mother, and felt a little tremble at her sudden embrace. His hand lightly touched the spot she'd pressed her head against.

"Sir?" said the clipboard man. "Are you ready?"

Samuel was about to say yes when he heard a name he recognized— a name that abruptly popped out of the airport's ubiquitous and usually ignorable noise. It came from the television overhead: *Guy Periwinkle.*

Samuel looked up to see if he'd heard correctly, and that's when he saw him, Periwinkle, on TV, sitting in the studio, talking to the anchors. Under his name it said *Packer Campaign Consultant.* They were asking him what drew him to the job.

"Sometimes the country thinks it deserves a spanking, sometimes it wants a hug," Periwinkle said. "When it wants a hug, it votes Democrat. I'm hedging on it's a spanking moment right now."

"It's time to go now, sir," the man with the clipboard said.

"One second."

"Conservatives tend to believe more than the rest of us that we need a spanking. Read into that whatever you want." Periwinkle laughed. The anchors laughed. He was a natural on television. "Right now the country sees itself as a poorly behaved child," he continued. "When people vote, what they're really doing, way deep down, is externalizing some childhood trauma. We have reams of paper showing this."

"It's really time to go now, sir." The man with the clipboard was getting impatient.

"Okay, fine," Samuel said, and he let himself be escorted away from the television, toward the exterior doors.

But just before leaving, he turned around. He turned in time to see his mother collect her belongings on the other side of security. And she didn't look for him, she didn't wave at him. She simply gathered her things and left. And thus Samuel endured, for the second time in his life, the sight of his mother walking away, disappearing, and not coming back.

| PART NINE |

REVOLUTION

Late Summer 1968

1

THE CONRAD HILTON ground-floor bar is separated from the street by panes of thick, leaded, plate-glass windows that muffle all but the closest sirens or screams. The Hilton's front entrance is guarded by a phalanx of police officers, who themselves are being watched over by a great many Secret Service agents, all of whom are making sure anyone coming into the Hilton is registered and unthreatening: delegates, their wives, candidate support staff, the candidates themselves, Eugene McCarthy and the vice president, they're here, as are some minor artist-type celebrities, Arthur Miller and Norman Mailer being the two that at least a couple of the cops recognize. The bar itself is full of delegates today, and the lights are appropriately low to accommodate the privacy needed to lubricate the political process. Small packs of intense-looking men in booths talk quietly, make promises, trade favors. Everyone has a cigarette and most have martinis and the music is jazz and big-band stuff—think Benny Goodman, Count Basie, Tommy Dorsey—at a volume great enough to obscure nearby conversations but not so loud that anyone needs to shout. Television over the bar tuned to CBS News. Delegates walking around the bar and seeing friends and slapping hands and backs because roughly the same people come to these things every time. Ceiling fans twirl just fast enough to draw the cigarette mist up and scatter it.

Outsiders to the political process sometimes complain that real decisions happen in dark smoky rooms, and this is one of those rooms.

Two guys at the bar that absolutely no one approaches or fucks with: mirrored sunglasses, black suits, obviously Secret Service, off duty, watching the news and sipping glasses of something clear. The buzz in the room dies down momentarily when a hippie breaks through the police line and sprints down Michigan Avenue and gets himself tackled right outside the plate-glass windows of the bar, and all the patrons inside—everyone but the two Secret Service guys—stop and watch the scene made wavy by the leaded glass as the police officers in their baby-blue uniforms descend on the poor guy and club him on his back and legs while inside the bar nobody can hear a thing except maybe sometimes old Cronkite talking on CBS and Glenn Miller playing "Rhapsody in Blue."

2

WAY UP ABOVE THEM, on the top-floor suite of the Conrad Hilton Hotel, Vice President Hubert H. Humphrey wants another shower.

This will be his third shower of the day, and his second since returning from the amphitheater. He tells the maid to run the water and his staff looks at him queerly.

They were at the amphitheater this morning so Triple H could practice his speech. His staff likes to call him "Triple H," but the Secret Service agents refuse, usually calling him "Mr. Vice President sir," which he prefers. They were at the amphitheater so he could stand at that podium and imagine the crowd and visualize his speech and think positive thoughts like the management consultants told him to do, to imagine the crowd in that vast space, that huge space big enough to hold every resident of his hometown plus many thousands more, and he was up there mentally going through his speech and savoring the applause lines and thinking positive thoughts and repeating "They *want* me to win, they want *me* to win," but all he could really think about was that smell. That unmistakable smell of animal feces, with an under-sweetness of blood and cleaning agents, that cloud hanging over the stockyards. What a place to have your convention.

The smell still lingers on his clothes, even though he's changed clothes. He can still smell it in his hair and under his fingernails. If he can't get rid of this smell he thinks he's going to go crazy. He needs another shower, to hell with what the staff thinks.

3

MEANWHILE, one story underground, Faye Andresen stares at shadows on the wall. This jail, it turns out, is not the official or permanent city jail but rather a makeshift holding pen that looks like it was quickly erected in a storage room of the Conrad Hilton Hotel. The cells are made not from iron bars but from chain-link fencing. She's been sitting on the floor ever since the last of her panic attacks, which had consumed her for most of the night. She had been photographed and fingerprinted and dragged to this cell and the door was locked and she pleaded into the darkness that there'd been some terrible mistake and wept at the thought of her family discovering she was arrested (for, oh my god, *prostitution*) and the terror quaked through her body and all she could do was curl up in a ball in the corner and feel her own rigid heartbeat and persuade herself she was not dying even though she was convinced that this is what it felt like, to die.

And after the third or maybe fourth attack, a strange calm came over her, a strange acceptance, maybe exhaustion. She was so tired. Her body rang from a night of spasms and tight dread. She lay on her back thinking maybe she'd sleep now, but she just stared into the darkness until the first dull glow of dawn slunk into the room through the basement's lone egress window. It is a gray-blue light, sickly looking, like the light of deep winter, dispersed and faded and occluded by several panes of frosted glass. She can't see the window itself, but she can see its light cast on the far wall. And the shadows of things that pass by. First a few people, then many people, then many people marching.

Then the door opens and that cop who'd arrested her last night—big crew-cutted guy who still is not wearing a badge or name tag or anything identifiable—walks in. Faye stands up. The cop says, "Basically you have two choices."

"This is a mistake," Faye says. "A big misunderstanding."

"Choice number one: You leave Chicago immediately," the cop says. "Or choice two: Stay in Chicago and go on trial for prostitution."

"But I didn't *do* anything."

"Also you're high. Right now you are abusing illegal narcotics. Those red pills you took. How do you think your daddy's gonna feel when he finds out you're a hooker and a doper?"

"Who *are* you? What did I do to you?"

"If you leave Chicago, this whole thing will go away. I'm trying to put this as plainly as I can. You leave, no harm done. But if I ever catch you in Chicago again, I promise you'll regret it for the rest of your life."

He gives the cage a shake to test its sturdiness. "I'll give you the weekend to think about it," he said. "See you when the protest is over."

He leaves and locks the door behind him and Faye sits down and stares again at the shadows. Above her, the big parade is fully under way, is what she thinks seeing the forms cast on the opposite wall. Thin shadows that look like snapping scissors held upside down are almost certainly legs, she thinks. People marching. The city must have backed down, issued a permit. Then a rumbling and associated large window-blocking shadows she assumes are pickup trucks, their beds filled with student protestors, she imagines, waving their homemade peace flags. She's glad for them, that Sebastian and the others got their way, that the biggest demonstration of the year—of the *decade*—is happening after all.

4

BUT THE SHADOWS ARE in fact not those of parading students. They are those of National Guard troop carriers filled with soldiers holding rifles tipped with bayonets. There is no parade. The city has not backed down. The shadows that Faye sees are cast by cops moving this way and that to contain the surge of screaming demonstrators massing across the street. In case any of them have designs on parading, the troop carriers have cages of razor wire attached to their front grills to show them just how unwelcome they are in the street.

They all gather in Grant Park, the many thousands of them, where Allen Ginsberg now sits in the grass cross-legged palms raised to the universe listening. Around him young people scream and revolutionize. They place their spit curses on police-state USA, the FBI, the president, petty materialist sexless soulless bourgeoisie killers, their bombs death-dropping on farmers and children a billion tons. *It's time to bring the war to the streets,* says one nearby bullhorned youth. *We're gonna shut down Chicago! Fuck the police! And anybody who's not with us is a bourgeois white honky pig!*

Ginsberg trembles at this. He does not want to take these children to war, misery, despair, bloody police nightsticks and death. The thought barb-wires his guts. One cannot react to violence with violence—only a machine thinks like this. Or a president. Or a vengeful monotheism. Imagine, instead, ten thousand naked youths carrying signs that say

POLICE DON'T HURT US
WE LOVE YOU TOO

Or crowned with flowers sitting cross-legged waving pure-white flags chanting glory nirvana poems to their holy Maker. This is the other way to react to violence—with beauty—and Ginsberg wants to say this. He wants to say to the bullhorned man: *You are the poem you are asking for!* He wants to soothe them. *The way forward is like water.* But he knows it isn't good enough, isn't radical enough to calm the wild appetite of the young. And so Ginsberg strokes his beard, closes his eyes, settles into his body, and answers in the only way he can, with a deep bellow from the bottom of his belly, the great Syllable, the sacred sound of the universe, the perfection of wisdom, the only noise worth making at a time like this: *Ommmmm.*

He feels the hot holy breath in his mouth, the lifted-up music breath released from his lungs and his gullet, from his guts and heart, his stomach, his red blood cells and kidneys, from his gallbladder and glands and the long spindly legs he sits on, the Syllable issues from all these things. If you listen quietly and carefully, if you are calm and you slow down your heart, you can hear the Syllable in everything—the walls, the street, the cars, the soul, the sun—and soon you are no longer chanting. Soon the sound settles into your skin and you are simply hearing the body make the sound it has always made: *Ommmmm.*

Children with too much education have problems with the Syllable. Because they do their thinking with their minds and not their bodies. They think with their heads and not their souls. The Syllable is what remains when you get out of your mind, after you minus the Great You. Ginsberg sometimes likes to pair them up and touch his hands to the

tops of their heads and say "You're married" to make them think about
what happens next, on the honeymoon; for all their talk of free love, they
need desperately the debauch of other bodies. They need desperately out
of their own brains. He wants to scream at them: *You are carrying lead
souls!* He wants them to lob their haunted heads into bliss devotion. Here
they are trying to murmur the Syllable and getting it all wrong. Because
they treat it like a lab rat or a poem—break it apart, dissect it, explain it,
expose the viscera. They think the Syllable is a ritual, figurative, a sym-
bol for God, but they are wrong. When you're bobbing in the ocean, the
water does not *symbolize wetness*. The water is simply there, lifting you
up. That is the Syllable, the universe's deep bellow, like water, omnipresent, endless, perfect, it's the touch of God in the loftiest place, the most
exalted place, the eminent, the pinnacle, the highest, the eighth.

Ommmmm, he says.

5

AND ABOVE THEM ALL a helicopter screams north now at the news of
some impromptu illegal cavalcade on Lake Shore Drive: a company of
girls marching and shouting and raising their fists in the air and high-
stepping it right down the middle of the road slapping their palms on the
windshields of cars exhorting the drivers to join them on their procession
south, which the drivers universally do not do.

The chopper reaches them and points its camera at them and people
watching this on TV—people like Faye's father and Faye's several burly
uncles, who are all gathered right now in a living room in her little Iowa
river town two hundred miles distant from Chicago but linked to it via
television—they say: *They're all girls?*

Well, yes, this particular cluster of protesting student radicals are, sure
enough, all girls. Or presumably so. Several are wearing handkerchiefs
over their faces so it's hard to tell. Others have these haircuts that make
the uncles say, *That one looks like a man.* They're right now watching
on the best TV owned among them—a twenty-three-inch Zenith color

console as large as a boulder that comes to life with an electric *thwump*—
and they want their friends and wives to see what they're seeing. To hear
what they're hearing. Because what these girls are yelling? They are yelling crazy shit! They are yelling "Ho! Ho! Ho Chi Minh!" and stabbing
their fists in the air at each syllable, just completely ignoring all the cars
honking at them, not even moving for oncoming traffic, just daring these
cars to run them down like bowling pins, which the uncles wish they'd
do. The cars. Run the girls down.

Then they look at Frank sheepishly and say *I'm sure Faye's not there*
and Frank nods and everything is real quiet and awkward until one of
the uncles breaks the tension saying *You see what that chick is wearing?*
and they all nod and make various sounds of disgust because it's not like
the uncles think all women should dress like debutantes, but come on.
These girls make those girls who protested outside Miss America look
like Miss America. Because, okay, here's an example: This leader girl that
the cameras keep showing because she's in front of the horde and seems
responsible for the forward-moving progress of the horde, here is what
she's wearing: First? Army jacket, which the uncles agree is so low-down
disrespectful, patriotism-wise, which is point A. Point B is that army
jackets are not form-fitting or flattering for girls because they are made
for a man. And this girl knew she'd be on TV and this is how she wishes
to present herself? In a jacket inappropriate to her gender? Which leads
them to point C, which is that she probably *wants* to be a man, secretly,
on the inside. Which they think, okay, fine, draft the bitch like a man and
send her to Vietnam like a man and let her hump it through the jungle on
point duty watching for trip wires and unexploded ordnance and snipers
and then we'll see how much she's loving on Ho Chi Minh.

Bet she hasn't showered in days, one of the uncles says. How many days?
Six days is where they put the over/under.

The news identifies this leader girl as someone named Alice who, the
news says, is a well-known campus feminist, and the uncles huff and
snort and one of them says *That figures* and they all nod because they
understand exactly what he means by that.

6

THE CONRAD HILTON'S FIRST-FLOOR BAR is called the Haymarket, and this seems historically significant to at least one of the two Secret Service agents sitting at the bar right now nursing his nonalcoholic drink.

"Like, as in, the Haymarket Riot," says Agent A———. "The Haymarket Massacre? Anything?" To which Agent B———, whose chin hangs over the glass of club soda he really wishes had bourbon in it, shakes his head. "Nope," he says. "I got nothin'."

"It was in Chicago? Eighteen eighty something? Workers striking at Haymarket Square? It's pretty historic."

"I thought Haymarket Square was in Boston."

"There's one here too. It's northeast of us, about two clicks."

"What were they striking for?" asks B———.

"An eight-hour workday."

"God, I'd love one of those right about now."

A——— shakes his glass and the bartender fills it. His preferred off-duty drink is this thing involving simple syrup, lemon juice, and rose water. You can't always find rose water in most places, but the Haymarket Bar, it turns out, is well stocked.

"What happened," A——— says, "is that they were demonstrating, the workers were, marching and picketing, and then the police showed up and attacked them, and then a bomb went off."

"Casualties?"

"Several."

"Perp?"

"Unknown."

"And you're bringing this up now because?"

"Because don't you think it's a coincidence? That we're the in the Haymarket Bar? Right now?"

"Riot central," says B———, pointing with his thumb behind them, toward the thousands of protestors currently gathered beyond the plate-glass windows.

"That's what I'm saying."

"A real hedley-medley out there."

Agent A——— looks sidelong at his partner. "A real hugger-mugger, you might say?"

"Yep. Gone all topsy-turvy."

"A sincere higgledy-piggledy."

"Yessir, one hundred percent hurly-burly."

"A pell-mell."

"A ribble-rabble."

"A skimble-skamble."

They smile at each other and suppress a laugh. They clink their drinks. They could do this all day. Outside, the crowd churns and boils.

7

AND WHERE THERE LOOKS to be an oval-shaped cavity in the crowd is actually the spot where dozens are sitting. They're watching Allen Ginsberg or joining him in his *ommmm*ing, his head-bopping, clapping, his face uplifted like he's receiving messages from the gods. To the anxious and terrified crowd, his chanting is barbiturative. In its monotony and resolve and purpose, it is the verbal equivalent of being held tenderly by a nurse who really cares. Those who join him singing *Ommmm* feel better about the world. This is their armor, the spoken sacred Syllable. Nobody would strike someone sitting on the ground singing *Ommmm*. Nobody would gas *them*.

Around Grant Park, this calm, this peace has rippled out to the far borders. Protesters standing there lost in the crowd screaming at the cops and maybe digging up chunks of sidewalk to throw at the Conrad Hilton Hotel in a spasm of loose rage and wildness because *they're just so angry at all of it* when someone touches their shoulder from behind and they turn to find these gentle soothing eyes made tranquil and serene because they themselves were touched by the person behind them, and they in turn by the person behind them, one long chain leading all the way back to Ginsberg, who's powering this whole thing with his chanting's great voltage.

He has enough peace for all of them.

They feel part of his song pour into them, and they feel its beauty, and then they *are* its beauty. They and the song are the same. They and Ginsberg are the same. They and the cops and the politicians are the same. And the snipers on the roofs and the Secret Service agents and the mayor and the newsmen and the happy people inside the Haymarket Bar bopping their heads to music they cannot hear: all of them are one. The same light threads through them all.

And thus a calm comes over the crowd in a slow circle around the poet, moving outward from him like ripples on water, like in that Bashō poem he loves so much: the ancient pond, the still night, a frog jumps in.

Kerplunk.

8

GIRLS STILL MARCHING SOUTH. White girls, black girls, brown girls. Close-ups on their faces now. Chanting, yelling. There are, in the uncles' opinion, three kinds of girls: long horse-faced girls, and wide muffin-faced girls, and bulging bird-faced girls. This girl at the front of this march, this Alice person, has a lot of horse in her, they think. (Ha-ha, *a horse in her,* ha-ha.) Mostly horse, but a bit of the bird too. What they can see of her face, anyway, that part of her not covered by sunglasses or ratty hair. Two parts horse face, one part bird face is where they'd plot her on the 3-D map of girl faces.

Except she is carrying a weapon, which puts her in a whole other category. Girl faces just look different when they're all violent like that.

Actually almost all the girls in the crowd are carrying weapons: two-by-fours, some with these evil-looking rusty nails sticking out of the swinging end; and rocks and chunks of pavement; and iron bars and bricks; and bags with unknown contents, but their guess? Shit and piss, plus menstrual blood. *Gross.* The TV says there's rumors of radicals buying huge amounts of oven cleaner and ammonia, which sounds like bomb-making material even if the uncles are not a hundred percent sure of the chemistry of this. But if anyone would be carrying oven-cleaner explosives it would be one of these girls because, they figure, girls have routine access to such things.

CBS has cut away from old Cronkite for a moment and is just showing all this live and unedited. And most people tune in to CBS to hear old Cronkite deliver his assessment about things, but the uncles' opinion about it? About not seeing Cronkite right now? They think *good*. The guy's gotten a little soft lately, a little lefty too, and arrogant, all these puffed-up pronouncements from the top of Mount Journalism or something. They prefer their news from the source, undiluted.

Case in point: girls walking south in the middle of the street. This is action. This is news untouched. Especially now as a cop car rolls up and instead of dispersing like they ought to the girls actually attack the cop car! Jabbing at the siren with baseball bats! Breaking the windows with rocks! And the poor cop leaps out the other side of the car and holy cow is that boy running! And even though it's only girls he's running from there's like a hundred of them and they mean business. Then the girls all gather on the car and it looks like a bunch of ants surrounding a beetle ready to devour it. And the leader horse-faced girl yells *Heave-ho!* and they actually tip over the police car! It's the most amazing thing the uncles have ever seen! And the girls all cheer at their job well done and then continue marching and chanting and the cop car's siren is still blowing but instead of at full volume it's like a demoralized and sad siren sound. It moans and whines in this low, pitiful way. It sounds like an electronic toy whose batteries are just about dead.

And now girls are yelling after the cop, yelling "Here piggy piggy! Oink, oink! Soo-ee!" And this is about the best thing the uncles have seen on television in a month.

9

THE CONRAD HILTON HOTEL is nowhere near the convention. The Democratic National Convention will happen at the International Amphitheater, down on the grounds of the Union Stock Yards, about five miles south of here. But the amphitheater is completely inaccessible: A barbed-wire fence surrounds it; National Guard troops patrol the grounds; every manhole cover has been tarred shut; roadblocks at every intersection; even airplanes are banned from flying over it. Once the delegates are inside the amphitheater, there would be no reaching them. Hence the protest at the Hilton, where all the delegates are staying.

Plus there's the matter of the smell.

It's all Hubert Humphrey can think about. His staff is right now trying to tell him how the peace-plank debate will go, but it's like every time he turns his head he can smell it again.

Whose idea was it anyway to hold a convention next to a slaughterhouse?

He could sense them, smell them, hear them, the poor animals huddled and dying hundreds per hour to feed a prosperous nation. Trucked in as infants, trucked out as parts. He could smell the hogs insane with fear, the hogs hanging from hooks, their stomachs opened in cascades of blood and pig barf. The smell of bright raw ammonia used to clean the addled floors. Creatures in their death-fear releasing cries and stink glands, a terror both audible and olfactible. The chemical breath of a million aborted animal screams, aromatized and blooming into the atmosphere, a sour, meaty vapor.

The perfume of slaughter is at once nauseating and fascinating. The way the body is tuned to another body's loss.

A pile of manure that rose even above the barbed-wire fences, *fifteen feet tall,* dropped tepee-shaped in a fit of copromania, sitting raw in the sun and cooking. Like some kind of ancient evil bubbling up out of the Pleistocene. An organic mud that tanged the air and locked itself in fabric and hair.

"What kind of abomination is that?" Triple H asked, pointing at the shit cone. His security men laughed. They were the sons of farmers; he was the son of a pharmacist. His only encounter with this kind of biology came after it was processed and pulverized. He wanted to stuff his nose in his own armpit. The smell was more like a weight than a gas. It felt like the whole moral rot of the world taking shape and form right here, in Chicago.

"Somebody light a match!" said one of the agents.

The smell is on him still. The maid says the washroom is ready. *Thank god.* At this point a shower is more analgesic than anything else.

10

FAYE IS IN JAIL roughly nine hours before the ghost appears.

She is kneeling, hands clasped, facing the far wall where shadows flicker by, and she asks God for help. Says she'll do anything, anything at all. Please, she says, rocking, whatever you want. And she does this until she feels dizzy and she begs her body to let her sleep, but when she closes her eyes she feels like one big long plucked guitar string, all shaky and furious. And so it's during this in-between state of being too exhausted to stay awake but too agitated to fall asleep that the ghost appears to her. She opens her eyes and senses a presence nearby and looks around and sees, on the far wall, illuminated by the window's dull blue light, this *creature*.

He looks like, maybe, a gnome. Or a small troll. Actually he looks exactly like the figurine of a house spirit her father gave her so many years ago. The *nisse*. He is small and round, maybe three feet tall, hairy, white-bearded, fat, caveman-faced. He leans against the wall with his arms crossed and his legs crossed and his eyebrows raised, looking at Faye skeptically, as if he doesn't believe in her existence rather than the other way around.

She might have otherwise panicked at this sight, but her body is so tired.

I'm dreaming, she says.

So wake up, the house spirit says.

She tries to wake up. She knows the thing that usually pulls her out of dreaming is the realization that she's dreaming, which has always frustrated her; dreams, she thinks, are best when you know they're dreams. Then you can act without consequence. It's the only time in her life that is worry-free.

Well? the ghost says.

You're not real, she says, even though she has to admit this does not feel like a dream.

The house spirit shrugs.

You spend all night praying for help and when help finally arrives, you insult it. That is so typical of you, Faye.

I'm hallucinating, she says. Because of those pills.

Look, if I'm not wanted here, if you've got this situation under control, then best of luck to you. There are plenty of people out there who would appreciate my help. He points a stubby finger toward the window, the outside world. *Listen to them,* he says, and just then the big basement room is crashing with sound, the discordant and overlapping voices of people pleading for help, asking for protection, voices young and old, male and female, as if the room were suddenly a radio tower picking up every frequency on the dial all at once, and Faye can hear students asking for protection from the cops, and cops asking for protection from the students, and priests asking for peace, and presidential candidates asking for strength, and snipers hoping they won't have to pull the trigger, and National Guardsmen staring obliquely at their bayonets asking for courage, and people everywhere offering whatever they can in return for safety: promises that they'll start going to church more, that they'll be better people, that they'll call their parents or children soon, they'll write more letters, give to charity, be kind to strangers, stop doing whatever bad things they are currently doing, quit smoking, quit drinking, be a better husband or wife, a whole symphony of kindnesses that might result if they are simply spared on this one ugly day.

Then, just as quickly, the voices turn off, and the basement is silent again, the last noise to fade being the low deep thrum of someone chanting: *Ommmm.*

Faye stands and looks at the house spirit, who is himself looking innocently at his own fingernails.

Do you know who I am? he says.

You're my family's house spirit. Our *nisse.*

That's one word for it.

What's another word?

He looks at her, his eyes black and sinister. *All those stories your father told you about ghosts that look like rocks or horses or leaves? Yeah, that's me. I am the nisse, I am the nix, not to mention various other spirits, creatures, demons, angels, trolls, et cetera.*

I don't understand.

No, you wouldn't, he says, and he yawns. *You guys haven't figured it out yet. Your map is just way off.*

11

NOW THE GIRLS HAVE SWITCHED from "Ho! Ho! Ho Chi Minh!" to "Kill the pigs! Kill the pigs!" and the uncles are *glued* to the television because the girls are full of confidence after their cop-car-tipping success and obviously feel indestructible right now because they taunt the various cops they see along their slow march south yelling "Hey piggy!" and "Soo-ee!" and stuff like that. And the reason this is unswitchoffable television and why the uncles keep yelling *Honey c'mere you've got to see this* and why they are considering calling all their buddies to make sure they're watching too is because the police? And the National Guard? *They're waiting for the bitches a couple blocks away.* It's like a trap. They're to the west of the girls' route waiting to flank them and drive into them and split open their wedge (ha-ha) and the girls have no idea this is about to happen.

The uncles know this because of chopper cam.

And right now they are just about as grateful to chopper cam as they are to their mother on their birthdays. And they wish there were some way they could record for all time what is about to happen and watch the chopper-cam footage over and over and maybe put it in a scrapbook or time capsule or shoot it into space on the back of a satellite to show the Martians or whoever the hell else is out there some pretty goddamn entertaining TV. And the Martians? The first thing they'll say when they land their flying saucers on the White House lawn? They'll say, *Those girls had it coming.*

About a hundred cops in riot gear wait for the girls, and behind them a platoon of National Guardsmen in gas masks, holding rifles with fucking daggers attached to the barrels, and behind them this monstrous metal thing with nozzles on the front like some kind of terrible Zamboni from the future that the TV folks tell them the purpose of, which is gas. Tear gas. A thousand gallons.

And they're waiting behind a building for the girls to come to them, and the uncles feel really present and edgy and almost like they're with the cops or something, and they think that this moment—even though the uncles are hundreds of miles away from it and all they're really doing is sitting on a couch watching an electronic box while their food goes cold—might be the best thing that has ever happened to them.

Because this right here is the future of television: *pure combative sensation*. Old Cronkite's problem is he's treating television like it's a newspaper, with all of print's worn-out obligations.

Chopper cam provides a new way forward.

Faster, immediate, richly ambiguous—no gatekeepers between the event and the perception of the event. The news and the uncles' opinion about the news are flattened into a simultaneous happening.

But the police are on the move now. Nightsticks out, riot helmets down, and running, *sprinting,* and when the girls understand what is about to happen their big march breaks apart, like a rock exploded by gunshot, pieces of it flying off in every direction. Some girls head back from the direction they came, only to be cut off by a paddy wagon and a squadron of cops who anticipated this very move. Others hop the barrier between northbound and southbound traffic and hightail it toward the lake. For most of the girls, the crowd is so thick there's nowhere to run. And so they trip over each other and fall and flail like a litter of blind puppies, and these are the ones the police reach first, bringing down their nightsticks on the girls' legs, the meat of their thighs, their backbones. The cops drop these bitches like they're mowing tall grass—a quick thrust and the girls bend and fall. From above, this looks like those slides from high-school biology textbooks of the immune system wiping out a foreign agent, surrounding it and neutralizing it in blood. The cops pour into the crowd and everyone gets mixed up together. The uncles see the girls' mouths moving and they wish they could hear the screams above the rotary noise of the chopper. The cops drag the girls to a paddy wagon mostly by their arms, some by their hair, some by their clothes, which gets the uncles momentarily jazzed up because maybe their hippie dresses will rip and they'll catch a little skin. Some of these girls are bleeding rivers from their heads. Or dazed, sitting on the road crying, or passed out on the curb.

Chopper cam looks around for that leader girl, Alice, but she took off south, toward Grant Park, to join with the rest of the hippies down by the Conrad Hilton, presumably. Which is too bad. That would have been fun to watch. The National Guard hasn't even gotten involved yet. They're watching and clutching their rifles and looking deadly as hell. The giant tear-gas machine, incidentally, is rumbling slowly south, toward the gathered masses at the park. The girls have for the most part dispersed entirely. A few run away on the lakefront beach, tearing ass across the sand in front of all these stunned families and lifeguards. Chopper cam is now heading south to cover whatever's going on in the park, and that's when goddamn CBS cuts back to old Cronkite, who looks all shaken and pale and has clearly been watching the same footage the uncles have been watching but has come to a radically different conclusion.

"The Chicago police," he says, "are a bunch of thugs."

Well fiddledeedee! How about that for bias? One of the uncles leaps out of his chair and places a long-distance call to CBS headquarters and he doesn't even mind how much this is costing him because any amount would be worth it to give old Cronkite a piece of his mind.

12

OFFICER CHARLIE BROWN, badgeless, anonymous, is sweeping the crowd for Alice, knowing Alice will be here, in this particular all-girl march, and he's swinging his nightstick and feeling, right now, as he connects with another hippie forehead, like Ernie Banks.

Like Ernie Banks the instant after he hits another home run ball, and there's that tiny interval before the crowd cheers, and before he trots the bases, before he even leaves the batter's box, before anyone can locate the ball in the air and extrapolate its path and understand that it will clear Wrigley's ivy, there must be this moment when the only person in the park who knows it's a home run is Ernie Banks himself. Even before he looks up to watch it fly away, there must be a moment when his head is still down looking at the point in space where the baseball was a heartbeat ago, and the only information he has is the information that travels up the bat and into his hands, a percussion that feels *just right*. As if the ball has offered him no resistance whatsoever, so purely did he strike its exact middle with his bat's exact middle. And before anything else happens there's this moment where it's like he has this secret he's dying to tell everyone else. He's just hit a home run! But nobody else knows it yet.

Brown is thinking about this as he clunks hippies on the head with his nightstick. He's pretending he's Ernie Banks.

Because it's hard to get a square, solid hit every time. It's a real challenge of athleticism and coordination. Brown figures three out of every four swings ends up a glancing blow, his nightstick vibrating complainingly. The hippies squirm. They cannot be trusted to stay still for a beating. They are unpredictable. They try to protect themselves with their hands and arms. They twirl away at the last second.

Roughly three out of four swings are these, he guesses. Misses. He's batting .250. Not as good as Ernie but still respectable.

But sometimes things line up. He anticipates the hippie's movements perfectly: the feel of the stick in his hand, the moist sound of the hippie's head, that hollow watermelon-thumping sound, and that moment where the hippie suddenly doesn't know where she is or what's happening to her, when she literally *does not know what just hit her* as her brain is up there sloshing around, and soon the hippie will tip over like a rootless tree, topple down and vomit and pass out, and Brown knows this will happen soon but it has not happened yet, and he wishes he could live inside this moment forever. He wants this moment captured in a postcard or snow globe: the hippie about to fall, the triumphant cop above her, his nightstick having clunked the hippie and then kept going in its arc of perfect swinging technique, and the look on his face would be like Ernie Banks after crushing another one to dead center: that giddy and gratifying pleasure of a job well done.

13

FAYE IS EXHAUSTED. She hasn't slept in more than a day. She's leaning against the wall with her back to the room and trying to keep it all together and she's just about crying from the effort.

Help me, she says.

The house spirit sits on the floor outside her metal cage. He picks at his teeth with a fingernail.

I could help you, he says. *I could make all this go away. If I felt like it.*

Please, Faye says.

Okay. Make me a deal. Make it worth my time. Entertain me.

So Faye promises to be a better person, to help the needy and go to church, but the house spirit only smiles.

What do I care about the needy? he says. *What do I care about church?*

I'll give money to charity, Faye says. I'll volunteer and give money to the poor.

Pbbth, the house spirit says, spit flecking off his lips. *You're gonna have to do better than that. Gonna have to leave some skin on the table.*

I'll go back home, Faye says. Go to junior college for a couple years and come back to Chicago after all this blows over.

A couple years at JuCo? That's it? Seriously, Faye, that's not nearly enough penance for how badly you've acted.

But what have I done?

Irrelevant. But if you'd like to know? Disobeyed your parents. Felt pride. Coveted. Thought impure thoughts. Plus, weren't you planning on having out-of-wedlock relations last evening?

Faye hangs her head, says yes, because there is no use lying.

Yes, the answer is yes. Plus you're high. Right now you are high. Plus you shared a bed with another woman. Do I have to keep going? Do you want to hear more? Do I even need to mention what you did with Henry on the riverbank?

I give up, she says.

The house spirit rubs his chin with a fat hand.

I should forget about this whole thing, she says. Go home and marry Henry.

The house spirit raises an eyebrow. *Go on.*

I'll marry Henry and make him happy and forget about college and we'll be normal, like everyone wants.

The ghost smiles, his teeth ragged and broken, a mouthful of stones.

Go on, he says.

14

NOW OLD CRONKITE is interviewing the mayor, the fatly jowled and thuggish dictator of Chicago. Cronkite is asking him questions live on the air but really the journalist's mind is elsewhere. He's barely paying attention. It doesn't matter. The mayor is as professional as they come. He doesn't need a journalist's questions to hold forth on whatever he wants to talk about, which is currently the extraordinary threats to the police and to ordinary Americans and to *our democracy itself* posed by outside agitators, the out-of-town radicals causing trouble in his law-abiding town. He really seems to want to stress the "out-of-town" stuff. Probably to emphasize to hometown voters that whatever problems his city is currently having are not his fault.

And anyway, even if old Cronkite were concentrating real hard and asking penetrating, difficult questions, the mayor would just perform that politician's maneuver where he doesn't answer the question you asked but instead the question he wished you had asked. And if you pursue this too much and insist that he did not answer the question, then you're the one who looks like a jerk. At least that's how it plays on TV. Badgering this very charismatic fellow who's been saying lots of words that at least seem *related* to the question. This is how it seems to the viewers anyway, who are splitting their attention between Cronkite and children running around and cutting the Salisbury steak at the center of their TV dinners. If you keep pestering the politician, you look like a pest, and America does not tune in to watch pests. It's a chilling thought, that politicians have learned to manipulate the television medium better than the television professionals themselves. When old Cronkite first realized this was happening he imagined the kinds of people who would become politicians in the future. And he shuddered with fear.

So he's ostensibly interviewing the mayor but he knows that his only real job here is to stick a microphone under his mouth so CBS News can seem balanced by providing a counter-narrative to the images of police brutality they've been showing for hours. So old Cronkite isn't really listening. He's watching, maybe. The way the mayor seems to hold his head as far back on his neck as possible, in the manner of someone avoiding a bad smell, and how this makes the part of his chin that on a rooster would be called a wattle press out and jiggle while he speaks. It is impossible not to stare at this.

So a bit of old Cronkite's mind is following this, watching the mayor's Jell-O face wriggle. But mostly he's thinking about something else: He's thinking about, of all things, flying. He imagines he's a bird. Flying over the city. At a height so great that everything is dark and quiet. This is occupying roughly three-quarters of Walter Cronkite's mind right now. He's a bird. He's a nimble flying bird.

15

FAYE IS IN HER DARK BASEMENT CELL cringing in anticipation of another panic attack because the house spirit's hot breath is right up next to her and he's holding the chain-link fence and pressing his face against it and his black eyeballs are bugging out and he's telling her exactly what he's going to need from her, which is vengeance and retribution.

But retribution for what?

She wishes more than anything that her mother were here to stroke her forehead with a cold washcloth and tell her she's not dying and hold her till she slept, and Faye would wake up in the morning blanketed and warm, her mother beside her having fallen asleep sometime in the night while watching over her.

Faye could use that tenderness right now.

Yes, but where was your father when you needed him, the ghost says. *Where is he now?*

Faye doesn't understand.

Your father is a terrible, evil man. You must know this.

Yes, I suppose. He kicked me out of the house.

Oh, it's all about you, eh? Jeez, Faye. Selfish?

Okay, then he's evil why? Because he works at ChemStar?

C'mon. You know what I'm talking about.

Faye's impression of her father is that of a mournful silence. Sometimes staring off into the distance. A man who keeps everything locked up within. Always some slight melancholy, unless he was telling her stories of the old country, stories about his family's farm, the only subject at which he seemed to brighten.

Faye says: He did something back home, didn't he? Before he came to the U.S.

Bingo, the ghost says. *And now he's being punished for it, and you're being punished for it. And your family will continue to be punished for it, to the third and fourth generation. Those are the rules.*

That's not very fair.

Hah! Fair? What's fair? How the universe works and your sense of fairness are very different things.

He's an unhappy man, Faye says. Whatever he did, he's sorry for it.

Is it my fault that just about everyone on earth by now is paying for some evil committed by a previous generation? No. The answer is no. It is not my fault.

Faye often wondered what passed before her father's eyes when he stared into the distance, when he stood in the backyard looking into the sky for an hour. He was always so maddeningly vague about his life before America. All he'd talk about was that house, that beautiful salmon-red house in Hammerfest. All other details were forbidden.

Alice told me something, Faye says. She told me the way to get rid of a ghost is to take it home.

The house spirit crossed his arms. *That would be rich,* he said. *I would love to see that.*

Maybe I should go to Norway. Take you back where you came from.

Oh I dare you. I double dare you! That would be seriously entertaining. Go on. Go to Hammerfest and ask about Frank Andresen. See how well that works for you.

Why? What would I find?

Probably better if you didn't know.

Tell me.

I'm just saying, there are some mysteries of the universe that ought to remain mysteries.

Please.

Fine. Fair warning? You won't like it.

I'm listening.

You will find that you are as awful as your father is.

That's not true.

You will find that you two are exactly alike.

We are not.

Go ahead. Try it. Go back to Norway. You've got yourself a deal. I'll let you out of jail right now. And in exchange? You go find out about your dad. Have fun with that.

And just then the door to the room pops open, and light from buzzing overhead fluorescent lamps spills in, and there appears, in the doorway, remarkably, Sebastian. With his bushy hair and baggy jacket. He sees her and comes to her. He has the keys to her cell. He opens the door and crouches down and takes her in his arms and whispers into her ear: "I'm getting you out of here. Let's go."

16

BY NOW THE MAYOR is practically lecturing at poor old Cronkite, who looks dispirited and withered and sad. There have been threats, is what the mayor's saying. Assassination attempts against all of the candidates, bomb threats, even threats against himself, the mayor. Old Cronkite doesn't seem to be looking at him but at a spot just past him.

"That true?" asks Agent B———. "About the threats?"

"Not true," says Agent A———. "Nothing credible."

They're watching in the Haymarket, on the television above the bar. The mayor is holding old Cronkite's microphone for him and might as well be interviewing himself. He says, "Certain people planned to assassinate many of the leaders, including myself, and with all of these talks of assassination and it happening in our city I didn't want what happened in Dallas or what happened in California to happen in Chicago."

The Secret Service agents feel bristly at him bringing up the Kennedys like that. They take small, measured sips from their mocktails.

"He's lying," says Agent A———. "Nobody's trying to assassinate him."

"Yeah, but what's old Cronkite gonna do? Call him a liar on live TV?"

"Old Cronkite doesn't seem to have his heart in this one."

"Checked out, passion-wise."

Quick break from the mayor's interview to a shot of Michigan Avenue to show what appears to be a real full-size military tank rolling down the street. On television, it looks like something out of World War II footage, like the liberation of Paris. The tank is rolling right in front of the Hilton, and they begin to feel its rumble in their bellies, and the assembled politicos in the Haymarket Bar gather close to the plate-glass windows to watch it rattle hugely by—all save for the two Secret Service agents at the bar, who are not surprised by the fact of the tank (it had been mentioned in the many "eyes only" memos leading up to the event) and anyway the Secret Service always maintain in public an air of unflappability and total discipline and composure, and so they watch the tank roll by on TV, unimpressed.

17

FAYE HAS BEEN PRAYING all night for a rescue, but now that a rescuer has come she hears herself telling him no.

"What do you mean no?" Sebastian says. He's crouching on the floor with his hands holding her shoulders like at any minute he's going to shake some sense into her.

"I don't want to go."

"What are you talking about?"

"Never mind," she says. Her brain feels fuzzy and swollen. She tries to remember what the house spirit had told her, but already it's fading. She can remember the sensation of talking to the ghost, but she can no longer remember what he sounds like.

She looks at Sebastian, at his worried face. She remembers they were supposed to have a date last night.

"I'm sorry I stood you up," she says, and Sebastian laughs.

"Another time," he says.

The clenching in her chest is releasing, her shoulders loosening, the bile in her stomach seeping away. It's as if her whole body is a spring after it's sprung. She's relaxing—this is what it feels like to relax.

"What was I doing when you came in?" she says.

"I don't know. Nothing."

"Was I talking to someone? Who was I talking to?"

"Faye," he says, putting his palm gently on her cheek. "You were sleeping."

18

ERNIE BANKS PROBABLY FEELS SOMETHING ELSE, too, whenever he hits a home run. Along with the sense of professional mastery, there's probably this other, uglier feeling—what would you call it? Payback? Retaliation? Because isn't one reason men are moved to greatness partly the need to respond in a grand way to the people who cut them most deeply? For Ernie Banks, it was the older and bigger boys who said he was too skinny. Or the white boys who wouldn't let him play. The girls who left him for smarter guys, bigger guys, guys with more money. Or the parents who told him to do something better with his life. The teachers who said he wouldn't amount to nothing. The beat cops who were leery of him. And because Ernie couldn't defend himself then, he defends himself now: Each home run is his retort, each sprinting impossible center-field catch part of his ongoing vindication. When he swings his bat and feels that delicious *thwack,* he must feel a powerful sense of professional satisfaction, yes, but he must also think: *I proved you fuckers wrong again.*

So that's an essential part of it, too. That's what's going on in Officer Brown's head right now. This is, in some ways, a reprisal. This is righteous.

And he thinks of those nights with Alice, those encounters in the backseat of his police cruiser, and how she wanted him to be violent with her, to shove her around and choke her and grab her roughly and leave marks. And how he felt bashful about it, demure, shy. He didn't want to do it. Felt himself incapable of it, actually. Felt like it required a different kind of man altogether: someone unthinking and brutal.

And yet here he is now, clunking hippies on the head. It turns out he had deep reserves of brutality that were, up till now, unprospected.

In a way, this makes him happy. He's a fuller and more complicated man than he thought he was. He imagines himself in dialogue with Alice right now. *Didn't think I could do it, did you?* he says as he clobbers another hippie. *You said you wanted me to be rough, well, here you go.*

And he imagines that for Ernie Banks the best home run is the one when the girls who broke his heart are in the stands to see it. Brown imagines Alice is here watching him, right now, somewhere in the fray, observing his new vitality and strength and brute masculine dominance. She's impressed. Or she will be, as soon as she sees him and sees that he's changed, that he's exactly what she needs him to be now: Of course she'd take him back.

He clunks a hippie on the jaw, hears that pregnant crunching sound, and there's screaming all around him and hippies running terrified and one of the other cops grabs Brown by the shoulder and says "Hey buddy, settle down a little" and Officer Brown sees that his own hands are trembling. They're quaking, actually, and he waves them in the air like they're wet. He feels ashamed of this and hopes that if Alice is indeed watching him right now she did not see that.

He thinks: *I am Ernie Banks rounding the bases—the very picture of calm, serene delight.*

19

IT IS REMARKABLE how quickly extraordinary things turn ordinary. By now the patrons of the Haymarket Bar do not even flinch when some thrown projectile strikes the plate-glass windows. Stones, chunks of concrete, even billiard balls—all have made their way through the air, over the heads of the assembled police line, and whacked against the windows of the bar. People inside have stopped noting them. Or if they do note them, they do so condescendingly: "The Cubs could use an arm like that."

The cops are generally good at holding the line, but occasionally a wedge of protestors breaks through and a couple of kids get beaten up right in front of the Haymarket windows and dragged to a paddy wagon. This has now happened so many times that the folks in the bar have completely stopped watching it. They ignore it in that strained way they walk by homeless men on the street.

On the television, the mayor is back with old Cronkite and the latter appears as penitent as ever.

"I can tell you this," the journalist says, "you have a lot of supporters

around the country." And the mayor nods like a Roman emperor ordering an execution.

"It's your basic jingoistic sucking up," says Agent A———. "Your basic
dezinformatsiya."

Outside, a police officer strikes a bearded man wearing the Vietcong
flag as a cape, strikes him with his rifle butt right in the middle of the
cape, sending the guy sprawling forward like he's diving into home plate,
face-first into the Haymarket's thick leaded windows with a dull crunch
that is eaten up in the bar by Jimmy Dorsey's sweet, sweet saxophone.

Old Cronkite is saying, "I have to compliment you, Mr. Mayor, on the
genuine *friendliness* of the Chicago Police Department."

Two cops descend on the bearded man at the window and clunk him
on the head.

"That is the look of someone who's given up," says Agent A———,
pointing at old Cronkite.

"Put him out of his misery, please," says Agent B———, nodding.

"You want to see what a fighter looks like when he knows he's lost?
There it is."

The bearded man outside, meanwhile, is dragged away, leaving a
smear of blood and grease on the window.

20

SAY A SEAGULL, old Cronkite thinks. He recently took in a game at
Wrigley and saw how, in the ninth inning, the seagull masses were drawn
from the lake to the stadium. The birds were there to clean up the pop-
corn and peanut scraps left under the seats. Cronkite was amazed at their
timing. How did they know it was the ninth inning?

If you saw the city from this view, seagull-view, way up high, what
would it look like? It would be quiet and peaceful. Families in their
homes, the blue-gray color of televisions flickering, a single golden light
in the kitchen, sidewalks empty but for the occasional stray cat, whole
motionless blocks, and he imagines soaring over it and noting that every-

where in Chicago that is not the few acres surrounding the Conrad Hilton Hotel is the most peaceful place in the world right now. And maybe *that* is the story. Not that thousands are protesting but that millions are not. Maybe to achieve the balance CBS is looking for they should take a crew to the northern Polish neighborhoods and western Greek neighborhoods and southern black neighborhoods and film *nothing happening*. To show how this protest is a pinprick of light in a much larger and gathering darkness.

Would this make sense to the TV audience? That a thing like a protest expands and draws everything into it. He wants to tell his audience that the reality they are seeing on television is not Reality. Imagine a single drop of water: that's the protest. Now put that drop of water into a bucket: that's the protest movement. Now drop that bucket into Lake Michigan: that's Reality. But old Cronkite knows the danger of television is that people begin seeing the entire world through that single drop of water. How that one drop refracts the light becomes the whole picture. For many people, whatever they see tonight will cement in place everything they think about protest and peace and the sixties. And he feels, pressingly, that it's his job to prevent this closure.

But how to say it right?

21

SEBASTIAN LEADS HER by the hand out of the small makeshift jail and into a completely gray and anonymous cinder-block hallway. A police officer hurries out of a room and Faye jerks back at the sight of him.

"It's okay," says Sebastian. "Come on."

The cop walks right by, nodding as he goes. They pass through a set of double doors at the end of the hall and into a space decorated lavishly: plush red carpet, wall sconces emitting a golden glow, white walls with ornate trim that suggests French aristocracy. Faye sees a sign on one of the doors and understands that they're in the basement of the Conrad Hilton Hotel.

"How did you know I was arrested?" she says.

He turns to her and flashes a rascally smile. "Grapevine."

He takes her through the belly of the hotel, passing police and reporters and hotel staff, all of them hustling to somewhere, all of them looking grim and serious. They reach a set of thick metal exterior doors guarded by two more cops, who nod at Sebastian and allow him to pass. And in this way they are delivered into a loading dock, and then into the alleyway, into the open air. The sound of the protest reaches them here as an indistinct howl that seems to be coming from all directions at once.

"Listen," Sebastian says, cocking his ear to the sky. "Everybody's here."

"How did you do that?" Faye says. "We walked right by those cops. Why didn't they say something? Why didn't they stop us?"

"You have to promise me," he says, grabbing her by the arms, "you'll never mention this. Not to anyone."

"Tell me how you did it."

"Promise, Faye. You cannot breathe a word about it. Tell them I bailed you out. That's it."

"But you didn't bail me out. You had a key. How did you have a key?"

"Not a word. I'm trusting you. I did you a favor, and now your favor back to me is to keep this a secret. Okay?"

Faye considers him for a moment, and understands that he is not the single-entendre student radical she had taken him for—he has mysteries; he has layers. She knows something about him no one else does, has power over him no one else can wield. Her heart swells for him: He's a kindred spirit, she thinks, someone else whose life is hidden and vast.

She nods.

Sebastian smiles and takes her hand and leads her to the end of the alley and into the sun, and as they round the corner she sees the police and the military and the blockade and beyond the blockade, the great teeming mass in the park. No longer shadows on the wall, she sees them now in detail and color: the soft baby-blue police uniforms; the bayonets of the National Guardsmen; the jeeps whose front bumpers are coils of razor wire; the crowd moving as a surging beast presently surrounding and taking over the statue of Ulysses S. Grant opposite the Conrad Hilton, the ten-foot-tall Grant on his ten-foot-tall horse, the crowd climbing up the horse's bronze legs and onto its neck and rump and head, one brave youth continuing up, climbing Grant himself, standing atop Grant's huge broad shoulders, teetering but erect, raising his arms in double peace signs above his head in defiance of the police who are right now noticing this and are ambling over to pull him down. This will not end well for him, but the audience cheers anyway, for he is the bravest among them, the tallest thing in the whole park.

Faye and Sebastian slip by the mayhem and into the anonymity of the crowd.

22

OFFICER BROWN CONTINUES to bust heads and around him the cops have removed their badges and name tags. They have pulled the visors of their riot helmets over their faces. They are anonymous. The news is not happy about this development.

Police are beating people with impunity, the journalists say on CBS News. They demand transparency. Accountability. They say the police have removed their badges and hidden their faces because they know what they're doing is illegal. Comparisons are made to the Soviets rolling into Prague earlier this year, running down and overwhelming the poor Czechs. The Chicago PD is acting like that, the journalists say. It's Czechoslovakia west. *Czechago* is a word it does not take long for someone clever to make up.

"In America, the government is accountable to the people, not the other way around," says a constitutional law scholar sympathetic to the antiwar movement on the subject of the anonymous police.

Officer Brown is whaling away, the most excited among all the cops to really clunk the hippies in vital and deadly places: the skull, the chest, even the face. He was the first to appear minus a badge or a name tag, and all the officers around him have lowered their visors and removed their name tags too, but not because they want to join him in his frenzy. Rather the opposite. They see he's going a little nuts now and they can't really stop him and the cameras are clicking away, attracted as they are to any moment of police brutality, and so all the nearby officers tuck away their badges and lower their visors because this fucker is asking to lose his pension, but they sure as shit won't lose theirs.

23

CRONKITE KNOWS this is his punishment for editorializing. Doing this interview with the mayor and serving up these cream-puff questions. It's because Cronkite called the Chicago police "a bunch of thugs," and he did it live, on the air.

Well, that's what they are! And that's what he told his producers, who said he'd made a *judgment,* which was wrong, since it was up to the viewers to decide whether the police were or were not thugs. He countered that he'd made an *observation,* which is what they paid him for: to observe and report. They said he'd expressed an opinion. He said sometimes an observation is inseparable from an opinion.

This was not convincing to his producers.

But the police were out there cracking open skulls with nightsticks. They were taking off their badges and name tags and lowering the visors on their riot helmets to become faceless and unaccountable. They were beating kids senseless. They were beating members of the press, photographers and reporters, breaking cameras and taking film. They even punched poor Dan Rather right in the solar plexus. What do you call people like that? You call them thugs.

His producers still were not convinced. Cronkite thought the police were beating innocent people. The mayor's office told them the police were *protecting* innocent people. Who was right? It reminded him of that old story: A king once asked a group of blind men to describe an elephant. To one of them, he presented the head of the elephant, to another he presented an ear, a tusk, the trunk, the tail, and so on, saying, *This is an elephant.*

Afterward, the blind men could not agree on what an elephant really looked like. They argued with each other, saying, *An elephant is like this, an elephant is not like that!* They fought each other with their fists, and the king watched the whole spectacle, and was delighted.

Probably as delighted as the mayor is right now, old Cronkite imagines as he lobs him another softball question about the well-trained and heroic and completely supported by the public Chicago PD. And the gleam in the mayor's eye is just about the most insufferable thing old Cronkite has ever seen, that sparkle the mayor gets when he's beaten a worthy opponent. And Cronkite is a worthy opponent indeed. One imagines there were lengthy phone calls between the mayor's office and the CBS producers, much debating, many threats, some kind of compromise was reached, and thus old Cronkite stands here extolling the virtues of men he called thugs not three hours ago.

You gotta eat a lot of shit in this job sometimes.

24

NEAR THE END of the day, just before sunset, there's a lull in the trauma. Police hang back sort of stunned and shamefaced. They have stopped raising their nightsticks and raise their bullhorns instead. They ask the protesters to please leave the park. The protestors watch them and wait. The city has the feeling of an injured child. A toddler will knock its head and, after a slight delay during which all the chaotic sense-signals resolve into pain, it begins to wail. The city is inside that delay now, between injury and lamentation, between cause and effect.

The hope is that the lull will persist. This is Allen Ginsberg's hope, anyway, that once the city gets a taste of this peace it won't want to fight again. Grant Park is calm now and he's stopped his chanting and *ommmm*ing long enough to move about the beautiful crowd. In his bag he always carries two things: *The Tibetan Book of the Dead* and a silver Kodak Retina Reflex camera. It's the Kodak he reaches for right now, the thing he's used to document all the luminous moments of his life, and this moment is luminous indeed. The gathered protestors all sitting and laughing and singing songs of joy and waving homemade flags with their cleverest slogans hand-painted on them. He wants to make a poem out of it all. His Kodak is a worn-out secondhand thing, but it's sturdy, its guts still sound. He loves its metal girth in his hand, the black grips rippled like alligator skin, the mechanical gear-noises as he advances the film, even the Made in Germany sticker stamped so confidently on the front. He snaps a photo of the gathered crowd. He walks among them, their bodies parting for him, their faces open to his. And when he sees a familiar face he stops and kneels: one of the student leaders, he remembers. The olive-skinned pretty one. He's sitting with a pleasant young girl with big round glasses who rests her head on his shoulder, exhausted.

Faye and Sebastian. They lean against each other like lovers. Alice sits behind them. Ginsberg raises his camera to his eye.

The young man gives him a wry, sidelong smile that just about breaks his heart. The shutter clicks. Ginsberg stands and smiles sadly. He moves on, swallowed by the vast crowd, the incandescent day.

25

THE POET WALKS AWAY and Alice taps Faye on the shoulder and winks at her and says, "So did you two have a good time last night?"

Because of course Alice doesn't know what happened.

And so Faye explains to her about the mysterious cop who arrested her and the night she spent in jail, how Faye doesn't even know the cop's name or what she did to deserve all that, how the cop told her to vacate Chicago immediately, and Alice is stricken because she knows right away it's Officer Brown. Of course it's him.

But she can't tell Faye. Not right now. How could she possibly admit in the middle of this crowd of protestors throwing angry insults at the police that she'd been having a pretty passionate love affair with one of these very cops? There's no way.

Alice hugs Faye tightly. "I'm sorry," she says. "But don't worry. Everything will be all right. You aren't going anywhere. I'll stick by you, no matter what."

And that's when the police gather on the edges of the park and announce via bullhorns: *You have ten minutes to clear this area.*

Which is a laughable request, because there's like ten thousand people here.

"Do they really expect us all to leave?" Alice asks.

"Probably not," Sebastian says.

"What are they gonna do?" Faye says, looking around at the great stubborn mass of humanity occupying the park. "Move us all by force?"

Turns out, this is exactly what they're going to do.

It begins with a soft pop of compressed air, a gentle-sounding and almost musical burst as a canister of tear gas is launched into the park. And for those who watch it come, there's a strange delay between seeing it and understanding what it means. It soars in its parabola up into a sky far too pretty to accommodate it, and it seems to hang in the air above them for a split second, a North Star to some of them, their compasses now pointing at this thing, this strange new flying fact, which then begins its descent, and the yelling and the screaming begin roughly *now* as the people in the projectile's landing zone start to accept what is coming right at them and understand this is the de facto end of their sit-in. The canister is already leaking its contents, leaving this tail of orange gas, a comet on a collision course. And when it lands it thuds into the grass like a golf ball and kicks up the turf and ignites. It spins and spews jets of toxic smoke as more little pops are heard coming from the direction of the Conrad Hilton and one or two more flying bombs come hurtling into the crowd, and this is how fast relative peace and order can fall into madness. The crowd starts running and the police start running and almost everybody in the park is simultaneously crying. It's the gas. The way it attacks your eyes and throat. How it feels like burning oil splattered right into your pupil, the way you can't keep your red swollen eyes open without the pain, no matter how much you rub them. And the coughing as sudden and urgent as drowning, that reflexive hacking that bypasses all willpower. People are crying and spitting and running anywhere there is not gas, which presents a basic problem of volume: The gas was fired—purposefully or accidentally, it's not known—so that it landed *behind* most of the crowd, which means the only way to avoid the misery of the gas is to run the other way, in the direction of Michigan Avenue and the Conrad Hilton and the vast police blockades, and so the volume problem is that there are way more people wanting to be on Michigan Avenue than there is currently space on Michigan Avenue for these people.

It's your unstoppable force meeting its immovable object, the body mass of ten thousand protestors running headlong into the teeth of the Chicago PD.

And Sebastian with them, towing Faye by the hand. And Alice watches them and understands this is *exactly the wrong way to go,* that the only direction where there are no police is back into the tear gas itself, the cloud that hugs the ground like an orange fog. She calls out to them to stop, but her voice—raw and ragged from the earlier chanting and now blown to bits by the gas—cannot be heard above the roar and screams of the crowd, all of them running, bouncing into one another, scattering. She watches Sebastian and Faye as the crowd collapses around them and she loses them in the mass. She wants to go after them, but something holds her back. Fear, probably. Fear of the police, one of them in particular.

She will go to the dorm and wait for Faye, she decides. And if Faye doesn't come back she'll stop at nothing to find her, which is a comfortable lie she tells herself to get out of the immediate situation. She will, in fact, never see Faye again. She doesn't know this yet, but she senses it, and she stops running. She turns back toward the protest, the park. And at that moment Faye is tugging on Sebastian's arm because Alice isn't with them. Faye stops and turns around. She looks back at where they came from. She hopes Alice's face will pop out of the chaos, but between the two of them is an orange cloud of gas. It might as well be a concrete wall, or a continent.

"We need to go," says Sebastian.

"Wait," says Faye.

Faces fly by her, none of them Alice's. People clip her shoulders, dodge her, keep running.

Alice is on the other side of the gas now. She can see the lake. She runs to it and splashes her face to calm the sting of the gas, and she slinks northward along the shore, where to avoid drawing attention to herself she ditches her favorite sunglasses and army jacket in the sand and pulls her hair back and tries to look for all intents and purposes like a normal bourgeois law-abiding kid, and this effectively puts an end to her protest career forever.

"We need to go *now*," says Sebastian.

And so Faye agrees, for Alice is gone.

26

HUBERT H. HUMPHREY in the top-floor presidential suite shower digs under his fingernails with the hotel's complimentary bar of Dove soap, which during his lengthy shower has slivered down from its original kidney-shaped girth.

The agents keep popping their heads in: "You okay in there Mr. Vice President sir?"

He understands there's much to do and little time to do it and taking a ninety-minute shower was not exactly on his campaign manager's itinerary. Still, he would have been worthless had he not gotten that stink off.

His fingers are beyond pruned and into this supersaturated territory where his skin looks like an afghan draped loosely over his actual skin. The mirror is opaque and slate gray by now in the humid, dense air.

"Yes, I'm fine," he tells the agent.

Only he's not fine, he realizes, as he speaks. Because there's a sudden tickle in his throat, a slight scratchy pain behind his Adam's apple. He hasn't spoken in an hour and a half and now that he's spoken he feels it, that first leading edge of illness. He tests his throat—his precious and golden throat, his vocal cords and lungs, these bits of him that are all he has to give as he addresses the country and accepts the nomination for president in a few days' time—he verbalizes a few notes, just a little solfège, a little *do, re, mi*. And sure enough he feels it, that spike of pain, that friction burn, that swelling on the soft palate.

Oh no.

He turns the water off and towels himself dry and robes up and crashes into the suite's main conference area and announces that he needs vitamin C *right now*.

When the group looks at him funny, he announces "I may have a sore throat" with the kind of gravity a doctor might use to say *The tumor is malignant.*

The agents look at each other uncomfortably. A few of them cough. One of them steps forward and says, "Probably not a sore throat, sir."

"How would you know?" Triple H says. "I need vitamin C, and I need it right this goddamn second."

"Sir, it's probably the tear gas, Mr. Vice President sir."

"What are you talking about?"

"Tear gas, sir. Your typical motivational weapon, sir, used to disperse crowds nonviolently. Irritating to the eyes, nose, mouth, and, yes, certainly sir, the throat and lungs."

"Tear gas."

"Yes, sir."

"In here?"

"Yes, sir."

"In my *hotel suite*."

"It came from the park, sir. The police are using it on the demonstrators. And today, you see, we've got an easterly wind—"

"At about twelve knots," adds another agent.

"Agreed, yes, thank you, a sturdy wind that pushed the gas back across Michigan Avenue and into the hotel and even, yes, up to the top floor. Our floor. Sir."

Triple H can now feel his eyes watering and burning, that feeling like when you're standing over chopped onions. He walks to the suite's large front windows and looks out at the park, which is a chaos of running, terrified youths and pursuing cops and clouds of orange gas.

"The police did this?" he says.

"Yes, sir."

"But don't they know I'm up here?"

And this is almost the breaking point for poor Hubert H. This was supposed to be *his* convention, *his* moment. Why did this have to happen? Why does it always have to turn out like this? And suddenly he's eight years old again back in South Dakota and Tommy Skrumpf is ruining his birthday party by having an epileptic fit right there on the kitchen floor, and the doctors take Tommy away and the parents take their kids home still carrying the unopened presents that were supposed to be Hubert's, and a small ungenerous part of him broke open that night and he wept not that Tommy might die but wishing that he would. And then he's nineteen years old and he's just finished his first year at college, and he got good marks and he likes it, college, he's good at it, and he's made friends and found a girl and his life is finally shaping up and that's when his parents tell him to come home because they're out of money. So he comes home. And then it's 1948 and he's just been elected to the United States Senate for the first time and at that moment his father up and dies. And now here he is about to be nominated for president, and all around him is fighting and tear gas and butchers and shit and death.

Why does this always happen? Why does he have to pay for any triumph with sadness and blood? All his victories end in sorrow. In some ways, he's still that disappointed eight-year-old thinking bad things about Tommy Skrumpf. He feels the sting of that day all the way to his marrow, still.

Why do the best things in life leave such deep scars?

Which is exactly the kind of self-destructive, negative-type thinking the management consultants were brought in to fix. He repeats his confidence mantras. *I'm a winner.* He cancels the order for the vitamin C. He gets dressed. Gets back to work. *Sic transit gloria mundi.*

27

OLD CRONKITE LISTING to his right, leaning on his desk in a manner that plays on TV as serious contemplation and the strong-willed constitution of a man whose job it is to deliver bad news to the country, leaning like this and cocking his head and staring into the camera with a pained look on his face, a kind of father's this-is-going-to-hurt-me-more-than-it's-going-to-hurt-you look, and saying, "The Democratic convention is about to begin"—then a long dramatic pause here for this next part to really sink in—"in a *police state.*"

Then adding "There just doesn't seem to be any other way to say it" for the benefit of his producers, who he can imagine are right now shaking their heads in the control van at his blatant editorializing, again.

But something needs to be said for the benefit of the viewers who are at home and plainly not getting it. The CBS switchboard has been going nuts all day. The most calls they'd gotten since King was shot. Well sure, Cronkite said, people are mad, the police are out of control.

Yes, people are mad, his producers told him, but not mad at the police. They're mad at the kids, they said. They're blaming the kids. They're saying the kids are *getting what they deserve.*

And it's true that certain protestors are not entirely, let's say, easy to like. They try to offend your sensibilities. They try to push your buttons. They are unkempt, unclean. But they are only a tiny part of the mass gathered right now outside the Hilton. Most of the kids out there look like normal kids, anybody's kids. Maybe they'd gotten themselves into something they didn't understand, swept up in something larger. But they aren't criminals. They aren't deviants. They aren't radicals or hippies. They probably just don't want to be drafted. They are probably just sincerely against the Vietnam War. And, by the way, who isn't these days?

But it turns out that for every poor kid shown getting his head drubbed by a nightstick, CBS gets ten phone calls in support of the cop who held the stick. Reporters got gassed in the street and then came back to HQ to find a telegram from a thousand miles away saying the reporters didn't understand what was really happening in Chicago. As soon as he heard this, old Cronkite knew he'd failed. They'd been covering the radicals and the hippies so much that now his viewers couldn't see past them. The gray areas had ceased to exist. And old Cronkite had two thoughts about this. First, anyone who thinks television can bring the nation together to have a real dialogue and begin to understand one another with empathy and compassion is suffering a great delusion. And second, Nixon is definitely going to win this thing.

28

IT IS BAD PLANNING on the part of the police to demand that protestors leave the park but give them no obvious way to do so. It is no longer legal to assemble in the park, but it is also illegal to cross a police barricade, and the park is barricaded on all sides. So it's your classic double bind. Actually, the only place not barricaded is a spot on the eastern edge of the park, by the lake, exactly where the tear gas landed, stupidly. So here they come, the protestors, because they have no other choice; there's nowhere else to go. The first of them flow onto Michigan Avenue and into the walls of the Conrad Hilton like runaway waves. They splash onto the concrete and brick and they're pinned there as the police recognize that something has shifted in the rhetoric of the day. The stakes have changed. The protestors—with their numbers and their new desperation—now have the upper hand. And so the police push back, crush them into the walls of the hotel, and swing away.

Sebastian and Faye are in there somewhere. He's squeezing her hand so hard it hurts, but she doesn't dare let go. She feels herself caught in this moving human river and pressed at all sides and sometimes even lifted off her feet for a moment and carried, a sensation like swimming or floating, before being dropped again, and the thing she's thinking about most right now is keeping her balance, staying on her feet, because these people are panicked and this is what ten thousand panicked people look like: like wild animals, huge and insensate. If she falls she'll be trampled. The terror she feels about this goes way beyond terror and into a kind of calm clarity. This is life or death. She squeezes Sebastian's hand harder.

People run with handkerchiefs on their faces, or with their shirts wrapped around their mouths. They cannot stand the gas. They cannot stay in the park. And yet it's becoming clear to them now that this was a mistake too, going this way, because as they get closer to the safety of the dark city beyond Michigan Avenue, the spaces they can fill are getting smaller and smaller. They are being funneled by heavy equipment and fencing and barbed wire and lines of cops and National Guardsmen thirty deep. And Sebastian tries to get to the Hilton's front doors but the crowd is too thick, the current too strong, and so they end up off target, carried to the side of the building instead, and up against the plate-glass windows of the Haymarket Bar.

That's where Officer Brown sees them.

He's been watching the crowd, looking for Alice. He's standing atop the back bumper of a U.S. Army troop carrier, several feet above everyone else, looking at the crowd, the baby-blue helmets of the Chicago PD, en masse, like a colony of agitated poisonous mushrooms, it looks like, from up here. And then suddenly a face pops out of the crowd, over by the bar, a woman's face, and he feels a surge of optimism that it's Alice, because it's the first time all day he's had any flash of familiarity, and the film that's been running in his head—that Alice sees him clubbing hippies and thus recognizes him for the brutal man she's always wanted him to be—starts running again until the face resolves itself and he realizes with crashing disappointment that it's not Alice he's seeing, it's Faye.

Faye! The girl he arrested just last night. Who should be in jail right this moment. Who is the very reason Alice left him.

Fucking *bitch*.

He leaps into the crowd and unholsters his club. He presses forward, shoves his way toward the plate-glass window Faye is trapped against. Between him and her are several lines of cops and a mass of stinking hippies trapped and flapping like tuna in a net. He shoulders his way through the crowd, saying, "Coming through! From behind!" And the cops are glad to let him go because that's one more guy between them and the front line. And he's getting closer to the boundary between the cops and the protestors, a boundary visible by the nightsticks in the air coming down fast like a typewriter getting all jammed up in itself. The closer he gets, the harder it is to move. Everything seems to *heave,* like they are all part of one great, sick animal.

And at that moment a squad of National Guardsmen—one of them carrying an actual *flamethrower,* though, thankfully, not using it—carves through the protestors on Michigan Avenue, effectively flanking them, cutting them off from the rest of the herd, and so this small group by the Conrad Hilton finds itself trapped: police on one side, National Guard on the other, hotel walls behind them.

There is nowhere for them to go.

Faye is crushed against the plate-glass window, her shoulder pressed hard into it. Any harder, she thinks, and it'll pop, the shoulder. She's looking into the Haymarket Bar, through the window that seems to wobble and creak, and she sees two men in suits and black ties staring back at her. They sip their drinks. They seem to have no expression at all. Around her, protestors squirm and duck for cover. They get clubbed in the head, get jabbed in the ribs with the blunt end of a nightstick, and as they go down they are dragged to paddy wagons, which seems to Faye preferable. Between a knock to the head and going to the paddy wagon, she'll take the wagon. But she can't even turn here, much less go to the ground, such is the tightness of the bodies pressing into her. She's losing hold of Sebastian's hand. There's someone between them now, another protestor between Faye and Sebastian doing exactly what they're doing, which is to say trying to flee, putting off the beating as long as possible.

This is simple and irrational survival kicking in. There's nowhere to flee, yet they flee anyway. And Faye has to make a choice right now because if she keeps holding on to Sebastian's hand like this, her elbow might break where this guy is pressing into it. Plus she's such an easy target like this, her back to the cops. If she turned around maybe she'd be able to duck out of the way of their wild swinging. So she makes the decision. She lets go of Sebastian's hand. She lets his sweaty fingers slide away, and as she does so she feels him grasping for her harder, really clamping down, but it's no use. She's free. Her arm snaps back to her and the man between them collapses into the plate-glass window—which trembles at the impact, and sounds a sharp crack like boots on ice—and she turns around.

The first thing she sees is the cop bearing down on her.

They lock eyes. It's the cop from last night, who arrested her at the dorm. His is the first face she sees in that way someone's face seems more illuminated when they're staring right at you. That face, that awful man who last night wouldn't look at her as she cried in the backseat of his police cruiser and she pleaded with him and urged him to let her go and she stared at his reflection in the rearview mirror and he didn't say anything except, "You are a whore."

And how he found her again, here, now.

His face is psychotically calm. He swings his club quickly and emotionlessly. He looks like someone out trimming the grass, feeling nothing about it except that it needs to be done. And she looks at his big brutal body and the strength with which he swings his nightstick, its speed as it dashes into heads and ribs and limbs, and she knows her plan to avoid a police beating by athletically dodging it was both naïve and impossible. This man can do whatever he wants. She can't stop him. She is powerless. He is coming.

And what she does here is try to get really small. It's the only thing she can think of. To become the smallest target she can. She tries to shrink into herself, draw in her arms and duck her head and bend at the knees and waist to get below the level of the people in front of her.

A posture of supplication, it feels like. All her alarm bells are going off, and she feels the panic attack starting as it always does, with that iron weight in her chest like she's being squeezed from the inside. She thinks *Please not now* as the cop continues to punish whoever happens to interrupt his path to Faye. And the protestors yell "Peace!" or "I'm not resisting!" and they hold up their hands, palms out, surrendering, but the cop clobbers them anyway, in the head, the neck, the belly. He's so close now. Only one person stands between him and Faye, a young wiry man with a big beard and camo jacket who is very quickly getting the message and trying his best to squirm away, and Faye's lungs are locking up and she's feeling that head-rush dizziness that makes her all trembly and unsteady, and her skin feels cold and wet, and the sweat erupts out of her, so quickly is her forehead damp, while her mouth is chalk-dry and gummy so that she can't even tell the cop not to do whatever he's going to do—all this happening as she watches him shove aside the camo-jacket guy and press into the crowd so that he's within range of Faye, and he's trying to angle his body so he can get to her, trying to raise his weapon in all that human chaos, when from behind them they all hear two pops, two light pops that sound like someone's hand beating the open end of an empty bottle. And before today a sound like that would have had no meaning, but now the protestors are all veterans at this and they know: that sound means tear gas. Someone behind them has fired more tear gas. And the crowd reacts to this—the sound and then the inevitable smoke cloud that erupts a second later—predictably: They panic and surge away from it, a wave of bodies that reaches Faye just as the cop lunges for her, and all of them at the same time crash into the plate-glass window together.

This, finally, proves too much for the window to bear. This is well beyond its tolerances.

The window doesn't even really crack so much as explode sharply everywhere all at once. And Faye and the cop and the great rush of protestors pushing themselves against it all collapse and tumble backward into the people and smoke and music of the Haymarket Bar.

29

THE DAY HAS THUS FAR BEEN so unusual that it takes a moment for the patrons of the Haymarket Bar to recognize something has happened that is even more unusual. The plate-glass window shatters and in tumble protestors and cops and great sharp shards of glass, and for a moment they simply watch this happening as if they're watching the television above the bar. They are mildly fascinated. They feel drawn to it, yet also separate from it. They are spectators, not participants.

So for a few moments as the protestors and cops all wrestle around regaining their lost balance in this scrum of humanity on the black-and-white-tiled Haymarket floor, people in the bar watch with a passive interest, like: *Wow.*

Neat.

Wonder what'll happen next?

What happens next is that the tear gas leaks in and the cops get extremely pissed off and pile through the new opening in the side of the bar and sprint from the lobby because the thing that was never supposed to happen in Chicago has now happened: The delegates and the protestors are in the same room, together.

Their orders were very clear on this point: The delegates were to be met at the airport, right as they stepped off the plane, taken in police cars to the Hilton, taken in big buses with military-grade escorts to the amphitheater and back—shielded, bubbled, cut off from the hippies because *the hippies are trying to disrupt and threaten our democracy,* which is what the mayor said every day in the newspapers and on television. (The protest leaders' responses that a democracy has ceased to be democratic when its representatives must be shielded from the people they represent went for the most part unreported and for sure unanswered by the mayor or his press office.)

Anyway, here they come, the police, red-faced and running, moving as quickly as allowed by jangling heavy utility belts full of weapons. And this is about the time that things get very real for the patrons of the Haymarket Bar. Coughing and crying suddenly because of the gas, clipped by running police or errant billy clubs, they realize they are not really spectators to this event; they are now part of it. This is how quickly the reality outside the bar penetrates and obliterates the reality inside the bar: with a simple pop of glass. The bar is now an extension of the street.

The front lines have shifted.

How long, they wonder, before the lines shift further? How long before their hotel rooms are at risk? Their own homes? Their families? For many of them, the protest was mild street theater until this moment, when they themselves are getting gassed. They think of bricks perhaps someday flying through their own windows, or they think of their daughters growing up and getting seduced by bearded long-haired smoke-smelling men, and even the most pro–peace plank among them stand back and let the cops do their brutal work.

So it's all chaos, in other words. Chaos and panic. Faye lands hard on her side and under several other bodies all clacking heads and jaws together and she's seeing stars and fighting to regain the wind that was knocked from her when she landed on the floor. She tries to focus on little things, to see through the green-purple starry screen of her vision to the checkered floor, the bits and chunks of glass around her, some sliding like hockey pucks as they're kicked and battered by the melee now occupying the bar. It all feels very far away. She blinks. She shakes her head. She sees the feet of police as they run toward her, the feet of patrons as they run away. She runs her fingers over her own forehead and feels a lump the size of a walnut growing there. She remembers the cop who was a moment ago coming after her, and sees him lying faceup, halfway in the bar and halfway out.

30

HE'S NOT MOVING. He stares straight up. What he's seeing is the jagged edge of the plate-glass window—what's left of it—about eight feet above him, an equator in his field of vision. North of it is the tin ceiling of the Haymarket Bar. South, the sky, a hazy vaporous dusk. When he fell, he twisted and turned and crashed down backward and felt a bolt of pain at the landing. He's lying perfectly still and thinking about what he feels now. Nothing, is what he feels.

Around him, police jump through the broken window and into the bar. He feels like he needs to tell one of them something, though he doesn't know what. Just that something doesn't feel right here. And he doesn't understand what's going on but he senses that it's important— more important than the delegates or the hippies or the bar. He tries to speak to them as they leap around him, over him. His voice comes out small and thin. He says "Wait," but none of them do. They crash into the bar, where they yank hippies off the floor and eject them onto the street, where they club the hippies and maybe even a few delegates too because it's dark in there and hard to tell the difference when you're swinging like that.

31

SEBASTIAN HAS GOTTEN to his feet and finds Faye on the floor and yanks her up by the arm. She's feeling light-headed, queasy, she would like nothing better than to sit down at one of the Haymarket's comfortable-looking plush booths and sip some tea with honey and then maybe sleep—oh my god how she wants to sleep, even now, right here at the violent center of the world. She's still seeing stars. She must have hit her head pretty good.

Sebastian pulls her and she is compliant. She lets herself be pulled. Not toward the front door, where several of the other protestors are running, and not back out onto the street, but deeper into the bar, back to the farthest corner, where there's a pay phone and a pair of bathrooms and one of those silver swinging doors with the round window that leads into the kitchen. This is where they go, into the Hilton's industrial kitchen, which is currently enfrenzied with room-service orders—the guests at the hotel being terrified to leave the grounds and so getting all their meals on-site, delivered—and dozens of white-aproned, white-hatted men stand over griddles that crackle with porterhouse steaks and filet mignon, over sandwich stations building hoagies of improbable height, over table services polishing wineglasses to a perfect smudgeless clarity. They see Sebastian and Faye and they don't say a word. They keep on working. Not their problem.

Sebastian ushers her through the loud and busy kitchen, all the way past the grills with leaping fire and burners cooking sauces and pastas, past the dishwashing station and the dishwasher himself, his face in a cloud of steam, and beyond to the back door, through the door and into the trash area, the dumpster with its sharp sour-milk and old-chicken smells, and beyond that into the alley, away from Michigan Avenue, away from the noise and tear gas, and away, finally, from the Conrad Hilton Hotel.

32

OFFICER BROWN IS STILL on his back in the broken window well of the Haymarket Bar and he's beginning to understand that he cannot feel his legs. He fell and he landed on something sharp and felt a stabbing pain near his kidney and now he feels nothing. A spreading chill, a numbness. He tries to stand but cannot. He closes his eyes and he swears he's trapped under a car. That's how it feels. But when he opens his eyes again there is nothing visibly trapping him.

"Help," he says to no one, to the air, at first quietly but then with more urgency: "Help!"

The bar has been cleared of hippies by now, and the guests have all retreated to their rooms. The only people who remain in the bar are two Secret Service agents, who amble up to him now and say "What seems to be the problem, officer?" with a kind of lighthearted chumminess that disappears as soon as they try to help him get up and can't and their hands come away bloodied.

At first Brown thinks they've injured themselves on the broken glass beneath him. Then he realizes the blood is not theirs. That's his blood. He's bleeding. He's bleeding a lot.

But he can't be bleeding.

Because nothing hurts.

"I'm okay," he says to the one agent who has sat down next to him, one hand pressing firmly on Brown's chest.

"Sure thing, buddy. You're gonna be fine."

"Really. It doesn't hurt."

"Uh-huh. You stay right where you are and don't move. We're getting you some help."

And Brown notices the other agent now speaking into a walkie-talkie about an officer down, send an ambulance immediately, and it's the way he says the word *immediately* that makes Brown squeeze his eyes shut and say "I'm sorry, I'm sorry," not to the agent above him but to God. Or the universe. Or whatever karmic powers are out there right now deciding his fate. He apologizes to all of them—for his encounters with Alice, for cheating on his wife, for cheating on his wife in such an ugly way, in the dark, in alleyways, in his car, he's sorry he didn't have the will to stop it, nor the discipline, the self-control, he's sorry for this, and sorry that he's repenting only now, after it's too late, and he's aware of the spreading coldness in his lower half and he senses (though he cannot feel) the sharp shard of plate-glass window currently penetrating his spinal cord, and he's not sure what exactly has happened to him but feels that whatever it is, he is sorry—that it happened, that he deserved it.

33

CHURCHES ACROSS CHICAGO have opened their sanctuaries, as sanctuaries. Youths arrive teargassed and beaten. They are given water, a meal, a cot. After the violence of the day, some of them almost weep at these small kindnesses. Outside, the riot has splintered, broken down into fragmented fighting and scuffles in the street, a few cops chasing kids into bars and restaurants, into and out of the park. It's not safe to be out there right now, and so youths show up in ragged pairs at places like this: old St. Peter's on Madison Street downtown. They don't even gossip with the other protestors, all of them having endured roughly the same day. They sit penitently. Priests give them bowls of warmed canned soup and they say "Thank you, Father" and they really mean it. The priests give them warm washcloths for their eyes, red from the gas.

Faye and Sebastian sit in the front pew quiet and uncomfortable because there's so much to say and they don't know how to say it. They stare at the front altar instead, the elaborately inscribed stone-and-wood altarpiece of St. Peter's in the Loop: stone angels and stone saints and a stone Jesus hanging on a concrete cross, his head looking straight down, two stone disciples below him, just under his armpits, one looking up at him with a face of anguish, the other looking at his own feet, ashamed.

Faye touches the lump on her head. It has stopped hurting, for the most part, and now feels simply *fascinating,* this strange alien growth, this hard marble under her skin. Maybe if she plays with this thing she can resist asking the questions she is dying to ask, questions that have begun forming these last twenty minutes, as they've sat here, out of danger now, as she's collected her thoughts and begun looking at the evening rationally and logically, these questions have settled upon her.

"Faye, listen—" says Sebastian.

"Who are you *really?*" she says, because she cannot resist asking, no matter how fascinating her bump feels.

Sebastian smiles a sad smile. He looks at his shoes. "Yeah. About that."

"You knew your way around those buildings," Faye says. "How did you know that? And that key. You had the key to my cell. And how did you know those cops in the basement? What is going on?"

Sebastian sits there like a child being scolded. It's like he can't even bear to look at her.

Behind them, Allen Ginsberg has now found his way to this church. He walks quietly in and goes from tired body to tired body blessing people in their sleep and placing his hand on the heads of the conscious and saying *Hare Rama, Hare Krishna* and shaking his head the way he does, so his beard looks like a tight shivering mammal.

A month ago, a Ginsberg appearance would have drawn a lot of attention. Now he's become part of the scenery of the protest, one of the protest's many colors. He walks around and the kids give him weary, exhausted smiles. He blesses them and moves on.

"Are you working for the police?" Faye asks.

"No. I'm not," Sebastian says. He leans forward, clasps his hands as if in prayer. "More like *with* the police. It's nothing official. Actually I'm not even working with them. It's more like we work alongside each other. We have a certain understanding. A certain accommodating relationship. We both understand a few simple facts."

"Which are what?"

"Primarily, that we need each other."

"You and the police."

"Yes. The police need me. The police *love* me."

"What happened out there today," Faye says, "did not look like love."

"I provide heat. Drama. The police want reasons to crack down on the radical left. I supply those reasons. I print that we're going to kidnap delegates or spike the drinking water or bomb the amphitheater and it makes us look like terrorists. Which is exactly what the police want."

"So they can do what they did tonight. Gas us and beat us up."

"In front of the TV cameras, with people cheering them on at home. Yes."

Faye shakes her head. "But why help them? Why encourage all this . . ."—she waves her hand around at the bloodied youths now occupying the sanctuary—"all this madness, this violence?"

"Because the more the police crack down," Sebastian says, "the stronger our side looks."

"Our side."

"The protest movement," he says. "The more the cops beat us up, the more our argument seems correct." He leans back into the pew and stares blankly forward. "It's actually pretty brilliant. The protestors and the police, the progressives and the authoritarians—they require each other, they create each other, because they need an opponent to demonize. The best way to feel like you really belong to a group is to invent another group to hate. Which is why today was fantastic, from an advertising standpoint."

Behind them, Ginsberg is walking up and down the many pews of St. Peter's, quietly blessing those who are sleeping there. Faye can hear his monotonous voice singing Hindu songs of praise. She and Sebastian stare at the altarpiece, the saints and angels in stone. She does not know what to think about him. She feels betrayed, or maybe more accurately she feels like she *should* feel betrayed—she has never thought of herself as part of Sebastian's movement, but there are many people who do, and so she tries to feel betrayed on their behalf.

"Faye, listen," Sebastian says. He puts his elbows on his knees, breathes heavily and looks at the floor. "That's not entirely the truth. The truth is, I couldn't go to Vietnam."

The lights in the sanctuary are dimming now, the trickle of protestors through the front doors has stopped. All over, people fall asleep in twos and threes and fours. Soon the church is lit only by candles on the altar, a soft orange glow.

"I told everyone I was in India this summer," Sebastian says. "But I wasn't. I was in Georgia. At boot camp. They were going to send me to Vietnam until a guy came offering this deal. An official at the mayor's office, who could pull some serious strings. He said print these certain kinds of stories and we'll get you out of the army. I couldn't bear the thought of going to war. So I took the deal."

He looks at Faye, his face pinched. "I'm sure you hate me now," he says.

And, yes, maybe she *should* hate him, but she feels herself softening to him instead. They are, she realizes, not that unalike.

"My dad works at ChemStar," she says. "Half the money that sent me to college came from making napalm. So I guess I'm in no position to judge."

He nods. "We do what we have to do, right?"

"I probably would have taken the deal too," Faye says.

They stare at the altar until a thought crosses Faye's mind: "So when you said you saw my *maarr*?"

"Yes?"

"You said you learned that word from Tibetan monks."

"Yes."

"While you were in India. But you weren't in India."

"I read about that in *National Geographic*. It wasn't Tibetan monks. I think the article was about an aboriginal tribe in Australia, now that I think about it."

"What else have you lied to me about?" Faye says. "How about our date? Did you ever really want to go on our date?"

"Definitely," he says, smiling. "That was the real me. I really wanted that. Promise."

She nods. Then shrugs. "How would I know?"

"But there's one thing, actually, one more little lie."

"Okay."

"It's not technically a lie I told *you*, per se. More like a generalized lie I told everyone."

"Let's hear it."

"Sebastian is not my real name. I made that up."

Faye laughs. She can't help it. The day has been so ridiculous that it seems proper to add one more lunacy on top of it. "This is what you think of as a *little* lie?" she says.

"Call it a nom de guerre. I took it from Saint Sebastian. You know, the martyr? The police needed someone into whom they could shoot their arrows. I supplied that target. I thought it was apt. You don't even want to know my real name."

"No, I don't," Faye says. "Not yet. Not right now."

"Let's just say it's not a name that would rally the troops."

Ginsberg has reached them now. He's crisscrossed the entire sanctuary, gone up and down all the pews, and he finally comes to them. He stands before them and nods. They nod back. The church is so quiet, all noise coming from the poet himself, his metal necklaces scratching and banging together, his murmurs and blessings. He places a hand on their heads, a soft warm hand, a gentle touch. He closes his eyes and whispers something incomprehensible, like he's casting a secret spell on them. When he stops he opens his eyes and removes his hands.

"I just married you," he tells them. "Now you're married."

Then he shuffles off, humming quietly to himself.

34

"PLEASE DON'T TELL ANYONE what I've told you," says the man she knows as Sebastian.

"I won't," she says, and she knows this is a promise she can keep, because she's never going to see any of these people again. She will, as of tomorrow, no longer live in Chicago, no longer study at Circle. The knowledge of this has hardened around her during the day. She's not aware of having made a decision; it's more like the decision has been there all along, already made for her. She does not belong here, and all that has happened in the last day proves it.

Her plan is simple: She will leave at dawn. While everyone sleeps, she will slip out and leave. She will stop at her dorm. She will walk up to her room and she will discover her door wide open, the lights on inside. She will find Alice sleeping in her bed. Faye will not wake her. She will tiptoe to her bedside table, very slowly open the bottom drawer, and take out a few books and Henry's proposal letter. She'll quietly leave, stealing one last glance at Alice, who without her black sunglasses and combat boots looks human again, and gentle and vulnerable and even pretty. She will wish good things for her, in life. Then Faye will leave—Alice will never even know she was there. Faye will catch the first bus back to Iowa. She'll stare at Henry's letter for about an hour before exhaustion finally takes her and she sleeps the rest of the way home.

This is the plan. She will escape at first light.

But that's still hours off, and here she is in Chicago, with this boy, in what is feeling like a moment outside time. The dark and quiet sanctuary. The glow of candlelight. She doesn't want to know Sebastian's real name because, she thinks, why ruin it? Why ruin the mystery? There's something delicious about his anonymity. He could be *anyone*. She could be *anyone*. She knows she will be gone tomorrow, but she is not yet gone. Tomorrow will be full of consequences, but this moment is consequence-free. Whatever happens right now will happen without repercussion. It feels delicious, being on the edge of abandonment. She can act without worry. She can do what she wants.

What she wants is to take his hand and lead him into the shadows behind the altar. What she wants is to feel his warm body on hers. What she wants is to be impulsive—impulsive like she was with Henry on the playground that night that seems a lifetime ago. And even as she does this and presses her mouth to his and he resists a little and whispers "Are you sure?" and she smiles at him and says "It's okay, we're married now" and they collapse on the tile floor together, she's aware that she's only partly doing this because she genuinely wants to. She's also doing this because she wants to prove something to herself, that she's changed. Because after you go through a trial by fire aren't you supposed to come out a changed person? A different and better person? And this day was indeed trying, and she would prefer not to be the same person she was before, with the same petty worries and doubts. She wants to prove that she's gone through the terror of the day and now she's stronger and better, even though she doesn't know if she really is. How can one tell when one becomes a stronger and better person? Through action, she decides. And so this is her action. She takes off his jacket, then hers. They sit yanking off their shoes and giggling because there is no way to remove tight shoes in a manner that's sexy. This is her great demonstration, to herself and to the world—

she is changed, she is a woman, she is doing womanly things and she is doing them fearlessly. She unbuckles his belt and slides down his pants until he is poking nicely out of them. And even the posters from her high-school home economics class have no power over her now, because she can feel the grit on her skin, and this man's smell right now is a mixture of sweat and smoke and body musk and tear gas, and her feeling about this is that she wants to devour him, and he wants to devour her, and if she's really honest it feels delicious and liberating rolling around dirty together on these sparkling clean and smooth floors, God's floors, where if she looks up she can see the stone Jesus directly above her, his head hanging so that at this angle it seems like he's looking right back at her, her terrible God disapproving at what she's doing in his holy house, and she loves it, loves that it's happening right here, and she knows that tomorrow she'll return to Iowa and return to being Faye, old Faye, she'll come back to her real self like a soul that's been traveling outside its body, and she'll say no to college and yes to Henry and she'll become a wife, a strange new creature who will keep locked within herself the knowledge of this night. She will never speak of it, even though she will think of it daily. She will wonder how she is capable of being such different people: the real Faye and the other one, the brash and aggressive and impulsive Faye. She will long for this other Faye. As the years mount and her days become cluttered with chores domestic and infantile, she will think about this night so often that it will begin to feel more real to her than her real life. She'll begin to believe that her existence as wife and mother is the illusion, the façade she's projecting to the world, and this Faye who came alive on the floor of St. Peter's, that's the real one, the authentic self, and this belief will hook so deeply inside her, will pierce her so completely that eventually it will take over. It will become too powerful to ignore. And by then it will not seem like she's abandoning her husband and child; it will seem like she's retrieving the real life she abandoned in Chicago many years ago. She will actually feel good about this, about being true to herself, her real self. It will feel like she's found the one true Faye—at least it will feel like that for a while, until she begins to long for her family and all the confusion returns.

In the story of the blind men and the elephant, what's usually ignored is the fact that each man's description was *correct*. What Faye won't understand and may never understand is that there is not one true self hidden by many false ones. Rather, there is one true self hidden by many other true ones. Yes, she is the meek and shy and industrious student. Yes, she is the panicky and frightened child. Yes, she is the bold and impulsive seductress. Yes, she is the wife, the mother. And many other things as well. Her belief that only one of these is true obscures the larger truth, which was ultimately the problem with the blind men and the elephant. It wasn't that they were blind—it's that they stopped too quickly, and so never knew there was a larger truth to grasp.

For Faye, the larger truth, the thing that holds up every important episode in her life like a beam holding up a house is this: *Faye is the one who flees.* The one who panics and escapes, who fled Iowa to avoid disgrace, who will flee from Chicago and into marriage, who will flee her family and who will eventually flee the country. And the more she believes she only has one true self, the more she flees to find it. She's like someone trapped in quicksand whose efforts to escape only make her drown faster.

Will she ever understand this? Who knows. Seeing ourselves clearly is the project of a lifetime.

These thoughts are far away from her now. Now everything is simple: She is a body in congress with another body. And his body is warm, and pressing all over into hers, and the taste of his skin is like salt and ammonia. At dawn she will begin using her head again, but for now it is this simple—as simple as *taste.* She is a body perceiving the world, and all her senses are filled.

35

THE ONLY OTHER PERSON in the church who knows what they are doing is Allen Ginsberg, who is sitting cross-legged, leaning against a wall and smiling. He could see them duck behind the altar, could see their candlelit shadows, could hear the familiar jangle of a belt undone. This makes him happy, these kids enjoying their exhausted and soiled flesh. Good for them. It reminds him of that sunflower poem he wrote so long ago—what is it, ten years? Fifteen? No matter. *We're not our skin of grime,* he had written, *we're golden sunflowers inside, blessed by our own seed & hairy naked accomplishment-bodies growing into mad black formal sunflowers in the sunset . . .*

Yes, he thinks. And as he closes his eyes and lets sleep come, he feels satisfied and delighted.

For he knows he was right.

PART TEN

DELEVERAGING

Late Summer 2011

ONCE AGAIN, Faye had lied to her son.

Once again, there was something she felt too ashamed to tell him. In Chicago, at the airport, he had asked where she planned to go, and she lied to him. She said she didn't know, that she'd figure it out in London. But in fact she knew exactly where she was going: as soon as she discovered she'd be traveling alone, she resolved to come here, to Hammerfest, Norway. Her father's hometown.

The way her father had described it, the family's home in Hammerfest was a resplendent thing: on the edge of town, a wide three-story wooden house with a view out to the ocean, a long pier where the family could fish for an afternoon and come away with a bucketful of arctic char, a field in front that waved golden with barley through the summer, a small pen for the animals—a few goats, sheep, a horse—the whole spread marked by a line of beautiful blue-green spruces that caught so much snow in winter that the snow sometimes fell off them in great loud *thwumps*. The house was repainted every spring a bright salmon-red after the winter elements dulled the previous year's coat. Faye remembers sitting at her father's feet listening to this and fully internalizing this vision of her family's ancestry and later adding to it in her mind, putting a jagged mountain range in the background, covering the beaches with the volcanic black sand she saw once in *National Geographic*—whatever other beautiful thing she encountered in some movie or magazine, any place that seemed to be rural and idyllic and foreign, they all became this place, the home in Hammerfest. It drew together all her fantasies by slow childhood accretion. It became the depository for all the best things, and eventually her image of it was equal parts Nordic and French countryside and Tuscan fields and that great scene in *The Sound of Music* of singing and spinning in the grassy Bavarian hills.

The real Hammerfest, Faye discovers, does not look like this at all.

After a quick flight from England to Oslo, and another flight in a de Havilland that seemed too big for its propellers to keep up, she lands in Hammerfest to find a rocky, hardscrabble place devoid of any growing thing except the hardiest and prickliest of shrubs and thicket. A place that whistles with the wind of the arctic circle, a wind that carries on it a sweet petrochemical vapor. For this is an oil town. A gas town. Fishing boats are dwarfed by massive orange container ships taking liquid natural gas and crude oil to refineries that dot the coastline, to round white storage and distillation tanks that look, from the air, like mushrooms sprouting from some dead thing. Offshore platforms drilling reservoired gas are visible from town. No fields of gently swaying barley but rather empty lots with discarded equipment rusted and petrolic. Rocky hills, craggy and covered with lichen. No beaches but rather a bouldered and inaccessible cliff side that looks like the aftermath of an accident involving dynamite. The houses painted brightly in yellows and oranges are more a bulwark against the dark winter than evidence of actual cheer. How could this be the beautiful place she imagined? It seems so foreign.

She had thought she'd find somebody at the tourist office who could help her, but when she said she was looking for the Andresen farm they looked at her like she was out of her mind. No Andresen farm, they said. No farms at all, they said. So she described the house and they said that house wouldn't exist anymore. The Germans would have destroyed it in the war. They destroyed that specific house? They destroyed *every* house. Faye was given a pamphlet for the Museum of Reconstruction. She said she was looking for a place with a fair bit of land and maybe some spruce trees and a house that faced the water. Might they know where she could find a place like that? They said that could describe a lot of places and told her to walk around. Walk around? Yes, it's not a big city. So that's what she's doing. Faye walks Hammerfest's perimeter looking for something that matches her father's description, a farm at the edge of town with a view of the water. She passes flimsy square apartment buildings that seem huddled together for warmth. No fields whatsoever, no farms. She moves out farther, where the terrain is stony, weedy, the only plants able to survive are those that root into the rock itself, hard crunchy grasses that go dormant during the two months of darkness that come during winters above the arctic circle. Faye feels like a fool. She's been walking for hours. She had actually thought she knew what to expect here, she had actually believed in her own fantasy. All these years and still she's making the old mistakes. She finds a path of trampled-down grass that leads over a nearby ridge and she follows it, lost in dismal thought, saying out loud at roughly every second step, "Stupid. Stupid." For that's what she is, stupid, and every stupid decision she's ever made has led her here, to this stupid place, alone on a chalk-dusty path at the godforsaken end of the world.

"Stupid," she says, staring at her feet, climbing the path that leads steeply uphill and over the ridge ahead, thinking that coming here was stupid, looking for the old house was stupid, even her clothing is stupid— little white flat-soled shoes totally inappropriate for hiking over tundra, and a thin shirt she hugs around herself because even though it is summer, it is brisk. Just a few more stupid choices in a life full of them, she thinks. It was stupid to come here. It was stupid to get back in contact with Samuel, whom she felt responsible for after abandoning him to Henry, which was also stupid. No, that wasn't stupid, but marrying Henry in the first place was stupid, and leaving Chicago was stupid. And on and on it goes as Faye continues up the hill, tracing back her long line of bad decisions. What had started it? What put her on the path to this stupid life? She doesn't know. When she looks back on it, all she sees is that old familiar desire to be alone. To be free of people and their judgments and their messy entanglements. Because whenever she got tangled up with someone, disaster always followed. She got tangled up with Margaret in high school only to become a town pariah. And with Alice in college only to be arrested and plunged into violence and mayhem. And with Henry only to wreck the child they had together.

She had been relieved at the airport when Samuel's name appeared on the no-fly list. She feels bad about this now, but it's true. She felt these opposing emotions: joy that Samuel no longer seemed to hate her, and relief that he wasn't coming with her. For how could she have endured the entire flight to London with him—a whole ocean of questions? Never mind traveling with him and living with him wherever they ended up (he seemed to prefer Jakarta, for some reason). His need was too much—it was *always* too much—for her to bear.

How could she tell Samuel that she was going to Hammerfest because of a silly ghost story? The one she heard as a child, the story her father told her about the *nisse* on the night of her first panic attack. The story had stayed with her all this time, and when Samuel mentioned Alice's name, she was reminded of something her old friend told her long ago: The way to get rid of a ghost is to take it home.

Which is stupid, such superstition. "Stupid, stupid," she says.

It's as if she really is haunted. All this time she thought maybe her father had brought some curse from the old country, some ghost. Only now she thinks maybe she's not haunted but rather *she's the one doing the haunting*. Maybe the curse is her. Because every time she's gotten close to someone she has paid for it. And maybe it's appropriate she's now here, in the remotest part of the world, alone. Nobody to get tangled up with. No more lives to destroy.

She reaches the top of the ridge lost in thought, brooding on these bitter things, when she becomes aware of a presence. She looks up to see a horse standing in the path, maybe twenty feet ahead, where the ridge begins sloping back downhill to a small valley. She flinches and exclaims a surprised *"Oh!"* when she sees it, but the horse does not seem startled. It is not moving. It is not eating. She does not seem to have interrupted anything. It's eerie—like it's been expecting her. The horse is white and tensely muscled. Its flanks occasionally shiver. Big round black eyes that seem to consider her wisely. A bit in its mouth, reins around its neck, no saddle. It stares at her as if it's just asked an important question and is waiting for her to respond.

"Hello," she says. The horse is not afraid of her, nor is it friendly. It is simply that Faye occupies its whole attention at the moment. It's actually a little creepy, the way it seems to be waiting for her to do something or say something, though she does not know what. She takes a step toward it, and the horse has no reaction. She takes another step. Still nothing.

"Who are you?" she says, and even as she says it the answer bursts into her head: It's a nix. After all these years, it has appeared to her, here, on a ridge high above the frigid harbor, in Norway, in the northernmost city in the world. She has found herself in a fairy tale.

The horse looks unblinkingly straight at her as if to say, *I know who you are.* And she feels herself drawn to it, wanting to touch it, to rub her hand along its ribs and bound onto it and let it do whatever it wishes to do. It would be a fitting end, she thinks.

She comes closer, and even as she reaches up to pet the beast's face, still it does not flinch. Still it waits. She touches it on that spot between its eyes, that spot she always thinks will be softer than it really is, the skull so close to the surface there, all thin fur and bone.

"Were you waiting for me?" she says into its ear, which is gray and black and flecked silver and looks like a porcelain teacup. She wonders if she can leap onto its back, if she can manage the jump. That would be the hardest part. The next part would be simple. If the horse began galloping, it would reach the nearby cliff in maybe a dozen strides. The fall down to the water would take only seconds. It amazes her that after such a long life, the end could come that quickly.

Then Faye hears a sound, a voice carried on the wind from the valley below. A woman is down there walking toward her, yelling something in Norwegian. And beyond her, just past her, is a house: a small square thing with a deck in back that faces the water, a path down to a rickety wooden dock, a big garden out front, a few spruce trees, a small pasture for a couple of goats, a couple of sheep. The house is gray and weathered, but in the places that are protected from the wind—under the eaves and behind window shutters—Faye can see the lingering color of old paint: salmon-red.

She almost falls over at the sight. It's not how she imagined it, but still she recognizes it. It's familiar, as if she'd been here many times before.

When the woman reaches her, Faye can see she's handsome and young, maybe Samuel's age, with the same striking features she sees all the time in this country: fair skin, blue eyes, long straight hair that delicate color halfway between blond and cotton. She's smiling and saying something that Faye does not understand.

"This must be your horse," Faye says. She feels self-conscious about using English so presumptuously, but she has no alternative.

The woman does not seem offended, though. She cocks her head at this new information and seems to process it for a moment, then says, "British?"

"American."

"Ah," she says, nodding, as if this solves some important mystery. "The horse wanders off sometimes. Thank you for catching him."

"I didn't really catch him. He was standing here when I found him. It's more like he caught me."

The woman introduces herself—her name is Lillian. She's wearing gray herringbone pants of some sturdy-looking material, a light blue sweater, a wool scarf that looks homemade. She's the very picture of unassuming Nordic style—restrained and elegant. Certain women can wear a scarf effortlessly. Lillian takes the horse by the reins and together they all begin walking back down toward the house. Faye wonders if this might be a distant relative, a cousin, for this is almost certainly the place. So many of the details match, even if the version her father told was exaggerated: not a field in the front yard but rather a garden; not a long line of spruces but only two; not a great pier over the water but instead a small flimsy-looking dock perhaps large enough for a canoe. Faye wonders whether he was self-consciously lying and puffing it up, or if, in the years since he left, in his imagination, the house really did grow in its proportions and majesty.

Lillian, meanwhile, is pleasantly making conversation, asking Faye where she's from, how she's enjoying her travels, where she's gone. She suggests restaurants to try, nearby sights to see.

"This is your house?" Faye asks.

"It's my mother's."

"Does she live here too?"

"Of course."

"How long has she lived here?"

"Most of her life."

The garden out front is wild with life, a great efflorescence of bushes and grasses and flowers thick and barely domesticated. It's an eccentric and rowdy garden, a place where nature has been encouraged to its messy ends. Lillian leads the horse into its pen and closes a rickety gate that she secures with a bit of twine tied in a knot. She thanks Faye for helping return the animal.

"I hope you enjoy your vacation," she says.

And even though this is what Faye has come here to find, she's feeling tongue-tied and nervous now, not sure exactly what to say or how to proceed, not sure how to explain everything.

"Listen, I'm not really on vacation."

"Oh?"

"I'm looking for someone. Old family, actually. Relatives of mine."

"What's the name? Maybe I can help."

Faye swallows. She doesn't know why she's so anxious saying it: "Andresen."

"Andresen," Lillian says. "That's a pretty common name."

"Yes. But, you see, I think this is it. What I mean is, I think my family used to live here, in this house."

"Nobody in our family was named Andresen, or moved to America. Are you sure you have the right town?"

"My father is Frank Andresen? When he lived here he went by Fridtjof."

"Fridtjof," Lillian says, and this seems to take a moment to register as she looks up in concentration trying to access why that name sounds familiar. But then suddenly she finds it and she looks at Faye and her stare feels piercing.

"You know Fridtjof?"

"I'm his daughter."

"Oh, my," she says, and she grabs Faye by the wrist. "Come this way."

She leads Faye into the house, first through a pantry full of vegetables elaborately canned and pickled and labeled, through a warm kitchen where some bready thing is baking, the air smelling of yeast and cardamom, and into a small living room with squeaky wood floors and wood furniture that seems antique and handmade.

"Wait here," says Lillian, who lets go of Faye's wrist and disappears through another door. The room she's left in is cozy and richly decorated with blankets and pillows and photographs on the walls. Presumably family photos, which Faye studies. None of the people here look familiar, except for certain of the men who have a quality around the eyes that Faye recognizes from her father—or maybe she's imagining it?— a familiar kind of squint, a familiar way with the eyebrow, the slight wrinkle between the eyes. There are lamps and chandeliers and candles and sconces all over, presumably to light the place brilliantly during the interminable winter darkness. A big stone fireplace occupies one wall. Another wall is filled with books with unassuming white spines and titles Faye does not recognize. A laptop computer that seems anachronistic in the otherwise old-fashioned room. Faye can hear Lillian speaking through the door, speaking gently but quickly. Faye does not know a single word of Norwegian, so the language is only a phonic event for her, its vowels sounding a little flat, almost like German spoken in a minor key. Like most languages that are not American English, it seems to move too fast.

Soon the door opens and Lillian returns, followed by her mother, and when Faye sees her it's like she's looking into a mirror—in the eyes, and the way they both hunch at the shoulders, and the way age has played out on both their faces. The woman recognizes it too, as she comes to an abrupt stop when she sees Faye and they stare at each other for a moment, not moving. It would be clear to anyone watching that they're sisters. Faye can see her father's features play out on the woman's face: his cheekbones, his eyes, his nose. The woman cocks her head, suspicious. She has an unruly mass of gray hair tied up at the top by a ribbon. She's wearing a plain black shirt and old blue jeans, both dotted with the evidence of many domestic chores: paint and spackle and, on the jeans, on the knees, mud. She is barefoot. She is wiping her hands clean with a dark blue rag.

"I am Freya," she says, and Faye's heart leaps. Every ghost story her father told her, every one involving a beautiful young girl, this was the name he gave her: Freya.

"I'm sorry to bother you," Faye says.

"You are Fridtjof's daughter?"

"Yes. Fridtjof Andresen."

"You're from America?"

"Chicago."

"So," she says to nobody in particular, "he went to America." Then she gestures toward Lillian, "Show her," and Lillian fetches a book from a shelf and sits on the couch. The book is an antique, yellowed brittle pages, two flaps of leather protecting its cover, a clasp on the front. Faye has seen one of these before: her father's Bible, the one with the family tree on the inside filled with exotic names he used to show her and cluck disapprovingly at because they were all too cowardly to make a better life for themselves in America. And the Bible in Lillian's lap is just the same sort, a family tree on the front two pages. But whereas her father's stopped at Faye, this one shows the full blooming of the family here in Hammerfest. Lillian, Faye can see, is one of Freya's six children. Grandchildren fill the next line down, a few great-grandchildren below that. It's a flourishing that takes another sheet of paper to fully accommodate. And above Freya's name are her parents' names: Marthe, her mother, and another name, blacked out, inked over. Freya shuffles toward them and stands in front of Faye and bends to point at that spot.

"This was Fridtjof," she says, her fingernail pressing a crescent into the page.

"He's your father too."

"Yes."

"His name is erased."

"My mother did that."

"Why?"

"Because he was a . . . oh, how do you say it?" She looks at Lillian for help with the word. She says something in Norwegian and Lillian nods in comprehension and says, "Oh. You mean, *coward*."

"Yes," Freya says. "He was a coward." And she watches Faye, waiting to see what kind of reaction this will bring, whether Faye will be offended by this, and Freya is tense and maybe waiting for an argument she seems perfectly willing to have.

"I don't understand," says Faye. "A coward. Why?"

"Because he left. He abandoned us."

"No. He immigrated," Faye says. "He tried to make a better life for himself."

"For himself, yes."

"He never mentioned he had family here."

"Then you don't know very much about him."

"Will you tell me?"

Freya breathes heavily and looks at Faye with what feels like impatience or disdain.

"Is he still alive?"

"Yes, but his mind is going. He's very old."

"What did he do in America?"

"He worked at a factory. A chemical factory."

"And did he have a good life?"

Faye thinks about this for a moment, about all those times she saw her father alone, keeping his distance from others, desolate, in his own self-made prison, standing for hours in the backyard staring into the sky.

"No," she says. "He always seemed sad. And lonely. We never knew why."

Freya seems to soften at this. She nods. She says, "Stay for dinner, then. I'll tell you the story."

And she does, over bread and a fish stew. It's the story Freya's mother told her when Freya was old enough to understand it. It begins in 1940, the last time anyone heard anything about Fridtjof Andresen. Like most young men in Hammerfest, he was a fisherman. He was seventeen and had recently graduated from the dockside work given to children, the cleaning and gutting and filleting. He now worked on the boat, which was an all-around better job: more lucrative, more fun, so much more thrilling when they'd drag up whole big nets of cod and halibut and the evil-looking, foul-smelling wolffish, which everyone universally agreed was better to catch than to gut. Whole days spent out on the water, losing track of the days because in the summer in the arctic the sun never sets. And feeling proud of the mastery he achieved with his trade's various tools, the buoys and nets and kegs and lines and hooks stored in the hull just so. His favorite thing was sitting lookout atop the highest mast because he had the sharpest eyes on the boat. He had a gift; everyone said so. He spotted the schools of blackfish that steered into the bay all summer long, and seeing a boiling spot on the water he yelled "Fish-o!" and all the men would roll out of bed and put on their caps and get to work. They'd lower the rowboats, two men per craft—one to handle the oars, the other, the net—and they'd spread the net between them and he'd direct the whole operation from up top until the school reached them and they'd encircle the fish and hoist the whole churning mass of them triumphantly into the boat. There was power in that, their control over the wild sea, feeling unstoppable even while they sailed too close to jagged shores that would doom their ship to sinking if they weren't such capable sailors.

Fridtjof could spot the fish better than anyone in living memory. He had the sharpest eyes in town, and he bragged about this constantly, whenever they were in port. He said the ocean was a piece of paper only he could read. He was young. He had a bit of money. He spent time in bars. He met a waitress named Marthe. It might not be accurate to say he fell in love with her. More like they were both feeling certain common teenage longings and they made themselves available to satisfy them. The first time they made love it was in the hills near her family's house, after he'd waited for the bar to close and walked her home and they lay in the tough grass under a gray-white sun. Then she showed him around the land, the big house painted salmon-red, the long pier over the water, the long line of spruce trees, the field of barley. She loved it here, she said. She was a charming girl.

That was the summer the war came. Everyone thought Hammerfest was too remote to be of any concern, but it turned out the Germans wanted the city to disrupt Allied shipping to Russia, plus it would serve as an effective resupply base for their U-boats. The Wehrmacht was coming, was the word that spread up Norway's coast, from dock to dock, boat to boat. There was talk on Fridtjof's ship of escape. They could make it to Iceland. Start a new life there. Or keep going. There were ways to get from Reykjavík to America, some said. But what about the submarines? They wouldn't bother their little fishing boat. But what about the mines? Fridtjof would spot them, they said. It could be done.

Fridtjof wanted to believe what some of the older men said, that the Germans were more interested in the docks than in the city, that they would leave everyone alone as long as there wasn't a resistance, that their fight was with Russia and Britain, not Norway. But rumors had been spreading about happenings in the south: surprise attacks, burned villages. Fridtjof didn't know what to think. On their next landing in Hammerfest, the crew would make a decision: stay or go. Anyone who wanted to stay was free to do so. Anyone wanting to risk the voyage to Iceland would bring all the supplies he could manage.

The only one who didn't have a choice was Fridtjof. Or at least that's how it seemed to him, when the older guys took him aside and said they needed his eyes. Only he could spot the mines that made the waters out beyond the islands so treacherous. Only he could read the swirls and eddies that signaled the presence of a U-boat. Only he could see the shapes of enemy ships way out there on the horizon, far enough away to avoid them. He had a gift, they all agreed. They'd be dead without him.

That night he waited for the bar to close and went to see Marthe. She was so happy to see him. They made love in the grass again and afterward she told him she was pregnant.

"We'll have to get married, of course," she said.

"Of course."

"My parents say you can live with us. We'll inherit the house someday."

"Yes. Good."

"My grandmother thinks it's a girl. She's usually right about these things. I want to name her Freya."

They made plans for most of the night. In the morning, he told her he was voyaging out to hunt cod to the northeast. He told her he'd be back in a week. She smiled. She kissed him goodbye. And she never saw him again.

When Freya was born, she was born to an occupied city. The Germans had come and removed most families from their homes. Soldiers lived in the houses now, while everyone else crowded into apartment buildings or schools or the church. Marthe shared a single flat with sixteen other families. Some of Freya's earliest memories were from this time of hunger and desperation. They lived this way for four years before the Germans withdrew. On that day, in the winter of 1944, every living soul in Hammerfest was ordered to evacuate the city. Those who did fled to the forest. Those who didn't were killed. The Germans burned the city to the ground. Every structure except the church. When the people returned, there was nothing left to return to but rock and rubble and ash. They lived through that winter in the hills, in caves. Freya remembers the cold, and the smoke from the fires they burned, smoke that kept everyone awake coughing and hacking. She remembers vomiting spoonfuls of acid and ash into her hand.

In the spring they emerged from shelter and began rebuilding Hammerfest. But they did not have the resources to make it what it once was. That's why the city looks in places the way it looks now, cheap and anonymous, a testament not to beauty but to resilience. Marthe's family rebuilt their house as best they could, even painting it the same color, that same salmon-red, and eventually, when Freya was old enough, Marthe told her the story of Fridtjof Andresen, her father. Nobody had ever heard from him after the war. They assumed he fled to Sweden, like so many others did. Sometimes Freya would go out to watch the fishing boats, imagining him on top of one searching the ocean for her. She'd daydream about his return, but then the years went by and she grew up and had her own family and she stopped wishing for his return and started hating him, then stopped hating him and began simply forgetting him. Before Faye arrived, she hadn't thought about her father in years.

"I don't think my mother ever forgave him," Freya says. "She was unhappy most of her life, angry with him, or with herself. She's dead now."

It's just past seven o'clock and the sunlight pouring into the kitchen is slanted and gold. Freya slaps her palms on the table and stands up.

"Let's go to the water," she says. "For sunset."

She brings Faye a coat and on the walk down explains that sunsets are a precious thing in Hammerfest because they get so few of them. Tonight, the sun sets at eight fifteen. A month ago, it was setting at midnight. In another month, it will get dark at five thirty. And one day in mid-November, the sun will rise at around eleven o'clock in the morning, set about half an hour later, and that's the last they'll see of it for two whole months.

"Two months of darkness," Faye says. "How do you bear it?"

"You get used to it," she says. "What choice do you have?"

They sit on the dock in silence drinking coffee and feeling a cold breeze coming off the water and watching a copper-colored sun set over the Norwegian Sea.

Faye tries to imagine her father sitting high above the water, perched on the uppermost mast of a fishing boat, the wind reddening his face. What it must have been like for him, in comparison, at the ChemStar factory in Iowa—turning dials, recording numbers, doing paperwork, standing on the flat, dull earth. And what would he have been thinking as they left for Iceland, as he watched Hammerfest recede from view, leaving behind a home, a child. How long would he regret it? How big would that regret become? Faye suspects he regretted it forever. That the regret became his secret heart, the thing he buried most deeply. She remembers him as he was when he thought no one was looking, staring off into the distance. Faye always wondered what he was seeing in those moments, and now she thinks she knows. He was seeing this place, these people. He was wondering what might have been had he made a different decision. It was impossible to ignore the similarity of their names: Freya and Faye. When he named her Faye, was he thinking about the other daughter? When he spoke Faye's name, did he always hear the echo of this other name? Was Faye just a reminder of the family he left behind? Was he trying to punish himself? When he described the home in Hammerfest, he described it as though he'd actually lived here, described it as though it were his. And maybe, in his mind, it was. Maybe next to the actual world was this fantasy, this other life where he inherited the farm with the salmon-red house. Sometimes those fantasies can be more persuasive than one's own life, Faye knows.

Something does not have to happen for it to feel real.

Her father was never more animated, never happier, than when he spoke about this place, and maybe even as a child Faye recognized this. She understood that part of her father was always somewhere else. That when he looked at her he never really saw *her*. And she wonders now if all her panic attacks and problems had been elaborate attempts to be paid attention to, to be seen. She'd convinced herself she was haunted by ghosts from the old country because—even though she didn't understand it in these terms—maybe she was trying to be Freya for him.

"Do you have children?" Freya asks, breaking the long silence.

"A son."

"Are you close?"

"Yes," Faye says, because, once again, she's too embarrassed to tell the truth. How could she ever tell this woman that she did to her son what Fridtjof did to her? "We're very close," she says.

"Good, good."

Faye thinks about Samuel, and seeing him in the airport a few days ago, saying goodbye to him. She had found herself, at that moment, overcome with a peculiar need: to press herself into him, to feel him physically *there*. It turned out, the thing she missed the most was his heat. Those long years after she left the family, what she longed for more than anything was that human warmth, how Samuel would climb into bed on those mornings when another of his nightmares terrified him, or how he'd press into her when he was running a fever. Whenever his need was great, he'd come to her, this little cauldron, this hot humid ball. She'd press her face into him and smell his little-boy smell, like sweat and syrup and grass. He ran so hot her skin would dampen where it touched him, and she imagined his core burning with all the energy his body would need for its growth to manhood. It was that warmth she craved suddenly in the airport. She has not felt such a thing in a very long time. Mostly she's chilled—maybe because of the pills, her anxiety drugs, her blood thinners and beta-blockers. She's always so cold these days.

The sun is down now and they're staring at a purple sky. Lillian is in the house lighting a fire. Freya sits listening to the rushing water. To their right, up the coast, is an island where in the gathering darkness Faye can see a bright tongue of light.

"What is that?" she says, pointing.

"Melkøya," Freya says. "It's a factory. It's where they take the gas."

"And that light?"

"Fire. It burns all the time. I don't know why."

And Faye stares at the smokestack venting its orange flame into the night and all at once she's transported back to Iowa, she's sitting with Henry on the shore of the Mississippi River and she's looking at the fire coming out of the nitrogen plant. She could see that fire from anywhere in town. She used to call it the lighthouse. That was so long ago it feels like a different life. And at the sudden recall of this long-dormant memory, Faye begins to cry. Not a hard cry, but a light and delicate one. She thinks about what Samuel would have called it, this crying—a Category 1— and she smiles. Freya either does not notice the crying or pretends not to notice it.

"I'm sorry I got him and you didn't," Faye says. "Our father, I mean. I'm sorry he left you. It's not fair."

Freya waves at her, dismissing it. "We managed."

"I know he missed you a great deal."

"Thank you."

"I think he always wanted to come back. I think he regretted leaving."

Freya stands and looks out at the water. "It's good he stayed away."

"Why?"

"Look around you," she says, opening her arms to the house, the land, the animals, to Lillian and the fire she's building and the Bible with its exhausting family tree. "We didn't need him."

She extends her hand to Faye and they shake, a formal gesture declaring the end of this conversation and the end of Faye's visit.

"It was very nice to meet you," Freya says.

"And you."

"I hope you have a nice stay."

"I will. Thank you for your hospitality."

"Lillian will drive you to your hotel."

"It's not far. I can walk."

Freya nods and begins making her way toward the house. But then a few steps up the path, she stops and turns to Faye and looks at her with these knowing eyes that seem to pass straight through her and access every secret she has inside.

"These old stories aren't important anymore, Faye. Go back to your son."

And all Faye can do is nod her head in agreement and watch as Freya ascends the rest of the way and disappears into the house. Faye lingers a moment on the dock before leaving as well. She follows a path up the ridge, and when she reaches the top, at precisely the place she met the horse, she looks back down into the valley at the house, now lit warm and golden, a thin tendril of blue smoke drifting from the chimney. Maybe this is where her father stood. Maybe this is what he remembered. Maybe this is the vision that passed before his eyes those nights in Iowa when he stared into nothingness. It would be a memory that sustained him his whole life, but it would also be the thing that haunted him. And that old story about the ghost that looks like a rock comes to her now: The farther from shore you take it, the heavier it becomes, until one day it gets too heavy to bear.

Faye imagines her father taking a small piece of earth with him, a memento: this farm, this family, his memory of it. This was the *drowning stone* from his stories. He took it to sea and took it to Iceland and took it all the way to America. And as long as he held on to it, he just kept sinking.

2

WHY HAVE HOSPITAL ROOMS begun to look like hotel rooms, is something Samuel wonders as he looks around at this hospital room's beige walls and beige ceiling and beige curtains and industrially sturdy carpet whose color could be described as tan or wheat or beige. Paintings on the walls designed to be inoffensive and forgettable and un-upsetting and so abstract they do not remind anyone of anything. Television with a billion channels including FREE HBO, according to the little cardboard sign on the dresser. A fake-oak dresser with a Bible inside. The desk in the corner with the many ports and outlets is the "wireless workstation" with a Wi-Fi password printed on laminated paper crinkled and splitting at the edges. A room service menu where you can order things like chicken-fried steaks and french fries and milk shakes and have them delivered anywhere in the building, even the cardiac wing. The remote control Velcroed to the television. The television bolted to the wall and angled toward the bed so that it's like the television is watching the patient and not the other way around. A book of nearby Chicago attractions. The couch along the far wall is actually a hide-a-bed, which is something anyone will realize if they sit on it too quickly and bang into its hard metal architecture. A digital clock radio with green numbers currently blinking midnight.

A doctor in the room, thoroughly bald, explaining the case to a group of medical students. "Patient's name, unknown," he says. "An alias he goes by is, um, let's see, *Puh-wan-edge*?"

The doctor looks to Samuel for help.

"Pwnage," Samuel says. "Two syllables. Rhymes with *ownage,* but with a *p.*"

"What's *ownage?*" says one of the students.

"Did he say orange?" says another.

"I think he said porridge."

The doctor tells the students they are lucky to be here today because they may never see a case quite like this again, and indeed the doctor is considering writing an article about this patient in the *Journal of Medical Oddities,* which the students would be invited to co-author, of course. The students look at Pwnage with the same bemused appreciation they might have for a bartender preparing them an elaborate drink for free.

Pwnage has been sleeping for three days straight. Not in a coma, the doctor has pointed out. Sleeping. The hospital is nourishing him intravenously. And Samuel has to admit that Pwnage looks better, his skin less waxy, his face less bulbous, the splotchy rashes all over his neck and arms now faded to more or less normal human textures. Even his hair seems healthier, more (and this is the only way Samuel can think of describing it) *well-attached.* The doctor is listing the various medical conditions the patient presented upon admission to the emergency room: "Malnutrition, exhaustion, malignant hypertension, kidney and liver malfunction, dehydration so far along that frankly I'm not sure how the patient wasn't hallucinating more or less all the time about water." The students write this down.

The doctor's head and face and arms have achieved a really impressive sharklike hairlessness. The medical students carry clipboards and they collectively smell like antiseptic soap and cigarettes. A heartbeat monitor connected to Pwnage by a series of wires and suction cups is not beeping. Samuel stands with Axman and keeps looking at him with these quick sidelong glances that he hopes Axman won't notice. Samuel has heard Axman speaking over the computer hundreds of times from their many raids together but has never met him in person, and he's feeling that dislocation you feel when the visual does not match up with the aural, like when you see a radio personality's face for the first time and you think: *Really?* Axman's voice has that whiny, nasally quality that makes him seem, online, like he must be one of those ninety-pound bepimpled nearsighted sissies who are the very quintessence of the online gamer stereotype. His reedy voice is the phonic equivalent of a punch that does not hurt. The kind of voice that makes it sound like his mouth was stuffed into his sinus cavity a long time ago by bullies.

"—and cardiac arrhythmia," the doctor is saying, "diabetic ketoacidosis, diabetes, which he probably didn't even know he had and which he definitely was not managing in any way and which made his blood about the same thickness and consistency as instant pudding."

The real-life Axman turns out to be stylish and dashing—his tight-shorts-and-tank-top combo, and his tanned arms that are muscular but not gaudily so, and his sockless boat shoes, and his moderately curly hair begging to be playfully tussled, it all seems like he dressed from some instruction manual given only to young hip gay men. Pretty soon he's going to discover sex and then he'll wonder why he ever spent so much time playing video games.

"So we were all there," Axman is saying, "on the cliffs above Mistwater Cape. You know the place?"

Samuel nods. It's a spot on the *Elfscape* map, the southernmost point of the western continent, the place Pwnage apparently had his near-terminal medical crisis. That's where Axman found him, his avatar, naked and dead, and he noticed Pwnage's prolonged AFK status, which stands for "away from keyboard," which Pwnage almost never was, Axman knew, away from his keyboard. So Axman called the real-life authorities, who went to investigate and saw through the front windows Pwnage slumped unconscious before his computer.

"I told everyone to meet at Mistwater," Axman says in a semi-whisper so as not to interrupt the doctor. "I posted it online. 'Candlelight vigil for Pwnage.' We had a pretty good turnout. Maybe thirty people. All elves, of course."

"Of course," Samuel says. He has the feeling one of the attractive female medical students is right now eavesdropping on their conversation, and he feels that embarrassment he feels whenever someone from the real world discovers this is what he does with his spare time: plays *Elfscape*.

"All these elves standing there with our lit candles. And except for one guy in the back who was break-dancing and not really taking part, it was a somber and beautiful and mournful scene."

"—and a rash on his arm that looked alarmingly similar to, but thankfully was not, necrotizing fasciitis," says the doctor. The dome of his bare head shines. It makes the room feel bigger in the same way a large mirror might.

"But so here's the thing," Axman says, and he's now gripping Samuel's shirt and pulling lightly at it to keep Samuel's attention and to express his own agitation. "I posted plans for the vigil online, in the Elves Only forum. But it turns out there were some trolls who saw it too."

"Trolls?"

588 | THE NIX

"Yeah, orcs."

"Wait, trolls or orcs?"

"Orcs who were trolling. You know what I mean. Some orc-playing players saw the news about the candlelight vigil and reposted it in the Orcs Only forum, which of course I didn't see because I don't read their forums because I'm honorable like that."

The reason the heartbeat monitor is not beeping is because heartbeat monitors in real life do not beep, Samuel decides. That must be a Hollywood affectation, a way to report to the audience what's going on inside the patient's chest. The heartbeat monitor attached to Pwnage just slowly prints a jagged line onto a narrow piece of paper that's spooled up like something inside a cash register.

"So unbeknownst to us," Axman says, "while we're gathering on the cliffs above Mistwater Cape, the orcs are hiding in a cave to the north. And right in the middle of our ceremony, which I should stress was, with the exception of the guy who was break-dancing and then later took off all his clothes and jumped around a lot, really somber and beautiful and quiet, right in the middle, right as I'm making a speech about what a great guy Pwnage is and how we're all hoping he gets better soon and urging people to write get-well cards to him and giving out the address of the hospital so that they can write actual real paper cards, all of a sudden all these orcs rush out of the trees and start murdering us."

The attractive medical student seems to be chewing on her pencil either to suppress the smile or outright giggle generated by eavesdropping on this particular conversation. Or because she's a smoker and that's one of those oral-fixation unconscious-tic things that smokers tend to do. The doctor's head has the buffed quality of a new bowling ball still wrapped in its protective sheath.

"So all of our orc alarms start going off and we all turn around to fight them," says Axman. "Only we can't fight them. Do you know why we can't fight them?"

"Because you're all holding candles?"

"Because we're all holding candles."

That the doctor does not even have eyebrows or eyelashes is an unsettling quality it takes Samuel a few minutes to identify. Before that, it was like the guy looked off for a reason he couldn't quite put his finger on.

"So this orc starts fighting me," Axman says, "and I instinctively swing at him and hit him, but of course I hit him with a candle, which does like zero damage and causes him to ROFL over and over. So I open my control panel and select the character screen and select the candle and then locate my sword in my inventory screen and then double-click to switch them and the game says *Are you sure you want to trade items?* and all this time the orc is chopping me in half slowly with his ax, swinging away casually and I'm just standing there like a tree totally helpless to stop him, and I'm all like to the game *Yes I want to trade items! Yes I'm fucking sure!*"

At Axman's sudden outburst the doctor and the students look over with these expressions of disdain that communicate how quickly he'd be thrown out of here had he not saved the life of the patient they're going to write a quirky journal article about.

"So anyway," says Axman, quieter now, "I ultimately don't have time to even switch weapons because I'm fully dead way before I get through the process. And so my ghost resurrects at the nearest graveyard and I run the ghost back to my body and respawn and you know what happens?"

"The orcs are still there."

"The orcs are still there, and I'm still holding a goddamn candle."

"—and lactic acidosis," says the doctor, stronger now, trying to talk over Axman, "and hyperthyroidism, urinary retention, croup." The doctor's allover hairlessness is beginning to seem clinical and not aesthetic, like he suffers from a genetic disorder the kids probably made fun of throughout his childhood, which makes Samuel feel a little guilty for staring.

"And this happens maybe twenty or thirty times," says Axman. "I get back to my body, respawn, and get killed within seconds. Rinse and repeat. I wait for the orcs to get tired of it, but they never do. I finally get so angry I log out and post a pretty big rant on the Orcs Only forum where I say the behavior of the orcs who crashed our vigil was reprehensible and immoral. I said all their accounts should be banned and they should personally apologize to everyone in our guild. This ignited a pretty big debate."

"What's the consensus?"

"The orcs said their maneuver was accurately orc-like. They said killing us during our vigil was in keeping with how orcs are supposed to act in the game world. I said sometimes the game world and the real world overlap in certain places where the real world should take precedence, like during a quiet vigil where friends are mourning for their seriously ill raid-leader buddy. They said their orc avatars don't know what this 'real world' is that I'm talking about and for them the *Elfscape* world is the only world that exists. I said if that's true then they would never have known about the vigil in the first place because they don't have orc laptops from which to access the Elves Only online forums, and even if they did, they could not comprehend what was written there because orcs cannot read English."

"This all sounds very complicated."

"It opened up this big metaphysical problem about how much of the real world you're bracketing when you're playing *Elfscape*. Most of our guild is taking the week off from raiding to think about the problem."

"Did you ever log on again?"

"Not yet. My elf is still on that cliff. Dismembered."

The doctor is saying, "I swear to god this is the first time I've ever seen a pulmonary embolism be the *least bad* thing wrong with someone. Compared to everything else going on here, the anticoagulant we administered for the embolism was an easy fix."

Samuel feels the little buzzing of his phone in his pocket that signals a new e-mail. He sees it's from his mother. Despite their agreement, she has written. He excuses himself and goes into the hallway to read it.

Samuel,

I know we said I shouldn't do this, but I've had a change of heart. If the police ask, please tell them the truth. I didn't stay in London. I didn't go to Jakarta. I went to Hammerfest. It's in Norway, the northernmost city in the world. It's terribly remote and sparsely populated. You'd think it would suit me. I'm telling you this because I've decided not to stay. I've met some people who have convinced me to come home. I'll explain later.

Actually, Hammerfest is no longer the northernmost city in the world, I just discovered. Technically it is the second-northernmost. There's a place called Honningsvaag that is also in Norway and slightly farther north that declared itself a city a few years back. But with a population of about 3,000 people, you can hardly call it a "city." So the debate rages on. Most folks in Hammerfest are friendly to anyone except people from Honningsvaag, whom they consider usurpers and bastards.

The things you learn, eh?

At any rate, Hammerfest is distant and isolated. It'll take me a few days to get home.

In the meantime, I want you to go find your friend Periwinkle. Tell him to tell you the truth. You deserve some answers. Tell him I said to tell you everything. He and I go way back, you should know. We met in college. I used to be in love with him. If you want proof, go back to my apartment. On the shelf, there's a thick book of poetry, the collected Ginsberg. I want you to look inside that book. You'll find a photograph. I hid it in there years ago. Please don't be angry with me when you find it. Soon you'll have all the answers you want, and when you do, remember that all I was trying to do was help. I did it clumsily, but I did it for you.

Love,
Faye

Samuel thanks Axman and tells him to send word once Pwnage wakes up. He leaves the hospital and drives quickly into Chicago. He enters his mother's apartment through the still-wrecked door. He finds the book and begins flipping through it, holding it upside down and shaking it. It has that old-book smell, dry and musty. The pages are yellowed and feel brittle on his fingertips. A photograph flutters out and lands on the floor facedown. On the back, it is signed: *To Faye, on your Honeymoon, love Al.*

Samuel picks it up. It is the same photograph he'd seen on the news, the one taken at that protest in 1968. There is his mother in her big round glasses. There is Alice sitting behind her all deadly serious. But this photograph is larger than the one he'd seen on the news, its field of vision wider. He realizes that the photo he thought he knew so well was actually only a fragment from this bigger photo, sectioned off, cropped to hide the man his mother leans against. But Samuel can see him now, this man, his bowl of black hair, the way he looks sidelong and cleverly at the camera, his eyes full of mischief. He is so young, and his face is half in shadow, but it's obvious. Samuel has seen that face before. It's the spitting image of Guy Periwinkle.

3

GUY PERIWINKLE'S OFFICE in downtown Manhattan is on the twentieth floor, southeast corner, overlooking the financial district. Two whole walls are made entirely of glass. The other walls are painted a neutral slate gray. A small desk in the middle of the room, a single swivel chair. There are no works of art on the walls, no family photos, no statuary or plants, nothing on the desk but a single sheet of paper. The aesthetic here is way beyond minimalism—more like monkish denial. The only decoration in the entire large space is a single framed advertisement for some kind of new potato-chip thing. The new chip is shaped like a small torpedo instead of the more traditional triangle or circle. The ad is dominated by a photograph of a man and a woman whose bug-eyed excitement to eat these chips might best be described as maniacal. A caption above them, written in bold three-dimensional-looking letters, says: DO YOU NEED TO LIVEN UP YOUR SNACK ROUTINE? This advertisement is roughly the size of a movie poster. It looks out of place in its lavish gold frame.

Samuel has been waiting for twenty minutes, walking around the room like a bean jumping in its pod, from window to advertisement and back, studying each thing for as long as he can before his agitation twists him up and he feels it necessary to pace. He'd left for New York directly from his mother's apartment. It is the second time in his life he's driven from Chicago to New York City, and the feeling of déjà vu is so powerful right now that he's feeling this low-level background dread: The last time he drove to New York, it did not turn out well. And it's impossible not to remember this right now, because as he stares out Periwinkle's office window he can see, a few blocks to the east, that old familiar building, the thin white one with the gargoyles near the top: the building at 55 Liberty Street. Bethany's building.

He stares at the building and wonders if she's there right now, maybe looking this way, in Samuel's direction, at all the ruckus below. For between Bethany's building and Periwinkle's, way down at street level, is Zuccotti Park—though "park" is a generous term for this small patch of concrete no larger than a few tennis courts, where protesters have been gathered for weeks. Samuel had waded through the crowd on his way into the building. WE ARE THE 99 PERCENT, their signs said. THIS SPACE OCCUPIED. From above, he can see the great mass of people, the fluorescent blue nylon bubbles of their tents, the drum circle on the outer edge, which is all he can hear of the protest from up here on the twentieth floor: the endless, unstoppable drumming.

He moves back to the advertisement. The new torpedo-shaped potato chips seem to come in their own special plastic serving cups with peel-away tops like yogurt. The way the couple stares at the chips in anticipation of eating them is so manic that it almost looks like terror.

The door opens and Periwinkle finally appears. He wears his usual tight gray suit and colorful tie—turquoise today. His hair is newly dyed and looks lacquered black. He sees Samuel looking at the potato-chip poster and says, "That advertisement tells you everything you need to know about twenty-first-century America."

He swings himself into the desk chair and swivels it around until he faces Samuel. "Everything I need to know to do my job is right there," he says, pointing at it. "If you can understand this ad's insight, then you can conquer the world."

"It's a stupid potato chip," Samuel says.

"Of course it's a stupid potato chip. It's that phrase I love: *snack routine.*"

Outside, the drumming swells and then dissipates by some improvisational musical logic.

"I guess I'm missing it," Samuel says, "the genius."

"Think about it. Why does one eat a snack? Why is a snack necessary? The answer—and we've done a million studies on this—is because our lives are filled with tedium and drudgery and endless toil and we need a tiny blip of pleasure to repel the gathering darkness. Thus, we give ourselves a treat.

"But here's the thing," Periwinkle continues, his eyes all aglow, "even the things we do to break the routine *become routine.* Even the things we do to escape the sadness of our lives have themselves become sad. What this ad acknowledges is that you've been eating all these snacks and yet you are not happy, and you've been watching all these shows and yet you still feel lonely, and you've been seeing all this news and yet the world makes no sense, and you've been playing all these games and yet the melancholy sinks deeper and deeper into you. How do you escape?"

"You buy a new chip."

"You buy a missile-shaped chip! That's the answer. What this ad does is admit something you already deeply suspect and existentially fear: that consumerism is a failure and you will never find any meaning there no matter how much money you spend. So the great challenge for people like me is to convince people like you that the problem is not systemic. It's not that snacks leave you feeling empty, it's that you *haven't found the right snack yet*. It's not that TV turns out to be a poor substitute for human connection, it's that you haven't found the right show yet. It's not that politics are hopelessly bankrupt, it's that you haven't found the right politician yet. And this ad just comes right out and says it. I swear to god it's like playing poker against someone who's showing his cards and yet still bluffing by force of personality."

"This isn't exactly what I came here to talk about."

"It's a heroic job, when you think about it. What I do. It's the only thing that America's good at anymore. We don't make the snacks. Our specialty is making new ways to think about snacks."

"So it's patriotic, then. You're a patriot."

"Have you ever heard of the Chauvet cave paintings?"

"No."

"They're in southern France. Oldest paintings ever found there. We're talking like thirty thousand years old. Scenes typical of the Paleolithic— horses, cattle, mammoths, that kind of thing. No pictures of humans but one depiction of a vagina, for what that's worth. The really interesting thing is what happened when they carbon-dated the place. They found pictures in the same room painted six thousand years apart. They looked *identical*."

"Okay. So?"

"So think about that. For six thousand years there was no progress and no evidence of any impulse to change anything. People were fine with the way things were. In other words, this is not a people experiencing spiritual desolation. You and I need new diversions nightly. These people didn't change a thing for sixty centuries. This is not a people tired of their snack routine."

The drumming outside escalates for a moment and then fades back into a kind of ominous tolling.

"Melancholy," Periwinkle says, "had to be invented. Civilization had this unintended side effect, which is melancholy. Tedium. Routine. Gloom. And when those things were birthed, so were people like me, to attend to them. So no, it's not patriotism. It's evolution."

"Guy Periwinkle, pinnacle of evolution."

"I understand you're trying to be sarcastic there, but a word like *pinnacle* doesn't make sense in an evolutionary context. Remember that evolution is value-free. It's not what's best, it's just what survives. I assume you're here to talk about your mother?"

"Yes."

"And where is she these days?"

"Norway."

Periwinkle stares at him for a moment, digesting this.

"Wow," he says, eventually.

"Northern Norway," Samuel says, "all the way at the top of it."

"I'm speechless, for I think maybe the very first time."

"She wants you to tell me the truth."

"About what?"

"Everything."

"I really seriously doubt that."

"About you and her."

"There are certain things that children let's say have the right not to know about their mothers."

"You met each other in college."

"What I mean is I seriously doubt she wants you to know *everything*."

"That was her word. That was the word she used."

"Yes, but did she mean it literally? Because there are certain things—"

"You met each other in college. You were lovers."

"This is what I'm saying! There are certain details, certain sexual things of a sexual nature—"

"Tell me the truth, please."

"Certain, let us say, racy particulars you and I would almost definitely agree we should be spared the embarrassment of, if you understand my drift."

"You knew my mother in college, in Chicago. Yes or no."

"Yes."

"How did you know her?"

"Biblically."

"What I mean is, how did you come to meet her?"

"She was a new student. I was a counterculture hero. Back then I went by a different name. Sebastian. Sexy, right? And so much better than Guy. You can't be a counterculture hero *and* a Guy. That name is way too average. Anyway, your mother sort of fell for me. It happened. And, yeah, I fell for her too. She was a cool girl. Sweet and smart and compassionate and totally uninterested in getting people to pay attention to her, which was unusual for my social circle back then, when even my friends' wardrobe choices had a kind of *Look at me!* subtext. Faye never bought into it, which was refreshing. Anyway, I published a newspaper called the *Chicago Free Voice*. It was the thing all the turned-on kids read. Your late-sixties version of an internet meme, to put it in terms you might understand."

"It doesn't sound like my mother to be drawn to something like that."

"It was a seriously influential newspaper. Really. You can read every edition at the Chicago History Museum. They'll make you wear these tiny white gloves to touch it. Or you can access it on microfiche. They've all been archived and microfiched."

"My mother is not exactly a people person. Why did she get involved with a protest movement?"

"She didn't intend to. She was more like dropped into the middle of it, so to speak. Do you even know what microfiche is? Or are you too young for that? Little black-and-white coils that you spool into this machine that blows hot air and goes *ka-chunk* when you turn the page. Very analog."

"She was dropped into the middle of it because of you?"

"Me and Alice and this cop who got involved, this guy with some serious jealousy-management issues."

"Judge Brown."

"Yes. That was unexpected, encountering him again. Back in '68 he was a cop who, I think, really wanted to kill your mother."

"Because he thought she was having an affair with Alice, whom he loved."

"That's right! That's right all the way down to the correct usage of 'whom.' Congratulations. Now keep going. Tell me what you know. Tell me about 1988. It's twenty years later and your mother finally leaves your father, leaves you. Where does she go? Tell me."

"I have no idea. She goes to live in Chicago? In her tiny apartment?"

"Think harder," Periwinkle says. He leans forward in his chair, his hands clasped and resting on his desk. "One moment your mother's in college, in the beating heart of the protest movement, the next she's married to your dad, the frozen-foods salesman, living his safe suburban life. Imagine how that must have felt for her after all the thrills and drugs and sex of which I'm not going to give you any details. How long could she last being Henry's housewife before it started burning her up, the decision she didn't make, the life she could have had?"

"She went to *you*?"

"She went to me, Guy Periwinkle, counterculture hero." He spreads his arms like he wants a hug.

"She left my dad for *you*?"

"Your mother is the kind of person who never feels at home no matter where she is. She didn't leave your dad for me, per se. She left your dad because leaving is what she does."

"So she left you too."

"Not as dramatically, but yes. There was some yelling, some disgust on her part. She said I was abandoning my principles. It was the eighties. I was getting rich. Everyone was getting rich. She wanted a life of books and poetry, but that wasn't my, shall we say, career trajectory. She wanted another chance to live like a radical, since she blew it the first time. I told her to grow up. I suppose this is what she meant by telling you everything?"

"I think I need to sit down."

"Here," Periwinkle says, getting up from his chair. He withdraws to the window and stares out.

Samuel sits and rubs his temples at what feels suddenly like a migraine or hangover or concussion.

"The drumming down there sounds like it's improvised and chaotic," Periwinkle says, "but it's actually on a loop. You just have to wait long enough for the repeats."

Samuel's feeling about all this new information is simply to be numb to it for now. He suspects he will be feeling something very powerful, very soon. But right now all he can really do is imagine his mother working up the courage to go to New York, only to be utterly disillusioned once she got here. He imagines her doing this and he feels sad for her. They are exactly alike.

"I suppose my big book contract wasn't some huge coincidence."

"Your mother was snooping on the internet," Periwinkle says. "She found out you were a writer. Or trying to be one. She called me and asked for a favor. I figured I owed her at least that much."

"Good lord."

"Bursts your bubble, doesn't it?"

"I actually thought I'd gotten famous on my own."

"The only people who get famous on their own are serial killers. Everyone else needs people like me."

"Governor Packer, for example. He needs someone like you."

"Which brings us to the present."

"I saw you on TV defending him."

"I'm on his campaign. I'm a consultant."

"Isn't that a conflict of interest? Working on his campaign while you're publishing a book about him?"

"I think you're confusing your role here with some kind of journalism. What you call conflict of interest, I call synergy."

"So the day my mother attacked the governor, you were in Chicago, weren't you. You were with him. At his fund-raiser. His grub-down."

"That is his delightfully folksy name for it, yes."

"And while you're there," Samuel says, "you also schedule a meeting with me. At the airport. To tell me you're suing."

"For totally failing to write your book. For completely fucking up the giant contract we gave you. A contract you didn't deserve in the first place, I should add now, since we're putting all our cards on the table and everything."

"And you told my mother about this, this meeting with me, this lawsuit."

"As you can imagine, she was pretty upset that she'd screwed up your life for a second time. She asked to speak with me, before I met with you. She wanted to talk me out of it, I'm guessing. I said okay, let's meet in the park. She asked to meet at the exact spot where, many years ago, police fired tear gas at us. Your mother is a nostalgic sap sometimes."

"And then you showed up with Governor Packer."

"That's correct."

"She must have truly despised that you were working for someone like Governor Packer."

"Well, let's see. She threw away her marriage for some vague liberal antiestablishment idealism. And Packer is the most pro-establishment authoritarian candidate, like, ever. So it's fair to say she was not pleased. She had the same reflexive hatred of him that most die-hard liberals do, comparing him to Hitler and so on, calling him a fascist. She just doesn't understand what I understand."

"And what is that?"

"Packer has the same stuff inside him as anyone else who runs for president. Left or right, they're all made of the same material. It's just that he's shaped like a missile instead of a chip."

The drumming outside slows for a moment and falls apart. Everything goes silent for a few seconds and then begins again with that familiar driving *thumpa-thumpa-thumpa-thumpa*. Periwinkle raises a finger. "There's the repeat," he says.

"You *wanted* all this to happen," says Samuel. "You wanted my mother to react the way she did."

"Some might call it a crime of passion, but I say I presented your mother with an opportunity."

"You set her up."

"In one moment, she had the chance to give you a story that would fulfill your contract, get herself off the hook for screwing up your life again, and give my candidate a much-needed visibility bump. Win win win win. You'll only be angry with me if you fail to see the big picture."

"I cannot believe this."

"Plus remember that I only masterminded it. Your mother was the one who actually picked up the stones and threw them."

"She wasn't aiming at Governor Packer. She was aiming at *you*."

"I was in his entourage, yes."

"And the photograph in the news? The one from '68, where she's leaning on you, at the protest. You had a copy of that."

"A nice present from a great poet."

"You cropped yourself out of it and gave it to the news. You leaked the photo and you leaked my mother's arrest record, which you also knew about."

"I was adding heat. It's what I've always done, what I've always been good at. I should say that your mother attacking me with rocks was a sincere gesture on her part. She really does, I believe, hate me. But afterward, the two of us agreed that in order to make the most of the situation, she should stonewall you completely. Tell you absolutely nothing. That way, you'd have no choice but to agree to my version of events. Speaking of which?"

Periwinkle fetched a book from the shelf behind his desk and gave it to Samuel. It was a plain white book, with black letters on the cover: *The Packer Attacker.*

"That's an advance copy," Periwinkle said. "I had my ghostwriters whip it up. I'm going to need to put your name on that book. Or else we'll have to move forward with that lawsuit of ours, unfortunately, for you. There's a piece of paper on my desk indicating such in bewildering lawyer language. Please sign it."

"I assume this book is not very kind to her."

"It savages her intimately, publicly. I believe that was *your* pitch. *The Packer Attacker.* Good title. Catchy without being smug. But I'm especially fond of the subtitle."

"Which is?"

"The Untold Inside Story of America's Most Famous Radical Leftist, by the Son She Abandoned."

"I don't think I can put my name on that."

"Most books of nonfiction are sold on the strength of their subtitles. You may not know that."

"I can't do it, not in good conscience. It wouldn't feel right, putting my name on that book."

"And what, ruin the reputation I invented for you?"

"Is she really America's most famous radical leftist?"

"We're selling it as a memoir. The genre allows a little wiggle room."

"It's just that the book now seems to me, you know, false."

"This is of course your choice. But if you don't put your name on that book, then we proceed with the court action against you, and your mother remains a fugitive. Notice that I'm not telling you what to do here, just illuminating two paths, one of which I hope is the obvious choice if you are not totally insane."

"But the book *isn't true.*"

"And that should matter to us why, exactly?"

"I feel like it would keep me up at night. I feel like we should resist printing outright false things."

"What's true? What's false? In case you haven't noticed, the world has pretty much given up on the old Enlightenment idea of piecing together the truth based on observed data. Reality is too complicated and scary for that. Instead, it's way easier to ignore all data that doesn't fit your preconceptions and believe all data that does. I believe what I believe, and you believe what you believe, and we'll agree to disagree. It's liberal tolerance meets dark ages denialism. It's very hip right now."

"This sounds awful."

"We are more politically fanatical than ever before, more religiously zealous, more rigid in our thinking, less capable of empathy. The way we see the world is totalizing and unbreakable. We are completely avoiding the problems that diversity and worldwide communication imply. Thus, nobody cares about antique ideas like true or false."

"I'll need to give this some thought."

"Maybe literally the last thing you should be doing right now is thinking."

"I'll let you know," Samuel says, standing now.

"The very worst thing you could be doing right now is examining the situation and trying to decide what is *right*."

"I'll call you."

"Listen, Samuel, really, voice of experience here? It's a terrible burden, being idealistic. It discolors everything you'll do later. It will haunt you constantly for all time as you become the inevitably cynical person the world requires you to be. Just give up on it now, the idealism, doing the right thing. Then you'll have nothing to regret later."

"Thanks. I'll be in touch."

4

OUTSIDE PERIWINKLE'S BUILDING, the sidewalks howl. The new concern for those currently occupying Zuccotti Park is that the police are threatening to enforce city ordinances that prohibit occupying parks. Police stand at the edges of the park and watch as protestors gather in a general assembly and talk openly about the pros and cons of obeying the police. So it's a tense day. Plus there's the thing about the drumming: People are complaining about it, the ceaseless drumming way into the night, neighbors mostly, families who live in the area and have kids with early bedtimes, and local businesses who up till now have been pretty cool about letting protestors use their bathrooms but are about to become way less cool unless the drumming stops pronto. On one end of the park is the drum circle, on the other end is the multimedia tent and speaker's platform and library and general assembly in what seems to be the superego to the drummers' id. Someone is discussing the matter of the drumming right now, a young man in a vintage-looking sport coat who says a few words and stops while those words are shouted by people closest to him, which are then again shouted by those in the next zone back, and so on in a great wave, a sound that begins quietly and then is quickly amplified and amplified again, like an echo traveling back in time. This is necessary because the protestors do not have microphones. The city has banned sound-amplification devices, citing public nuisance laws. Why they have not yet arrested the drummers is anyone's guess.

The speaker is currently saying he totally supports the drummers and thinks the protest should be an inclusive, big-tent, come-one-come-all type of affair and he understands that people express themselves politically in different ways and that not everybody feels comfortable up here talking rationally and democratically into the "people's microphone" and some people prefer their message take on a more let's say *abstract quality* than the policy proposals and talking-points papers and multistep manifestos this group has heroically written through a painstakingly slow consensus-approach apparatus and under incredible duress that includes constant police surveillance and media scrutiny and also talking above the sounds of the drum circle, he might add, but that's all fine and they should embrace diversity in all its forms and be thankful that so many different kinds of people have joined their protest but he's submitting a proposal that the collective occupying group ask the drummers if they'd knock it off at like maybe nine or thereabouts, nightly, please, because people have to sleep and everyone's on their last nerve out here and it's hard enough sleeping in tents on the concrete without the goddamn drumming all goddamn night. He submits this to the general assembly for consensus. Many hands are thrust into the air, fingers atwirl. In the absence of outright opposition, the motion seems to pass, until someone suggests they haven't heard from the drummers yet and we have to hear from the drummers because even though we might disagree with the drummers it's important to get everyone's perspective here and everyone's point of view and not be like fascist about it and quote-unquote *jam it down their throats* or something. Groans from many quarters. Nevertheless, an emissary is sent to the drum circle in search of a representative.

Samuel watches all this in a kind of dispassionate daze. He feels so separate from what's happening here, so alone and hopeless. These people seem to have a sense of purpose that he has completely lost. What do you do when you discover your adult life is a sham? Everything he thought he'd accomplished—the publication, the book deal, the teaching gig—he'd only gotten because someone owed his mom a favor. He'd never earned any of it. He is a fraud. And this is what being a fraud feels like: emptied out. He feels hollow. Gutted. Why don't any of these people notice him? He longs for someone in the crowd to see the haunted expression he's sure is playing all over his face right now and come up to him and say, *You seem to be experiencing overwhelming pain, how can I help you?* He wants to be seen, wants his hurt acknowledged. Then he recognizes this as a childish desire, the equivalent of showing your mom a scratch so she can kiss it. Grow up, he tells himself.

"On the matter of the police," says the speaker, switching topics while they wait for a drummer to stop drumming and speak to them.

"On the matter of the police," the crowd repeats.

Samuel wanders away, up Liberty Street, walks the two blocks to Bethany's old apartment building. He stands there staring up at it. He doesn't know what he's looking for. The building looks unchanged in the seven years since he was last here. He thinks it's disallowable that the places of life's most important moments continue going on looking like themselves, unaffected, simple facts that resist the imprint of the stories happening around them. The last time he was here, Bethany was waiting for him in her bedroom, waiting for him to break up her marriage.

Even now, he can't think about this without that familiar flood of bitterness and regret and anger. Anger at himself, for doing what Bishop wanted him to do; anger at Bishop, for asking him to do it. Samuel has relived that moment so many times, fantasized so often about it: He had read Bishop's letter and then placed it heavily on the kitchen counter. He had opened the bedroom door to find Bethany sitting on her bed waiting for him, her face dancing with the shadows cast from three bedside candles, their little amber glow the only light in that whole big room. And in his dreams, he goes to her and embraces her and they are together at last and she leaves the awful Peter Atchison and falls in love with Samuel and, for Samuel, everything about these last seven years changes. Like one of those movies about time travel where the hero comes back to the present to find the happy ending that was always impossible in his previous life.

When Samuel was a child reading a Choose Your Own Adventure novel, he'd keep a bookmark at the spot of a very hard decision, so that if the story turned out poorly, he could go back and try again.

More than anything he wants life to behave this way.

This is the moment he would bookmark, finding Bethany all beautiful and candlelit. He would make a different decision. He would not do what he actually did, which is to say "I'm sorry. I can't," because he felt it was his duty to honor Bishop, who was dead and therefore in need of honoring. It wasn't until much later that Samuel realized it wasn't Bishop he was honoring, it was Bishop's most disfiguring wound. Whatever had happened between Bishop and the headmaster, whatever haunted Bishop as a kid, it went right on haunting him overseas and into a war, and this was what compelled that letter. Not duty but plain old hatred, self-loathing, terror. And by honoring it, Samuel had failed Bishop once again.

Samuel didn't realize this until much later, but he had sensed it at the time, sensed he was making the wrong choice. Even as he took the elevator down, even as he walked away from the building at 55 Liberty Street, he kept saying to himself, *Go back, go back.* And even as he found his car and drove out of the city and drove all night through the Midwest darkness, he kept saying it: *Go back. Go back.*

The story had appeared in the *Times* a month later, on the wedding page, the marriage of Peter Atchison and Bethany Fall. A finance guru and a violin soloist. A nexus of art and money. The *Times* just ate it up. They met in Manhattan, where the groom worked for the bride's father. To be married on Long Island, at the private residence of a friend of the bride's family. The groom specializes in risk management in precious-metal markets. Honeymoon planned involving sailing and island-hopping. The bride is keeping her name.

Yes, he'd like to go back to that night and make a different decision. He'd like to erase these last several years—years that, as he sees them now, are long and indistinguishable and monotonous and angry. Or maybe he'd go further back than that, back far enough to see Bishop again, to help him. Or to convince his mom not to leave. But even that wouldn't be far enough to recover whatever it is he lost, whatever he sacrificed to his mother's brutal influence, that real part of him that was buried when he started trying to please her. What kind of person would he have become had his instincts not been screaming at him that his mother was moments from leaving? Was he ever free of that weight? Was he ever authentically *himself*?

These are the questions you ask when you're cracking up. When you suddenly recognize that not only are you living a life you never intended to lead but also you are feeling assaulted and punished by the life you have. You begin searching for those early wrong turns. What moment led you into the maze? You begin thinking the entrance to the maze might also be the exit, and if you can identify the moment you screwed up then you can perform some huge course correction and save yourself. Which is why Samuel thinks that if he can see Bethany again and resurrect some kind of relationship with her, even a friendly platonic one, then he might be able to recover something important, that he might be able to set himself aright. This is the state he's in, that this kind of logic makes sense, that he thinks the only answer right now is to go backward, to

essentially hit the reset button on his life—a scorched-earth maneuver he
is beginning to understand urgently needs to happen as he stands outside
Bethany's building and his phone buzzes with a new e-mail from his boss
that sends his spirits tumbling even further when he reads it—*I wanted
to let you know that your office computer has been confiscated, as it will be
presented as evidence in the Faculty Affairs trial against you*—and he hears
Bishop's voice in his ear on that day Samuel's mother left and Bishop told
him this was an opportunity to become a new person, a better person,
which is something Samuel wants to be, very much so right now. Better.
He walks into the building at 55 Liberty Street. He tells the guard in the
elevator lobby to please get a message to Bethany Fall. He leaves his name
and number. Says he's in town and asks if she would like to meet. And
about twenty minutes later as he's walking aimlessly north on Broadway
past the clothing boutiques of SoHo that leak dance music onto the sidewalk along with their air-conditioning, he gets a message from Bethany:
You're in town. What a surprise!

Turns out she's in a rehearsal that lets out soon and would he like to
meet for lunch? She suggests the Morgan Library. It's close to her, in
midtown. There's a restaurant inside. She'd like to show him something.

Which is how he finds himself on Madison Avenue in front of a palatial stone mansion, the former home of J. P. Morgan, American titan of
banking and industry. Inside, the place seems designed to make visitors
feel small—in stature, intellect, and pocketbook. Rooms with thirty-foot
ceilings elaborately muraled with images inspired by Raphael's at the Vat-
ican, the saints replaced here by more secular heroes: Galileo, for example, and Christopher Columbus. All surfaces are either marble or gold.
Three stories of shelving for the many thousands of antique books—first
editions of Dickens, Austen, Blake, Whitman—visible behind the copper
lattice that protects them from being touched. A Shakespeare first folio.
A Gutenberg Bible. Thoreau's journals. Mozart's handwritten *Haffner*
Symphony. The only surviving manuscript of *Paradise Lost*. Letters written by Einstein, Keats, Napoléon, Newton. A fireplace about the size
of most New York City kitchens, above which hangs a tapestry titled,
appropriately, *The Triumph of Avarice.*

The space feels designed to intimidate and diminish. It makes Samuel
think that the folks protesting the superrich at Zuccotti Park are about a
hundred years too late.

He's staring at a life cast of George Washington's actual face when Bethany finds him.

"Samuel?" she says, and he spins around.

How much do people change in just a few years? Samuel's first impression—and this is the best way he could explain it—is that she looks more *real*. She is no longer glowing with his fantasies about her. She looks like herself, in other words, like a normal person. Maybe she hasn't changed at all, but the context has. She still has the same green eyes, the same pale skin, the same perfectly erect posture that has always made Samuel feel a little slumpy. But there is something different about her, the way her face has creased about the eyes and mouth that does not suggest time or age but rather emotion, experience, heartache, wisdom. It's one of those things he recognizes in a blink but could not point out specifically.

"Bethany," he says, and they hug, stiffly, almost ceremonially, like how you might hug someone you used to work with.

"It's good to see you," she says.

"You too."

And because she probably doesn't know what to say next, she looks around the room and says, "Quite a place, isn't it?"

"Quite a place. Quite a collection."

"Very pretty."

"Beautiful."

They spend a useless moment staring at the room, looking at everything but each other. Panic surges up in Samuel—have they already run out of things to say? But then Bethany breaks the silence: "I've always wondered how much joy all this stuff really brought him."

"What do you mean?"

"He has the big names—Mozart, Milton, Keats. But there's no evidence of real fire. It's always struck me as an investor's collection. He's building a diverse portfolio. It doesn't say love."

"Maybe there were a few pieces he loved. He hid them from everyone else. They were only his."

"Maybe. Or maybe that's even sadder, that he couldn't share them."

"You wanted to show me something?"

"This way."

She leads him to a corner where, displayed under glass, are several handwritten musical scores. Bethany points to one: the Violin Concerto no. 1, by Max Bruch, written in 1866.

"The first concert you heard me play, I played this," Bethany says. "Do you remember?"

"Of course."

The yellowed manuscript pages look like chaos to Samuel, and not because he doesn't read music. Words have been written and then scribbled over, notes have been erased or x-ed out, there seems to be a first layer of pencil under the ink, and stains on the pages from what might be coffee or paint. The composer had written *allegro molto* at the top, but then crossed out *molto* and replaced it with *moderato*. The title of the first movement, Vorspiel, is followed by a lengthy subtitle that extends more than half the page and is completely obscured by squiggles and lines and doodles.

"That's my part," Bethany says, pointing at a clump of notes that seem barely contained by the five-line staff underneath. How this mess could turn into the music Samuel heard that night seems like a miracle.

"Did you know he was never paid for this?" Samuel says. "He sold the score to a couple of Americans, but they never paid him. He died poor, I think."

"How do you know that?"

"Something my mother told me. At your concert, actually."

"You remember that?"

"Very well."

Bethany nods. She doesn't press.

"So," she says, "what's new with you?"

"I'm about to be fired," he says. "What's new with you?"

"Divorced," she says, and they both smile at this. And the smile grows into a laugh. And the laughing seems to melt something between them, a formality, a guardedness. They are together with their disasters, it turns out, and over lunch at the museum's restaurant she tells him about her four-year marriage to Peter Atchison, how by year two she'd begun saying yes to every international gig offered to her so she wouldn't be in the same country as Peter and therefore did not have to acknowledge what had been plain to her from the beginning: that she was very fond of him but did not love him, or if she did love him she did not love him in that particular way that sustains the years. They were good to each other, but they were never passionate. In their final year of marriage she was finishing a monthlong tour of China and dreaded going home.

"That's when I finally had to end it," she says. "I should have done it much earlier." She points her fork at him. "If only you hadn't left that night."

"I'm sorry," Samuel says. "I should have stayed."

"No, it's good you left. That night, I was looking for an easy way out. But the hard way out was better, ultimately, for me, I think."

And he tells her all about his recent upheaval, beginning with his mother's odd reappearance—"The Packer Attacker is your *mom*?" Bethany says, which draws looks from other tables—and the police and the judge, all the way up to today's meeting with Periwinkle and Samuel's current dilemma involving the ghostwritten book.

"Listen," he says, "I think I want to start over."

"With what?"

"With my life. My career. I think I want to burn it all down. Reset it completely. The thought of going back to Chicago is unbearable. These last few years have been one long rut I need to get out of."

"Good," Bethany says. "I think that's good."

"And I know it's forward of me and presumptuous and really unexpected and all, but I was hoping you could help. I was hoping to ask you a favor."

"Of course. What do you need?"

"A place to stay."

She smiles.

"Just for a little while," he adds. "Till I figure a few things out."

"Conveniently," she says, "my apartment has eight bedrooms."

"I'll stay out of your hair. You won't even notice me. I promise."

"Peter and I lived there and never saw each other. It is definitely possible."

"Are you sure?"

"Stay as long as you need."

"Thank you."

They finish lunch and Bethany has to leave for her second rehearsal of the day. They hug again, this time tightly, as intimates, as friends. Samuel lingers for a while at the Bruch manuscript, studying its messy pages. It makes him happy that even the masters have false starts, even the greats must sometimes double back. He imagines the composer after he'd sent this manuscript abroad, imagines how it must have felt when he no longer had the music but only had his memory of it. The memory of making it, and the way it would sound when it was played. His money would have been drying up, and war was breaking out, and all he had at the end was his imagination and maybe a fantasy of what his life would have been like had things turned out differently, how his music would have filled the spaces of cathedrals on brighter days.

5

THE HEADLINE APPEARS one morning from the Bureau of Labor Statistics: UNEMPLOYMENT UNCHANGED.

Television news picks it up moments later, cutting into programming to deliver the startling report: Over the last month, the economy has added no new jobs.

It's the biggest story of the day. It is hard data that seems to crystallize this ambiguous, uncomfortable feeling people are having in the autumn of 2011, which is that the world is galloping toward ruin. Whole island nations are going bankrupt. The European Union is pretty much insolvent. Brand-name banks have been suddenly liquidated. The stock market crashed this summer, and most experts say it'll continue tumbling well into winter. The word on the street is "deleveraging"—everyone owes too much. The world, it turns out, has way more stuff than the world has the money to own. Austerity is very hip right now. So is gold. Money pours into the gold markets because things have gotten so bad people are questioning *the very philosophical legitimacy* of paper money. Certain views that paper money is a hoax propped up by a collective fantasy move from the fringes and gain traction in mainstream conversation. The economy has turned medieval, the only treasure now being *actual treasure*—gold, silver, copper, bronze.

It is a massive, unprecedented global contraction, but it's almost too large to grasp, too complicated to fathom. It's hard to step back far enough to fully see it, and so the news engages with its manifold parts—labor data, market trends, balance sheets—smaller episodes in the larger story, places where the phenomenon pokes out and can be measured.

Which is why the unemployment story gets so much attention. There is integrity in a solid number that an abstract idea like "deleveraging" does not have.

So a logo is made: *BIG FAT ZERO!* Elaborate and colorful graphs and charts are prepared mapping recent terrible employment trends. Anchors ask probing questions of experts, pundits, and politicians, who all yell at each other from their separate TV boxes. The networks gather "Americans off the street" to engage in "roundtable discussions" about the country's jobs crisis. It feels like a flying avalanche of coverage.

Samuel sits in front of the television flipping between the news networks. He's curious to see what they're talking about today and feels relief that it is this. Because the more the news obsesses on the unemployment numbers, the less time there is to discuss the day's other potentially big story, which is the release of a new book: *The Packer Attacker*, a scandalous biography of Faye Andresen-Anderson, written by her own son.

Samuel had stopped by the launch party the night before. It was part of the deal he'd made with Periwinkle.

"Don't feel bad about this," Periwinkle said after the requisite photographs were taken. "Smartest move you've ever made."

"I trust this will settle the matter with the judge?"

"I've already taken care of that."

Turns out, the same day Judge Brown discovered Faye Andresen-Anderson had escaped to Norway—which meant he was looking at an extradition trial that could last years—he got a phone call from the Packer for President campaign offering him a job: crime czar. The only catch was that he had to make the case go away. And so because the case against her had no hope of wrapping up anytime soon, and because the job of crime czar for a presidential candidate who carried around a gun seemed unturndownable, the judge agreed to these terms. He quietly slipped the case down some bureaucratic, jurisdictional, legal black hole and officially retired from his judgeship. His first policy proposal at his new job involved a serious curtailing of First Amendment rights for leftist protestors, a proposal enthusiastically endorsed by Governor Packer, who was hoping to score some easy points among conservatives who just loathe what's happening with this whole Occupy Wall Street thing.

Samuel can hear them every day, the Wall Street protestors. He wakes up and has his coffee and writes well into the afternoon in a big leather chair next to a window that looks down at Zuccotti Park, where the protest seems to have real staying power. They're going to be sleeping there until winter, obviously. Bethany had given him his choice of room, and he had chosen this one, on the west side, with a view of the protest and, in the evening, the sun setting over the country. He's grown to enjoy the drumming, especially now that the drummers have agreed to drum only during reasonable daylight hours. He's fond of their rhythms, their ceaseless forward momentum, the way they can go for hours without a single pause. He tries to match their discipline, for he has a new project, a new book. He'd told Periwinkle about it after he was free of his contractual obligations.

"I'm writing my mother's story," Samuel said. "But I'm writing the true story. The actual events."

"Which events in particular, I'm curious to know," Periwinkle asked.

"All of them. It's going to include everything. The whole story. From her childhood to the present day."

"So it's going to be like six hundred pages and ten people will read it? Congratulations."

"That's not why I'm writing."

"Oh, you're doing it for the *art*. You're one of those now."

"Something like that."

"Names will have to be changed, you know. Essential identifying facts altered. I wouldn't want to have to sue you again."

"Would it be for libel or slander? I can never remember the difference."

"It would be for libel *and* slander, plus defamation, invasion of privacy, scurrilous statements, loss of reputation, loss of business, personal anguish, and violating the competitive works clause in your contract with us. Plus lawyer fees, plus damages."

"I'll call it fiction," Samuel said. "I'll change the names. I'll be sure to give you a really silly one."

"How's your mother?" Periwinkle asked.

"I wouldn't know. Cold, I imagine."

"Still in Norway?"

"Yes."

"Among the reindeer and northern lights?"

"Yes."

"I saw the northern lights once. In upper Alberta. I booked a trip with this outfit called See the Northern Lights! I had wanted the northern lights to fill me with wonder. And they did. They filled me with wonder. Which was a big letdown because they exactly matched my expectations of them. They did exactly what I'd paid for. Let that be a lesson to you."

"A lesson about what?"

"Writing this big epic book of yours. And what you expect it to accomplish for you. Let the northern lights be a lesson. It's a metaphor, of course."

Samuel isn't sure what he's trying to accomplish. At first he thought if he gathered enough information he could eventually isolate the reason his mother left the family. But how could he ever really pin it down? Any one explanation seemed too easy, too trivial. So instead of looking for answers, he'd begun simply writing her story, thinking that if he could see the world the way she saw it, maybe he'd achieve something greater than mere answers: Maybe he'd achieve understanding, empathy, forgiveness. So he wrote about her childhood, about growing up in Iowa, about going to Chicago for college, about the protest in 1968, about that final month she was with the family before she disappeared, and the more he wrote the more expansive the story became. Samuel wrote about his mother and father and grandfather, he wrote about Bishop and Bethany and the headmaster, he wrote about Alice and the judge and Pwnage—he was trying to understand them, trying to see the things he was too self-absorbed to see the first time through. Even Laura Pottsdam, vicious Laura Pottsdam, Samuel tried to locate a little sympathy for her.

Laura Pottsdam, who at this moment is feeling really great about life and the world because her jerk of an English professor has been fired and replaced by this hapless grad student and her failed plagiarized *Hamlet* paper has disappeared into the academic mists, so this is all super cool and this whole episode totally confirms what her mother has been telling her since she was a kid, which is that she is a powerful woman who should get what she wants and if she wants something she should GO FOR IT, and what she wants right now are a few Jägerbombs to celebrate justice: The professor is gone, her career is saved. And she sees in this a glimpse of her future, the inevitable successful future laid out in front of her like a runway for an F-16, a future where if anyone tries to get in her way she will blow them to smithereens. This thing with the professor was her first big test, and she passed it. Spectacularly. This is most especially true when Laura's S.A.F.E. initiative gains serious traction and some awesome shout-outs on the nightly news and in meetings of the Board of Regents, and her friends start telling her she should run for student senate next semester, which she's like *No frickin' way* until the Packer for President campaign comes to campus and Governor Packer himself wants to do a photo op with Laura because he's super impressed with her efforts on behalf of hardworking Illinois taxpayers everywhere, saying, "Something must be done to protect our students and our wallets from these unproductive liberal professors in outdated fields." And during the press conference some reporter asks Governor Packer what he thinks about Laura's gumption and pluck, to which this totally famous presidential candidate responds: "I think she should run for president someday."

So she switches her major. No more business communication and marketing. She promptly enrolls in the two majors she decides will most help her for a future possible presidential bid: political science and acting.

Samuel does not miss teaching students like Laura Pottsdam, but he does regret how he taught them. He winces at it now, how much he looked down on them. How eventually he could only see their flaws and weaknesses and shortcomings, the ways they did not live up to his standards. Standards that shifted so that the students would never meet them, because Samuel had grown so comfortable being angry. Anger was such an easy emotion to feel, the refuge of someone who didn't want to work too hard. Because his life in the summer of 2011 had been unfulfilling and going nowhere and he was so angry about it. Angry at his mother for leaving, angry at Bethany for not loving him, angry at his students for being uneducatable. He'd settled into the anger because the anger was so much easier than the work required to escape it. Blaming Bethany for not loving him was so much easier than the introspection needed to understand what he was doing that made him unlovable. Blaming his students for being uninspired was so much easier than doing the work required to inspire them. And on any given day, it was so much easier to settle in front of his computer than to face his stagnant life, to actually face in a real way the hole inside him that his mother left when she abandoned him, and if you make the easy choice every day, then it becomes a pattern, and your patterns become your life. He sank into *Elfscape* like a shipwreck into the water.

Years can go by in this manner, just as they had for Pwnage, who, at this moment, is finally opening his eyes.

He's been sleeping for a month—the longest sustained "nap" ever recorded at the county hospital—and now he opens his eyes. His body is well-nourished, and his mind is well-rested, and his circulatory and digestive and lymphatic systems are more or less flushed out and operating normally, and he doesn't feel that ringing headache and clawing hunger and stabbing joint pain and muscle tremor he usually feels. Actually he doesn't feel any of the background pain that has been his constant companion for so long, and what this feels like to him is a *miracle*. Compared to how he usually feels, he decides he must either be dead or on drugs. Because there's no way he could possibly feel this good if he weren't on some serious drugs, or in heaven.

He looks around the hospital room and sees Lisa sitting on the couch. Lisa, his beautiful ex-wife, who smiles at him and hugs him and who's carrying under her arm that tattered black leather notebook in which he'd written the first few pages of his detective novel. And she tells him that several packages have arrived from a big-shot New York publishing house with all this paperwork for him to sign, and when Pwnage asks her what the paperwork's for she grins at him and says, "Your book deal!"

For this was another of Samuel's conditions to Periwinkle, that Periwinkle publish his friend's novel.

"And what is this novel about?" Periwinkle had asked.

"Um, a psychic detective on the trail of a serial killer?" Samuel said. "And the killer turns out to be the detective's ex-wife's boyfriend, I think, or son-in-law, or something."

"Actually," Periwinkle said, "that sounds *amazing*."

Pwnage once told Samuel that the people in your life are either enemies, obstacles, puzzles, or traps. And for both Samuel and Faye, circa summer 2011, people were definitely enemies. Mostly what they wanted out of life was to be left alone. But you cannot endure this world alone, and the more Samuel's written his book, the more he's realized how wrong he was. Because if you see people as enemies or obstacles or traps, you will be at constant war with them and with yourself. Whereas if you choose to see people as puzzles, and if you see yourself as a puzzle, then you will be constantly delighted, because eventually, if you dig deep enough into anybody, if you really look under the hood of someone's life, you will find something familiar.

This is more work, of course, than believing they are enemies. Understanding is always harder than plain hatred. But it expands your life. You will feel less alone.

And so he's trying, Samuel is, trying to be diligent in this odd new life he has with Bethany. They are not lovers. They may one day become lovers, but they are not lovers yet. Samuel's attitude about this is: Whatever happens, happens. He knows he can't go back and relive his life, can't change the mistakes of his past. His relationship with Bethany is not a Choose Your Own Adventure book. So instead he will do this: He will clarify it, illuminate it, try to understand it better. He can prevent his past from swallowing his present. So he's trying to be in the moment, trying not to let the moment get all discolored by his fantasies of what the moment ought to be. He is trying to see Bethany as she really is. And isn't that what everybody really wants? To be seen clearly? He'd always been obsessed with a few of Bethany's qualities: her eyes, for example, and her posture. But then she told him one day that the feature she shared most closely with Bishop was her eyes, and so whenever she stares into a mirror at her eyes it makes her a little sad. And another time she told him her posture had been drilled into her by the endless Alexander Technique lessons she endured for years while other kids her age were playing on swing sets and running through sprinklers. After Samuel heard these stories, he could not go on thinking the same way about her eyes or posture. These things were diminished, but what he realized was that the whole was greatly expanded.

So he is beginning to see Bethany as she is, for maybe the first time.

His mother, too. He's trying understand her, to see her clearly and not through the distortion of his own anger. The only lie Samuel ever told Periwinkle was that Faye had stayed in Norway. It seemed like a good lie to tell—if everyone believed she was in the arctic, then nobody would bother her. Because the truth is she returned home, to that little Iowa river town, to care for her father.

Frank Andresen's dementia was pretty far along by then. When Faye saw him the first time and the nurse said "Your daughter's here," he looked at Faye with such wonder and surprise. He was so thin and skeletal. There were red spots on his forehead rubbed raw from scratching and picking. He looked at her like she was a ghost.

"Daughter?" he said. "What daughter?"

Which is the kind of thing Faye would have chalked up to battiness if she hadn't known better, if she hadn't known there might be more to that question than simple confusion.

"It's me, Dad," she said, and she decided to take a risk. "It's me, Freya."

And the name registered somewhere deep down inside him and his face crumpled and he looked at her with anguish and despair. She went to him then and gathered his fragile body in her arms.

"It's okay," she said. "Don't be sad."

"I'm sorry," he said, looking at her with an intensity unusual for a man who had spent his life avoiding the gaze of other people. "I'm so very sorry."

"Everything turned out well. We all love you."

"You do?"

"Everyone loves you so much."

He looked at her very closely and studied her face a long time.

Fifteen minutes later the whole episode was lost. He caught himself in the middle of some story and looked at her pleasantly and said, "Now who are you, dear?"

But the moment seemed to shake something loose in him, seemed to uncork something important, because among the stories he'd tell now were stories of young Marthe, taking midnight strolls under a dimly lit sky, stories Faye had never heard before and stories that embarrassed the nurses because it was clear the walks were postcoital. Something seemed to lift inside him, some burden let go. Even the nurses said so.

So Faye is renting a small apartment close to the nursing home and each morning she walks over and spends the whole day with her father. Sometimes he recognizes her, but most of the time he doesn't. He tells old ghost stories, or stories about the ChemStar factory, or stories of fishing the Norwegian Sea. And every once in a while he'll see her and by the look on his face she understands that he's really seeing Freya. And when this happens she soothes him and hugs him and tells him everything turned out well, and she describes the farm when he asks about it, and when she describes it she does so grandly—not just barley in the front yard but whole fields of wheat and sunflowers. He smiles. He's picturing it. It makes him happy to hear this. It makes him happy when she says, "I forgive you. We all forgive you."

"But why?"

"Because you're a good man. You did the best you could."

And it's true. He did. He was a good man. As good a father as he could be. Faye had simply never seen it before. Sometimes we're so wrapped up in our own story that we don't see how we're supporting characters in someone else's.

So this is what she can do for him now, comfort him and keep him company and forgive and forgive and forgive. She cannot save his body or his mind, but she can lighten his soul.

They talk for a while and then he needs to nap, sometimes falling asleep mid-sentence. Faye reads while he sleeps, making her way once again through the collected poetry of Allen Ginsberg. And sometimes Samuel phones her, and when he does she'll put the book away and answer his questions, all his big terrifying questions: Why did she leave Iowa? And college? And her husband? And her son? She tries to answer honestly and thoroughly, even though it's frightening for her. It is literally the first time in her life she is not hiding some great piece of herself, and she feels so exposed that it's close to panic. She has never before given herself over to anyone—she'd always parceled herself out little by little. This bit for Samuel, some small part for her father, barely anything for Henry. She'd never put all of herself in just one place. It felt too risky. Because her great and constant fear all these years was that if anyone ever came to know all of her—the real her, the true deep essential Faye—they would not find enough stuff there to love. Hers was not a soul large enough to nourish another.

But now she's trusting Samuel with everything. She answers his questions. She holds nothing back. Even when her answers make the panic boil up within her—that Samuel will think she's a terrible person, that he'll stop calling—still she tells him the truth. And just when she thinks his interest in her must be exhausted, just when her answers prove that she's a person unworthy of his love, what actually happens is quite the opposite. He seems *more* interested, calls *more* often. And sometimes he calls to talk—not about her ugly past but about how her day went, or about the weather, or the news. It makes her hope that someday soon they'll be two people encountering each other sincerely, without the disfigurement of their history, minus all her immutable mistakes.

She'll be patient. She knows she can't force a thing like that. She'll wait, and she'll take care of her father, and she'll answer her son's many questions. And when Samuel wants to know her secrets, she'll tell him her secrets. And when he wants to talk about the weather, she'll talk about the weather. And when he wants to talk about the news, she'll talk about the news. She flips on the television to see what's happening in the world. Today it's all about unemployment, global deleveraging, recession. People are panicked. Uncertainty is at an all-time high. A crisis is looming.

But Faye's opinion is that sometimes a crisis is not really a crisis at all—

just a new beginning. Because one thing she's learned through all this is that if a new beginning is really *new,* it will feel like a crisis. Any real change should make you feel, at first, afraid.

If you're not afraid of it, then it's not real change.

So banks and governments are cleaning up their ledgers after years of abuse. Everyone owes too much, is the consensus, and we're in for a few years of pain. But Faye thinks: Okay. That's probably the way it ought to be. That's the natural way of things. That's how we'll find our way back. This is what she'll tell her son, if he asks. Eventually, all debts must be repaid.

ACKNOWLEDGMENTS

THE EVENTS of 1968 described in this novel are a blend of historical facts, eyewitness interviews, and the author's imagination, ignorance, and fancy. For example, Allen Ginsberg attended the Chicago protests, but he was not a visiting professor at Circle. And Circle did not have dorms in 1968. And the Behavioral Science Building wasn't opened until 1969. And my depiction of the Grant Park protest does not follow the exact chronological order of things. And so on. For more historically accurate accounts of the '68 protests, I would recommend the following, which were invaluable to me during the writing of this novel: *Chicago '68* by David Farber; *The Whole World Is Watching* by Todd Gitlin; *Battleground Chicago* by Frank Kusch; *Miami and the Siege of Chicago* by Norman Mailer; *Chicago 10* directed by Brett Morgen; *Telling It Like It Was: The Chicago Riots* edited by Walter Schneir; and *No One Was Killed* by John Schultz.

In addition, I am indebted to the following books for helping me to portray the time period in (I hope) a convincing way: *Make Love, Not War* by David Allyn; *Young, White, and Miserable* by Wini Breines; *Culture Against Man* by Jules Henry; *1968* by Mark Kurlansky; *Dream Time* by Geoffrey O'Brien; and *Shards of God* by Ed Sanders.

Some of the words given to Allen Ginsberg in this book were written by him first in his essays and letters, collected in *Deliberate Prose: Selected Essays 1952–1995* edited by Bill Morgan, and in *Journals: Early Fifties Early Sixties* edited by Gordon Ball.

For the great Norwegian ghost stories, I am indebted to *Folktales of Norway* edited by Reidar Christiansen and translated by Pat Shaw Iversen. The *nix* is the Germanic name given to a ghost that, in Norway, would actually be called the *nøkk*.

My information about panic attacks comes from *Dying of Embarrassment* by Barbara G. Markway et al. and *Fearing Others* by Ariel Stravynksi. For insights regarding desire and frustration, I am indebted to *Missing Out: In Praise of the Unlived Life* by Adam Phillips.

For his research on the psychology and behavior of MMORPG players, I am grateful to Nick Yee and his Daedalus Project. My thinking about the four kinds of challenges in video games was aided by Phil Co's *Level Design for Games*. Pwnage's various brain disorders came from Nicholas Carr's blog *Rough Type* and the article "Microstructure Abnormalities in Adolescents with Internet Addiction Disorder" by Kai Yuan et al., published in *PLoS ONE,* June 2011.

Feminine hygiene ads in Faye's home ec classroom are from the website Found in Mom's Basement at pzrservices.typepad.com/vintage advertising. Certain Laura Pottsdam details were plucked from a couple of amazing calls to the *Savage Lovecast* by Dan Savage. My description of the Molly Miller music video owes a debt to Andrew Darley's *Visual Digital Culture*. Some information regarding Circle's brutalist architecture comes from Andrew Bean's Wesleyan University honors thesis, "The Unloved Campus: Evolution of Perceptions at the University of Illinois at Chicago." The argument for a reproductive boycott is excerpted from an article in *Ain't I a Woman* 3, no. 1 (1972). The letter to the editor that Faye reads in the *Chicago Free Voice* is excerpted from an unpublished letter to the *Chicago Seed* donated to the Chicago History Museum. Sebastian's information about the *maarr* comes from Franca Tamisari's "The Meaning of the Steps Is in Between: Dancing and the Curse of Compliments," published in *The Australian Journal of Anthropology,* August 2000. Allen Ginsberg's "Eat Mangoes!" story is from *Teachings of Sri Ramakrishna*.

Thank you to the staff at the Chicago History Museum for their assistance. For supporting revisions on this novel, a big thank-you to the Minnesota State Arts Board and the University of St. Thomas.

Thank you to my editor, Tim O'Connell, for his exceptional guidance in shaping the story, not to mention his Periwinkle-like enthusiasm and zeal. Thank you to all the great people at Knopf: Tom Pold, Andrew Ridker, Paul Bogaards, Robin Desser, Gabrielle Brooks, Jennifer Kurdyla, LuAnn Walther, Oliver Munday, Kathy Hourigan, Ellen Feldman, Cameron Ackroyd, Karla Eoff, and Sonny Mehta.

Thank you to my agent, Emily Forland, for her wisdom, patience, and good cheer. Thank you to Marianne Merola, and all the wonderful folks at Brandt & Hochman.

Thank you to my family, my friends, and my teachers for their love, kindness, generosity, and support. Thank you to Molly Dorozenski for her counsel after reading lengthy early drafts.

And finally, thank you to Jenni Groyon, my first reader, for helping me find the path through ten years of writing.

picador.com

blog
videos
interviews
extracts